W9-AGZ-877

WITHDRAWN

A DEEPER WILD

by William L. Sullivan

Yours truly
George Müller

A DEEPER WILD

by William L. Sullivan

Navillus Press
Eugene, Oregon

In memory of Elsie Jane Brownell Sullivan

© 2000 by William L. Sullivan

All rights reserved. No part of this book may be reproduced in any form without written permission from the publisher.

Published by the Navillus Press
1958 Onyx Street
Eugene, Oregon 97403

www.Oregonhiking.com

Printed in USA

FIRST EDITION

Frontispiece: Joaquin Miller, circa 1872.

Or why , or when, or whence I came;
mistaken and misunderstood,
I sought a deeper wild and wood.

—Joaquin Miller, *Songs of the Sierras*

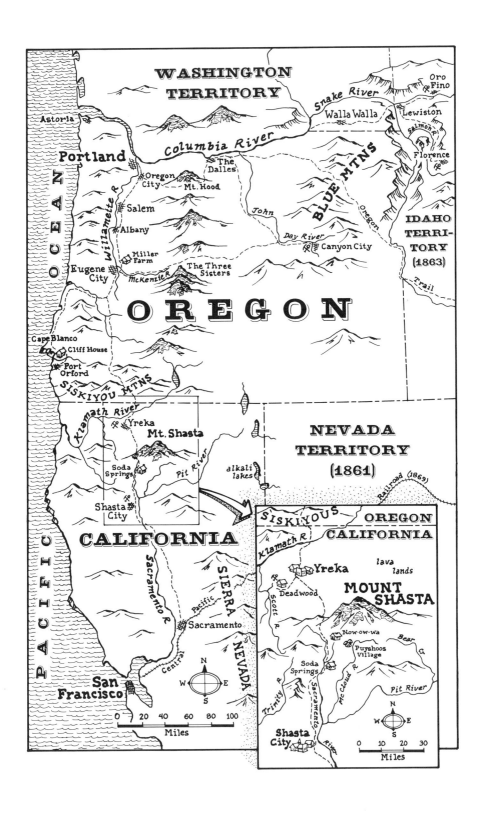

Contents

Introduction

Joaquin Miller, the American West's first world-renowned writer, galloped to fame in the England of 1872 as the swashbuckling "Poet of the Sierras."

Miller set the London literary scene on its ear by appearing for poetry readings outfitted with a sombrero and spurs, howling like a coyote. He amazed Browning and Tennyson with tales of dusky Indian maidens and lassoed bears. He was introduced to Queen Victoria as the frontier's greatest writer of all time. His success set the stage for Mark Twain, Bret Harte, and others to try their literary luck abroad—and inspired Buffalo Bill Cody to capitalize on the public's hunger for flamboyant frontiersmen.

The most astonishing thing about Miller is that he was not lying. He had in fact been an outlaw, pony express rider, gold miner, county judge, Indian fighter, Civil War pacifist, newspaper editor, and horse thief in the frontier West. And while this resumé bedazzled audiences in Europe, the West itself was in an uproar over a more serious scandal: Miller had married a popular Oregon poet without admitting he already had an Indian wife and daughter in the California wilderness. When his white wife found out, she joined forces with legendary woman's rights activist Susan B. Anthony and denounced him from the stage—becoming the first pioneer Oregon woman to lecture in public outside a church.

In writing this historical novel, I have followed the record as closely as possible. Where facts exist, the book is an accurate history. Where gaps in the record cry out for speculation, the book is a novel. The newspaper articles, legal documents, and poems quoted within the book are sometimes shortened, but are otherwise verbatim. Chapter-by-chapter notes in the appendix identify sources and separate historical fact from fiction.

My intent has been neither to write a vilification, as has been done by

Miller's more vindictive biographers, nor to compose a glorification, as has been attempted by Miller's apologists.

I offer instead the story of a fascinating man and the courageous women who molded his life.

William L. Sullivan
Eugene, Oregon

PART ONE

Paquita

Chapter 1

Lonely as God, and white as a winter moon,
Mount Shasta starts up sudden and solitary
from the heart of the great black forests of
Northern California.
                                        —Joaquin Miller

Stars glimmered above Mt. Shasta's ghost-like silhouette as Ned Miller rode to the edge of the raging Sacramento River. He frowned at the whitewater. He had come so far that Mountain Joe's log cabin should be close. But where the devil was the ford?

When the young man finally spotted the mouth of Soda Creek among the shadows of the far bank, he ran his hand over his smooth jaw. He had not lost the trail in the dusk after all. The river had shifted its channel over the winter. All trace of the old, easy ford was gone. Ahead, the current roared against boulders, turning up great waves of frothing white.

Reason told Ned to pitch camp so he could search for a better crossing in the morning. But the river spoke to him with a different voice, alive with danger and beauty. It glinted through the dark forest like a defiantly drawn saber.

In Ned's eighteen years, he had chosen more than his share of difficult trails. He had walked from Indiana to Oregon beside a covered wagon. He had spent a year in the hardscrabble gold fields of the Northern California wilderness—a rough place in 1856, with the Gold Rush fading. Through it all, it seemed as if he had always been overshadowed by other men. Sometimes he blamed his schoolboyish features—gray-blue eyes, a tall, earnest forehead, and wavy blond hair. Or perhaps it was his name. He had been born Cincinnatus Hiner Miller. And although the frontier often recast such oddities into colorful nicknames, he had never yet been known by more than his plain boyhood handle, Ned—or worse, by his ungainly middle name, Hiner.

The thought steeled him. But he had never really considered turning back. He had quit the mines to seek a different kind of fortune with Mountain Joe. Working with the old packer had never been just another job. Wherever Joe went, adventure wasn't far behind.

Ned braced himself with a few deep breaths. He tucked the three precious books from his saddlebags firmly under his shirt. Then he tapped his spurs on the horse's flanks.

The roan gelding took one step into the cold, rushing water and hesitated.

"Hyah!" He urged the horse on, spurring with more determination. The horse threw back its head with a defiant snort.

"Dammit, Pache, move!"

When the horse only braced its legs against the gravel, Ned pulled his rifle from behind the saddle and fired into the air. The blast boomed off the canyon walls and echoed high up into the granite spires of Castle Crags. "Hyah!"

The startled horse leaped headlong into the swirling water.

Ned just had time to clutch the mane. The horse lunged again and was swept off its feet into the churning dark. Icy water foamed over the saddle and sprayed Ned's face. The chill shock gave him a shot of fear. He gripped the reins tighter and pulled back, as if to guide the horse through the dark. The wild rush of the river pulsed in his ears. But then he realized he had no choice but to trust his horse. With an effort, he fought back the panic and opened his fist. Now it would be up to Pache.

The horse pawed onward through the waves, swimming with just its head and flared nostrils shining wet in the starlight. A black snag stabbed past in the dark. Sharp, barren branches raked the horse's flank as they drifted past. Ned's heart raced at the narrowness of the miss. "Come on, Pache," he urged.

Suddenly a wagon-sized boulder loomed ahead, bucking the current into a glassy roll. Here the river suspended them for a moment, as if debating whether to dash them on into the rapids. Then, relenting, the waves shunted them aside into a bubbling plain in the shadows of the far shore.

When the horse found its footing Ned let out a whoop of success. "Good boy, Pache!" He shivered with the thrill of the ride, and felt the horse shivering too.

With yet another whoop, he rode the dripping horse up the bank. From here the welcome glow of a campfire flickered through the trees in the direction of Joe's cabin.

But as soon as he saw the hut—its single window dark, its rock chimney smokeless—he knew there had been trouble. Spilling from the open door was a shambles of looted supply sacks and cooking gear.

Alarmed, he spun in his saddle toward the light.

There, in the shadows behind the campfire, stood an enormous, buckskin-clad Indian, leveling a long hunting rifle at him.

Ned's mouth was suddenly dry, his voice gone.

The Indian clicked back the gun's hammer.

Ned silently cursed his carelessness in firing his own rifle by the river. It would be useless without reloading. Nor was there hope of escape from the giant Indian at this range. Grimly, Ned dropped his weapon to the ground.

At the same moment a cracked voice cried from a shed by the corral, "Bandits! You hold 'em, Charley, I'm—I'm—" and an old, long-haired mountain man stumbled out, pulling a fringed buckskin jacket onto one arm and holding a pistol with the other.

"Mountain Joe!" Ned cried, flush with relief.

"The hell—" The old man stopped. "Ned Miller?" He squinted, scratching his bushy, white-streaked beard. "What the Sam Hill you doin' howlin' through the woods like some kind of Joaquin?"

When the strange Indian lowered the gun, Ned hazarded a smile. He wiped the river spray from his brow. "Reckon I'm looking for a job. For a minute there I thought you'd been ambushed, Joe."

"I did too." Joe grunted and spat to one side. "Damn. Coulda stood a good bandit." He took the heavy, octagonal-barreled rifle from the big Indian and lumbered off toward the log cabin muttering, "Give Charley your mount. I'll scare up some grub. We'll jawbone about jobs tomorrow."

"Joe—" Ned began. But the old man was already gone.

Ned let out a long breath. He eased down from his horse, aware that his every move was still being watched by the Indian.

Ned had seen Indians before in the boomtowns of Northern California, but none had been permitted to carry a gun. They were short, with pointed hook noses and almond-shaped eyes—not at all like this commanding man. This Indian stood even taller than Ned, with a broad nose and a strangely familiar, haunted look in his dark eyes.

Ned took off the horse's wet saddle. The Indian waited, motionless. This might be one of the volatile Modocs Ned had heard about. Still, all the Indians he had known could speak Chinook jargon. He ransacked his memory for a Chinook greeting.

"*Klahowya*," Ned ventured, holding out the horse's reins.

Charley took the reins. Before turning toward the dark corrals, he replied, "Pleased to meet you, Ned."

*   *   *

When Joe returned from the log cabin Ned demanded, "Who is this Indian?"

The old man handed him a hunk of dried meat and squatted by the fire on short, springy legs. He took a swig from a flask hidden in his shirt and wiped his mouth with a buckskin sleeve. "Take a drink?"

"But why've you got an Indian here?"

Joe aimed the flask at him. "I said, Take a drink?"

Ned sighed. The man could not be hurried. He tipped back the whiskey for a fiery gulp.

The old man nodded approvingly and pushed back his broad-brimmed felt hat. "I got reasons for Charley. Now you tell me how come you're hootin' in here like a locoed coyote. Last I seen, you was all fired up 'bout the gold mines."

Ned shook his head. "I finally threw in my pick and rode off."

"Partner troubles?"

"Not so much that. I just had to try something else—I don't know what. It's like there's something gets a hold of me."

Joe stroked his beard and smiled into the fire. "Maybe it's 'Joaquin' after all." He drawled the name quietly until it was "Wah-keen."

"What do you mean?" Ned shivered in his wet clothes. He had heard Joe tell hair-raising campfire tales about Joaquin Murietta, the long-dead Mexican bandit who haunted American miners as the "Ghost of the Sonora." But if there was a connection between this vengeful ghost of Old California and his own restlessness, Ned couldn't see it.

Joe took an ornate gold watch from his ragged buckskin jacket and began winding it thoughtfully. "Oh, I reckon you're not the only one gits that 'Joaquin' itch. You just git it more reg'lar than most. Like in Oregon, when I found you high-tailin' it from your pa's homestead."

"All I had then was gold fever." Ned laughed, but the memory of his Oregon boyhood was unsettling. He had hung so eagerly on the words of the farmers returning from the '49 Gold Rush. He had thrilled to their stories of easy wealth. By the time he actually reached California the first flush of adventure was gone and the easy gold had been panned out. The mines that remained were hellish camps hacked into the canyons, squalid ore factories blighting the wilderness.

"You never had gold fever," Mountain Joe scoffed.

Ned looked into the fire. Perhaps Joe was right, and the gold had been an excuse all along. A deeper call had drawn him to follow Joe even then. The moguls of the mining camps held the keys to metal wealth, but Joe was the unlikely guardian of the frontier's greater treasure: adventure and renown.

Ned nodded toward the cabin. "Come on, let's go in so I can dry my gear."

"Hell, Ned, I never do a campfire in a shack. Too much trash in there anyway."

"What did we build the cabin for if you're going to live outside?"

The old man grunted. "I git too damn cooped up in houses. After all them years trailin' pack stock up from Arizona, I gotta see stars at night."

Ned sighed and pulled off his wet boots. "Next you'll be telling me you're already tired of running a horse ranch."

"Tired?" Joe raised his bushy eyebrows. "Ranchin's like gittin' a foot caught in a short-chained beaver trap. No tired to it. But a man'd chew his goddam leg off to git loose."

Ned was propping up his boots to dry by the fire when he saw a stony face in the flickering shadows between the trees: the Indian. The uneasiness he had felt before crept back. He shot a glance to Joe.

"Don't git your fur up over Charley," Joe said. "Best vaquero I ever found. Understands animals like nobody else."

Ned lowered his voice. "Where did you run across him?"

"Oh, he's usually up around Shasta somewhere, with the Wintus." Joe spat away from the fire. "Digger Injuns, folks call 'em."

"Are they at war?"

Joe shook his head, frowning. "Folks say Diggers're too lazy to fight. Truth is, there's nobody to fight with up there yet. No gold on Mt. Shasta, so white men mostly steer clear of it."

"But if the tribe's so isolated, how'd he learn to speak English?"

Joe turned to the face in the shadows.

The big man hesitated, then stepped forward into the firelight. Long, black braids fell over his broad chest. For a moment his lips only tightened. Then he lowered his eyes. "I am not of the tribe. I am not an Indian."

Ned stared at him in astonishment. "You're what?"

Mountain Joe put his hand on Ned's shoulder. "Charley's pa was from Scotland. Hell of a Hudson's Bay man, he was. Old man McCloud packed enough bales of beaver pelts out of these mountains to put a stovepipe hat on every liar in England. Got a squaw from the Puyshoos—that's Charley's band of Wintus up on the McCloud River."

"What happened to him?"

Joe pulled at his big beard. "Reckon he moved on. Named the river after himself 'fore he pulled up stakes, though."

"Why aren't you one of the tribe, then?" Ned asked the big man. "You sure look Indian enough."

Charley replied, "To whites, yes. But look at me, Ned." He straightened himself to his full height. He was every inch of six foot four. "The Wintu are short and dark. To them I am white."

Ned looked again at the young man. Now he recognized the strangely familiar look in Charley's mild eyes: the shadow of loneliness. And he thought he understood why Mountain Joe had taken in both Charley and him. They were each riding trails on the edges of their worlds.

Chapter 2

An Indian girl with ornaments of shell
Began to sing . . . . There fell
A sweet enchantment that possess'd me as a spell.
                    —Joaquin Miller

Dawn had scarcely lit the window of the one-room log cabin the next morning when the sound of boots broke into Ned's dreams.

Joe was pacing the dirt floor, scowling out the window with each circuit of the room. "Summer pasture's what we need, Ned," he exclaimed.

"How's that?" Ned rolled his head groggily. He caught sight of the huge Indian sitting across from him and was suddenly awake, remembering the night before.

"Pasture!" Joe said. "Stock've been bottled up in this canyon all winter pickin' the range to the bone."

Charley stopped lacing his tall, beaded moccasins, and looked up thoughtfully. "The snow should be off Now-ow-wa, the valley between here and the McCloud. It has deep grass. The Puyshoos might not be too angry if you put only a few horses there for the summer."

"*Injun* land?" Joe moved his jaw as though chewing the thought. "Hell, it's worth scoutin' out. If we get crackin', we can ride to the pass on Shasta 'fore breakfast." He grabbed some saddlebags off a wall peg and kicked open the door. "Comin', 'Joaquin?' Or ain't explorin' Injun territory the kind of job you had in mind?"

To Ned, this sounded like the trumpet call of adventure he had ridden so far to hear. He threw off his blankets and began pulling on his tall miners' boots. "Round up Pache, old-timer."

* * *

The morning fog swirled across the steep ridge, leaving the three riders afloat in clouds. Joe's black mare rose above the misty chaparall of manzanita , his fifty-caliber Hawken across the saddle. Gnarled madrone trees sank into the fog behind the gray outline of Charley and his horse.

It seemed to Ned that the shadows of the land about them were drifting—but that he, for once, was on a steady path. With each step of the horses he felt more distant from the shabby mining camps and closer to the heroic frontier world that lived in Mountain Joe's campfire tales.

As they rode upward into the wilderness, the fog thinned overhead. The low sun appeared as a faint red disk through the mysterious white. Then the fog melted and the red ball flashed in Ned's face. To the south, pink-struck cloudtops filled the Sacramento River canyon like snow on a frozen sea. The spires of the Castle Crags and the thousand black ridges of the Klamath Mountains sailed like distant ships above the billows. Ned was just turning to Joe to exclaim at the scene when he saw the mountain.

The great cone towered into the sky, its writhing glaciers turned to rivers of fire by the sun. Overhead, crimson cloud banners and belts of gold streamed from the summit.

"Shasta," Charley said.

The mountain took up half the sky. Ned felt as though it could crush him, or exalt him, at will.

Joe swung down from his saddle and tied his mare to a stunted fir in the alpine meadow. "Grandest damn volcano in the West."

Ned dismounted as if in a trance. Charley, who had been watching him, now crouched beside him amongst the meadow flowers. The big man spoke in a low, earnest tone very different from his usual aloof manner. "Here the spirit's power is very strong."

Ned looked up, eyes narrowed. The mountain's beauty had in fact struck a strange chord within him, and this made Charley's tone all the more disturbing. "What spirit is that?"

"Kusku. My mother's tribe says this is where he created the world."

"And how do they say the world began?" Ned asked.

Charley slowly moved his hands before him in a circle, as if for an incantation. "They say Kusku used a rock to grind a hole in the sky. He pushed snow and ice through the hole until he built up the mountain. Then he climbed down and planted trees all around by putting his finger on the ground. The sun melted some of the snow, and water ran down to make the rivers. After that he made fish for the rivers out of the small end of his walking stick."

Mountain Joe hunkered across from them, listening.

Charley picked up a handful of dry fir needles and let them fall. "They say Kusku made the birds by picking up leaves from below the trees and blowing them into the air. Then he made the other animals out of the rest of his walking stick, saving the big end for the *wemir*—the grizzly bear—the biggest of all. Back then the *wemir* was so strong that even Kusku was afraid of him. So Kusku hollowed out the mountain to make a safe wigwam. He built a fire inside. That's what heats the mountain's hot springs. Sometimes you can even see its smoke blowing from the mountain's top."

Charley looked down at his hands. "At least that's what the Puyshoos say."

Mountain Joe spat to one side. "Beats hell out of a lot of stories I've heard."

Ned looked at him. "I thought you said Mt. Shasta was just a volcano."

"Oh, I reckon there's somethin' to the old tales, too. Nothin' you could stake down an' stare in the eyeball, you understand. Just somethin'." The old man opened his gold watch thoughtfully and heaved a sigh.

For an instant the sunlight touched the back of the watch, highlighting an elaborate engraving. Ned caught the old man's ragged buckskin sleeve. "Is that a picture of Shasta?"

Mountain Joe held out the gold timepiece. "Reckon so."

Ned read a small inscription below the etching of the mountain and whistled. "*Captain John C. Frémont.* How—"

Joe closed the watch in his weathered hand. "Me an' Kit Carson joined on as scouts for Frémont's expedition back in '43. We got almost to Shasta 'fore the Modocs attacked, buzzin' up out of hidden lava caves like yellowjackets. We lost some good men in that fight. I led the ones that were left 'cross the Sierras in snow so deep we damn near had to tunnel through. When we got to San Francisco Frémont told me, 'Joe, no man alive knows more about the mountains than you. This watch has been with me through all my expeditions, an' now I'm givin' it to you so it can stay in the mountains with the man who knows 'em best.'"

A wind off the mountain blew back the meadow's larkspur and anemones. A hawk wheeling overhead screamed.

Ned thought: then the tallest of all Joe's tales was true. Had Charley sensed that, too, with his talk of spirits? Could it be that the three of them were even now being moved by the same unseen force?

Joe cleared his throat and began tightening his saddlebags. "Better git ready for ambushes east of the pass, 'Joaquin.'"

* * *

The three horsemen rode on through the pass to Now-ow-wa, a valley more beautiful and silent than any Ned had ever seen. Dark floes of pines swept down from the slopes of the mountain, gradually thinning into green meadows. A silver creek meandered across the grasslands and disappeared into a cleft in the jumble of foothills that rimmed the valley on three sides.

As the three rode down through the pines, a ruffed grouse suddenly started out of the brush, beating the air with brown wings. A mule deer bounded stiff-legged before them, then turned to snuff the air, long ears pricked, before fleeing into the woods. As the riders neared the valley's floor, warmer breezes carried the sweet fragrance of sunny pine boughs and wildflowers.

Ned closed his eyes and filled his lungs with the perfumed air. Floating across the stillness, he imagined he could even hear the music of a distant song. Almost involuntarily he reined in his horse. The others stopped too, as if they also had to listen. To Ned's surprise, the enchanting voice was now even clearer.

Gradually Charley smiled. "The Puyshoos are in Now-ow-wa," he said. "I should have known. It's early camas-time."

Charley's pony led them out of the forest into a broad meadow. There, a dozen dark-haired Indian women bent hip-deep in lush grass and blue, star-like camas blossoms. An Indian warrior put down his bow when he saw Charley and spoke a salutation in a language Ned could not understand. When Charley dismounted and the two solemnly embraced, Ned was struck by how different they were: while Charley was tall and broad as an oak trunk, the other was short and sinewy, with angular bones and a hardened expression.

After the two had talked in their Wintu tongue, Charley turned back to Ned and Mountain Joe. "This is Akitot, my mother's nephew. He has come with the women from the McCloud camp this morning to watch them during the first harvest of new camas bulbs."

Ned was only able to mutter a distracted reply. His attention had long since strayed to the little band of women and girls shyly grouped about their camas baskets. One dark-eyed young girl in particular—perhaps the one who had been singing?—had ventured to cast Ned a fleeting smile that had caught him by surprise and sped his heart. She was small like the others, not even five feet tall, but with full, jet-black hair that fell in two thick braids over her fringed deerskin dress to a thin sash at her waist. But what sent a flame of desire through him was the astonishing sight of her slender legs—smooth brown skin bare all the way up to the knees. None of the Wintu women seemed to know or care about the floor-length Victorian fashions of white society. The wild freedom of the girl was almost as intoxicating to Ned as her beauty. She lifted her face again: a full mouth, high cheekbones, and mysterious dark eyes.

Ned hardly heard the discussion that Charley interpreted between

Mountain Joe and Akitot. When he fully returned to his senses, the little band of Indians was drifting across the meadow to the east and Mountain Joe was saying he'd like to bring a dozen horses up to Now-ow-wa for the summer, if only there were a way to keep an eye on them.

"I'll do it," Ned volunteered.

"How's that again?"

He had wanted adventure, and now here it was. "I'll watch the stock here for the summer if you want. I said I was looking for a job."

"But this here could be risky, picketing stock on Injun land. I was figgering you'd rather work down in Soda with Charley an' me."

"We'll keep in touch." Ned smiled across the meadow. "Have you ever seen such a good place to build a little cabin?"

The old mountain man scratched his head. "Well, if that don't beat all."

* * *

The memory of the dark-eyed Wintu girl haunted Ned during the weeks that followed. When he returned to the summer pasture at Now-ow-wa with the string of horses, the wind in the trees seemed to sing the enchanting Indian melody he had heard before. After he had begun felling and barking trees for the small cabin, he found himself sitting on a log for hours at a time, gazing across the wildflower meadows, picturing the girl with such clarity that he was able to recall even the details of her dress: the red leather ties on her braids, the white shell earrings against her brown skin.

The memory made him ache with desire. He found himself wanting to know all about her—how she lived, what she thought, how she spoke—and most of all, if she had been struck by the sight of him, too. How different, he thought, the Wintus' fragile, unspoiled life must be from the gritty, gold-grubbing routine in the mining camps! Like a wild bird's song drifting above the clamor of a busy city, she seemed to be calling him to a purer, better world, folded in the arms of the mountain wilderness.

More than once he saddled his horse and rode up into the scrub-covered foothills towards the McCloud River. Each time, however, he stopped at the summit of the ridge. From there he could see the winding channel four miles beyond, where the McCloud cut into the forests fanning out below Mt. Shasta. At the edge of that plain, where the river entered the narrow chasm that led it through the foothills, was the Wintu village: a clearing in a sharp bend of the river, overhung with a wisp of blue smoke.

But how could he go there? What would he be able to say when the warriors came out to meet him? Charley had made it clear that none of the Puyshoos band spoke English, or even Chinook jargon. Besides, he didn't know the girl's name. All he knew about her was what he had read in her dark eyes.

One time when he rode up to the ridge a new and sobering thought struck him: Did he really want to fall in love with an Indian woman?

Even supposing that the insurmountable barriers of the village and the language were somehow lifted, what then? Would he take her home to Oregon? Ned's lips tightened at the thought. He had only to picture walking her past the settlers in Eugene City to know how difficult that would be.

Or did he want to stay with the girl in the wilds, where public censure could not reach? Ned recalled that Charley's own mother had married a Hudson's Bay trapper. Such things were common among the mountain men who lived apart from civilization. And yet, lovely as this mountain valley was, he was reluctant to exile himself completely from the world below. When he had run away from his parents' Oregon farm he had dreamed of returning one day cloaked in fame—perhaps even to become a senator should Oregon win statehood. Those ambitions weren't dead.

Had he imagined he could love her for a while and then simply leave her behind? He knew this unchivalrous behavior was also common among the mountain men. But the thought of cheapening his passion left him ashamed. He swore to himself that he was made of nobler stuff.

He gave a long sigh, realizing now what he had to do. This adventure was tempting him down a dangerous side road, far from his grander ambitions. He would have to put the girl out of his mind.

As he led his horse back down from the ridge, he wondered how emotions could have clouded his thinking for so long.

When he reached the meadow, Ned's spirits rebounded a bit at the sight of Charley's Indian pony tethered in front of his half-finished cabin. Here was the distraction he needed to take his thoughts off the girl. He galloped up to the fresh-cut log ends that marked the cabin's door opening and swung down from the saddle.

The big half-Indian looked up from the embers of Ned's morning fire. "*Klahowya*, Ned."

"So what brings you up here, Charley?"

"Joe wanted to check on the vaquero he hired." Charley's look was solemn. "He won't think you have built much in these two months."

The tone wasn't sharp, but it stung all the same. Ned sat in the window opening and looked out toward Mt. Shasta. Charley was right. Considering how little time it took to watch the horse herd he should have finished the log cabin long ago. He had even decided to build it with a wigwam-style smoke hole in the roof so he wouldn't have to stop to build a chimney. But how could he tell Charley about the longing that had tormented him? Joe would surely have no sympathy; he often said he would rather be kicked about by mules than by women. Ned frowned, thinking again how foolish his distraction seemed.

"Joe sent supplies," Charley said, nodding toward a leather pack beside the doorway.

"Did he?" Ned perked up. He had nearly run out of food. He opened the pack, but only saw pouches of gunpowder and bullets. "Where's the food?"

Charley shrugged. "He thought you'd get meat by hunting."

Ned dug deeper in the leather pack, hoping Joe had included at least a small sack of beans or flour. When he found one of Joe's flasks at the bottom, he gave a wry smile. The old mountain man obviously considered whiskey more important than flour. Ned uncorked the bottle and took a dizzying drink for the old-timer's sake. Whiskey, he thought, would probably be Joe's prescription for woman troubles, too.

He handed the bottle to Charley. "Take a drink?" The strict laws against giving liquor to Indians and half-breeds mattered nothing to him here.

Charley turned the bottle over thoughtfully in his big hands. "Spirits," he said quietly. "I wonder what the Puyshoos would say if I told them white men keep their spirits in bottles."

Ned almost smiled again, but a chill wind blew through the cabin's unchinked cracks, and he shivered.

"The Wintu tribes say the world is alive with spirits," Charley continued, almost to himself. "But they say we can only see their masks. Every coyote is just another mask for the spirit of Coyote himself, every raven a mask for the spirit Raven. Trees, rivers—everything hides spirits."

"Even Mt. Shasta," Ned suggested, recalling the legend Charley had told.

Charley shot him a scrutinizing glance. "Even the masks of Kusku." Then he looked into his hands. "The Puyshoos say the white man alone has no spirit. They say the things he makes are dead—the things he touches die."

"And what do you think?" Ned asked. "You're part white."

Charley was silent a long time. Finally he said, "My spirit doesn't live in either the red or white worlds. Still, I know the white world isn't dead."

"How can anyone know that?"

"You know it too, Ned. Today even I can feel your spirit struggling. I felt it ride all the way down from the ridge. I felt it cross the meadow." Charley gave Ned an unblinking gaze. "The Indian never needs to question who he is or why. He learns of the real world in the masked spirit dances. But the white men are lost in a dance where even the masks are wearing masks. I know—"

Charley paused and lowered his eyes. "I know nothing, really. But I think most white men live only in a world of masks, unaware of the powerful spirits beyond. It's just that you, Ned, are different."

Ned turned his gray-blue eyes to the mountain framed by the window. Charley's words rang through him like a bell. He *had* felt the pull of a spirit within him—hadn't it been the drive that had guided him all his life, even to this lonely mountain valley? Perhaps it really was beckoning him to choose one of the many masks before him to play his part in its mysterious dance. But he wanted more than to dance through life to an unseen musician's tune!

Charley drank from the bottle and handed it back. Ned set the flask on the only shelf he had yet built in the cabin, beside the three books he kept there. *The books.*

He ran his hand along the leather backs. If there was a spirit waiting for him, he thought, it spoke to him also in the words of poets. Even on the darkest days in the mines he had been able to find some bright scene in the two thin volumes of Browning and Byron—the only books he had taken from his father's bookshelf in Oregon. But why did the magnitude of the beauty in poems fall so far short of the glory he could feel radiating from Mt. Shasta?

Charley's voice came from behind, as if it were his own thought: "Most white men are afraid to learn the power of the world's spirits."

Ned's hand stopped on the third book—the ledger where he secretly worked on his own poems. Now he realized his goal must be greater even than to describe the mask of the spirit that had drawn him into the frontier.

He wanted to find and know the spirit itself. If he could do that, the world would be at his feet.

*   *   *

The next day Ned fried up the last of his flour as a small, doughy biscuit. He ate it hungrily and then sat by the cabin's empty window, trying to sketch Mt. Shasta in his poetry journal. It was the first entry he had made in a month. He frowned at the scratchy lines. The demon in the mountain obviously would not let itself be caught in a trap made of paper. His drawing looked like two mountains instead of one; the steep cone of Shastina, a butte high on Shasta's western shoulder, was somehow out of proportion. And now clouds were blowing in from the west to obscure the view. In frustration he tore out the page and threw it into the fire smoldering in the middle of the cabin floor.

As he watched the fire, the memory of the beautiful girl began creeping back unbidden, like the gnawing of his hunger. Ned paced the unfinished cabin, alarmed by the drift of his thoughts. The remedy, it seemed, was to keep his mind busy elsewhere.

He decided to hunt for a deer. Taking up his hat, rifle, and powder pouch, he ducked out the doorway. He jumped the creek and strode off quickly into the foothills toward the McCloud. He had long avoided hunting in that direction. The deer would have had time to collect there, imagining themselves safe.

Only after Ned was well on his way did he have second thoughts. A faint wind had sprung up behind him from the west, and he feared it might betray him by carrying his scent ahead.

Soon his suspicion proved correct. A doe bolted from a cluster of cottonwoods just out of range, lifting her nose toward Ned and trotting up toward the ridge indifferently.

"Damn!" Ned said. Still, it looked like a good deer, and she wasn't moving fast. He decided to follow, hoping she would stop at the bunch-grass just over the ridge.

Ned crested the windy summit in time to see a flash of the deer's black-tipped tail disappearing into the forest at the head of a gulch. *Damn it all!* But now that he had come so far, he wasn't going to turn back.

Now Ned began to hunt in earnest, creeping silently down toward the McCloud, sneaking ahead of the deer to try to cut her off. But each time he thought the deer would surely be in his sights, she bounded ahead over the dry brush and turned, just out of range, as if waiting for Ned to continue his pursuit.

By this time he was close to the McCloud itself, so he decided on a new strategy. Stealthily, he climbed to a rocky point overlooking the larger canyon. Here he crawled to the edge of the cliff and rested his rifle barrel on the rock, sighting in on the field below, where the creek he had been following entered the canyon. Anything coming out of the canyon would have to pass before his gun.

He did not have to wait long. The deer ventured out and stopped in full view, with her ears pricked toward a new sound.

But Ned's finger hesitated on the trigger. He had heard the sound as well: the clear tones of the Indian song that had been echoing in his memory all summer. Ned scarcely noticed when the deer bounded across the canyon, for walking along a narrow trail beneath him was the Indian girl, singing her enchanting melody while an older woman tapped the rhythm against a basket.

Lithe and graceful as the deer he had hunted, the girl dipped in mid-song to catch up some pine cones alongside the trail and drop them into a basket on her hip. Then she tossed a cone toward the woman's basket, missed, and flashed a smile framed by long, black braids.

"Paquita!" the woman chided as they walked out of sight down the canyon.

Ned closed his eyes to hold the vision fast. She was even more beautiful, more alluring than he remembered.

Ned covered his face with his hands. The old doubts and arguments flew past him like night birds: the bonds to his family in Oregon, his dreams of fame and fortune.

Then he opened his eyes again. A conviction was growing within him, like a wind gathering to a storm. He felt it lift him above the wild canyons, bracing him with the power to bridge worlds. On the frontier, the path to greatness was never straight, nor well traveled.

Had he ever really tried to escape the girl's dark spell? Wasn't she the one he had been hunting after all?

Chapter 3

An Indian summer-time it was, long past,
. . . and God had cast
Us heaven's stillness.
                    —Joaquin Miller

In the lingering Indian summer of that year, dogwoods and maples speckled the forests about Now-ow-wa with their crimson fire. Black bears grew fat and lazy eating huckleberries in the high meadows. It was a season when all of nature seemed to be holding its breath in anticipation of the winter storms to come.

Ned drove the horses back down to Soda Springs with his emotions and plans still in turmoil. He arrived just ahead of Charley, who swung down from his Indian pony and told Joe, "I've just been to the Puyshoos' village."

Ned raised his eyebrows. "You have?"

Charley continued to the old mountain man, "The chief wants to meet with you during the tribe's autumn festival tomorrow. Worrotatot didn't say what he wants to talk about, but it must be serious. They rarely have whites at the festival."

"Fair 'nough. Sounds right neighborly of him," Mountain Joe replied.

The news left Ned uncertain, but his voice spoke out with surprising conviction, as if with a will of its own. "Could I come with you?"

Charley cast him such a penetrating and inquisitive look that Ned distractedly began rubbing a spot on his sleeve.

"I suppose you could come. You have also been their neighbor."

                              * * *

Ned didn't know what to expect from the autumn festival, but in the morning he took care to look his best. He polished his tall black boots, put on a clean cream-colored shirt thas was open at the collar, and combed the blond locks that now fell nearly to his shoulders. Charley, too, brushed down his buckskins and plucked the few whiskers growing on his big, square chin. In Indian fashion he scorned a razor and instead used two small, flat rocks as tweezers to pull out the hairs. Only Mountain Joe made no noticeable preparations, other than to slip a flask of whiskey into his saddlebag.

On the way they stopped at Now-ow-wa to unpack the flour, beans, and other supplies Ned had insisted on tying to the backs of their saddles. "Beats me what the hell you're goin' to do up here all winter," Mountain Joe muttered and rode his horse ahead, splashing across the creek.

Ned knew how little Mountain Joe concerned himself with women. Instead, he fell back beside Charley, who would have to translate for him if he ever hoped to meet the Indian girl.

"Charley?" he asked.

"Yes?"

Ned cleared his throat. "Have you ever heard of a Wintu name that sounds like 'Paquita?'"

"It's the name of my mother's niece. How do you know it?"

Ned told him about the deer he had hunted toward the McCloud River, and of the woman he had overheard talking to a dark-eyed girl—the same girl they had seen earlier digging camas. When he finished, Charley looked at him evenly.

"So that's why you're staying at Now-ow-wa."

A part of him still wanted to deny it. But it wasn't the part that controlled his voice. "Yes, it is."

"As far as I know Paquita isn't married—that's lucky for you. On the other hand, she's one of Chief Worrotatot's granddaughters."

"Then it will be difficult to see her?"

"Not that. But she'll be expensive."

"Expensive! Can a chief's granddaughter be bought?"

"You certainly can't get her for nothing. I imagine Worrotatot himself would have to set the price. It'd be best to wait until the end of the festival to discuss it with him, though."

Ned's head reeled. He had only wanted to meet the girl, and now suddenly Charley was suggesting she be bought. Indian courtship did not rely on romance as much as he had expected. The whole business seemed too quick—too callous. "Honestly, Charley. The girl's only seen me once in her whole life. What if she doesn't want to be sold?"

The horses reentered the pine forest and Charley pushed a branch aside. "That would be her concern, not yours. My mother Ahatnika told me she didn't want to be sold to McCloud at first. Later, she learned to like the ways of the whites so much she wanted to raise me like one. If

Worrotatot had listened to her at first, she wouldn't have been happy later. It works best for the Wintu when men decide these things. How would a woman be able to bargain for a good price? How would a woman know when a man could afford a second wife?"

"You mean a man can buy all the wives he wants if he has enough money?"

"Not quite. The Puyshoos trade more freely with some tribes than others. Also, a man won't sell a daughter to someone he believes is unworthy. That's why I suggest you wait until the end of the festival. After the feast will come the competitions. If you can do well then, the chances are greater that Worrotatot will bargain reasonably."

"Competitions?" Ned said. "What kind of competitions?"

Charley only replied, "You will see."

* * *

A couple of half-wild Indian dogs raced up, snarling at the three riders before they had even come in sight of the village. A word from Charley, however, sent the dogs retreating with their ears back. When the horses reached the rimrock overlooking the river, Ned's heart beat faster. Below, within a silvery bend of the stream, stood a cluster of about thirty dome-shaped bark-and-mat huts.

"Is that all the bigger it is?" Ned asked. In his imagination, the village had loomed much larger.

"Each family only needs one *cawel*," Charley said.

To Ned the cluster of huts seemed a natural part of the river scene, as if the village had grown there on its own. The thought brought a different question to mind. "Charley, what does the tribe use for bargaining? Not gold, I suppose."

"No, not gold."

"Then what? Wampum?"

"Whatever they need." Charley shrugged and turned his attention to the trail, leaving Ned to wonder just what kind of price he might be asked to pay—if he were allowed to bargain at all.

The horses picked their way down through a break in the cliffs and clopped toward a dusty open area in the middle of the village. Ned craned his neck, hoping to spot Paquita, but couldn't see any girls her age. Ahead, several sharp-voiced old women were hurriedly driving a band of naked, wide-eyed children into a large central *cawel*. Finally the only tribespeople left in sight were a group of men, headed by a single old Indian. The old man was short and powerfully built, with shoulder-length black hair and a wrinkled face. He wore a mountain lion skin over his shoulders. Unlike any Indian Ned had ever seen, he had a thin black beard on the end of his chin.

Charley spoke in his Indian tongue with the old man. Then he announced, "This is Worrotatot, chief of the Puyshoos. He thanks you for accepting his invitation, and offers you places at the feast."

"Tell the chief me an' Ned are honored to share his grub as friends—an' to parley with him if he ever gits 'round to that too," Mountain Joe said.

When Charley translated this, the bearded chief seemed satisfied. Ned and Joe gave their horses to a waiting man and followed the chief to a large circle of stones. There the chief sat cross-legged on the ground. Mountain Joe squatted on his springy legs. Ned tried twice to fold his long legs like the chief's, knowing he should make a good impression on Paquita's grandfather, but finally had to settle for pulling his knees up in front of him.

The men of the tribe joined them in a large ring on the ground. The group ranged from naked boys of ten or twelve to withered, white-haired men. Most wore only frayed strips of blankets like narrow skirts around their waists. Several had tight-fitting brimless basketwork caps to keep their shaggy black hair in order.

Ned whispered to Charley, "Where are the women?"

"Preparing the food," Charley replied. "They'll eat in the *cawels* with the children when we're done."

Ned's face showed his disappointment. He had come to the festival to see Paquita. "It's awful quiet for a festival. Not much laughing and dancing."

"The dancing comes later. And as for laughing, everyone here is old enough they don't have to show pleasure with laughter." Charley tilted his head toward five old women approaching with heavy baskets. "The chief's wives. Remember, Ned, accepting food is a sign of respect among the Puyshoos."

The women, adorned with strings of beads and shells, walked around the ring, tipping their baskets to offer food to each of the men. The Indian men began eating as soon as their hands were full, grunting approvingly. A hunchbacked old woman held one of the thickly-woven baskets in front of Ned. Inside were a pile of white patties about the size of hands. Smiling, he took one and nodded. It had a texture like dried mush and was flecked with pieces of ash, but smelled somewhat like mashed potatoes. He saw Mountain Joe take a patty and bite into it hungrily.

"What is this?" Ned asked him.

"Camas cake, Ned. Fella gets to miss this stuff. Hell of a kind of grub to make without a squaw. Damn roots grow a foot and a half down, and you gotta bake 'em three days in a fire pit. I was stakin' the trip on gettin' some of this, I reckon."

Ned took a wary bite, and was just deciding it was rather starchy and bland, when another woman came by. This time he recognized the basket's contents as dried fish—apparently sun-dried, with a dizzying smell that made him suspect it had rotted first. He took the smallest piece and set it beside him casually. However, a scrawny man across from him gave him a puzzled look, and held up a slab of the odoriferous fish, patting his stomach heartily. Ned flushed, remembering how important it was to show respect for the tribe's food. He smiled, patted his stomach, and looked in desperation toward the next food basket.

The next basket held some little fruitcake-like loaves. They smelled delicious. To make up for his hesitation with the other foods, Ned tried a large mouthful. It was crunchy, with a wonderful nutty flavor he couldn't place.

"Charley, this is really good," he said.

"Yes, isn't it? Acorn bread with dried grasshoppers."

The bite stuck in Ned's throat. With a weak smile he laid the loaf next to the dried fish. For a moment he debated what to do with the grasshopper parts still in his mouth. There was no polite way to spit them out. If he wanted to win Paquita, he could not insult the tribe. Clenching his hands about his knees, he forced the insects down.

Just when Ned was beginning to despair of finding enough to eat, the baskets of huckleberries and jerked elk meat came by, and he took handfuls of these familiar favorites. Then the women left the baskets in the middle of the ring and withdrew. Other than a few small boys who quickly finished the huckleberries, the men now seemed to be holding back, as if they were already anticipating some more important event.

Soon Worrotatot stood up and led the way to another small field near the river. This, Ned realized, would be the site of the afternoon's competitions—where he would be expected to prove himself to the tribe. Colored feathers fluttered from short poles staked in the grassy field.

Ned still hadn't seen Paquita. "Won't the women at least get to watch the competitions?" he asked Charley.

Charley waved the question away. "They're eating in the *cawels.*"

Three men, gaudily arrayed in masks and shell ornaments, began beating a deep, solemn rhythm on a log drum. The bearded chief raised his hands and spoke to the sky. Then, suddenly, the crowd of men erupted in shouts. They dashed into the field toward the poles and yanked them from the ground. The young warriors paired off, defiantly holding the poles crosswise between them. Everywhere they began a kind of one-on-one tug-of-war, straining and gritting their teeth until one or the other was thrown onto his back.

To Ned's embarrassment, he and Joe were left with the old men. These unathletic elders were lining up black and white sticks in the dust, as if for some tamer kind of game.

Mountain Joe guffawed, "Well, I'll be jiggered. These old guys play bones." The old mountain man fell to the game, which seemed to involve guessing the arrangement of several concealed sticks. Ned watched in frustration as the old men began betting in rapid, confusing play. He wanted to impress the tribe, but how?

Finally Charley returned from the tug-of-war competitions, accompanied by the same stern warrior Ned had seen guarding the camas gatherers that spring.

"Ned," Charley said, "This is Paquita's brother Akitot. He has asked to challenge you in the footrace."

Ned sized up the lean young man by Charley's side. He had an angular face with a stony expression, and a fire in his eyes that suggested this was no idle dare. But if Paquita's brother had hoped to discredit him, Ned thought, he had chosen the wrong challenge. Ned had always been a good runner and had longer legs than any man in the tribe.

"A footrace?" Ned smiled. "Tell him that's just what I need. Where should we run?"

"The race follows the river trail all the way around the village and returns to the race rock." Charley pointed to a stone among a cluster of young men. "Worrotatot will drop a feather to signal the start."

"I'll be ready," Ned smiled. He stripped off his shirt and warmed up by jogging in place. Several boys stopped to watch him, surprised perhaps by the whiteness of his pale chest. Ned made the most of the chance for an exhibition of high spirits, puffing out his chest and shaking down the muscles in his long legs. He enjoyed the thought that Paquita might be watching him as well, through the chinks of a *cawel* wall.

The dozen runners lined up, each backed by friends giving encouragement and making bets. Only Ned stood alone at the line. He smiled to Akitot, who answered with an earnest nod.

The tribe's black-bearded chief dropped his feather and the runners took off toward the trail.

Ned estimated the course would be about a mile, and since he didn't know the trail, he decided not to take advantage of his long stride to pull ahead right away. He felt sure he could pass the leaders when he chose. So he positioned himself behind Akitot, thumping loudly with each step of his tall boots while the other runners ran barefoot, and almost silently. The trail flashed by in a blur of willows, with the whitewater of the

McCloud keeping pace. Ned rounded the first bend taking deep, even breaths. When he thought the others would surely begin to slow down, however, they showed no sign of tiring.

Ned was also surprised that so many logs lay across the trail. He hurdled the first awkwardly and wrenched his knee with a small stab of pain. He tried to keep his pace, but Akitot was already out of sight up the trail, and several others sprang past him, light-footed as deer.

The final stretch across the peninsula was a tiring uphill climb. The last of the other runners passed him by without slackening pace at all. When at last the course turned downhill, Ned was too exhausted to stride out ahead as he had planned.

He arrived at the starting rock, panting and coughing, to find Akitot waiting with a faint smile on his lips. Although nothing was said, Ned felt the weight of humiliation as he stooped over to catch his breath. How was he going to impress the tribe if he finished last?

Then he had an idea. He waved Charley closer. "Tell me, Charley, does anyone in this tribe besides you know how to ride?"

"Of course. Many of the warriors have become good horsemen."

"I haven't seen their stock, though."

Charley hesitated. "The Puyshoos have only had horses for a few years, since they first bought them from the Achomawis on the Pit River. Unfortunately, the last winters have been hard for the tribe and the snows have been deep." His voice dropped. "The horses didn't survive."

Ned pressed on. "Then Akitot can ride?"

"Yes."

"If you'd loan Akitot your pony, I'd challenge him to run that same course again on horseback."

Charley nodded. "All right. I'll tell him of the challenge."

The race was quickly arranged. At Akitot's request, the horses were to be raced bareback. Charley's spotted pony and Ned's roan gelding were brought to the field and unsaddled. Ned grabbed the mane with his left hand and swung his booted leg over the gelding's tall back. "Ready when you are," he told Akitot.

Akitot mounted almost as swiftly and brought the pony up even with Ned. Then Worrotatot slowly raised his arm and let the feather drop.

"Hyah!" Ned cried, digging into the horse's flanks with his boot heels. The horse shook and bolted forward like a startled elk. This time Ned did not intend to trail Akitot at all. He had to win for Paquita. He pulled ahead and reached the river first. "Hyah!" he cried again, ducking the overhanging branches that whipped past like a gamut of willow switches. The hooves thundered around the bend in the river, leaving sparks and dust

for Akitot's pony, close behind.

Suddenly the first fallen log loomed ahead, broad as a barrel and waist high. Here the danger of falling would be great even with a saddle. Ned clutched the horse's neck and dug in again with his heels. The horse sprang, flew a silent second, and then landed with a jolt. But the horse broke stride while Ned was struggling to keep his balance. Akitot's pony leapt smoothly over the tree and took the lead.

"Damn!" Ned said, pulling up behind Akitot as the two again sped down the trail. Now he hoped Akitot would falter over the last two jumps, but the Indian rode low like a jockey, his black hair flying together with the pony's long mane. Finally, as they neared the hill that would take them back across the peninsula, Ned knew it was time to break for the lead. "Hyah!" he shouted. His powerful roan stretched its haunches in an uphill gallop that brought him almost up with Akitot. They crested the hill and pounded down the far side. Ahead, Ned could see Mountain Joe waving his hat. The tribe was scattering to make way. Ned put down his head and gave his horse one last kick. With a final effort, the horse closed Akitot's lead.

"*Ee-Haw!*" Mountain Joe hollered as the two pounded into the clearing side by side. "Now *them's* high doin's!" He caught the roan as soon as Ned slid off. The horse shivered, and Joe let it roll in the dust.

"Did I win?" Ned asked, still dazed.

"Don't reckon you lost, Ned. Call it a dead heat, myself. Sure kicked dust to beat hell, though."

Ned wiped his forehead and shook his head with disappointment. He had given the race his best try, and it had not been good enough. With a sigh he held out a hand to Akitot.

The Indian stiffened at the gesture, evidently unfamiliar with the concept of a handshake. Then he spoke rapidly in Wintu with a sharp, formal tone.

Charley translated. "Akitot congratulates you on your horsemanship. He says it is rare for a white. He also asks if you will join in the final competition of the day."

Ned looked at Akitot skeptically. Hadn't he been tested enough? "What's supposed to come next?"

"Archery."

"Archery?" It almost seemed to Ned that he had awakened some grudge that made Akitot determined to challenge him where no white man could be expected to surpass an Indian. Still it would not look good to decline. Wearily, he followed to the archery range, wishing that love could somehow grant him a miracle.

Most of the men were already wearing quivers over their shoulders and carrying three-foot-long, double-curved bows. The quivers were made from otter skins, complete with heads and tails, and sprouted bouquets of feathered arrow stocks. From the somber expressions of the men, Ned could tell this competition was the most important of all.

It also looked like the most difficult. The archers stood fifty paces from the target, a pine cone suspended from a branch by a long string. Before each shot, the cone was set swinging.

Young and old alike, every Indian male took his turn, arcing two obsidian-tipped arrows into the soft dirt bank behind the target. Many did not hit at all, and they received only a solemn silence. Those who managed to send the pine cone spinning won nods and a few spare words of praise.

Akitot, for his turn, hit the pine cone both times. His face betrayed neither pride nor pleasure, however, as he turned and handed the bow to Ned, adding a few words of Wintu. Ned looked to Charley for a translation.

Charley shrugged. "He said it is a good bow."

Ned shook his head and gave the bow back to Akitot. "Tell him I have a better one."

It was only a few paces to the rock where Ned's saddle and rifle had been left. He could feel the tribe watching with curiosity as he poured powder into the rifle barrel, added a cap and ball, and rammed it in place. Then, deliberately, he strode back to the archery range and leveled the long barrel at the distant pine cone.

The shot's blast shook the village like the thunder of an unexpected storm. When the smoke from Ned's rifle cleared, the men of the tribe saw that the pine cone had not merely been hit—it had been blown to dust.

* * *

It was evening before Ned finally caught sight of Paquita, among the dancers who stamped and sang their way about the fire. She wore egret feathers on her ankles. The white plumes curved up her slender legs nearly to her knees, shivering as her small brown feet traced the throbbing one-two drum beat. It was almost more than he could bear, watching her sway gracefully in her fringed deerskin.

By then, however, Ned realized his chances of winning her had grown maddeningly bleak. He may have weathered the challenge of the competitions, but what hope could there be after that afternoon's disastrous parley between Worrotatot and Mountain Joe?

The old chief had called them into his *cawel* shortly after the competitions. Charley had come as interpreter, and a very old man by the name of Witillahow, or "Quick Fox," had also been there, his narrow chest draped with necklaces of shells and blue feathers. For a long time they had sat silently about a fire, passing a small hardwood pipe of dried manzanita tobacco.

Finally the chief had spoken. "The salmon did not come again this year." He had paused to let the significance of this settle. "We wove the willow trap in the river narrows as always. When we didn't catch any fish, we asked our shaman why." The chief had nodded toward the old man with the necklaces and feathers.

Witillahow had spoken in a high, cracked voice. "I called upon my guardian spirit power, Blue Jay, to say what angered Salmon. He said there was an evil spirit far to the south. I asked our cousins the Narshoos about this, because they live in that direction. They said Blue Jay was right. They said the great river in Noorkan Charook, the valley to the south, runs thick with mud because of the white man."

Chief Worrotatot had then looked earnestly to Mountain Joe. "There were no fresh fish at the harvest festival. That is a bad sign. It means the tribe will be hungry this winter. When will the white man let the river run clear again?"

Mountain Joe had shaken his head sadly. "I wish to hell I could tell you. Reckon the miners'll keep sluicin' up dirt as long as there's color in their pans. Could be years."

When Charley had translated this, the two old Indians had seemed greatly disturbed. Worrotatot had run his hand over his thin black beard. "We could wait these years for the salmon to return if we had game. But you saw we had no fresh venison for the autumn festival either. In the lower valleys the white men have killed the herds of elk. Even on the mountain the deer are afraid of guns and won't come within an arrow's flight of our warriors. Last winter the tribe survived by slaughtering the horses. This winter we will have nothing."

At this point the chief had again paused—an uncomfortable pause for Ned, who had then understood the grim reason for the Puyshoos' lack of horses. He had also realized that his own hunting in Now-ow-wa had contributed to the tribe's appalling hardships.

Then the chief had turned to Mountain Joe. "The white man's guns are more powerful than our arrows. They could kill enough game to feed the tribe this winter. Where can we trade for these guns?"

Mountain Joe had wrinkled his brow and grunted. "Hell, Charley could've told you it ain't legal to sell an Injun firearms." He had coughed and spat out the entranceway of the *cawel* before adding, "Folks've gotten funny 'bout Injuns and guns since the Modoc troubles. Hell, I can't even hand Charley my rifle without some dunghead miner waggin' 'bout sheriffs and such. Seems folks nowadays're changin' ever'thing that used to be good enough. We're just lucky you ain't hauled off to the reservations like they was up in Oregon."

Again the chief had stroked his beard. "Then what the Achomawis to the east tell us about the moving of tribes is true. I believed them when they said there will also be hunger on the Pit River this winter, but I had doubted that the whites would want them to live with the canoe Indians by the ocean. This news unsettles my heart. When McCloud came to our tribe the whites were our friends. Now it seems that angry whites have come. Maybe they will go away again. I don't know. I don't even know why they are angry. I only know I must feed the tribe."

Mountain Joe had looked at the ground, blinking his eyes and shaking his head sadly. "Damn it all," he had muttered. "Reckon you know as much as anyone."

The discussion had ended inconclusively with that reply, Ned recalled. Worrotatot had asked them to stay for the remainder of the festival and Mountain Joe had grunted his acceptance, but Joe had been too restless after that to watch the Indian dance for long. He left several times to check on the horses, only to return with the smell of whiskey on his breath.

Ned watched the dancers and sighed. Then he felt a tap on his shoulder. It was Charley, motioning for him to follow. "Worrotatot has asked to speak with you alone."

"What for?"

"Buying a wife."

When Ned returned to the large *cawel* he was surprised to see Akitot sitting tensely beside the old chief at the fire. Again the tobacco pipe was passed. Even though Ned did not inhale the thick smoke, his head began to hum from its effect.

The chief began the conversation, with Charley as interpreter. "I'm told you want Paquita."

Ned nodded cautiously. Were these people intending to mock him? Would they attempt to punish him for contributing to their hardships? Or was there yet hope of winning Paquita?

The chief said, "You should deal with her father, but his spirit no longer wears a mask. Akitot, her brother, will deal for her instead."

Ned had not expected this. Of all the tribe, his rival in the competitions seemed the least likely to bargain. He turned to the short warrior, but saw no emotion in his hardened features.

"It's usual to set a price in blankets," Akitot said. "But we don't need blankets. We won't be cold this winter, we'll be hungry. We need the white man's guns. Paquita's price is three rifles like yours, with gunpowder, caps, and bullets to last the winter."

The bluntness of the offer stunned Ned. For a hundred dollars worth of guns and ammunition, the girl could be his wife. His heart raced crazily. Then he remembered: illegal guns. If he agreed, he would risk being caught and tried for selling arms to the Indians. Still, the tribe needed guns in order to feed itself in the coming winter. And one look at Akitot's cold stare told Ned that no other trade would convince the warrior to sell his sister to a white man.

For a heartbeat Ned hesitated at the brink of a decision he knew he could never take back. It was only an instant, yet it seemed the longest moment of his life. Finally, his voice low and dry, he said, "All right."

*   *   *

When the moon came up that night, Mountain Joe, Charley, and Ned saddled up for the ride home. As they passed the chief's long *cawel*, Ned caught a glimpse of Paquita, partly hidden in the entranceway, watching with one of her long black braids held to her lips. When Ned flashed a nervous smile her way, however, she disappeared into the shadows. By now she must know, Ned thought. Did her shyness mean she liked him, or that she mistrusted him? Or maybe that she feared him? And had she been told the price he had been asked to pay? The unanswered questions tormented him and left his stomach churning. But now there was only one way he could know.

"Joe?" Ned asked as they rode out of the village.

"Yup, Ned?"

"Do you think when we get back to Soda we could settle for my work this summer?"

"If you need the money, I reckon."

"Yes," Ned said. "I'll need it."

*   *   *

At the general merchandise store in Shasta City two days later, Ned handed the clerk a list. The man's eyebrows went up. "How old are you, son?"

"Twenty-two," Ned lied, squaring his shoulders to carry the extra years more easily.

"Well, this here's more firepower than a young guy like you can use, ain't it?"

Ned tried to make his voice sound resolute. "Me and my partners are wintering over back in the hills. We'll be doing a lot of hunting."

The man next to Ned at the counter chipped in with a booming voice, "Probably fighting Injuns, too." He was a big man with a white-streaked beard and big white eyes. "You keep it up, boy," he said, extending a hand for Ned to shake. "The name's Sam Lockhart, from over on Pit River. All us settlers are stocking up there, too."

Hesitantly Ned shook his hand. "You are?"

"Only way to be sure these days. Hell, the Army won't do nothing till the varmints are already on the warpath."

Lockhart's fierce white eyes turned to Ned, filling him with a flash of fear. It was an unnaturally probing stare, as if Lockhart already knew he was actually a gun runner, and was looking straight into his heart for proof.

As soon as the clerk returned with the rifles, Ned paid quickly, tied his purchases behind his saddle, and galloped out of town.

That night he slept by a chilly campfire, far from the main trails, in a forest haunted by the questioning calls of owls. He awoke with a start, long before dawn, in a cold sweat. He shivered, thinking of the guns, the tribe he hardly knew, and the wilderness he was entering, perhaps forever.

A coyote's yipping cry echoed across the valleys like distant laughter. A feathery mist began creeping through the forest, grayed by the coming day.

Ned blew into his cold hands, wondering if he was making a mistake after all, blinded by love. Marrying into a remote Indian tribe seemed more a recipe for obscurity than greatness. But when he thought of Paquita, and the spirit of beauty he had felt in Mt. Shasta, he knew he must go on.

* * *

The shadows were already lengthening the next day when Ned rode alone into the Puyshoos' village. This time the snarling Indian dogs followed him all the way down from the rimrock. Charley was not there to call them off—just as Charley would not be there to translate the words and moods of the people. Ned had tried to think of all the ways his bargain with the tribe could go wrong, and had given up when he had lost count. Now, as he rode past the strangely silent *cawels,* he began the frightening list again.

Ned stopped in the village's deserted central clearing, still accompanied by the barking dogs. He could feel the eyes of the Puyshoos watching him from all sides. The urge to turn around and gallop free swept over him with a chill, but he fought it back.

Finally Akitot stepped out from a cawel and took the reins without a word. Ned dismounted and untied the rifles nervously. Akitot inspected the guns with a surprisingly knowledgeable manner. Ned wondered where he had learned to handle firearms; the rest of the tribe seemed to know so little about them. At length Akitot nodded with satisfaction and carried the rifles into the chief's large cawel. Ned waited uneasily by his horse for a long time before Akitot reappeared in the entranceway, motioning for him to follow.

As Ned was about to step down into the hut, fear suddenly stopped him. What if this was an ambush? He had left his unloaded rifle on his horse. The Indian massacres he had heard about flashed pictures in his mind of war paint and tomahawks.

With his hand on the hilt of his bowie knife he stepped down into the cawel. Inside he was relieved to find the chief's wives busy preparing a meal nearly as large as the autumn festival's feast. Worrotatot and several other men were already sitting in a line on one side of the fire. Akitot led him to a mat in front of the baskets.

Ned sat down uncertainly. Worrotatot and the others wore stony expressions that betrayed nothing. Did they despise him for buying his way into their midst, or did they admire his courage? Glancing from face to face, Ned began to suspect the tribe was feeling a contradictory blend of both emotions. And why not? From one moment to the next he himself was lurching between fear and excitement. He recalled Charley explaining why adults did not laugh at Wintu celebrations. Celebrations, Charley had told him, were solemn because they marked transitions in the course of life. And inside, all of life's transitions contained as much loss as joy. Certainly this nervous gathering was charged with loss, joy, and much else besides.

The sweet, smoky aroma of jerked elk meat and dried huckleberries reminded Ned that he hadn't eaten all day. Still, he resisted the urge to eat from the baskets before him, waiting for a signal to begin. If he wanted to learn the tribe's ways, he would have to learn to follow their lead.

Soon a group of women and girls stepped down into the cawel, as lightly and cautiously as herons. They sat in a line opposite the men on the other side of the fire.

Ned's heart leapt when Paquita herself finally appeared in the entranceway, surrounded by the reddish light of the evening. She wore a fur headdress tipped with raven feathers. Smaller feathers adorned her ears. Her dress, fashioned from the white hide of an albino deer, twisted slightly as she stepped, accenting the curve from her bare knee to her hip. All the desire Ned had felt for her surged back in a rush. When she sat opposite him, he was dizzy with happiness. Now at last it seemed certain that the feast honored the two of them. Yet how strange, Ned thought, that this could be his wedding—a silent ritual in a wilderness hut!

"Paquita!" he dared to whisper.

She lowered her eyes as if she had not heard. Then, at a single word from Akitot, she began to offer food to the women on her right and left. With a start, Ned realized he should follow her example. He too began passing the baskets to his left and right. The men were soon consuming what seemed to be enormous amounts of food, even though Ned still had nothing. When the baskets finally returned Ned reached for a piece of meat. Akitot, however, caught his arm firmly. A stern shake of his head made it clear that Ned was not to eat at all. Ned was about to object when he noticed Paquita also was not eating. She sat with her hands in her lap, her mild eyes admonishing him to be patient.

When at last the frustrating meal was over, the women stood and lit pitch torches from the central fire. Then, singing in a high-pitched monotone, they danced Paquita out of the cawel into the dark. For a long time the men neither moved nor spoke. The women's song faded and vanished beneath the evening call of crickets.

The silence that followed left Ned afraid that he had mistaken the purpose of the ceremony after all. He wished he could talk with someone—to ask these people what they intended.

At length an old man raised himself on weak legs and lit a pitch torch. The other men soon followed his example. Then they began dancing around the fire, waving their torches and stamping their feet to a low chant: "Oh, ah, no, ah." Finally they took Ned by the shoulders. He let them guide him through the entranceway, hoping they would lead him to Paquita.

Outside, the air was crisp and the sky black. The chanting warriors surrounded Ned, slowly moving him away from the village and into the forest. The flickering torchlight on the pine trunks made the forest seem like a huge, pillared cavern with countless confusing side passageways.

Finally Ned spotted the glow of the women's torches, surrounding a cawel ahead in the trees. For a moment he was afraid Paquita was no longer among them. But when he neared the cawel, torchlight caught the white of her albino robe. She was seated cross-legged inside, as still as an Oriental ivory statue.

Ned's heart beat so hard he was afraid the others would hear it. His legs had gone weak.

Akitot took him by the shoulders and set him down on a fur robe beside her. Then, one by one, the men and women laid their torches in the middle of the dirt floor to build a cheering blaze. After that the dancers suddenly fell silent and disappeared into the forest.

Ned swallowed hard. He was so nervous he hardly dared to look at

Paquita. For the first time, he was alone with the girl he had dreamed about for so long. Even though he did not understand the details of the ceremony that had just been performed, he knew Paquita was now his bride.

He was married. And he knew he was in love. But he wondered what strange thoughts must be in her mind, a girl of perhaps sixteen who had never seen a carriage or a book—who was now alone in a cawel with a husband she could neither understand nor talk to.

Ned cleared his throat.

She looked at him, startled.

He pointed to her slowly, nodding and saying, "Paquita." Then he pointed to himself and said, "Miller."

Paquita hesitated. Then she shook her head. "Kibo," she said.

Perplexed, Ned pointed to himself again. "Kibo?" he asked.

She nodded.

So, Ned thought, apparently the Puyshoos already had their own name for him. If he was going to be married to one of their tribe, it seemed only reasonable. Somehow it was reassuring, too, to think she had already given him a Wintu name.

But now Paquita was looking down again. Ned decided it was time to try the only Wintu word he knew, the word he had asked Charley about the morning he had set out for Shasta City—the word for "love."

"Paquita?" he asked softly. She lifted her dark eyes. "Kibo *hinna* Paquita," he said.

Suddenly her eyes twinkled in the firelight and she broke into a shy smile—the same fleeting smile that had caught Ned's heart months before at Now-ow-wa. The smile now melted him again with a flood of joy. He put his arms to her, and sensing no resistance, pulled her to him in a gentle embrace that thrilled him with the soft pressure of her breast under the white dress.

Ned lifted her chin to kiss her full lips, but at this she pulled back with surprise. Didn't the Wintus know about kissing, Ned wondered? He puckered his lips again to show her what he intended. She gave him a quizzical look, and tried to imitate him with a little pouting expression that made Ned suppress a laugh. Then, while she still held her lips puckered, Ned swiftly kissed her on the mouth. This time her surprise hid behind a flustered smile.

Now Ned held up his hand seriously, as if to say he would show her how it really ought to be done. Holding her in his arms, he met her lips with a long and warm kiss that seemed to Ned to be the end of a long loneliness.

When he finally released her, she swayed a moment, catching her breath. Then she cast a searching glance up into Ned's gray-blue eyes. "Kibo *hinna* Paquita?" she asked.

Ned nodded. Nothing had ever been more true.

Paquita untied the leather thong at the front of her deerskin dress. With a wiggle of her shoulders the white leather slid loose to her waist, revealing a warmth of smooth brown skin Ned had never dreamed could be so rich and real. She had unveiled herself with such casual grace that Ned's breath stopped short.

Paquita gave him a curious look, as if to wonder that he had never seen a woman without clothes. And how could he admit it? A moment earlier he had been the guide, confidently demonstrating the art of the kiss.

With a small smile, Paquita lay back in the bearskin floor robe, her dark nipples tipping the firm roundness of her young breasts like an invitation to a warm land of peace and beauty.

Ned drew a tremulous breath, half afraid that he might do something to make this intoxicating dream vanish.

With a laugh she caught his hand and gave a gentle pull.

He lay down to meet her, glad for once to be led.

Chapter 4

We saw an elk . . . with lifted antlers stand . . .
A sturdy charging line with crooked sabers drawn.
—Joaquin Miller

The wild geese strung their ragged, honking V's past Mt. Shasta, following summer southwards for the third time since Ned had left Oregon. Beargrass plumes had lost their lilied blossoms, leaving the meadows posted with empty sword-like stalks. Chill winds scattered the puffs of mountain dandelions.

But this October melted in Ned's memory with a warm glow. The scenes were framed in the flush of young love—riding two to a horse across the divide to Now-ow-wa, a green Eden in the mountain's embrace; waking up warm and sleepy from the bear robes in the little log cabin to find the meadow sparkling with frost.

In the weeks that followed, Ned and Paquita were alone together, with time to learn each other's ways. Ned turned to a fresh page in his journal and began a dictionary of Wintu words, determined that he would learn Paquita's language. Paquita marveled at the way the quill marks could give paper such a perfect memory. Ned guessed she saw writing as a kind of sorcery unsuited for a Wintu woman, for she refused every offer to try the quill, even to draw a picture.

At first Paquita set about the business of preparing food on her own. She seemed surprised when Ned showed an interest in acquainting her with a different type of cookery. The cast-iron pot was clearly a curiosity. She watched as Ned filled it with dry beans and water. Then she took the pot, but instead of putting it on the fire, she set it on the dirt and began dropping hot rocks into it—after the Indian fashion of boiling water in watertight cooking baskets.

On some days Paquita would go on walks to gather pine nuts, acorns, or berries. She smiled with embarrassment when Ned went with her through the forests and meadows to help gather food she would like. Gradually, Ned even grew fond of the Indian dishes. Acorn bread was better, he thought, now that grasshoppers were out of season. Mashed pine nuts rivaled hazelnuts for flavor. And there was one incomparable dessert made from russet berries whipped into a pink froth almost like a kind of tart ice cream.

Once the snows came, however, the supply of fresh food all but stopped. The valley became a vast sea of white—smooth as an empty china bowl. Even deer became harder to hunt. Ned had cut no winter hay for his horse, and so was forced to take it down to the pastures at Soda Springs. The trek back to Now-ow-wa was a long, cold trudge through a land of deepening snow.

Then the weather turned sharply colder, until the surface of the snow crackled and sharp six-sided flakes materialized in the air. Puffing great clouds of steam, Ned sawed and chopped frozen firewood to stack under the cabin's eave. Inside, Paquita worked deerskins until they were soft, and sewed them into tall moccasins using laces of deer sinews.

The days quickly grew darker. Howling storms dumped foot after foot of powdery snow across the valley. Finally the snow lay six feet deep. Pines sagged with the weight, transformed to ranks of alabaster spires. The cabin's door and window peered up at the dark sky out of billowed drifts, like entrances to a marble cave. Only the cabin roof remained bare, steaming from the constant fire inside.

For Ned, the cabin seemed a world beyond time, where his happiness with Paquita made all futures possible. In the evenings he wrote poetry and smoked a pipe of kinnikinnick. At first he imagined the long winter hours would be a time he could teach Paquita the language and culture of the whites. But to his surprise, it was Paquita who did most of the teaching, sharing the skills and knowledge of the Wintu.

Ned studied the lists he had made of Wintu words and gradually became fluent enough that he and Paquita could talk about all manner of things. One evening she showed him how to make snowshoes from vine maple withes, tying them together with horsehair and wrapping them with buckskin.

Another evening, when the log walls shook from the force of the storms outside, Paquita insisted they sit by the fire and tell each other stories to take their minds off the dark of winter. She told him her favorite Wintu tales of Coyote, the trickster god. Often as not, the bungling Coyote of her stories would end up misplacing his eyeballs or eating his own tail by mistake, and Ned couldn't help but laugh. In turn, Ned invented his own tales of gold miners, gamblers, and vaqueros. She listened with wonder and bemusement, stopping him often to ask questions about the things he struggled to describe in Wintu. What was an elephant? Was it the same as a locomotive?

When she gave him a heart-melting smile at the end of a well-told tale, it seemed to Ned that the winds outside really did stand still. In those moments he realized how much the harshness of the winter had deepened their love, and how much he had grown to need her.

In the blackness of the early mornings he sometimes awoke to the deep rumble of avalanches resounding across the valley. He thought of Kusku, the stern spirit of the beautiful mountain, carelessly shrugging great glaciers and forests loose, and he held Paquita close.

*   *   *

The snow had settled to a three-foot pack and Ned reckoned that it was February when an Indian warrior snowshoed down to the log cabin, looking gaunt and cold. Although Ned did not recognize him, it had been so long since he had seen a visitor that he invited him in directly. If the man was surprised to hear Ned speak in heavily accented Wintu, he did not show it. He squatted by the fire, accepted some biscuits from Paquita, and washed them down hungrily with a tea Paquita had made from boiled lichens.

Only after he had finished the biscuits and lit a pipe was he ready to talk. "Kibo," he said to Ned, "the Puyshoos no longer have food."

"No food! But they have the guns."

"There are only three guns and a hundred empty bellies. The great-grandmothers have stopped eating." The man cast a solemn glance full of meaning to Paquita, then back to Ned. "Worrotatot has called the warriors to join in one last great elk hunt before our strength is gone. The hunt must begin soon or the cold rains will come, making the snow too weak for travel. Worrotatot asks if you will bring your gun."

Without hesitation Ned reached for his buckskin coat and rifle. "Of course we'll come." He could not sit by while the tribe starved. A moment later, however, he began to reconsider. Paquita's people had always acted so guardedly toward him. Now they only wanted his gun. His return to the village would be yet another test. But it was a test he could not avoid.

In five minutes Ned and the warrior were outside with their snow-shoes on. As Paquita was about to close the door, Ned stopped her. "Wait. Go back and bring me that last sack of flour. The Puyshoos will need it more than we do." She obeyed, reappearing a moment later with the fifty-pound sack in a woven burden basket on her back. The pack's forehead strap strained against her brow. She fastened on her snowshoes but still sank into the snow as she climbed up from the door.

To Ned's surprise, she did not stop for him to take the load, but trudged past him, following the track eastward. Ned caught up with her. "I'll carry the flour," he said.

But Paquita continued on. "It would disgrace me before the tribe if my husband had to wear a burden basket. They would think you married a weak and worthless wife."

For three steep, uphill miles through the heavy snow Ned watched the small young woman struggle bravely onward with a strength he had never known she possessed. Finally he could bear the sight no longer and hefted the flour sack to his shoulder, returning it to Paquita only when they came within view of the village.

* * *

In Worrotatot's long cawel Ned found the warriors of the tribe busy preparing for the hunt. Several men were using antler tips to chip obsidian into large hunting arrowheads. They held the glassy rock firmly against pieces of thick leather on their thighs as they worked. Other men stood near the fire, steaming branches and running them through grooved stones to make arrow shafts that were straight and free of kinks. Akitot was helping a young warrior apply deer sinews to the back of his finely curved yew bow. Ned listened carefully to the men's low voices, straining to understand the Wintu words. Now he realized how slowly and carefully Paquita spoke for his sake. These men obviously did not care for him to know what they said.

"I see you have learned to follow the Wintu tongue," Worrotatot said beside him.

Ned turned with surprise to the bearded chief; he had not heard him approach. "Yes, a little."

"It must be hard to learn. Few white men are able."

Ned shook his head. "Actually, it is not very hard. The Wintu do not use many words."

"It doesn't take many words to tell the truth."

This wasn't what Ned had meant. He tried to explain. "The white men often have ten words for your one."

"Yes," the chief replied with solemn significance. "The white men need them."

* * *

In the morning a cold rain pelted the *cawels* from a low, dull sky. The elk hunt had to be postponed. Sullen women divided the flour and baked it into hard biscuits on hot rocks. The following morning the rain continued unabated, packing the snow down even further. The warriors spoke darkly of possible causes. They pointedly left Ned behind that evening when they went to the sweat house to purify their spirits.

At first Ned was angered by this exclusion—as if he could have brought on the bad weather. But when he saw the purification rite he was not sorry to have missed it. The sweat house was a two-foot-tall, grave-like tunnel, visible only as a slight mound under the snow. The warriors crawled in through small square openings at either end and built a smoky fire inside. When they finally crawled back out their naked bodies were streaming with sweat and ashes. Then they marched through the snow to the river and plunged into the icy current before returning to the village to put on their clothes.

No one spoke during the purification ordeal, and even Paquita was curt with Ned that night. "The tribe is starving," she said simply. "They must do what they can."

On the third day, when rain still lashed the hungry camp, the chief called for Witillahow, the shaman. This time Paquita brought word that Ned was to join the men in the chief's *cawel* for the ceremony.

"Does that mean they're finally going to trust me?" Ned asked. He wondered bitterly if anyone had ever had such difficult in-laws.

She tilted her head with a tentative nod. "Now that they suspect you are not the one who angered the spirits, they are looking elsewhere. Please, help them."

Ned was at the chief's *cawel* when Witillahow arrived. Ned was taken aback to see the old shaman's naked, loose-skinned body. His bony frame was decorated with jagged stripes of paint and a wealth of jangling bracelets and necklaces. He carried a coyote skull rattle and wore a heavy beaked mask over his head. The mask had been carved into a horrific black grimace, and was surrounded by blue jay feathers. Together with two other heavily painted men, Witillahow raised his hands before the fire a long time. Then, slowly, they began to chant.

A pipe was passed around the ring of watching men as Witillahow started to dance, lifting his bony feet cautiously. Soon the chant spread among the men and grew louder. Even Ned joined in, caught up in the dance's hypnotic rhythm. Gradually the shaman and his helpers danced more and more wildly about the fire. They stamped their feet faster and harder until at last Witillahow was pounding the ground with a fury that seemed impossible for such an old man. Ned stamped and chanted his encouragement along with others, sharing in the tribe's release of anger at the rain.

Then suddenly Witillahow stopped. He loosed an unearthly scream toward the roof, put his hand into the gaping beak of the mask, and withdrew a live green frog that he apparently had been keeping all this time inside his mouth. "You!" he shouted. "You have called the clouds!" With a single motion he skewered the frog on a sharp stick and stabbed it into the fire. Then he resumed the dance with a redoubled frenzy, furiously gesticulating and thrashing the air. He writhed on the ground and gnashed his teeth until he spat blood at the watching men. Ned was swept up in the spectacle, the need of the tribe throbbing through him like a heartbeat. While that rhythm drummed it seemed there were no individuals—only one great tribal animal that was starving and raging and scared.

When the old shaman finally collapsed, unconscious, the helpers had to carry his frail body away.

* * *

In the morning the rain had stopped. The wet snow had frozen so hard overnight that it could bear weight. Ned walked out on the newly crusted snow and studied the broken, retreating clouds, wondering if Witillahow's frantic display really could have stirred the spirit world. The old shaman had focused the tribe's energy into a single cry for help. Perhaps even the gods beyond the sky had heard that desperate shout.

The sun had scarcely streaked the clouds when the fifteen warriors chosen for the elk hunt began assembling in the village. Ned joined them, and they promptly set out in single file, their snowshoes hanging over their shoulders. Worrotatot led off northwards along the McCloud River. Akitot and the two other warriors with rifles followed directly behind the chief.

After several miles of rapid walking on the crusted snow Worrotatot announced, "We'll cross here." Ned had to hide his skepticism, for the McCloud was thirty yards wide and quite swift at this point—certainly not fordable at any season, much less after a February rain. Nonetheless, the chief led them to a jam of drift logs that had piled up in the current. After an hour of climbing and crawling through icy water on mostly submerged logs, the crossing was accomplished.

On the far side they found elk sign—both inch-long pellet-like droppings, and saplings that had been rubbed or chewed barkless. Hooves had packed a narrow trail that wound up the canyon like a sled run.

"It has been a week," Akitot said sullenly, turning a pellet with his moccasin. "The rain let them escape."

Ned's heart sank at this news. The other men were far hungrier than he, and starving men could hardly hope to close a week's lead on a herd of elk. He shivered, his feet numb from the river crossing. He wished he could give his gun to one of the others and turn back to warm himself by Paquita's fire. But he knew he couldn't abandon the hunters, no matter how hopeless their cause. He looked at the cold, swift river, and was glad the horrible crossing lay behind him, a barrier to retreat.

Worrotatot surveyed the faces of the men, as if he too sensed their discouragement. "There is no honor in dying in a *cawel,*" he said curtly. Then he turned and led the way up the elk track at a faster pace than ever.

By nightfall they had reached the upper falls of the McCloud, where the white river roars over a basalt cliff, pounding itself into mist in a green pool below. Here the old chief called a halt. The men took refuge under the snowy boughs of several spreading fir trees for the night. Ned unpacked his biscuits, only to discover that no one else had brought provisions. After he had shared, there was just enough to leave him feeling hungrier than ever.

In the night the cold was intense. A fire was out of the question; the smoke would cause the tree to dump its load of snow onto the small dry patch of snowless ground where they sat. The Indian men huddled together in the animal skins they had worn and were soon asleep. Ned, however, was too cold to sleep. He shivered through the interminable hours of the night, moving his toes to keep them from freezing, and counting the tortured minutes until he lost track of numbers. His mind raced backward to confront him with astonishingly vivid memories from what seemed like former lives—watching his rosy-cheeked mother standing up from the hearth with a steaming roast chicken for the Sunday table; cutting sheaves of wheat with his brother John on a scorched August afternoon.

When the black clouds turned dark gray, Ned wondered if he had dreamed after all. He stretched his stiff muscles by walking quickly up and down through the light layer of new snow. Most of the other men went to the river as soon as they awoke. There they broke the ice around the waterfall's misty pool and swam briefly before putting on their clothes.

The hunt resumed without food. The elk trail turned away from the river, following a creek that Worrotatot said would lead to high meadows and springs. Now the elk sign became much fresher. The Indians again increased their pace at this encouragement, and Ned fell behind. The cold stabbed through his wet buckskin clothes as he walked, making each step an agony. Thick flakes of snow began to drift down from the low sky. He blinked the snow from his eyes and struggled on, afraid he might lose sight of the hunters marching rapidly through the deep snow ahead.

Finally, at the lip of a high valley, the chief called a hasty council. Ned staggered up to join them, out of breath.

Akitot said, "The elk must be weak from winter. They are very close."

"But we are also weak, and the snow is giving way," another man countered.

Worrotatot spoke. "We will put on snowshoes. At my signal everyone will rush forward at once."

Silently the men tied on their snowshoes and spread out through the forest. In his exhaustion, Ned stumbled over a log and sprawled into the deep snow. He pulled himself back onto his feet, gritting his teeth against the numbing cold. Then he braced himself against a tree, knowing he must summon a last reserve of energy for this final chase.

When the old chief lowered his arm, Ned and the others charged forward into a meadow. Their snowshoes thumped softly as they kicked up the snow in a long line. Far across the snowy plain were the dark shapes of the herd, obscured at times by the rising steam of hot springs along the base of a ridge. Long before the hunters were within range, a bull elk with a rack of antlers like a rocking chair threw back his dark muzzle and sounded a long, whistling blast. When the men were still only halfway across the meadow the herd was on its feet, scattering into the brisket-deep snow in great fourteen-foot leaps.

The desperate hunters rushed on. At a hundred yards Worrotatot's arrow silently arced into the shoulder of a fat cow. Instantly the rifles cracked and a hail of arrows descended on the retreating herd. Ned had been too exhausted to aim well. He reloaded and took a second shot, but it only broke the leg of a young elk that already carried an arrow in its back. By the time he could reload again, the herd had bounded out of sight over the ridge. One bull, however, stopped at the top for a defiant look back. Ned fell to his knee to steady the barrel, knowing this was his last chance to hit his mark.

The rifle boomed. The great bull elk dropped. Slowly, limply, its dark brown body slid down the steep slope, leaving a thin red streak to the rockpile where it finally came to rest.

Wearily Ned let his gun barrel droop to the snow. He looked to the others, wondering if now, after all the deprivations he had shared with the tribe, they might accept him. He had been with them to the brink of death. Perhaps now he might win a word of praise.

The old chief nodded. "You are right, Kibo. It is a good bow."

* * *

In all, twelve elk had been slain, weighing six hundred to a thousand pounds each. Worrotatot announced that the entire tribe would spend the next three days with the business of preparing meat. Two of the men went to bring the women from the village while Ned and the others made a temporary camp by the welcome warmth of the hot springs.

By the first night the hunters had already quartered the animals and hung them from trees. They built fires to roast the elks' hearts and livers for a spirited feast in celebration of the successful hunt and the assurance of the tribe's survival. Long into the night the warriors took turns standing before the campfire to retell legends, history, and tales of adventure from other hunts. Even Ned took his turn, practiced from the evenings he had told stories to Paquita, For once it seemed he was almost one of the tribe.

Shaggy coyotes, their eyes gleaming just beyond the ring of firelight, came as if to listen to the tales, only to howl in long yipping cadences when they discovered that the tallow was safely heaped near the fires and the meat hung out of reach.

On the second day the women arrived. They turned the elks' intestines inside out, rinsed them in the hot springs, and stuffed them with cuts of tenderloin. Paquita roasted one of these long wilderness sausages for Ned, who pronounced it more flavorful and juicy than any meat he had ever tasted.

By the third day the carcasses had been so carefully stripped that the bones were left for the wolves and coyotes. The women packed the piles of meat into their burden baskets for the trek back to the McCloud. There was a satisfied look in their faces as they hefted the packs. Ned felt good that he had been on the hunt to help feed Paquita's people. He had been as one of them.

But then everyone stopped.

A lone figure was approaching on snowshoes from the east. It was an Indian man, not of the Puyshoos tribe. He wore a green woolen coat and a beaded headband with a single black feather.

At once a group of Puyshoos warriors hurried across the plain to meet with the strange Indian, exchanging quick words in solemn tones.

"Who is he?" Ned asked as he neared the group.

Worrotatot motioned him away with a frown. "Go back with the others."

Ned folded his arms defiantly, neither retreating nor coming closer. From where he stood, the words he could overhear seemed to be in a language he could not understand. The conversation grew surprisingly heated and was punctuated with unsettling glances toward Ned and the women. Finally Akitot took a black feather from the stranger, and, without a single word of farewell, left with him across the fields towards the east. Then the Puyshoos men returned to the women as if the mysterious visitor had never appeared.

"What did the man want?" Ned asked Worrotatot. The old chief only shook his head as he passed.

Ned asked Paquita, "Where is your brother going?"

She shrugged and lifted her load for the trip.

"Don't you care what happens to Akitot?"

"Yes, I do," she replied. But she would say no more, and remained strangely silent during the long march back to the village.

Ned was left with the disturbing memory of the Indian's ominous final glance—at him, a white man among the Puyshoos.

Chapter 5

Above I have heard is where they will go,
The ghosts of the people rhythmically swaying,
Above I have heard is where they will go,
Rhythmically waving dandelion puffs,
The ghosts of the people rhythmically swaying.
                                        —19th century Wintu song

A week after the elk hunt, Ned hiked over the pass to Soda Springs to restock his supply of flour. By then the spring thaw was well underway. Down in the Sacramento canyon the river was brimming with snowmelt.

Mountain Joe gave a start when Ned's long-haired head peered in the door of the log cabin.

"Didn't mean to surprise you," Ned said.

"Didn't mean to be surprised. You jus' looked like a ghost I knew."

Ned smiled. "Not Joaquin Murietta's again?"

"Nope. Ned Miller's. We figgered you'd be one gone beaver by now." Joe's earnest tone made Ned's smile evaporate.

"How's that?"

Joe grunted. "Well, I'll be damned. Whole state's bustin' out their rifles an' you stand there like you ain't heard."

"Heard what?" What's happened?"

"Seems the Injuns up an' massacred all the settlers over on the Pit River."

"But I was just hunting elk with the Puyshoos less than fifteen miles from there."

Joe's bushy eyebrows rose up under his hat. He cast a glance to Charley by the fire.

The half-Indian looked up hopefully. "Perhaps they weren't involved with the Achomawis after all."

"Reckon them settlers are dead 'nough, though," Mountain Joe said.

"Fifty-sixty of 'em. All but Jed Sims an' Sam Lockhart—they say they was out cuttin' wood when it started."

"How long ago was this?"

"Three-four days now since Lockhart an' Sims made it to Yreka, half froze an' 'bout starved to death. From what they say they must've gone right by your winter camp. That's why I reckoned the Injuns'd cleaned you out. Anyways, Sims is roundin' up a comp'ny of volunteers. He'll head back there pronto with blood in his eye."

Ned was staggered. The strange Indian he had seen after the elk hunt must have been bringing word of the massacre. Had the tribe debated murdering him as well? How could Paquita have known and said nothing? The thought brought up a flurry of conflicting emotions. At first his love for Paquita and his trust of the tribe rose up like a proud defensive wall. But then he felt a frightening flutter of doubt, recalling the times he had been surprised by the Puyshoos' silent ways. Could they have helped the Achomawis slaughter the Pit River settlers? "Still, Joe, it's hard to believe—"

"Have to, Ned, if you listen to Lockhart."

Suddenly Ned thought: Lockhart. That was the name of the fanatic Indian hater he had met while buying guns in Shasta City. Such a man might have exaggerated his report—maybe fabricated the whole thing—to create an excuse for a retaliatory strike. And once the volunteers were on their way they would attack any Indians they met, innocent or not. Paquita's tribe might be driven to war before the facts were known.

"Has anyone actually gone to take a look at Pit River since Lockhart was there?" Ned asked.

"Don't reckon. Sounds like a good place to steer clear of to me."

"Then I'll have to go myself."

"To the Pit River?" Joe made chewing motions while he studied Ned with his small eyes. "Sometimes, Ned, you git me out an' out buffaloed. Why in the Sam Hill would you want to do a fool thing like that?"

"Until I find out what's really happened and who's responsible, it won't be safe at Now-ow-wa. It shouldn't be too hard to look things over without being seen. I know the country as far as the headwaters of the McCloud and there's enough timber to hide out in."

Charley stood up. "I'll go with you. I too want to be sure the Puyshoos were not involved."

Joe pulled off his big hat and scratched his shaggy head. "Well, hell. You two've got as much sense as a coupla locoed mules. Who'd want to run out between a pack of wild Injuns an' a comp'ny of volunteers? Just beats me which side would git your scalps first."

Ned stood firm. "I'm still going."

Joe chewed some more and looked to Charley.

The big man lowered his gaze. "It is my mother's tribe."

Joe blew out a long breath. Then he frowned out the window. Finally he took down the octagonal-barreled hunting rifle over the mantle, and handed it gruffly to Charley. "Here. You'll need this."

*   *   *

Early the next morning Ned and Charley set out on foot, knowing that horses would make stealth impossible. The patchy snow was still crusted from the night's chill, allowing them to set a fast pace.

"The Puyshoos do not need to know of this," Charley said, with a glance to Ned.

Ned nodded. They would avoid the Puyshoos' village. The days since the elk hunt had been strangely unsettled there. Many warriors had come and gone; Paquita had been ill, from the sudden diet of meat, she claimed. He wanted to think that there had been no massacre at all, that the Puyshoos were blameless—but what if he was wrong?

They crossed the McCloud on a logjam well south of the village and headed for the ridgecrest of the foothills. There the deeper snow would slow them, but they would not be seen.

By the time the sun had swung behind them to a perch atop the distant peaks of the Klamath Mountains, they had covered more than twenty miles. Ned's legs ached from the pace of their trek. His tall moccasins were soaked from the thawing snow. Everywhere the spring sun had coaxed drips and rivulets from the heavy snowpack.

At last they stood on the eastern end of a long ridge. From there the sun's last rays projected shadows in a red pall across a vast valley Ned had never seen before—a wrinkled plain of sagebrush and juniper that stretched towards the forbidding lava flats, cinder cones, and playas of the desert beyond. This eastern slope of the mountains was clearly a much drier world, cut off from the Pacific's storms. Greenish, snake-like shadows on the arid plain marked the courses of the Pit River and its tributaries, Fall River and Bear Creek.

"I reckon what we're looking for is out there," Ned said. "But where?"

"There are only a few ranches." Charley pointed to a canyon that seemed to be at their feet. "Bear Creek was the Achomawi summer camp. The whites had kept them from it for years. Perhaps there."

Ned looked into the canyon with misgivings. For an instant the dark gulch reminded him of a snake pit, exuding danger and warning. "Should we camp here or go down tonight?"

They exchanged a glance. Charley's eyes said what Ned already knew:

that time was not on their side. Without another word, they set off down the hill.

The canyon that had seemed so close proved to be much farther than they had thought. Night fell quickly about them, but a cold, gibbous moon appeared, casting a ghostly light through the sparse forest. They slid most of the way down the hill's snowy north face before reaching patches of bare ground.

After several hours Charley held up his hand. "I can't go on without rest."

"You reckon it's safe to build a campfire this close to the Achomawis?"

"No. We shouldn't camp. It's best to travel at night."

Without further explanation, Charley sat cross-legged, rubbing his feet and rocking gently while he sang a low, wordless song.

"Charley?" Ned asked. When he received no response, Ned leaned against a tree trunk to wait out whatever ritual Charley had undertaken. In the meantime Ned's aching muscles began to shiver violently. His wearied mind circled fitfully toward dreams. He thought of Paquita, warm in their bearskin bed. He wished he were safe beside her again, out of this cold forest of unseen terrors.

After half an hour Charley looked up. "I am ready now."

With this announcement they started again, By then Ned's wet moccasins and buckskin pant legs had frozen stiff in the night air, and chafed his legs at every step.

They reached the bend of a small river as dawn was streaking the sky with trails of blood-red clouds. "Bear Creek," Charley said.

"This is no place to stop," Ned said. Though he had hiked through the night and his limbs were leaden, he knew it was too dangerous to rest this close to their goal.

Charley nodded.

Soon the sun stabbed through the forest, portending another day of thaw. They crept ahead through the trees along the river with all the caution of a pair of Wintu warriors. When a deer bolted before them with a crash, Ned's heart leapt to his throat.

Finally the forest thinned. Ned slipped to the last rank of trees before a clearing, his heart pounding. Ahead, standing forlornly in the broad hay field, stood the charred frame of a wooden house. The dark shapes of a dozen dead cattle littered the field. His breath left him in a whisper: "Then it's true."

"Yes, but who did it, and where are they?" Charley whispered behind him.

"What tribe would leave cattle to rot?"

"Any of them. The Indians are hunters, not ranchers. They blame the white man's cattle for the shortage of elk."

For a full hour Ned peered out from behind his tree, watching for the slightest movement in the forest ringing the field. Then he whispered, "Keep low and follow me." With his rifle cocked, he began to cross the open field.

He almost stumbled over the first body, among the cattle. At the same time the nauseous stench of rotten flesh hit him and he took a step backwards with an involuntary groan. The naked corpse of the man had bloated and burst. Although the man's clothes were gone and most of his flesh had been stripped by animals, his boots lay nearby in the field.

"It has been at least a week," Charley said beside him.

Ned went on mechanically to the house. He stepped between the timbers where a wall had been. Broken plates projected from the blackened rubble like giant, scattered teeth. A half-burnt corpse lay heaped in the corner, clutching the charred remains of a thick book. He had only to push its surviving pages askew to see that it had been an ornate family Bible. Then he recognized the white sticks at his feet as the remains of a much smaller skeleton, its fragile, bubble-like skull lying an impossible two feet from the tiny shoulder blades.

Horrified, Ned covered his face with his hands. He had not wanted to believe it could happen so close to Now-ow-wa. Had these settlers been so different from his own family in Oregon? The thought gave Ned a rush of anger. Nothing this family had done could ever justify the slaughter of a mother and her baby in their home.

Then Ned plumbed the deeper terror: that the murderers might be the same silent people he had chosen to live among. He pictured the gaunt, desperate Puyshoos warriors from the elk hunt. Could they possibly massacre humans with the same chilling calculation? The Puyshoos struggled so hard for survival, and valued life so highly. Never had they shown themselves capable of brutality. And above all, there was Paquita's love—a rock upon which Ned felt he could build his trust. Surely the Puyshoos were innocent!

Finally Ned looked up to Charley with damp eyes. "What kind of tribe could do this?"

Charley shook his head. "If there were arrows I could tell you for certain it was the Achomawis. Still, this does not look like the work of Puyshoos."

Ned nodded, but he knew the company of volunteers would not spare the Puyshoos without irrefutable evidence. He spotted a small, roofless stone barn in a far corner of the field and grimly led the way there.

Perhaps it would yield the proof he needed.

Suddenly Charley clutched his arm and pointed. Across the field, several Indian men were disappearing into the brush along the riverbank. A cold chill swept through Ned's body. "Did they see us?" he whispered.

"If they have, other warriors will be here soon. The camp must be very close."

Ned looked about the field in desperation. "The barn! Come on!" He ran ahead, crouching.

The barn's roof had collapsed from the weight of the winter's snow, leaving a ring of stone walls that would stop bullets and arrows. With a few minutes' work, they managed to block the doorway and window with shingles from the broken roof. In each of the corners they rigged a kind of scaffold over the debris so they could stand and use their rifles to best advantage. Then they checked their guns and waited with trembling hands.

For the remainder of the day they manned the makeshift stronghold, keeping track of the hours by the sun's slow march across the sky.

Before long they regretted having brought no water into their fortress. Ned's mouth grew parched and his head throbbed. In the afternoon Charley offered to stand watch alone so that Ned might rest. But thirst and fear made it impossible for either of them to close their eyes. When dusk finally fell, Ned looked to Charley.

Charley tilted his head toward the west. "In the dark we could escape to the McCloud."

"No." Ned tightened his lips. "We came here for evidence. Before I go I want to see who is in the Indians' camp."

Charley wiped his mouth with his hand. "I too would like to see, but—"

He didn't have to finish. Ned knew Charley looked too much like a white to be safe. They would both be killed if they were discovered.

"Tonight will be our only chance," Ned said.

Charley replied with a grim nod of assent.

With his rifle ready Ned led the way to the riverbank, crawling through the shadows. Furtively they dipped handfuls of the cold water. Down-stream, the Indians' campfires were so close they could be seen as flickering red ghosts amongst the trees. Ned inched through the brush along the river, sweat beading on his face, until he was opposite the first of the fires. It reflected eerily from the smooth river and lit the red faces of a circle of Indian men. They wore the tattered coats and bloodied shirts of white men. Several had felt hats, with black feathers like the one Ned had seen Akitot accept after the elk hunt. One man was standing, sweeping his arm in some kind of gesture as he spoke.

Ned turned to Charley. Scarcely daring to whisper, he mouthed the words, "Can you understand?"

Charley listened. "No. It is Achomawi. Only Achomawi."

With a nod of his head Ned indicated that he had seen enough. As slowly and cautiously as stalking cats, the two retreated. Once they were out of sight Ned moved faster, and at the hay field he broke into a run, giving way to the fear that seemed to hang in the air like the fog shrouding the burnt farmhouse.

By sheer force of will they dragged themselves ten miles to the divide separating the Pit River Valley from the McCloud. Never had Ned felt so utterly hollowed by hunger and so drained by lack of sleep. In the final miles he began to imagine he could hear a distant laughter, as if Kusku or Coyote were watching from the hilltops, amused by their plight. Ned shut out the sound and trudged onward with blind resolve.

When they finally reached the pass, they rolled into their blankets and collapsed onto a bed of yellow needles at the foot of a gnarled pine tree.

*   *   *

The sun was already high in the sky when Ned was shaken from a stony sleep. Charley touched his lips with a finger and pointed west. Groggily, Ned raised himself from his blankets and rubbed his eyes. A half mile down the meadows toward the headwaters of the McCloud, something was moving.

Suddenly Ned was wide awake. "The volunteers," he whispered. The long, black string of mounted men was coming toward them, obviously heading for the Pit River divide. "Looks like they've already missed the Puyshoos village."

Charley nodded. "If the volunteers had been there we would see the smoke by now. But we must hurry. It was not good to camp in the pass. Now we must head for the ridge and hope they are blind to the tracks we have left."

"You go on," Ned said. "I'm going to stay and talk with them."

Charley stared at him, not comprehending. "Talk with them?"

"Of course. How else can I convince them not to attack innocent tribes?"

"You should talk with them alone, then, my friend. Alone you may have a chance."

"You mean you're leaving?" Ned asked.

"If I stayed they would hang us both." Charley shook his hand in a brief good-bye. Then he slipped across the meadow from tree to tree, avoiding the patches of snow until he reached the forested foot of the ridge, where he disappeared into the shadows.

For a moment Ned stared after him, taken aback by his parting words. The sound of voices, however, soon reminded him of the approaching volunteers. Resolutely, he stepped out from under the pine tree.

"Drop it, Injun!" The man on the first mule squinted down the barrel of his rifle at Ned's chest.

"Wh—"

"Drop it!" The man wore a blue Army cap and had bristling red sideburns.

Slowly, Ned let his rifle fall to the ground. "I—I'm not an Indian," he stammered.

The man looked up from the rifle sights. Several other riders came up behind him, pistols in hand. "Then what the hell are you doing out here in an Indian costume?" He held out his arm to the others. "Hold it, men."

Ned looked at his buckskin jacket and moccasins. "These are the only clothes I have left. I've been prospecting in the hills all winter. I just heard about the trouble at Pit River and thought I should come help."

"Help which side?" one of the men said. "What kind of white man would turn up in the Pit River Valley alive, anyway? He's one of 'em, Cap!"

The man with the Army cap kept his rifle aimed at Ned, but he stiffened to a more formal pose. "I am Captain Gideon S. Whitney of the United States Army, commander of the Pit River Punitive Expedition. What is your name?"

By now thirty or forty mounted men had drawn up to look at Ned. Several dozen pack mules were behind them, braying at the delay. "Cincinnatus Hiner Miller, sir," Ned answered, "but I go by the name of—"

"*Hiner!*" a sharp voice broke in. "That Injun's Hiner the Miner."

Astonished, Ned followed the voice. "Bill Hearst!" he exclaimed. It was one of the gold mining partners he had left almost a year before. The tough little '49er had obviously done well since then. He wore an expensive black hat and rode a horse several hands taller than the rest of the company's mules. Ned had never much liked Hearst, or Hearst's nickname for him, but now the man looked like a savior.

"You know this man?" the captain asked.

Hearst spat to one side. "He mined near Horsetown a while."

"'Vhat's dat?" a heavily accented voice came from the back of the group. "It's Hiner?" A big, puffy-faced blond man rode up through the crowd and broke into a big grin.

Ned smiled at this additional testimony from his mining days.

"Howdy, Swede."

The captain inspected Ned again. "Well, well. A prospector in hostile territory without pick or pan. If he hasn't turned traitor, he'll be wanting to join his friends, won't he?" The captain turned to Swede. "Reload those mules. See if we can get one free." Then he added to Ned, "I trust you can ride bareback?"

Ned was dazed; he had never considered joining the volunteers at all. Now the captain's rifle—still aimed at his chest—told him he had no choice. "Yes, sir," he finally sighed.

* * *

As soon as he could, Ned rode his mule beside the captain's and told of his reconnaissance mission the previous day, hoping his unfortunate enlistment might at least help to spare innocent tribes. "It's the Achomawis, captain. They're the only ones I've found in the valley."

The captain listened coldly, then gave a stiff reply. "And where have you learned this word, *Achomawis?* The tribe we are after is known only as the Pit River Indians."

"But that's their name—" Ned caught himself, "—among the mountain men."

"Is it really? We shall see." He waved Ned back with a gloved hand. "Return to your position, Miller."

The afternoon passed tensely for Ned, who now feared his every movement might confirm to the volunteers that he was an Indian sympathizer. Even Hearst, who had worked with him for months in the mines, watched him suspiciously. Only the big, good-natured Swede rode beside him, telling him of the bandit attacks and miners' strikes he had missed the past year.

At the burnt-out Bear Creek settlement the volunteers exploded in oaths of outrage and revenge. When Jed Sims discovered the dead man was Sam Lockhart's twin brother, he fell on his knees, sobbing into his hands.

Hearst put a hand on the man's shoulder. "We'll pay 'em back. Too bad Sam ain't with us to help. I reckon he was too shook up to come."

Jed Sims looked up, a fierce look in his eyes. "You're one of 'em thinks Lockhart went crazy, aren't you? Well, you'll see. He'll git back at them Injuns, an' better than this goddam expedition."

Captain Whitney ordered the bodies buried. Then he sent out scouts. Before long the captain confronted Ned. "The scouts have looked at the bend across the river where you said the Indians camped. They found no evidence of a campsite. Furthermore, they say there is snow in the trees encircling the area—without footprints."

"But that's impossible!" Ned cried.

"Is it, Miller? See for yourself."

With his heart in his throat, Ned waded his mule through the river. He did not need to look back to know he was being followed by the captain's cocked pistol. On the far side he tied the mule to a tree and studied the ground, desperately trying to remember what he knew of Indian ways. He paced around the perimeter of the area carefully before turning to the captain.

"Well, Miller?" The captain leveled the pistol at him with clear intent. "What do you have to say for yourself?"

Ned began cautiously. "I believe, sir, that your scouts have missed some details. This bush, for example." He kicked it aside. "It's been cut and left here to cover a fire. Under the fresh needles the ashes are still warm."

The captain inspected the spot. For a moment he seemed bewildered to find what Ned said was true. Finally he muttered, "Must have been here this morning. But how could they have left without making tracks?"

"They didn't. Over here, by the trees, is the set of moccasin tracks."

"*One* set of tracks..." the captain nodded grimly now that he saw them. "The old Modoc trick. Count on these damned volunteer scouts not to spot it. From the size of the footprints it looks like quite a number of Indians, too, all stepping in the same track."

"And from the smell of horse," Ned added, "I'd say they were going to their stock in that meadow through the trees. They probably heard our mules braying."

"Yes, I see." The captain cleared his throat. "We shall make ready to pursue them at once. And Miller—" he gave Ned an earnest nod, "I like your confidence. Tomorrow I'm going to try you out as one of our scouts."

"Yes, sir."

The captain mounted to leave, adding almost casually, "And if you have any ideas of leaving us, remember that desertion from the U.S. Army is a hanging offense."

* * *

For the next days Ned had no choice but to help lead the expedition on the trail of the fleeing Pit River tribe. Ned worried about Paquita, knowing that he was riding farther and farther away from her on a mission she might never understand.

When the scouts met the first evening to discuss strategy with Captain Whitney, Ned listened silently to the others' plans. Finally the captain turned to him. "All right, Miller, and what do you think?"

"I think we should follow exactly in the hoofprints of the Indians. The

Pit River earned its name from the Indians' camouflaged pit-traps."

The other scouts laughed until tears came to their eyes. "Pitt River is spelled with *two* T's, boy," one of them said. "It's named after William Pitt, the Englishman!"

The next day, however, the lead scout suddenly disappeared. After following his cries, the others were able to use a rope to rescue the man from a pit. But his mule, impaled on the sharpened sticks and antlers at the bottom of the ten-foot-deep trap, had to be shot.

The day after, Ned was lead scout.

At the confluence of Bear Creek and Fall River there had been a second, larger ranch. Here, great circular corrals made of long hayricks had been burned, leaving enormous rings of blackened posts. Hundreds of cattle littered the fields in various stages of foul-smelling decay. Ned noticed that many of the animals had been slaughtered and quartered with the same techniques the Puyshoos had used on the elk hunt.

Suddenly Ned recalled Worrotatot's words about the winter hunger among the Indians. Had starvation been the cause of the massacre, rather than revenge? But how could he have sympathy for the black-feathered Achomawi warriors he had seen near the ghastly ruins of the Bear Creek farmhouse? Nothing could excuse such crimes. Perhaps it was just as well that he had been forced to join the expedition. If he could help vent the volunteers' revenge on the guilty warriors, he reasoned, the Puyshoos and Paquita might yet be safe.

The following day Ned rode ahead to a basalt bluff overlooking the Pit River's mile-wide canyon. From there he finally sighted the tribe's horses—a herd of dark spots crowding the river's grassy bank. He counted as best he could and returned with the report.

"Two hundred head?" Captain Whitney frowned. "If they outnumber us four to one, why have they been retreating?"

"It could be just a little pack of Injuns," one scout suggested, "driving a big pack of stolen horses."

"More likely, they have inferior firepower," the captain said. "Load and check all weapons and prepare for an engagement."

The volunteers responded skeptically, grumbling about the number of Indian horses before them. When the command came to gallop, however, the men spurred their mules and charged down into the canyon, clutching their guns. At the river's edge they found fresh hoofprints on the trail upriver.

"Follow them!" the captain ordered, and the volunteers galloped on.

Half a mile farther, a long thicket of cottonwoods loomed from the sagebrush. Just as the captain was holding up his hand to urge caution, a silent volley of arrows launched from the thicket at the onrushing volunteers. With an agonized bray, the mule next to Ned's suddenly reared back, a feathered shaft through its neck. Ned pulled in his reins to wheel his mule about, firing his rifle one-handed as he turned.

The captain shouted, "Fall back, men!"

A hundred yards back the shaken volunteers regrouped amidst the sagebrush, cursing and spitting.

"Courage, men!" the captain shouted. "The Indians are only using arrows. That means they don't know how to use the rifles they stole from the settlers. All we have to do is keep out of arrow range and we're safe. Now spread out and open fire!"

With whoops of grim satisfaction the volunteers took up positions, struggling to keep their panicky mules in place. The men peppered the thicket with rifle and pistol shot, while the Indians' obsidian-tipped arrows thunked harmlessly into the ground or shattered on the rocks in the field. The roar of the guns shook the air. Ned's rifle grew hot in his hands. White clouds of gunsmoke drifted slowly over the sagebrush. The smoke made it impossible for Ned to pick out any specific target, much less one of the hidden warriors, but he kept firing with the others.

Gradually the rain of arrows slackened in the face of the withering fire. Finally Captain Whitney ordered, "Lower your guns!"

In the pause that ensued, Ned heard nothing but a high ringing in his ears. There were no more arrows.

The thicket still seemed somehow menacing. Ned and the other volunteers loaded their pistols and advanced tentatively, alert for the slightest movement in the trees. At the edge of the thicket they stopped again. Ned peered into the trees, half expecting knife-wielding warriors to spring out from the branches or the brush.

When they finally ventured into the thicket, Ned saw that the bark of the trees had been shredded by their hail of lead. In several places blood had splattered or dripped in the brush, but there were no bodies, no other signs of the Indians' stand. Even when they reached the far side of the thicket they found nothing but hoofprints.

"They're gone," one of the men said—rather stupidly, Ned thought, for it had become obvious to him that most of the Indians had left long ago. He guessed that only a handful of warriors had actually stayed behind to hold them at bay, and that these had succeeded in escaping on fast horses while the volunteers were still busy firing at the thicket. Ned was embarrassed, and a little bitter, that the volunteers had been so easily fooled.

Hearst spat. "Least we gave 'em one hell of a scare."

* * *

That night Captain Whitney posted a heavy guard about the camp, but the volunteers were in good spirits as they sat around the bonfire swapping stories. For once the rough group seemed to forget about Ned's buckskin garb and long hair. The common danger of the first battle had worked a subtle change. Men Ned had never known were now calling him by his mining nickname "Hiner" and including him in the never-ending discussions about where the Indians might be heading, or whether gold could be found east of Shasta.

"Now me," said a talkative, red-faced miner by the fire, "I think these Digger Injuns're fixin' to join with the Modocs up north."

"*Well* now," said another, "I reckon we'd sure as hell better call their hand before *then*. The captain who led the last battle up there's too dead to make them Modocs dance to our tune anymore."

Swede looked up. "Vhat happened to dat captain?"

"Passed in his checks, Swede. The government made him an Injun agent. One night all the soldiers was at a dance when the Injuns up an' kilt ever'body for forty miles. They cut out his heart an' ate it, thinkin' the heart would make 'em as brave as he'd been."

"Is *that* why they're called 'Diggers?'" a young miner asked in awe. "Because they cut out your heart?"

"It's sure not because they can work in the mines," Bill Hearst said, his eyes flashing in the firelight. "After I'd opened up a new quartz shaft last year a Digger came up begging for grub. I gave him a pick and showed him the face, but he just walked off."

"I thought they were called Diggers because they dug up roots," Ned said, trying to sound informative and not defensive.

"Hell no!" the red-faced miner by the fire interjected. "It's 'cause they dig up graves to steal the clothes right off the corpses. Yes, sir! Why, I've seen 'em runnin' around wearin' nothin' but a long white shroud straight out of the grave."

"I'll *bet* you have, Red," someone said, and a chuckle ran through the group.

Ned did not join in the laugh. Now that the volunteers were beginning to accept him as one of their number, he felt more than ever that he did not belong.

* * *

The most serious result of the battle proved to be the loss of five of the volunteers' mules. Ned helped reload the packs, but the extra burden made the supply mules lag farther behind each day. Their long ears, usually pricked forward, flopped back and forth as if wilted by the desert sun. What was worse, their hooves were getting severely cut by the sharp pumice and lava rocks that now had to be crossed. There were delays to renail or replace worn horseshoes, and one lame animal had to be abandoned in a grassy spot by the river, in the hopes that it would recover there.

Ned guessed the Indians were having similar difficulties, for they seemed unable to travel faster. One evening he undertook a scouting foray along the canyon's rimrock. When he returned he reported, "They're just five miles upstream. I could make out campfires and some kind of hide shelters. Their horses seemed to be farther down the canyon."

Captain Whitney met the news with a long, thoughtful silence. Finally he announced, "We will attack at the first light of dawn—on foot, so the mules won't give us away. We'll need to split into the three groups." He looked at the faces of the men around him. "You, Hearst. You'll take eight men to attack from the north. Your job is to scare off the Indians' stock so they can't ride on. Got it?"

Hearst nodded. "Yes, sir."

"I'll lead the main group of men up the canyon for a frontal assault. And the third group will flank them on the south, coming down from the rimrock. For that detachment—" Whitney's eyes swept the group again. He stopped at Ned. "Hiner, you've scouted that position. You'll take the third group. Now roll into bed. Reveille's at two."

That night Ned lay sleepless, thinking of his sudden assignment, and watching the huge stars that hung untwinkling in the still desert air. On the one hand, he thought, he had finally proven himself to the volunteers. There was a broad-shouldered feel to being the captain's lieutenant. But then he remembered proving himself to the Puyshoos just a few weeks before on the elk hunt. How would the tribe ever understand the charge he would lead at dawn? And when he thought of the numbers of Achomawi warriors he would face at close range, with just eight men at his side, he wondered if he would survive the charge at all.

* * *

"Up! Move! Roll out!" A big miner kicked the men out of their blankets. Slowly the volunteers assembled in the dark for a cold breakfast. Spoons shook in trembling hands.

"Men," Captain Whitney said, "You will come within arrow range of the enemy today. As armor, you will fold your blankets in half, cut a hole in them, and wear them like ponchos. Thick wool is quite capable of stopping the primitive kind of obsidian arrowheads these Indians manufacture."

Ned finished his breakfast quickly and cut up his bedroll with the others, even though he knew it would not stop an arrow. He had seen arrows pierce the much thicker hides of elk. Then the captain lined up the three groups single file. In the firelight Ned looked with renewed distress at his very small column of eight undrilled volunteers. The men looked back at him with a kind of desperate hope, as if they had forgotten entirely their earlier suspicions that Ned was a renegade.

"Details—march!"

The groups set off into the darkness. Ned led his men up a steep scree slope to the canyon rim. There, the moonlit tableland was only sparsely dotted with sagebrush, allowing them to move rapidly toward the Indian camp. Then, in silence, he picked a path down through a break in the cliffs.

Ned waved his men together behind a group of boulders. "We will wait here for Whitney's signal," he whispered. "Then we advance right to the edge of the camp. Pistols aren't much use at a distance."

The wait seemed interminable. The man next to Ned tapped the ivory handle of his revolver against the heel of his hand to settle the powder in the tubes. The gun clicked as he turned the chamber, checking that all six caps were still in place. The black sky on the eastern horizon gradually softened to deep purple and became fringed with a blush of dark magenta. Ned imagined he could see orange shadows shifting through the dark sagebrush near the river.

All at once a long crackle of gunfire split the air, echoing across the canyon.

"That's Whitney. Let's go!" Ned whispered. The group sprang out of hiding and ran forward. Fifty yards from the Indian encampment they collected behind a fallen tree and opened fire.

This time the Achomawis were not prepared for battle. Dark forms stumbled about, trying to find cover among the few low bushes along the riverbank. Some carried bundles, only poorly distinguishable in the dawn's dim light. They rushed in opposite directions, occasionally jerking and sinking in the whistling crossfire that met them from three sides. A few arrows splintered into the log in front of Ned, but more often the shrieking warriors would sprint toward the line of volunteers, knives in hand, to be riddled with volleys from the six-guns.

The engagement lasted just fifteen minutes. When the full light of morning revealed that the remaining Indians were no longer resisting, Ned held up his hand. "Hold your fire," he said. "We'll take the rest as prisoners."

"What for?" one of the volunteers asked. "They didn't take prisoners when they ambushed the settlers."

"I said *hold your fire.*" Ned turned his rifle toward the man who had spoken. The man lowered his pistol, watching Ned warily.

A moment later the gunfire from the other two groups of volunteers began to slow, stuttering like the end of a pan of popping corn. Finally, the guns fell silent.

The sound that remained was unmistakable—more chilling than anything Ned had ever heard before. It was the cry of a baby.

Dumbstruck, Ned followed the cry. The air was still thick with the acrid taste of gunpowder. Alone, he walked past the bodies of the warriors that had rushed the volunteers. Farther on, the dead people were not warriors. A woman lay twisted on her back, eyes frozen wide and mouth agape. An old man had fallen against the sagebrush he had uselessly hidden behind, embracing it with bony arms. Near him lay the bodies of two young children, streaked with red from the wet bullet holes in their arms and necks.

Ned found the baby in a bundle of blankets on a mat, thrashing its tiny hands and feet in the air while its face wrinkled into a defiant howl. He watched it incredulously, afraid to come any closer. Now he understood why the Achomawis had needed two hundred horses—why they had retreated so slowly before the punitive expedition. There had been families, grandparents, babies to move.

Suddenly an Indian woman rushed before Ned and threw herself across the baby, repeating a plaintive, unintelligible phrase. Ned realized she thought he had come to shoot the baby as well. He turned away, ashamed.

When the volunteers saw there were no more arrows, they approached the Indian camp with triumphant shouts. At the sight of the carnage, some became somber. The others, rougher sorts of men, pushed each other aside for the right to scalp the warriors, pulling up handfuls of black hair and sawing them loose with knives.

The few Indian survivors huddled in small groups. The women began the high, mournful wail of a death chant while the whimpering children stared about with the wide eyes of frightened rabbits. The only able-bodied Indian man still on the field of battle was a shaman, whom the volunteers discovered with headdress and rattle, performing a chant over a fallen warrior.

"Hang him," Captain Whitney said curtly.

"But he's unarmed," Ned protested. "He's a religious man, praying for the spirits of the Indians who've died." The blue feathers in the shaman's headdress brought back a vivid, startling memory of Witillahow and the Puyshoos.

"All the more reason to hang him," the captain replied. "If this tribe had been brought to a proper religion, our whole expedition might never have been necessary."

The shaman did not struggle when the men led him to a large juniper tree amid jeers and talk. The Indian held his feathered head high and closed his eyes as though he were beyond harm, in another world.

Ned walked away, feeling helpless and ill. The tribe he had helped to slaughter was agonizingly like Paquita's tribe. These were people with families and gods, doing what they believed was right, trying to survive.

He had to have time to think, or perhaps to stop thinking. He sat down heavily on the sandy bank of the river and wiped his face with his sleeve. But even there the bent body of a warrior looked up at him from the grass.

Then he saw the dead man's face, and Ned's heart almost stopped. It was Akitot, Paquita's brother, still wearing the black feather.

Ned was no longer able to hold back his tears. When he looked again at Akitot, he saw the rifle slung over his shoulder—one of the rifles Ned had bought in Shasta City. The empty ammunition pouches at Akitot's side explained why it had not been used to return the volunteers' fire.

In a sudden rage Ned took the gun and smashed it against a rock until the stock splintered and the barrel bent. Then he threw it aside.

How had it come to this? he thought. And why? At every step he had only done what seemed best, or what he had no choice but to do, yet now he had brought about the death of his brother. And Paquita—the thought frightened him—would she not see the blood on his hands? The Puyshoos might murder him if he returned. Would they be entirely wrong if they did?

Ned struggled to slow his galloping thoughts. The Puyshoos had spared his life so far. The tribe had actually tried to insulate him from news of the massacre, to protect him from the inevitable clash between Achomawis and whites. And the other warriors had argued with Akitot when he had left. Perhaps Paquita had suspected then that her brother would never return. Picturing her now, strong, yet fragile, Ned knew he must go back.

With that resolve, Ned began piling dead brush and driftwood over Akitot's body. There were enough campfires still burning along the river that the soldiers would not question him building another to ward off the morning chill. But that was not his purpose. He knew the Puyshoos believed cremation to be the only way to release a warrior's spirit. It would be important to be able to tell Paquita he had honored her brother with the Puyshoos' traditional last rites. He also knew Akitot was the sole evidence that the Puyshoos had been involved in the Pit River Massacre. The body must be burned.

When the pile stood four feet high, he touched a match to the dry limbs. The little flame caught and spread, gradually transforming the pile into a roaring funeral pyre. Heat hit Ned in waves with the changing wind. The smoke's sweet smell made his head swim. But Ned still stared into the flames, as if in a trance. Shimmering through the tongues of fire was the distant cone of Mt. Shasta, shining boldly in the morning sun.

It seemed to Ned that the vision danced in the pyre's heat with all the tenacity, courage, and mystery of the spirit he intended to release.

* * *

The captain issued an order to collect the Indian horses and turn the squaws loose.

"What about all the children?" a man asked.

"If any of you have use for an Indian orphan," the captain replied, "it would be an act of charity to take one into civilization and provide for it. I have known them to learn English and to put in good work."

Several men nodded agreement and began claiming the healthier looking children, setting them on spare horses. A few of the children submitted with a stunned meekness, as though they had expected to be taken as slaves. Others struggled until the men tied their hands. A group of women cowered nearby, wailing and pleading in their own language.

"You can't just take the children," Ned objected. "Many of them aren't orphans at all."

"We'll fix that," a man chuckled. He pulled a pistol and began firing into the sand at the squaws' feet. The terrified women jumped to dodge the shots. Then they ran into the desert.

The volunteers broke into hearty laughter.

"Back to Yreka!" one of the men shouted. "They'll throw one helluva celebration when we get back."

"Hurrah for the Pit River War!" several others cried.

"A campaign waged without the loss of a single man," Captain Whitney added, pride in his voice. Then he raised his arm and motioned forward. "All right soldiers, let's move out."

Ned followed with a heavy heart. He was ashamed to ride among these men. They had treated the people of the tribe like animals. Couldn't the volunteers see the pain in the children's eyes? Hadn't they heard the anguish in the women's voices? If only these men could spend a day living among the Puyshoos—if only they could talk with Paquita for an hour! Surely then they would see how wrong their treatment of these people had been.

The next day, when the company reached the foot of Mt. Shasta, Ned told the captain, "Reckon this is where I leave. I'm headed back to my prospecting."

"Here? On foot?" the captain asked. "Are you sure, Miller? This is rugged country. At least you'd better take one of the Indian ponies."

Ned shook his head and turned to go.

"Wait a minute, Miller. Where do you want the Army to send the pay you've earned?"

"I don't want my pay."

The captain studied him levelly. "You've surprised me more than once, Miller, and I'm rarely surprised. I think you have the instincts of a soldier. Let me know if you ever need a letter of introduction."

"And if you want a job in the mines," Bill Hearst put in, "Just look me up. I'm running a quartz mill at Deadwood now, near Yreka."

Ned hardly heard the offers. His thoughts were not on the world of the whites as he turned to walk alone toward the McCloud River.

*   *   *

Ned sat on the rimrock overlooking the Puyshoos' camp a long time before he worked up the courage to enter it. When he finally did, he found the camp ominously hushed. Paquita was not in her *cawel*, though her things were there. He went on. The Indian dogs peered out of an entranceway but did not bark. The central open area, muddy from snowmelt and footprints, was silent. He pursed his lips and looked about him. Then, reluctantly, he stepped down into Worrotatot's long lodge.

The bearded chief did not rise to greet him. Paquita's dark eyes followed him from where she sat. Neither spoke.

Ned sighed with resignation. "Then you already know what has happened on the Pit River."

"We know the whites have returned from there with many horses and slaves," Worrotatot replied. "Our dark dreams have told us the rest."

Paquita spoke cautiously. "Kibo—the dreams about Akitot—there was an empty mask—"

Ned lowered his gaze and gave a brief nod. "I built the pyre that released his spirit." Paquita bent forward, pressing her eyes tightly closed so that tears could not come. Gently, Ned knelt beside her and held her shoulders. "I could not stop an army of white men. I tried to make them understand, but they only saw that the white settlers had been killed. All I could do was keep them away from the people on the McCloud."

Gradually Paquita managed to open her eyes. "You are my husband," she said, forcing out the words. "You—are a good husband. Some spirits are released from their masks, and others are given new masks." With that, she tried to bring her tensed face to smile.

Puzzled, Ned looked to Worrotatot. The chief said, "Can you not see why you have been spared? Stand up then, Paquita."

When she had raised herself to her feet Ned still understood nothing. Then he realized her deerskin no longer quite fit, and he paled.

"It will be five moons," she said quietly.

Worrotatot said, "You are now one of us."

Chapter 6

Then clouds blew in, and all the sky was cast
With tumbled and tumultuous clouds that grow
Red thunderbolts . . . .
            —Joaquin Miller

A month of warm spring sunshine drove the snow from the foothills and breathed life into the meadows, healing the wounds of the long, cold winter. Ned returned with Paquita to the little log cabin in Now-ow-wa, a refuge of calm and love in the midst of storm. Paquita never again mentioned his role in the death of her brother. She seemed more solicitous and close to Ned than ever. But he knew the memory of the Pit River War still haunted them both.

In the heat of early August, when Paquita was great with child, she suddenly begged him to bring her snow. To please her he rode half a day high on Mt. Shasta. When he returned with a saddlebag of melting glacial ice Paquita was resting beside a wriggling bundle.

"The baby!" Ned exclaimed. "Are you all right?"

She nodded wearily. "It must be done alone."

"You wanted snow—"

She smiled faintly. "Only so your daughter and I could do our work alone."

He took her hand, marveling at her will. Beside her in the blankets a tiny, wrinkled face peered up at him. Ned bent near the little face, awestruck. It seemed incredible that this miniature person, balling its fists and blinking, could be his flesh and blood—the miraculous proof of his love. Pride and happiness swelled in his chest. The child had dark hair and dark eyes like the Wintu, but her skin was nearly as light as his own.

"She will be as beautiful as her mother," he announced. "What will we call her? The prettiest name I can think of is Paquita, and that's taken."

Paquita lowered her eyes. "She is Cali-Shasta."

"The lily of Shasta." Ned looked again at his fair-skinned daughter and thought: she will be like a wildflower, a child of the mountain's spirit. In all the poems he had written in his quest to find and know that beautiful, elusive spirit, nothing had captured its powerful allure so perfectly as this delicate, dark-eyed infant.

* * *

Cali-Shasta's first months at Now-ow-wa were shadowed by dark news from the Puyshoos village. First a warrior disappeared during a hunt. Then a pair of women failed to return from their root-gathering.

"What do you think is the cause?" Ned asked the Puyshoos man who brought the news. "Could it be grizzlies, or rattlesnakes?"

The man shook his head. "It's an evil spirit. Witillahow has spent many nights asking his guardian powers for help. He has not yet gotten an answer."

Ned shook his head doubtfully. "Well, I don't believe in evil spirits."

Paquita looked at him. "You only believe in good ones? We will be safer if you keep near Now-ow-wa."

Through the fall it was easy to please her by staying within the valley—hunting, dreaming, and writing more poems in his journal. Sometimes the rhymes would fall neatly in place, building verses to match the beauty of his mountain valley. Then he would chuckle, thinking he might have sneaked onto a little-used path to greatness after all. Between the luck with his writing and the health of his beautiful baby daughter, the future hinted at more promise than it had for years.

But by November supplies were running low, and Ned had to bring his horse down to pasture along the Sacramento. He saddled up and rode to Soda Springs.

In the forest a chill wind moved the trees' shadows. The branches clicked and whispered. He couldn't help but remember the stories of the evil spirit. If the evil didn't exist, then what had happened to the people missing from the tribe? He thought of Paquita's warning to stay near Now-ow-wa, and cocked his rifle.

When Ned reached Soda Springs Charley was alone in Mountain Joe's cabin.

"Where's Joe?" Ned asked.

Charley shook his head. "Mountain Joe was very drunk last month."

"Well, that's hardly news."

"He was *very* drunk." Charley held out his broad hands. "He gambled away the ranch to a Yankee traveler."

"*What?*"

Charley nodded. "I decided to work for the new owner, in order to live near the tribe. But Joe loaded his black mare with prospecting supplies."

"You mean he just rode off?" Ned felt empty and alone. Mountain Joe had been his guide to the gold country, and then again to Mt. Shasta. More than that, Joe had been his link between the civilized and frontier worlds—a friend who understood that great deeds and grand ambitions grew best under the wilderness' starlit skies. It hurt to think he had left so abruptly.

"Did he say where he was headed?" Ned asked.

"He mentioned Canada. Something about turning a few dollars out of the Fraser River gold rush."

Ned sighed. This did sound like Joe. No doubt the old mountain man had been glad enough for an excuse to roam again. Joe had never cared for his settled life on a horse ranch. His home was the whole unfenced sweep of the West, two thousand miles wide. And even in that vast country, Joe cut a large enough swath that he never disappeared for long. Sooner or later, Ned knew, their paths would join again. But that didn't ease the emptiness he felt now. He had lost a trusted friend at a time when friends seemed scarce.

Ned was glad Charley had remained. "Then I reckon you'll be the one to sell me my winter supplies."

"Actually, no. You'll have to talk to the new owner."

Ned found the short, clean-shaven businessman working on the corrals. The man only laughed when Ned asked for credit to buy supplies. "How do you intend to pay back credit? They say there's no gold in the creeks on Shasta."

"I guess that's true." Ned really didn't have a way to earn money. For a moment he regretted refusing his Army pay.

"Well, then." The businessman's tone was curt. "Anything else I can do for you?"

Sullenly Ned tied Pache's reins to the corral fence. The roan gelding had been his companion for nearly three years. It would hurt almost as much to lose Pache as Joe. But perhaps it was fitting to say good-bye to them both at once. What choice did he have? He could only hope to meet them again in better days.

"Want to trade for a first-rate horse?"

*   *   *

The snowflakes fell fine and cold throughout that winter, frosting every needle of every tree rimming Now-ow-wa. Ned was glad for the sparkling white blanket that wrapped the beautiful mountain valley. Snow, he hoped, would isolate them from the troubles of the outside world.

One day late in January Ned took down his rifle to hunt for deer. On and on he walked, until finally a buck stepped in front of him, almost as if on purpose. He lifted the rifle's cold, heavy barrel and squeezed off a single shot. Without so much as a cough the animal bowed its head, bent its legs, and lay down in the snow as if to sleep. Ned approached uncertainly, though he had seen the shot slap into the deer's chest. It was harder than usual to bring himself to slit the buck's throat and drain its lifeblood. He muttered the Wintu words of forgiveness. Then he made the cut, his hands red and warm.

Without Pache to carry the load, Ned had little choice but to drag the deer home five miles over the snow. When Paquita saw the red trail he had left to their door, however, she shook her head. "A trail of blood is a bad sign, Kibo. It will bring evil."

"We're snowed in. No evil can reach us here. Don't worry, Paquita," Ned said, waving off her fears. He skinned the meat, cinched it with a rope, and hoisted it to the ceiling to cure in the fire's constant smoke.

That evening, after Ned and Paquita had finished a dinner of venison liver, little Cali-Shasta tried to crawl for the first time. She rolled off her bear rug at the far end of the cabin with a lonesome cry and began to creep toward them.

At once both young parents were on the floor, offering encouragement. "Come on, Cal! Crawl to Papa!" Ned urged.

Paquita helped the baby pull its pudgy knees forward one at a time. Cali-Shasta's naked rear wobbled uncertainly in the air and flopped to one side. Paquita smiled to Ned at the failure. "Maybe she isn't ready. She is only six moons old."

"Let's trade places," Ned suggested. "You wait by the window and I'll get behind her with this great big grizzly *wemir*."

"What *wemir*?" Paquita asked, puzzled.

"This one back here. You better watch out for him!" Ned crept along the dark wall making spooky growling sounds like a bear.

Cali-Shasta flashed a smudgy grin at her father and got back up on her knees. Ned growled closer. The baby squealed and took off crawling on all fours.

When he finally caught up with Cali-Shasta, her dark eyes sparkled and she threw her little arms about his neck.

"I knew you could do it, Cal," Ned whispered.

Later, when the little one had been put to bed, Ned kissed Paquita and pulled her toward their furs. She slipped her deerskin robe off with a dip of her shoulder, but sat leaning against the log wall, pensively untying her long braids.

"What is it?" Ned asked.

"I've been thinking," she said. "Sometimes a happy day makes me sad. Is that strange?"

"A little, perhaps. Why should you be sad?"

"I don't know. I think of the memories such days will leave—later."

"Later?"

"When you've gone back to your own people."

Ned was shaken. He sat up, frowning. "What makes you talk like that? I've fathered your child and learned your language. Why should I want to be anywhere but with my *mahala,* my wife?"

"I think about your other people, and I wonder what they're like. You're always writing in your books. You say it's only stories, but if the stories aren't for me, then they must be for the others." She straightened, shaking her black tresses from her smooth, bare shoulders.

Her words gave Ned pause. Of course he couldn't write his poems in Wintu—Paquita's people didn't use a written language. But by striving to capture the frontier's spirit in English, had he subtly aimed his thoughts at a distant audience? It was as if Paquita had ventured into his soul and had stumbled across the ambitions lurking there.

"There is no reason to worry, my Paquita. I only write the poems to remind me how much I love you." He put his arms around her slender brown waist and laid his head softly against her.

She ran her fingers over his long, wavy hair. "The writing will make it so you never forget?"

"Yes, Paquita. I will always love you," he said.

She held his head tight against her. When he wanted, she allowed him to lay her back into the deep furs.

*   *   *

A splintering crash and an icy wind woke Ned from stormy dreams. A wild voice boomed from the door in the bright morning light. "Hell, I wouldn't believe it if I hadn't seen it with my own eyes. A white man sleeping with a Digger squaw!"

The gray dawn framed huge, white-eyed Sam Lockhart in the ruined doorway, a strange grin stretching his white-streaked beard, and an ugly shotgun barrel drooped toward Ned. "Nothing but a goddamned traitor, running with the Injuns that murdered my brother. Put on your boots so I don't have to kill you like one of them Injun dogs."

Cali-Shasta broke into a frightened wail. Paquita could understand only the stranger's violent tone, but she scrambled to rush the baby aside.

"You're making a mistake," Ned stammered. With horror, he realized it must have been Lockhart who had been hunting the Puyshoos. Lockhart was the evil spirit responsible for so many disappearances. Now this madman had discovered Now-ow-wa. A cold sweat of terror broke out on his face and hands. If only he could reach the loaded rifle hanging by the door! He pulled on his pants, intentionally stumbling closer.

"Like hell I am!" Lockhart roared, spotting the gun. With one hand he took it down and emptied the barrel onto the floor. Then, with a swing of his heavy arm, he smashed it against a wall and flung it out into the snow. He jabbed his shotgun at Ned's chest.

"Hold it, Lockhart." Desperate, Ned groped for an argument the man might understand. "Killing a white man's murder. They'll track you down if you shoot me."

Lockhart lowered the gun a trifle. "Hell, you're just a no-count squaw man."

Ned pushed on, recalling now that Lockhart's twin brother had died on the Pit River—no doubt the event that had pushed Sam to his lunatic course. "I tried to save your family on the Pit River, Sam. Only an outlaw would kill a man who tried to help him."

Lockhart spat contemptuously.

"You've got to have a judge and a trial, or they'll come after you."

"A judge?" The word seemed to filter through Lockhart's turbulent consciousness slowly. "There ain't a judge between here and Yreka."

"Then you'd better go there and settle with the law first. You don't want to hang for shooting a white man by mistake. Put down the gun, Sam, so we can talk about it."

"And give you time to tell the Injuns?" Lockhart's white eyes shifted nervously while he thought. Regardless of how many Indians he must have gunned down, he had evidently never pulled the trigger on a white man before, and it obviously made him uneasy. He spat out a violent oath. "Wish to hell you was just an Injun, so I wouldn't have to bust a gut to see you dead. Now git your squaw to pack me some grub, and make it fast."

Paquita was still huddling against the far wall, trying to keep the baby from attracting the intruder's attention. She looked grateful when Ned spoke to her in Wintu.

"This white man's name is Lockhart. He wants you to get him provisions for a journey. He thinks I—"

"Cut the Injun talk!" Lockhart bellowed, jabbing Ned again with the gun.

Trembling, Paquita packed a leather bag with biscuits and venison. Lockhart took it with one rough hand and stuffed it inside his shirt. "Move," he grunted to Ned.

When they were outside he turned to aim the shotgun back at Paquita, still standing in the doorway.

"Kill her and you'll be dead before you can reload," Ned warned.

Slowly, Lockhart swung the muzzle back to Ned. "So git moving. And keep your hands on your head or I'll blow it off."

As they shuffled off through the shallow snow, Ned turned to say a final word to Paquita. But Lockhart only prodded him on. "Git!"

* * *

It was fifty miles to Yreka, and Lockhart seemed to have the stamina of a pack mule. When night fell they were nearly halfway to their goal. Lockhart bound Ned's hands and feet and tied him securely to a tree. Then Lockhart dozed off beside a campfire.

For hours Ned struggled against the ropes, thinking of Paquita and the baby. His mind tumbled through the choices he would face if he did break free of his bonds. Should he try to steal Lockhart's gun while he slept? Would it be wiser to escape to Paquita and take her to the Puyshoos village so the tribe could plan revenge? Or perhaps he should simply go on with Lockhart to Yreka where the law could bring him to justice for his murders?

When morning finally approached, Ned sagged against his bonds, exhausted and hungry and shivering from the cold. He had succeeded only in wearing painful red slashes in his wrists and hips.

When Lockhart awoke he marched Ned mercilessly the remaining twenty-five miles. Ned's bound hands were bloodless and numb, tied behind his neck for the entire trek. When he finally staggered onto the windy streets of Yreka, Ned was so tired and hungry he could hardly keep upright.

Sam pushed him into the courthouse just as Judge Rosborough was leaving.

"What's this, Sam?" the judge asked with surprise.

Ned began to talk, but Sam rammed the gun into his back. "I found me this boy living with the Diggers. I reckon he's the one what riled 'em up to kill my brother."

The judge sized up the two bedraggled men. "This requires an investigation, Sam. We'll look into it in the morning."

"What!" Sam sputtered. "Hell, I brang this varmint halfway 'cross the county so you can do your judgin'. Get it over with and string 'im up."

"Law takes time. Still, I suppose we can jail your suspect until the hearing." The judge led the way to a windowless room. He pushed Ned inside and locked the wooden door with a key at his waist. "That'll hold him for the night, Sam."

"Like hell it will. If this is all the better jail you got, I aim to sleep here with a chair leaned against the door and my shotgun cocked."

"Very well." Shortly afterwards, the judge's footsteps echoed down the hall.

The darkness in the cell was almost complete. Ned searched the walls carefully, but found no means of escape. Hollowed by fatigue, he slumped in a corner, where his worry for Paquita and his fury towards Lockhart seethed like a lake of lava. Futile, fragmentary plans surfaced and submerged in confusion. At one moment he could see her face before him as if by firelight, and then again the shadow would come—the shadow of the evil spirit that did exist. Finally, after endless hours, the images swirled down into a troubled dream.

He was running in the dream, running toward the sun, as if his goal lay just behind that blindingly bright disk. At times there were others chasing after him. Some were angry, some pleaded with him to stop, but one by one they faltered and sank back among the faceless crowds. Only when he was sure he had outrun them all did he dare to turn and look back. And he saw with horror that he was still being followed—by an ineradicable trail of red.

* * *

When Judge Rosborough returned in the morning he listened to Ned's side of the story. "This is easy enough to clear up, Sam," he said. "If Miller here fought the Indians with the Pit River Punitive Expedition, he wouldn't have been against you." He called in Red, a miner from the expedition who now worked in a brewery down the street.

Red swaggered into the courtroom and grinned. "You got yourself Hiner, all right. Helluva lieutenant in the war."

"Looks like you'll have to let him go, Sam." The judge tapped his gavel and waved him from the room. "Case dismissed."

Lockhart's face turned red and his white eyes flashed. He shook a crooked finger at Ned. "Listen, Miller, you stay away from them Injuns, hear? 'Cause if you go back, I'll *know* you're in cahoots with 'em, and I'll find you." He stormed out of the room, shotgun in hand.

The judge unlocked Ned's manacled hands silently.

"You're a man of the law," Ned said. "Isn't there some way Lockhart can be stopped? He's gone mad, killing any Indian he can find."

"Do you have specific evidence to prove that?"

Ned hesitated. "I don't, but the tribes have—"

"Then there's nothing you can do. Under California law, no white man can be convicted of a crime on the basis of testimony by an Indian."

"Well, can't you at least arrest him for trying to kill *me*? You just said I was innocent."

"Now hold on," the judge retorted gruffly. "I never said you were *innocent*. I said we'd have to let you go. All that means is we're going to give you another chance. Nobody explained what you were doing living with the Indians. As far as that goes, Sam's right—if we were to find you aiding a tribe that harbored criminal elements again, your case just might need a reevaluation."

Ned withdrew his hands from the manacles and backed away. He had forgotten that Yreka had celebrated the Pit River volunteers' slaughter of the Achomawi tribe. A jury here would more likely acquit a murderer than an Indian. "Of course, your honor," he said, reaching for the door. He was not going to find justice in Yreka.

* * *

He took the first road out of town and found himself stumbling through the town's wind-blown cemetery. There his legs finally buckled, weakened from three days without food, and he collapsed amidst the snow-flocked tombstones. Only then did he wonder where he had thought he was going. He had no money, no horse, and no rifle. Going back to Now-ow-wa would be suicide: Lockhart would be waiting for him. Then what?

Exhaustion closed his eyes, and his mind began to jolt and rumble down its own hellish spiral track towards a black, grinning mask.

When he opened his eyes again, he could not say how long he had lain on the frozen ground. His hands and feet were numb, but his head was clearing. Standing uncertainly, he saw the pale, distant peak of Mt. Shasta. Surely, he thought, Paquita and Cali-Shasta would go to stay with the tribe until his return. As long as they stayed there they would be safe. Sam Lockhart, however, had to be stopped, and the law was not going to do it. If only he had a horse and a rifle, he could confront Lockhart himself. But where could he get the money to buy a horse?

He looked below, at the men and wagons heading west on the trail up Greenhorn Creek. Hadn't Bill Hearst offered him a job at a mine in that direction once, at Deadwood? If he went there, he could thaw out and beg something to eat. Then maybe he could earn the horse and rifle he needed to meet the Puyshoos' evil spirit head-on.

Chapter 7

I want you to know, all you animals,
Open your eyes.
Find this man who killed this animal.
Find out what happened to this animal who is our friend, and whom
This man killed.
We'll go out to meet him . . . .
—Modoc prayer to a slain animal

It was snowing when Ned arrived in the mining town of Deadwood, twelve miles west of Yreka. Mechanically, he dragged his frozen feet in time with the rhythmic din of the steam-driven stamp mills. The valley was a moonscape of tailings and plank shacks. Where the sludgy dribbles of Deadwood Creek and McAdam Creek met, a dozen relatively elegant buildings huddled together, as if in defense against the desolation around them.

Ned drifted toward the hotel, a two-story structure whose brickwork and cast-iron ornamentation bespoke sudden wealth. An old man with a shiny bald head rocked slowly on the porch, seemingly unaffected by the cold. He was a strangely misshapen old-timer with a crooked jaw, skewed shoulders, and one eye considerably larger than the other. As Ned approached, the man hunched over a meerschaum pipe and puffed assiduously.

"You wouldn't know whereabouts I could find Bill Hearst's operation, would you?" Ned asked.

The old man studied him a minute, squinting with the eye that would close enough to squint. "Reckon that's the mill up the crick. But you'll find Hearst in thar if you want him." He pointed his pipe's amber stem toward the hotel saloon.

Ned nodded his thanks and pushed past the heavy wooden door. Inside was a strange world of warmth and luxury, with chandeliers, thick

Persian carpets, and trim-bearded men in dapper black suits. Ned brushed the snow from his long, tangled hair and ragged buckskins, and continued resolutely to the bar. Hearst was there all right, wearing a bowler hat and a stickpin made from a huge lump of gold.

"Howdy, Bill," Ned said.

Hearst spun about and glared. "Who are you?"

"Why, I'm Miller. You remember, Hiner Miller. You used to mine with me and Swede."

Hearst frowned, obviously displeased by the sight of this ragged man. "If you're looking for Swede, he took off for the beach mines in Oregon."

"No, I came to see you."

"Me? What do you want?"

"A job, I reckon, if you've got one."

"A job!"

Ned was a bit bewildered by Hearst's gruff tone. "Don't you remember, on the Pit River expedition? You told me to look you up if I needed work. Now I reckon I'm about as busted flat as a man can be. I haven't eaten for three days."

Hearst grunted and waved him away. "Talk to Tom Bass, the pit boss. Every morning at six he tells if he's hiring."

"Thanks. I'll do that," Ned said. Then he added tentatively, "You wouldn't have an advance for a meal and a bed, would you?"

"Don't push it, Miller," the wiry '49er said, his voice on edge. "That Pit River business was damned near a year ago. Now move on."

Hearst turned his back. Everyone else in the bar watched Ned as he retreated toward the heavy door.

On the hotel's chilly porch again, Ned heard a quiet cackle. "Found him, didn't you?" It was the bald old man.

"Yeah, but he's changed."

"Gold fever. Made big money for a time. Now his mine's goin' downhill. Makes a fella stingy." The man's big eye bugged up at him like an old toad's. "You look hungry, son, and it's gonna freeze mean tonight. Where's your shack?"

Ned looked away. "Don't have a place yet."

"Then you might as well use mine till you get a stake. I don't use it no more and there's no sense in your freezin'." He got up, leaning heavily onto a pine burl cane. "Follow me."

"That's mighty decent of you, but where will you stay?"

"Hotel. Guess the girls there are soft-headed or somethin'. Anyhow, they look after me since I got run through the flume."

"You ran the flume?"

"Yeah," the man grinned as he hobbled on, revealing jagged gaps from broken teeth. "We was hydraulickin' back on Hardscrabble Butte when a loose hose kicked me into the slurry, sent me down head first with the rock. Reckon it 'bout broke every bone I had. Ground me down smooth as a worn quarter dollar." He stopped, pointing with his cane to a board shack dug into the hillside. "There she is. A good kick's the only key you'll need. And there's grub if the rats ain't got it."

"Thanks again, Mr.—"

"Baboon, son, Old Baboon. No mister to it anymore." He turned and hobbled silently back toward the hotel.

*   *   *

In the morning Tom Bass, a growling boss with a white scar across his nose and cheek, reluctantly put Ned to work beside a mineshaft derrick. His job was to lead the pinto horse that hauled buckets of ore up the shaft with a rope and pulley. When there was enough, Ned was supposed to cart the rock into a shed and dump it into the stamp mill. There, the two six-hundred-pound iron pistons of the battery pounded out the ore, shaking the entire mine with each deafening crash. The mind-numbing work continued twelve hours a day, six days a week. But Ned thought: the horse, the rifle, Paquita. How he ached to be with her and the baby again! He put in harder work than he had ever done, knowing money would be the key to his return.

The wages were set at ten dollars a week, which was low enough, but the first payday only brought Ned seven dollars. Bass explained curtly that he would earn full pay after he "learned the trade." In the next weeks, the quality of the ore declined, and the paychecks shrank still further. Once there was no money at all; the mine's gold shipment to Yreka had been robbed by the renowned Australian outlaw Neil Scott. "Wanted" posters in town spread pictures of the square-jawed Scott—the most feared of the many Sydney penal colony convicts shipped to California by the British.

Ned counted and recounted the few dollars he saved, but there was never enough. The long, springless winter seemed to hold him trapped in the valley mines. He decided to hold out a few more months, until the snowpack around Mt. Shasta melted enough for horse travel.

During that lonely winter Ned lived for the Sundays when he could sleep in, write in his journal, or amble down to the hotel to swap stories with Old Baboon. On one such day he was dangling his feet over the edge of the porch while he tried to start a journal entry. He had only written "Deadwood, Mar. 2, 1859." Nothing else seemed to come. Somehow the poetic fire he had felt in Now-ow-wa had flickered low in this desolate mining town. He looked up for inspiration and found Old Baboon staring over his newspaper at him with his one large eyeball.

Suddenly the old man pulled the pipe out of his mouth. "I've been wonderin'," he said. "Is that 'Hiner' your born name or did some fool make it up?"

Ned put down his quill. "Actually, it's my middle name. Pa named me Cincinnatus because he was from Cincinnati, and Ma picked Hiner because that was the name of the doctor when I was born." He paused, then returned the question with a grin. "Hiner's not so bad. How did you get a name like Old Baboon?"

The old timer sank back into his rocking chair. "Baboon," he muttered. "There's a story. Back in Pennsylvania I was Peter Bablaine, sure 'nough. But when I stepped off the boat in 'Frisco they knocked an 'r' off my first name as quick as you'd knock a tile hat off a judge. Then it was *Pete* Bablaine. So I packed into the mines at Dogtown and danged if they hadn't somehow ripped off the whole front of my name and lost the thing. That left me with *Bablaine*.

"After that I can't rightly recall just where I lost the rest. Must've just wore off and washed down with the tailings till all I had left was *Bab*. Now I never reckoned Bab was much to go on, and I was gettin' to wonderin' how much more I could lose without bein' out and out *nameless*, when that hydraulic hose hit me and I woke up in the county hospital."

He stuck out his crooked jaw fiercely. "That's when I picked up my stubborn streak. Hair fell out, too. The hospital women started callin' me *Old* Bab. When I finally git back to camp, though, Snappin' Andy takes one look at my beat-up face and calls me Old Baboon. Well, that was that, I reckon. You can shuck your name around just so long. When it finally sticks, there's no arguin' with it."

With a decisive nod he returned to his newspaper, allowing Ned to record as much of the tale in his journal as he could remember. After a minute, however, Old Baboon interrupted him with a grunt. "S'pose you saw this 'bout your Oregon bein' made a state."

Ned dumped his journal and looked at the paper. There was the article, saying President Buchanan had finally signed the bill, after years of roadblocks. The Southern states had long protested that another slave-free state would tip the balance in Congress toward the North. Ned sat back, imagining the celebration the news of statehood would bring back home. And as always, the thought of home made him think guiltily of his other home—of Paquita and the baby.

"Politics!" Baboon humphed. "Can't even get away from it out here.

It's enough to drive a man into the territories."

"You, Baboon? What would you do out there?"

"Prospect, I reckon. Ain't too old yet. There's a lot of gold left out there, Hiner. Folks just ain't looked the right places."

* * *

The months ticked past, filled with disappointment and delay, until finally Ned sharpened his quill by candlelight in Old Baboon's dugout cabin to pen what proved to be the last entry of his California journal:

> *July 13, 1859.* Every day the summer gets hotter. In half a year of tortuous work I have only saved 39 dollars and 50 cents, not enough to buy a horse. Still I *must* leave Deadwood and return to Paquita.
>
> The Hearst-Bass diggings are three weeks behind in payroll. Hearst is making his usual promises, but the Mexican pick-swingers at the face say we are out of "bonanza" (clear skies) and into "borrasca" (storm). Chinamen have started to buy the old claims and work the tailings, and Baboon says that's a sure sign it's over here. He says we may never get our back pay.
>
> By my figuring, Tom Bass has cheated me out of $80 altogether, either by "paying" in notes, by counting days crooked, or by paying with ore that's so poor even he can't use it.

Ned stopped writing and looked up grimly. He had already decided to balance that ledger before dawn. The mine's pinto gelding was worth about eighty dollars. And he had grown attached to Niño. He figured the horse would settle his account with Bill Hearst and company. He also figured Hearst would raise hell when he found out. But by then Ned planned to be well out of town.

After blotting the ink he closed the journal and packed it in his catenas, the Mexican-style saddlebags he had bought in town. He checked his newly purchased rifle. Then he blew out the candle and closed the door hard behind him.

* * *

The pinto at the mine knew Ned so well it let itself be saddled in the dark without a whinny. When the tack was in order and cinched down tight, Ned slipped to the corner of the stable to peer anxiously across the grounds. As usual, Hearst had left a guard. Ned could see him now, swinging his shotgun as he walked past the dark framework of the derrick. There was a creak of hinges as the man disappeared into the equipment shed to check on the stamp mill.

Quickly Ned returned to the horse. "Here's our chance, Niño," he whispered, swinging into the saddle. He clicked his tongue and the horse stepped smartly onto the main road to town.

Ned had one last call to make in Deadwood before he left. He threw pebbles at the second story window of the hotel until Old Baboon finally stuck out his bald head angrily.

"Shh!" Ned called. "It's me!"

"What the hell—"

"I'm on my way, old pardner. Doesn't look like I'll be back anytime soon, so I thought I'd better pay the rent on your shack now." He tossed a twenty-dollar gold piece into the window.

Baboon, still half asleep, rubbed his hand over his shiny head. "There ain't no rent on my shack."

But Ned had already spun the horse about. With a nod and a wave he bolted into the night.

*   *   *

It was careless of Ned to sleep late in his Yreka hotel room the next morning, but it seemed a pleasure he had earned. Even after he awoke he lay with his hands folded behind his head for a lazy hour, smiling comfortably at the ceiling. He had done well after all. He owned a horse, a rifle, and a bit of cash. Most important, he would be with Paquita again soon. He had even be in time for the baby's first birthday. He sat up and pulled on his boots, gazing dreamily out the window.

That was when he saw the six men on horseback riding up to the courthouse. Ned's heart began to thud. Leading the troop was Hearst's minion, the scar-faced Tom Bass. If they had already assembled a posse, the charge could be nothing less than horse theft.

Stumbling over his own feet, he rushed down the stairs. He tossed the hotel clerk a two-and-a-half dollar piece and hurried out the back way to the livery. There he handed the stable boy a dollar, almost expecting some burly sheriff to clap him in manacles for coming to claim the mottled, red-and-white horse. Now he regretted the distinctive pattern—it would be too easily recognized.

Ned left town on back streets, trotting the pony as briskly as he dared. His heart was pounding, but outwardly he tried to appear calm. At the edge of town he struck out cross-country for the forests surrounding the mountain. The main trail would have been much faster, but he could not afford to be seen heading toward Shasta.

At first he was grateful for the low cloud cover that blew in from the west, burying the hills and hugging the treetops with wisps of fog. But by afternoon he had to admit he was lost. All of his landmarks—even Mt. Shasta—had disappeared into the swirling white clouds. At one point the steep black face of a rugged lava field loomed up before him. He skirted around it and found himself in a strange valley. When night fell he continued at a walk, heading from clearing to clearing in the hopes of finding a creek or some other clue that might lead him to Now-ow-wa.

Just before dawn the clouds broke. A moon-silvered patch of mountain slope shone through the gap like a beacon. By the time the sun rose out of the desert, burning the last fog into a rosy haze, Ned had already found his way to the head of Now-ow-wa.

Caution kept him from galloping wildly down the middle of the meadow. The smoke drifting above the log cabin seemed too carelessly thick to be from an Indian fire. Could it be Lockhart, using the cabin as his hideout? Ned checked that the powder in his rifle was dry and the cap in place. He left the horse in the trees and stealthily worked his way toward the log cabin.

When he was just thirty paces away the door began to open. Ned held the rifle ready. Suddenly, near the bottom of the door, a little tousled head poked out.

"*Yapiton!*" Cali-Shasta squealed. "A white man!"

Paquita stepped into the doorway. "Kibo!" she cried.

Ned tossed his rifle aside with a grin. He ran to her and spun her around off the ground in his embrace. When he finally set her down she held her flushed face to his chest. "Kibo, I knew you would come back."

"I've ridden all night to return to my Wintu princesses." He swept off his broad felt hat grandly and kissed Paquita gently. Then he strode to greet the dark-haired toddler in the doorway. But the naked little girl toddled past him to hide behind her mother's legs.

"*Yapiton?*" the child asked.

Paquita nodded. "Your father, Cali-Shasta."

Ned lowered himself to one knee. "When I last saw you, you'd just learned to crawl. Now look how big you've grown!" He fished a moment in his pocket and withdrew a shiny piece of gold ore. "Come, here's a pretty rock I've brought just for you. I had to travel far away and move most of a mountain to find it."

The rock was streaked with colors and quartz crystals that flashed in the sun.

Cali-Shasta cautiously held out her hand for the beautiful rock. She gave Ned a respectful glance, as if this treasure more than explained why someone might travel far. "Pretty," she said.

Ned marveled to Paquita, "She talks."

"A few words, yes."

Ned looked again at his dark-haired daughter. "I'm your Papa. Can you say 'Papa'?"

The little girl twisted away shyly and shook her head.

Paquita smiled. "She'll learn. Come in now, Kibo. I'll serve you a warrior's feast."

Inside, while Paquita prepared a festive breakfast, Ned leaned back in his old chair and stretched out his feet, enjoying the thought of being home at last. This was where he had first heard the whisperings of the Wintus' spirits—where he had struggled with his first poems about the beauty and adventure of the frontier. It felt good to be with his family again.

But his ease was disturbed by the memory of Sam Lockhart—the reason he had been forced to leave Now-ow-wa months ago. "Paquita, I expected to find you in the Puyshoos village. Aren't you afraid Sam Lockhart will come back?"

Paquita shook her head. "Once our shaman Witillahow knew the evil spirit was using Lockhart's mask, he could invent dances and chants to combat it. Then there were no more attacks."

"But where *is* Lockhart? I've got a score to settle with him."

Paquita shrugged. "Charley says he's gone to look for gold in the east."

"Then I'll have to track him down there," Ned said, frowning. "That man is a danger."

"Why? Why burn yourself up with revenge for Lockhart? It's the evil spirit that you hate, and that spirit is still here. A spirit doesn't leave when its mask leaves. Until the spirit itself is gone, it will always take on new masks, new Lockharts. It's better to trust Witillahow. He knows about these things."

Ned studied Paquita silently for a moment. Of course, he realized, she was right. With Lockhart gone there was no reason they couldn't slip back into the familiar, idyllic life of the lovely mountain valley. Except—but he thrust the thought of Tom Bass' posse out of his mind. They had been easy to shake.

"Sometimes," he said, "I think you understand more than all of the whites put together. How is it you can be so wise, and yet so young?" He held her head in his hands marveling at her lovely dark eyes.

Before he could kiss her, however, a shot cracked outside, followed by the angry whine of a ricochet and a cry from the baby.

Instantly Ned ducked to clutch Cali-Shasta, afraid she had been hit. There was no blood. She was only startled. But fear left Ned chilled. He peered out the cracks between the wall logs and counted the rifle barrels—one over the woodpile, one behind a rock, and two others behind trees.

"If you surrender, Miller, it'll make things a whole lot easier," a voice shouted.

Paquita whispered anxiously, "What do they want?" She crawled closer and took Cali-Shasta.

Ned edged toward the window. He yelled outside, "Don't shoot. I'll—I'll come out unarmed."

"What is it?" Paquita asked. "What did you tell them?"

He turned to her but suddenly found it hard to meet her eyes. What could he say to her? His only thought was a painful one: that this posse was a greater danger even than Sam Lockhart.

"I—I have to go," he stammered in Wintu. "I don't know how they followed me here."

Paquita lowered her eyes. Ned put his arms around her and embraced her tightly.

Then he held Cali-Shasta's little hands, studying the features of her impish face. "Your Papa has to go away again for a while," he said.

"More?" the little girl asked, holding up the shiny ore in her hand.

Ned eyes grew damp at the innocence of the question. All she knew of fathers was that they went away in quest of treasures. He nodded.

"Come back?" Cali-Shasta asked.

"I promise, Cal." Ned felt a lump in his throat. "I'll come back and make everything right again. I *promise*."

"We'll give you to the count of five, Miller," the voice outside bellowed.

While the voice outside began its count, Ned stood up and swept his gaze around the cabin he had built endless summers ago, when he had first been in love with Paquita. It struck him that the log walls had grown dark with smoke and age since then. Only the window was unchanged, still framing the lonely, lofty mountain to the north. Time and fate might toss their lives about like autumn leaves. But Mt. Shasta would always be there.

As soon as Ned stepped outside the rifles surrounded him like the spokes of a wheel. Tom Bass, his scar red with anger, wore a satisfied sneer. "Sheriff Bradley here has a warrant for your arrest, Miller. Says you're a horse thief. Now I didn't believe it, you understand, till I found you and my horse right here in Squaw Valley where he said you'd be."

"I never—"

"Save it for the jury." Roughly, Bass twisted Ned's hands behind his back and tied them as tightly as he could. When he was done, the men set Ned on the pinto horse and tied its reins to the sheriff's saddlehorn.

After some discussion it was decided to take Ned south to Shasta City, since the new jail at Yreka was not yet finished. Bass and Sheriff Bradley said they could handle the job, so they let the rest of the posse return the way they had come.

Just before the sheriff led off towards Soda Springs Ned dared to ask if he could at least fetch his journal from the cabin. "It's not much—just one book," he said, glancing back toward the cabin's dark window, wishing for one last glimpse of Paquita and his daughter.

Bass' reply was dry. "You won't need no books where you're goin'."

Chapter 8

. . . an adobe prison stood
Beside a sullen, sultry town,
With iron eyes and stony frown.
　　　　　—Joaquin Miller

Ned did not remember the trip well. At a farmhouse that night they bound his chest and stomach so tightly to a chair that he vomited repeatedly. The taut ropes seared like hot iron. The night was a long, waking nightmare, haunted by self-incriminations. He had been a fool to think the posse wouldn't know about Now-ow-wa. But he had wanted so desperately to believe he could go back—that he could live with Paquita and Cali-Shasta as if nothing had happened. Toward morning Ned's tortured half-dreams turned to the hellish night half a year ago when Lockhart had held him prisoner. It almost seemed as if that nightmare had never really ended. The wild-eyed phantom of Lockhart glared at him and roared with satisfaction.

The following day a sweltering July sun sent the temperature soaring. By noon the world had boiled into a seething blur. Finally Ned could no longer keep his head up. He slumped to one side and fell from the saddle into the manzanita brush, landing heavily on his shoulder. The jolt brought him back, moaning, to a dizzying state of semi-consciousness. His captors cinched his bonds tighter and tied him back on like a sack of grain, leaving his head to thump against the horse's flank with each step. When the grim troop passed the first shacks on the outskirts of Shasta City, blackness closed over Ned altogether.

* * *

Ned awoke to the stench of sweat and urine. He lifted his aching head from the plank bunk, trying to figure out where he was. He stared at a dirty adobe wall carved with names. It explained nothing. Above, a window let in a single square beam of sun. There were bars in the opening. Bars. Suddenly he remembered and sat up with a start.

Across the cell another prisoner sat slumped on a bunk, his feet on a stool and a slouch hat tipped over his face. At first Ned thought he might be asleep, but then the man lifted a hand to play a card on the solitaire game on his bunk.

Ned rubbed his hands over his face, still trying to clear his thoughts. "Were you here when they brought me in?"

The man played another card but did not answer.

"Looks like they really built this place," Ned went on. "Don't reckon anybody's going to break out of here."

The man slowly looked up. Ned's heart stood still. "Neil Scott!" he whispered. The infamous outlaw was just as hard-jawed and stocky as his picture in the wanted posters. Ned remembered that Scott was the "Sydney duck" who had robbed the Hearst payroll and murdered a guard without flinching.

The red-haired Australian gave the slightest sign of a smile. "Yeah?"

"Nothing," Ned added quickly. "I mean, I've seen your picture before."

"Is that so?"

Ned's voice dropped a note. "In Deadwood." With a chill he realized that he, too, was in prison for robbing Hearst—though the circumstances had been far different. The law, in its blindness, had thrown him together with a cold-blooded killer.

A key rattled in the door, and Ned jumped. A man with a mustache leaned his head in. "Visitor for you, Miller." He pulled out the key and let in a tall, thin man in a black suit.

The visitor nervously shifted a top hat in his hands. "Good day, Mr. Miller," he said, offering Ned a weak smile. "I am H. T. Ferguson, your court-appointed attorney." His voice rose uncertainly, as if he had asked a question.

"Pleased to meet you."

"Yes. I regret that the citizenry has taken such an active interest in your legal affairs, but as a result the grand jury has already met and handed down an indictment. Here, I've brought it with me. Of course, this only means your case will come to trial as soon as time permits. A day or two, depending on—" he glanced at Scott, "—other pending matters."

Ned took the paper from him and read through it carefully.

THE PEOPLE OF THE STATE OF CALIFORNIA against HINER MILLER. In the Court of Sessions in the County of Shasta, July Term, A.D. 1859.

Hiner Miller is accused by the Grand Jury of the County of Shasta by this Indictment of the crime of Grand Larceny, a felony committed as follows—

That the said Hiner Miller at the County of Shasta on the 10th of July A.D. 1859, one gelding horse of the value of Eighty Dollars, one saddle of the value of Fifteen Dollars and one bridle of the Value of Five of the property, goods and chattels of one Thomas Bass then and there being found then and there feloniously and willfully did steal, drive and take away, contrary to the statute in such case made and provided and against the peace and dignity of the People of the State.

Names of witnesses	District Attorney
THOMAS BASS	JOHN D. MIX
WILLIAM KAPPEL	

A true indictment by D.D. Horril, foreman Gr. Jury, July 19, 1859.

"But this *isn't* true," Ned objected. "The horse wasn't stolen at all—it's mine by right of the two months of back pay Bass owes me for working at his mine. And anyway, it was in Siskiyou County, not Shasta, it happened on July 15, not the 10th, and I've never heard of this 'witness' William Kappel!"

The lawyer cleared his throat and took the paper back. "If you want an exhaustive defense, you should expect to provide the proper fees. Now, you entered here with a credit of sixteen dollars—you'll find a receipt for it with your file; I have accepted it in lieu of my usual initial fee of twenty dollars, but perhaps you have other assets or family who might be interested in your defense, and if that is the case, I—"

At this point Scott dropped a foot heavily to the floor. "Get out."

"Pardon?"

"I said *get out* before I wring your neck." Scott moved to the edge of the bunk menacingly.

The lawyer's thin lips began to flutter. "Look, Mr. Miller, perhaps we can discuss this later, when we won't be disturbed?" He nodded timidly at Scott and suddenly fled for the door. The jailer locked it behind him.

Ned turned reproachfully to Scott. "What'd you scare him off like that for?"

"Bloody buzzards rob you blind." He returned sullenly to his card game.

"But he knows law."

"Didn't you hear the bastard? 'Town folks taken an interest in your case.' Know what interest they got in a horse thief? Town ladies prob'ly already gettin' picnic baskets ready for the hangin'."

Ned paled. "I suppose you've got a better plan?"

Scott gave his half-smile again. "When *I* swing, it won't be because I sat in some jail waitin'."

"But—"

"Jus' siddown an' shuddup. You play Seven-Toed Pete?"

* * *

There was a rustle in the dark cell that night. Ned opened his eyes to see Neil Scott's stocky form raise itself from the opposite bunk and take a step toward him.

Ned sat up with alarm. "What the—"

Scott hissed. "Shut your bloody trap, will you? It's time to get to work."

"What do you mean?"

Without answering, Scott pulled the stool to the small window. He scratched his fingernail across the bars. In the moonlight Ned could see what looked like dirt fall from slits across the bars, revealing a row of saw kerfs. "You fill the saw cuts with spit an' adobe every mornin'," Scott explained. "Makes 'em look jus' like rusty bars to the bleedin' wardens."

"How did you get the saw?"

"I brung it with me. Always good to keep a notched watchspring sewn in your shirt." Scott uncoiled the makeshift hacksaw and set to work on the last of the five bars, moving his short but powerful arms swiftly.

An hour passed while Scott toiled single-mindedly with the metal, refusing all offers of help. He stopped only once, when a wagonload of drunks rumbled down the street singing and swearing. Finally he coiled the spring up carefully and inserted it into a slit in his collar. Then, hanging from the window like a gorilla, he began to ram the bars with the heel of his boot. Straining and sweating, he bent out one after the other.

When at last the bars were splayed out like the thin fingers of an iron hand, he turned to Ned. "I don't want you wakin' up the town, now. I plan to be sixty miles from here by dawn an' I don't want no mob o' wardens chasin' after me." He began to squeeze out over the black stubs of the bars.

"Wait, Scott," Ned said. The outlaw was so obviously skilled at escape that Ned had reluctantly decided it would be best to stick with him—at least for a while. "Tomorrow the county's going to be crawling with sheriffs no matter what, and I don't have any place to hide out. How about if I go with you just until things quiet down?"

"Bloody likely I'd drag along a galah like you."

"I'm a fast rider, and a crack shot with a rifle. I reckon it'd be safer going together, wouldn't it?"

Scott snorted contemptuously, about to jump down onto the sloping roof outside. Then he stopped, as if struck by a second thought. "Aw, hell with it. If I don't keep an eye on you, you'll be caught in ten minutes an' have us both strung up by noon." He made a face and spat. "Well, c'mon then. But remember, you double-cross Neil Scott an' your hide ain't worth scratch."

Ned crawled out the window after him and dropped to the roof. Crouching, they crept to the eave and sprang to the steep hillside behind the jail. Ned was ready to run up the moonlit hill and out of town, but Scott waved him into the shadows. Silently he led the way behind several buildings and past a drunk asleep in a back street. Finally they reached the door of a livery. "Take a fast one, kid," Scott whispered. "You'll need it."

The warm, rich smells of horses and leather filled the dark stables. Once Ned's eyes adjusted he could see the big animals, some lying, some asleep on their feet. He smiled to himself. The third horse from the door was the pinto gelding. He rubbed its nose gently, whispering, "Well, Niño, looks like you're mine after all." The pony sniffed him quietly, registering no surprise at finding an old friend in the stall.

Scott's choice, however, let out an angry snort as he was trying to put on a bridle. A moment later, footsteps creaked down a set of wooden stairs and a lantern was thrust into the room. Ned dived into the hay, not daring to breathe. A pair of boots crunched through the straw as the lantern advanced down the stalls. Ned heard his heart pounding. There was a flicker as the lantern turned. Then the boots slowly retraced their steps.

As soon as it was quiet again, Ned saddled hastily and led the pinto outside. After a minute's wait Scott appeared at the door with a sleek white horse.

"Is that the best you could find?" Scott scowled.

"Niño's plenty fast."

"I hope so for your sake, kid. C'mon." He rode out into the moonlight and up the hill.

Ned hesitated. Was it really wise to follow Neil Scott? The outlaw had one of the blackest reputations in all of Northern California. The man was a savage—a ruthless murderer. Perhaps, Ned thought, it would be safer to strike off on his own.

Ned looked over his shoulder at the dull gray roofs and empty streets of the town. In a few hours, he knew, the streets would be alive with scores of mounted men riding out in search of the two escapees. He had underestimated the deputies' tracking skills once before, when they had found him at the log cabin in Now-ow-wa. This time he wasn't in familiar country. The posses knew the land around Shasta City better than he did.

And this time they would be shooting to kill.

"C'mon, Niño," he said, kicking his heels to follow Scott up the hill.

Chapter 9

Go, traverse Trinity and Scott,
That curve their dark backs to the sun:
. . . have they not
The chronicles of my wild life?
My secrets on their lips of stone?
                                    —Joaquin Miller

Ned had to ride for all he was worth to keep sight of the apparition galloping ahead through the moonlight. First Neil Scott raced west past Whiskeytown. Then he left the main trails and climbed over Mad Mule Mountain into the wilderness along the Trinity River. Finally the outlaw turned north and rode sixty grueling miles to the trackless headwaters of the Trinity in the black forests of the Scott Mountains. There, when the sun was already high in the sky, their exhausted horses smelled the lush grass of Scott Valley. Hunger kept the sweat-drenched horses trotting downhill toward the meadows.

"How far are you going?" Ned asked. "Deadwood's hardly twenty miles away. People could recognize me in these parts."

Scott grunted. "Reckon they know me, too. To some of 'em this here's Neil Scott Valley, they know me so bloody well. Trouble is, they can only find me when they ain't lookin'."

Scott rode on until the trail crossed a small creek. He stopped in the middle, looking carefully in all directions. Then he turned his horse downstream. In the creekbed the hooves left no tracks.

They waded down the creek a mile to the Scott River. From the creek's mouth Ned could see the river ahead was split into two channels, surrounding a long, densely-forested island with a moat of swift water. Scott tilted his head back and let out the long, yipping howl of a coyote. A moment later the call was answered by a howl from the island. Scott spurred his horse into the river.

The shack in the trees was so well hidden that Ned only saw it when they were almost there. A rifle barrel in the window turned to follow them. A voice called out in a thick Australian accent, "Neil, you old bastard! Say—who's the bloke with you?"

"Just a kid. Busted out of Shasta jail with me."

After a moment's hesitation, the rifle was pulled in and a fair-haired man appeared at the door. He was thin and delicately built, quite unlike Scott. His pale cheek carried the red stripe of a recent wound. "So who the hell are you?"

Ned dismounted, but hesitated to offer his hand, unsure whether outlaws held with such formalities. "Ned Miller," he said.

"Dave English," the man replied. "I guess if you lit out with Neil you'll probably pass. He and I don't split up very often." He turned to Scott. "Bring any tucker? I've been pressed for eats since I holed up here."

Scott shook his head. "I can't pack in no supplies with a posse behind me."

"Well, I hope you're better at shooting squirrels than I am, 'cause I'm not going out on the trail until this cut heals." English felt the wound on his cheek tenderly. "How were you figuring on feeding this new bloke, anyway?"

"Buggered if I know. Don't have to, eh?" Scott took a rifle off the wall and conspicuously began loading it.

Ned saw it was time to speak up. "I'm good at hunting game. Lend me a rifle and I'll have grub up in a couple hours."

English looked to Scott. "I'm awful hungry, mate. Best you let him try."

Scott said nothing. He clicked the hammer of his rifle, as if weighing the options. Then he took down a second rifle and laid it on the shack's only table. "All right, kid, you go ahead an' find us dinner. But remember, Neil Scott's gonna be bloody well right behind you all the time."

*   *   *

By sundown Ned had bagged a fat grouse. He knew it wouldn't go far among three hungry men, so he put it into a stew with lots of roots and blueberries. When he served it up, Neil Scott poked out a white root with his knife and turned it over. "What the hell's this?" he asked.

The Wintu name for the root was on the tip of Ned's tongue. Instead he said, "In the backwoods we call them 'mountain potatoes.' Sometimes that's all a mountain man'll eat."

Scott took a bite and made a face. "Ya ask me, it ain't worth a Digger Injun's breakfast." He pulled a jug out from a nook in the wall and sloshed a liquid into the stew pot. Then he put the jug to his lips and tilted it back a long while. Finally he set it down and wiped his mouth with satisfaction, loudly exhaling the smell of brandy. "Reckon it'll be better now," he said.

English borrowed the jug next. When he had drunk, the nervous tension that had kept his slight frame taut began to slacken. Speech began to pour out, as if it had been bottled up for ages. "So where are you from, Miller?" He tipped back the bottle again.

"Well, I—"

Suddenly English set the bottle down and belched.

Ned hesitated. When the lean outlaw drooped back on his stool to drink yet again, Ned went on. "I was born—"

"The hell you say!" English sputtered his brandy, and Neil Scott pounded the wall with his huge fist until the shack rocked.

"Neil and me were born, too—in bloody Liverpool." English licked the brandy from his lips, his eyes closed as if to picture that British seaport. He frowned. "We met in the prison there when we were just tykes."

Ned began, "How did you—" but was cut off by an ominous growl from Scott, who had tipped his chair back against the table.

English nursed the bottle. "No secret. Neil's father flogged him to make him work in the factories. The old man threatened him with a gun till he accidentally shot himself. So Neil was in for murder."

Scott growled again, staring into the stew pot.

"Me, I ran away from an orpha— orpha—" he drank another swig, as if to lubricate the word. "I ran away. Then I took up with a gypsy show, learned to do costumes and pick pockets. Got run up for petty theft. Petty's right." English laughed. "I slipped out of there in a week, dressed up like a warden. Then they sent me to Australia. So I couldn't escape. That's where Scott and I met again."

Scott was growling with a lower tone now, and still staring in a strangely absent manner. English leaned back, talking a little faster than his tongue seemed able to go. "Oh, sure, we took up th' deal. Y'know. The wardens give ush a free trip to Shan Francisco. If we never come back. Ha! You think we want to see Aushtralia again? But no one had work for th' likes of ush in Frishco. That's when Neil figgered out gambling. Me, I went back to my ol' routine. Coshtumes, light fingers. It'sh a different bloke each time what nips their gold. That'sh what they think. Until—" he winced, eyes closed, drawing the red wound on his cheek into an arch. "Never been shot at b'fore. An' now . . ."

English's head had been rolling. Finally he sank to one side and his tongue gave up its struggle.

The cool air of evening had settled over the island hideout. Now Ned could hear from Scott's steady breathing that he too had long been sleeping, even though he was frowning sternly at the stew pot with his eyes wide open.

Ned waved a hand uncertainly before Scott's gaze. Without so much as blinking, the wide-eyed outlaw began to snore. For a moment Ned was tempted to use the moment to slip away from the hideout. But where would he go? Into the arms of the posses that would be scouring Northern California for him?

He sighed and stirred through the pot for the last of the grouse. Scott and English had hardly touched the food, even though they must have been famished. Ned guessed they were used to flour and beans. After listening to English talk, he knew why they had not been able to stock up on such food. Their last robbery had failed. It would take time before they dared to venture out again.

*   *   *

During the hot days that followed, Ned's main concern was convincing the outlaws he was of more use to them alive than dead. His knowledge of wild edibles was his only high card. Hunger forced Scott and English to give him enough freedom to hunt and gather along the riverbank. Still, there could be no talk of trust. As long as Ned knew the location of the hideout, he figured Scott eventually wanted him dead.

One afternoon, while the outlaws fitfully dozed after an unsatisfying dinner, Ned noticed a discarded scrap of paper among the empty biscuit tins in a corner. The blank paper made him think of the journal he had been forced to leave behind with Paquita and Cali-Shasta. That book had contained an unfinished poem, a verse describing how he could travel the world without finding the beauty he had discovered in Now-ow-wa. He had labored over the poem during the final weeks he had mined at Deadwood, full of longing for his Wintu wife and daughter.

Now, suddenly, the final verse sprang full grown into his head. It was as if the spirits of the wilderness had reached inside him and written the words on his soul—as if his unjust banishment had allowed the simple perfection of Now-ow-wa's peace and beauty to glow its brightest.

Trembling with excitement, Ned picked up the ragged scrap of paper. He smoothed it as carefully and gently as if it were a carrier pigeon with a message to the outside world. Perhaps, he thought, this poem would somehow endure, winning the acclaim he felt destined to achieve. He took a blackened stick from the fire, sharpened it against a rock, and set to scratching the words in tiny gray letters.

"Bloody hell!" a voice growled behind him. Neil Scott sprang from his chair like a cougar. He knocked Ned to the ground and snatched away the paper.

Angrily Ned scrambled to his feet. "Damn it, Scott, why'd you—"

Scott cut him short with a glare. Then he held the paper to the light, turning it different directions uncertainly. "Take a look at this, Dave. What the hell's it say?"

Roused from his nap, Dave English rubbed his eyes. He took the scrawled text and read aloud.

> "If I should go out in the world,
> On life's broad sea set sail;
> If I should go where waves are hurled. . ."

"Bloody hell!" Scott interrupted. He grabbed Ned by the collar. "It's an escape message. You were gonna put it in a bottle and throw it in the river."

"No, I swear it. It's just a poem. See, it rhymes."

Scott tightened his grip until the collar strangled Ned. "So it's in code, eh?"

Ned mouthed a wordless denial, struggling for breath in the outlaw's iron grip.

English mused, "Actually, Neil, it does rhyme. 'World'—'hurled.' A trifle clumsy, to be sure."

Scott grunted. "What're you saying?"

"Looks like it is some sort of poetry, mate. Nothing wrong with that."

"You sure it ain't trouble?"

Ned tried to signal agreement, but lack of oxygen left him too weak to do more than flop his arms.

"Well," English went on, "it reads a bit rocky for my liking. Still I reckon it's harmless enough."

"Huh." Scott loosed his grip. Ned sank to the floor, writhing for breath. Then Scott swept his arm through the air, in a single motion crumpling the paper and throwing it into the fire.

"Wait!" Ned managed to gasp. But already the flames were taking the words. At the same time he realized his own memory of the long, final verse had dimmed. Only a hazy rhyme or two remained from the sharp, earlier vision. The poem was gone.

Anger flared through Ned for an instant. He balled his fists, but tried to hold back. He knew if he challenged these rough men they would kill him. Nor could he really expect to explain his loss to them. All he could do was try to preserve the emotion he had touched in the lost verse.

"Don't try no more tricks, kid," Scott growled. "Just work on finding us some decent tucker."

* * *

As the days wore on, the Australians grumbled louder about the meals Ned concocted from roots and berries. Even when Ned brought in venison they continued to argue. English grew nauseated if he ate meat three meals a day, but Scott became livid at the sight of boiled "Digger Injun" roots. Finally one morning he hurled a stack of mashed root-cakes out the door, roaring, "That's the bloody limit. We gotta have flour and beans and bacon. One of us is goin' in to town."

English quickly raised his hand to his scar, feeling it gently.

"Well," Scott demanded, "who'll it be?"

"I can't go till I've healed," English said. "And you'd be recognized. Why don't we disguise Miller and send him in?"

"The kid? He'd just botch a holdup and lead the bloody wardens after us."

Ned weighed the idea. If the disguise were good enough, he might be able to play a bluff hand in Deadwood. Most of all, however, he relished the thought of time away from the outlaws—even if it would be just a few hours. He had been cooped up in the cramped hideout with these coarse men for what seemed like years.

"I wouldn't have to rob the food," Ned suggested.

"What are you saying, kid?"

"I could buy it."

"*Buy* it?" Scott frowned at him, as if letting this idea sink in. "Hell, that might be the only way. Dave, you change the kid into some kind of get-up. I'll stake 'im for the ante." He slapped three gold pieces on the table and stalked off, scowling.

When he was gone, English opened a small leather-bound trunk filled with wigs, clothes, and bottles. For a moment he studied the contents thoughtfully. Then he squinted at Ned with an artistic eye. "We'll have to get rid of that scraggly beard of yours. Do you know any Spanish?"

"Spanish? A little, I guess. Just what I've picked up from the passing vaqueros. Why?"

"I've got a set of togs that'll fit you out finer than Joaquin Murietta." English fished out a black wig, a mustache, a striped serape, and a sombrero. In a minute he had arranged the gear on Ned. On his tall, square-shouldered frame it had a striking effect, augmenting the wild look of his buckskins and moccasins. "Well, if it ain't the bleeding Ghost of the Sonora," English marveled.

"*Buenos dias, gringo,*" Ned said with a smile. "I buy some beans, *si?*"

English grew serious. "You buy all you can carry. Take my horse and be back in five hours. Just make sure you're not followed, 'cause if you come a gutzer on this job, Neil and I will track you down and see you pay the reckoning."

Ned pocketed the gold coins. "I'll be back."

* * *

Ned galloped nearly two hours down the Scott River trail to the edge of Deadwood. Then he slowed the horse to a lazy walk. The town seemed to match the pace. Idlers sagged on wooden kegs or stumps in the shade of dusty plank shacks along the main street. The town looked even more dusty and tired than when he had galloped out in the middle of the night three weeks before. He shook his head as he thought of those weeks, and how they had unjustly turned Hiner Miller into a man wanted for the gallows, an accomplice to two of the most notorious outlaws in California.

He hitched the horse at the dry goods store and walked boldly in. He handed the clerk a crumpled list with a silent nod. Just as silently, they filled the order and figured the bill.

Ned had already cinched the purchases on behind his saddle and had one foot in the stirrup when he hesitated. The act had gone too smoothly to be gratifying. He still had plenty of time, and a pocketful of the outlaws' gold. He decided to take a drink before heading back.

Smoothing his new black mustache he crossed the broad street to the brick hotel. Old Baboon was rocking on the porch, smoking his meerschaum despite the hot sun. "*Buenos días,*" Ned said as he passed, but the old man just squinted at him with his one big eye.

At the ornate bar, he tossed a gold coin on the counter and ordered tequila. Cautiously, he looked around. The town was no longer wealthy enough to fill a fancy saloon on a workday afternoon. He tipped his sombrero back and relaxed, savoring the irony of his second visit to this bar.

Footsteps creaked on the hotel stairs. Looking tired and old, his bowler hat and gold nugget stickpin missing, Bill Hearst walked down to the bar. With a weary sigh he ordered a brandy smash.

When the drink came, Ned chipped a coin onto the counter. "*Señor,* I pay for this one." He raised his tequila. "To the hearts of gold." In a single draft he drained it.

Hearst hesitated. "Do I know you, mister?"

"No, *señor,*" Ned said, wiping his mouth and turning to leave. "Not at all."

Hearst gradually followed him to the doorway. He leaned against the cast-iron door jamb as Ned crossed the street and untied his horse. Hearst was still watching when Ned trotted his horse past on the way out of town.

*   *   *

The next day Ned was cooking again, pouring dried beans into a big pot of water by the fireplace. For once he was alone in the hideout. The outlaws had been in such high spirits after that morning's pancake breakfast that they had gone to watch the road south for miners returning from the mountains with ore or dust.

Ned went out into the sun in front of the shack and punched down some bread dough rising under a cloth. Just as he was about to go back in, two large deer leapt out of the manzanita and bounded past the front of the cabin. Beads of water shook from their fur.

Ned paused, thinking for a moment like a Wintu. Something must have spooked those deer across the river. Possibly a bear. Possibly a wildcat. He checked his rifle and stepped out back. Niño was sniffing the air. He stalked toward the river bank.

But he had hardly stepped out onto the river's gravel bar when Hearst's sharp voice barked out, "That's him, sheriff!" A pistol cracked, zinging a bullet into the gravel at Ned's feet.

Ned saw the sheriff begin to raise his rifle, hardly a hundred yards downstream. Almost before he could think Ned had pulled up his own rifle and fired. In the same moment the sheriff dropped his gun and clutched at his leg just above the knee.

Ned watched the man in disbelief. Now, on top of all the other charges, he had shot and wounded a sheriff.

"Damn you, Hiner!" Hearst bellowed. He sent a bullet whistling past Ned's ear.

Ned dodged back into the brush and ran for his horse, followed by a hail of curses. He threw on the saddle, tightened the cinch, and rode to the upstream tip of the island. He splashed into the river with his rifle over his head and drove the horse up through the woods to the trail.

But when he reached the trail he stopped, unsure which direction to turn. To the south were Scott and English, and the shortest route through the mountains to Paquita. To the north was the trail to Oregon. He gritted his teeth, looking first one way and then the other. It seemed as though the cloth of his life was being ripped apart before him, and he was left to cling to whichever torn edge held the most promise.

A shot rang out behind him. He made his choice—there was no choice: Oregon. He jerked the reins to the north, setting his spurs in the pinto's flanks. "Hyah! C'mon Niño!" If he could outrun them seventy miles to the border he would be safe.

At a breakneck gallop he covered the ground to Deadwood in scarcely an hour. He pulled his slouch hat down over his face and galloped through Main Street, only tipping his head up as he passed the hotel to yell to Baboon, *"Hasta la vista!"*

At the far edge of town he glanced over his shoulder in time to see a line of dust rising from two dark dots galloping behind him in the distance. He knew the horsemen must be Hearst and the wounded sheriff. In minutes they would have a posse mounted on fresh horses.

Ned's heart pounded in his throat. Niño was just a pony—no match for the lawmen's sturdy horses in a long race. He could only hope to outrun the posse on the strength of Niño's fiery spirit. He hunkered down in the saddle and dug his heels into Niño's flanks. The pony shivered and streaked a dozen miles down Greenhorn Creek to Yreka. Froth blew back from the horse's flared nostrils. Sweat dripped from its flanks and plastered Ned's buckskins to his aching legs.

They raced through Yreka's dusty streets. Men looked up in bewilderment as the wild-eyed rider in buckskins galloped past the courthouse, dodging wagons and dogs. A woman crossing the street clutched up the hem of her long dress and dived for the boardwalk. Shouts followed Ned as he banked around a corner and tore out of town to the north.

Still Niño galloped on. Another grueling hour of heat, dust, and strain brought them exhausted to the Klamath Canyon. They galloped down from the rim and charged aboard the Klamath River ferry.

"Push off, man!" Ned shouted at the astonished ferryman.

"Have to pay the fare first," the man replied.

Cursing, Ned ransacked his pockets in vain.

"You in trouble, mister?" the man asked suspiciously.

"Here, damn it all," Ned said, pulling out his rifle.

The ferryman paled and fell back against the rail, hands up.

"It's my fare, damn it," Ned said, holding the gun out stock first. When the ferryman still hesitated, he repeated, "I said *there's my fare*. Go on, take it. Hell, the rifle's worth *twenty* fares. Get moving, man! I can't be out to hurt anybody if I'm giving my gun away!"

Reluctantly, the ferryman took the firearm and set the boat across. On the far side Ned again urged Niño on with his spurs, and though the pony had already given more than seemed possible, it was as if Ned's desperation tapped a deeper reserve of strength. For most of another hour the loyal pinto steadfastly loped uphill into the Siskiyou Mountains. Only then, where the trail crested at the Oregon line, did the half-dead animal stagger to a stop and collapse on the ground to rest.

Ned fell on his knees beside the panting pony. "We made it, Niño. Good boy." He unbuckled the saddle to let the horse roll in the dusty gravel of the mountain pass. Then Ned wiped the sweat and the dust from his own face, rose stiffly to his feet, and turned to look behind him into California.

The sun's last rays had transformed the distant cone of Mt. Shasta into a blazing volcano, draped with rivers of fire and haloed with an aura of magenta. The world beyond lay dimmed by the twilight to an indistinguishable black morass below Shasta's spectral peak.

Tears started to Ned's eyes. Somewhere out there, he knew, were Paquita and Cali-Shasta. Would they understand how much he loved them? The thought of leaving them on their own made his throat tight with anger and guilt. But he had shot a sheriff, and he was charged with stealing a horse. Wherever he went in that dark land a posse would not be far behind. Worse yet, he had led the law to the outlaws' hideout, so that Scott and English—if they lived—would be waiting with their revenge.

He was a liability to Paquita, and to her tribe. He could not go back now, and bring them new suffering. But then it seemed he had never been able to go back—he could only go further on.

It was as if a great black door were swinging closed behind him. Six years had passed since he had left the sleepy farmlands of Oregon in search of gold and adventure in the wilder frontier of Northern California. The greatness he had dreamed of finding had taunted him and finally laughed in his face. He was leaving behind unfinished business—with his Wintu family, with Lockhart, with Mountain Joe's legacy, with Neil Scott, and with the law. Someday, he knew, he would be called to account for every bit of it.

If he couldn't return to Paquita and Cali-Shasta in California, perhaps he could bring them to Oregon? His heart clung to this hope. Yes, he would send for them as soon as he was settled.

But what could he do to establish himself in Oregon? The skill he had studied most was the art of living on wild roots and berries—not a very useful talent in a city. Perhaps he could turn to his writing? There must be some respectable trade that would give him a foothold. He couldn't bring Paquita until he had a place of his own.

With a deep sigh, he turned to look north into Oregon. A cool evening breeze met him from the gentle valleys below, as if from a different world. What would he do down there, among the farmers? How could he fit in, a failed gold miner with a bent for poetry and a head full of wild memories? What would he tell his parents that he accomplished in these six years? And how could he face his brother John, to whom he had bragged of returning to Oregon in glory?

Wearily, he brushed down Niño's coat and strapped on the saddle.

Then he led the pony down the grassy trail into Oregon, certain only of one thing: the spirit that had brought him to this lonely pass still whispered within him. Despite all the disappointment and loss, that haunting ambition for greatness still dared to speak. For once, Ned wondered if he should still listen.

Chapter 10

*Or did I have a double, and was it the other self who was
at college? And is it not possible that I am even now the
original and only real Joaquin Murietta?*
—Joaquin Miller

"Teacher!" A fat boy on the back schoolbench jabbed his hand into the
air.

Ned winced at the word. Though he had taught in the one-room
country schoolhouse near the Columbia River for most of a year, he had
never gotten used to the job. He was still taken aback whenever he
glanced in a mirror and saw his own short, slicked back hair, his white
starched collar, and the mandatory black suit, as stiff and grim as an
undertaker's.

"Teacher, can we go home early today?" the fat boy whined. "My pa'll
tan me if the hogs ain't slopped."

Ned fought back an urge to boot this lummox back to his farm.
Sometimes it took an effort to keep in mind the point of being a teacher:
to widen these children's horizons, to open their eyes to the beauty of the
world.

Ned unwrapped a thin parcel, the surprise he had ordered with his
own money many months ago. Surely this would catch the students'
imaginations. "Today I've brought a treat to finish up the day—a new
book."

The dozen schoolchildren leaned forward to see. It was rare enough
to have books in the classroom at all. For many of their lessons, they had
to copy the texts arduously onto slates. A pig-tailed girl in the front row
asked, "What's it about?"

"Well, it's a new story by a popular American writer named Longfellow. It's a poem about an Indian family far away in the East." The warmth
in Ned's voice showed how much he admired this verse. The first time

he had opened "The Song of Hiawatha" he had been astonished by the lyric rhythm, the epic scale of the saga, and the depth of its insight into Indian culture. Now he held out the thin book. "We'll use it to practice reading aloud. Why don't you start, Evelyn?"

The pig-tailed girl took the book uncertainly. She studied the first page and screwed up her face, as if this would help her decipher the letters. Then she started to read.

"By the shores of Gi— of Gi—" she faltered. "What's this word, Mr. Miller?"

"Gitche Gumee."

"Gitchy *what?*" the girl asked. The boy sitting next to her snickered.

"Gumee," Ned replied irritably. "It's the name of a lake. Go on."

"Oh." Evelyn put her freckled nose back to the page. "By the shining Big Sea Water stood the wigwam of No— of No—"

"Of Nokomis. Very good." Ned nodded to the girl's neighbor. "Obadiah? Would you like to read next?"

Obadiah squirmed, obviously recognizing this as a punishment for his earlier mirth. He was a good reader, but now he spoke in an odd, halting voice that gave the verse a faintly moronic tone:

> There the wrinkled, old Nokomis
> Nursed the little Hiawatha,
> Lulled him into Slumber, singing,
> 'Ewa-yea! my little owlet!'

Someone hooted like an owl—perhaps the fat boy in the back row?— and the class broke into laughter.

"Quiet!" Ned shouted, red-faced with anger and humiliation. The children's lack of discipline was bad enough. He had never had the heart to whip them, and as a result he had endured the sting of countless mental lashes in class, from minor hesitations to subtle taunts. But by mocking the great literature of the age they had wounded him much more deeply.

The children lowered their heads, as if they knew they had finally pushed him too far. The boys glanced to each other and then to the rack of willow rods on the wall.

For once Ned was tempted to use the switches. But how could he punish them for being children? Now he realized the mistake had been his own. He had expected too much from them. No one in the sleepy Oregon farmlands surrounding his lonely schoolhouse seemed to understand his love of poetry. Perhaps he had been wasting his time here all along.

The class still held its breath.

Ned took back the book of poetry from the boy in the front row. With a sigh he said, "Class dismissed."

Instantly the schoolroom was a blur of coats and grins and squeals.

As soon as the last child had gone Ned slammed the book down on the bench. He unbuttoned his stiff white collar and paced the room, angry with himself for having been trapped in this cold clapboard prison in the first place. He wasn't the kind of man who could live in a cage, working for a salary in a dead-end job. Like his old guide to the frontier, Mountain Joe, he needed room. He needed to gamble for higher stakes if he was going to play the game at all. How could he have forgotten that?

He opened the potbelly stove to put in more wood. A puff of smoke billowed up into the room, spreading the smell of memories. Campfires. Log cabins. *Cawels.*

A year and a half had passed since his return to Oregon, yet already his tumultuous life in California seemed part of a distant, shadowy world. Paquita! By the smoldering fire he could almost feel her presence, a ragged shadow in his heart, like the flickering shadows in the stove cast by a small, stubborn flame.

When he had left California he had been able to think of little else but the beautiful black-haired woman and the bright-eyed daughter he had been forced to leave behind. He had carefully laid out a daring plan to slip back across the border to bring Paquita and Cali-Shasta north with him. But as the months crept past, doubts had gradually dulled the sense of urgency. It wasn't easy picturing Paquita in the Oregon towns. She knew no English. She knew only the ways of the Wintu. How could he bring her to Oregon, where the townsfolk would laugh at her clothes, her manners, and her beliefs? Schoolchildren would be sure to spit at Cali-Shasta and taunt her as a half-breed. Perhaps Paquita wouldn't agree to come at all. She was a practical woman. She would know that the Oregon women would scorn her. Memories would still be vivid from the Pit River War, when whites had slaughtered her brother along with the Achomawis. Paquita had never asked to leave Now-ow-wa. The tribe was there. That was her home.

Still Ned had not altogether given up on his plan. Men usually didn't marry until they were well established. Perhaps if he could earn enough money it wouldn't matter what people thought. If only he had a couple thousand dollars! Then he could buy a house in town and a business of his own. Perhaps then he could convince Paquita to come to Oregon, and they could ride north with their heads held high.

The thought of money made Ned so angry that he slammed the stove door shut. As long as he was working for fifty dollars a month in the school he was more likely to sprout wings and fly than to save up thousands of dollars.

He went back to his teacher's desk, beside the narrow cot where he slept each night, and took up a letter that had arrived earlier that day. It was in the fastidious hand of his brother John. Though John was five years his senior, they had often been close, with a long history of rivalries and confidences. Ned had planned to save the letter to help pass the lonely evening. But now he tore it open, hoping for distraction.

> Eugene City, Oregon
> April 7, 1861
>
> Dear Ned:
>
> I suppose even in your country schoolhouse you have heard the reports from the Portland assayer's office about the newly discovered gold mines on the tributaries of the Snake River. I have been discussing the reports daily with a group of men of this city. There are three of us who have concluded the time is right to begin a mining venture.
>
> We are preparing to set out as soon as possible, and intend to stay in the territories at least through the fall. However, the group is actively seeking a fourth partner—someone who can provide technical knowledge about gold mining. Your name has come up because of your experience in California. Would you consent to join us?
>
> Please reply with the next post.
>
> Yours,
> John

Ned looked up from the letter at his plank-walled room. He pondered the irony: John, who had always made a virtue of following their father into farming and teaching, now was eager to join the latest mining stampede. Ned, the prodigal son who had rushed off to the gold fields as a boy, now sat in a schoolhouse, a teacher. He managed a grim smile. Always the same, he and John. And yet, always exact opposites.

The switch had not been an easy one. Eighteen months before, Ned had ridden into Eugene City wearing dirty buckskins and shaggy hair, with nothing but the horse beneath him to show for his years in California. All he could tell his family of what he had left behind were fanciful tales of gold mines and mountain camps. They didn't want to hear about Indians. They only seemed to care that he settle down to classes at the local college, preparing for a decent job.

The whole town had left him disoriented. Eugene City had grown from a sleepy hamlet of two hundred to a city of two thousand, dizzy with politics and fashion. He marveled at the wasp-waisted, hoop-skirted, button-shoed creatures that hobbled to church on Sundays, pale beneath their parasols. Sickliness was the latest vogue, and his little sister Ella, who had always been thin and weak, now had suitors—a line of young thinkers and dandies who conversed with her on vegetable diets, water cures, and atheism. They explored plaster heads for phrenological insights, read the Koran, and attempted to "magnetize" each other with hypnosis to reach the spirit world.

At Ned's college, Unionists and "States' Rights" lecturers hissed at each other like steam boilers building pressure. Twice already the pro-South college administration had seen their school burned to the ground by a secret "Union University Association" of pro-North fanatics. Finally, when news arrived that the radical Lincoln had been nominated for President, the frenzied college president took a gun downtown, accused the Republican newspaper editor of leading the Union University Association, shot at him, and fled to Virginia. The scandal forced Columbia College to disband in mid-term, leaving its new fire-proof stone building half-built.

With Columbia College closed, the money Ned had borrowed to pay his board and room came due. Finally he had accepted one of the teaching jobs his father kept finding for him. Ned knew he had to earn a living, and what other work had his poetry studies prepared him for? Besides, there was still Paquita, and the hope that money might one day pry open the door that had slammed so hard behind him in California.

Now he looked again at John's letter, and smiled. Here was a new mask to try on for size. A mining expert. An adviser to his learned older brother. This time he would be more than just another greenhorn pickswinger. Who knew what opportunities awaited in the gold strike east of Oregon? At least it would give him a gambler's chance at the money he needed. And gold fever was the perfect excuse for breaking away from his classroom in the farm fields. After all, he was meant to be something more than just a schoolteacher!

Ned's heart sped just a bit at the thought of the distant wilderness. It was as if his ambitious muse had awakened from a long sleep. The old spirit was humming a faint but familiarly alluring melody from its haunts on the frontier. It was time to see if he had forgotten how to dance to that tune.

*   *   *

When Ned arrived at the Portland docks two weeks later, paperboys were selling extras in the muddy streets. Their sing-song message sent a chill up Ned's spine: "It's *war!* Civil *war!* Fort Sumter falls to rebel guns!" He had not really believed war would come. The center of the whole controversy, whether federal or state laws should prevail, did not seem worthy of war.

The river steamer belched smoke and sparks. As Ned waited for his brother, watching the crowd of pack-carrying men surge aboard, he thought: it is a good time to leave for the territories. Politics would mean little in the gold mines.

Finally Ned spotted his older brother, balancing a duffel on his big square shoulder like a bag of grain. John's wavy dark hair was still parted down the middle like a teacher's. When he saw Ned he smiled and pushed up his wire-frame spectacles.

"There you are, Ned. Ready?"

"You bet." Ned shook hands with his brother and was introduced to the two mining partners following behind. He recognized them as medical students from Columbia College. Apparently they had been unsuccessful in establishing practices. Ned would have liked to think this was because of their reputations as hot-headed pro-North Republicans, but he knew the cause was less political. People simply did not trust doctors under thirty, regardless of how long they could grow their mustaches.

"It looks like you brought an awful small pack," John said. "Are you figuring on buying your equipment in Walla Walla?"

"I won't need much gear." Ned said. He had his own plan for striking it rich in the gold country. He had tried mining once and had learned a few lessons. One was that miners rarely got wealthy, but the suppliers always did. He planned to keep his options open for a while.

John shrugged. Then he straightened his spectacles uneasily. "Hard news today."

Ned nodded.

"Hurrah for Honest Abe," one of the medical students broke in. "Oregon voted Lincoln in to stand up to the Southerners, and now he's doing it, by God."

Ned gave the man a cold look, already regretting that John had brought along partners. Oregon had been so badly divided over the recent election that Lincoln had won the state by a mere 270 votes.

"I just hope he'll let the South go in peace," Ned told the medical student.

John raised his eyebrows. After a moment's silence he straightened his spectacles again. "I see it's a mistake we haven't talked about this before, Ned."

"You never talk politics."

"It is time people spoke up, Ned. The South has earned its war."

Ned bristled; his brother's voice had the tone of a teacher reprimanding a pupil. "I saw war when I was in California. It's too terrible for anyone to earn."

In reply, John cast a meaningful glance to the two medical students.

The ship's steam whistle split the air with a warning blast. Ned only stared at his brother. How could he favor the war? For an instant Ned was about to turn and walk away. But there was only the schoolhouse waiting behind him, and a whole territory ahead. His brother, and his promise to help, could not be abandoned now.

"Board!" a sailor cried.

Ned shouldered his small pack and silently pushed through the men jostling aboard. He crossed the gangplank and made his way to a crowded railing before John caught up with him.

"Ned." John took his arm. "I know you haven't always agreed with the family, but when war comes, people need to stick together. Can you see that?"

Ned stared out over the river, torn by a volatile mixture of resentment and loyalty, thinking how difficult family unity could prove to be.

"Well?" John asked.

Before Ned could reply, the ship's big paddlewheel began to churn the water white, backing the ship out into the choppy Willamette.

*   *   *

Within a day the sternwheeler had left the rain of Western Oregon behind. Ned's spirits rose when he saw the proud white peak of Mt. Hood emerge from the clouds like a sentinel on the road to the wild territory to the east.

The steamboat docked at the falls of the Columbia River. There the army of miners had to portage, hoisting their gear on their shoulders for the hike to the upper dock. Shaggy-haired Indian fishermen stood on rickety platforms in the midst of the falls, watching the roaring whitewater and skillfully spearing the huge salmon that leapt up through the spray.

Above the falls a smaller steamship took the miners eastward for a night and a day into a desert country of brown plateaus where the wind blew hot and the nighttime skies blazed with stars. Finally the crowded shipload of miners disembarked on the bank of the Columbia for the overland trek to Walla Walla, the gateway to the new mining district some were already calling "Idaho."

John led the way through the crowd to catch up with a wagon. "Say, driver," John called. "Take a dollar for giving us a lift to town?"

The driver turned. He was a long-jawed man, wearing a blue cap and a blue uniform with brass buttons. "Sure, mister, I reckon. I'm going as far as the fort, a half mile shy of town."

John tossed his duffel onto the pile of flour sacks in the wagon and hopped in after it. He waved to the others to join him.

As Ned was climbing aboard he recognized the long wooden boxes loaded underneath the flour sacks. "Coffins!" He cast a cautious glance toward the driver. "The war can't be out here already."

"Maybe not, but there's trouble enough."

"Indians?" John asked, knitting his brow.

"Just one: Cherokee Bob, a half-breed from Georgia. He's one of them secessionists that've been making it hot for us soldiers from the Army garrison. Reckon they think the whole Washington Territory's somehow gonna up and join the South."

"Have they attacked the fort?" John asked.

"No," the driver smiled grimly. "That's not the way they work. They're really nothing but a pack of gamblers and outlaws what've drifted in with the miners. But a guy can't walk through town in a uniform without one of 'em picking a fight. Last week they took on a half dozen soldiers at the opera house."

"Can't you get the sheriff to lock them up?"

"Ha! He's secesh too. Why, he was the one what started it at the theater. Between acts everyone was getting a drink and yipping it up like usual when Sheriff Porter comes up to some privates and says, 'Dry up there, you brass-mounted hirelings, or I'll snatch you bald-headed!' That's the way they always pick fights, calling us 'Abe Lincoln's hirelings' or 'Sam's sons.' Anyway, the soldiers hadn't been particularly rowdy and they told him so. That was enough of an excuse for the sheriff to jump on 'em. They tried to defend themselves, and suddenly Cherokee Bob's on 'em like a crazy man with a knife in one hand and a revolver in the other. Next thing you know there's two men shot dead and a couple pretty badly cut up."

"Where's this Cherokee Bob now?"

"He shot Sheriff Porter through the legs by mistake, so he's skipped town for now. I just hope he don't show up again before I get my transfer back to Missouri."

Ned gave him a sour look. "So they're sending you back to the war, huh?"

"Yeah, all of us regulars'll be going back East. They figure they can man a garrison like this out in the territories with a bunch of green recruits. Glad I won't be around to see it, though." He turned to his four passengers with a confiding tone. "This place has been crawling with trouble since they found gold. If I were you I'd travel together with some well-armed men. That's why I picked you fellas up—to have a couple of friendly guns along."

John frowned and looked at Ned. "I only brought this old Allen pistol," he whispered, hauling an ungainly gun out of his duffel.

"A pepperbox!" Ned guffawed. "Who knows what you'd hit if you fired that thing?"

"It *does* misfire, and I haven't very good aim anyway, with my spectacles." He paused, then added, "Isn't Walla Walla where the Indians massacred the Whitman missionaries?"

"Yes," Ned replied, "but Lewis and Clark came through here once, too, and they were treated well by the Indians."

"I'd still feel better if we pushed right on to the mines."

"As you like," Ned said, although he suspected Walla Walla would be the more promising spot to make money. After all, every ounce of gold from the mines passed through the town, and some of it was bound to stick there.

Before the wagon driver pulled up within sight of the fort, Ned and the others had to get off, since the driver wasn't supposed to take on riders. They paid their dollar fare and began the hike. The dusty track led them toward a collection of tents, tepees, and plank buildings about a mile ahead. Walla Walla lay in a treeless plain, baking in the midday May sun. A steady wind swirled dust into the air from the dry land.

At a corral on the edge of town they stopped to look at saddle stock. John picked out three of the sturdiest pack mules for himself and his two partners. With the experienced eye of a farmer John checked every animal's teeth and hooves. He glowered with disapproval when Ned insisted on buying a quick-footed Nez Perce pony.

"What do you think you came out here to be?" John asked. "An Indian scout? A racehorse jockey?"

Ned swung smoothly up into his saddle, remembering Niño, the brave little pony that had helped him outrun a California posse nearly two years ago. "We'll see."

*   *   *

Forty miles and two days later they had crossed the windswept desert plateaus to the Snake River, amid an incessant stream of men and pack animals on their way to the mines. The masses of gold-seekers huddled against the wind on the riverbank, where the Clearwater joined the Snake, waiting for the ferry to Lewiston.

Ned had never seen a more sickly, discouraged-looking town than

Lewiston. The tent city shuddered under the dust and sand blown down the windy canyons like volleys of shot from an unseen army. The town looked as if it had started down from the mines in the mountains above, ragged and discouraged, and had sat down in the forks of the river to wait for the ferry. It looked to Ned as though it ought to move on—as if it wanted to move on, as if it really would move on, if the wind kept blowing and the unseen army kept up the cannonade.

The buildings in Lewiston were made of white muslin stretched over frameworks of poles. The tents billowed before the wind, their walls punctured in places by airborne debris. Occasionally a ragged, shredded wall flapped angrily. Even the doors were not wooden, but only made of cloth stretched taut over rectangular frames. There were no windows, since the cloth roofs let in diffused daylight. As night fell, the tents of the town took on a ghostly yellow glow from the oil lamps within. The streets had no other light than this eerie, dim shine.

They arrived at dusk and stopped at a long tent with the neatly-printed lettering, "Hildebrandt's Hotel." The German proprietor showed them to a cluster of cots behind a stack of sandbags.

"It iss best you sleep behind sand. Stray bullets travel far in a city of tents." Then the bushy-mustachioed German dropped his voice to a whisper. "Keep your valuables in a roll under your heads. Sleep vith your pistols cocked. Thieves."

"We're only staying the night," John said quickly. "Then we'll be going on to Oro Fino." All day he had talked about the town whose name meant "fine gold."

"Oro Fino? Do not stop on the vay. Cherokee Bob's men run all the stations on the Clearwater. Even now they are taking inventory of your goods and are writing out phony bills of sale. Tomorrow they are riding ahead so they can show you the bills of sale at the stations, take your things, and call you the robbers."

The German caught his breath and looked behind him. "But please, do not mention my name. Ve are not yet organized. There are not yet enough of us." He took a step back, then again raised his voice to a normal tone, smiling broadly. "Velcome, gentlemen. *Gute Nacht* and sleep vell."

* * *

In the morning John admitted he had hardly slept at all. When they reached Oro Fino without incident two days later, however, John wondered out loud if the German innkeeper had been lying about the dangers of Idaho.

As soon as Ned saw Oro Fino, a ragtag scattering of tents along a wilderness canyon, he could tell that the peak of the gold rush had already passed on. For several days he led the others up and down the creekbed, searching for a worthwhile claim. Along the way he explained how the sluices, long toms, and rockers sifted gold from the black sand in the creek gravels. All the claims for sale had been worked clean, but the camp was full of rumors of gold strikes far back in the hills. On the third day they heard that a group of prospectors was leaving to scout the Bitterroot Mountains into Montana. John and the two medical students decided to join them.

"The way I see it, Ned," John said by the campfire that night, "there will be less likelihood of Indian or outlaw trouble away from the mining camps. And we're more likely to find a good claim by traveling through virgin land with a group of prospectors than by waiting here, where it's all been worked over."

"Possibly."

There was a silence as they stared into the flames.

"Then you will come with us?" John finally asked. The others looked to Ned as well.

"I came with you this far to teach you what I'd learned in California about mining. The truth is, I learned that miners don't get rich. The real fortunes are made by the outfitters and packers who supply them. That's why I'm thinking I'll head for Walla Walla."

John rolled one hand in the air, as though he were clarifying an issue for a student. "You have to understand, Ned, that things were a lot different back when you were a boy running away to California. Down there you were by yourself and there weren't any big discoveries left. Here we're still all together and the country is just being opened up. It would be a shame if you split up our group now."

Ned recognized the same argument in this speech that his older brother always used: John wanted Ned to bow to the will of the group, to finally become another good family boy—like him. Only this time it was easy to turn the argument on its head. Wasn't John as blinded by gold fever as he himself had been seven years before? John had left their father to plow and plant the family farm alone, and now he was about to march into the trackless wilderness with little more than a gold pan and a dream of easy wealth. In some ways, John was the seventeen-year-old dreamer Ned had once been. But John was also the plodding conservative Ned might have become if he had never left home. John was a part of himself, and that made it plenty difficult to let him go.

One of the medical students tugged a long mustache. "Besides, these mining towns are lousy with rebel sympathizers. If I were you I'd stick with honest Union men."

Ned frowned. "That kind of 'honesty' is burning down the whole country, the same way the Union University Association burned down Columbia College back home."

John straightened his spectacles. "Perhaps even fire is needed to burn out a greater evil."

"What are you saying?" Ned felt a sudden foreboding.

John cleared his throat. "Now that we're headed for the mountains, you might as well know. The three of us have been members of the Union University Association from the first."

Ned stared at his brother in disbelief. It was hard enough to think John supported a bloody war in the east. But it was worse to know he had condoned arson in Eugene City. And why hadn't John told him before now?

For a moment Ned felt anger rising inside him, ready to burst out in a stream of accusations. But then he caught himself. He, too, had kept secrets. He had never told his brother the whole story of his years in California—and the Wintu family he had been forced to leave behind. In a way, John's revelation only confirmed how similar they were. The difference, Ned now saw, was that John had committed his offense in the name of war, not peace.

The campfire crackled between them, slowly reducing the flaming argument to a mute ember.

Ned shook his head. "Good luck in the mountains, John."

Chapter 11

WANTED—Young, skinny, wiry fellows not over 18. Must be expert riders willing to risk death daily. Orphans preferred.

—1860 newspaper advertisement
for the Pony Express

Two days later Ned's Nez Perce pony clopped down the main street of Walla Walla. Ned sized up the saloons, hotels, and outfitters as he passed them by. But he shook his head at each of the storefronts in turn. If he was going to win fame and fortune on the frontier, he needed a higher stakes game.

Then he came to a tiny office with "Mossman's Express" in gold letters on the glass. A small placard in the window read, "Rider Wanted."

The pony express! That was the kind of free life he had learned to love from Mountain Joe. Of course there were dangers. Pony express riders traveled alone. Everyone had heard stories of holdups, Indian attacks, and sudden storms. But what could the Idaho wilderness throw at him that he hadn't already faced in the Northern California frontier? This was the chance he had been looking for.

He dismounted, brushed the dust from the wrinkles in his black suit, stuffed the pant cuffs into his tall leather boots, and strode through the doorway, already planning his strategy.

Isaac V. Mossman was a short, overweight man with dark, curly hair. His small black eyes studied Ned. "Yes, I lost my rider last week," he said. "Seems every time I send a rider out to pick up dust from a fresh strike, he gets gold fever and quits. Now, you—how can I be sure you'll stick with it?"

"Make me your partner," Ned replied evenly. It was a gamble, but an express business can't live long without a rider, and he guessed from the girth of the expressman's paunch that Mossman was loath to climb up in the saddle himself. "You could run the office while I ride the route. I've got a fast pony and I know the route to Oro Fino."

"Make you a partner? Pah!" the short man sputtered. "Here I've got offices in Lewiston and Oro Fino and four stations along the way with fresh horses. All you've got is one pony."

Ned shrugged and turned for the door.

"Wait!" Mossman said, rising from his chair. When Ned stopped, the portly expressman sank back, his dark eyes avoiding Ned's gaze. "Thirty percent of receipts if you can make it to Oro Fino and back in two and a half days."

"Forty."

Mossman shifted uneasily in his chair. "One third and that's it. Take it or leave it. Look, mister, how the hell do I know you can even ride?"

"Miller, Ned Miller." He offered a hand. "And don't worry."

The expressman gave a defeated sigh and shook his hand. "All right, Miller, you're on. The mail's five days late as it is. Can you ride out tonight?"

"Fine. Just fill me in on the details."

Mossman leaned back and blew out a long breath. "Well, it's a bit like the Pony Express between Missouri and San Francisco. You heard of them?"

"Of course."

"We're filling a gap in the U.S. Mail service. The government only takes mail as far as Walla Walla. Beyond that, people have to pay us."

Ned nodded. "Do we charge the same as the the Pony Express to California?"

"No, no. Their operation's on an entirely different scale. They've got eighty riders, spread out halfway across the continent. That's why they have to charge five dollars for a letter. We've just got the one rider, but then we'll take a letter to Oro Fino for ten cents. Even a newspaper only runs two bits."

"And that's profitable?" Ned asked.

Mossman grinned. "The profit's not in taking mail to the mines, Miller, it's in bringing back the gold. We charge one percent to carry gold dust by pony to the Wells Fargo bank here in town. That one percent adds up fast."

"But carrying gold also adds to the risk."

"It's risky as hell, Miller."

A tickle of fear ran up Ned's back. He wondered if the previous pony express rider had really left because of gold fever, as Mossman said, or if he had been ambushed by bandits. Ned studied Mossman again. The man's expression was somber, as if to say that some questions were better left unasked. Ned knew the dangers. High profits always came with high risks.

"All right," Ned said. "What's the schedule?"

Mossman laid out a map and pointed out the route drawn in red. "You leave the office here at closing time each Monday and Thursday. Gallop twenty miles to pick up a fresh horse at a relay and then gallop another twenty miles to the Patoka Station. That way you'll be crossing the open desert in the evening when it's cool. Stay overnight at Patoka with the old Nez Perce stationmaster before heading on into Lewiston at dawn. That'll keep you out of the Lewiston hotels. Too damn many robberies there. Then if you gallop straight on to a relay on the Clearwater—there's cottonwoods along the river so the heat's not too bad—you should be in the Oro Fino office tomorrow at two o'clock."

Ned nodded, trying to appear confident. In fact, the route Mossman expected him to cover in twenty-one hours had required four days to travel with John. It would be possible only if he galloped hell bent for leather—and if he wasn't stopped by thieves or rattlesnakes or thunderstorms or Indians. He cleared his throat. "Two o'clock tomorrow. How do I handle business at the Oro Fino office?"

Mossman explained the routine of sorting mail, accepting deliveries, and giving receipts. Then he unlocked the safe and dragged out a pair of leather express catenas. Their compartments bulged with sheaves of letters and newspapers. Finally he took a brace of Navy revolvers off a peg on the wall. "You'll want these along, too. The main trail's almost safe when there's a good string of summer miners around, but don't get caught out there alone without a fast horse and a pair of good shooting irons." Mossman pulled a pocket watch out of his vest and clicked his tongue. "Already past five. Better get cracking, Miller. You'll have to hustle to hit Patoka before dark."

Ned loaded his pony with the bags and touched her flanks with his spurs. Then he waved a farewell salute to his new partner and galloped off down the main street, determined to make a success of his new career. John had never let him forget the humiliation of returning empty handed from six years in the California gold mines. This time it was John who was likely to come back empty handed from his prospecting. Ned swore to himself he would stick with the pony express until he could return rich.

* * *

Darkness was rapidly falling across the desert when Ned reached the point on the trail where he thought the Patoka Station ought to be. The treeless tablelands stretched out around him as if drawn taut by the twilight glow silhouetting the horizon. The sagebrush flats seemed as vast and directionless as the buffalo prairies of the Great Plains he had crossed on the Oregon Trail as a boy. He reined in his horse and stopped for a moment, listening for any sound that might help direct him. A cricket chirped cautiously. Far away a coyote's song floated out across the twilight sea of sage. Ned shivered. The station had to be near, but he might never find it in the approaching darkness.

Just then his horse snorted, shaking its mane impatiently. With a wry smile, Ned dropped the reins and tapped the horse's flank. Of course the relay horse would know where to find its oats. And in fact it trotted purposefully for several minutes until it reached the head of a small canyon. Below, Ned could see a light—a lantern on a pole. The horse made its way to a plank lean-to, where an old Indian man appeared from a nearby tepee to give it grain and hay.

Ned stood with the catenas over his shoulder while the white-haired man unsaddled the horse and brushed it down. Ned told the Indian all about his new partnership with Mossman and his difficulty finding the station at night.

When the Indian was done with the horse he turned to Ned as though he had only just noticed him. "*Nika wake kumtux,*" he said. "*Boston wawa wake kloshe.*"

Ned reddened. Even he knew these few words of Chinook Jargon: 'I not understand. English language not good.' Since the Indian still stood watching him, Ned patted his stomach and suggested, "*Muckamuck?*"

Silently the old man led the way into the tepee, where the two sat cross-legged on elk hides by a small fire of gnarled sagebrush branches. The Indian spread several purple pemmican cakes before Ned and retired to the far side of the fire, watching Ned motionlessly.

Ned had tried pemmican years before, on the Oregon Trail. He had watched Shoshone women pound jerky into a paste and mix it with elk fat and huckleberries to make the cakes. Now he was hungry and it tasted good.

After dinner Ned had some time on his hands and he was curious about the mail he had carried, so he decided to take a closer look at the bundles in his catenas. He flipped through the letters. The return addresses were from Texas, Virginia, Boston, and even Europe. An unsettling number of the letters hailed from Northern California. Although it made sense that California miners would drift north to the new mines in Idaho, Ned didn't want his troubles with the law brought here to haunt him again. Already, those festering, unjust charges had cost him his Wintu family.

The sudden thought of Paquita brought tears to his eyes. Sitting by the fire in this Nez Perce tepee his longing for her hit him harder than ever. Here he was, carrying mail, yet it was impossible to send her a letter. She had no address, and she couldn't read. It seemed he could only communicate with her through his memories.

Damn! He felt like he had been living on memories too long. Angrily he yanked a newspaper out of the catenas and threw himself into the distant news for the sake of distraction.

The newspaper was from Port Orford, a little mining and lumber settlement on the southern Oregon coast. Evidently some beach miner who had come to Idaho subscribed to the paper for news from home. The sheet had eight tight columns of print: folksy local notices and grim news reports of war mobilization efforts back East.

But there was also a poem in a corner of the front page. Gradually Ned began reading it with genuine interest. The verse was the lament of a young, chestnut-haired girl sighing on the bluffs above the sea, pining away for her lost sailor suitor. In vain she watched the waves for the bright sails of the ship that would bring her love and take her away with him, leaving the melancholy, rain-swept shore behind. The poem was signed "Minnie Myrtle," to which the editor had added the sobriquet, "Sweet Singer of the Coquille."

On an impulse, Ned took out the paper and quill he carried for writing express receipts. In a minute he had dashed off a witty little poem as a kind of reply in verse—an ode from an express rider in the Idaho wilderness to a kindred poetic spirit by the sea.

Suddenly he stopped, guiltily realizing what he had done. He had wanted to take his mind off Paquita, but in his loneliness he had allowed himself to begin fantasizing about a Port Orford poet. What did he really know about this Minnie Myrtle? She might well be a decrepit spinster or a married shrew. But in his mind's eye he had already turned her into the longing, chestnut-haired girl in her poem. Worse, he had dressed up this dream with the very qualities Paquita lacked: ivory skin, erudite English speech, lofty manners, and lacy petticoats.

He knew it would be fairest to Paquita if he simply burned the poem he had written about the white girl. He held the paper out to the fire. But he couldn't quite let it go.

Slowly, counter arguments fluttered nearer, like moths approaching the firelight. Maybe this would prove to be the best poem he had yet written. Even if Paquita were here she wouldn't ask him to burn it, just as she had never cared about any of his verse. And how long did he expect to punish himself for leaving her behind in California? The "crimes" that had forced him to leave hadn't been his fault then and shouldn't make him feel guilty now. Surely there was nothing wrong with allowing himself to think normal thoughts about a female poet, if only to ease the loneliness of the frontier.

Ned looked again at the verse he had penned. All he wanted was that someone, somewhere would read what he had written and think a tender thought about another hopeful poet. If Minnie Myrtle were at all like the girl in her poem, perhaps she would.

He took up the pen again, signed his verse "C. H. Miller," wrote the name of the Port Orford paper on an envelope, and sealed the poem inside to be mailed.

Now the weariness of the long ride hit him. He stretched out and covered himself with a fur for the night. If he was going to succeed with the pony express, he knew he would have little time for poetry.

* * *

Ned worked harder in the summer of 1861 than he had ever worked before. Each week he galloped almost continuously for five days and then fell exhausted onto a cot in the back of the Walla Walla office to sleep around the clock. Twice already he had put off Cherokee Bob's hoodlums in the streets of Lewiston by firing warning shots into the air to draw a crowd—the only sure protection in a town where the law was controlled by Bob's syndicate of thugs. On another occasion Ned had outrun a band of Nez Perce hotbloods who had been lurking on the cliffs above the Clearwater. And once, after a long gallop in the shimmering heat of August, a relay horse had collapsed underneath him dead, leaving him on foot in a remote desert canyon.

Mossman's Express doubled its receipts under the new partnership, even though Oro Fino was producing less gold than in previous months. When the winds of winter arrived, some of the miners who had spent the summer prospecting the mountains began to drift down to Walla Walla, mostly with empty pockets. Ned heard that his brother John had crossed into Montana for the winter, but he had no way of knowing if the report were true.

It was a Thursday afternoon, and Ned was watching the Walla Walla office, getting ready for his evening ride to the Patoka Station, the day a wild-eyed young man in a red shirt burst in the front door.

"Where is it?" the man shouted, and threw himself halfway across the counter to grab Ned by the shirt.

In the first instant of panic, Ned thought he was about to be strangled and robbed. But the young man seemed too crazed even to be a robber. Ned freed himself from the man's grip with a powerful twist and quickly drew a cocked pistol at the red shirt. "Back off and calm down or I'll blow off your arm. Now what the hell are you talking about?"

"The *gold strike*, man! Where is it?"

Before Ned could speak again, another man had run in through the open door. "Miller! Have you heard any—"

Three more men knocked him down in the middle of his sentence, as they rushed in, shouting. Then two more men charged in through the door. Finally, an entire mob of loud, jostling miners pushed into the little express office, so that Ned could only make out fragments of what was being said: ". . . bigger than California. . ." ". . . I heard from a man who's seen . . ." ". . . the express always knows first . . ."

"*Shut up!*" Ned bellowed, but no one seemed to hear. Finally he could think of no other way to get the men's attention than to fire his pistol into the ceiling.

The sudden roar of Ned's big Navy revolver left the room in a stunned silence. He aimed the barrel of the smoking six-shooter at the faces in the crowd. "Now, all of you, get out."

"But you've gotta know where—" the red-shirted man began.

Ned cut him short. "I don't. This is an express office, not a rumor mill. If you want gold strikes, go look in the hills like everybody else."

Some of them men turned and rushed back out the door. Others left more slowly, grumbling that they had been tricked by yet another unfounded rumor. When all the men were gone, Ned mopped the sweat from his brow, thinking just how vulnerable he was to a holdup. Perhaps because he so often carried pouches of gold in his saddlebags, he had begun to treat the yellow metal casually, and with a touch of disdain. Considering the money he was earning each month as an express rider, it seemed foolish to chase after rumors of gold strikes for a few thimblefuls of yellow powder.

Five minutes after the crowd had left, a hunched-over man limped into the deserted express office. The man wore a big felt hat pulled down over his eyes and a thick scarf about his chin. He half-carried and half-dragged a leather knapsack in behind him, glancing about as if he thought he were followed. With an effort he hefted the bag to the counter. Then he flipped back the bag's flap and loosened the drawstring.

"There you be, Hiner. See if you can't get this to Wells Fargo for me. I'm goin' back to Pennsylvania, I am. Gonna quit the mines for good this time."

Ned stared into the open bag, speechless. It might have been filled with wheat, from the shape and color of the grains. Only he knew it was not. It was the largest pile of gold he had ever seen. Fifty pounds if there was an ounce. It was enough to buy half the town.

"Hiner," the old man cried, in a harsh, cracked voice. "Don't you know me? That's gold, and I know where there's bushels of it." The old man pulled off his hat to reveal a bald head and a bug eye.

"What! Baboon?" Ned was even more astonished to see this old California friend than he was to see the gold. In Deadwood the old man had helped him out of a tight spot more than once. But he had seemed an arthritic old codger, absolutely incapable of the secretive adventuring required to unearth this scale of bonanza in the wilderness. For an instant Ned recalled slipping out of Deadwood by night, tossing Baboon a hard-earned twenty-dollar gold piece on the way. Now here was a thousand times that treasure. The sheer magnitude of the man's sudden wealth left Ned bewildered. He stammered, "I—I beg your pardon, I suppose I should call you Mr. Bablaine."

"No! Baboon. Old Baboon; that's my name. Old Baboon."

Ned collected his wits enough to lock the front door. When the ancient miner clapped an arm about his shoulder, Ned felt a little more at ease. "An old friend's a sight for sore eyes out in these parts, Baboon. But I never reckoned I'd see you out here."

"Didn't take me for the travelin' type? I always told you back in Deadwood how there was loads of gold left to be found. Well, when word came of the mines in Idaho, the girls at the hotel fitted me out and I went to find it."

"But where did you—I mean, *thousands* of men have been doing the same thing, looking."

"So they have." Baboon seemed more relaxed with the door locked. He tipped back in a chair, fished his old meerschaum pipe out of a pocket, and began to stuff the bowl with tobacco. "There's luck to it, too, I reckon. When I got to Elk City in the hills south of Oro Fino, I could smell the place was gonna go bust, so I threw in with about two dozen men tryin' to make it through to Shoshone Falls. No trail there, and bad mountains, heavy timber."

He stopped to suck on his pipe and drive the smoke fiercely through his nostrils like steam through twin-valves.

"I reckon they only took me along to do an old man a favor, so they were a mite surprised when all but nine had turned back, and I was still with 'em. When we finally got worn out and discouraged, and down to half rations, we tried to get back by what looked like a shorter route. After nine days of scramblin' through mean underbrush and fallen timber we came out on a little prairie. We found signs of game there, and since we were out of grub, we turned the horses out on the grass and set out to replenish with the rifles. Only *somebody* had to stay to keep camp. And since I was just a fool old man, they left me."

Here Baboon fired another double-barreled volley of smoke at his boots. "We had our blankets spread by a little stream that was tight up against the tamarack at the edge of the prairie. Now, any farm back home in Pennsylvania would've shown 'bout as many 'indications' to most gold-hunters as you could see from that camp, but I had some time on my hands, so I took up a pan, stepped up to where a fallen tree had thrown up the dirt, filled the pan, and washed it out."

He squinted until his one bug eye narrowed as far as it would go. "There was *half a handful* of gold in that pan. Everywhere I looked there was a layer of gold dust 'bout an inch thick between the turf and the granite bedrock. When the others got back there was nine of us that knew about it, and we all swore not to tell. But, seein' as how we're all sworn, they've taken the first opportunity to rush off and tell their friends an' relatives."

There was a pause as Baboon stuck out his crooked jaw. "Now me, there wasn't nobody I could tell, so I figgered I'd tell you. Besides, there were some rough men on the trail got wind of me, been waitin' for me to show up at the Wells Fargo bank. Looked a helluva lot like Neil Scott, one of 'em did."

"What!" A chill ran through Ned at the mention of the Australian bandit's name. Scott had sworn to track him down if Ned led the law to their hideout. Now, as a pony express rider, Ned was doubly vulnerable to the outlaw's vendetta. It was hard enough for him to dodge Cherokee Bob's growing band of cutthroats. Bandits were swarming to the gold fields like yellowjackets to honey. "Are you sure Scott's still alive?"

"Them Sydney ducks don't kill easy. Figgered you'd want to know he was in these parts, seein' as how you stepped on his toes pretty bad back in California. You got a safe?"

Ned nodded uneasily.

Baboon put his hat back on and stood up. "Just lock up that bag a spell, then. See it gets to the bank in my name, won't you, Hiner?"

With that he ripped down the map that was tacked up beside the counter and drew a crooked line south and east from Oro Fino, to a blank spot near the Salmon River. Then he gave Ned a single nod and was gone.

*   *   *

It was nearly two weeks after that singular event that Ned actually set out for the gold field near the Salmon River. In a way he regretted having waited so long, especially when he saw that a dusty trail had already been beaten across the desert plateaus south of Lewiston toward the new El

Dorado. But Baboon's warning about Neil Scott had kept him from rushing off into unfamiliar territory alone. Nor had he wanted to break his promise with Mossman to keep up his share of the partnership. Even now, although he had brought a little mining gear along, he carried freshly-painted signs for a new office. "Mossman's and Miller's Express," one of the signs stated, while the other was a listing of rates.

This was a business trip. Mossman had been insistent about opening the new office, and had belittled the danger of Neil Scott's revenge. "You've got Cherokee Bob's men buffaloed," Mossman had crowed. "Why should this Australian be any different? Besides, you joined on as partner saying you wouldn't quit when the going got rocky. Well, so it's rocky. If we can open a run to this new gold strike, we'll turn profits so fast your head will spin."

Finally Ned agreed to go, if only because he had sworn to himself he wouldn't give up on the pony express until he had earned a sizable stake. Still he brought along an extra pistol and a great deal of additional caution. He had never had a chance to explain his sudden departure from Scott's hideout in California, and he didn't relish the idea of a confrontation now.

The trail wound southeast of Lewiston sixty miles into the rugged pine forests of Idaho's central mountains. After a stretch along the rushing Salmon River, the route took off cross-country at Slate Creek, heading five thousand feet straight up a precipitous ridge before finally dropping into the high mountain meadow Baboon had described.

It was an arduous trail, leading to one of the most remote regions of the entire territory. Yet when Ned arrived at this unlikely-looking plain, there was already a small city by the name of Florence there, with the tents and gear of a thousand men. The stream where gold had been first discovered, now known as Baboon Gulch, was a beehive of men, shoveling and panning and building rockers.

Ned picked a side creek not far from the others and washed out a few dozen grains of gold. Satisfied that the ground was good, he built four corner cairns and left his pick in the middle with the name "Miller" scratched in the handle. That would be sufficient for the claim to be legal at any miners' court of inquiry. This accomplished, he rode into the makeshift town to see about finding a suitable location for an express office.

The streets of Florence were unusually narrow and crooked for a frontier town. Ned learned when he stopped at one of the tent saloons that the streets had been laid out in a conventional gridiron pattern one afternoon the previous week by a Dr. Furber, who had named the town

Florence after his daughter. However, by the next morning so many new tents had popped up randomly on the townsite that it had been easiest just to let the streets snake around them. The same Dr. Furber now operated the most prestigious establishment in town, the Hotel Florence, at the skewed intersection of the two widest streets. Ned drank up, thanked the barkeep for the information, and made his way through the brown grass still growing in the streets, heading for the Hotel Florence's huge tent.

Dr. Furber was a middle-aged gentleman with a touch of gray in his hair. He looked up from the counter in his makeshift hotel and nodded as he listened to Ned's request. "An express office? Just the thing we need to put our town on the map. Sure, I'll take mail for you here at the hotel desk. Just hang your sign outside and I'll bet we'll have enough to fill a saddlebag before long."

"What kind of rent will I have to pay you for your trouble?"

The doctor waved the thought away as if it were a passing fly. "It's a good draw for the hotel. Make a few weekly runs, see how it goes; then we can talk about rent."

More than satisfied with the doctor's conditions, Ned left him paper for the receipts and a box for the money, and wired his express sign on the outside of the tent.

When Ned returned the next day, however, there were only a handful of letters waiting. Ned frowned. "Why aren't there any gold dust shipments?"

Furber smiled. "This is your first run. Once your express has proven itself, you'll get more than letters to carry."

Outside, the shouts of a distant crowd had been gradually growing louder. "I'll ride first thing tomorrow," Ned assured him.

He stepped out of the tent and peered down the crooked street toward the sound of whoops and cheers. Slowly the source of the commotion came into view around a curve. First Ned saw four teams of mules, all harnessed together in a single train. Then came a large two-wheeled cart—evidently the first vehicle that had managed to reach Florence over the steep and treacherous mountain trail. What had sparked a spontaneous celebration, however, was the load: a small steam-powered sawmill. A sawmill meant the miners would no longer have to whip-saw boards to make their rockers and sluices. It would even be possible to erect wooden buildings that would be warmer and stronger than tents during the coming winter.

Ned pushed his way into the throng of bobbing heads that had surrounded the cartload of machinery. A man in front of him called back,

"The old muleskinner's already sold it. There'll be lumber tomorrow." Ned stood on tiptoes and caught a glimpse through the crowd of the buckskin-clad driver. He hardly saw more than a slouch hat and a huge bushy beard, but he knew in an instant who it was.

"Mountain Joe!" Suddenly Ned began plowing into the thick of the crowd with wild enthusiasm. Ever since the old packer had left California without saying goodbye, Ned had hoped to meet up with him again. It was Joe who had first led him into the wilderness and taught him the ways of the wilds. It was Joe who had understood his ambition for greatness. Now Ned's heart beat as if he were meeting a long-lost father.

The old mountain man squinted up, his small brown eyes nearly lost behind the underbrush of white hair and beard. "Well, blast my dog's tail to the bone, if it ain't Ned Miller. What the Sam Hill you doin' out in this neck of the woods?" He looked much older and more tired than Ned remembered him. "Stand me for a drink, Ned? I'm busted flat an' thirstier than a prairie dog on a cactus."

"You bet, Joe," Ned said, slapping him on the back and leading him out of the crowd. The raspy sound of Joe's voice gave Ned a warm, easy feeling he had not felt for years. "It's been ages since I saw you last. How've you been?"

"Still slappin' leather, I reckon."

"That was some rig you hauled in. But I sure don't see how you could be short on money after selling it."

Joe spat into the dead grass. "Had a string of bad luck in Lewiston. Wound up gamblin' with a man named Plummer, turned out to be a sharp—profesh, you know. One of the scaliest critters in Cherokee Bob's pack of bandits. Gave me a drink an' played the ol' shell game till I turned up a wee bit shy. Had to bet him I could freight a mill to Salmon just to clear my goddam name." He looked up and gave a cackle. "Whupped the bugger, didn't I, Ned?"

"At least you broke even."

"Hell, that's still broke, I reckon." Joe glanced about and lowered his voice. "What riles me is I had to pack in that mill for Cherokee Bob's gang. This town's already lousy with the varmints. They'll bleed this camp dry if someone don't stop 'em."

The two found a tent saloon and ordered drinks at a whiskey keg. For most of an hour they sat in the grass in front of the tent, swapping tales from the adventures they had been through in the past years, Ned in Oregon, and Mountain Joe in the mines of British Columbia. Joe shook his head when he heard of Ned's brief stint at college. "Last I heard you was goin' back to live with them Injuns. Whatever happened to that squaw of yours? What was her name? Paquita."

Ned looked down. "There was some trouble. I had to leave her behind."

"Musta been tough. That girl had an eye could melt a man."

Ned glanced up at him, surprised. "I thought you said women were more trouble than mules."

Joe lifted a bushy eyebrow. "They are. Mules I figgered out long ago. So what happened?"

Ned sighed, not wanting to explain the horse-thieving episode, and the rest of his California troubles. "Plans got changed on me."

"Mebbe best thing for her, Joaquin."

"What do you mean by that?" Had Joe heard about his brush with the law?

Joe chewed a moment, as if trying to find the right words to explain. "It ain't easy leavin' gold in the ground. But sometimes that's where it fits in best."

This was a different, still more sobering argument: The less contact the Puyshoos had with white civilization, the better off they might be. Could it be that Paquita would be happier among her own people, without him? Ned noticed a wistful look in Joe's eyes, and he wondered if the old mountain man had once made the hard decision to pass up a chance at love for similar reasons.

"What about Charley?" Joe asked suddenly, as if to change to subject. "You heard from Charley?"

"He was working at Soda Springs when I left."

Joe nodded. "Reckon he's still there, then. He used to trail to heck an' gone with me, but he always went back to that big white mountain." He pulled his gold watch out of a pocket in his buckskin jacket and tapped the engraving of a mountain on its back. "Shasta. I'll have to go back there someday. You will too, Ned."

"I suppose so," Ned replied, with a new touch of uncertainty. It was getting harder to picture himself together with Paquita at Mt. Shasta again.

"Oh you will, Ned. It's like the salmon. The toughest smolts grow up in the wildest streams. They move on to bigger and bigger water, finally roam the sea for years if they make it that far. But even the biggest old king Chinook out in the ocean hears the call of that little wild stream where he started out."

Ned weighed Joe's words, wondering if they were meant to balance the earlier warning about leaving Paquita. Usually the old packer had a knack for cutting into the most complicated subjects with a wit as sharp as his hunting knife. This time it seemed there was no simple answer. One the one hand, Ned did feel a powerful urge to return, like a salmon longing for a memory. On the other, he worried that he and Paquita really might not be good for each other after all that had passed. Besides, he felt like he hadn't swum out to see the ocean yet. After a pause he asked, "Is that where you're headed next? Back to Shasta?"

Joe grunted and put the watch away. "Naw. Might stay here a while. Want to keep an eye on them Cherokee Bob bandits. Got a score to settle with them."

Ned shook his head. "That would take a helluva lot more firepower than we've got. This isn't just a couple bandits, like in one of your tales. It's a whole web of outlaws. I've been dodging them for months."

"Reckon so. Still, I aim to stay. Mebbe I'll think of somethin'. Besides, from what they were sayin' in Lewiston, gold dust jumps out of the ground at you here. I figger that'll be worth watchin' for a spell anyways."

"I've got a claim off Baboon Gulch," Ned offered. "You're welcome to camp there with me tonight and work it while I'm gone. I've got to leave with the express in the morning, and I won't be able to keep out claim jumpers by myself."

Joe gave another grunt and drained his glass. "All right, Ned. Let's have a look at this camp of yours. Mebbe that'll keep my mind off bandits a spell."

* * *

As soon as they arrived at Ned's claim, Joe took charge of laying out the camp and fixing the dinner with the same gruff efficiency that had always been his style on the trail—hacking up the bacon with his bowie knife and spitting into the pan to see if it was hot enough to crisp the fat. Then, when the stars had worked their way through the pale mountain twilight, Joe heaped pine limbs on the campfire until it blazed and crackled. He borrowed Ned's whiskey flask and squatted by the fire on his springy legs, drinking with great satisfaction and passing the bottle back.

That evening Ned counted himself content for the first time in what seemed like ages. Sitting with his old guide to the mountains again, by a pine campfire under the stars—all that was missing were the tales.

The tales! He had almost forgotten how much he had come to love this evening entertainment with Mountain Joe. Had Joe changed so much that he no longer told his tales?

"Come on, Joe, you're sitting there like a bandit cut out your tongue," Ned chided. "Can't you give me a story about the old days or something?"

"The old days? I reckon they're gone, Ned," the old man muttered, shaking his head. "Nowadays these goddam miners are ever'where. They look at the mountains an' all they see is rocks. To a reg'lar mountain man they're alive with all kinds of doin's. Course now it's been twenty years since the last big rendezvous, so I reckon most of the old Rocky Mountain trappers an' packers have taken the one-way trail. Makes an old man wonder what he's still around for."

Ned knit his brow. He knew Joe did not launch into his storytelling without an introduction, but never had he sounded so despondent. Ned searched for the appropriate cue to get him back on track.

"With the old-timers gone, I suppose you're about ready for young guys like me to take over telling the old tales."

Joe's bushy eyebrows shot up. "Farm boys! Tellin' the old tales? Why, next you'll be sayin' you can remember when the forest fire of '23 took out half the Rockies!"

"Was that the time you were with Kit Carson?"

"No, that was when Jedediah Smith an' me was trapped in Jackson's Hole between the Snake River an' a wall o' flames. You mean to say I never told you that one?"

Ned shook his head.

Mountain Joe borrowed the flask for another swig and wiped his weathered face with a stiff buckskin sleeve. These preliminaries finally completed, he began the story.

"I remember Jed an' me hid out under a ledge right on the riverbank. Behind us the ragin' fire was drivin' ever'thing that could move into the river. First came a swarm of little critters—rabbits, squirrels, an' such, all crowdin' the bank an' climbin' out on the willows until the branches would bend into the river an' the critters would float away.

"Next thing Jed gives a holler an' pulls out his rifle. Rattlesnakes! They were slithering down under our little ledge by the score. I knew they was just runnin' from the fire, so I held Jed's arm to keep him from shootin'. Them snakes crawled right over the toes of our moccasins, but then, sure enough, they all sort of flattened out their bodies an' slid out onto the river like a swarm of crooked canoes."

"Amazing," Ned commented, making a mental note to save the image of swimming rattlesnakes. If he ever found time to write again, the picture would make a powerful poem.

"It got worse," Joe went on. "When the fire was damn near on top of us, then came the *bears*. First a posse of little black bears hunkered down together by the water, lookin' back over their shoulders like a bunch of bad dogs told to leave home. Well, after they'd swum for it, there was just the grizzlies left. They kicked up a terrible ruckus, rearin' up on the ledge above us, snarlin' an' growlin' back at the fire like they was gonna scare it away. It was gettin' so hot our eyebrows shriveled right up, but still them bears wouldn't budge. Finally I stuck my head out an' saw their fur had *burst into flames!* They let out a roar that shook the rocks, and then, one by one, jumped right over my head into the river like a row of howlin' fireballs."

Ned smiled his appreciation, for it had truly been one of Joe's more spectacular campfire tales. At the same time he had to resist a strong temptation to ask Joe how he and Jed Smith could possibly have escaped the fire themselves. Skepticism was against the unspoken rules of a tall tale performance.

After a pause, Joe added, "Ol' Jed an' me would of been in trouble that time, too, if a cloudburst hadn't come in. They do that ever' afternoon up there, an' that's what we'd been countin' on."

Then Mountain Joe gave a serious nod to Ned. "You take a turn now, Ned. I aim to rest my jaw a spell."

"What—you want *me* to tell a tale?"

"Aw hell, what you said there a while back got me thinkin'. I can't go tellin' the old stories forever. Go on, take a crack at it. You spend enough time yakkin', you might as well learn to put it to some use."

Ned scratched his short beard. It was one thing to tell stories—he could do that—but it was something else to come up with a tale for a master of the art like Joe. Ned had spent most of his time in college studying poetry, not tall tales.

"I guess I could tell you about the time my brother John and I helped tree a bear," Ned suggested.

"Sounds toler'ble," Joe said. "Let's hear it."

"Well," Ned began, clearing his throat cautiously, "there were a lot of black bears in the Willamette Valley when my family first got there in the fall of '52. In fact, after the missionaries gathered in the Indians, I guess the bears had things pretty much their own way. My brother and I hunted them to keep down their numbers. We were too poor to have guns, so we'd usually just chase the bears out into a field and lasso them on horseback."

Ned glanced to Joe to make sure he would accept this stretch.

Joe grunted earnestly. "An' then what?"

"Well, then our Pa needed the horses to plow, so we had to hunt on foot with Ed Parrish. His father was a wealthy missionary, you see, and he had a gun of his own. The day he treed a bear, Ed's plan had been simple enough. Ed was supposed to march up the bottom of a canyon with his gun while John and I flushed game off the slopes.

"So we all got started, and before long I heard a shot. There was a long silence. Then, suddenly, I heard this high, wild voice coming out through the tree tops down in the canyon, 'Come quick! I've treed a bear! Come and help me catch him! Oh, Moses! come quick and—and—and catch him!'

"John and I came tearing down the hillside, but we couldn't find Ed anywhere. Then we heard another wild yell, this time from away up in the branches of an old maple. When my eyes got used to the dark I could see the leaves rustling. And it looked like Ed was rustling too. He had treed a bear, sure enough. The bear was right behind him, wounded pretty badly, but still just alive enough to chase Ed out a limb where he couldn't reload. As long as the bear was growling, we couldn't talk Ed into climbing down over him.

"Time went on and it got to be dusk. Finally he called down, 'Boys, I'm going to come down on the laz ropes. See if you can't tie yours together and throw an end up here.' Soon as we did, he crawled down like a spider and ran out of that canyon like a spooked horse.

"When John and I went back the next day to get our ropes we found the bear dead near the root of the old mossy maple. The skin was a beautiful one, but even though Ed had earned it he let us keep it—on the condition that we never remind him of how he had 'treed a bear.'"

As soon as Ned finished the story he glanced to Joe, but the old mountain man was shaking his head.

"That's 'bout what I figgered," he said somberly.

"Well, what did you figure?" Ned asked.

"I thought you had it there, the way you got started good. But then the thing turned all sissy. How the Sam Hill did you expect to get a good tale out of a little boy bein' scared of a little bear?"

Joe threw out his hands to emphasize his criticism. "A roarin' good story don't have to be so darned long-winded, neither. It's just got to have some more guts. Now take the one 'bout Pegleg Smith—there's a tale."

"I've never heard that one," Ned said flatly, refusing to show that he had been hurt by Joe's complaints.

Joe told his story to demonstrate the point. "All right, listen to this: I was up past Coeur d'Alene the time a Flathead scout blew up Smith's kneecap just for target practice. Ol' Smith dragged that danglin' leg around till it started turnin' green, but he wouldn't let nobody touch it. Finally he just sits himself down, notches his knife blade, hones it down razor sharp, an' saws the thing off himself, right through the bone. Then he drags himself to the fire pit, sears the stump, an' sets to whittlin' a wooden leg just as calm as calm.

"There, you see?" Joe said, and gave a short cackle. "Course a farm boy like you could never tell the likes, I reckon."

Now this was a challenge Ned could not pass by and keep his self respect. He took a drink from the whiskey flask and wiped his mustache.

"Well," he began, looking thoughtfully out over the fire, "actually it does remind me of a man named Ted McGuire who used to live near our farm in Indiana."

"So it does, huh?" Joe asked doubtfully.

"Yes, it does," Ned replied. "You see this man McGuire worked for a year on the *Ohio Belle,* a steamboat out of Cincinnati, till her boiler burst and he found himself hanging in a cottonwood tree, missing an arm and some hair and a number of other things. By the time he came back to the farm though, they'd fitted him out well enough that he looked all right. Then we set off for Oregon and he wanted to come along, so Pa let him ride up ahead of the family wagon as a scout.

"Well, everything went fine till just before Fort Kearney, when a Sioux war party with a hundred warriors swept down off a bluff and surrounded us. Pa never carried a gun, being raised a Quaker you know, so he surrendered without a shot. I guess he thought it ought to make the Indians more lenient, but the chief said we all had to be scalped anyway. He said Ted was going to be the first to die and came up to him with an ugly-looking tomahawk.

"I never have seen a man with such nerve. Even when that Indian had his hatchet raised over Ted's head he just stood there like he didn't care. He just pulled off his wig and said, 'If my scalp's all you want, here, take it.' Then, while the Indian was staring at all that loose hair, Ted took out his false teeth and said he might as well take them too. When Ted popped out his glass eye the chief jumped a foot in the air, yelling that they'd caught a pack of devils by mistake. They took off at a hard gallop and never bothered us again."

During this story Mountain Joe had been watching Ned with raised eyebrows. When Ned finished, Joe mused silently for a minute, making chewing motions with his jaw. Then he muttered, "Well, don't that beat all! You *can* tell a toler'ble tale."

The old mountain man wrinkled his brow and tugged on his beard a few minutes in silence. At length he said, "Don't reckon I'd heard of beatin' an ambush quite that way before. The only way I know that could top it is the *slow echo.*"

Ned had never known Mountain Joe to have to think so long before starting a story. And this itself was a kind of praise.

"The slow echo?" Ned asked, genuinely curious to hear what Joe had come up with.

"You mean I never told you 'bout how I learned to throw echoes with the Navajos down in the Arizona badlands?"

Ned shook his head.

"Well, I got to practice it a lot up in the Fraser River Canyon while I was stuck on a wagonload of high-grade ore with the suspension bridge out. Took 'em weeks to get the danged bridge fixed. While I was camped there I'd sit an' throw my voice kinda slow-like across the canyon. Fact is, I got so good I could holler in the evenin' before turnin' in, an' the echo'd get back just at the crack of dawn to wake me up like a reg'lar alarm clock."

Ned nodded with all the seriousness he could muster. "Well, I'll be."

"That's right. So when the bridge was in, word got 'round that this bandit Wabash was fixin' to lay for me at The Narrows, 'cause he knew I'd be takin' the high-grade through 'bout an hour after leavin' camp. I made like I didn't give a hang, an' told ever'body I'd be leavin' camp all by myself at seven sharp. But that night I snuck over the bridge to The Narrows an' threw my voice. Then I went back to camp an' got some shut-eye. In the mornin' I drive my wagon on over, an' out jumps this Wabash character, armed to the teeth an' snarlin' like a lynx. Me, I just tip my hat. An' sure 'nough, right on time there's the echo behind him, sayin', 'Drop it, Wabash, or I'll blow the back of your head to buzzard feed.' He didn't know whether to shit or go blind. So I just picked up his gun an' took him in to town."

By the time Joe finished his tale the campfire had burned down to a glowing pile of red embers, with a pair of blue-edged flames hanging phantom-like above the coals.

Ned watched the evanescent flames, and sighed. "You're right, Joe. There's an awful lot I've left to learn from you."

Chapter 12

*The snow deepened rapidly, and it soon became necessary
to break a road. For this service, a party of ten was formed,
mounted on the strongest horses; each man in succession
opening the road on foot, or on horseback, until himself and
his mount became fatigued.*

—John C. Frémont, report of the
1843-44 expedition to California

The winter of 1861 hit harder than the Idaho miners had thought possible. Blizzard after blizzard swept over the mountains, driving hundreds of discouraged men from the faltering mines of Oro Fino. The larger companies that remained raised wages to four dollars a day, but still could not attract workers. After a New Year's blizzard left seven-foot drifts over the Clearwater Canyon trail, Ned made his last run into Oro Fino, a day late, and closed the office there for the season.

The conditions in Florence were even more desperate, but with one important difference: there was gold. For every man who left, two trudged in over the mountain to take his place. They shoveled off the snow and chipped down into the frozen ground with picks, or built bonfires on the claims to warm the gold-rich earth. The dark winter days along Baboon Gulch ended by the light of candle lanterns, as cold, gaunt men weighed out their shares.

The earnings were often staggering—as much as three hundred dollars per man per day. Miners kept loose gold in bags as if it were so much sand. They carried pounds of the yellow flakes with them into the Florence saloons and stores, but there wasn't much to buy. The steep trail over the mountain was impassable for pack mules all of January and February. Supplies had to be carried over the mountain on men's backs, and as a result freight costs soared from a few cents to a dollar a pound. A sack of flour cost a hundred dollars, a slab of bacon eighty dollars if it could be bought at all.

With a tenacity that amazed his partner, Ned continued to ride the mail into Florence against increasing odds. Even under the best of conditions the round trip required eight grueling days on the trail. Now Ned often returned two days late, or three. One particularly cold afternoon in early March, as Ned was cinching on the catenas for yet another run, Mossman shook his head. "If you make it through this time, Miller, double the rates to four percent." The express charges for gold had already been doubled from one percent to two, but Ned only nodded. When the risks were highest, the profits deserved to climb. Already he had laid away nearly a thousand dollars. If he could earn another thousand he would have enough to scoff at schoolteaching jobs when he returned to Oregon. He spurred his horse and galloped down the snowy street.

The snow was hip-deep at the Patoka Station, and lay draped over the roof of the dark stable like a cold feather tick. It had melted away from the tepee, however, where a warm orange glow promised Ned a chance to thaw his stiff fingers. That night by the fire he had time to read through the newspapers in his catenas. Although it had been months since he had written his little poem, he picked up the Port Orford paper first. To his surprise, the short verse sat staring back at him from the page.

"Ee-HAW!" he whooped. "I'm published!" It was the first time he had ever seen his byline in print, and the crisp, proud "C. H. Miller" gave him a heady thrill. Ned rocked back with a big grin at his literary victory. In his delight he even pointed out the poem to the solemn Nez Perce stationmaster and tried to explain with a few clumsy Chinook words that it was his. The old Indian stared at the paper without any sign of comprehension, then looked suspiciously at Ned.

Undeterred, Ned read through his verse again. Now he saw it had gained by its long round-trip journey. The editor had added an italic notice: "The author of the above is advised that we (and our young poet Minnie Myrtle) should like to hear more such rhyme.—ed."

The note left Ned aglow with a mixture of pride and curiosity. Of course it was promising that the editor requested more of his work. But it was even more interesting that Minnie Myrtle, the poet who had originally inspired his reply, wished to see another of his poems. And the editor called her young. She was no spinster. Perhaps she really did resemble the pining, chestnut-haired girl of her verse.

Ned looked up at the tepee's shadowy walls and listened to the rush of the wind across the snowy wastes outside. It felt somehow comforting to imagine that this young woman might even now be sitting in a warm seaside cottage, rereading his verse by lamplight.

He thought again of Paquita, but with less guilt than before. After all, there was no conflict here. He couldn't write letters or poems for Paquita because she couldn't read them. It made sense to write instead for Minnie Myrtle, who obviously appreciated his literary efforts.

With a smile Ned fetched pen and paper from the catenas and set to composing another poetic missive to the "Sweet Singer of the Coquille."

* * *

It took two more days for Ned to reach the Slate Creek Station, a small shack he had built by himself on the Salmon River. A band of Indians wintering nearby had readied his relay horse for the ride into Florence, but he did not take it. He had been forewarned by miners trudging down from the mountain that no horse could survive the trail now. The freezing nights had left a crust on the snow that was only firm enough for men to walk on; horses merely sank to their bellies with each step. If they did not die of exhaustion, they bled to death when the icy crust cut their struggling legs.

In the morning Ned tossed the catenas over his shoulder and resolutely started up the mountain on foot. As he climbed, he passed men staggering under the weight of ten-gallon liquor barrels and sacks of flour. Here and there, where footsteps had broken through the crust, abandoned packs and bundles marked the route, like curses strewn along the mountain's icy face.

Ned reached the rutted, frozen snow of the streets of Florence as night was beginning to fall. Unnoticed and exhausted, he made his way to the little wooden office of Mossman's and Miller's Express, next door to the imposing clapboard silhouette of the Hotel Florence. He unlocked the door, stamped the snow off his boots, and tossed the catenas on a chair. For a moment he just stood in the doorway, watching the quiet streets. Florence was one of the richest towns on earth, but it looked as though it had already suffocated under the snow, lost in the Idaho wilderness. With a sigh, he reached up and pulled a small bell rope.

At once the street erupted into life. Crowds of men charged out of saloons whooping and whistling. Up and down the streets the call roused the remainder of the settlement: "Mail's in!"

For the next two hours Ned was besieged in the tiny office by a torrent of faces and names, all eager for news from the outside. Only when the catenas were finally empty did the rush subside. Then, wearily, Ned finished his paperwork and gathered what he needed to camp for the night on the claim with Mountain Joe.

While Ned was locking the door, he listened to the violin music and laughter drifting out of the Hotel Florence. Through the brightly lit windows he could see gay paper decorations and red, white, and blue bunting draped between the wall sconces. From the frozen street where he stood, it seemed to Ned that he was looking through a magic glass at a different world. Inside, a table set with linen and silver held trays of unimaginable luxuries: wine, cheese, and exotic hors d'oeuvres. Well-dressed men waltzed past with elegant ladies on their arms. Although the town had fewer than a dozen female inhabitants—mostly the wives of merchants and mining barons—it was evident that the hotel had seen fit to sponsor an elaborate ball, perhaps to convince the wealthy citizens of the town that they had indeed become rich, despite the hardships of the long, bleak winter.

As Ned watched the ladies swirl past, with gems at their low-cut collars and ruffled flounces on their long dresses, the longing to join them in that warm, elegant ballroom was almost overpowering. How long had it been since he had touched a woman's hand, much less held a woman in his arms? He found himself imagining the smell of perfume mingling with the sweet aroma of the ballroom's candles.

At length Ned sighed, knowing he would not be welcome. After four long days on the trail, his clothes were ragged and smelly. His hands were dirty and coarse. All that waited for him was a swig of whisky at the tent on his claim. But he told himself that one day he would know that grander world too.

Ned was about to walk past when the hotel door burst open. Dr. Furber stepped into the doorway, roughly escorting a finely-dressed couple out onto the porch. "I'm sorry," the doctor said firmly. "I've met with the committee and we won't have it. The ladies insist. Good night." He closed the door behind them adamantly and did not reply when the expelled party-goers cursed and kicked at the door. Finally the two stormed across the street toward a saloon. As the woman passed by, picking up the hems of her satin hoop-skirt, Ned observed with surprise that she had painted her lips and eyes.

When Ned reached the claim he recounted what had happened at the hotel.

"'Tain't good," Mountain Joe said gruffly. "An' it all comes from them damn women. Them an' all the damn bandits, anyway."

"You know who they were?"

"Sure. That was Cherokee Bob's whore Cynthia. Won her off a gambler in Lewiston. When he opened up a saloon here last month he brung her along. Course soon as Furber started billin' the ball she made a fuss 'bout bein' as good as anyone an' wanting to go. So I reckon Bob tried to send her."

"Cherokee Bob wasn't with her, though."

"That thievin' snake? You'd never see his face at dress-up doin's like that. He'd rather sit in his saloon thinkin' up new ways to skin the miners. No, he prob'ly sent Cynthia with one of the littler coyotes in his pack. Problem is, he'll be madder'n blazes now, an' he's 'bout as clear-headed as a buffalo bull. He an' Furber have been rivals since they staked out businesses on opposite sides of the street. I don't like it, I can tell you. Things can happen when a townful of folks is hungry too long."

"Is it really that bad? Looked like the hotel had plenty of food."

"Mebbe Furber cached a box or two of fancy eats, but ever'where else, it's thin trappin's. The town's starvin'."

"You haven't been going hungry, have you Joe?"

"Me? Hell, I don't eat much anymore. Gettin' old, I reckon. It's tough on the young bucks, though. Butcher's been out of sheep for a month. Last week I was a mite surprised to see he had a little meat again—an' it didn't taste like skunk or dog or even porcupine, so it sold pretty high. But then a horse turned up missin' an' they found the hide under some tailin's on the butcher's place. They would've strung him up for horse thievin', too, if they hadn't been so hungry. 'Sides, the man who'd lost the horse owed the butcher a bill long as your arm."

Ned shook his head. He was glad no one in town knew he himself had once been accused of horse theft. "What about money? Is the claim still producing?"

Mountain Joe rubbed his neck as though he had a kink in a muscle there. "Oh, the claim's good enough. Hell, Ned, I ought to be rich by now. It's just I never cared much for diggin' around like that. Too old to learn how, I reckon. And when I do get some dust together it lasts 'bout as long as a snowball in hell down at them saloons."

"Well, we've still got the camp, the claim, and a crackling fire. How about telling one of the old tales?" Ned suggested.

"Not tonight," Joe muttered, shaking his head. He stood and gathered his bedroll.

"Why not?" Ned had never known Joe to refuse so resolutely.

"Trouble's comin'. Gotta think."

"What kind of trouble?"

But Joe just shook his head. "Need a plan."

* * *

A line of men were already waiting at the express office door when Ned arrived the next morning. Mountain Joe had insisted on coming along with his big hunting rifle, saying that a lot of miners would be wanting to ship out gold and it would be a good idea to have an extra gun on hand, just to watch the door. He pulled a chair outside, tipped it back against the wall, and sank its legs down into the snow, sitting with the ridiculously long, octagonal rifle barrel slanted across his lap at what seemed a careless angle.

Joe was right about the gold shipments. A few of the men had brought letters, but mostly they had gold. They carried it in pokes and pouches and even old socks. One by one they set their treasure on the counter and watched critically as Ned poured it into the shiny brass pan of the scales, ran his finger through the grains to check for purity, and balanced it up carefully against the little cylindrical weights in the opposite pan. Then he poured the dull yellow dust back into the bag, tied it closed with a wire, and sealed it with a lead stamp. He entered the quantity into his ledger and scratched the owner's initials into the lead seal. "That's four percent ad valorem, you know," he said, but no one held out for a lower rate. They knew if the gold could be brought to the outside world it would be worth a hundred times more than in supply-poor Florence.

By noon Ned saw he was going to have to close the books and turn people away. His ledger already showed receipts for an astonishing twenty-five thousand dollars in gold—over a hundred pounds of nuggets and dust—and he was beginning to wonder if he could possibly carry it all over the mountain on his back. Before he could make an announcement, however, the office mysteriously emptied by itself. First there was a whispering among the men, and then they all simply vanished out the door.

Ned put down his quill and scratched his head. He went to the door, but didn't see anything out of the ordinary. Mountain Joe was still tipped against the wall with the muzzleloader aslant on his lap. The old mountain man had pulled his beat-up slouch hat down and even looked like he might have nodded off. Dr. Furber was on the porch of the Hotel Florence, quietly talking with a bowler-hatted hotel guest. The street, however, was ominously vacant.

Then Ned saw Cherokee Bob. The huge man filled the doorway of his saloon across the street. He leaned against the door jamb, slowly spinning the chamber of a six-shooter. Leisurely he pushed off with a hip and began to crunch through the dirty, trampled snow to the middle of the street. Though his neck was hunched, he stood taller than any man Ned had ever seen. His long, black hair swayed across his massive shoulders with each step.

"Get out of the street, Joe!" Ned whispered.

"Just let an old man sleep a spell," Joe muttered, immobile.

"Furber!" Cherokee Bob bellowed, his pistol raised. Doctor Furber turned, taken by surprise, and lifted his hands while the hotel guest dived for cover. For a second Cherokee Bob just sneered, showing a crooked row of teeth. Then the pistol cracked in a sudden cloud of white. Ned heard the slug slap into Furber's stomach. The blow knocked the doctor backwards half a step and buckled him over. Before he hit the porch, however, there was an even louder retort.

When the smoke from Cherokee Bob's pistol cleared in the cold air, his eyes were oddly glazed. A liquid red flower had bloomed on his chest, and he fell backwards into the snow like the trunk of a cut tree.

Mountain Joe sat unmoved with the big rifle still across his lap, a wisp of smoke drifting away from its muzzle. "I reckon I'll be ridin' back to Walla Walla with you this time, Ned," the old man said dryly.

Ned stared at him with wide eyes. "But you—" Ned was too frightened and stunned to complete the sentence. In broad daylight Mountain Joe had gunned down Cherokee Bob, the ringleader of Idaho's most powerful outlaw gang. The old packer had obviously settled his score with Cherokee Bob's bandits, but what would he do now? There wouldn't be a safe hiding place in the entire territory.

"Hope the doc pulls through," Joe muttered.

Furber! The thought of the doctor jerked Ned's thoughts away from Joe and himself. Already a crowd was gathering around the fallen doctor on the hotel porch.

A waiter from the hotel held out his arms. "Everyone stay back until we find out what's happened."

Furber lay bent on the porch with his hands pressed to his stomach. Through gritted teeth he managed to say, "Damn it, I'm shot. That's what happened."

"Get a doctor!" someone shouted.

"Furber *is* the doctor," another man said.

With a chill, Ned realized this was true. Furber himself was the only one with the knowledge that might save him from blood loss and gangrene—if only he could stay conscious long enough to explain the process. "As long as he can talk, he'll have to tell us what to do."

Furber groaned. "He's right. Inside. Put me on a table. And fetch the butcher."

"The butcher?" Ned wondered if he had heard the man right.

Pain seized the doctor's face momentarily. Then he nodded. "Surgeon. Bullet's lodged beside my stomach. Hurry. I'll tell him how to cut it out."

"I'll get the butcher," a miner volunteered. Other men formed a ring around the doctor to carry him inside.

So many people had flocked to help the doctor that Ned saw he was no longer needed. He ran to the other cluster of men in the street to see what had become of Cherokee Bob.

Bob was not yet dead, although the snow was red all around him and blood choked out of his mouth as he tried to form words.

"Wh— Who done it?"

Ned looked around the ring of faces anxiously, fearing that any one of the men might point out Mountain Joe. The old packer still sat in his tilted chair, but now squinted lazily up at the sun, as if to wonder how much past noon it was getting to be.

A tall miner in a red shirt put his head forward. "Why, don't you reckon Furber just beat your draw, Bob?"

"He—he didn't have no gun."

The miner lowered his voice. "Any skunk that'd draw on an unarmed man deserves what he gets." Still more quietly, he added, "Glad *I* didn't have to give it to him, though," and he shot warning glances to Ned and Mountain Joe.

The advice was clear: this town wouldn't be safe for them long. Ned knew they would have to leave at once. He also knew Mountain Joe would never be able to hold off the bandits alone. Together, they might have a chance.

Bob gagged on his blood and rolled his head to one side, where he caught sight of Ned—the express rider. For a second a kind of gloating recognition seemed to cross his face. Then a shudder ran through his huge body, and he was still.

*   *   *

Half an hour later Ned and Mountain Joe were trudging up the mountain outside of town, their pistols capped and ready. Their back-packs bulged with the most valuable gold shipment the express had ever carried. Ned had abandoned the claim and had left his express office keys at the Hotel Florence. The hotel waiter had told him that the stoic Doctor Furber had directed his gunshot wound surgery without anesthetic, and was expected to live. The waiter also said Cherokee Bob's body had been laid out on the bar of a saloon while his lieutenants argued over who should replace him as boss. It was just the delay Ned needed to gain a head start in his escape. He knew Bob's gang of murderers and thieves never waited long to avenge a death. He also knew the heavy gold shipment would slow his retreat with Mountain Joe—leaving them all the more vulnerable to ambush.

As Ned trudged on, breaking through the snow's crust every few steps because of the weight of his backpack, a vivid memory confronted him of the day he had fled California. Then, too, he had feared the wrath of the outlaws he had left behind. But now that adventure seemed a mere lark by comparison—a morning's fast ride on a sunny summer day. Here he faced four long days of the hardest kind of trek through the snow-bound Idaho wilderness to reach the Walla Walla office—where Cherokee Bob's gang still might try to kill him. And now he remembered Old Baboon's warning that Neil Scott and Dave English were in Idaho too. It seemed danger was everywhere.

When Ned and Joe finally reached the summit of the ridge it was late in the afternoon and the sky had grown dark with an approaching storm. Mountain Joe had kept up well, considering that his short legs put him at a disadvantage. But Ned noticed that Joe's red, wrinkled face was streaming with sweat, and his legs had begun to shiver with fatigue. It was still ten miles to the Slate Creek Station—and five thousand feet down.

They both knew there was no choice but to push on, and so they did, half staggering, half slipping down the crusted snow of the mountain's west face, sometimes sliding for hundreds of yards with their heavy backpacks of gold skittering along the frozen snow behind them.

By the last light of day, as the first snowflakes of the coming storm began to fall, they arrived at the shack by the Salmon River and collapsed onto the dirt floor with their packs.

*   *   *

Ned awoke the next morning to the smell of coffee and campfire smoke. He opened his eyes to see Mountain Joe hunkered by a fire on the floor.

"Nice place you got. Wood's wet, though. Smokes a lot."

Ned rubbed his eyes. "How long have you been up?"

"Oh, I don't know," Mountain Joe said, fiddling with the fire. Then he added, almost to himself, "Don't know if I did get much shut-eye. Hear too many damn voices in the wind."

Ned was fully awake now, remembering their sudden flight and the risk of pursuit. The Slate Creek Station was isolated, but it was just where Cherokee Bob's gang would expect them to be. Already the bandits could be closing in on the cabin—or more likely, staking out positions for an ambush on the trail ahead.

"If the snow's not too bad we should get moving," Ned said. "The Indians down the river have got the horses—the regular horse and the relay."

"Yeah, I reckon we'd best keep movin' a spell."

There was a foot and a half of new powder snow outside, with more falling, but Ned thought the horses could get through. The trail along the

Salmon River had been packed down over the course of the winter by miners, deer, and elk. Although the night's snow had nearly filled the packed channel, a crease along the new powdery surface still showed where the path ran. With dismay he realized Cherokee Bob's men could have ridden ahead on this trail in the night, and their tracks would have been covered without a trace.

When Ned brought the horses Mountain Joe walked around them, feeling their protruding ribs and shaking his head. "Stock could use a good grainin'," he said.

Ned put on the saddles and bags without answering. Of course what Joe said was true. But there was nothing to be done. Even the Indian caretakers were not at fault. There was no grass. Nothing but trees showed over five feet of snow. And the grain and hay that had been put up in the fall had been exhausted by the unexpectedly long winter.

"Breakin' trail's hard work for a hungry horse," Joe said.

"We'll just have to take turns and hope they hold out," Ned replied, climbing into the saddle. "Come on. I'll lead out first."

The storm kept up all that day, hurling thick snow at them from the dull clouds to the west. They pulled down their hats and spurred the horses to keep them walking. Ned's fingers grew numb from holding the cold metal of his rifle as he rode, but he wanted to keep the weapon handy. At the first relay station, Joe took the fresh horse. Ned's mount took the rear and continued unwillingly, its left flank completely flocked by the cold, dry snow.

In the afternoon the trail climbed up from the Salmon River, through cold canyons on the slopes of Craig Mountain. "Mighty fine spot for an ambush," Joe said over the howl of the wind.

As if in reply, the distant cries of men met them from the canyon ahead. Ned looked to Joe anxiously. Joe gave a grim nod, cocking his heavy hunting rifle. "Ready for 'em, Ned?"

But already the cries were changing to a strange wail. "Listen." Ned peered ahead into the storm.

"Could be a trick."

Ned nodded. Cautiously he rode onward into the swirling snow to investigate.

First he saw the smoke. Then, around a curve in the trail, he saw a half dozen men huddled against a cliff. The men wore the thin, ragged red shirts of California miners. Although they had built a small fire, their bare hands were blue.

"Hey, someone came!" one of the men yelled, and the others joined him, hobbling on stiff feet toward Ned and Joe.

Ned did not yet lower his pistol.

"Mister, don't go and shoot us now," the first of the men said, hands in the air. "We're just cold and hungry."

Ned blew out a long breath. This was almost worse than meeting bandits. Obviously these miners had set out on the trail toward the gold fields unprepared for winter travel. Now, afoot in a fierce blizzard, without food, proper clothing, or shelter, the miners wouldn't have to make many more mistakes to meet an icy death. Ned knew he should stay and help them through the storm, but he really didn't have enough supplies to share. Worse yet, Cherokee Bob's gang would catch up with them if they stopped here.

Ned tossed the miners a pouch of jerky from his bag. "I'm sorry. We'd take you on to the next station, but our horses aren't strong enough."

The man tore open the pouch greedily. "Thanks, mister. I reckon as long as we've got the fire, we'll make it. What we really need is to find the three men who left here this morning, trying to break through to Lewiston."

Ned pursed his lips. A sinking feeling told him the three men who had left the fire had already made their last mistake. "We'll keep an eye out for them." He looked to Joe, who nodded solemnly, and urged his horse on.

By nightfall, Ned and Joe reached the next station without seeing a trace of the lost men. The thought weighed heavily on Ned's mind as he thawed his fingers by a small fire.

Joe scratched in his big white beard. "I reckon they'll find them three miners in the spring," he said, watching the fire. "There's a lot worse ways to go than freezin'. They say it's just like goin' to sleep. 'Tain't cold at all."

Despondently, Ned nodded. "That's what they say."

* * *

The news spread through Lewiston the next morning as Ned and Joe were still riding down into the cold, windy town: the pony express had made it through from Florence with its heaviest shipment of gold ever.

Pistols cocked and within reach, Ned quickly took care of business at the little express office while Mountain Joe saw to saddling fresh horses. He had felt the hungry eyes of the townsfolk watching the heavy saddlebags. It would be safer to ride through the storm toward the Patoka Station than to guard a hundred pounds of gold very long in Lewiston. He especially did not want to be on hand when the town's collection of thugs found out about their bandit chief. So far no one in Lewiston seemed to know that Cherokee Bob was dead, but that bombshell was sure to hit soon.

Ned and Joe rode quickly to the Snake River landing. The ferryman charged them double the usual fifty-cent fare, complaining about the drift ice in the river and the shortage of travelers in bad weather. "Truth is, Miller, I've only put across two other gents all day. Friends of yours, I reckon."

Ned raised an eyebrow. "Friends? Who were they?"

The ferryman shrugged. "Didn't say their names. Short fellas on Indian ponies. Talked like Britishers. Said they were looking for you."

The news sent a chill up Ned's spine. He pressed the ferryman for more details, but the man swore he had been too busy watching for ice in the river to notice anything else about the horsemen.

On the far shore, Mountain Joe gave Ned a piercing look. "*Do* you know them riders?"

The two sets of hoofprints ahead of them on the bank were partially covered by windblown snow. "Maybe," Ned said. He had matched the ferryman's description against his memory of Neil Scott and Dave English, and it fit far too well for comfort. "If I do, they're no friends."

"With Cherokee Bob's gang?"

"No. Worse, I'm afraid."

"*Worse?*" Joe chewed the thought a moment. "What the hell kind of varmints you got yourself tangled up with?"

"Australian gents I tripped up in California."

"Well if they're plannin' to lay for us out here, they sure must not give a hang 'bout freezin' to death."

"That's what I don't understand," Ned said. "If they meant to ambush us, why ride off ahead into a blizzard when they could just as well try it in town?"

Joe shrugged. "Maybe they wouldn't be any more comfortable sittin' on all that gold in Lewiston than you were." Joe spat into the snow. "No matter. I say let 'em come. Long as we're two an' two, it's even odds. Ain't you up to seein' an even bet?"

"Don't think we have much choice," Ned replied. Turning back would only leave them facing the gun barrels of a different and larger set of enemies. He loosened his belt and stuck a pistol in it. Then he led the way up to the plateaus.

The blizzard thickened as they rode, reducing the juniper snags and boulders along the slope to indiscernible dark forms. Ned eyed the shapes suspiciously, half expecting them to spring to life and attack in a hail of lead. On the higher flat ground the wind bit harder and the snow lay deeper than Ned had expected. At times the drifts were brisket-deep, so that the horses could only bring their heavy loads forward with exhausting, slow lunges.

It was late afternoon, and the weary horses were puffing rapid, erratic clouds of steam when they finally neared the Patoka Station. Nonetheless Ned refused to ride directly to the station, in the direction their approach would be expected. Instead he spurred his horse on another mile around the end of the canyon, so they could approach from the far side.

Only then did they ride to the edge to look below. There Ned and Joe were quiet a long time. The wind howled behind them, curling a dust of white flakes out over the dark canyon. There was no lantern visible below, and no fire smoke from the tepee, even though the cold was intense.

"Reckon your friends've been here already," Mountain Joe said with a tired voice.

Ned swallowed hard. If the Nez Perce stationmaster were alive, there would certainly be a fire. "I suppose they must be waiting for us down there now."

Mountain Joe swept his small dark eyes across the view. "Nope. Over there." He pointed across the canyon to the far rim, where two brown dots were slowly bobbing towards them. "We been standin' out here 'gainst the sky like signposts, an' now they're comin' over to read us. What's your move, Ned? Wait or run?"

Ned's heart pounded in his throat. There was no mistaking the two dots as horsemen, even though they were still nearly half a mile away. If he held his ground now there would be a gun battle, the only sure outcome of which would be two, or three, or four dead men. On the other hand, by riding on toward the next relay shed, twenty miles distant, they might be able to avoid bloodshed altogether. And if the outlaws were on Indian ponies as the ferryman said, they should be no match for the longer-legged, stronger express horses.

Ned reined his horse to an about-face. "Let's take 'em for a ride. We'll lose 'em on the way to the next shed." Mountain Joe followed Ned out into the deep snow of the vast, white plateau without reply.

It was mid afternoon, but the temperature had already begun to plummet, working with the bitter headwind to sculpt their beards into masks of snow and ice. At the top of a slight rise Ned stopped to rest the horses, and saw behind that the horsemen had reached the near side of the canyon. They, too, had halted. He watched them huddle together a minute, as if in discussion, and then continue onward. Grimly, Ned set on as well.

A few miles further Ned again looked back through the storm, and felt his first shot of uncontrolled fear. Instead of falling behind, their pursuers had gained on them considerably. They might only be riding Indian ponies, but they didn't have the gold shipment to weigh them down, and they didn't have to break trail. Now Ned realized how seriously he had miscalculated. But the decision to push on could not be changed. There was nowhere to hide, nowhere safe on the vast white plain in the freezing fury of the blizzard. And now he was convinced it *was* Scott and English—if only because of their maddening determination. He spurred his horse until its flanks left a trail of red spots in the snow. Mountain Joe followed silently, and indeed the wind had become so strong that talk could scarcely have been heard.

In another hour the shivering horses finally foundered in the ever-deepening snow. At once Ned's fears rushed in upon him with a wave of pure panic. The sun, which had been but a dim glow all day, had set, leaving the seething clouds a uniform twilight gray. The plain about him was unbroken by tree or rock, an identical white in all directions. Though the two outlaws were hidden by the thickly falling snow, he knew they must be close on their tracks—perhaps already within rifle range.

Ned jumped from his horse and tried to yank it forward into the snow, breaking the trail with the weight of his own body. The exhausted animal, however, fell to its knees. He and Mountain Joe were just reaching for their pistols when they heard a voice shouting through the dark, thickening snowstorm.

"Miller!"

Ned and Mountain Joe looked at each other.

"Give it up, Miller!" the faint voice called.

Ned dropped his reins. Behind him were the guns of the outlaws; ahead was an impassable, trackless wasteland of snow that now seemed as though it would swallow them all. "Let's face them, Joe." His pistol shaking in his numb hand, he turned around and slowly began to walk back in the direction of the outlaw's voice. Ned squinted into the storm, trying to discern the shapes of the men who had followed all this way to kill him. But what frightened him most was the feeling that he didn't hate these men enough to kill them—that perhaps he wouldn't be able to pull the trigger if he saw them first. Perhaps—

"Drop it, Miller. You too, old man." The sudden, growling voice behind them was clear and close. With a horrible sinking feeling, Ned realized Scott had outflanked them and gotten the drop on them from behind. He slowly raised his hands, doubting that even this would save him from being shot. Then he turned around.

To his astonishment, Neil Scott did not even have his pistol drawn. The stocky Australian hunkered before them like a wary, half-frozen bear, his red hair and beard a mass of ice.

"Hell's to pay, Miller!" Scott growled into the fierce wind. "We gave up on the gold an hour ago, an' just been trying to catch up. I tell you, hell's to pay! If we don't keep our heads level, we'll all go down the flume together like spring salmon. English, get up here!"

At this, Dave English appeared out of the storm in the other direction, shivering as he led their horses. He was as pale and sorry-looking an outlaw as Ned had ever seen.

Scott growled, "All right, Miller. Which way do you reckon's the bloody station?"

Ned began an indecisive reply, not yet fully adjusted to the idea that Scott wanted to cooperate rather than murder him. "Well, I—"

English broke in, "You wandered too far north. You blokes got us turning back on our tracks."

Ned objected, "We followed the sun. Tell them, Joe."

"Blast that old bugger," English said. "Neither of you galahs know—"

Finally Scott silenced the group with a gruff growl and a wave of his arm. He studied the faces a moment, and then, as if resolving to take all into his own hands, said, "We bloody well better stick together—stick together, and follow me. I'll shoot the first bloke who don't, and send him to hell a-flukin'."

With that he shoved his way to the front and led on, whipping the horses brutally until they staggered to their feet and stumbled forward. The others followed numbly, silently leaving their fates in the hands of this violent Australian, whose iron will seemed only strengthened by adversity.

It grew dark, the most fearful darkness Ned had ever seen. Suddenly Scott called a halt, cursing like a madman. "*Hell* with the bleedin' station!" he roared. "Come up here with your horses, and cut off the saddles!"

"If we cut them off we can't—" Ned began.

"Shuddup!" Neil took out his six-shooter and shot Ned's horse through the head. The animal jerked and collapsed into the snow.

"My God, man, that was Star!" Ned stood stunned with outrage. "Have you gone crazy?"

Scott swung the pistol to Ned. "I'm makin' a shelter out of the bodies what ain't helpin' us. Are you one of 'em?"

Ned gritted his teeth to keep from saying more. It was true that the exhausted horses could no longer help them travel. He recalled that the Puyshoos tribe had once eaten their horses to last through a harsh winter. Scott's cruelty was born of the same desperate will to survive. But it hurt Ned to see his relay horse die by this man's hand.

Scott turned the pistol back to the remaining horses, shoved them as close together as possible, and shot them down, throwing away his pistols as he emptied them. Then he tossed the saddles on the pile. "Now we take the horse blankets and huddle together on the heap. The heat from the horses'll help. But keep awake, all of you, or you'll never see the dawn." Scott flared his nostrils and balled his fists till the knuckles were white. His wild eyes fell on Ned. "All right, Miller," he said grimly. "Keep the party lively now, won't you, an' tell us how you sicced the bleedin' wardens on us back in Scott Valley. That'll get some hot blood flowin'."

The cold wind had set Ned's teeth chattering. "I didn't tell the law. It's just I'd worked in Deadwood before, and the mine owner saw through my disguise. He must have tracked me back. I—" He paused, and looked to Mountain Joe, who hardly seemed to be hearing what was said. Ned lowered his head. "I shot the sheriff and led the posse north."

Scott's eyes narrowed. "You were the bloke who shot the warden?"

English said, "I told you, Neil. I told you you're not the only galah who's taken a bad rap."

"Shuddup! We'd have gone after the gold anyway."

Their quarreling gave Ned courage. "Sure, you'd have killed Joe and me for the gold, but that wasn't enough. You had to murder the old Indian back at the Patoka station, and then chase us all off into a blizzard."

English, cowering in his blanket, shook his head, whimpering like a child. "We didn't kill anyone. If there was an Indian at that station, he'd taken off long before we ever got there. I told Neil we should go back to Lewiston, but he didn't listen. He never listens. He just went on and on till we couldn't turn back, and now we're goners—I know it, we're goners now."

English began to cry, but Scott smacked him with the back of his fist. "Shuddup. You ain't dyin' unless I wring your neck."

No one spoke for a long time. Ned pulled his wool blanket up over his head, but the wind still cut through the cloth mercilessly. He could tell the small amount of body heat rising from the dead horses would not last long. Already, drifting snow had banked up behind them, leaving here a hoof and there a wide-eyed horsehead exposed. When he closed his eyes to shut out the scene he saw instead the dark forms of uncomplaining Wintu warriors huddled beneath a pine tree—a chill memory from an elk hunt many winters ago. Now he wished he could set aside his suffering, as the Wintu had apparently done. But nothing he could do or think seemed to lessen the slash of the fiercely cold wind.

Ned did not remember how many hours of that interminable night had passed before he turned the opening of his blanket into the wind and saw that Mountain Joe's blanket had fallen onto the snow about his waist.

With horror, he shook the old man by the shoulders until the snow fell from his hair and his eyelids flickered open. "Joe! Wake up! You've dropped your blanket."

Dreamily Mountain Joe nodded, lifting a gray hand to his eyes. "I—I'm all right, just tired as an old mule, I guess."

Ned threw the blanket back around him and embraced the old man to try to keep him warm. It surprised him to feel what a thin frame his friend had.

Joe gave a soft laugh. "No, no. Lemme alone. Just gettin' old, I reckon, old an' tired." He closed his eyes gently. Quickly Ned shook him awake again. This time Joe opened his eyes wide with a start. "Wha—? Oh, Ned, it's you. Good, now mebbe you can unpack the stock so we can turn in."

"What are you talking about? We've shot the horses."

Joe seemed not to hear. "An' wind up my watch, too. You know, in my pocket. My hands're too damn stiff."

Ned felt inside Joe's buckskin jacket for the cold metal. The watch had stopped, but he wound it anyway.

"Frémont gave me that 'cause I knew the mountains," Joe muttered, and snorted contemptuously. "Ha! Nowadays the mountains're overrun with folks I don't know nothin' about."

Ned began to put the watch back in Joe's buckskin, but the old man shook his hands excitedly. "No, no! You take it, Ned. I can't even wind it anymore. You take it with you to the mountains. Take it back to Shasta where it belongs. You'll do that for me, won't you?"

"Sure, Joe, but you—"

Mountain Joe interrupted with his hand. "Too tired to jawbone 'bout it all night. Just keep it now." The old man pulled his blanket around him tighter and turned so Ned's protests were lost in the howl of the wind.

For a moment Ned held the watch in his hand uncertainly, but then an icy gust of wind hit and he put it in his breast pocket, huddling deeper into his blanket.

* * *

Scott shook Ned awake in the morning. The fearful storm had passed, but it was still cold and lightly overcast. A vast plain of white snow stretched before them. "Come on, get up," the scar-faced outlaw growled. "There must be more'n twenty miles yet to town." Ned stood up with difficulty. His lower legs were numb and responded only distantly to his commands. Likewise his hands and the tips of his ears and nose felt strangely leaden.

"You too, old timer," Scott said, kicking the huddled form next to Ned.

Mountain Joe, however, did not get up. Instead, the old man slowly tipped backwards and rolled down over the frozen horses into the snow.

Ned gave a startled cry. His mouth was open but would not form words. Before he could move, his head began a giddying spin.

*   *   *

Later Ned could not remember if he had really blacked out when he had seen that Mountain Joe was dead, or if his memory had simply erased almost half of the rest of that day. He regretted not having a final farewell to remember the old mountain man by. The last image, of the little man rolled face-down into the snow, was a cruel one, and he would have liked to know they had left him in a more honored fashion, perhaps laid next to the catenas of gold. In any case, he knew he had not remained unconscious for the entire day, because he did remember tramping with Scott and English in the bright sunshine, using sagebrush branches and leather strips for snowshoes.

In the memory, Ned imagined they were walking across a long, misty cloud, and were not on the earth at all. There was little to dispel the notion. The makeshift snowshoes were virtually soundless. There was nothing to see but sky, sun, and snow—all a dazzling, burning white.

As the sun climbed higher, an aching snow blindness dulled the glittering flakes from white to soft purple. Great dark shapes started up before his eyes when he blinked. When the snow darkened to a near-black in the afternoon there was almost no sensation in any part of his body. His thoughts grew strangely detached. A series of waking dreams took over his benumbed mind, each more realistic and detailed than the last.

Finally, when he staggered over a low rise with Neil Scott, half dragging the frail form of Dave English between them, he did not see the smoke rising from the chimneys of Walla Walla. Instead he saw before him a chestnut-haired girl on a bluff beside a curving ocean shore, and he smiled at the warm touch of a sea breeze.

*   *   *

At first there was only a sound—the sound of dripping water. Then Ned opened his eyes cautiously. His head throbbed with a tingling pain. Gradually he noticed his arms and legs tingling too. He was on a cot in the back of the Walla Walla express office. The cot creaked as he raised himself painfully onto an elbow.

Isaac Mossman's curly-haired head appeared beyond the counter. "Miller! You're awake!"

Ned rubbed an aching hand over his face and groaned. "How long have I been lying here?"

Mossman stumbled in his hurry to come to Ned's side. "Three whole days. Even the doc couldn't bring you around. How do you feel?"

"Like I've been through a buffalo stampede." A fearful memory swept through him, and he knit his brow.

Mossman seemed to read his thought. "Don't worry about the shipment. The fellow who brought you in said we'd find it all next to a dead man at the first relay station. I organized a search party to break trail back to the station two days ago. They've already recovered the gold and brought back the body."

Ned covered his face with his hands. Then the dream about Mountain Joe was true. And the iron man Neil Scott—he had left the gold behind in order to save Ned's and English's lives. Now Ned remembered the story English had told him long ago in the California hideout, of the young Neil Scott, who had been falsely accused of his own father's murder. Never again would he doubt that the heart of a man, however misunderstood he might be, was good.

Ned sat up painfully. "The old man—did you—did you bury him?"

Mossman nodded. "No one knew who he was, so I had him put in a corner of the cemetery. He didn't have anything of value on him."

Ned managed to whisper, "Thank you."

"Did you know him?"

"Yes, I—he was my friend." Ned limped to the window so that Mossman would not see the tears dampening his eyes. Joe was gone, and with him, an irreplaceable part of Ned's life. The frontier had lost a bit of its magic forever. All that remained of his steadfast backwoods mentor were memories, a handful of tall tales, and the gold watch softly ticking in his breast pocket. It seemed to Ned that the friends and places he had loved in his youth were slipping away—first the Soda Springs ranch, then Now-ow-wa, then Paquita and Cali-Shasta, and now Joe. Perhaps it was time to begin building a world for himself that would not slip away.

Outside, water dripped from bare roofs. Men, stripped to the waist, were digging a gutter to divert a muddy creek that ran down the middle of the street.

"What happened to the snow?" Ned asked incredulously. Had he been unconscious that long? The snow that had buried the land was gone.

"The Chinook wind hit town just about as you came in."

"What's a Chinook wind?"

"Don't you know? It's a warm wind that brings the thaw. Usually comes down out of the Rockies. Funny thing, though—this time she came up the Columbia Gorge, right off the ocean."

"Off the ocean," Ned muttered, with the flickering memory of another dream in the snow.

"Yup, since the wind hit after that last blizzard, everything's been melting. Rivers are high and a lot of trails are washed out, but the mines are freed up. People will be moving around again, so I suppose the express rates will have to drop."

Mossman hooked his thumbs on the belt about his portly midsection and looked out of the window with Ned. "I want you to take a good rest, though, to make sure you recover properly. You've been mighty sick, Miller."

Ned watched the gullying meltwater, thinking of the painful memories Idaho now held, and the very real threat of revenge from Cherokee Bob's gang. "How much does my share of the express receipts come to now?"

"We turned a pretty penny on that last run. I'd say there's over three thousand dollars in your name."

Three thousand dollars! It was more than most miners or schoolteachers could scrape together in a decade. Surely it would be enough to launch him on a steadier course to greatness than the ones he had followed so far. "Could you weigh it out for me?"

"Certainly. You need the gold now?"

Ned turned to face his partner. "I'm thinking I'll quit the express altogether."

Mossman's lips tightened. "Aw, now don't go breaking up our partnership, Miller. We've been doing so well. Besides, how am I supposed to find another rider?"

"Put your 'Rider Wanted' sign back in the window."

The stocky expressman sighed. "I don't suppose I can talk you into staying on?"

"No—I reckon I'll be going down to Oregon for good this time."

"I understand." Mossman put his arm on Ned's shoulder fraternally. "And to tell the truth, I don't blame you either. Young guy like you ought to buy his own business, settle down in some decent town."

Ned stared out the window again. "Yes," he said. "That's what I aim to do."

Chapter 13

Here, on the river, at the head of navigation, is Eugene City—a dear, delightful town among the oaks, but slow and badly hide-bound. It needs a good shaking up; wants someone who has the courage, and is enough its friend to tell it of its sins.
                                    —Joaquin Miller

Two weeks later, when Ned rode his shiny black express horse into the flooded streets of Eugene City, the little bag of gold he carried seemed a greater burden than any shipment he had hauled through Idaho's mining country. This time it was his own money, and his future hinged on how it was spent.

Three thousand dollars! The thought of it had fanned his ambitions to a flame. For once in his life, he had a real chance to establish himself, to finance whatever dreams he chose. But at the same time, the whisperings of his conscience had grown to a raucous chorus, shouting conflicting advice: Send for Paquita! First gamble for real wealth! No, help out your family instead! Try your hand at poetry again! Dedicate yourself to opposing war! Invest in a safe business!

Already guilt had made him part with two hundred dollars. He had stopped by his parents' farm, a dozen miles north of Eugene City. Worry had hung in the air of the little, rundown farmhouse like smoke from a smoldering fire. His mother Margaret had wrung her thin hands and chattered on nervously about all manner of unimportant things. His father Hulings had rocked in his chair for a long time, silent except for an occasional coughing attack that left him looking weak and old.

Gradually Ned had learned the truth. Last summer his sister Ella's illness had worsened. There had been trips into town to see the doctor, and expensive medicines to buy. Hulings had mortgaged the farm to find the money, but after the harvest had failed, he had fallen behind in the payments. Hulings blamed the poor weather and the poor soil, saying he seemed to have chosen the rockiest, least fertile corner of the entire Willamette Valley for his donation land claim. But Ned knew there was more to it, and he felt ashamed. His father had grown old, yet none of his boys had helped with the farmwork that fall. He and John had been in Idaho. His baby brother George had wanted to help, but he was only eight—too young to be anything but another burden.

Ned had easily paid off the farm's mortgage with a small portion of his pony express money. But he knew the debt was only symbolic of a deeper problem. His parents were no longer happy on the farm. They were too tired to put in the long hours anymore. Unless something was done the crops would lose money again in the coming fall, and in the fall after that. He had considered doing the farmwork himself, but had rejected the idea. It was too much like being a teacher—another chore, another rut. There must be grander opportunities in the city for a young man with cash in hand.

Now, riding into Eugene City, Ned noted wryly that opportunity and trouble always seemed to go hand in hand. The great blizzard and thaw in the mountains had left Willamette River floodwaters swirling three feet deep across the town. The river rippled out from the oaks along the millrace, eddied about the isolated clapboard houses on the edges of town, flowed past the porches of the buildings along the half dozen built-up streets, lapped at the four tall columns of the courthouse, and then spread out across the plains to the west, leaving only Skinner's Butte untouched, a grassy green island in the sparkling sea of mud.

"Hey, mister!" a man's voice woke Ned from his thoughts. "You're riding right down the middle of my flower bed!" A man in a gray cap was untying a rowboat full of tables and chairs from the submerged porch of a house.

Ned blinked down at the muddy waters with embarrassment and began to offer an apology, but the man replied, "Forget it, forget it. I reckon you're just new in town is all."

"Not really, but I've been gone a few years. I just got back today."

"You're coming back? Now's a hell of a time to come to Eugene City, friend. I'm just getting out."

"Floods don't last forever," Ned said. The town had never flooded before, and Ned thought it unlikely to happen again soon. He had seen the unusual snowstorms that had triggered the high water.

The man waved a hand toward the two-story house behind him. Waves sloshed in and out of broken first-floor windows. "Well, I've been living upstairs there for two weeks. I reckon I'm about fed up with sitting in a cold room, eating cold food. Now I'm heading out to camp on Skinner's Butte till I can find some dry land. Say, you want to buy a house?"

Ned had been about to ride on, but he stopped to take another look at the man's house. After all, he *did* need a place to stay. The frame house had white clapboard sides, a gable roof, and a single brick chimney. There were blue shutters on the windows and a shed-roof porch in front. Gray stripes marked the various levels of the flood.

"Maybe," Ned said. The house would be big enough to hold both him and his parents, and it was close to town, too—Fifth and Oak, kitty corner from a small store. Perhaps this was the first of the opportunities the flood of 1862 might open up. "What are you asking?"

"Wouldn't turn down three hundred dollars."

Ned considered. The high water probably hadn't done much more than fill the house with mud. "How about two hundred?"

"What? Are you crazy, for a two-story house?" The man laughed a moment, and then said, "Two-fifty."

With a smile, Ned dug five fifty-dollar gold slugs out of an inner pocket and held them out in his palm.

The man snapped his fingers and rowed over for a closer look. Now Ned could see his clothes were soaked and water dripped from his mustache and hair. The man stood up to see the coins better, rocking his boatload of furniture precariously.

"You got it, mister," the man said. He pulled paper and ink from a drawer in one of the tables, wrote a three-line deed, signed it, and traded for the money with a handshake. "You can have anything left inside, 'cause I don't plan on coming back. This town's getting too Republican anyway." His eyes narrowed. You aren't one of them pro-North types, are you?"

"No, I'm an anti-war Democrat, and I thought Lane County was run by Democrats."

"Well, the county still is, but only because they were elected back before the war. Now there's so many crazed abolitionist Republicans in town it's worth your life to talk States' Rights." He set his oars in the oarlocks seriously. "I reckon I wouldn't have cared when the flood washed out my store and my house—I'd have stayed on if it weren't for politics. There's an election four weeks away, and I don't want to be around if the Republicans take over."

"Where are you going?"

"Hills out west," the man replied, already pulling on the oars and turning the boat toward the butte. "That end of the county still has plenty of Democrats. You can fly the Stars and Bars out there, and that's more than you can do in Eugene City." The man nodded his gray soldier cap and leaned into the oars. "We're getting up a Confederate militia to defend ourselves, too."

Ned folded the deed uneasily, watching the rowboat cut across the floodwaters. What the man had told him about Eugene's politics had touched a sore spot. He had seen copies of the two town papers while riding the express, and he knew the rivalries still existed that had led to the collapse of his short-lived alma mater, Columbia College.

The Civil War debate had split him and his brother when they were in Idaho. That argument still rankled. Ned had never had a chance to convince John of the importance of peace over war. Returning to Eugene City made him want to get the issue off his chest once and for all. Maybe people would listen to him here. During his brief college days he had been chums with both of the town's newspaper editors—Newt Gale of the *State Republican* and Andy Noltner of the *Democratic Register*. They had both seemed reasonable, well-lettered men. Perhaps if he wrote guest editorials they would print them.

With a sigh, Ned turned his horse toward the house he had just bought. He swung down into the waist-deep water with a splash, tied the horse to a porch post, and waded in through the front door to inspect his bargain.

The parlor resembled a seacoast grotto. Half full of murky water, the room was lit by an eerie undersea shimmer of rippling sun reflections from the windows. He pushed waves across the room as he waded, bobbing the flotsam in the corners. He passed the open doors to two back rooms and climbed dripping up the stairs. His boots sloshed as he walked to the front gable window. There he leaned against the sill to look out across the town below, framed by a rectangular pane.

Buildings and trees peacefully dotted the plain's broad, still lake. But on the far shore, above the domed steeple of the courthouse, the brooding sandstone ruins of Columbia College glared back at him, a reminder of the tensions that had torn the town in half. Ned knew if he stayed in Eugene City as an outspoken Democrat he would be thrust into the continuing battle. Perhaps, he thought, it was time to hold his ground.

* * *

A month passed before Ned finally decided how to spend his pony express gold.

Day by day he watched from his gable window as the floods retreated and the puddles dried in the spring sun. The oaks and maples, held back by the long winter, burst into leaf, while the garden beds in the yard put up a waving crop of daffodils. The street mud dried in a stiff pattern of wheel ruts and hoofprints, rattling the buggies pulling up to Brumley's store across the intersection. Farmers cared little about the bumps, driving their big draft horses and mud-stained wagons down Fifth, hauling sacks of seed wheat for the spring planting.

Ned took a deep breath of the fresh air from the window and turned. His sister Ella had recovered sufficiently from her illness to oversee the renovation of the two upstairs bedrooms—one for Ma and Pa, the other divided for herself and little George. Her artistic touch was evident everywhere: in the gay flower-print curtains, in the colorful feather tick quilts, and in the neat but sparse arrangement of four-poster beds, spiral wool-rag rugs, and coal oil lamps with hand-painted glass shades.

Ned was proud of his sister's skill, but worried how frail she remained. There might be more medicines to buy and doctor bills to pay. He had only been home a month, and already the family relied on him for money. The thought made Ned uneasy about his decision.

He stopped by a dresser mirror to straighten the black cravat of his crisp, three-piece suit. He checked the time on Mountain Joe's gold watch—linked to his vest button by a new, draping chain. Then he descended the stairs.

"Ella, you've done a magnificent job with the upstairs," he said when he found her reading a book in the parlor.

She turned her face up, shaking a loose strand of blond hair out of her eyes. "It's really a beautiful house once it's tidied up, Ned. Of course, there's a lot left to be done downstairs. I feel a little guilty you had me leave your room for last."

Though her long dress was fashionably layered with ruffles, Ned could tell she was still alarmingly thin. "There's no need to work on it anytime soon. I think you deserve a rest." His sister had so much promise, yet had such a frail constitution. She looked up at him with admiring eyes—a look that startled him with the sudden memory of Paquita's bright-eyed glance. The two young women were so different: one pale and thin, the other robust and dark. But both had anchored a tether of guilt and love in his heart. It almost seemed that by protecting Ella now he might make up for the years he had roamed the wilderness, neglecting his Oregon family. Or was he trying to make up for neglecting his "other" family—Paquita and Cali-Shasta?

He pushed the thought from his mind and continued to the front porch. There he found his father standing in the sunshine with a shovel in his hand. "Say, son. I've been thinking about fruit trees. In the corners of the yard. What do you think?"

Ned joined him on the top step and hooked his thumbs on his vest pockets. "Sure. Let's get a bunch and plant them all along the fence."

Hulings nodded, but then he cleared his throat, and this set off one of his coughing fits. When at length he straightened up he added in a cracking voice, "Good idea. You could even buy some land on the edge of town and put up an orchard. Apples are easy to grow and pears sell high. Couldn't make a safer investment."

It was not the first time Hulings had dropped heavy hints about Ned's money. Three weeks ago he had talked up barley farming. Then it had been a livery operation. Then dry goods. Each time Ned had felt himself twisting inside, as if he were trying to escape a wrestling hold.

"Pa, sometimes a man has to take risks."

"What?" Hulings' face darkened. "Now's no time to gamble."

Ned braced himself to confront him. "What about when you were young? You risked everything coming out here to Oregon."

"Land's never a risk! Oregon's full of good land and trees. That's what I'm trying to tell you, son. You have to reach out and take it while you've got the chance."

"I want more from my chance than a rocky farm."

Hulings tightened his lips, obviously hurt. What could he say? The farm he had built had failed.

"I'm sorry, Pa," Ned said, softening. "But nothing's completely safe. I took a risk on the pony express, worked hard, and it paid off. Now I need work I can believe in. I need a chance to leap into a bigger world."

Hulings shook his head. "The world's already too big. You'll wish you'd bought fruit trees."

"Get a dozen and I'll help plant them," Ned said, putting his arm on his father's shoulder. "And tell Ma I'll be back for supper." Then he went on down the steps and toward the street.

"I hope you're not thinking about that bankrupt newspaper," Hulings called after him. "There's better ways to get your name in print, you know."

Ned stopped. "I'll be all right, Pa. Trust me."

Hulings sighed and shook his head."

*   *   *

It was one of those beautiful, fresh days of early summer that made Eugene City seem the greenest, most pleasant spot on earth. Birds flitted about in the maples outside the blacksmith shop. A striped cat rolled on the sunny plank sidewalk and yawned. At Eighth Street Ned paused by a stile in the courthouse lawn's white board fence, enjoying the calm of the smooth expanse of green, already well recovered from the flood.

Ninth Street was much livelier by comparison. As soon as Ned rounded the corner he could see two small crowds of men on opposite sides of the street. One group had collected on the porch of the *State Republican's* office. Ned recognized editor Newt Gale among them, somewhat taller and stouter than the rest. Though he was still young, Gale had a balding head and a full beard. He stood with his arms crossed and a slight smile on his lips.

Ned walked directly to the other side of Ninth, where men were carrying chairs, desks, and trays of type out onto the sidewalk from the low, square-fronted building that housed the rival *Democratic Register.* Among the workers was the owner, Andy Noltner, a short man with a smooth chin and a huge, bushy mustache. He spotted Ned and greeted him somberly. "I guess you heard we're folding up."

"Yes, after the election there's—"

"Well, the auction isn't till noon." Suddenly he caught sight of the crowd across the street. "Sweet Jesus, will you look at those vultures? Excuse me." He raised his voice. "Gale, why don't you and your gooneys clear out? Don't you have stories to cover or something?"

Gale smiled back broadly. "Are you kidding? I've been waiting to cover this story for years. I don't want to miss a minute of it."

Noltner muttered. "Christ, it's bad enough without a pack of Republican fanatics breathing down my neck. Look, Miller, if you want to kill some time till noon you can help move this stuff out. Everything goes."

"Wait a minute," Ned said, trying to slow him down. "I've been thinking about your paper closing. Maybe you're being a little hasty."

"Hasty? You know what it's like to lose an election and have half your advertisers pull out, just so they can butter up the new commissioners? Do you have any idea what it takes to run a paper?"

"Maybe I do and maybe I don't. What *would* it take to get your paper back in print?"

"Oh, about a thousand dollars loose change and a new editor, that's all."

Ned nodded. "Then I wasn't so far wrong." His father's warning still rang in his ears, but wasn't the whole trick of investing to buy low, when sellers were desperate? Where else could he get into a business for a thousand dollars? And it wasn't just a matter of seeing his name in print. How was he going to make the jump to a literary career if he didn't apply his writing skills? Besides, he would still have more than half of his pony express gold as a reserve.

Ned took a deep breath and took the plunge. He pulled a small leather bag out of his suit pocket and held it out to Noltner. "There's four pounds of gold dust, and I'm your editor. Now, what do you say we start moving all this stuff back in?"

Noltner stared from the bag to Ned open-mouthed. "You're not serious."

"I am."

"You know what you'll be up against if you start that press again?"

"I do."

"It'd be like swimming upriver and trying to take the whole damned current with you. Only a crazy man would try."

"I've been called worse. But if enough crazy men stand up for peace, we might just shut this war down."

Noltner pulled thoughtfully on one end of his long mustache. Then a strange, boyish gleam kindled in his eyes. He muttered to himself, "If I hired back the typesetter we could print Saturday without missing an issue."

Noltner cast a sidelong glance at the crowd across the street. "Come on inside where these hyenas aren't watching, Miller, and shake the hand of another crazy man."

In the dark, musty office the two men worked out the details of a plan to revive the *Democratic Register* under a new masthead that was to read: "A. Noltner & C. H. Miller, Proprietors." While the workers fetched the furniture in off the sidewalk, Noltner gave his new partner a tour of the establishment.

There were only three rooms. In front was a desk by the door for taking subscriptions, notices, and advertising. The middle room, banked with counters and cases of type, was dominated by the press. The ungainly machine hunkered in the middle of the floor like a cast-iron monster, with a flattened head, its mechanical hands full of ink rollers, and an enormous flywheel under its arm. It was not immediately clear to Ned where or how the thing actually printed newspapers, and Noltner did not lend either encouragement or instruction by calling it "Sukey" and cursing it for breaking down weekly since the floods.

The back room was actually a narrow, shed-like addition, where a single, cluttered desk sat in the light from four dirty windowpanes. "Here's where I used to do all the editorials, but if we're going to get this paper rolling again I'd better be out drumming up advertisers." He pulled a quill and some paper out of the top drawer and cleared a spot for them on the desk. "All right, Miller. You say you're an editor—let's see some writing. Show us what you can do for the Democracy."

Noltner left him there, alone in the back room. Uncertainly Ned approached the desk. A wind outside rattled a loose window pane, tapping it back and forth in its dingy frame.

Ned sat down. For a long time he contemplated the blank sheets of paper on the desk, not knowing where he should begin. How could he start to fill those vast empty pages with the thoughts that raced through his head, seemingly without beginning or end? For years he had dreamed of having a genuine writing desk. He recalled the wintry Now-ow-wa log cabin where he had wrapped rags around his hands to warm them while he wrote poems in a notebook on his lap. He remembered writing furtively in outlaws' hideouts and Nez Perce tepees. Always he had struggled to find a place and a time to pen his ideas. But now, when ample blank paper lay before him in his own newspaper office, he was at a loss.

Finally he shoved the paper aside in frustration and grabbed one of the notes that littered the desk. It was a telegram. Most of the papers on the desk proved to be telegrams of different dates, sent to Sacramento on the new transcontinental line and relayed north as far as the telegraph office in Yreka, where the wires ended. From there the messages had been sent by stage—a four-day trip, even running day and night.

He looked through the hand-written dispatches and saw they were almost entirely news from the Eastern war. New Orleans had fallen to Farragut. Memphis had fallen to Union gunboats on the Mississippi. General Grant's army had narrowly escaped annihilation at the Battle of Shiloh, and tens of thousands had died on both sides. McClellan was preparing Federal troops for an advance on Richmond, the Confederate capital.

Ned looked up at the dirty window and tightened his lips. The war itself was the enemy. The key issue was not secession—although it did seem undemocratic to force states into a Union. Certainly the issue was not slavery; even Lincoln was rejecting the radical abolitionists' demands to free the slaves. The issue was war.

Ned reached for the quill and began to write.

There is a pleasure in war. It yields a certain wild, intoxicating pleasure—for a time at least—that few of the inexperienced can resist. The stirring martial music of the fife and drum; the pomp and magnificence of the marching companies; the glitter and show of the burnished arms and gay uniforms of the regiments arouse the pride and energies of the young farmer, mechanic, or merchant; his heart is filled with aspirations never felt before. It matters but little what the cause may be, or where the war is to be waged, just so the call is made it is promptly answered by the volunteer.

But now that we have had a war of one year or more, let us pause and look at the effects. We need not enumerate the multitudes that have fallen in battle, or mention the cities destroyed or fields laid waste, for as long as the public mind remained healthy and vigorous, the country might be repeopled and cities rebuilt, but we see in the civil war of but one year's duration, (and it is only begun) that the public mind is almost entirely demoralized. The minister enters the pulpit and prays for the outpouring of seas of blood to wash out the dark sin of slavery. The yeomanry of the North have caught the contagion from the preacher and politician and almost groan with disappointment when they hear of a bloodless victory. Alas! Our country revels in the intoxication of blood!

News reaches us of a great battle. The Administration has won the victory, at least so we must publish; the eager people inquire how many killed? We answer thousands; they are wild with delight. Their minds have drunk the most baneful poison to the moral man, and they only arouse from its influence long enough to listen for something more terrible. Yet this will not always last. Americans will awake—there *must, there will* be a reaction. In that reaction, which the noble old Democracy is struggling to bring about, is the only redemption for the Union.

—C. H. Miller, *Democratic Register*

* * *

The summer of 1862 did not exist for Cincinnatus Hiner Miller, or if it did, it consisted of a dozen issues of tight, typeset columns, stacked against the bitter opposition of the authorities and of Republican papers from all over the fledgling state of Oregon. Ned threw himself into his newly-found calling with such determination and energy he soon had no time to help work on the Fifth Street house or its garden. From dawn to dusk he worked only with his quill at the cluttered, backroom desk, swept up in a maelstrom of opinions, news, ads, and insults that increased in intensity for the three months the government allowed his little four-page weekly to exist.

Ned had expected that his eloquent opening editorial would draw fire from Newt Gale's paper across the street, the *State Republican*. He knew Oregon journalism's trademark was its reckless mud-slinging. But Gale's editorial that week ignored the *Democratic Register* altogether. Instead it acclaimed the Republican victory in the local county election as if the fragmented Democratic party had already ceased to exist.

UNION TRIUMPH.—The ignorant mass of deluded followers of low party hacks and designing, unprincipled political hucksters are at last foiled in the county of Lane, and decently and triumphantly defeated. While the Union *arms* are gloriously triumphant in the Atlantic States and Mississippi Valley, we have with unfeigned joy to record a less magnificent, but not less glorious triumph of Union *votes* in Oregon. Lane County has at last concluded to *right about face,* and march to the music of the Union. As soon as it was ascertained that we had carried Lane County by a Union majority of 60 to 100 votes, it was determined to celebrate the glorious victory by firing 34 guns, which was done in approved style, winding up with three cheers for success, and three times three for the old flag and the Union. Poor show for secesh in this neck of the woods.

—J. Newton Gale, *State Republican*

When Ned read this bombast from the *Republican,* he sat back in his chair. He had already prepared an editorial exposing prominent Republicans, who had sent threatening letters to Democrat farmers before the election, warning that a "traitorous" vote might cause the government in Washington to withdraw their donation land claim patents. Since ballots were not secret in Oregon, the threat that the poll books might be used as evidence against a man had been real enough, and probably had changed some votes. Still, all of Ned's political and moral arguments against the Republicans would be useless as long as Gale could discard any Democrat as a "party hack" or a "huckster." He decided to add the following comment at the conclusion of his prepared editorial:

> Oregon presents some quaint characters to be sure. Far from the least curious among them is a class that the world calls editors, but the members of that class usually nominate each other as dolts, doughfaces, cabbage-heads, squibbs, and such like decorous titles. The *Republican* is run by a Gale, a very light and harmless Gale. He says the earth is as round as a pancake and is seven stories high—he aspires to the seventh.
>
> —C. H. Miller, *Democratic Register*

Newt Gale's reply appeared shortly thereafter:

> C. H. Miller, formerly of Mossman & Miller's Express to Salmon, has now the editorial charge and is also assistant publisher of the *Democratic Register*. Personally we have the best of feelings towards the editor, and hope that experience and a careful study of the public sentiment of this community will lead him to improve the tone of

the paper, which has not yet been known to give indications of joy at Federal victories or regret at rebel successes.

—J. N. Gale, *State Republican*

But Gale evidently could not resist a broader swipe, and also ran the following column:

It is reported that Florence precinct, Washington Territory, at the late election, gave a thousand secesh majority, and that there were not over three hundred legal voters in the precinct. It is also reported that Lewiston and Walla Walla gave rebel majorities. This strange result is accounted for by the fact that a multitude of loafers, thieves, robbers, and gamblers always rush into the mines to prey upon the miners, and they are nearly all secessionists.

—*State Republican*

Ned read this column with disgust. People in town would see the intended connection—that he was just back from Walla Walla, that he was clearly "secesh," thus that he was likely to be mixed with disreputable sorts. It gave him no motivation to pen a similar smear in reply.

Instead, he sorted through the stack of mail at his desk irritably—exchange newspapers, dispatches, subscriptions. Then his eye caught a small envelope that seemed somehow different, perhaps because his name had been written on it with such a flowing, elaborate hand. He opened it and glanced for a signature. Instantly his irritability disappeared.

It was from Minnie Myrtle, the poet for whom he had composed several sentimental verses in the Port Orford paper. She had discovered his name in the *Democratic Register* and wanted to thank him for his thoughtful rhymes and to wish him well in his new post. She included a stanza about the lonesomeness of a young singer whose ballads were heard only by the tall firs and the crashing sea, and invited him to devise another poetic reply, adding that mail could reach her directly under the name Theresa Dyer, as "Minnie Myrtle" was only her *nom de plume*. "And, if you wish, you might include a small likeness, since a picture is a kind of poem too, is it not?"

After Ned had read and reread Minnie Myrtle's enticing letter, he found his quill only wanted to write poems. The "Sweet Singer of the Coquille" had chosen to pick up a correspondence he had begun from Idaho with no more hope than one might have from a letter left adrift in a bottle! Perhaps this lonely poet on her windswept seacoast really was a kindred spirit—someone who would understand the desire and ambition of his verse. But who was she really?

When the need to turn out copy for the coming newspaper deadline finally became urgent, Ned was forced to set aside his unfinished, only semi-coherent poetic scribblings to "M. M." But he still could not summon the angry adrenaline needed to write editorials. Local news, advertisements, and mining reports had piled up on his desk. Now he lunged into these with an unusually wild and free pen:

RUNAWAYS.—Sunday a team broke loose at "Bristow's Corners," ran as far as the stage barn and up Eighth Street to the fence around the public square and tore to pieces a buggy tied up there. There were only two runaways on Monday. A farmer in town whose horses took a dash around the block, and Vich Behven's dray horse, not to be outdone by a team from the country, started out and mowed down nearly all the signs and awnings as far as Bristow's.

NEW DISCOVERY: Know all men, women, young ladies, and boys, J. A. Winter has perfected a process by which he can take pictures without showing the freckles. This is a distinction sought for in vain for a long time. Come along in before the roads get too bad to travel.

CORRESPONDENCE FROM JOHN DAY'S MINES.—The following extracts are from a letter from A. A. Smith, Esq., from Eastern Oregon:

"I am now on John Day's river and in a mining country, in my opinion, as extensive as California has been, but probably not so rich, though more evenly distributed through the mountains. I think there will be as much gold taken out of the Blue Mountain Range as there has been out of California, and do the men who get it out more good. For the next two years I think there will be room for 20,000 men in the mines that have already been discovered, which will pay from one-half ounce to three ounces per day. We have the quietest time here of any mines I was ever in. Sundays we have church and Bible class—three preachers within a mile."

Dr. J. C. YOUNG, late Prof. of the Univ. of Penn., can be found at his private Medical Office and Hospital, No. 751 Clay St., S. F.

Dr. Young addresses those who are suffering under the afflictions of private diseases, whether arising from impure connection or the

terrible vice of self-abuse. Devoting his entire practice to that particular branch of the profession, he feels warranted in GUARAN-
TEEING A CURE IN ALL CASES.

YOUNG MEN, especially, who have become victims of solitary
vice, that dreadful, fascinating, and destructive habit, which fills
thousands of sickrooms with paralytics and consumptives, and
hundreds of untimely graves with its unguided victims, should
consult one who will cure them for a moderate compensation.

As the week's deadline drew near, Ned still had no editorial. He read
the *Republican* for inspiration, but Gale appeared to have likewise lost
interest temporarily in the larger debate, confining himself to a rebuke of
the local movement to incorporate Eugene City, saying there were less
expensive ways of banishing the common nuisances, "loose hogs and
grog shops," than by setting up a city government.

Smiling, Ned turned to the San Francisco papers. There he found his
topic, and began the painstaking process of coaxing an unwilling editorial
onto his blank paper.

We have lost all confidence in the Administration telegraph,
though our sable friends may shriek "treason" at the announcement.

The monopoly of news asserted by the Federal Executive has
produced a very natural result of throwing complete discredit upon
the accounts that reach us through the channels of the Northern
Government. The *Times*, indeed, has made no small cackle over the
premature slaughter of Gen. Beauregard, and contends that it is base
ingratitude on his part to insist upon being not merely alive and well,
but absolutely victorious, after the Northern press had so decently
and circumstantially announced his death and defeat.

—C. H. Miller, *Democratic Register*

* * *

Another deadline behind him, Ned whistled his way from the barber's
shop to the Daguerrean photographic studio on Willamette Street, nodding recognition to passersby. When he caught a glimpse of himself in a
store window he stopped to smooth his blond mustache. The barber had
removed his thin, fuzzy sideburns, leaving a trim beard about his chin.
His hair flowed back from his high forehead in dramatically handsome
waves, still shiny from the barber's tonic.

He bounced up the step to the photographer's office and announced
his intention to have a small daguerreotype taken. A large, balding man
with sideburns like slipped earmuffs took him earnestly by the arm and

led him through the exhibition gallery in the front room, trying to persuade him to order something larger, as long as he was going to sit for one at all. Ned surveyed the array of large portraits and panoramas, but shook his head. It had to be suitable for sending through the mails.

The photographer smiled, with an "Ah" of comprehension, and led the way to the studio. There he showed Ned the backdrops available for an extra charge: Niagara Falls? An Italian balustrade? The columns of a ruined Greek temple, perhaps? Ned waved them all away, saying he only wanted a good likeness.

With a humph the photographer showed him to a plain chair and began to arrange large mirrors so the sunshine of a skylight glared into his face. Then he adjusted a pair of calipers on a stand so they pinched Ned painfully behind the ears. The man explained that the calipers would keep Ned's head from moving for the two minutes the lens had to remain open.

It was late in the day when Ned returned to the office of the *Democratic Register*, still in far too good a mood to be prepared for what he found. Andy Noltner handed him a handwritten paper and spoke gruffly. "A dispatch came from San Francisco while you were out. I wrote you an editorial about it." From his sullen eyes it was clear he was frowning; his bushy mustache drooped over his mouth, hiding any expression that might have been there. "The federal soldiers have orders that would let them bust up the paper and beggar us anytime they want. So much for free speech." He kicked a wastebasket on his way out of the office, leaving Ned to read the editorial alone:

> General George Wright, commander of the Military Department of the Pacific, has issued the following intolerant and proscriptive orders:
>
> "Whereas, it having come to the knowledge of the undersigned that there are certain persons either holding office under the Rebel Government, or aiding or abetting the enemies of the United States, and that such person or persons are owners of real estate or personal property within the limits of this military department; it is hereby declared that all such estates or property are subject to confiscation for the use and benefit of the United States."
>
> The real interpretation of these orders, we presume, can be thus set forth: every citizen who shall oppose the policy or doctrines of the Administration; who does not favor a war for Abolition; who believes and declares that the President has violated the Constitution; who thinks and asserts that members of the Cabinet and

commanding generals have been privy to Treasury frauds and speculations; and who refuses or fails to vote the straight Republican ticket, shall be deemed disloyal, and an aider and abettor of the rebellion, and shall, therefore, be arrested and imprisoned, and his property be confiscated, and no sale made by him to be of virtue or effect.

General Wright is generally wrong.

—A. Noltner, *Democratic Register*

During the following week Ned watched the Republican papers carefully, but they avoided any editorial comment on the confiscation issue, almost as if it were simply another part of the war effort. In fact, the Confiscation Act had first been suggested by the Republicans as a way to keep wealthy Southern landowners from supporting the rebel cause once their plantations were behind Union lines, but now confiscation seemed to be threatening anyone who opposed war. Why else did the military announce confiscation orders for California and Oregon, where there were no army lines? Why weren't the Republican papers talking about the constitutionality of taking property without due process? Gale, for one, merely treated the issue as a news item, casually noting that confiscated property might eventually be returned to a person's heirs:

Washington, July 17. A bill passed both Houses yesterday removing the President's objection to the Confiscation bill. The Act is so amended as to not work the forfeiture of the real estate of the offender beyond his natural life.

—*State Republican*

Ned and Andy Noltner met in the back room and discussed their options late into the night. Andy puffed nervously on a cigar. Their paper still was not clearing a profit worth mentioning, he said. Financially, it would be best to sell before the government impounded the press. On the other hand, they were not really in the red, and federal soldiers were not likely to march into town to arrest them—they would have to come from the Vancouver garrison, and that would surely lead to an ugly battle with armed Lane County Democrats.

Ned, for his part, was adamant that finances were not the only issue. Part of the reason he had bought into the paper was to speak against the war, and that is what he intended to do.

Andy chewed his cigar and squinted at Ned before he gave his reply. "Then you'd better roll up your sleeves, Miller, 'cause we're going to have us one hell of a fight now."

* * *

The next issue of the *Democratic Register* hit the streets of Eugene City with its editorial guns still blazing. From the telegraph's contradictory war dispatches it was clear the Northern armies had suffered a crushing defeat in their attack on Richmond, and Ned made the most of it.

> The Atlantic news of the last ten days is far from encouraging to the Federal area. McClellan has withdrawn from James River and returned to the Potomac with his army dwindled down to less than one-half its original size by death in the camp and on the battlefield, and the spirits of his remaining troops broken by disappointment and defeat. The Confederates made no attempt to attack McClellan while withdrawing from their country, which goes to substantiate their declarations that they only ask to be let alone.
> —C. H. Miller, *Democratic Register*

But the Republican papers of Oregon were not about to leave C. H. Miller's paper alone—not when the military had spoken in their favor. The *Sentinel* in Cottage Grove printed the following comment:

> THE DEMOCRATIC REGISTER.— Why this treason-reeking sheet is permitted to live is something of a wonder to loyal men.
> —*The Sentinel*

Ned fired back an immediate reply:

> Why do Republicans insist that the REGISTER should not be permitted to live? If its statements are false, why not expose them? If its arguments are unsound, why not destroy them? And if its principles are false, why not meet them like men? They will only be the more easily overcome. The truth is, the leading Republicans feel galled and harassed by the REGISTER exposing the treachery, foul and black-hearted villainy of the corrupt, usurping Administration. But, instead of admitting these facts like men or meeting and confuting them like honest journalists, they go whining to the vile authorities at Washington, like overgrown children, fastened to their mother's apron-strings, and ask old Abe to come to their assistance.
> —C. H. Miller, *Democratic Register*

Each week Ned wrote the editorials as though they might be the last, for the war was deepening. Word arrived that some eastern states were now forced to draft men to fill their quotas. The federal government had begun to pay its debts by simply printing Treasury notes, or "green-backs." Ned fired yet another dangerous editorial at the Republican government—this time for continuing its war even after its Treasury was depleted and its volunteer recruits dead.

> Let no man deceive himself into the belief that drafting will not be resorted to on this coast, as soon as the powers that be feel safe in doing so. Already contracts are being made for shipping troops to the east by way of Panama. It is no argument to say that it is poor economy for the government to ship troops to the Atlantic. What cares our Administration for expense when it can grind out green-backs enough in one day to buy the Pacific Coast, if it can only make us believe they are "legal tender?"
> —C. H. Miller, *Democratic Register*

Salem's *Oregon Statesman* quoted Ned's editorial with the following comment:

> The name of the miscreant and traitor who uttered the above quotation is C. H. Miller. As soon as his one-horse paper is busted up he will be found skedaddling to the Southern Confederacy.
> —Asahel Bush, *Oregon Statesman*

Furious, Ned resolved to fight fire with fire. If these foul-mouthed Oregon editors only understood tough talk, he'd show them he could beat them at that style, too:

> Traitor do you say? You cowardly, perjured, lantern-jawed, green-eyed Yankee—traitor to what? You talk of traitor—you who have for ten years been a traitor to the best interests of our infant State for the sake of filling your own greedy pockets. You who today stand a perjured traitor before the party that made you what you are. You who are this hour the blackest traitor that the valley can boast. Scream "traitor" because a man dares to hope for the return of the peace and prosperity of our country? Go, humble your "diminished head" in gunny sack and ashes, for no other penance can save the perjured villain that bestrides the editorial tripod of the *Statesman*.
> —C. H. Miller, *Democratic Register*

                                    *   *   *

"Take a rest, Miller," Andy said, shaking his head. "If you don't go home to bed, that cold of yours will blow up into full-scale pneumonia. Seems like you haven't slept for days."

"I'm waiting for the mail," Ned sulked, and noisily blew his nose.

"Aim that howitzer at General Grant," Andy said. "You'd shorten the war."

The bell above the office door tinkled. Ned jumped up, but his fever had left him so dizzy he nearly blacked out. When he regained his balance he flipped through the stack of mail that had been left on the front counter. A small envelope fell from the pile with a clink. Instantly he grabbed it up and disappeared with it toward his backroom desk, leaving Andy Noltner shaking his head at the jumbled heap of newspapers and letters left behind.

Ned locked the door behind him so he would not be disturbed. Then he slit open the envelope with his pocket knife, carefully unfolded the elegantly-penned letter, and slid a small, rectangular metal plate out of its tissue wrapping.

The photograph of Minnie Myrtle left him breathless. Never had he expected the poet from Port Orford to be so beautiful. She leaned against the back of a chair, gazing at him wistfully with eyes as large as moons. A wealth of dark, wavy hair swirled about her brow and cascaded down her back, leaving a delicate curl like an earring to frame her cheek. Her pouting mouth was small and her Roman nose prominent, but she wore such a romantic, longing expression . . .

Ned had begun to drift into a feverish trance when a violent sneeze shook him back to his senses. He blew his nose again, leaned the photograph against the back of his desk, and picked up the unfolded letter with a shaky hand.

> Dear Mr. Miller—or shall I say Ned?
>
> How lovely to find your little verse and your photograph in the mail! Am I mistaken, or did I glimpse beneath the elegant rhyme of the Eugene City editor a daring glint of the pony express rider's keen eye and wit? Alas, my own photograph is but poor repayment!

The words left him with a glow that added to the heady fever of his cold. He rubbed his eyes and lavished another look at the longing debutante in the photograph. She seemed to be gazing back at him. But what did she see, he wondered? She wasn't interested merely in the staid editorialist, nor even the struggling poet, judging from what she had written. What had caught her fancy was the wilder, impulsive spirit below the surface—the flamboyant pony express rider of the frontier. He held onto that thought as best he could, accustoming himself to the idea. It gave him a dizzy, broad-shouldered feeling. Yes, he could be that person too.

In his fever, the room began to spin. He lay his head on the desk and closed his eyes, intending to rest only for a moment. But exhaustion pulled him toward sleep—toward the deeper darkness beyond the letter.

*   *   *

In the dream Ned stood beside the crashing ocean. He could sense someone was there, waiting for him. But he was startled all the same when a familiar voice spoke.

"Howdy, old man."

Ned turned about and gaped. The shadowy figure of a young man was leaning against the ocean bluffs. A slouch hat hide the man's face, but he wore the same style of fringed buckskins Ned himself had worn in California years ago.

"Who—?" Ned began. His words froze when the young man lifted his head. An eerie fear crackled through Ned. Impossibly, the face was his own—younger perhaps, and with his mouth drawn up in a dry look of disdain, but as clearly Ned Miller as if he had looked in a mirror.

Ned stared at the apparition, speechless. His heart beat faster. He knew what he was seeing was part of a dream he had wanted to avoid. "Go away," he said, as evenly as he could manage. "You don't exist."

The young man took off his slouch hat and ran a hand through his wavy hair, just as Ned himself often did when puzzled. "Well I reckon you've got me there, old man." The apparition spoke with a wry tone Ned knew all too well. "If I don't exist, I can't go away."

Ned closed his eyes tightly, hoping this would dispel the dream. But when he opened them the figure was still there.

"It's OK, old man. This is a bad dream for me too." The young man pushed off from the cliff. As easily as if he were crossing a room he wiped out the seascape with a sweep of his arm and sat on the edge of Ned's desk.

"Fancy dress," the young man said, idly fingering the photograph. "Pretty poetry, too. But I bet she's no better in bed."

Ned felt his face flush even hotter. He stood up and crossed his arms. There seemed no choice but to confront the apparition on its own terms, with words. "Is that why you're here?"

The young man took over the chair and leaned back, putting his tall miner's boots up on the desk. "Just look at this place: clapboard walls, glass windows. You've even got a regular two-story city house with a picket fence, all painted white. Still I can't shake the feeling you're forgetting something."

"Damn it all, you know why I had to leave Paquita."

The young man raised an eyebrow. "Touched a nerve, did I?"

"Look, I loved her. I'll always love her. But I couldn't have stayed in California. There was a posse after me for horse theft and attempted murder. Now-ow-wa was the first place they would have looked. Paquita didn't need any more grief. As it was, I only escaped hanging by sheer luck."

"That was two years ago," the young man reminded him. "The posse's gone and Neil Scott's in Idaho. You could go back."

"California won't drop those charges so fast. I took enough law at Columbia College to know that," Ned said. "Besides, a lot of things have changed for me since then—and for Paquita too, I'll bet. By now she's probably settled into a routine. I'd just disrupt things. She's a resourceful woman. And she's got the tribe—they always take care of their own."

The young man smiled sourly.

"Don't give me that look," Ned said. "It's not just that I don't wear buckskins any more. Now-ow-wa is a paradise—but it's a paradise I've lost."

"You could bring her here."

"Oh hell." Ned blew out a breath. "The woman's never even seen a city. She'd hate it, and it would hate her. You want that?" Andy Noltner had told him just the other day of a *Register* subscriber who lived with an Indian wife outside Eugene City. People spat on the poor woman when she dared to come into town, and no shopkeeper would serve her.

The young man put his feet back on the floor and looked straight at Ned. "You made a promise."

Ned turned away. It did hurt, remembering the Wintu wedding. He had loved her so much then it had seemed anything would be possible. But time and misfortune had returned them inevitably to their own worlds.

"Well?" the young man demanded.

Ned still looked away. "I couldn't even speak Wintu then. We weren't able to make any hard promises." He wished the boy hadn't forced him to say these truths out loud.

"Clever, old man," the younger version of Ned said sarcastically. "But that's not the promise I meant."

"Then what?"

The young man deepened his voice and spoke in Wintu, "Your Papa has to go away again for a while."

"Cali-Shasta!" Ned said.

"Five years old by now, I suppose."

The thought staggered Ned. Among the Wintus, the child would be considered nearly half grown. "I suppose she wouldn't remember me at all by now."

"Or your promises?"

Ned glared at him. "That's not what I meant. I haven't forgotten. I'll go back one day. I'll see everything's made right." He looked away again, realizing how weak his words sounded. "How is the girl doing?"

The young man shook his head. "I don't know. I left California when you did."

"We left together?"

"Of course. When a spirit puts on a new mask it doesn't throw the old ones away. They just become part of the baggage people carry around."

"You're a mask. An old mask."

The young man nodded slowly. "An old mask. Your spirit called me back when you saw her."

Ned turned to the desk and looked again at the tintype photograph. Minnie Myrtle's long hair fell in curls on a shiny gown. Surely, he thought, it wouldn't be fair to compare her to Paquita. They were different people, from different cultures. He was a different person now too. He had mourned his love for Paquita long and well. Now it was time to admit that his life with the Wintus was irretrievably lost. He had a right to build a new life—to find new happiness. And no ghost was going to stand in the way.

Ned turned to the boy, no longer afraid. "I won't need you again."

"You will," the young man replied with a smirk. "But I won't come." Then he tipped his slouch hat and sank into the shadows of the dream, leaving nothing but an uneasy ripple in Ned's heart.

*   *   *

In its next issue the *Democratic Register* ran a poem where the editorials should have been:

INSANE

Insane, did you say? Yes, gone insane!
Drove mad, some say, by a love affair,
While others say by a fevered brain—
And others, again, by too much care;
Maybe the first, maybe all combined,
But he's crazed, I know; why I cannot guess,

For what should dethrone a young man's mind,
We little know and care still less.

. . . But still 'tis a pity he's gone insane.
—C. H. Miller

* * *

In the following week Ned spent his nights writing sheaves of poetry, pouring out the emotions unleashed by Minnie Myrtle's letter. The startling memory of his feverish dream gradually dimmed. The unsettling nightmare did not return. Now his goal was clearer; his purpose set. He rewrote, merged, trimmed, and polished the verse, hoping to have one special poem perfect in time for the Friday night deadline.

By day, however, business forced him to perform the increasingly grim task of preparing news and editorials for the upcoming issue:

> The news from the John Day mines is still encouraging. Several of our citizens have gone and a good many are preparing to go. They all go the McKenzie road.
>
> ROBBERS HUNG AT LEWISTON.—On the 9th, three robbers were hung at Lewiston. They had robbed two brothers named Berry, between Florence and Lewiston, were pursued and captured near Walla Walla, carried back to Lewiston, and there taken out by a vigilance committee and hung. The names of these men were Nelson Scott, David English, and Wm. Peoples. Another man was found hanging to a tree on the road between Lewiston and Walla Walla.

Ned stopped at the telegram announcing the deaths of Neil Scott and Dave English. It saddened him to think the world would applaud the news. Scott had been the most feared outlaw of the Pacific Coast. He had also saved Ned's life. Someday, Ned swore, he would proclaim to the world that even the heart of the most despised outlaw could be good. But not yet. Now Ned somberly laid the telegram aside, saving his thunder for the editorial he had yet to write.

> The Administration papers of Oregon denounce us for opposing drafting, yet they, with self-conceited wisdom, carefully avoid saying a word for or against the atrocious order, and why? Because they well know it is miserably unpopular even among the most rabid Republicans. Come, don't be intimidated. Oregon is yet a free country. Let us hear your views on the practical application of Treasury notes, Confiscation bills, and drafting orders in Oregon.
> —C. H. Miller, *Democratic Register*

*   *   *

The night was muggy in the pressroom. Ink rollers hummed and machinery clanked as the sweating pressboy cranked the flywheel in the shadowy lantern light. Andy Noltner pulled sheet after sheet off the relentlessly rocking pressbed. Ned worked feverishly to keep pace, stacking the papers to dry and buttering the press's ink-plate with black paste from a can. He had rolled his white sleeves up to his biceps. Ink and sweat streaked his face.

When Andy finally pulled the thousandth copy from the sticky black type, the first light of the summer dawn was a dull glow in the window. The pressboy unlocked the type, washed it with thinner, and began to break it down into the type cases. Andy set to folding papers for the morning mail pick-up.

But Ned did not help fold yet. He took one of the dry papers from the rack to his backroom desk, where the letter he had written was waiting unsealed. Taking care not to smudge the ink, he folded the newspaper smaller and smaller. When it was finally small enough to fit the envelope, all that showed on its front was a bit of the masthead and a short poem.

MIDNIGHT PENCILINGS
I am sitting alone in the moonlight,
In the moonlight soft and clear,
And a thousand thoughts steal o'er me,
While penciling, sitting here;

Away in the hazy future—
Afar by the foaming sea
I am painting a cot in my fancy—
A cottage, and "Minnie," and me.
—C. H. Miller, *Democratic Register*

And he swore: if she dares to answer, I'll marry her.

Joaquin Miller, about 1870 (photo courtesy Lane County Historical Museum).

Left: Castle Crags, over-looking Soda Springs on the Sacramento River of Northern California.

Below: The young Poet of the Sierras at the Soda Springs cabin. Romaticized illustration from Miller's Unwritten History: Life Amongst the Modocs *(1873).*

Above: Romanticized illustration of Joaquin Miller's departure from Paquita and Cali-Shasta, from Unwritten History: Life Amongst the Modocs *(1873).*

Left: Mount Shasta.

Above: The earliest known photograph of Eugene City, Oregon, about 1865. The Miller house is in the foreground at the far left. (Photo courtesy Lane County Historical Museum)

Left: The earliest known photograph of C. H. (Joaquin) Miller, about 1868. (Oregon Historical Society photo 100160)

Below: Cape Blanco, the westernmost point of Oregon, lies four miles north of the Dyer home where Joaquin Miller met Minnie Myrtle.

Theresa (Minnie Myrtle) Miller, about 1870.
(Oregon Historical Society photo 100161)

THE DEMOCRATIC REGISTER

"EVERY ATTEMPT TO EXERCISE POWERS BEYOND THESE LIMITS [THE CONSTITUTION] SHOULD BE PROMPTLY AND FIRMLY OPPOSED."—WASHINGTON'S FAREWELL ADDRESS.

$2.50 PER ANNUM. EUGENE CITY, OREGON, SATURDAY, AUGUST 9, 1862. VOL. I, NO. 22.

The Democratic Register. PUBLISHED EVERY SATURDAY, BY NOLTNER & MILLER. A. NOLTNER, C. H. MILLER, PROPRIETORS.

Democratic Register.

C. H. MILLER - - Editor.

EUGENE CITY, SATURDAY, JUNE 28.

The War—Its Effects and Final Result.

There is a pleasure in war. It yields a certain wild intoxicating pleasure—for a time at least—that few of the inexperienced can resist. The stirring martial music of the fife and drum; the pomp and magnificence of the marching companies; the glitter and show of the burnished arms and gay uniforms of the regiments, arouse the pride and energies of the young farmer, mechanic or merchant; his heart is filled with

The Democratic Register.

INSANE.

Insane, did you say? Yes, gone insane!
Drove mad, some say, by a love affair,
While others say by a fevered brain.
And others, again, by too much care;
Maybe the first, maybe all combined,
But he's crazed, I know; why, I cannot guess.
For what should dethrone a young man's mind,
We little know and care still less.

Yet still 'tis strange that the man is crazed,
For he had a cheerful and brilliant mind,
And oft I have heard his genius prais'd,
And his name with the gifted and good entwined.
But his thoughts are wild and wandering now,
While he talks sometimes in a mournful strain
Of blasted hopes and a broken vow.
Poor boy, 'tis a pity he's gone insane!

EUGENE CITY REVIEW.

C. H. MILLER, - - Editor.

EUGENE CITY, SATURDAY, JAN. 3, 1863.

Freedom of the Press.

With this number of the REVIEW we again hoist the almost hallowed name of Democracy to the head of the paper. We never ceased to deprecate the high-handed usurpations of power that forbid Democratic papers equal rights with other journals to mail facilities at all times and places, but we lived and labored in the hope that re-action would set in in the minds of a majority of the people that would warn the powers that be of the folly and danger of too far trespassing the sacred rights of a free people. We believe the Administra-

Above: C. H. (Joaquin) Miller was editor and co-owner of the Democratic Register *and* Eugene City Review *during the Civil War. The editorials he wrote for peace left him accused of treason.*

Below: While in San Francisco 1863-64, both Joaquin Miller and Minnie Myrtle freelanced for the literary magazine the Golden Era, *but Minnie's work was accepted more often.*

The  Era.

SAN FRANCISCO, CALIFORNIA, SUNDAY, FEBRUARY 1, 1863. VOL. XI.—NO. 9.

THE GOLDEN ERA.

[Written for the Golden Era.]

LOVE STORIES.

BY MINNIE MYRTLE.

I have been listening to one of those pretty, pathetic love stories, of blushes, and sighs and tears, and broken hearts etc. read in the sweet, low tone of little sister Ell. Wonder why young people like these stories so well. They are always popular just as they contain the complement of "casting down eyes," and "tender sighs," blushes and an Elysian of happiness in the ending. I remember how I used to smuggle candles in my bedroom, and read of nights; and when reading was forbidden, with what fascination I pored over the productions of some prolific-brained novelist, and how sad, or joyous I felt over some non-existing event. Nature never grows old, love is ever new, and this is why love stories always are, and always will be read.

La Grand passion! Where is there a wedded man or woman but have sometime in their life, before they vowed to "love, honor etc," (not afterwards, of course) been deeply distractedly in love? If there is any I pity them; if they

in a sombre traveling dress, not at all suitable for church. She arose slowly, threw back her veil, and revealed a hard cold-looking face, not at all warmed by the love of God, and a pair of black eyes looking straight at the pulpit. Several of the old brethren greeted her with "that's right, sister! tell us what the Lord has done for you!"

"I wish first tell you what brother Esperdene has done for me."

I looked at our brother. He was ghastly pale, and I wondered at his distressed, appealing expression, as he looked at the woman. She continued, with the same disagreeable look:

"I wish to recount some of the labors of brother Esperdene before he came to your 'moral vineyard.' He came to a little village in this State about six months ago, and remained there some two months: and during that time he won the affections of a wealthy and respectable girl, married her, obtained possession of her property, and then vanished."

The woman paused. Brother Paul's face was perfectly haggard. The woman went on in a moment, and said she had proof, that two officers were waiting her commands without, and finally that she was the wronged woman.

The Golden Era.

SAN FRANCISCO.

JOSEPH E. LAWRENCE, } JAMES BROOKS, } Proprietors.

SUNDAY MORNING .... JULY 19, 1863.

Answers to Correspondents.

CINCINNATUS.—Cape Blanco, is, we should judge, a romantic spot. Freedom and flowers and cool butter-milk, with the blue-stocking companionship you hint of, is provocation sufficient for the sighs of a man of any appreciative size. The lines have something of the free sweep of the sea-waves about them. Rewash in.

Above: The house Joaquin Miller built for Minnie in Canyon City, Oregon.

Left: The Canyon City house has been moved to the center of town, where it serves today as a museum.

Below: Canyon City in about 1900, thirty years after the Millers left. (Oregon Historical Society photograph CN021645)

Above: An 1860s store for Chinese gold miners near Canyon City survives as the Kam Wah Chung Museum in John Day, Oregon.

Right: The gold rush store includes a Chinese shrine.

Below: The kitchen of the Kam Wah Chung store in John Day.

In the Circuit Court of the State of Oregon for Lane county.

Theresa Miller pltff }
vs.
C. H. Miller Deft. } Suit in divorce:

I admit that I have stated to her Attorney Mr. Ellsworth that I have not treated her as a wife for one year past & do not intend to do so in the future. I do not claim ... both the custody of the younger child

Subscribed & Sworn to before me this 18th day of April 1870.

C H Miller

Left: Excerpts from the divorce proceedings of C. H. (Joaquin) Miller and Theresa (Minnie Myrtle) Miller. (Courtesy Oregon State Archives)

Below: The daughter of Joaquin and Minnie, Maud Eveline Miller, in about 1873. (Oregon Historical Society photo 100162)

Minnie Myrtle assisted women's rights activist Susan B. Anthony (above) during her Oregon tour in 1871, and reported on Anthony's lectures in a relatively radical women's newspaper, the New Northwest (below).

The New Northwest.

FREE SPEECH. FREE PRESS. FREE PEOPLE.

VOLUME 1. PORTLAND, OREGON, FRIDAY, SEPTEMBER 29, 1871. NUMBER 23.

Upper left: Joaquin Miller, about 1872. (Oregon Historical Society photograph 100158)

Upper right: Joaquin Miller, about 1876. (Oregon Historical Society photograph 100724)

Left: Joaquin Miller, about 1905. (Oregon Historical Society photograph 65375 by Lee Moorhouse)

PART TWO

Minnie

Chapter 14

You called me, and I came home to your heart.
The triumph was—to reach and stay there.
                    —Robert Browning

Minnie worried about the letter she had written. She gazed across the waters of the Elk River, remembering the wording she had used.

"Purty weather, Miss Dyer, ain't it?" a voice broke into Minnie's thoughts.

With an effort, she smiled at the bowler-hatted miner leading his horse down the road to the river's grassy bank. "Mr. Nubia. Yes, very nice weather. Shall I take you across?"

"I'd like it if you called me Alf."

She knew he had not come up from Port Orford merely to cross on her ferry. He wore the same mismatched plaid suit and vest as always. His nose was sunburnt from working on the beach.

"Well, Alfred, shall I take you across?"

"It just wouldn't seem right to make a young lady work on a purty day like this." Nubia's callused hands fidgeted nervously, as if they did not know where to hide.

Minnie pretended distraction, tipping her yellow bonnet to hide her eyes. She thought again of the letter. *I'm writing amidst wildflowers, by the edge of the little lisping river that curls past the house to the sea. Spotted fishes drift lazily through—*

"When I woke up this mornin', I knew it warn't no day to shovel sand. Even though I've hit a big streak of black dirt, an' it's sure to pay now."

"Really? How wonderful for you."—*through the rippled waters. It's said a dreamy trail winds over the mountains to the sea here. If you came to see me, I would ferry you in my little boat across—*

"Miss Dyer?" The miner startled her by suddenly dropping to one knee and clutching his rough hands to his chest. She had feared this, that her politeness would lead to yet another proposal.

"Oh! Are you hurt?"

The miner looked at her blankly. Then he poked a thumb at the breast pocket of his plaid vest. "I reckon I'm hurting here, Miss Dyer."

Desperately Minnie searched for diversion. Hoofbeats? She scanned the road up the bluffs across the river and made out a tiny dot. "Oh, excuse me. I'm afraid I have to take the ferry across."

She stood, straightened her yellow dress, and began walking down toward the cable spanning the river, glad for once for the task of winching the little raft across. But she stopped at the bank, suddenly uncertain. The hoofbeats were alarmingly rapid. She watched the horseman crest the bluff and charge down the road toward the ferry landing at a furious gallop, leaving a long cloud of dust.

For an instant a fearful thought crossed her mind: the rider might be an Indian. What she had read of red men gave her chills. But no—as the rider drew nearer she could see he was wearing a black suit and a broad felt hat.

The rider's big, black horse galloped to the far shore, its coat frothed with sweat. The steed reared into the air, flaring its nostrils with a piercing whinny.

"Hyah!" the stranger cried, and—to Minnie's astonishment—spurred his horse straight over the bank and into the river.

The man swam his horse across the stream and leapt from the dripping saddle. Then he bowed before her, sweeping the ground grandly with his broad felt hat. "Minnie Myrtle—even poetry fails me before your divine beauty."

"Ned Miller?" she gasped. "I—I thought you were in Eugene City!"

"When a goddess calls? I have neither slept nor eaten since your letter arrived." Ned's heart was pounding so hard he felt his whole chest must be shaking. For days his only thought had been to reach this longing poet with the romantic curl framing her cheek, and now she stood before him, more beautiful than he had imagined.

"But it's a five-day ride from the Valley!"

For the first time Ned looked into her eyes—brown and wide with wonder—and felt a warm strength spreading through him. "I'm afraid your pony express rider crossed that 'dreamy little trail over the mountains' in less than two."

The man with the bowler hat cleared his throat. "Pardon me, mister."

Minnie remembered the beach miner with a start. "Oh, Ned, this is Alfred."

"Ah!" Ned said, without releasing her gaze. "Your brother, I presume."

The awkwardness of the situation made Minnie hesitant. "No, actually Mr. Nubia has taken the liberty to drop by from town."

"From town?" Ned raised himself to his full height. He knew at once from Nubia's stiff, waxed mustache and starched-collar shirt that the man had come courting. Ned spoke directly into the man's face, "If he's from town why isn't he making tracks for town?"

Nubia faltered, "Well, I reckon a guy has a right to—"

"Loitering, is it? Disturbing the peace of an honest young woman? Get on your way, you overstuffed dandy, or I'll fill your feet with lead!" With dramatic flair, Ned pulled a six-shooter from his belt and brandished it at Nubia's mining boots.

The miner paled and fell back to his horse.

"I said, move on!" Ned cocked his pistol.

"Don't shoot! I'm moving!" The terrified suitor scrambled up into his saddle. He whipped the horse with his bowler hat, glancing back anxiously as he galloped up the road.

"I apologize for the disturbance, Minnie," Ned said, putting away the gun.

Minnie was speechless. She didn't know whether to be outraged or impressed. This impetuous rider from Eugene City acted more like an outlaw than the poet she had envisioned from his letters. Never had any of her admirers from the coast's mines and logging camps shown *this* kind of fiery spirit on her behalf.

She felt like telling him off and sending him packing. But that would be awkward, too, since she *had* encouraged his visit in the first place. She had been so bored by the narrow-minded backwoods louts from Port Orford. It had been so refreshing, so hopeful, when the poetic letters had come, with their unspoken promise of a better, more intellectual life somewhere far away.

She blushed and looked at her hands to avoid the gaze of his deep, blue-gray eyes—deeper and far more handsome than his photograph had shown. "I'm sure I didn't expect you so soon, or so suddenly," she said.

When he only smiled in reply she suddenly felt hopelessly flustered. "We live on the other side of the river," she said, and gave a short, musical laugh. "Unless you'd prefer to swim again, I could ferry you."

* * *

Cliff House, where the Dyer family lived, was a mile beyond the ferry landing. Ned walked up the road with Minnie, leading his horse with one hand and gesturing with the other as he entertained her with tales from the pony express. Only her poetry, he confided, had given him the strength to brave the blizzards, bandits, and Indian attacks of Idaho. She listened politely, but turned her head away at the frequent praise, hiding her eyes with the brim of her bonnet.

When she did so, Ned had a chance to look over the young woman he had ridden so far to see. Although her hair was tied up underneath the yellow bonnet, the loose dark curl from her photograph had fallen coyly to the clear, pale skin above her collar. She was shorter than he had imagined from her picture, and quite slender. The light yellow dress she wore was drawn wonderfully tight about her narrow waist. A row of tiny white buttons down the dress's front accented the modest curves and continued to the dress's hem, which she kicked lightly at each step with the tips of her small, pointed shoes.

After his long ride through the wilderness, the young woman seemed as elegant and alluring to him as a Roman empress discovered among the barbarian provinces. The curve of white buttons, the spotless yellow hem that briefly caressed her dainty ankle at each step—these graceful minutiae were more arousing to him than any overt display she might have affected. Still, he worried that such a genteel young lady might not really be as attracted to wild pony expressmen as her letters suggested. He had swum the river and brandished his six-gun to play the part. Now he questioned his own brashness, but it was too late to change roles.

Ned managed to keep up a conversation about her poems until they reached the top of a bluff. There he abruptly stopped, struck by the panorama that had suddenly come into view. Before him stretched the Pacific Ocean, broad as the sky. In the foreground, perched boldly on the grassy bluff, stood a gray shingled house with heavy shutters and a dormered roof. On one side of the house the bluff ended in a dramatic cliff, high above the winding river, and the long curve of the beach. A flock of white gulls whirled up from the dunes, screaming as they rode a breeze rich with the fishy tang of the ocean. To the north a weathered spruce forest clung to the lip of the bluff. From there the shore arced grandly out into the sea, culminating in a massive, green-topped headland with tall cliffs. At sea, the shallows of a reef mottled the waves the colors of sapphires and emeralds, while a score of craggy islands lay scattered about, miles from shore, as if some giant had tossed the ragged rocks carelessly beyond the surf.

"Small wonder that your poems are so beautiful, when you live in the midst of such grandeur," Ned said, and turned to Minnie. "I had never seen the ocean before this very moment. Still, it is the lesser of the wonders I have first seen today."

Minnie reddened again and was glad when her little sister Emily suddenly came running out of the house to meet them, her apron strings and hair flying. She was perhaps thirteen, but small and boyish. "Hello, Theresa," she sang to Minnie with feigned casualness, obviously eager to meet the man her sister had brought home.

Minnie looked stern. "Emily, I want you to take Mr. Miller's horse to the stable, if you please. It has had a long, hard trip and is sure to be wanting oats and hay."

"Certainly," the girl replied, taking the reins of the black stallion while she eyed the newcomer.

"Minnie," Ned began, and then looked down at his hands. "I reckon I should call you Theresa, or Miss Dyer, actually. But I feel your pen name suits you better. May I say Minnie?"

"If you prefer." In fact, she rather liked the idea of dropping her prosaic first name, at least temporarily. "Could you wait here a moment, though? Before I invite you in, I need to give my parents a chance to make your acquaintance."

"It would be my honor."

Minnie stood him on the porch and vanished inside. Ned waited nervously, shivering in his wet clothes. After several minutes she returned with what Ned thought seemed a mismatched couple. Minnie's father filled the doorway—a large, elderly seaman with a bad limp and bushy gray beard. He wore a captain's cap and tugged smoke out of a short pipe in his teeth. Mrs. Dyer, on the other hand, was small and fairly young, judging from her relatively smooth skin and the way she nimbly untied her ruffled apron.

"Father, Mother, this is Ned Miller," Minnie said, carefully keeping her voice matter-of-fact. "You remember, the editor from Eugene City I mentioned."

"Well," the old captain said. "He's a bit ragged. I wonder how long he'll stay on."

"George!" Mrs. Dyer exclaimed with exasperation, and came up to take Ned by the arm. "Why, your clothes are soaked! Come inside; we'll find something dry. And you must be famished. I hear the trail to the Valley is simply impossible—no farms on the way at all."

Ned let the kindly woman take him into the kitchen. There the nervous energy that had driven him on during his grueling, non-stop ride finally began to ebb. He had not eaten or slept in two days, and now the aroma of fish and potatoes cooking on the wood range left him weak in the knees.

Mrs. Dyer took command, sending Minnie out of the room while Ned put on dry clothes from the captain's closet: floppy slippers and a pair of short, baggy trousers. To Ned's surprise, Mrs. Dyer did not turn her back as he disrobed, but rather collected the wet clothes as casually as if she had been his own mother. Later, when Mrs. Dyer announced dinner, Minnie's sister Emily and an even smaller sibling by the name of Robert helped carry steaming platters of food out to a large oak table. They cast furtive glances at Ned's ill-fitting, borrowed clothes, and giggled whenever they felt they were out of earshot.

At dinner Ned forced himself to take only modest portions, not wanting to appear as starved as he felt. Instead he talked, telling the wide-eyed children about the tremendous snows of Idaho and the devastating floods of the Willamette Valley.

After dinner the women and children retreated to the kitchen, leaving an uncomfortable silence over the table between Ned and Minnie's father. The captain tipped back in his large, spindle-back chair and lit his pipe, evidently waiting for Ned to speak. For his part, Ned's lack of sleep was about to conquer him after the meal. He struggled to keep his eyes open and his head clear enough to think of a conversation of mutual interest. Finally, in desperation, he said, "Your house has a beautiful view, Mr. Dyer."

"Judge," the old man said, with a puff of smoke.

"Pardon?"

"Judge Dyer. I am the local justice of the peace."

Ned was failing fast; the drowsiness of the dark, smoky room was almost unbearable. "Yes, sir," he said. Resolving not to fall asleep at the table in front of Minnie Myrtle's father, he summoned enough energy to stand up and say, "Excuse me. I think I'll have to lie down."

Mrs. Dyer returned from the kitchen in time to hear this and to see Ned tottering beside the table. She drew in her breath sharply. "Why, yes, I think you'd better." She led him to a small guestroom at the back of the house. There Ned finally gave way to his exhaustion. When Mrs. Dyer let go of his sleeve he collapsed face first onto the straw mattress and was instantly asleep.

*   *   *

That evening by the fireside Minnie's father frowned and put down his newspaper when his wife brought up the subject of their newly arrived guest. "You think he's *what?*"

"Interesting," Mrs. Dyer repeated, without stopping her knitting. "And certainly a fine-looking young man. Really, it's rare enough that we get visitors with a cultural background here on the coast."

"So now it takes culture to show up in wet pants and fall asleep at the table?" He poured himself a glass of sherry and shook his head. "No, I won't lower the flag when this one ships out."

Upstairs in the girls' bedroom the same topic was keeping Minnie and her sister awake, even though the candle had long since been blown out. Emily giggled uncontrollably, recalling how her father's baggy pants had reached only to Ned's hairy calves. She pestered Minnie to tell how Ned had got his pants wet in the first place. At length Minnie decided she would never be allowed to sleep unless she relented, so she described Ned's arrival at the ferry.

Rather than quieting her sister, however, the story made Emily even more excited. She sat in the middle of her bed and pulled her nightgown tight over her knees with a suppressed squeal. "You mean, he scared Alf Nubia away with a revolver?"

"Shh!" Minnie glared at her disapprovingly, but with little effect.

"And he rode all the way from Eugene City and swam the river just for *you?* Isn't it *romantic?*"

"Don't talk nonsense. He might really have hurt someone. I thought it was very ill considered."

"And to think he rides the pony express, and writes poems about you—it's enough to make you want to *die!*"

"Oh, really. Emily, you don't know anything about it."

The young girl put her chin in the air defiantly. "Maybe I know more about him than you think."

Minnie pulled up her covers without answering.

The little girl looked impish. "I looked in his saddlebags when I took his horse to the stable."

"Emily! You didn't!"

"I *did*. And you know what he had?"

Minnie shook her head and closed her eyes. "I don't want to know."

"*Gold!*"

Minnie opened her eyes. "So? Lots of people carry gold when they travel."

"But that's *all* he had—one big bag of gold dust—more than *I've* ever seen before. I tell you, he's *rich!*" Emily gave a smug nod and crawled back under her covers.

Before long the young girl had fallen asleep, but Minnie lay in her bed, in the square of moonlight cast from the dormer window, listening to the whispered roar of the ocean. The rumble of the waves seemed to rise up out of the ground, filling the house with crashes and silences. All she had seen and heard that day tumbled over and over through her memory. There were so many unresolved questions about him, so many things that could be interpreted different ways. She watched the silent moon drift into a web of thin night fog off the land, and she sighed, wishing she knew just what to think of him after all.

*   *   *

When a bright ray of sun finally prodded Ned out of his deep sleep it was late in the morning. He stretched, threw open the window of his room, and breathed deep the exhilarating salt breeze. Sleep had left him marvelously refreshed and eager to see what the day would bring.

He poured a pitcher of water into a basin and washed up as best he could. Then he changed the baggy pants he had worn all night for his own, which he found dried and ironed on the back of a chair—evidently the work of Mrs. Dyer. He took it as a good sign that Minnie's mother seemed solicitous, especially after Judge Dyer's cool reception. As he was combing his hair at a dresser mirror, he heard horses trotting up the sandy road to the house. He frowned, fearing it might be more of Minnie Myrtle's local admirers. He decided it would be best to make himself visible soon to show any competitors that the young lady already had company that day.

But when he reached the front hall he found Minnie talking with a couple who proved to be only her aunt and uncle from up the river. They had brought baskets for gathering the September crop of wild huckleberries on the headland, and were disappointed that Minnie could not come along as planned.

"I'm sorry, Auntie Ev," she said. "I'm afraid my first duty is to help entertain Mr. Miller. Why, I don't even believe he's had breakfast yet."

"Oh, that's all right," Ned put in cheerfully. "It'd be a shame to miss the huckleberries. Besides, my brothers claim I'm the world's fastest huckleberry picker. Why don't we both go along?"

"You'd really like to?" Minnie asked.

"Of course."

Aunt Ev brightened. "Come then, Theresa. We could use the extra hand, and it's rare enough we get to meet one of your beaus."

"Mr. Miller is not a beau. He's a visiting editor," Minnie explained curtly, but her cheeks reddened nonetheless. She excused herself while she went inside to extract reluctant permission from her father and a full picnic basket from her mother. This accomplished, the harvest excursion could begin in earnest.

At the front of the small procession, Minnie's lanky uncle and bonneted aunt led their horses down the dunes to the beach. Then came Minnie, wearing a broad white hat with a lilac ribbon that matched her print dress. She rode primly on her white mare's single-stirruped sidesaddle. She kept her face toward the sea, trying not to encourage Ned unnecessarily, even though he was riding almost at her side and was making the expedition lively with all manner of light compliments, clever tales, and quotations from the poets.

Minnie found she had to smile, however, when they reached the hard sand at the edge of the waves and he reared his stallion back in a mock heroic pose, citing Browning in ringing tones,

> Boot, saddle, to horse, and away!
> Rescue my castle before the hot day!

With an imaginary saber in hand, he charged forward, racing over the black-streaked sand where the waves had left lacy arcs of foam. He returned through the soft sand nearer the bluff, where driftwood logs lay beached, grayed by the salt and the sun. Rather than ride around the uplifted roots of one great gray log, he spurred his stallion and cleared the high trunk in a spray of sand. Then he pulled up beside Minnie with a laugh of delight.

"You're certainly a confident horseman," Minnie said, stifling her smile.

"Confidence alone will never give me the grace of a rider like yourself. I'll bet you ride on this beach every day." When she did not deny it, he added, "I tell you what—if you're up to it, let's gallop ahead to the cape. It's not more than a mile or two, and in sight of your aunt and uncle all the way. 'I'll gallop, you'll gallop, we'll gallop all three.'"

"If that's Robert Browning again, you've stretched the verse pretty far," she chided. "Who's the third galloper?"

"My heart, of course."

"Oh, really!" Minnie shook her head, but she also shook her reins, urging her mare to join the run. At first the horses cantered ahead. When they broke into a gallop, Minnie called, "Not too fast. I'm not a pony express rider, you know."

They sailed along the beach together at an easy pace, accompanied by the shimmering golden reflection of the sun on the waves. A miniature battalion of sandpipers fled before them, marching their stilt legs in formation left, then right, before finally taking wing in a wheeling, peeping retreat. Farther on, a single white sea gull flapped alongside the horses, eyeing one and then the other. Ned mimicked the curious bird, flapping his elbows and ogling back at it until Minnie could hold back her mirth no longer and broke into a silvery laugh. While Ned was still clowning, a larger-than-average wave unexpectedly sent a thin, flat sheet of white under the hooves of his horse. Minnie laughed anew to see Ned's startled expression when his stallion kicked up a sparkling spray of salt and foam.

"Your horse wants to take you swimming again!" she called.

Ned held up his hands to show he had not gotten wet. "Just make sure you stay on this side of the ocean or I'll have to swim it yet."

The beach narrowed, squeezing between the bluff and a thumb-shaped rock in the surf. Then the sand ended altogether at the base of the cape. Beyond, the headland presented a nearly vertical face of rock to the sea, but above them the bluff was broken to form a brush-covered slope. When Minnie's aunt and uncle arrived, they all dismounted and led the horses up a steep trail to a ridge that formed the narrow neck of the peninsula. To Ned's surprise, they did not turn inland at this point, but rather climbed west along the ridge toward the tip of the cape. Just when he thought they were surely about to come to the barren sea cliffs, the ridge suddenly opened onto a marvelously green plateau from which the world disappeared precipitously on all sides. Magic seemed to be the only thing keeping the secret field suspended above the waves.

The horses were let loose to graze, and Minnie invited Ned to walk about the edge of the meadow for the view. To the north the shoreline alternated long beaches and green headlands in diminishing succession toward a distant, sharp horizon. Almost at their feet, the waves of the Pacific crashed upon the cliffs. A handful of rocky islands teemed with shiny brown dots that Minnie insisted were actually very large sea lions.

At the tip of the headland Minnie stopped and gazed out over the blue. "You can't go farther west anywhere in the United States," she said. "I suppose you knew that."

"No, I didn't."

"It's true. Cape Blanco is the country's westernmost point. When I was younger I used to stand here and imagine I was at the prow of a gigantic clipper ship bound for the Orient." She smiled wistfully at the thought. "I'd watch for the spouts of the gray whales. Somehow that made it easier to believe I was really at sea."

"Was your father a clipper captain?"

Minnie continued walking along the edge of the headland. "No, just a fisherman. And to tell the truth, I haven't been on the ocean since he brought us here and sold his ship. We all were told Port Orford would be the new San Francisco then." She shrugged. "Some people still believe it will be. But I don't anymore."

By now they had come far enough to look south down the beach they had traveled that morning. The white curve of sand stretched a couple miles past Cliff House, and ended with a small headland, a few tiny buildings, and a bay where toy sailing ships sat at anchor. Minnie held out her slender arm to the town, a tone of irony in her voice.

> And lo, the city of Marseilles,
> With all her ships behind her, and beyond,
> The scimitar of ever-shining sea
> For right-hand use, bared blue against the sky.

"A pretty image," Ned commented. "Is it your own verse?"

"No, Elizabeth Barrett Browning's."

"Browning's wife? I've never read anything of hers. But if she can write like that I suppose she'll outshine her husband yet."

Minnie gave Ned an odd look. "She died last year. I'd have thought you'd know." She turned again to the ocean thoughtfully. "It's a pity, too, that you haven't read her work. I, for one, find it has much more insight and feeling than her husband's. The Barretts were several steps above the Brownings socially, you know."

"No, I guess I didn't."

"Oh, yes. They had to elope. She was always ill, but her father was an impossible tyrant and wouldn't even let poor Robert Browning visit. Finally he just stole her away from her sickbed and took her to sunny Italy. Can you imagine? They lived in Florence in perfect happiness for fifteen years. Her health improved there too, and she wrote the most beautiful poetry of her life."

"Theresa!" Minnie's uncle was holding up a basket and shouting to them. "Don't you think you'd better start picking?"

"Oh, my!" Minnie said, blushing to think they had wandered away for so long. She picked up her skirts and hurried through the meadow to the patch of huckleberry bushes in the middle of the field.

When Ned caught up with her she was already plucking the small blue berries. He took a basket and knelt on the other side of a low bush from her, but did not pick. He whispered,

> There be none of Beauty's daughters
> With a magic like thee;
> And like music on the waters
> Is thy sweet voice to me.

"Ned!" Minnie objected, not looking up.

"Byron's my favorite poet, I think. Do you like him too?"

Minnie smiled. "My parents forbade me to read him. They said he was evil."

"Then you don't know his work?"

She answered in a confiding whisper. "They never said *why* he was evil, so I decided to find out for myself. I asked a beach miner to get me a copy, and I read the whole thing secretly at least a dozen times. It's frightfully beautiful, and hardly naughty at all."

"He was a genius, I'd say, with the courage to fire his poems right at the heads of critics and kings. A kind of literary outlaw—always haunted by his own wild past."

"His wild past? I know he was born with a lame leg. Was there more?"

"Who knows what all he did to get banished from England, or what drove him to it? His father, Mad Jack, was insane, they say."

Minnie drew her hand to her mouth. "Oh! But Byron himself was a nobleman, wasn't he?"

"His mother raised him a commoner. When his uncle died unexpectedly, he became Lord Byron of Newstead Abbey, with a seat in the House of Lords. Grandest of the grand, yet an outcast in his own land."

"I still think his poetry is beautiful." She picked berries for a while, then crossed her hands on the basket handle, looked out over the headland, and sighed.

"What is it, Minnie?"

"Oh, I was just thinking. This is the first time in my life I've been able to really talk about the great poets. At school they hardly even knew who Longfellow is. But with you—" she looked flustered for a moment, for she did not really want to praise Ned, regardless of how unexpectedly pleasant his company that day had been. She caught sight of his empty basket and quickly shifted the subject. "Why, Ned Miller, you haven't picked a single huckleberry! And you said you were so fast."

"I thought it'd be fairest to give you a head start," he replied with a wink. He set his broad basket under a bush and combed his fingers swiftly through the overhanging branches, raking handfuls of berries and leaves loose. Minnie watched skeptically as he moved from branch to branch, rapidly filling the basket.

"All those leaves are going to make terrible preserves," she admonished.

"Only if I leave them in." He spread his large, red bandanna in a hollow on the ground, and held the basket above it. Then he tossed the berries several feet in the air and caught them in the basket. As he did so, the brisk sea breeze carried the fluttering green leaves away like winnowed chaff.

Minnie clapped her hands and laughed. "Bravo! Where did you ever learn to pick like that?"

"Oh, I learned that trick from an Indian tribe in the mountains." Though his tone was casual, he reddened slightly at the thought of his Wintu years.

"Really? I had no idea the Indians were so clever. All the ones near Port Orford were taken away to the reservation years ago. It must be fascinating to study their ways—but dangerous too, I imagine."

"Terribly dangerous! The red men have learned some of the darkest mysteries of nature, but they guard their secrets with poison-tipped arrows. Some people say I was lucky to escape with my life." He belittled the incident with a wave of his hand, but the sudden memory of his life with Paquita was powerful. What an impossibly distant, unreal life that now seemed! For a moment he swept his eyes across the island-dotted horizon, letting the pleasant sunshine and the salt tang of the sea bring him back to the present.

"Let's not talk of such things—that was all so long ago and far away. Now I'm vexed by a mystery of a different kind."

Minnie asked, "And what might that be?"

Ned came closer and touched her hand. "It might be a beautiful poet with great, captivating eyes and an irresistible charm." He lifted her small hand and kissed it tenderly.

"Ned!" she protested, but did not draw her hand away. His warm voice and gallant gesture held her with a power she had never felt before. Her pulse raced, leaving her flushed and confused. When he then lifted his face and met her eyes, the moment left a picture in her heart that she was to remember for the rest of her life: the two of them amidst September wildflowers—so high atop the cliffs that the churning ocean seemed an endless sweep of untroubled azure.

* * *

The following day was Saturday, and Minnie spent the afternoon preparing for the dance that was to be held in town that night. Ned made himself useful by sawing and splitting nearly a cord of firewood, a chore that was gruffly recommended by Judge Dyer.

After the dinner dishes were done, the Dyer women hurried about the house in one last flurry of hats and shawls, and then boarded the buggy the old captain had readied in the yard. Ned spruced himself up as well as his limited wardrobe would allow and rode his black stallion behind them down the road to the ferry.

It was a five-mile trip through the twilight to Port Orford, a sleepy little plank-and-shingle town lining the edge of a crescent shaped beach. Dark ships rocked at anchor in the small bay, their tall masts and web-like rigging swaying with the waves. A pier stretched out into the surf from a large sawmill. The smell of fish and woodsmoke pervaded the main street, where lights already glowed from the saloons and from the dance hall in the upstairs of a big, wood-frame hardware store.

Ned tied up his horse at a rail while the Dyers hurried into the dance hall; the dance wouldn't start for a while, but the women wanted to prepare their hair and dresses after the buggy ride. The dimly lit town gave Ned an uneasy feeling. He wished he could stop somewhere for a couple of stiff drinks. He even paused in the open doorway of a loggers' bar, but passed on, not wanting to have the smell of whiskey on his breath. As he left the light, however, a deep voice called out, "Hiner!"

The name made Ned jump. Who could know him here? He turned and saw a huge, dark shape lumbering out the bar toward him. In the doorway the shape became a puffy-faced blond man, wearing an awkward black suit several sizes too small for him.

"Swede?" Ned asked incredulously.

"Ya, Hiner, so it *is* you!" He held out a mammoth, dirt-creased hand and pumped Ned's arm vigorously. "It's been long since ve mined back in Horsetown, eh? Vhat you doing in Port Orford? Looking for a yob?"

"No, I'm just visiting the Dyers, a family north of town. These days I work as an editor for a newspaper in Eugene City."

"Yiminy!" Swede laughed. "You write newspapers? And to think I can hardly read them."

Ned put his hand on the Scandinavian's massive shoulder. "It's good to see you again, old friend." Swede had always been an untroubled soul, even in the midst of the Pit River Indian War, and earlier, when they had worked together on a mining claim. Sometimes it seemed to Ned that he had left only enemies among the California miners. It was good to remember he had had friends in those hellish canyons as well. "So how about you, Swede? What brings you up to Oregon?"

"Me? I come up here to mine beaches, but the gold sand gave out on me, so I got a yob as a timber faller." Suddenly Swede slapped his palm to his forehead. "I've been yakking here outside! Vhat do you say I take you in and buy you a drink?"

"Thanks, but I'll have to pass." Ned glanced at his pocket watch. "I've got to be at the dance pretty soon."

"Me, too. That's vhy I need the vhiskey—for courage, you know."

Ned smiled. "I don't reckon you need to be afraid."

"Only of the vomen, Hiner. Only of the vomen."

While Swede went back for his drink, Ned went on to the upstairs dance hall. The room was lit with candles in tin sconces on the walls, and was decorated along its length with wreaths of greens and flowers. At the far end was a platform for the musicians—a fiddler, a harpist, and a cornet player. But what Ned noticed most was the crowd. There were roughly forty men, most of them ungainly and uncomfortable in their go-to-meeting clothes. But there were hardly a dozen women, and many of these were grandmothers or children who would not make suitable dancing partners.

Ned hadn't finished his count when the fiddler drew his bow across the strings—apparently a signal to the crowd—and the men stepped forward to choose the few available partners. Ned was left behind to watch as a bullhorn-voiced caller at the front of the stage directed the couples through the opening "Grand March."

Minnie was clearly in her own element now. She walked primly about the hall with a radiant yet slightly aloof smile that beamed alike on her partner and on the other dancers. Her dark hair was tied back in an intricately-plaited bun, and she wore a shiny, rustling dress trimmed with lace-edged flounces.

At the conclusion of the "Grand March" the women curtsied and returned to their chairs on the right-hand side of the hall. Ned was not about to be left behind again. He quickly strode across the floor and bowed. "May I have the pleasure of the next dance, Miss Dyer?"

"Why certainly, Mr. Miller. I'm glad to see we didn't lose you on the way after all."

"Partners for a square dance!" the caller announced. Soon the fiddler was sawing away at a lively tune, and the caller was singing out instructions that kept skirts whirling and faces flushed: "Swing around the circle, balance all—Now swing your partner, don't let her fall—Meet your corner with a do-si-do—And ladies chain till you get back home."

Ned had never done much dancing before, but he followed the others with a natural smoothness that belied his effort. On the difficult steps Minnie whispered enough encouragement and advice that he made it through the set in good form. And what fun it was! Whirling about with his arm around her waist, thrilling to the sparkle in her eyes when they rejoined hands at the end of the circular chain of passing partners. It was only when he had bowed his thanks and returned to the crowd of men that he realized his dance with Minnie had left a certain tension in the hall. There was no mistaking the glares of the miners and loggers for whom Ned was unwelcome competition.

For the next hour or so the dance went smoothly, with quadrilles, Virginia reels, waltzes, and square dances. Ned joined in as many of the different numbers as he could, but it became increasingly difficult for him to win a partner. Several times he found his way through the crowd of men blocked by shoulders and scowls. A touch of anger welled up in him, but he kept it tightly capped. Rather than shove his way through and risk a commotion that would only upset Minnie, he sat out a few dances next to Swede, who clapped his big hands to the music but never did muster the courage and speed required to ask a woman onto the floor.

Once, when Ned did succeed in asking Minnie, the caller announced a polka. Ned looked sheepish, and admitted with a whisper, "I've never done a polka—what do I do?"

Minnie clicked her tongue. "Never polkaed? It's just a fast waltz with a hop at the end of each measure. It's easy."

The musicians struck up a fast-paced 4/4 introduction and the couples began sailing about the hall. Quickly, Minnie took Ned's left hand in hers, put his other hand on her waist, and marched him through the steps, whispering, "One, two, three—hop; one, two, three—hop."

At first Ned hopped the wrong direction and stumbled. He reddened to hear a ripple of coarse laughter spread through the men's side of the room over his obvious misstep, but he did not falter again. He and Minnie were already wheeling smartly among the couples when the caller started singing out the words to the rollicking polka rhythm:

> Come, girls, come and listen to my noise:
> Don't you marry the Oregon boys.
> For if you do, your fortune it'll be,
> Johnnycakes and venison is all you'll see.
>
> They'll take you to a side-hewed wall
> Without any windows in it at all,
> Sandstone chimney and a button door,
> A clapboard roof and a puncheon floor.
>
> When they go milkin' they milk in a gourd,
> Strain it in the corner and hide it with a board.
> Some gets little and some gets none,
> And that's how things in the Oregon run!

The polka concluded with laughter and general merriment among the couples. Ned mopped his brow and bowed, saying, "That was wonderful fun, Minnie. I'm only sorry I'm such an awkward beginner."

"Really, Ned, you dance very well," Minnie replied, fanning her face with her hand. "I'm sure I've never enjoyed a polka more."

Ned retired from the floor with a warm glow and a light step, ignoring the poorly concealed animosity of the men he passed. When he reached his spot next to Swede, however, he was met by a boy nervously turning a hat in his hands. "Excuse me, mister. Is that your black stallion running loose in the street?"

Ned's face clouded. "I'm sure I tied him up." He quickly made his way through the crowd and down the dark stairs. At the door he recognized the silhouette of his stallion trotting up the dirt street. He cursed. It was the first time the horse had given him any trouble. He pushed angrily out the door.

Suddenly he found himself sprawled in the dirt beyond the porch. He spun around onto one elbow to see what had tripped him. Three tall shadows were standing by the door.

"Well, well," one of the shadows said, sauntering forward and tipping back a black bowler hat. "He's as clumsy on the street as he is at a dance, ain't he, boys?"

Ned scrambled to his feet, his heart racing. Angry and embarrassed that he had been caught off guard so easily, he stood his ground before the three advancing men.

"Surely you remember me?" one of them asked. "Alfred Nubia. We met a couple days back. Too bad you can't wear your gun to a dance."

Ned resisted the urge to bolt for his horse—the humiliation of abandoning Minnie at the dance would be too great. But he also knew the odds were against him in a street fight with three men. He aimed for a gap between two of the men and lunged back toward the door. A fist in his stomach stopped him short. As he doubled over, sick with pain, another fist caught him in the face with a flash of red. He staggered back, warm blood dripping from the corner of his mouth.

"He don't act like a poet at all, boys," Nubia said dryly. "See if you can't straighten him out, Jack."

Ned channeled his rage, knowing he was in for the fight now. Quickness and clear thinking were his only advantages. At least he could try to give them more than they had bargained for. When the man took a swing, Ned ducked and rammed him aside with a shoulder. That left Nubia in the clear. Ned landed a hard-driven fist somewhere soft under his black bowler and sent him sprawling backwards with a howl of pain. Before Ned could press his advantage, however, the third man's foot caught him in the stomach with a tremendous kick, buckling him backwards against a porch post. Ned's head slammed into the post with a thud. For a moment everything seemed to freeze, and a distant numbness ran through his body that left his jaw slack.

Now the first man was back, grabbing the front of Ned's shirt to keep him from sliding to the ground. He took an angry punch at Ned's sagging head, and was about to give the other man a chance to do the same, when there was a creak of heavy footsteps on the stairs.

"Hiner? You catch that hoss?" Swede's white face peered out the door and his brow wrinkled. "Hey. Vhat's—"

The first man responded by dropping Ned and taking a swing at Swede. The big Scandinavian took the blow squarely on the chest. He stared at the spot with some bewilderment, as though no one had ever really dared to slug him before.

When the second blow came, Swede stopped it dead with the flat of his massive hand. But at the same time he began to make a portentous rumbling noise in his throat, a strange angry sound, like a long-quiet volcano at the brink of an eruption. His face stiffened. Slowly he balled his thick fingers into an enormous fist and brought it down like a sledgehammer on the man's head. The man crumpled silently to the ground.

The other man began to back away, but Swede caught him by the coat. "So now you vant to run avay, do you?" he said, picking him up as though he were a disobedient schoolboy. Swede lifted him wriggling over his head, turned him around, and hurled him against the plank wall of the store. Alfred Nubia, who had watched this display of angry strength wide-eyed, now scrambled up off the ground and ran.

As quickly as Swede's face had hardened, it softened again, almost to a look of sadness. He pulled a whiskey flask from his coat and knelt beside Ned's limp form. Gently, he lifted his friend's head and tried to pour some of the liquid into his mouth. The sting of alcohol on Ned's cut lip jolted him out of his daze. He rubbed his painfully throbbing eyes and looked up at a blurry crowd of people coming down the stairs from the dance hall.

"Say, what's all the ruckus?" a voice asked.

Swede nodded to the two unconscious men. "These two guys vere picking a fight."

Ned cleared his throat with a wheeze and put his hand on Swede's arm. "Thanks, old friend." It hurt to move his jaw. A sick ache burned in his stomach and his head. But he was proud he hadn't backed down before the thugs. And he felt a stronger bond than ever with Swede, who had stood by his side.

At that moment a startled cry came from the stairs. "Ned!" Minnie rushed past the others to his side. "Oh, Ned, what happened?" She held his head and daubed at his cut lip with her handkerchief.

Ned smiled painfully. "I bumped into three of your admirers." He cast a glance toward the street. "Swede here helped me with two of 'em. Looks like Nubia took off. Left his bowler, though."

"Oh, Ned, they've hurt you! How *could* they?" She held his head close to her.

Judge Dyer hobbled down the stairs and surveyed the scene briefly. "Well, mates, looks like we'll be heading home now. A couple of you boys can see about catching Mr. Miller's horse. Theresa, see if he can ride."

"Papa! He can't! We'll have to take him in the buggy with us."

Ned managed to sit up, determined to prove himself to Minnie's father and to them all—the whole town. Summoning what seemed to be his last strength, he staggered to his feet, leaning heavily against the porch post. "There's no room, I'm sure," he said, his words slurred. "The Judge is right. I'll be fine, sir. If you lead the way, I can ride."

Judge Dyer tightened his lips, as if taking the measure of the battered young man before him. "Good," he said. "Then let's go."

Ned had little memory of the trip home. For Minnie, however, it was a long and painful voyage. All the way back she kept turning around in the buggy's cushioned seat, her heart in her throat, to watch him riding in the moonlight. To her, he was more than a brave, passionate man suffering for her hometown's ignorant jealousy. He represented the spirit of poetry she loved—the spirit Port Orford would never understand.

Ned sagged in his saddle with his cut lip held open and his eye swollen shut. While his horse plodded on, he rode with his head sunk forward, and could not see Minnie watching him, her pale cheeks wet with the streaks of her tears.

* * *

Minnie spent much of the following day nursing Ned's cuts and bruises as though they were much more serious wounds. When he did not eat well at dinner, she suggested a short walk in the fresh air to restore his vigor.

Ned was glad for a chance to get out of the house with her, even though his loss of appetite had nothing to do with the injuries of the previous night. He had spent the day tormented by the realization that he would soon have to return to Eugene City. He had left the *Democratic Register* in a time of crisis. He suspected he was wearing out his welcome with Minnie's parents. It was time to choose one of the speeches whose planning had caused him so much anguish.

Minnie held Ned's arm as they walked along the grassy bluff above the dunes, watching the flaming sun flatten against the horizon and ignite the clouds with crimson. Cape Blanco's bold arm reached out into the

golden sea, as if to gather in the islands drifting there before the sun.
      Ned recited grandly,

> And this in that land where the sun goes down,
> Where gold is gather'd by tide and by stream,
> And life is a love and a love is a dream;
> Where the winds come in from the far Cathay
> With odor of spices and balm and bay,
> And summer abideth with man alway.

Minnie held Ned's arm tighter. "I remember you once told me the ocean inspired what I wrote. Don't you feel that it helps you too?"

"Perhaps. I reckon there's as much inspiration in the mountains and the rivers, though, and I'll have that again soon."

"You don't mean you're about to leave?" Minnie's voice showed her surprise.

"Oh, yes. Very soon, I hope." Ned's matter-of-fact tone had a certain mysterious quality to it.

"Ned! If you leave now, I'll think you hate me for what happened at the dance. Please stay a few more days at least."

Ned looked out at the sunset. "I don't know. I was thinking you might be glad when I go back to Eugene City."

"How could you possibly think such a thing?"

"Oh, I can imagine it," Ned replied. "Assuming that you're willing to come with me as my wife."

Minnie's mouth opened with astonishment. The look in Ned's eyes left no doubt that he was serious now.

He held both her hands and spoke earnestly. "Will you marry me?"

Minnie's head reeled. A proposal after only three days! Hadn't she turned away a dozen suitors who had wooed her longer and promised her more? But the past three days had been more dramatic, more exciting than three years with the others. And the shining, unspoken promises of this gallant young editor—who seemed to achieve whatever he willed—made all other hopes cheap by comparison.

"Yes," she whispered, suddenly voiceless.

"Ee-HAW!" Ned whooped, holding her hands at arm's length and dancing her around in a circle.

Then he suddenly stopped and took a step back with a sober expression. "Do you really mean it?"

She nodded.

Solemnly he held out his arms, and she came into his strong embrace, letting him press her against his broad chest until she could feel the rapid beat of his heart against her own.

* * *

It seemed to Minnie that so much happened in the next two days she never did have time to sort out all her thoughts and emotions, even once she was really on the trail to Eugene City.

First there had been the argument with her father, who had thrown his newspaper on the floor when he had heard Ned wanted to become his son-in-law. Minnie had surprised even herself by standing up to him and threatening to elope if he wouldn't consent to the wedding.

Then there had been the moment of realization while packing her saddlebags that she would never be Theresa Dyer again. Not only was she losing her name, but almost everything else had to be left behind as well. By the time she had packed her diary, her notebooks, and a single change of clothes, the little saddlebags for the trip were full.

And then there was the whirlwind of emotion surrounding the wedding itself—the brief parlor-room ceremony by a somber Judge Dyer, the lavish wedding breakfast by her excited mother, the mumbled congratulations of Ned's ungainly best man, Swede, and the pan-banging chivaree all the way to the ferry by Emily and Robert.

Now she was overwhelmed by a confusion of firsts: her first night away from her family, her first ride through the mountains, her first trip alone with a man, her first day as Mrs. C. H. Miller—whoever that might turn out to be. Everything had happened so fast!

Ned's thoughts were markedly different from his bride's that day. As he rode ahead, whistling "Sweet Betsy From Pike" to the firs along the trail, he composed a series of one-act plays in his mind, each anticipating the wedding night to come.

When afternoon finally gave way to dusk, Ned stopped by a mossy-banked forest stream and suggested cheerfully that it would be as romantic a spot for a honeymoon camp as they could find anywhere.

"I—I've never camped outside before," Minnie admitted with a quavering voice.

"Well, we'll just fix things up snug," Ned said. He made a kind of nest among the fallen leaves with their blankets, produced a dinner of wedding breakfast leftovers from his saddlebag, and gathered firewood for a roaring blaze to burn through the night.

The darkness settled down through the trees behind the fire. Ned slipped his arm around Minnie's shoulders to keep her warm, but she still shivered. At first he regaled her with some of Mountain Joe's wild campfire tales, but after it had grown quite late, he began to praise her soft eyes instead.

At this point he had anticipated that she would simply melt toward him. But she was strangely stiff and reticent. In fact, when he started idly unlooping the tiny buttons on the back of her dress, she caught his arm with a small startled cry.

Ned gave her a bewildered look. "What is it? Aren't we married now?"

"Yes, but *Ned!*"

"But what?"

Minnie bit her lip, apparently unable to answer this straightforward question.

For a moment Ned wondered if she were angry with him. But that hardly seemed possible. She had been so happy and attentive until now. After all, this was her wedding day, and everything had gone as smoothly as she could have hoped. Nor did it seem convincing that her aloofness was due solely to a fear of the woods, what with the security of Ned's guns and the enormous campfire he had built to chase out the shadows. The only other explanation for her coolness was modesty, but Ned found this a little puzzling too. This same young woman had penned such passionately romantic verse for newspapers that he himself had blushed to read it.

Eventually Ned tried again with a different approach. "It's been a long day, Minnie. Don't you think it's about time to turn in?"

At this, Minnie stood up stiffly and straightened her hair. "All right. I suppose it is late. If you would just hang up one of the blankets, I'll start getting ready for bed."

"Hang up a blanket? What for?"

"As a dressing screen."

Ned blew out a long, exasperated breath. From Minnie's aloof stance, however, he could tell this was not a point that could be profitably debated. So he shook out a big wool blanket and tied it between two trees.

"Well, what now?" he asked.

"Now you wait on the other side, of course!"

Reluctantly, Ned ducked underneath to the side away from the fire, where he took up a position on a damp log.

He sat on that log for half an hour, growing more and more impatient. The blanket was tightly woven and perfectly opaque, so he couldn't see anything in that direction. Minnie neither spoke nor hummed, so there was little to hear but an occasional rustle. He *could* see the saddlebags on the ground if he leaned to one side. At first this offered little entertainment.

After what seemed like a very long time, a white hand unbuckled one of the saddlebags and took out a number of things he did not see clearly. Then, one by one, articles of clothing appeared, neatly folded, on top of the open bag. First there was the dress, with its countless tiny buttons undone. Then, after considerable rustling, the petticoats landed beside the bag like a pile of white foam. Again there was a very long pause, and then a ribbed corset appeared, replete with laces and straps. Ned thought it looked like an ungainly thing for a woman to wear, and found himself comparing it to a burro's backpack. Next came a light lacy garment which he concluded must be some kind of additional undershift. Then came a black, unbuttoned shoe, followed at length by its mate and finally two white knit stockings.

All this clothing seemed amazingly cumbersome and involved to Ned, but even after he assumed there could be nothing else for her to take off, there still was no sign his frustrating exile was over. Finally his impatience got the better of him.

"Minnie?" he asked.

"What is it, Ned?"

For a moment Ned sought an appropriate reply to this simple, yet somehow absurd, question. "The fire has about burned down, Minnie—do you think I could come out and put on some more wood?"

"All right," said the nervous voice.

Ned peered out. Minnie was standing by the fire in a long white nightgown, diligently running a comb through her beautifully wavy, waist-length hair.

"For a while I almost thought you'd forgotten me back there," Ned said.

He took an armload of wood and put it on the fire, sending a column of frantic red sparks skittering up into the darkness. Then he brushed off his hands and stepped up behind Minnie, who was still combing her hair.

"I didn't forget *you*," he said, and put his hands on her waist.

Minnie pulled away with a start. "Ned! I'm not through combing my hair."

"Oh, for God's sake!" Ned said. "Look, I'm going to bed. You can do as you please." He turned, tore down the blanket with a single angry sweep of his arm, and took off his jacket and shirt.

He had just reached for his belt buckle when two trembling white hands slowly began to slide about his waist.

As Minnie pressed herself cautiously against his strong, bared back, she managed to whisper, "I didn't forget you either, Ned."

Chapter 15

Reader, did ever you try to fly from your own thoughts?
—Minnie Myrtle Miller, *Eugene City Review*, 1862

Disheveled and sore from the journey, Minnie rode into Eugene City beside her husband. More than anything else she desired to retire in privacy, to bathe, and to begin sewing a presentable wardrobe to replace her two smelly calico dresses. She was so tired, aching from so many unmentionable saddle bruises, that she had a hard time appreciating the pretty house Ned presented so proudly at Fifth and Oak. Instead her gaze stopped at a delicate young woman leaning out the upstairs window. The frail girl waved to them excitedly and called back into the house, "Ma! Pa! Ned's home!"

Disoriented, Minnie looked to Ned. "Who on earth?"

He responded without any sign of embarrassment. "That's my sister Ella."

"You never told me you even *had* a sister!"

"Well, I didn't know you had one either until I came to Cliff House and met Emily. You'll find Ella's a lot quieter, and more your age."

"But—" Minnie faltered, not knowing where to begin. He had told her so much about the charming house, with its white picket fence and its garden. How could he have failed to tell her about these people? "For God's sake, Ned! Your sister isn't going to live in our house, is she? And what about your parents? I thought they lived on a farm somewhere."

"They used to. Now my family has the bedrooms upstairs. Of course we'll have our own room downstairs. Plenty of privacy. Honestly. Think of them as guests."

"But you never said we'd have to share—" Minnie's tired voice was cut short by the bang of the front door.

In an instant a wiry, white-haired woman was bustling around them.

"Thank heavens you're safe! We've been worried sick, Ned, what with you vanishing like that for most of two weeks, and your horse gone. What were we to think? I've kept things together as best I can, but your father's had his coughing fits again and little George caught the stomach flu and of course Ella's too tired to—" Her chatter suddenly stopped when she came face to face with Minnie.

Minnie returned the white-haired woman's stare with a shell-shocked smile, intensely wishing this sudden mother-in-law would smile back and admit she lived someplace else.

Ned broke the standoff with a small laugh. "Minnie, this is my mother Margaret. Mother, this is Minnie, my wife."

Minnie nodded slowly, as if afraid a sudden movement might shatter her ceramic smile.

Hulings wheezed as he hobbled up the walk from the house. "Wife did you say? By jingo, Ma, I told you it was something of the kind." He winked at Ned. "Reckon you were born with the bit in your teeth, son. Here, let me take those horses." He reached for the bridles but suddenly bent over coughing.

For the next few minutes Minnie was distantly aware of being introduced to little George, who ran about between people like her own brother Robert, and of exchanging courtesies with the consumptive-looking but tastefully dressed Ella.

Through it all there was Mrs. Miller's annoying patter. "Well I never! How did you meet my boy in the first place? What do your parents think of all this? I didn't realize there were actual families living along the Coast, you only hear about Indians and explorers out there, you know. Did you attend a regular school for white people? Are you sure you're well? You don't look at all—"

Finally Minnie took the woman by her bony hand, smiled with all the poise she could muster, and said, "Thank you for your concern, Mrs. Miller, but as you can see I have had a difficult journey, and I must *insist* on resting before we get to know each other better."

Margaret Miller fell silent, visibly taken aback.

In the ensuing pause Ella offered a tentative hand to Minnie. "Could I perhaps show you inside?"

* * *

Thimbles on the fingers of her left hand, Minnie shoved the needle up and down as she stitched a strip of lace to the mountain of blue cloth heaped beside her on the bedroom floor. It had been a week since she had made her debut in the Eugene City stores to buy the material, but her ears were still burning from the experience. In one shop a pair of frilly old ladies had gossiped about her loud enough for Minnie to overhear that her small black hat was a "curious heirloom" and her dress was made from "klootchman calico"—as if it were the same plain cloth handed out to Indian squaws on the reservations! She had turned strawberry red and had marched directly out the door toward Brumley's store, which, after all, was much closer to the Miller house. But even there the clerk had the most peculiar tone in his voice as he said, "Ah, so you're Mr. *Miller's* wife. Then I'm afraid we don't carry credit."

The rhythm of sewing helped ease her tension almost as effectively as writing, she thought, and wasn't sewing the first step toward setting up her new life? How could her poetry win respect unless her person warranted respect?

The only writing she had done so far was a single short story—a Scottish romance about a young woman novelist—and a single letter to her mother. The letter had been cautiously optimistic: her husband was kind and good, she had written, although he was still too busy with the newspaper to spend much time at home. She had not mentioned her several misunderstandings with the senior Millers. Instead she had written about her immediate rapport with Ella, who shared an appreciation for art and literature.

Minnie finished sewing on the lace, clipped the loose threads, and tried on the dress. When she stepped into the parlor, Ella looked up from reading. "Oh, it's lovely!" she exclaimed.

"Do you really think so?" Minnie stood on tiptoe before the parlor mirror. "What it needs now is a blue hat. That old black thing of mine is impossible."

"I'm afraid there's still no millinery in Eugene City. The closest is Abigail Duniway's shop in Albany."

While Ella was talking, footsteps sounded on the porch. Through the window they could see Ned, looking downcast, shaking the rain from his coat.

Ella glanced to Minnie and whispered, "Oh! I've left the tea kettle on." She slipped to the kitchen. Minnie let her go, grateful that Ella, of all her new in-laws, sensed that she and Ned needed some time and space to themselves.

When Ned opened the door and hung his coat on a peg Minnie arrayed herself before him in the new dress. "Well, Ned, what do you think?"

The sight lifted his spirits. With a smile he caught her by the waist and swung her once about. "I think you're the best news I've had all day."

"No, I mean the dress. I just finished it."

"What? You created this gorgeous contraption yourself? You're a genius, Minnie."

"Don't you think it needs a new hat from Albany?"

"New hat?" He sighed, and his smile deflated. "I reckon money's going to be tight for a while."

"Ned, what's happened?"

He handed her a paper from his pocket and sank into a chair. "There's the telegram from San Francisco. General Wright himself has closed the mails to the *Democratic Register*."

"They're not going to shut down the paper, are they?"

"Not in so many words. But over half our subscriptions are by post. And just in case we couldn't take the hint that free speech is dead, the general sent along his instructions for enforcing the Confiscation Act."

Minnie read aloud from the telegram,

> Everywhere the local police and the troops shall act in common for the suppression of disloyal speech and action. At an early date General Wright will appoint a military commission, to consist of three officers, who will take cognizance of all cases presented to their notice on this coast. It will be their duty to decide what punishment is due to persons who utter any treasonable language, who publish sentiments that are disloyal to the Union and the flag, or who by their acts discover that their affections are with the Confederacy of Jeff Davis rather than with the government that our fathers established.

She looked up. "This is war hysteria."

"It goes on," Ned said. "The military court isn't going to allow defense lawyers, or writs of habeus corpus, or a jury either."

"That doesn't sound constitutional," she objected.

"Oh, there's no question it's illegal. These fanatical Republicans never did like the Constitution."

Minnie handed back the telegram. "If they arrested you, they'd have to arrest hundreds of other people too."

"The general's got that figured out. Here, he added this little piece of news: 'Directions have been given for the immediate construction on Alcatraz Island of a prison for political offenders. There is plenty of prison room already there for no small number, but it is the intention to be quite prepared for whatever the future may bring.'"

Ned crumpled the paper and tossed it toward the fireplace. "So much for law. So much for trying to stop war. Damn it all if I can see a way to keep printing a paper when the federal army's got a gun to my head."

A depressed silence settled between them. At length Minnie spoke up.

"Don't they only object to your writing about politics?"

"Only the politics! That's why I bought into the paper in the first place."

"Oh, *really? From* what you told *me* it was for the *poetry.*"

Ned was a little surprised by Minnie's sarcastic tone. He had heard the tone once or twice before—always in moments of stress—but he kept wishing it were only his imagination.

"Well, poetry too, of course," he said. "I suppose the army wouldn't close us down if we just ran poems, but we wouldn't sell many papers either."

"The *Golden Era* in San Francisco only publishes literature, and they have lots of subscribers," she reminded him.

"San Francisco's a heck of a lot different from Eugene City."

"We could write most of the things ourselves until the paper caught on and other writers started contributing. I already have a story you could use."

Ned knit his brow. "I'm afraid my partner's sure to veto a paper filled with nothing but poetry. He's a bit hard-nosed about profit. But we *might* be able to put out a 'neutral' paper for a while—something just tame enough to pass the federal censors. They'd let us print telegraph news reports from the South, for example, if we dropped the editorials."

"And that would leave room for poems," Minnie suggested.

"For a while anyway," Ned conceded. He smiled at the thought of startling sleepy Eugene City with a dose of literature. "Of course we'd have to change the paper's name, but anything would be better than letting the Republicans think they'd forced us out of business."

He lifted his coat off the peg by the door. "I think I'll go back downtown and hunt up Andy before he closes shop."

"Will you talk to him about poetry?"

"Andy Noltner only knows two languages: politics and money. If I can translate poetry into one of those, we'll talk about poetry. And Minnie—" he paused, realizing he had been a little too abrupt with her. "I hope you wear the new dress tonight. I'll be back by seven. I don't want to miss anything special."

Minnie didn't know exactly what this was supposed to mean, and hardly had time to ask; he was already on his way out the door. She did manage to touch his arm and say, "Good luck, Ned."

Her touch was light, but it stopped him with a warm sensation of pride and love. It struck him now how hard she had been trying to help and please him. Perhaps a smaller newspaper would be better if it gave them more time together.

He kissed her on the cheek and whispered, "See you at dinner."

After the door clicked behind him, Minnie smoothed the front of her smart blue outfit and sighed. Then she drifted back to the bedroom, where she took her old black hat out of its box on the dresser. She turned it over in her hands and thought: perhaps it would be enough just to add a few feathers.

At the very least, Minnie decided, the new dress would make her look more like the woman of the house. It rankled her that Ned's mother had not immediately relinquished that role. Ned owned this house, so his wife ought to run it, not his mother. Of course, the girlish dress she had worn from Port Orford hadn't helped. But Margaret Miller seemed to have a deeper jealousy, especially when it came to running the kitchen.

The thought reminded Minnie of Ned's odd parting words. It almost sounded like he was *expecting* something special for dinner. She decided to start work in the kitchen at once. Besides, it would give her an excuse to confront Mrs. Miller with the new blue dress. In it, Minnie could feel herself radiating the same kind of self-assured power that had made her the belle of Port Orford dances.

She tossed aside the old black hat, walked down the short hall, and opened wide the door to the kitchen.

Margaret Miller glanced up from a chopping board by the big cast-iron wood stove, chicken blood on her hands, and went back to her work. "Kitchen's no place for a frilly outfit like that."

"I cook with an apron," Minnie retorted, but felt her face flush with resentment. How could she let this white-haired woman cut her down so easily? Already she had heard herself answer with an apology. Now she straightened her shoulders and added, "Besides, I hadn't planned chicken. Tonight is eggs and potatoes."

Mrs. Miller shook her head. "You can't serve a man breakfast for his birthday dinner."

"Ned's birthday? Are you sure?" Could that have been the "special" event Ned had hinted at? If so, why on earth hadn't he simply told her? Was she supposed to guess? Now she didn't even have a present!

"Honey, I'm his mother. Not likely I'd forget September 27. That's why I'm fixing my boy's favorite dinner, fried chicken and cake."

Minnie quickly organized her thoughts, trying to find a way to keep her authority. If it was indeed Ned's birthday, she would have to put off the egg dinner until tomorrow. But what did she know about frying chicken? She had always avoided cooking with hot oil, and the sight of the bloody, partly dismembered bird made her shudder. "All right, you fry the chicken. I'll bake a spice cake."

"A spice cake? Are you sure, honey?"

The skepticism in Mrs. Miller's tone made Minnie stiffen. "Yes, I'm sure." She tied on an apron. Then she poured flour and sugar into a bowl, grated in cinnamon and nutmeg, and began adding eggs.

"Don't forget the baking powder," Mrs. Miller commented.

"I wasn't!" Minnie raised her voice in exasperation—partly because she *had* forgotten the baking powder. She had watched her mother make this kind of cake countless times, but had only made it once herself. How much to add? She spooned some of the powder from a can, considered a moment, and then spooned in some more. At least the wood stove was already fired up. Obviously Mrs. Miller had been planning to bake. Minnie poured the batter into a greased pan, slid it into the oven with a mitt, and hurried back to her bedroom to write out a birthday poem for Ned. That would have to serve as her present to him.

Thirty-five minutes later, drawn by the wonderful spicy aroma of her baking, she returned to the kitchen to check the cake. The smell brought back memories of Thanksgiving, when spice cake crowned the celebrations at Cliff House. Then she opened the oven door, and her heart sank. The cake was perfectly browned, but it resembled an exploded volcano. A lip of crust hung over the edges of the pan. The center had collapsed into a gaping crater.

"Too much baking powder," Mrs. Miller laughed.

Minnie gritted her teeth. How could her mother-in-law be so heartlessly aggravating? "Not at all." Minnie managed to contain her anger. She set the collapsed cake defiantly on the table. "It's supposed to serve as a bowl for a fruit filling."

"In a spice cake?"

"Yes." Desperately she tried to back up this fiction by thinking of fruit that would be in season. Apples would be too plain and strawberries were long since unavailable. If only she had a jar of preserves from the blueberries they had picked on Cape Blanco! But wait—hadn't Ned mentioned he liked blackberries too? "Yes, I'll need to buy some blackberries."

"No, no," the white-haired woman protested. "I've already spent the last of the weekly household budget on the chicken. You'll have to make do." She took a stack of plates and left to set the table.

Minnie glared after her. The nerve of the woman—spending the last of the week's money! Why did she think she should control the grocery money anyway? Tonight, Minnie vowed, she would tell Ned in no uncertain terms that she wanted to be in the charge of the household budget. Money was power, and Mrs. Miller was using it unfairly to keep Minnie feeling like an unwelcome guest.

"Dinner!" Mrs. Miller called from the dining room.

Minnie looked at her cake in despair. Quickly she took a knife and trimmed the lip's crust, crumbled it into the cavernous center, and sprinkled the whole thing with powdered sugar. It would have to do. It was fine.

Still she worried about the cake all through the meal. She hardly touched the fried chicken, although Ned ate four pieces, laughing and talking about his plans to rename the newspaper. Finally Ned's sister cleared away the plates and blew out the kerosene lamps. "Time to sing, everybody!" Ella said gaily.

Minnie joined in singing "Happy Birthday," but her heart was in her throat. She lowered her eyes, afraid to watch. Would Ned ridicule her cake? The kitchen door opened and, in the shimmer of twenty-three tiny candles, little George carried in a cake—but it wasn't hers!

Ned smiled. "Oh, you've made my favorite, with whipped cream." He blew out the candles amid applause and handed Minnie a knife. "Here, you do the honors."

In a daze, she cut a slice. It was a four-layer vanilla cake with whipped cream and blackberries. Was this why the oven had been ready to bake before dinner—because her mother-in-law had just *finished* baking? Then why hadn't Mrs. Miller said anything? Had she only wanted to humiliate her? Minnie looked up and saw Mrs. Miller beaming across the table triumphantly. "But—" Minnie could think of nothing else to say— "But I thought there was no money to buy blackberries."

Little George laughed. "*Buy* blackberries? Why would anyone do that? Bushels of 'em grow wild all along the river."

Minnie's hand was shaking. She set down the knife unsteadily. Suddenly she felt she was a stranger in this place. All these people had known each other for years. Somehow she must have stumbled into their dining room by mistake. Of course there was Ned. She had Ned. But this wasn't yet her home. Perhaps it never would be. Had the entire marriage been a mistake? But how could she go back to Port Orford and admit to her father that he had been right?

"Minnie, are you all right?" Ned asked.

"Excuse me." She stood up shakily. "I'm afraid something didn't agree with me. Perhaps it was the chicken. I'm not used to such greasy foods." She turned a weak smile on her mother-in-law. "You go on with dessert, please."

"Are you sure?" Ned asked.

"Yes, yes. I'll be fine." But as she stood and opened the door to the dark kitchen, she wasn't sure. The sultry kitchen was dimly lit with a flickering orange glow from the joints in the cast-iron stove. It seemed a hellish place—a place where she did not *want* to rule.

She looked first for her cake, determined to throw it out. But it was no longer on the counter where she had left it. Had someone put it away? Then she heard a scraping of metal on the back porch. At the screen door she could just make out the shaggy shape of the neighbor's dog, pushing her cake pan across the floor with its muzzle as it ate.

Minnie's stomach wrenched sideways inside her. She turned back to the dark sink and vomited, hating with all her soul the oily aftertaste of Mrs. Miller's fried chicken.

*   *   *

Winter descended on Eugene City with endless cold rains that kept doors closed and hearth fires smoking. Ned came home late most days from the office or the saloons, met Minnie at the door with a tender kiss, and greeted the family. He was so caught up in his work for the freshly renamed *Eugene City Review* that he was able for a long time to mistake the quiet at home for peace.

Minnie had lived in the house nearly four months before he discovered the extent of the frustrations building in his young wife. He had been looking through the dresser for his gloves when he noticed the book among the clothes in Minnie's drawer—a diary he had never seen. It fell open at his touch to the most recent page. There she had written, in the beautiful looping hand he knew so well, about a life he obviously did not know. She wrote of quarrels with his mother, of being assigned to do the laundry for the entire family, and of being rudely ordered out of the kitchen. On one day Minnie had even composed a bitterly humorous, satirical one-act play about Hulings and Margaret.

Ned was relieved that the diary entries about himself were sympathetic and even touching. But a few had a disturbingly defensive undertone.

> *December 5, 1862.* Andy has started filling the *Democratic Review* with his politics again. Poor Ned has little choice but to go along. It seems Eugene City only has a handful of true literature lovers. Ned tries so hard and gets so little credit here. He says column space will be so tight my new Scottish romance may have to be serialized. Blame the war!
>
> *December 19, 1862.* Hurrah—Ned finally bought us tickets to a dance! The Globe Hotel's "Anniversary Ball" is almost a month away, and I don't have the foggiest idea what anniversary it is, but who cares? For months, while the paper was printed with "red ink,"

Ned wouldn't buy us tickets to anything. I think the poor dear about ran out of alternatives for Saturdays. Before the rains set in, we would walk to the Willamette and "waltz" (read: hike through brush) to the music of the rippling waters. Lately we lit candles in the attic bedroom and gave dramatic readings of plays, taking all the parts ourselves. It's fun—and the price was right—but it's less poetic, somehow, knowing Ned's parents are downstairs trying to interpret every creaky floorboard. I tell myself I should be happy with Ned wherever we are, but it's hard in this house, haunted by the living. Ned and I are so seldom together alone.

Ned replaced the book in the drawer uneasily. Of course he loved Minnie, and they had wonderful long talks about all kinds of things—but it disturbed him to know she was keeping a side of herself hidden. Perhaps she sensed that the issues in her diary were the subjects of arguments that should never be. Perhaps now that he was aware he could head off her unrest. Perhaps with time she would grow more at ease. Or perhaps she was only letting her dramatic storytelling ability spill over onto secret pages.

He decided it would be best if he had not found the diary at all.

* * *

In January John came home. Ned had not seen his brother since they had gone their separate ways at Oro Fino a year and a half before. As they now walked down Willamette Street together John's look was somber. He had grown quieter than ever during his stay in the mines. At first Ned thought it was John's lack of luck in Montana that had made him so strangely serious. But John shrugged away his failure to find gold with unfeigned indifference. Then Ned wondered if John was upset by Ned's sudden marriage. But John praised Minnie both as a wife and a writer, and only regretted that she did not get along better with their parents.

At the end of Willamette Street Ned suggested they walk up Skinner's Butte. After a short climb they reached the grassy hill's crest and sat on the dark rocks there. For a long time they looked out silently across the fields and the town. To the north the Willamette Valley spread until it vanished at a flat horizon. To the east the dark canyon of the McKenzie River led up through the foothills to a distant white peak. To the south, across the town, lay the ruins of Columbia College. Ned remembered sunny days when he and John had been students there, and had hiked up to this same spot on the top of the butte to read, and to talk. But then the college had burned with the first flames of the war. Now the sky was cold and overcast, and he shivered.

"I hear your paper has resumed its political attacks," John said.

"Yes, it was quite a gamble at first," Ned admitted. "We had to call General Wright's bluff, knowing even he had started to see it was unconstitutional to censor what we put in the mails. Besides, we'd lost a lot of subscribers running so much poetry. I just hope we won't lose more when we have to raise rates. What with the price of paper during the war I don't know if we'll ever turn a profit again."

"I suppose you've seen the bills posted by Governor Gibbs calling for a hundred volunteer soldiers, too."

"Sure! And to be paid in *greenbacks*. I've got an editorial set in type right now blasting the whole idea of sending Oregon men across a continent to war. I figure there's a good chance they simply won't go."

"Well, then you're wrong."

"How's that?"

John pushed up his spectacles and cleared his throat. "I am going to volunteer."

Ned felt the blood drain from his face. "*You*, John?"

"Look, Ned, it's time somebody woke you up. You've picked yourself the worst damn wrong-headed career you could by running that Democrat paper. The *family's* Republican—the whole *state's* Republican! The country needs to *unite* now, not fall apart. Don't you remember how we all hated slavery back on the Indiana farm? Have you forgotten the time the hired Negro man at the next farm was kidnapped and sold into slavery down the river?"

"But—but the war's not about slavery! That's all *Lincoln's* talk, and he only started it as a trick to whip up the abolitionists. They just want to fill the army with Negro infantry to go die on the front lines. The war's about states' rights and the Constitution, and that's where the South's right."

John said nothing, but closed his eyes and breathed out slowly, full of anger.

"If you turn soldier, John, you'll just get yourself killed," Ned said. "You're the one picking a wrong-headed career. You'll break our parents' hearts if you never come back."

John stood up and offered a strong, callused hand. "Good-bye, Ned. I'll be leaving for Vancouver tomorrow."

Hesitantly, Ned took the hand and shook it. "Is that all you have to say?"

"No, I have one more thing to say. People told me my brother had become a traitor and a coward. Those are hard words, Ned, but I can't see any way of proving them wrong. Until I do, that will be the rock that sinks our friendship. We might still be brothers, but keep this in mind: you have stained our family's reputation with a blot the rest of us will always be working to eliminate."

For once, Ned had no ready reply. How could he describe the peace and beauty he was really fighting for? How could he convince John that his uphill struggle to stop the war was *right*, and nobler than firing bullets at people, and a truer measure of success?

After an unsatisfactory pause that only betrayed how unfinished their conversation remained, John turned away, his expression carved in stone, and began to walk down the hill by himself.

Ned watched him go, anguished by his inability to say or do anything that might stop him. He couldn't change what John believed—it seemed he couldn't change what *anyone* believed, no matter how much of himself he threw into the little newspaper.

When John reached the streets of town and disappeared among the porch-roofed sidewalks, Ned ran his hand over his face. He remembered the arguments and reconciliations that marked off his times together with John like knots in two entwined ropes: in Indiana, on the Oregon Trail, the night he had left for California, the last day at Columbia College. John had always been the conscience of the family, trying to balance Ned's impetuous ambitions with the weight of his leaden conservatism. Now the balance was finally lost, the ropes at their last knot. His closest brother was gone. Was it his own fault after all? Why else had his life filled with so much anger and frustration, when he had thought he was working for peace and beauty?

Ned remained on his rock, adrift in his ponderings, until the twilight brought the first drizzle of another cold night. Then, sighing, he pulled out his watch and glanced down to see—not its face, but its back. There, in the gold, was the shiny engraving of Mt. Shasta, the gift Mountain Joe had given him on an even colder, more desperate night in Idaho. It was as if Joe had known that the memory of that hallowed mountain might guide him through his darkest hours. Ned closed his eyes, remembering the poems he had written in his Now-ow-wa log cabin long ago, looking up through a glassless window at that great, snowy peak. Entranced by the mountain's power, he had vowed to find and know the spirit of beauty. Had he lost sight of that goal, distracted by masks?

Of course, masks! How had he forgotten? The subtle ways of the masked Wintu spirits stood in stark contrast to John's mechanical, or-dered world. And from that more distant perspective, causes were deeper than they seemed; spirits could animate numberless masks. He remem-bered his half-Wintu friend, Charley, explaining that even Mt. Shasta was only a mask for Kusku, Creator of All. And Witillahow, the tribe's ancient shaman, who had known that the murderer Lockhart was only a single mask, a single manifestation of a much deeper, pervasive evil power. What was the shame in leaving behind an old mask when the world was full of new ones he had yet to try? In his rage he had built himself a mask of angry words, but perhaps that was not really the way to change what was unjust and ugly. Angry words, if they were heard at all, seemed to lead only to more anger. He needed a subtler, more peaceful power.

Decrying ugliness had not succeeded; in the future he would try proclaiming beauty instead. Eugene City had not listened; he would not waste his words there again.

He slid the watch back into his pocket. It was time to seek a wider, grander stage for his work. It was time to risk another adventurous leap into the unknown.

*   *   *

Minnie dropped her diary and gaped when Ned burst into the bedroom, dripping wet, to announce that they were going to San Francisco.

"Ned! I'd love to take a trip, but—"

"Not just a trip, Minnie. We're going to live there."

The words made her heart jump. The thought of trading her confinement under the Miller roof for the literature and elegance of San Francisco seemed too sudden and wonderful to be true.

"But what about the newspaper?"

"I'll sell my share and let Noltner run it. There's no future in a town like this anyway. In San Francisco we can keep writing poems till the papers cry uncle and *have* to make us famous. How about leaving tomorrow?"

Minnie began to laugh and cry at once. "You're teasing!"

"Then next week, perhaps—you're right, we'll do it in style. That will give you time to get everything ready, a new story for the *Golden Era* if you like, and I'll have time to buy tickets for a ship out of Port Orford. We could even have a grand farewell party."

"I think you're serious—are you?"

"Perfectly."

"Oh, Ned, if only you *would* take us away! I know we could be happy again." She threw her arms around him and hugged him with her eyes closed tight, as if that would help make it all come true.

*   *   *

To Minnie, the next ten hectic, whirlwind days seemed to undo all that had gone wrong—to spool back time to their giddy wedding day—and then to launch their honeymoon as she had always dreamed it should be. They threw a ball at the Miller house to say good-bye to everyone they knew in Eugene City. Then they rode their horses five days back over the Coast Range trail to Port Orford and gave another gala reception at Cliff House. Finally they waved farewell from the railing of a sleek, tall-masted schooner bound for California.

Minnie breathed deep the wonderfully familiar salt air, blissfully proud of Ned, her pony express prince who had whisked her away from her provincial home—this time, in the right direction. The schooner sliced through the waves, sending sprays of saltwater up at the screaming gulls. She squeezed Ned's arm and gazed into his deep, gray-blue eyes, thinking that now she loved him more than ever. The unhappiness she had suffered made the chance to start over in San Francisco seem all the more wonderful—and hadn't he proven his love by hearing her silent pleas?

He kissed her as they stood there by the railing, alone on the deck of the sailing ship. Then she cocked her head with a coy smile and said, "I have a secret."

"Ah, a woman of great mystery!"

"A little, perhaps." She shook her dark hair in the evening wind. The setting sun caught it with highlights of red and gold.

"Come, my love, surely you can trust me."

She put the tip of her tongue in the corner of her mouth for a moment, as though she were uncertain. Then she stood on tiptoe and whispered in his ear, "I *think*—you're going to be a father!"

The words caught Ned off guard. For an instant a look of confusion swept across his face. Quickly he replaced it with a smile. "Well! That *is* a surprise." He drew her into his arms to conceal a slow flush of guilt.

Over her shoulder he could see the gray coast of California shrouded by a low fog. Rising above it, far inland, gleamed the tip of Mt. Shasta, pink in the afterglow of the day. A lump rose in his throat as he recalled the great black forests surrounding that distant peak, for he knew that somewhere in that beautiful, lost world, he too had a secret—a secret that could shatter the happy, hopeful new life Minnie saw stretching ahead—a secret he must never let her share. He was already the father of a dark-eyed child.

Chapter 16

The stars came out . . . shyly, timidly, as on tiptoe. I saw them come out while it was yet day, twinkle a bit, and then go back, as if afraid.
—Joaquin Miller

For four days the schooner sailed south along a coastline of high white cliffs and narrow beaches, with only a few brief freight stops at the ragged villages that clung to the wild Northern California shore. Then one morning a gap opened in the bare, brown mountains as if by magic. The crew reset the sails and turned sharply east, riding the tide in through the Golden Gate to the calm waters of San Francisco Bay.

The city sprawled down over the hills to meet the bay with a ring of wharves and a forest of masts. Minnie and Ned began a lighthearted competition identifying the types of ships, but it ended in laughter when Ned threw up his hands at Minnie's expertise. Having grown up on the coast, she easily spotted brigs, barks, and clipper ships with flags from ports around the globe, while Ned could only point out a sternwheeler and say he reckoned it was a riverboat come all the way from Sacramento.

They docked at a large floating quay and descended the gangplank with a sense of excitement that made Minnie twirl her parasol over her shoulder. Ned gallantly offered his arm and led her up to the street. There he hailed an open carriage and gave the driver two dollars in gold.

The cab man stared at the extravagant overpayment in astonishment. "*Where* to, did you say, sir?"

"Everywhere!" Ned replied, with a wink to Minnie. "Show us the town."

"Yes, sir. I'll do my best." The driver fetched their trunk, climbed onto his box, and shook the reins. They passed a couple of blocks lined with lavishly decorated warehouses of ornamental brick and wood, and then turned onto Montgomery Street. Suddenly they were in a world so opulent and busy that Minnie caught her breath. Horse-drawn omni-buses and trolleys on steel-rail tracks shuttled up and down the middle of the street amidst swarms of carts and wagons. Strings of parked buggies lined the stone curbs, while broad rivers of bobbing silk top hats and bowlers coursed down the board sidewalks on either hand.

"Is this some kind of holiday?" Ned asked.

"Naw," the driver replied. "Folks are just out trading silver mine stocks. There's more bonanza news every day from the Comstock Lode in the Nevada Territory."

Block after block they passed under the shadow of three- and four-story buildings with elegantly sculptured cast-iron facades or ornate bay windows. Minnie marveled at the shop windows that seemed to display every imaginable ware—even ready-made dresses and the new birdcage-style wire hoops that could be worn instead of petticoats.

Ned spread out his arms across the back of the cab's seat as if he rode in taxis every day, but his casual manner hid a touch of claustrophobia. He couldn't help craning his neck at the buildings that loomed like canyon walls above the street. He had never been in a city one-tenth this large. The sheer mass of structures and people was almost overwhelming after his years on the frontier. He had wanted a wider, grander stage, but suddenly he realized how hard it would be to make himself noticed on such a bewilderingly crowded theater. Part of him was excited by the challenge. Another part of him wished he had stayed in Oregon, where he had become a relatively large frog in an admittedly small pond.

The driver called out the names of landmark buildings as they passed: the Lick House, the Wells Fargo & Company office, the U. S. Mint, the City Hall tower, the Opera House, the California Theater. Then he drove on into Chinatown, where the streets suddenly diminished to alleys full of Chinese men with long braids, who loudly hawked trays of fried meats in clamoring singsong syllables. "We call this here the miniature Celestial Empire," the cab man said over his shoulder.

"It looks like some kind of awful Indian reservation for the Chinese," Minnie said, shocked. The transition from the wealthy downtown district had been startlingly abrupt.

"Maybe it'd be safer to tour some other part of town instead," Ned suggested.

Obligingly, the driver took them to Nob Hill, only a few blocks from the flats of Chinatown, but worlds apart. The horses leaned into their harness to drag the carriage up the steep streets. Lavishly ornamented homes stood stacked behind the sidewalks staircase-fashion. Ned cocked his head back and forth as if to see each one properly as they passed, until

Minnie laughed and chided, "Really, Ned. You're clowning like a sea lion."

Finally the carriage stopped in front of the posh International Hotel. The ground floor housed an immense public buffet restaurant. Signs advertised free clam chowder, dried meats, biscuits, and cheese for the price of whatever alcoholic beverages one might choose to drink with them. Ned peered through the open doorway at the polished wood furniture, silver fittings, marble counters, and white-jacketed Negro servants. He was afraid there must be some additional hidden cost with the food. "We'll dine later, driver," he said.

"You bet, sir," the driver said. "But I brought you here because I figured you'd be looking for lodgings."

"Lodgings? Here?" Ned shook his head and gave the huge hotel a supercilious wave. "These public-houses are all alike. Can't you find us some rooms with *character?*"

The driver, attempting to follow these vague instructions, showed them to increasingly less wealthy neighborhoods. At length he frowned, "I'm afraid we're getting into the old part of town."

"Old enough to have character?"

"Oh, I reckon it's old enough. Back in '49 they cut down the hills inland and filled in the bay to deep water—added four blocks all along the waterfront. So this all's nearly thirteen years old."

"Wait a minute," Ned said, spotting a sign in a shabby three-story house. "There's a room to let. I'll be right back."

He sprang out, leaving Minnie and the driver stopped awkwardly in the middle of the dirt street while he popped up to the door. Hardly three minutes later he was back. He swept off his hat, offered Minnie his hand, and said, "The artists' studio awaits."

"You've already rented it?" Minnie exclaimed.

"I heard the muses whispering to me all the way up the stairs. A good sign, don't you think?"

Minnie flushed with exasperation that he had not even consulted her first. Still, there was nothing to be done for it now. She sighed, "All right, let's see it," and hoped for the best.

Cautiously, she followed him up two creaking flights of stairs to a small landing. There he suddenly picked her up in his arms, pushed the door open with his foot, and carried her across the threshold. He whirled around and set her down before the back window, with its view across a jumble of shake-roofed housetops to the masts of the wharves.

"Well?"

Minnie regained her balance with her hand held gingerly on her stomach. "Ned, be careful!" She looked about the garret apartment's two sparsely furnished rooms, with their slanting ceilings and the single pot-bellied stove. At once she knew the apartment would prove dim and small when the time came to make room for a nursery. Still, it would be their own, unshared, and it was in San Francisco. All other considerations paled beside these two.

"Well, it does have *character*," she said as cheerfully as possible.

* * *

The next day, while Ned was in town buying some basic supplies, Minnie set to the happy task of arranging the apartment, planning in her mind's eye the decorations and furnishings that would turn the garret into an artists' bungalow. She had just decided that curtains for the bare windows should be at the top of her list when the door flew open and a woman backed in carrying an enormous armload of fabric.

"Oh, sorry! Didn't think anyone was home," the woman apologized. "You must be Mrs. Miller. I just washed and ironed the curtains. My last tenant must have smoked three pipes at once. Left them as gray as a smokehouse wall." She laid the bundle across a table and extended her hand. "Claire Wheaton, your landlady. Call me Claire."

"I'm Theresa," Minnie said, and immediately wondered why she had chosen to give her real name instead of her pen name. Perhaps now that Ned called her Minnie all the time, she was ready to reclaim a little of her older identity.

"Well, Theresa, let me help you hang these up. I hear you're going into hiding."

"I beg your pardon?"

The landlady laughed. "Just an expression. Never could understand why folks don't want to see a woman in public when she's in a delicate condition."

It took Minnie a moment to realize the landlady was talking about pregnancy. "It doesn't show already, does it?"

"Just the glow on your face, dear. You've got a month or two before anyone but another woman would notice." She threaded a rod through the curtain's loop and set it on the hooks atop the window. "Shouldn't stay indoors even then. You'll need exercise if you're going to keep up your strength."

"Thanks," Minnie said—as much for the encouragement as for the help with the curtains. "Actually, I've been thinking of sewing a large coat so I can take walks."

"Good for you. Never had children myself, but Lord knows I've got more reason to stay in hiding than you do." The landlady brushed off her hands as she walked to the door. Before she left, she winked. "Let me know if I can help with anything else, Theresa."

Although the landlady's visit had only lasted a few minutes, Minnie found herself musing about it for hours. On the one hand, Mrs. Wheaton seemed as sympathetic a neighbor as she could have hoped for. But there was an air of mystery about the woman as well. She had said she was hiding from something. What might it be? A criminal past? She didn't seem to be married, but then how had she earned the money to buy such a large building?

Minnie amused herself by sketching out the plots of novellas about Mrs. Wheaton and the secret pursuers from whom she had to hide. In one story, Claire was the renegade madam of an underground San Francisco brothel. In another, she was a glamorous Southern spy. Minnie paused, licking the tip of her pencil as she looked out the curtain-framed window toward the docks. Then she smiled and chose the spy story. It would almost write itself.

* * *

A week later Ned and Minnie were making their way through the throngs on Montgomery Street to the office of the *Golden Era*, manuscripts in hand. They turned on Clay Street and were suddenly at their destination: No. 543, Brooks & Lawrence Publishers. Minnie straightened her black feathered hat nervously, wishing she had a less outmoded chapeau to wear in such a famous newspaper office.

Ned hesitated at the intimidating brass-handled door, too. He was trying to work himself into the proper frame of mind by recalling the time he had ridden into Walla Walla, barged into Mossman's pony express office, and demanded not merely a job, but a partnership. Courage had won him a place back on the Idaho frontier. But how much bravado would he need to take a San Francisco newspaper office by storm? Finally he cleared his throat, cinched up his cravat, and went in.

Inside was the most gaudily carpeted and gorgeously furnished office Ned had ever seen. He strode purposefully to the nearest desk and held out his hand to a man with a great dark mustache. "Howdy—is your name Brooks or Lawrence?"

The man left Ned's hand hanging in mid-air. "My name is Bret Harte. And who are you?"

"Cincinnatus Miller, just down from Oregon with my wife Minnie here." He withdrew his hand to introduce the young woman behind his shoulder. "We're looking for the editor of the *Era*, you see."

Harte was visibly unimpressed. "Colonel Lawrence is in conference. If you're here about subscriptions—"

"No, no." Ned pulled the manuscripts from his pocket. "It's poems we've come about. We're writers."

"I see. You could have sent them by post as well, but since you're here you can put them in the contributors' box outside."

"Outside?"

"By the door, if you would." Harte returned to his paperwork.

For a moment Ned stood there indecisively. Then he caught sight of an ornate side door with "Col. Joseph Lawrence" in gold letters across its frosted glass window. The door swung open as he watched and a slender young man with drawn, boyish features backed out, evidently concluding an interview.

"Look here, Mr. Harte," Ned said. "I reckon your editor's free now—why don't we just take this in ourselves like the other fellow there?"

Harte rose irritably to bar Ned's path. "Unsolicited manuscripts *must* go in the box. Once you have established a name, as Charley Stoddard has, you might also speak with the editor."

"Stoddard? Never heard of him."

Harte gave him a disgusted look. "Perhaps you'd recognize the pseudonym 'Pip Pepperpod?' For years *he* submitted his work anonymously through the slot without once blustering into the office. I advise you to do the same."

Ned fumed and turned on his heel. When he was once again on the broad wooden sidewalk he muttered, "Hell with them! There's thirty-seven other newspapers in San Francisco, aren't there?"

"Yes," Minnie said, dropping her manuscript into the box on the wall, "but none of them has the literary reputation of the *Era*."

Ned considered this a minute, then slipped his paper into the same slot, stiffly offered Minnie his arm, and stalked off.

* * *

In the months that followed, the *Golden Era's* eight pages of tight print were the chief source of weekly news at the Miller lodgings on Folsom Street. What its columns contained buoyed or depressed the two young poets' spirits as directly as fluctuation in the stock market might affect the hopes of two different shareholders.

A small celebration followed the publication of Minnie's sketch, "Love Stories," but two issues later, when the Correspondents' Column gruffly dismissed Ned's first poem, the smiles disappeared. The editor not only refused to print the verse, but published the rejection notice, noting that although "Oregon" was probably the longest verse on the coast, it suffered from forced rhymes and a "drowsy effect." Ned decided at once to change his *nom de plume* and to try again. He had first written as

"Agricola"—the farmer. Now he would be "Cincinnatus."

The next week, however, it was not Ned's poem, but rather Minnie's that saw print. This time the editor added a note to Minnie's verse. "'Encamped' makes a favorable impression. Keep it up and you need not fear rejection." Ned toasted his wife's success with a tin cup of whiskey. He blamed his lack of enthusiasm on the war news: the South had finally really lost Stonewall Jackson, and the North had passed a general conscription act to fill its Army.

Ned's whiskey cup was refilled more and more often as the balmy spring stretched into the equally balmy summer of 1863. The May 17 *Era* ran "May Bell," another of Minnie's romances. On May 24 there was "Before the Voyage" by Minnie Myrtle. May 31 and June 7 brought friendly notices to Minnie Myrtle in the Correspondents' Column. June 14 saw *another* Minnie Myrtle poem in print, and still Ned had nothing but rejections.

In the depth of one whiskey-soaked night, Ned even sketched out a battle epic in response to the *Era's* call for Fourth of July poetry—precisely the kind of writing he had pledged never to do. When, on July 5, the *Golden Era* actually printed "The Siege of Vicksburg" by Cincinnatus, Ned felt little enthusiasm. As far as he was concerned the only victory lay in the short editorial praise of Cincinnatus' effort, ending with the words, "consider us asking for more."

* * *

Minnie was alone, reading a letter from her mother, the day the argument broke out in the apartment downstairs. At first she stifled her curiosity, trying hard to ignore the muffled voices. She felt a little guilty that she had fantasized entire stories about the landlady's secret past. She wasn't about to stoop to eavesdropping, particularly because she really would have to put her ear to the floor to understand what was being said, and pregnancy made such a pose awkward. Instead she squirmed in search of a more comfortable sitting position—her unborn baby was kicking up a row, too—and spread the letter on top of her taut belly, as if to put a lid on the commotions below.

> Port Orford, Oregon
> July 8, 1863

Dear Theresa,

What wonderful news! It's hard to believe I'll really be a grandmother! I just wish you were closer to home now, there's so much I want to know. Are you eating well? It's so hard when you feel ill, but so important. I'm glad your writing is going well, I mount all the clippings in a scrapbook I've put on display in the glass cabinet. Everyone here is thrilled for you. Meanwhile, *don't* go out walking in the hot summer sun, no matter what your neighbor says! If you swoon, the baby won't get proper circulation. Besides, San Francisco is such a large and dangerous city compared to—

A crash and a thin scream from downstairs interrupted her reading, as if to underscore her mother's words. Minnie bit her lip, afraid that the argument in the landlady's apartment really had gone too far. But what could she do? A drunken man was roaring, and a door slammed. Finally the sound of rapid footsteps on the staircase brought Minnie to her feet, her heart speeding with alarm.

There was a furtive knock on the door and a female whisper: "Theresa! Please let me in!"

Minnie anxiously peered through a crack in the door. Cowering on the landing was Claire Wheaton, bruised about the head, her clothes torn, and blood in her gray-streaked hair. Aghast, Minnie quickly pulled the woman inside and locked the door behind her. "Claire! What on earth has happened?"

The woman sank into a chair and, for a while, only stared at the wall, her bloodied lips quivering. Minnie set about washing and bandaging the wounds as best she could, horrified at the extent of her injuries. Obviously, Claire had told the truth about her need to hide. And although Minnie still did not know who the persecutors were, she felt ashamed that she had speculated so light-heartedly about them in her fiction.

Another door slammed downstairs. Minnie waited tensely, afraid whoever it was might try coming upstairs too. But all was quiet. After several minutes the landlady managed to stammer, "Thank you, Theresa. I can take over the bandaging now."

"Are you sure?"

"I was a nurse once." The landlady gave a long, tremulous sigh, obviously trying to steady her nerves.

"Would it help if I brought some tea?"

"Please. Alfalfa tea, if you have it. It helps stop bleeding."

When Minnie returned with the steaming cup she dared to repeat her question. "What happened, Claire?"

This time the landlady was able to answer, her head sinking with shame. "My husband. I moved here to hide from him, but it's no use. I should have stayed an Army nurse. There I was safe."

"Why did you give up being a nurse?"

The woman stared into her hands. "The contract doctors ran the hospital. 'Iowa butchers,' they called them. Between battles they would cut off young men's toes for a price to help them avoid the draft. And when the wounded came back from the field, the doctors were paid by the operation. Because they made fifty dollars for an amputation and only a dollar for putting on a bandage, they took off arms and legs even for flesh wounds."

"How awful!"

The landlady nodded. "I helped some of the soldiers marked out for amputation escape. But then I was discovered and had to escape myself, both from the Army and from my husband."

"Why from your husband?"

"Yes, why?" The woman managed a weak but grimly ironic smile. "After all, he was the one who ran away from me, years ago. But now every time I get a new start in life and build up something worth having—like the house here—he finds me and gets drunk and gambles it all away."

"Can't you *do* something?" Minnie found the thought of such a husband terrifying.

Claire shook her head. "No. Nothing. Legally, everything a wife has or earns belongs to her husband." Then she took Minnie's hand. "You don't know how fortunate you are, Theresa, to have a husband who doesn't beat you."

* * *

By mid July Ned was determined finally to see the editor of the Golden Era in person, for he had decided it was time to come to grips with the matter of his literary success. He hadn't yet told Minnie just how desperate their financial situation was. His pony express gold was nearly gone. Everything in San Francisco had proven more expensive than he had planned. Six months here, living like paupers in a garret, had cost more than six years might have cost in a remote frontier settlement. What stung hardest of all was that he had fared so much worse in San Francisco's literary world than Minnie.

All the way down Montgomery Street Ned clutched the manuscript of his latest poem, "Cape Blanco," envisioning the obstacles he would have to overcome, the obstinate words he might have to speak in order to achieve this one goal.

As a result, he found himself unprepared when he pushed past the elegant door of the Era's office, crossed the room unchallenged, rapped unhindered on the frosted glass of Col. Lawrence's private office, and was promptly met by a monocled, kindly-looking old gentleman who asked him to come in and have a seat while he finished some business at hand.

Bewildered, Ned came in and had a seat.

An auburn-haired young man with huge bushy eyebrows already occupied one of the overstuffed leather chairs in the editor's office. During the time Ned waited, the editor exchanged only a few words with this man—enough to give Ned the impression that he was some kind of columnist from a newspaper in the Nevada Territory. The business at hand seemed primarily to involve puffing thick clouds of cigar smoke up toward the high ceiling by turns.

At length the editor turned his monocled eye from his first guest to Ned, asking simply, "And what may I do for you?"

Ned came forward with his papers. "I'm Cincinnatus Miller. I've brought a new poem."

"Ah, yes, you did that battle epic, right?" The editor took the papers and began to peruse them casually, simultaneously making a fluttering introductory gesture with his hand between Ned and the columnist. "By the way, this is Mark Twain, another of our new contributors."

While the editor was occupied reading his story, Ned offered the columnist his hand. "Twain, is it? I don't recall seeing your work in the *Era*."

"I write over in Washoe, mostly. And the name's really Clemens, Sam Clemens—the Twain business is just a recent alias to throw creditors off the track." He disappeared under a puff of cigar smoke, and Ned let the conversation lapse, nervously watching the editor read.

At last Lawrence looked up with his verdict. "All right, Cincinnatus, I think we can run this Blanco thing in the Correspondents' Column, if you'll let us print your cover letter with it."

"The cover letter? Why that?"

"It mentions that you're married to Minnie Myrtle. Is that true?"

"Yes."

"Well, that fact will suffuse your verse with sufficient interest to our readers to warrant its publication." The editor laid the papers aside. "Will that be all then?"

This was the most crushing blow of all for Ned: to have his work accepted solely on the basis of his *wife's* name. It left him fumbling for the words he had come prepared to speak with much more conviction. "Actually, I did want to ask—don't you pay your regular poetry contributors? My resources are otherwise growing mighty thin."

"Pay you for poetry!" The editor frowned. "There isn't a paper on the Pacific Coast that pays for unsolicited poetry." Then he stood up and suddenly donned a polite smile to signal the discussion was at an end. "Now if you gentlemen will excuse me, I do have a deskful of copy left to examine. Mr. Twain, I trust we are in agreement about the extent of your columns. Cincinnatus, it has been a pleasure meeting you."

In the outer office Twain clapped Ned on the shoulder. "Damn good try. These editors are always trying to get me to write for nothing, too."

Ned sighed. "Reckon I've about spent up my savings. It's starting to look like I'll have to leave San Francisco to find some other line of work, at least for a while." He glanced at the bushy-eyed columnist dejectedly. "*Do* you make writing pay?"

"A little. It's still nickel and dime stuff. Never sold a poem, though. They say it takes a gold mine to run a silver mine; I reckon it'd take a silver mine to run a rhyme mill."

When they reached the plank sidewalk, Twain jerked his head toward Montgomery Street. "I'm heading back to the Lick House—buy you a drink?"

"Sure," Ned replied. He rather liked the man's broad, folksy manner, but suspected writing was a sideline for him. Perhaps he had made his fortune in the Nevada silver boom. As they started off together down the crowded sidewalk, making their way past women in large hoop skirts and men reading newspapers beside cast-iron lamp posts, Ned said, "If you don't mind my asking, how do you make writing pay?"

"Humor columns, mostly."

"Humor columns! That pays the bills?"

Twain gave a slow laugh. "Anybody in this state who says he writes for a living is probably just a good liar. Mostly, writing's a bad habit you've got to support some other way."

"Well, I reckon that's true," Ned admitted. They crossed Clay Street behind a creaking wagonload of beer barrels. On the next sidewalk Ned confided, "I've tried a lot of ways to make ends meet—gold mining, horse ranching, schoolteaching, newspaper editing, you name it. Problem is, the only job I actually made money at was the pony express, and it was riskier than blazes." He studied Twain from the side. "How about you?"

"Oh, my training was varied enough," Twain mused, pulling on one end of his enormous moustache. "But it's no string of dazzling vocational successes either. First I was a grocery clerk, for one day, but I consumed so much sugar I was relieved from further duty by the proprietor; said he wanted me outside, as a customer. After that I studied law for a whole week. Then came a job as a bookseller's clerk, which was fine until the customers bothered me so much I couldn't read with any comfort.

"Since I came out to Washoe two years back I've been a private secretary and a silver miner and amounted to less than nothing in each. No, I reckon before I got stuck with newspaper work the only trade I'd ever much liked was riverboating. I was a good average St. Louis and New Orleans pilot, too, and wages were two hundred fifty dollars a month with no board to pay and nothing to do but stand behind a wheel."

"That's almost as much as I made riding express. Why'd you quit?"

"Maybe you haven't been reading the war news. Vicksburg's fallen. The Mississippi's been blockaded for two years. The riverboats may never run again."

"Yes, the war, of course." Ned frowned. "I suppose you're for the South, coming from the Mississippi River and all?"

They passed a cast-iron fountain that doubled as a watering trough for horses. Twain idly flipped in a copper penny. "Back in Missouri folks mostly were, but there was a lot of confusion about it. They got up a home guard militia and I joined it for a spell without ever knowing which side it *was* on. They weren't sure enough about the thing to come out and say, but I think it leaned awful Southish. Didn't stay long enough to find out. I took the stage west and they haven't caught up with me yet."

"I wouldn't count yourself safe here. Now the federals have their Conscription Act they could start up a California draft anytime."

"True, true. Course I live in the Nevada Territory, remember. No conscription in a territory. Sometimes it pays to step back a pace when you find yourself in the middle of a barroom brawl."

They had reached the Lick House, and Twain held open the hotel door for Ned. "Just like it pays to step back a pace when the job you want doesn't click first time around."

* * *

The Millers' last week in San Francisco began when Ned got a letter from his parents in Eugene City. His brother John, serving under General Meade, had been shot through the chest at the battle of Gettysburg, and was in a makeshift military hospital.

Ned stuffed the hated envelope in his pocket, sat down before the garret window, and pressed his eyes tightly closed to hold back the tears. He pictured his proud, bespectacled brother among the waves of blue troops sent to stop General Lee's advance into the northern States; felt the lead ball that broke through his lungs; heard the moans of casualties in fields where wagons came for the gruesome harvest of the not-yet-dead; smelled the stench of the hopelessly wounded packed together on the straw floor of a barn "hospital."

Ned was sure his brother was dying. Worse, he would die unreconciled, leaving Ned with an ineradicable guilt, a poison, a shadow in his heart that might yet have somehow passed on.

Ned pounded his knee. Damn the letter! Hadn't it been the letter he had been dreading most all along, the worst of all possible accursed letters? He stared out over the rooftops tight lipped.

Or was there perhaps one letter which would be worse? The one that would come to say *he himself* must enlist in a war that should never have been fought. He could imagine the envelope now, with its federal seal on the back. Inside would be cold government words about the medical examination he knew he would pass, about the substitute conscript he knew he could not conscionably enlist, and about the three hundred dollar waiver-of-service fee he no longer had the resources to pay. John was dying meaninglessly. Next they would want him. The order must never be allowed to come.

Minnie watched his silent deliberations without knowing what was in his letter. She approached him uncertainly, eight months of pregnancy making her sway with each step. Gently she put her hands on his shoulders. "What is it?"

He ran his hands over his face. "Look, Minnie, we're going to have to leave San Francisco."

Minnie froze. "Why?"

Ned turned aside. "I've—I've run out of the money I saved from the pony express. I'm going to have to put off writing for a while and find other work."

"Couldn't you do that here? You could work for one of the daily newspapers, maybe, and I could earn some money by taking in sewing."

"No, I need to get back to the mountains again, back to the gold mines where I can make enough to really write poetry. I can't do that here, not yet."

Minnie drew back, dismayed by a new worry. "*What* gold mines?"

"Well, there's the John Day River mines out in Eastern Oregon. That's frontier, with plenty of opportunities still. Canyon City—the main town—should be a few years old by now. I read a bit of law in college. I could maybe start a practice there, make a steady living."

"But Ned, there's the baby, and the *Era* has been publishing my work almost weekly. You don't really expect me to ride off to a gold mining camp *now?*"

"The *Era* accepts work by mail, and babies can grow up anywhere. Besides, I'm sick of this dried up town. It'll feel good to get back to country where there's room to breathe."

Suddenly Minnie could hold herself no longer and stomped the floor. "Don't you ever think of anyone but yourself?"

Ned stood to confront his wife, but did not return her angry tone. "I will do what is best for both of us. We start packing tomorrow morning."

Minnie retreated a step, instantly regretting the rashness of her outburst. As a wife, of course, she had no right to defy her husband's decisions, even if he robbed her of all she had enjoyed in the past six months—the cosmopolitan atmosphere of San Francisco, the independence of their Folsom Street apartment, and the bright literary career just opening before her. She remembered how much more Claire Wheaton had suffered. She also recalled the landlady's grim advice, to be thankful her husband didn't beat her.

Minnie was not afraid Ned would strike her for her defiant words, but she did fear the strength of his will. It was the same power that had once driven him to Port Orford to woo her there, and she had admired it then. She had been overwhelmed by it then. But now it was the enemy, an unpredictable force that could impulsively send her husband racing after frightening, dark dreams. Once it had driven him out of Eugene City, sweeping her along to the beautiful literary world of San Francisco. Now it was abruptly destroying that life, and she had no means of defense. Would women ever have weapons to fight a husband's tyranny?

Finally she whispered, "If we have to leave, I want to stay in Port Orford until the baby is born."

Ned's determined look softened. "All right, Minnie. Maybe that would be best. I can go on alone to Canyon City to get things settled there for you. Your mother will be more help with the baby anyway."

This kind of separation was not what Minnie had intended at all. She turned away, but Ned caught her gently by the shoulders. "Don't be angry. It will be hard enough without that too. Please." He pulled her into his embrace, and she tolerated it, her head against his chest.

As he stroked her long dark hair, he thought: it is even harder for me to leave San Francisco in defeat. But I will return someday—and I will return in triumph.

Chapter 17

I am conscript—hurried to battle
With fates—yet I fain would be
Vanquished and silenced forever
And driven back to my sea.

—Minnie Myrtle Miller

While Ned traveled on to the mines, Minnie stayed in Port Orford nearly a year.

For Minnie, the first weeks were the worst of all. The baby was late. Every day Minnie grew wearier of her awkward, distended body, and more resentful that Ned would abandon her at such a time. She sat upstairs in her room at Cliff House, aching helplessly in a dozen places, watching the afternoon fog creep in along the cape until it enveloped the house in a bottomless white. It was as if the chill obscurity of Oregon were slowly, inevitably extinguishing the last warm glow of the literary life she had enjoyed in San Francisco.

"A scoundrel, that's what he is," Judge Dyer said at dinner one evening. "What kind of man would go gallivanting off to the mining camps when his wife needs him?"

Minnie bit her lip, afraid that she had no ready answer. But she didn't want to encourage her father either, for fear he would boast he had been right about her marriage all along.

Mrs. Dyer waved her hand as if to belittle her husband's words. "George, honestly. You should talk. You were at sea most of the time when the children were small."

Judge Dyer straightened in his chair. "But at least I was there when they were born."

"Perhaps you've forgotten you were trolling in the Farallons when I went into labor with Emily." Mrs. Dyer passed a plate of potatoes around the table. "Seconds, anyone?"

The judge roughly took the dish and set it down on with a firm clunk. "Perhaps you've forgotten I was out working, earning the money that built this house and put the food on your table."

"And so is Ned," Mrs. Dyer replied. "He used up nearly everything he had supporting Theresa in San Francisco. Now if a man needs to earn a great deal of money in a short time, I'd say a gold mining town in Eastern Oregon is as likely a prospect as any. And until that country's a bit more settled, it's not really a place for a young woman."

The controversy made Minnie's stomach churn. She put her hand to her forehead, trying to steady her emotions. She had been through this wrenching debate a hundred times on her own. She didn't need her parents bringing it out at the dinner table.

"Those gold camps are no place for honest young men, either," her father said.

Mrs. Dyer asked, "What do you mean by that?"

"Just what I said. The real reason that boy is hiding out in the wilderness is to run away from the war. Truth is, he got scared when his brother was shot at Gettysburg. Now he figures he can dodge the draft in Canyon City. Isn't that about the size of it, Theresa? The boy's a coward."

"Stop it!" Minnie angrily slammed her silverware down on the table so hard that the water glasses sloshed. Her father had gone too far. Perhaps Ned had flaws, but cowardice was not among them. Suddenly a red flame of love and pride crackled through her. On the verge of tears, she surprised herself by throwing the words back in her father's face. "Ned is braver than you'll ever know! Do you think it was easy, fighting for peace in Eugene City, with the Army threatening to shut down his newspaper? Do you think it was easy, riding the pony express through Idaho, battling wild Indians? I am *proud* that he stands up for what he believes, even when—" Tears had begun to stream down her face, making each word a struggle. "Even if—"

Minnie buried her head in her hands. Through her trembling fingers, she noticed with dismay that water was dripping from her chair. Curiously, it did not seem to be from a spilled water glass. Nor from her tears. A strange fear gripped her. "Oh, God!" she wailed.

"Theresa! What is it?" Her mother was at her side in an instant. As soon as she saw the puddle, she held Minnie by her shoulder and turned a chilly glance to Mr. Dyer. "Fetch the doctor from town."

Judge Dyer sat with his mouth open. "What! Now?"

"Gallop, you old fool. This is partly your doing, getting her worked up. Her water's broken."

"Her—" He stood, tipping his chair over backwards. Suddenly at a loss for words, he gave an awkward salute. Then he stumbled to the door. In a moment they heard his footsteps running across the yard to the stable.

* * *

After the painful night of half-delirious, grunting, sweating labor—after Eveline Maud Miller's first pitiful cry—Minnie found her life so radically changed that her former existence seemed a distant dream.

The doctor explained that the baby cried so much because it had a touch of colic. He assured Minnie that this was quite normal. But nothing seemed normal to Minnie anymore. She walked the screaming baby about the house, nursed it, burped it, washed it, diapered it, and walked it again. Had she ever really had the leisure to sit down and write? It seemed impossible that she had actually complained of boredom during her pregnancy! Now she could hardly think three thoughts in a row before little Maud broke in with her plaintive squall, like an alarm bell clanging inside her skull.

Serenity came in snatches. Late at night, when mother and child had finally exhausted each other, Maud would hiccup herself to sleep. Minnie rocked on silently, a feather tick across them in the bentwood chair, gazing out the window at the moonlit arcs of surf. By then her thoughts no longer had words. An indescribable, happy weariness settled upon her, muffling the need for names.

When Ned's almost illegibly scrawled letters finally started arriving through the slow and unreliable postal system of the mining camps, she puzzled over each sentence, rereading them by bits and pieces for days. It was as if the words had been penned on a different planet.

Canyon City, Oregon
November 3, 1863

Dearest Minnie:

This village counts 10,000 men, but it is a terribly lonely place without you. The hardest part is not knowing if you and the baby are still all right. Please write again!

Creek claims were all taken before I arrived. Some of the best paydirt is on the sagebrush terraces now. I have staked there for a starter. Flume water costs $3 a foot! Still, I have already bought a lot and I'm saving money to build a first-rate house. I tell you, Minnie, there's greatness ahead here. I'll open my law practice tomorrow.

I wish I could bring you now, but the mountain passes to Eastern Oregon are snowed up. I'm told they won't be clear again until June. By then I'll have things all ready, and the baby will be old enough to travel better.

Twice a week I am at the head of the line when the express wagon rolls in from The Dalles with the mail. Please write soon to

Your loving husband,

Ned

Walking the baby, Minnie managed a steal a glance at the letter each time she passed the table. Did he say June? That meant he'd be gone another *seven months!* Where was she supposed to get the money for baby clothes until then? And what kind of a place was Canyon City, anyway? She didn't know what it meant for water to cost three dollars a foot, but it strengthened her suspicion that the whole region was a ghastly sagebrush desert.

The next time she glanced at the letter she wondered about the phrase "I've already bought a lot." A lot of water? Or did he mean a lot in town, for building the house? And what on earth did he mean by "greatness"? Just what kind of future was he imagining out in his remote wasteland, anyway? The man didn't seem to care that he had ripped her away from her literary hopes and left her dependent on her parents' charity.

Between interruptions for baby chores, Minnie managed to pen a quick letter. She fired off her questions one staccato sentence at a time. She didn't realize just how much frustration her fragmented prose carried until Ned's reply arrived nearly six weeks later.

Canyon City, Oregon
December 12, 1863

Sweet Singer of the Coquille!

I have reread your letter a hundred times, pondering each word like a riddle. How I wish I were there to stroke away the worry from your brow! I've drawn up plans for a beautiful, elegant little house for you here. Of course I haven't forgotten San Francisco. That is why I am giving up mining. Law is surer work. I know what you'll say: I only took one law class at Columbia College. Well, that is more than most attorneys in this town can claim.

Minnie paused, struck by a sudden, inexplicable sense that something was wrong in Canyon City—something Ned was not saying. His factual tone sent a shiver up her spine. The mines were full of dangerous men—men who might have known him from the gold fields of Idaho or California. Could he be in trouble? Or was it something else? For the first time, she wished she were there, just to know.

In the months that followed, while winter storms shook the house and pounded rain against the tightly shuttered windows, Minnie sewed baby clothes from worn-out gingham dresses, wondering more and more about her husband and Canyon City.

* * *

Ned was worried that winter, too. When June finally arrived, he trotted a pair of horses up the sandy road toward Port Orford, his heart pounding with a fear that something was wrong in Cliff House. Minnie's letters had been so aloof, so questioning—not at all like the carefree poetic missives she had written before their marriage. He knew Port Orford was full of Minnie's former suitors. But it wasn't merely the threat of another Alfred Nubia that worried him. What if there were some subtler problem—a misunderstanding that couldn't be frightened away by brandishing a six-shooter? After all these months, he longed to sweep Minnie into his arms. But he couldn't help remembering the time long ago when he had triumphantly returned to Paquita from a winter in the Deadwood mines, unaware that he was being shadowed by Hearst's posse. What kind of ambush might be lying in wait for him now?

When Minnie heard the clopping hooves she was standing in the yard, watching the baby sit unsteadily on a blanket. Minnie looked up, her heart in her throat. She hadn't expected to feel such a rush of love at the sight of her husband. For months she had resented Ned, almost hated him for leaving. Then she had gradually grown proud of her independence. But now she realized how much of her had been torn away when he left.

He did not gallop up like an outlaw, as he had two years before. His eyes were older now, perhaps sadder. He swung down from the horse and held out his muscular arms with a cautious, pleading look.

"Minnie?"

She ran to his arms and held him tightly. "Ned! You're all right?"

He closed his eyes with relief. "Now I am." As he stroked her dark brown hair he whispered, "Lord, how I've missed you."

"I've missed you too," she said, relieved by how comforting it felt to hold her head against his chest. "I'd begun to wonder—to wonder if—"

He touched his finger to her lips. Then he kissed her in a long and passionate embrace that temporarily buried the doubts they had unearthed in each other's letters. When Minnie finally came up for air, her chest rapidly rising and falling, she dimly heard a cry of protest from behind.

"Oh! The baby."

Ned tipped back his hat and grinned. "Well, look what else I missed."

He had not been sent a picture of Maud, and found himself oddly surprised by the little girl's fair, curly hair. Then he realized his mental image had been of his other child. His half-Wintu daughter with dark, straight hair. Cali-Shasta.

To hide a flush of guilt he gave a small laugh. "Hello, you must be Maud. I'm your Papa, and we're going to be friends." He picked her up and swung her lightly into the air.

When the baby squealed uncertainly, Ned said, "There, there. We'll get along famously, you'll see. For starters, I've bought presents for you and your Mama."

"Really?" Minnie asked, her eyebrow raised. Ned had never bought her a present before. Money had always been in short supply. Perhaps he really *had* done well in Eastern Oregon. Or perhaps time had taught him generosity.

"But of course." He set the baby at her feet and rummaged in his saddlebags. Then he laid a box before each of them. "Open them and see for yourselves."

Minnie helped the baby fumble with the smaller of the two boxes until they uncovered a tiny bonnet. While Maud was waving this gleefully, Minnie opened hers. Inside was an elegant blue hat with a profusion of satin ribbons and silk flowers.

"Oh, Ned, it's beautiful!" She threw her arms about him.

"It's from that Duniway's Millinery you talked about—most expensive chapeau in the store."

Minnie tried it on, embarrassed. "You shouldn't have, Ned."

"That's just so you and Maud can knock their eyes out in Canyon City."

Minnie hesitated at the name of the distant town. "Do you really think it's a place to raise a family? I've heard there were Indian attacks."

"It's perfectly safe. Since my last letter I captained a whole company of volunteers and sent them Paiutes high-tailing it into the desert. We won't be bothered by them again, I reckon."

"I don't know, Ned. Why not settle in a civilized town like Salem instead? Or even Portland?" She knew the Army had recently dropped plans to conscript Oregon men for the war, so even this no longer could explain Ned's fondness for a frontier camp. "Why Canyon City? It's so—so remote."

"That's where the big opportunities are, Minnie. I'm making a name there, and earning good money. Soon we'll be able to write all the poetry we want."

"But how can we take Maud on a journey like that?"

"Easy. I've got a cradle all rigged up for her." He pointed to a basket suspended by a framework of willow poles over the front of the spare horse's saddle. "She'll ride finer than a Nez Perce papoose."

"For a month?"

"It's hardly a three-week trip, Minnie. Through some of the prettiest country in the world."

She smiled uncertainly. Ned's expansive, salesman-like tone had begun to reawaken old doubts. She had ridden through some of Ned's "pretty country" while crossing the Coast Range on their honeymoon two years ago, and it had been pretty rough. On this trip they would also have to cross the Cascade Range. It was loftier, and probably much wilder.

"What about the house?" she asked at length. "Is it really finished?" After living in shared houses and a rented garret, the lure of a new house all her own glinted brightly.

"Complete with porch and garden. It sits right on the side of a hill overlooking town, with sunflowers all around the fence."

It sounded lovely. But Minnie couldn't help remembering their lovely house in Eugene City—and her shock when she first realized it was already occupied by four Millers. "It's not a log cabin, is it?"

"Minnie, really! Even a lawyer wouldn't put a witness through this tough an interrogation."

"I suppose you're right. I'm sorry." She put her arms around his waist and held herself against him again. But then she leaned her head back. "Does that mean it *is* a log cabin?"

Ned had to laugh. "No, it's built fancy with top-grade sawmill lumber."

"Glass in the windows?"

"Yes, of course. I swear, Minnie, everything's ready at Canyon City, just waiting. All we have to do is go."

Minnie sighed. She had waited so long for Ned's return that she had grown used to thinking of the trip as something in the hazy future. "Then I guess we'll have to go."

* * *

A week later they were on the trail. At Minnie's insistence Ned bought an extra pack mule to carry clothes and housewares she feared might not be available in the Canyon City stores. Minnie herself rode sidesaddle, keeping one eye on the trail and the other on the baby, who slept most of the way, rocked in the basket above the saddle horn.

When they stopped in Eugene City, Margaret Miller's chilly smile reminded Minnie of the humiliations she had suffered living with her in-laws. Nor did it help when Ned's parents whisked their curly-haired granddaughter into the dining room to feed her applesauce and whipped cream, as if Minnie weren't fit to care for their first, precious grandchild.

To avoid a confrontation, Minnie occupied herself nearby, idly flipping through the newspapers on the table. To her surprise, a recent letter from Ned's brother fell from the stack. "Didn't John die at Gettysburg?" she asked.

For once Margaret Miller began chattering to her with obvious pleasure. "Thank heavens, no. It turned out that first crazy Army report was all mixed up. John was a little hurt in some skirmish in Maryland—wounded through the lungs, it's true, but he's recovered nicely. Not enough to return to farming, you understand, so he's enrolled in a college of—what do they call it?—dental surgery back in Baltimore, and he's turning out to be a brilliant medical student. Imagine! Our son John, a dentist!"

Minnie agreed it was a twist of good fortune. When she asked Ned about it, however, he merely gave an oddly indifferent shrug. And then when she read the part of John's letter about Ned—"my Confederate brother"—she saw the coldness. And she thought: how silly for two brothers to start up their own little war over politics and ambition!

After Ned had bought an additional pack mule to carry a load of fruit trees, rose bushes, and law books, they headed up the long, black canyon of the McKenzie River toward Eastern Oregon. For four days they forded creeks and circumvented fallen logs on the poorly-blazed trail, riding through a dripping rainforest of Douglas fir giants—trees like pillars supporting a distant green sky.

"All our things are getting soaked," Minnie shivered as she shook the water from her dress's hem. "I'm almost looking forward to the desert on the other side of these mountains."

"It isn't a desert."

"No?"

"Well," Ned hedged. "It's not a full-fledged forest either. You'll see."

Maud began to cry and Minnie called a halt to breastfeed her. While they sat on a log, Minnie pointed toward a damp bundle of long, narrow cloths behind her saddle. "Maybe you could help with those."

"You want me to wash diapers?"

"No, I've already washed them. They just won't dry in this rain. Maybe you could build a fire. I only have one dry diaper left."

Ned considered this. If they stopped to dry diapers over a fire in this weather, they'd lose half a day of travel time. Suddenly a vivid memory from his years at Now-ow-wa gave him an inspiration. He mounted his horse and assured her, "I'll be right back."

When he returned fifteen minutes later, he carried an armload of cattails.

"What on earth?" Minnie asked.

"These will make one dry diaper last for days."

"Cattails?"

"Sure." Ned broke open one of the cattail stalk heads and spread a fluffy layer of seed-down on the dry diaper. "Cattail fluff's absorbent. So instead of changing the whole diaper you can just change the fluff."

"A disposable diaper!" Minnie laughed, delighted. "Where on earth did you learn a trick like that?"

He blushed and managed a small shrug. "Reckon I just thought of it." He remembered the time atop Cape Blanco when he had shown Minnie the Wintus' speedy method of picking huckleberries. He had explained away his skill as something he had picked up while risking his life in hostile Indian country. But his knowledge of Wintu diapering traditions would be harder to explain.

*   *   *

On the fifth day out from Eugene City the trail suddenly led straight up the steep canyon wall, climbing three thousand feet without a switchback to what Ned promised would be the crest of the Cascade Range. Minnie endured the difficult climb, imagining there would be pleasant mountain meadows at the top. However, when they reached the pass, she was appalled to see only a moonscape of black lava. The jagged rock on either side of the crudely leveled trail dropped off into black chasms or rose up in grotesque shapes, with nowhere a tree or blade of grass.

"Where did all this awful rock *come* from?" Minnie asked.

Ned held out his arm to a row of three white-capped mountains looming beyond the lava. "From the queens of the Cascades—the Three Sisters. They're volcanoes, like all the peaks from Mt. Shasta to Canada."

Minnie looked at the volcanoes, wondering if they might yet be dangerous, and she drew her cloak tighter.

Their camp that night was beside a jewel-like lake, walled in by the flows of rock. Ned returned happily from a driftwood search around the lakeshore with a few small sticks and a tiny, triangular rock chip. "Here's a piece of luck, Minnie—an arrowhead! The Indians must make them up here, near the obsidian fields on the mountains."

Minnie held little Maud close. "You call that lucky? What if Indians came here *now?*"

Ned chuckled as he built the fire. "Oh, don't worry about that. Most tribes don't even make arrowheads anymore now that they've all got guns. In fact, that was just the problem out in Canyon City this spring."

"Wh— What was the problem?"

"Why, guns," Ned said, the firelight flickering on his face. "The Paiutes got a hold of some rifles and figured out how to make iron bullets by cutting up wagon end-gate rods. Instead of hunting deer with the guns, they thought it'd be easier to come down to Canyon City and steal a hundred head of stock. The town got up four or five dozen volunteers—and chose me captain, since I'd fought in the Pit River War. So I sent a scout to check things out. He must not have been very careful though. Never saw him again."

"Ned, I—" Minnie faltered.

"What is it?"

"I wonder if you should talk about such things in front of the baby. You'll frighten her."

"Maud?" Ned looked puzzled. "She can't even say 'Mama.' How do you figure she can understand what we're saying?" He shrugged and went on, while Minnie huddled nervously by the fire.

"We followed the Paiutes' tracks south into a genuine desert. We found the stock grazing by a salt flat, between clumps of rabbit brush—no Indians in sight, but a trap nonetheless. The Paiutes had been crouching behind the bushes all the time. We had to retreat and hole up on top a ridge, trading fire till we were down to ten rounds of ammunition per man. The Indians kept charging up at us, riding drooped on the side of their horses so all you could see of them was a foot and a rifle barrel. But they were losing horses that way. Finally they left half the stolen stock in the canyon and headed for the hills. They haven't been back in Canyon City since."

"But—you mean the Indians are still out there? Aren't the people in the town terrified?"

"Not a bit. The miners all called the campaign a terrific victory. Why, before I captained the volunteers I had trouble filling my law practice. Now, C. H. Miller's the busiest attorney in town."

The baby had fallen asleep in Minnie's arms, but Minnie herself was wide awake. Every flickering shadow in the lava seemed to conceal lurking savages. Only after Ned had gone to bed, leaving her alone by the embers of the fire, did she finally crawl into the blankets, still holding Maud tightly against her.

* * *

The country east of the Cascade summit looked more like desert to Minnie the farther they went. The first day down from the pass they rode through a sparse, dry forest of ponderosa pine. The second day they traversed a juniper-dotted plain. By the third they had begun to climb a barren, nameless range of mountains that consisted chiefly of basalt precipices, loose rocks, and what Minnie thought must be excellent hiding places for rattlesnakes. The afternoon heat rose in shimmering waves that made her head swim. Finally she rested in the shade of a steep canyon wall.

She leaned her head against the rock with her eyes closed. "We've run out of cattails. Diapers dry fast in this heat, but God knows when I'll have enough water to wash again. I can't believe people really live out here."

"There's thousands in Canyon City. Mostly a good bunch of men, too."

"How many women are there?"

Ned hesitated. "Well, not a lot. A couple of the town merchants have wives, I reckon."

"I will want to meet them," Minnie said, wiping her forehead with her handkerchief.

"Yes, of course," Ned said, already tightening the harness to continue the trip.

On the far side of this second, drier mountain range they reached the John Day River. It could have been the Jordan River to Minnie, she was so glad to see the cool, sandy-bottomed stream, where she could finally wash. Huge yellow cottonwood trees lined the river as it meandered through a slot-shaped canyon flanked by layered basalt cliffs.

The following day the canyon opened into a long, trough-shaped valley, with yellow meadows crowding the slopes of sagebrush away from the riverbank. A few pine trees dotted the dust-brown hills on either side, but to Minnie it still looked like a wasteland.

Finally Ned pointed ahead to a side stream. "Canyon Creek," he announced.

Even from a mile away, Minnie could see men crowding the creek's banks like ants swarming along a trail of dribbled honey. Everywhere the land had been turned inside out and littered with tents, junk, shacks, and tools. Minnie drew herself up in her saddle when the grizzled, mud-spattered miners stopped their work to watch her pass, greeting her husband as "Hiner" or "Cap'n," and poking each other into doffing their slouch hats. After Ned and Minnie had ridden up the creek two miles, its canyon began narrowing between steep hills, squeezing together a string of tent saloons, board shacks, and plank buildings.

"Does this mining camp have a downtown at all?" Minnie asked.

"This is it," Ned replied. He pointed out the three stores, the French Hotel, and the little courthouse. "I run my law business upstairs from the post office down the street here."

"Top o' the mornin', ma'am," a drunk with a slurred Irish accent sang up to Minnie from the street. He fumbled with his cap and drooled as he staggered past.

Ned glared after him. "Don't mind Bill Cain. He's harmless." But Minnie had already formed a first impression of Canyon City and its inhabitants. She was quite sure she had worn her elaborate blue hat for nothing.

It came as a surprise, then, when Ned stopped at the post office to check his mail and a smartly-dressed woman came out of the express office up the street, picking up her skirt and waving as though she were greeting an old friend.

"Hello!" the woman called brightly. "You must be Hiner Miller's wife. *Everyone* has been talking about your coming and bringing the *darling* baby. Oh—I haven't told you who *I* am yet. Sarah Eckelhoff. My husband rides the route to The Dalles and I keep the office."

"How very nice to meet you," Minnie smiled. She liked the way the woman had tied up her hair to frame her pretty features with a shiny blond sweep. Her fashionable dress was nicely tiered with ruffles. And she was certainly cheerful. "You may call me Theresa, if you like. I've heard there aren't many women in town, so I hope we will be friends."

"We'll simply *have* to, Theresa." She smiled again, but then a shadow of confusion crossed her face. "Forgive me, but we'd been expecting a *Minnie*. I suppose Mrs. Miller decided not to come?"

Minnie laughed. "One and the same. Minnie Myrtle was my pen name for the *Golden Era*."

"Oh—I feel so foolish."

"Don't, Sarah. I confuse a lot of people that way." She added, "I hope you'll come visit us once we're settled, if you're not too busy in your office."

"I'd *love* to come by. And don't worry about me finding time! I just close the office whenever I want to step out. Sometimes it makes the men wait, but you know men—they always do."

She laughed disarmingly, and Minnie joined her, though she was a little surprised a woman with such an unusually responsible job could treat it so casually. She couldn't help remembering Claire Wheaton, the businesswoman in San Francisco who had been terrified of her husband. This Canyon City expresswoman seemed a happier acquaintance. Sarah positively radiated confidence.

In a minute Ned returned from the post office, tipped his hat to Mrs. Eckelhoff, and led the way up Main Street to their new home. The dirt road wound up a steep side gulch toward a few scattered hillside shacks.

"Why do they call such a small side road 'Main Street?'" Minnie asked.

"Beats me. It just goes up to the cemetery."

"Oh!" Minnie put her hand to her collar.

At a bend in the road Ned opened a gate in a board fence and proudly held out his hand toward a rickety one-story frame cabin set in a yard filled with sunflowers.

"This—?" Minnie began, all of her forebodings rushing in upon her. "This is *it?*"

"Built it myself." He tied the horses to a crooked log that served as a porch post.

She dismounted in a daze. With the crying baby clutched to her hip, she stepped onto the creaking porch and pushed open the plank door. The hot, shut-up stench of rat urine hit her like a horse's hoof in the stomach.

Bravely, she went inside. The sparse furniture had been nailed to-gether from stumps and boards. Through the cracks in the floorboards she could see the dirt below. Except for three windows in the two small rooms, the walls were bare. The tin wood stove was no bigger than a hatbox. Neatly stacked about the edges of the floor—in rows, as if with pride—were mining tools, boxes of books, and dishes.

All this was awful enough, but when she looked in the closet-sized bedroom at the back of the house, she found a mattress of writhing straw, alive with the rats' nest she had been dreading from the first.

Her face ashen, she staggered back to the door. Then, deaf to her husband's explanations, she collapsed on the rickety front step and cried.

Chapter 18

Ah, Sun-flower, weary of time,
Who countest the steps of the Sun,
Seeking after that sweet golden clime
Where the traveler's journey is done.
                                    —William Blake

When Minnie had dried her tears she announced, "I won't allow the baby inside a place this filthy."

Ned quickly suggested, "I'll clean out the mattress."

"You'll scrub the whole house out, Ned Miller. Or don't you even have soap and water out here? I don't see a well."

"No one has wells in Canyon City. We just fetch water from the ditch at Main Street."

"And soap?"

"I figured you'd make some."

Minnie blew out a breath. Making soap was among the least pleasant of a frontier wife's traditional chores. "No time for that now. Just buy some at that dry goods store in town. I don't care what it costs. And while you're at it, get some milk and eggs."

Ned hesitated. "They don't have much fresh food."

"Just go!" Minnie shouted.

As soon as he had retreated toward town, Minnie arranged a quilt on the porch for the baby and began work on washing the diapers properly. She hauled heavy buckets of water for the task from the ditch along Main Street. Then she split firewood for the little stove, brought the diapers to a boil, and lugged the great, steaming washtub outside. Finally she wrung and rinsed the scalding cloths three times each before hanging them to dry on the fence.

While Minnie was working, the baby began crying from hunger. At length the cries made Minnie set her work aside. She sat on a stump that served as a chair on the porch, unbuttoned her dress, and offered Maud her pale breast.

As she sat there, rocking to soothe the baby, she was simply too tired to think very far in any direction. The house was an appalling disappointment, but what could she do? Run off screaming into the desert? And although she was weak with hunger, she couldn't face yet another meal of dried trail food. She had glanced at the bags of food on the front room's floor. Discounting all that was rotten or infested with insects, only beans remained.

So she rocked, looking out across the garden paths her husband had lined with upended whiskey bottles and rocks of weirdly-colored mineral ores. She watched the ranks of tall sunflowers nodding their yellow heads toward the distant yellow sun. At least, she thought, the flowers had been a nice touch. Before the baby had nursed to sleep, Minnie herself had drifted into a gently rocking dream.

*   *   *

That night Minnie awoke in bed, in the dark, without knowing where she was. She jerked back in alarm at the sight of the stranger lying beside her in the bed—a bearded man with hair curling over his ears.

Then she gave a short sigh. It was her husband, of course. They had not shared a bed for nearly a year. Had they changed so much in that time? Somehow he seemed more distant. He didn't discuss his law work with her the way he had once discussed poetry. And she was not a girl anymore. She had become a mother, a woman. Was it her imagination, or did Ned really show no regret at having missed most of the baby's first year?

She got out of bed to check on Maud. Then she swept her hand under the dark bed, searching for the customary chamber pot. There was none. Reluctantly, she put on her shoes for the walk to the outhouse.

The floorboards creaked as she groped through the two small, unfamiliar rooms. In the front yard, drying diapers fluttered like ghosts. Overhead the heavens stared down at her with huge untwinkling stars.

Ned had built the outhouse on top of an abandoned mine shaft. He had told her this before, chuckling that it would never fill up. But now the thought of the excavation hidden below the flimsy little building left Minnie frightened. A cold, sour draft from the hole made her suspect the old mine had other entrances, perhaps far away, where wild animals or bats might go to find shelter. More terrifying still, might it be possible to fall through the crude seat, or for the whole structure to collapse?

Sitting in the intense cold, she searched nervously for paper—and found only a pile of rocks beside her. Now she recalled Ned saying paper was in short supply in the mining camps. But for God's sake, did he expect her to use rocks instead? For a moment she vengefully considered going back to the house to use some of the paper he had filled with his poems. When, humiliated and disgusted, she finally dropped a rock down the hole, it fell a long time before thudding ominously far below.

She banged the shabby outhouse door quickly behind her. As if in reply, a coyote's howl drifted down from the hilltop cemetery. Fear gripped her again. The animal's insane, yipping siren sounded like the warning cry of a land possessed by angry spirits—a land where she was a vulnerable intruder, dangerously ignorant of the secret evils at work all around her. Suddenly a louder, much closer animal howl split the night. Was it inside the yard? An unearthly terror pricked up the hair on Minnie's neck.

She clutched her nightgown tightly about her and raced back into the house. She slammed the door and leaned against it, panting unevenly.

In the morning, she vowed to herself, she would confront Ned.

* * *

When morning arrived, however, the voluptuous aroma of hot coffee and sweet woodsmoke nudged her from a dark, fading dreamscape. Sunshine lit the curves of the warm, billowing feather comforter. In the other room, a sonorous voice hummed "I Am As Happy As a Big Sunflower."

Minnie stretched to one side, pulling the comforter with her, and blinked the sleep away. Ned was cooking breakfast on the woodstove in the main room. Maud sat beside him on a blanket, contentedly gumming a big brown pancake. The table had been carefully set with a red gingham cloth and a blue bottle holding an enormous yellow sunflower.

She remembered planning to demand changes from Ned. Now it would be harder.

"Aha! The Sweet Singer awakens." Ned saluted her with a spatula.

Minnie crawled out of bed, pulling the comforter with her. She walked into the main room in her nightgown and stood there uncertainly, still holding the comforter.

Ned set down his spatula, sensing something was wrong. "What is it, Minnie?"

She hesitated. Finally she said, "There's no paper in the outhouse." At once she hated herself for this vast simplification—this retreat.

"I'm sorry. I'll try to get some old newspapers from town today." Then he held his hand out toward the table. "There's honey for the pancakes if you'd like."

She sat at the table and slowly looked around at the room. He had scrubbed the floor until it shone. In the morning light the house was neither as small nor as primitive as she had remembered. Finely fluted moldings framed the windows and doors. A large oak bookshelf on the back wall held leather-bound books by her favorite poets. A small writing desk by the front window had an ink pot, quills, a ribbon-bound stack of her letters from Port Orford, and a folded copy of the *Golden Era*.

Had she simply been too tired from the journey to notice these details the day before? Perhaps with enough effort she could yet turn this house into a real home. On this sunny morning, warmed by the tender, gallant side of Ned she loved so much, everything seemed possible. With time and courage, she suspected she could overcome even her fears of the night.

But then she recalled her vague but worrisome doubts about Ned himself. His letters had been almost too effusive. And more than once she had caught him looking at Maud with a strangely guilty, faraway expression—as if he really were hiding something.

"Ned." She turned to face him. "Is there something you're not telling me?"

The question had come so unexpectedly that he almost dropped a frying pan. For a fearful instant he wondered if she already knew about Paquita and Cali-Shasta, if this was how the good life would end. But how could Minnie possibly have found out about the Wintus? More likely she was thinking of something else altogether—perhaps something as simple as the shortage of paper!

"Not telling you? About what?"

Minnie shook her head, embarrassed that she had expressed the thought aloud. Maybe she had been mistaken. Maybe the fault was hers. She hadn't really given Canyon City much of a chance. He had worked so hard to give her a place they could call their own, even here, where most people lived in much smaller shacks. Certainly she no longer wanted to share a house with her parents—or worse, with his. "I don't know. I guess things have been hard for both us."

"I know." He knelt beside her and kissed her behind the ear. "This house just needed a princess to make it a palace."

"Honestly, Ned," she said. But his tickly nuzzling had spread a happy glow through her that forced her to smile. And a moment later she had dropped the feather comforter in exchange for his strong embrace.

* * *

Several days later when Minnie was sweeping the front step, she saw Sarah Eckelhoff walking up from town, wearing a frilly hoop skirt and carrying a dainty parasol. Minnie had longed for company, but now she groaned at her lack of preparation. She had only put on a single petticoat that morning. Her drab housedress hung over her thin hips practically straight to the floor. Still, there was nothing to be done for it now. She hurriedly tidied up the room and her hair, and set a kettle on the stove.

"Yoohoo! Theresa! Anyone home?" Sarah waved a gloved hand outside the front window.

"Come in, Sarah," Minnie smiled. "I'm just making tea. Have some?"

"Thank you." The blond woman looked for a place to sit. Finally she arranged her skirt carefully on a stump chair.

Minnie blushed. "I'm sorry things are so dreadfully primitive here."

"Oh, *I'm* used to it, dear. It must be such a shock for *you*, after San Francisco."

"Actually, we lived there less than a year."

Sarah smiled. "I'll wager even your Port Orford was more civilized than Canyon City."

"I feel like you know all about me already."

"Small towns, dear. We haven't much news."

Minnie brought the tea. "Then tell me about yourself. That will give our friendship a fair start."

"A lovely idea. Let's see . . ." She swirled her tea, thinking. "I married Manfred in Kansas—he was running a stage line there, too. But the *trouble* we had! Between the pro-slavery men and John Brown's anti-slavery Jayhawkers there were vigilante murders and house burnings all the time. We took the overland stage to California—*Lord*, what an awful ride—and Manfred got a job in Sacramento, you know, with that first little railroad down there? *Never* let your husband hire on with a railroad! Anyway, when news came about these gold strikes here in Oregon I just *jumped* at the chance to run our own stage business again."

"It almost sounds like it's *your* business, not your husband's!" Minnie laughed.

"In a way, it *is*," Sarah replied seriously. "He may run the business, but I run *him*—you know, we women have our ways, don't we?" She smiled quickly and then suddenly asked, "Have you ever been magnetized?"

"Pardon?"

"Magnetized. You know."

"Well," Minnie faltered. "I don't think so."

Sarah set down her tea cup and put her hand on Minnie's. "I'll bet you've been magnetized without knowing it, then. Magnetics is what gives women our spiritual power over men. Just last night I charged myself into a trance and had a vision that your spirit and mine were close, so I'm *sure* you've left the physical plane before."

A Deeper Wild

"Really?" Minnie had read of such things happening. Most of the newspapers had columns about spiritualism, but she had doubts. "How do you do it?"

"I have a medallion." Sarah unbuttoned her collar and pulled up a heart-shaped iron pendant from the cleft between her breasts. The medallion was marked with zigzag thunderbolts. "It even works to control *savages*. Sometimes I wish the Indians would come right into town so I could just *take over* their spirits."

"Oh!" Minnie put her hand to her throat. The last thing she wanted to see in town was an Indian.

"Does that startle you? They're men, too, you know. I think it's kind of *exciting*. Imagine—not long ago I heard some Indians sneaked up on an immigrant woman along the Malheur River while her husband was out hunting. They were coming for the shiny copper pans in her dish rack, but she took a tent pole and sent them running. Next day the chief came back and offered the husband five hundred dollars to swap wives, because she was so brave."

She slid the medallion back to its place. "If it had been *me*, I might have gone."

"Sarah! Not really."

"Why not? When I married Manfred I had the preacher leave out the word 'obey,' just like Lucy Stone and the women's rights people back East. Of course you're the only woman in town I'd tell *that* to."

"I haven't met the other women yet," Minnie admitted regretfully.

Sarah smiled and brushed the sweep of blond hair back from her eyes. "It won't take long. There's Madame Fleurot, wife of the owner of the French Hotel. *Tres charmante*, but no more spine than a jellyfish. She *lives* to dote on her husband. She has a *winch* in her bedroom to tighten her corset so she can wear those French costumes. You know what *I* think, I think she and 'Monsieur Fleurot' are so much alike they're guilty of psychological incest."

"Heavens! Do you think?"

"No doubt. If they have children, they'll be deformed, or idiots, I'm sure. The Fleurots aren't related *physically*, of course, but their temperaments are disgustingly identical. There's sin in that as much as in the others."

"What others?" Minnie was beginning to wonder what the other women in town *were* like.

"The harlots at the hurdy gurdy house. They're the only others, you know. And you can't talk with those girls. Every one of them, morally insane. Really! They belong in an *asylum*, not a house where they can sell themselves."

"Oh, my!" Minnie swept up the baby playing quietly at her feet and held her on her lap. "There must be other women."

"Not yet. But I'll bet there will be soon. Manfred brought in the first load of Chinamen last month to help build a ditch to Prairie Diggin's. If things go like they did in California, they'll bring the China slave girls too before long. Then we'll not only have prostitution, but slavery, too."

"How awful. There must be some way to stop it."

Sarah straightened and opened her handbag. "It's a long struggle, Theresa, but I'm glad to see you're right-minded about it. I think it's a woman's duty to uphold the morality of her community. And I'm sure you'll agree the first stage of moral depravity is drunkenness. That's why I've brought along these pledge cards today. Liquor ruins good men and worsens the bad, I always say."

Minnie blinked, trying to follow this new twist of the conversation. "Well, yes. That is true. And it must be a problem here. The first man I saw on the streets downtown was a drunk."

"Probably Bill Cain. Who knows what that man might achieve if he were free from the devil alcohol? I'm taking these temperance pledge cards to every saloon in the city that will let me in. Perhaps you could help and give one to your husband?"

"Of course." Minnie took the card with some embarrassment. "I only wish I could help your project more, but with the baby—"

"I understand. And such a *darling* thing it is, too." Suddenly she stood up. "Well, I must be going. I fancy there's a line waiting at the express office."

Minnie barely made it to the door in time to hold it open for her. "Do come visit again soon. You've no idea how I'll look forward to it."

She watched Sarah walk back down Main Street, and then sat on a stump by the stove. There were still the chores waiting for her. But perhaps they would seem easier now, knowing she had at least one person in town to talk to. To be sure, Sarah was startlingly unconventional—even eccentric—but she had all the makings of a sympathetic friend.

Then Minnie caught sight of the card in her hand. It pledged the bearer to "total abstinence from all alcoholic beverages and other intoxicating consumables." She smiled dryly to think of presenting it to Ned, and dropped it into the stove. But as she watched it flare up and curl black, she felt a touch of regret—a sudden, bold feeling that maybe she ought to have stood up to him after all.

She closed the stove and looked out the window at the strange, barren brown hills above Canyon City, wondering if Ned even knew he had won a battle. Despite the difficult life he had led her to, she still loved him. There would be time to smooth Ned's rough edges later. For now, they were both struggling. She would do her part, and give this rugged frontier life her best shot. Perhaps it would only be a few months before they had enough money to return to the literary world of San Francisco. That shining dream hung before her like a guiding star.

* * *

Fall did not bring the warm rains Minnie recalled from Port Orford, but only cold, clear skies with a hard frost every night and the threat of snow. On one chill afternoon Minnie decided she could not put off the hated job of making soap any longer. Certainly the grease bucket was full enough, and after the weeks of pouring water into an ash hopper in the back yard, the kettle below the hopper was overflowing with lye.

She built a fire outside and put the kettle of lye on to boil, trying all the while neither to breathe the ghastly fumes, nor to catch her long dress on fire, nor to let young Maud crawl into the hot coals. Gradually she added the grease, stirring and checking the infernal brew's consistency. When the bubbles belched to the surface like splatterings in a mud pot, she poured the kettle out into a coopered bucket, where the soft soap would remain until it was used.

She had not yet cleaned up from this unpleasant work when she heard bellows and shouts coming up the hill on Main Street. She glanced over the fence. Her husband was trying to drive a cow before him and wheel a heavily loaded wheelbarrow at the same time. She might have laughed at his awkward situation—having to alternately wheel the barrow and abandon it to chase the cow back onto the road—if she hadn't immediately guessed her husband's plan.

"Hey, Minnie!" Ned hollered, heading the cow off so it trotted into the yard. He caught its short tether with a lunge and tied it to the fence, then wiped his brow. "Here's the fresh milk and eggs you wanted. A man up Canyon Creek sold me his cow and chickens for fifty bucks. He said he was leaving for Portland for the winter."

"I didn't ask for livestock!" Minnie objected. She looked dubiously at the wheelbarrow, which held four cackling crates, and then back at the big, black-and-white Holstein. "Is the cow producing?"

"She just had a calf; they slaughtered it for veal." He rolled up a stump and fetched a pot from the porch. "Go ahead, give it a try."

"Ned! I've never milked a cow."

"Well, neither have I. Still, it can't be too hard, can it? Come on, I'll hold her for you."

Minnie hesitated. She knew it was supposed to be a frontier woman's job to milk the family cow. But she had never understood why. For some reason, even ranchers who worked with cattle all day left the milking to their wives. Now here was a cow. What's more, it had recently given birth. Minnie suspected it would be in pain, or perhaps even get sick, if it wasn't milked soon.

"I guess I can try," she said wearily. "Just be sure you watch Maud." She sat down, pushed up her sleeves, and cautiously reached underneath the cow's steaming flank to grab one of the swollen teats. Instantly the cow lifted a hoof and set it on the hem of Minnie's long dress. In her struggle to get the hem free, Minnie was twice swished by the animal's dirty tail.

"Maybe you have to talk soothingly to it," Ned suggested.

Minnie flushed red but did not answer. She hitched up her dress and took hold of the teats again. At first her small white hands accomplished nothing. But then, by closing off the top of the teat tightly with the grip of her index finger and then squeezing hard with her other fingers, she began to squirt dribbles of warm milk into the pan.

"There you go," Ned said. "Now I'd better get a fence up for these chickens."

"Ned!" Minnie called tensely, afraid to startle the cow, but even more afraid of being left alone beside the animal's rear hooves. And in fact the cow promptly lifted a dirty hoof, waved it a second over Minnie's dress, and splashed a large flake of manure into the milk pan. With an angry huff Minnie caught up the pan and dumped the dirty milk over the cow's black-and-white back.

Then, guiltily, she turned to face the reproach she expected from her husband. But he was already on the other side of the house, rattling lumber for his chicken coop.

Tears were starting to well up in Minnie's eyes. But then the cow turned its head and gave her what seemed to be a sympathetic—even encouraging—look. Dabbing her cheeks with her apron, Minnie stepped back to the cow. This time Minnie petted the smooth hair on its head. Then she wiped out the pan with another corner of her apron and began milking again.

Several weeks passed before Minnie finally realized why women in Oregon put up with milking the family cow twice a day—once in the pre-breakfast dark, and again after supper, when everyone else was sitting by the stove with a cup of coffee. A cow provided a woman with an acceptable means to earn a little money of her own. Every day there were three buckets of milk, which settled to leave three pints of skim-mable cream, which in turn could be churned to produce a single half-pound brick of golden butter. And butter, Minnie discovered, could be sold.

The first week that she took two extra pounds of butter to the store, hoping to exchange it for flour, she was surprised to see the clerk weigh out two dollars of gold dust. It only took a moment to realize she would be a fool to spend the gold on flour. This was money outside of the tight budget allowed by her husband. Instead she carefully poured the golden dust into an empty cod liver oil bottle, stoppered it tightly, and hid it in a cranny behind the bookshelf. Perhaps she would use it for a silk dress one day, or for copper cookware—she didn't yet know, but the slowly-filling bottle made her feel a little better during the hardships of that first winter in Canyon City.

The sale of eggs promised at first to be an even better money-maker. But it did not last. On the day of the first snow Minnie opened the chicken coop to find a rattlesnake curled up in the warmth of a nest where an egg should have been. Ned came and shot it, but the smell of blood must have brought the coyotes, for the next morning there was nothing left but feathers.

Minnie first used a little of her butter-and-egg money to buy material for a dress for Maud, and to buy wool to knit socks. It was cold and sunny that morning, with a wind that swirled the dry snow off the downtown streets. She carried Maud and her purchases out of Canyon City's "San Francisco Store," a small, pathetically misnamed dry goods emporium in the drab heart of the ramshackle mining town. Then she walked under the neighboring sign for "C. H. Miller, Attorney-At-Law" and headed for the Eckelhoff Express.

When the door's bell jangled, Sarah looked up from her deskful of account ledgers. "Theresa! How delightful. I've been meaning to come visit, but all my free time has been taken up with the temperance work, you know."

"Oh? And how is the work coming?" Minnie set Maud down. The little girl tottered uncertainly a few paces before plopping down to inspect a knot hole.

"Pretty well. I stand outside the saloons and talk with the men coming out or going in. Some of them are *very* interested in talking about it. You remember Bill Cain, that *hideous* drunkard? He's not only signed the card, he's found a job and is saving money for a fare to *Ireland*."

"That's certainly progress." Minnie shifted the packages under her arm, hoping Sarah would notice them.

"Why, you've bought *yarn*. What are you making?"

Minnie answered with a conspiratorial whisper. "You've inspired me to a little business venture. For ten cents I can knit a pair of wool socks that will sell for a dollar to the miners. If I can find enough time to work on it I hope to have enough money for a new dress by spring."

"Well, it's wonderful *you* can knit. I simply haven't the *patience* for it," Sarah replied, with less interest than Minnie had hoped. "When *I* need money I simply rearrange the books and take what I want from the receipts."

"Sarah! You don't really!"

"How else? Manfred would never give me money for the things I want. That's a woman's way, Theresa." Before Minnie could reply, Sarah quickly cleared her desk. "Now I wish I could stay to chat, but I've an account to discuss with a Chinese merchant in Tiger Town—it shouldn't be more than a twenty minute ride down to the John Day River, but I'd best be started before dusk."

Minnie had been startled to learn that Sarah routinely stole money from her husband's business, but she was even more surprised when Sarah stood up from behind her desk. Minnie's jaw simply dropped open. *The woman was not wearing a floor-length dress!* The hem scarcely came below her knees. Underneath were a pair of baggy white muslin pantaloons, tied tightly at the ankles.

"Oh! You have a Bloomer costume." Minnie had seen illustrations of the radical fashion in newspapers, but even in San Francisco she had never actually seen a woman wearing it.

"Of course. I don't wear long skirts at all for riding anymore. It's *simply* too impractical. You *must* have read about Amelia Bloomer and Susan B. Anthony in New York. It's irrational clothing that keeps women under their husbands' control. Why, Theresa, I'm surprised you don't wear short skirts yourself, what with working in the garden, and around open fires, and with those narrow doorways. You know this only took *five yards* of material to put together? That spring dress you've got in mind is probably some Great Pyramid thing that'll take *eighteen*."

"Well, yes, I suppose that's true." Minnie bit her lip. She couldn't take her eyes from the high hemline and the odd Turkish trousers. "But don't you have trouble with the wind catching up the skirt?"

Sarah tossed back her blond head and laughed. "If *that* is going to worry you, darling, just sew a little buckshot in the hem. I don't, but only because I can't *stand* the bruise marks it leaves on my legs. Now I really *do* have to close up the office."

Outside, Minnie saw that Sarah's horse did not have the usual ladies' sidesaddle. And in fact, Sarah climbed on like a man and rode down the street with her pantalooned legs actually straddling the animal.

Two miners gave a kind of appreciative yip as she rode past. Minnie overheard one of them slap his leg and say, "She's a fetcher even in them crazy britches. Did you see how they stretched tight over her knees? Whoo-haw!"

* * *

Ned sat at the long table in the front room, his quill poised over a sheet of paper like a heron waiting for a fish. He pursed his lips and twirled the feather in his fingers. His gray-blue eyes darted along the bookshelves for inspiration: a shelf of British poets, a shelf of American poets, and a shelf reserved exclusively for the B's—Burns, Byron, Browning, Blake, and the Bible. Ned pulled down the Blake and let it fall open. It was the most recent addition to the shelf and he still had doubts about the poet's reputation. Blake had been dead for forty years, but his works had only recently been rescued from obscurity by a group of radical London artists known as the Pre-Raphaelites.

He snapped the book shut and hollered into the bedroom, "Minnie, what's a rhyme for silver?"

"Just a minute, Ned. I've almost finished my new dress."

Ned humphed, scratched out the line, and took a drink from his whiskey flask. He was writing a new line when Minnie cautiously opened the door and stepped into the room in her new outfit. After a moment she cleared her throat.

Ned glanced her way enough to see the baggy white trousers. Suddenly he wrenched himself about in his chair. "What the—"

"It's a Bloomer costume," Minnie explained. "Easier to work in."

Ned ran his hand over his face. "For God's sake, don't wear it."

"Why not? Sarah Eckelhoff does, and she can ride a horse better because of it."

"I know. I've seen. But she's always taking up fads, most of them just as ridiculous. She'll have picked up some other cause by tomorrow. Don't make a fool of yourself by copying her."

"Well!" Minnie turned for the door. "I see. Nonetheless, I'll wear it or not, just as I choose."

She breezed back into the bedroom and began to putter about, straightening her sewing supplies, turning this way and that as if to show off her short skirt for Maud's benefit. The dress had a light, free feel to it that kept her bubbling along for several minutes with the kind of almost haughty, girlish air that had once teased the boys' hearts in the Port Orford schoolhouse.

Then she took a bucket to fetch water from the creek, and stopped. It was one thing to wear a Bloomer costume in the house, and something else altogether to take it out to Main Street. She sighed and set down the bucket. Then she went to the dresser to put the old housedress back on. Perhaps, she thought glumly, her husband was right after all.

*   *   *

Minnie pressed back the pages of her small diary on the kitchen table and wrote:

> *August 17, 1865.* More than a year has passed since I first arrived in this earthly paradise, and I think now I can fairly say it has been the hardest year I have yet lived. Most days I have been too tired to cry, too busy to give up. Small wonder, then, diary, that I have not written to you since winter! But now my webfoot Cincinnatus is out in his garden, taking Maud through the paths lined with his whiskey bottles, and I have a moment to catch you up.
>
> When spring came, I rejoiced to have the snow finally gone. Ned turned up most of the garden and planted it with vegetables, with wheat along the walks. He has his roses and his fruit trees, too, and flowers beside the house: peonies, wallflowers, pinks, sweet williams, honeysuckle, and of course the sunflowers. It is almost lovely, but the pleasantest part is that he will submit to watching the baby while he works outside.
>
> The Great War ended in April, and within a week Mr. Lincoln had been shot and was in a funeral car bound for Illinois. Of course that news failed to arouse the sympathy of this warm-hearted metropolis, just as the war did not unsettle things here, other than to add a brief population of refugees and deserters. Now the town is shrinking again because of the mines. Sarah says there are already as many Chinamen in the area as white miners. Apparently this is because the Orientals are content to sift through the deserted claims of others.
>
> The only news that has set the town abuzz this season concerns Bill Cain. It seems Mr. Cain kept getting into arguments even though he had taken Sarah's temperance pledge, and, they say, stuck by it. Finally, when his employer paid him in paper greenbacks instead of gold, Mr. Cain shot and killed the poor fellow. Ned dared to take the case when it came to trial, although everyone said it was hopeless. And then he really did lose . . .

Minnie stopped writing and looked out the window, remembering the electric atmosphere in town the day after Cain was sentenced to die. It had seemed as if all the shacks and tents along the creek bottoms had emptied out. Hundreds of men had poured through the narrow down-town and rushed past the house on Main Street that day, riding and walking up the hill as to a festival. Cain himself had been chained hand and foot to a buckboard for the trip. The sense of excitement had been so infectious that even Minnie had finally decided to walk up the hill with Maud.

Minnie had lingered at the back of the throng to keep the baby from seeing the gallows. Ned, as Cain's lawyer, had stood at the front wearing his handsome black suit. Sarah Eckelhoff, obviously mourning her lost temperance convert, had sat in her black buggy to one side, wearing a tight-waisted dark dress. When the workers at the wooden platform had unchained Cain, Sarah had suddenly rushed forward in tears. Ned had been the one who caught her and led her back to her buggy.

Remembering the scene gave Minnie a strangely disturbing feeling. She had covered Maud's eyes and turned aside just before the trap opened. That's why she had seen Ned at the black buggy, putting a comforting arm around Sarah. At that moment there had been a squeak of the hinge and a creak from the gallows rope. Then a deathly silence.

Minnie looked out the window, jealous at the memory. Why hadn't Ned comforted her with such solicitude during her year of hardships at Canyon City? In many ways he had been a model husband—gallant in public, passionate in bed, good with the baby. But something was miss-ing. When he wrote poetry, did he notice that she no longer had time to write? What did he do with all the money he earned? And why had he stopped talking about San Francisco? With every month that passed, the gleam from that distant beacon dimmed. When Ned mused instead about "greatness" on the frontier, it only reminded her of her old doubts.

Gradually she had convinced herself it was true: some kind of secret did lurk in his hazy past. At times she wanted to protect him with her love—to keep the unknown poison stoppered. At other times she thirsted to pull the cork and drink the deadly truth dry.

Outside the window, Ned's sunflowers hung heavy with ripening seeds. Summer had yet to bring its worst heat, but the yellow blooms already had given up following the sun across the sky each day. The weary stalks bowed their heads in the yard like rows of sympathetic mourners.

Chapter 19

*Of course I am often defeated, but sometimes I win,
and when I do triumph it is a glory worth winning.*
—Joaquin Miller

"If you look hard enough, darling, you'll find a skeleton in everyone's closet," Sarah Eckelhoff laughed.

Minnie laughed too, and it felt good. She was glad she had come downtown to pick up a package at the Eckelhoff Express. It gave her an excuse to get out of the house, take two-year-old Maud for a walk, and chat with Sarah. Who else could she confide in about Ned?

Sarah leaned forward to whisper, "Still, I think you're right about his past. Now my Manfred—he's always been just a babe in the woods. But Mr. *Miller?* For one thing, he's *older* than he lets on."

"Do you think?" Minnie glanced to little Maud to make sure she was still preoccupied, playing on a baggage cart. Then she whispered back, "What makes you say that?"

Sarah shrugged. "I heard a miner say he knew him from a place called Humbug Creek in California in '53. That would have been *thirteen years* ago. Your husband could be over *thirty* by now."

"I've only known him four years," Minnie admitted. Although she didn't believe Ned would lie about his age—why should he?—it did trouble her to learn he had spent so long in the mining country at a young age. "Sometimes I suspect he has enemies from before I met him. There's so much he doesn't talk about."

"Men never do." Sarah no longer bothered to whisper. "I tell you what. Let's both keep our eyes open." She hefted a bundle onto the counter. "Meanwhile, here's your package."

"Oh yes, I almost forgot. Maud?" Minnie motioned for the little girl to join her. "Come help Mama open it. Let's see what your grandma in Port Orford sent."

"Gammy presents?" Maud asked. She eagerly helped peel back the strings and canvas. Her face fell when she saw the bundle contained only clothes.

"Baby clothes." Sarah noted unenthusiastically.

Minnie nodded. "They were Maud's. I'll be needing them again soon."

"You're expecting? How lovely for you. Good time to check up on the father."

"That isn't why—" Minnie began.

"Well, why not? Remember, eyes open." Sarah winked and flipped open a ledger. "Thanks for dropping by."

Minnie had grown used to Sarah's abrupt ways, but she still felt a little slighted by this dismissal. Sarah usually didn't hurry back to her work. Minnie slowly gathered up the bundle and led Maud outside.

As Minnie walked back through town she wondered if there had been a warning in Sarah's words. No one knew more about the people in Canyon City than Sarah. Hundreds of customers passed through her express office each day. And although half the gossip Sarah repeated was probably invented—perhaps even by Sarah herself—there was usually some truth in it as well. The report of Ned's California mining work in 1853, for example, was too specific to be entirely a fabrication.

Minnie recalculated the numbers. If that date were accurate, Ned must have left Oregon at the age of fifteen. Eight years later he had started writing poems to her from his Idaho pony express route. What had he done in the meantime? Even counting his three months at college and the year she knew he had taught school, a huge gap remained. If Ned was hiding something, keeping her eyes open sounded like good advice.

Minnie walked more slowly down the street, lost in thought. Even if Ned didn't have a ghastly secret, it would be a relief to clear her mind of the troubling suspicion. The question was, how much would Ned tell her, and how much would she have to find out on her own?

* * *

That night when Ned dived headlong into the feather bed and began tickling her hip she caught his hand. "Ned, I've been thinking about Swede."

He popped his head out from beneath the covers, puzzled. "Sweet?"

"No, Swede. You remember. Your best man at our wedding."

"Oh, Swede." He scratched his head. "What about him?"

"It seems a shame we've lost track of him. How long have you known each other?"

Ned shrugged. "A long time. We worked together in California."

"At Humbug Creek in '53?"

She had his attention now. Ned twisted about in bed so he could see the outline of her face. It didn't tell him what she was thinking. "Did Swede tell you about that?"

"I suppose," she said, satisfied now that Sarah's information had been correct. "How many years did you work there with him? Six?"

Suspicion made his answer hesitant. "I don't know. I worked a lot of places."

"Like where?"

He sat up on one elbow. He had left his California years vague for good reason, and she had never seemed to care before. Suddenly she was exploring dangerous territory. "What's gotten into you, Minnie?"

"Nothing," she replied, but his response had already told her a great deal. Something was there, in the past. And she wasn't going to find out by asking him. She would have to do her sleuthing with Sarah's help. "I was just curious about you and Swede, is all."

He settled back again. "I think you'd be more curious about what I did at the courthouse today."

It was odd for Ned to talk about his work, and stranger still that he thought she would ask. "Why? What happened?"

He folded his hands behind his head. "You know how I've wanted the time to work on longer poems?"

"Yes." She had heard him complain that Byron and Browning had published entire books of poetry before reaching his age. It irked her that he never thought of her own abandoned writing career.

"Well, I've found a job with better pay and fewer hours than lawyering. It'll mean more time to work on poetry."

Now it was her turn to sit up in surprise. "You mean we're going to leave Canyon City?"

He chuckled. "No ma'am, we don't even have to move. They're making Canyon City the seat of a brand-new county, and I've filed to be its first county judge."

"What!" For a moment her hopes of leaving the Oregon desert had risen. But if he became a judge, they might be stuck in this plank shack for years. "Don't you have to be elected to a job like that?"

"I can win. People still remember how I captained that expedition against the Paiutes."

"But Ned! What about San Francisco?"

The name of that distant city rankled. Three years had passed since he had fled San Francisco, vowing to return one day in triumph. And he knew Minnie longed to go back. But he felt he needed to gather his strength before launching another attack on civilization.

Ned stroked her hair. "I haven't saved enough money for that kind of a move yet. That's why I'm running for judge. It'll mean better pay and steady hours. I thought you'd be glad."

In reply, Minnie clamped her arm on the feather tick and rolled her back to Ned. What did it matter what she said? He would do what he wanted anyway, just as he had when he left San Francisco and brought her here. Sometimes it seemed her only role in his plans for "greatness" was taking care of babies.

"Minnie? Don't be like that." He touched her shoulder with his hand.

She shook it away. "I'm tired." She would refuse him a night or two. It was small revenge, and she knew she would eventually give in. The loneliness was too great. But she was already cherishing the rebellious thought of subtly probing for The Secret.

* * *

As the seasons slipped past, Minnie did not find much time to pursue her investigation. First there was planning for the new baby. Minnie's mother, who had been so helpful when Maud was born, wrote that she could not travel so far to help again. This time, to Minnie's surprise and pleasure, Ned stood by her. When he discovered that the town's doctor— a man familiar with gunshot wounds and restorative tonics—had never actually attended a birth, Ned insisted he send for a nurse assistant from The Dalles. Ned ran the house as if it were a hospital for the birth, scrubbing floors, cooking meals, and even washing clothes. Then, after the tiny, wide-eyed George Brick Miller was born, Ned canceled all his law work for two weeks until Minnie was back on her feet. Was he merely making up for missing Maud's birth, Minnie wondered, or was he feeling guilty about something else as well?

Shortly afterwards, however, Ned won his election as judge of Grant County, and despite his promises he kept every bit of his law practice. He worked all day, and often stayed late in his office writing the longer poems he claimed might someday be publishable in a book. Minnie was left alone with her usual chores and the task of raising two small children. It was a lonely life in a city with a thousand miners, but almost no families.

One Tuesday afternoon Minnie was serving tea to Sarah Eckelhoff. Maud, now four years old, was playing on the plank floor of the house with her baby brother, quietly herding a cluster of pine cones as if they were farm animals.

"So have you learned anything new about you-know what?" Sarah asked.

The two women had talked so often about Ned's presumed secret that they had developed a kind of code for use when the children were present. Minnie replied, "Actually, I'm fairly certain there is a law charge in the *other state*. But the only way to check the records would be in person."

"Why not go there?" Sarah suggested.

"As if I could, with the children." Minnie rolled her eyes. "Why don't you?"

Sarah laughed. "No, if I were to travel, I'd want to see Kansas again."

Minnie was willing to let Sarah shift the conversation. They hadn't had genuine news about The Secret for a long time. Their detective work had become little more than a game—inventing fantasies, much as Minnie had once dreamed up romantic plots about her mysterious landlady in San Francisco. After all, whatever lurked in Ned's past must have happened such a long time ago it hardly mattered. Perhaps it was best forgotten. "Do you miss the Great Plains that much?"

"No, but I do miss the Kansans. I still take several newspapers to keep track of them." Sarah sipped from her cup of tea. "You know I was so glad to hear they're not going to let women vote there after all—it's *simply* the wrong way to go about winning women's rights. Voting jeopardizes that special relationship between women and men, don't you think?"

"Mmm." Minnie indicated her agreement, refreshing their tea cups from a pot. On the floor beside her, Maud was wiggling the pine cones closer to the baby and mooing.

Sarah continued, "Susan B. Anthony's suffrage campaign must have been something to see, though, what with her renting halls and speaking out in public."

"Did she really?"

"Oh, *yes*. She toured the whole state with George Francis Train. Now *there* I envy her."

"George Train?" Minnie mused. "I don't believe I know the name."

"Minnie darling, you really miss *so much* by not getting down to the express office to read the papers. George Train is probably the most handsome, talked-about man in the *country*. He does publicity for the Union Pacific Railroad—you know, the one building across the Rockies—when he's not involved in some scheme or other. He even claims to be running for *President*. My guess is he's head over heels in love with that crazy Anthony woman, even though she's plainer than a straight-backed chair. Why, he even offered her three thousand dollars to publish a women's rights newspaper—to be called *The Revolution*, no less."

"Good heavens! To be published by a woman? She turned it down, I imagine?"

"Not at all. I'd have brought a copy, but I refuse to subscribe. And now

Mr. Train's locked in a Dublin jail for smuggling explosives into Ireland. They've found out he's one of those secret *Fenians*, you know, who want to overthrow the British. It just goes to show, women should stay clear of politics. Dirtying one's hands with men's business only weakens a woman's *spiritual* power."

"Ma!" a voice on the floor squealed. "George is taking my cows!" The squeal rose to a wild screech as Maud shoved her baby brother backwards, scattering pine cones across the room. When George's head conked against the floorboards his startled expression melted into tears.

"Children, shame on you!" Minnie exclaimed. "Can't you behave when we have company? Maud, you go straight to the bedroom until I say otherwise. And I'm putting away the pine cones until you can play with them without arguing."

As Minnie rocked George on her lap to calm his cries, she noticed Sarah gazing out the window with a strangely satisfied expression. "I'm terribly sorry this had to happen while you were here."

"Oh, that's all right," Sarah replied, adopting her familiar smile. "Women control the world by controlling the children, I always say."

George began to nurse, and for a moment all was quiet.

"But you know—" Sarah began slowly, "there *is* a secret to controlling children." She lowered her voice to a whisper as she straightened her white gloves. "The Chinese have a special tonic—they say it's made from *rhubarb*—that can . . . actually . . . *prevent pregnancy*."

Minnie caught her breath. "That's just a story!" For years there had been rumors about contraceptive theories, even though most states had obscenity laws banning discussion of the topic in public.

Sarah gave a quiet laugh. "Oh, but it *isn't*. When my husband was organizing freight for the railroad coolies in Sacramento, I visited an old Chinese doctor by the name of *Hong Wo*. A spiritual man, with hollow eyes and fingernails *three inches long*. Believe me, Minnie, there is no greater power over men than the power to *control childbirth*."

"*You* don't—" Minnie whispered, not daring to complete the sentence.

"But yes I *do*. What do you think would happen if I had children? Manfred would have me busy with them all the time, of course. As it is, I have all the freedoms a woman could want."

"Don't you *want* to have children?" Minnie couldn't help wondering whether the rhubarb tonic really worked. Or perhaps was Sarah barren, and she didn't know it?

"I can have them when I *choose*, my dear." Abruptly Sarah rose and smiled. "Now I must be going. Oh, and I *do* hope you and your husband will be able to accompany me to see the Chinese New Year's parade

Saturday in Tiger Town. Manfred will be out driving the express, you know, but I'd *hate* to miss it. A merchant acquaintance of mine has a store there and promises us a pleasant evening."

Minnie's mind raced to encompass this sudden invitation. White people seldom ventured into the new Chinese settlement, but Sarah seemed so confident, and it would be nice to have an excuse to get out of the house for an evening. "What about the children?"

"Leave them with Madame Fleurot," Sarah smiled from the doorway. Since Minnie was still nursing the baby, Sarah let herself out.

*   *   *

Tiger Town was a jumble of more than a hundred shanties packed together at the confluence of Canyon Creek and the John Day River. In the Eckelhoff buggy, Ned, Minnie, and Sarah were riding toward the town on a road lined with tiny, immaculate vegetable gardens. Then Sarah called out, "Hang on! Here we go," and drove skillfully into the narrow, crooked alleyways of the Chinese city.

Festive paper lanterns lit the alleys amidst a haze of burning incense. Lines of drying clothes waved over the low roofs of the laundries. The shacks on either hand nearly scraped the wheels as the buggy turned sharply through the dark streets.

"Sure strange seeing a town without horses," Ned said.

Sarah nodded. "Manfred usually unloads his wagon at the edge of town. They don't know a *thing* about horses and actually *prefer* to send porters. Whoa! Here's a detour."

Suddenly she veered away from an alley blocked with piles of cattle bones and tin cans. "They don't waste *anything,* you know. Those bones are for *fertilizer.* They get tin and solder out of the cans."

Finally Sarah pulled up before the only stone building in town, a structure so new that its second story still seemed to be under construction. At once a Chinese man came out to meet them, bowing repeatedly. He wore a long, narrow beard and a colorful, sleeved robe. In the style typical of Chinese men, he had shaved the front half of his head and pulled the remainder of his hair into a rope-like, waist-length plait.

"I am deeply honored by your visit, Mrs. Eckelhoff. Could your husband not come?" the man asked. His flawless British accent astonished both Ned and Minnie.

"Manfred's busy so I brought some guests instead," Sarah replied. "Judge and Mrs. Miller—I'd like you to meet Kam Wah Chung. He's the merchant I talked about."

Ned managed to offer his hand. "Howdy, Mr. Chung."

"Yes, very good, thank you," the man said, smiling strenuously and bowing his way back from the offered hand. "Won't you please come in? I would be delighted if you would permit me to show you my store before we share dinner and watch the parade."

As they followed the Chinese man Sarah whispered, "He once studied at the English schools in Hong Kong. And he's called Mr. *Kam*, not Mr. Chung. They put the last name first."

"Ah, so that's it." Ned ducked through the building's low doorway. He noticed the shop was built like a fortress, with stone walls nearly two feet thick and double doors of plate metal. The few windows were small and battened with metal grates. Obviously the Chinese did not feel entirely at ease so close to Canyon City's rowdy American miners. The store was a refuge from stray bullets—and from the intentional potshots of jealous white miners who disliked the "Orientals" in Oregon.

Inside, candles lit a dim room. Incense and herbs heavily scented the air. One of the shelves displayed Chinese newspapers and books, another had religious miniatures built of bamboo or carved from jade, while still others were stocked with silk, firecrackers, and baskets. One entire wall displayed Oriental foodstuffs: tea, rice, birds' nests, duck eggs preserved in wax, and the ducks themselves, split and dried like cod for the journey from China. Mr. Kam took them to the counter where he kept his business records—a book listing when each Chinese laborer had been imported and which mine he worked for. A single grim page listed the dates corpses had been shipped back to China for burial. Posted about the counter were notices that he said related to the popular and profitable Chinese lotteries. On the wall behind he pointed out shelves jammed with ceramic pots of herbs, bark, powders, and liquors.

"Liquors?" Ned asked. "Your store sells everything else. Is it a saloon, too?"

Mr. Kam merely smiled and bowed, but Sarah said, "The alcohol's *medicinal* only. You'll never see a Chinaman staggering out of a bar. They have a *much* more refined custom. Perhaps Mr. Kam will show you after dinner."

Mr. Kam led them into the kitchen, a narrow back room with a wood stove, four crude bunks, and a plank table against the wall. The table was decked with a surprisingly ornate dinner setting of ceramic bowls. "Please, you are my guests," Mr. Kam said, handing each of them an orange.

"An orange! How very kind," Minnie said. She had not seen an orange since her stay in San Francisco. With her eyes closed, she smelled the exotic fruit. The pungent odor seemed to carry her far away to a rich land of palms and shady bowers. She almost wished she did not have to open her eyes to the dark back room of a Chinatown shop in the Oregon desert.

Ned held the rough straightback chairs as Minnie, and then Sarah, arranged their dresses to sit at the tiny kitchen table. Soon Kam began bringing them dinner from the woodstove: soup, egg rolls, chow chow, and tea. Ned's and Minnie's appetites, already reduced by the strangeness of the food, were further frustrated by the ceramic soup spoons and chopsticks.

After dinner, when the table had been cleared, the sound of several distant pops filtered in from outside. "Is that gunfire?" Minnie asked, alarmed.

Mr. Kam smiled. "Firecrackers. It is a sign for the paraders to gather. But we still have time for the gentlemen to smoke after dinner, if Judge Miller is interested."

"Sure," Ned shrugged. "What have you got here, cigars?"

Mr. Kam produced an ungainly water pipe that looked like a spidery candelabra. With a stick of kindling from the stove, he lit a small central cup.

Sarah nudged Ned with her elbow. "It's the charming tradition I told you about."

"Looks like some kind of peace pipe," Ned replied.

"What a lovely way to express it," Sarah said.

Minnie stiffened slightly. "It's opium, isn't it?" She did not want to offend their Chinese host, but she disliked the thought of the drug.

Sarah waved her objection away. "It's the same medicine everyone uses in laudanum."

Mr. Kam inhaled with closed eyes. Then he placed the pipe on the table before Ned.

"Go on, Judge, try it," Sarah urged.

A wisp of smoke wove upward in hazy loops, like the fleeting cursive script of a ghostly hand. Ned held the pipe's mouthpiece a moment, as if weighing it. Long ago in a Wintu *cawel* he had shared a strange pipe with Paquita's grandfather. The ritual had been a bridge between cultures. Was this so different?

Ned nodded to Mr. Kam. Then he put the mouthpiece to his lips and sucked a small sample of the smoke. It was sweet and warm, less bitter than cigar smoke. He was a little disappointed that it did not produce any noticeable effect.

Mr. Kam took another turn smoking from the opium pipe and pushed it back toward Ned.

When Ned declined this time, Sarah reached boldly for the pipe. "Here, let me try." Before anyone could object, she took a long, deep breath of the smoky drug.

Minnie blinked in astonishment at her friend's affrontery.

Mr. Kam's perpetual smile slipped momentarily to a shocked stare. When a crackle of firecrackers went off outside, Ned seized the distraction. "Isn't that the parade you mentioned, Mr. Kam?"

Their Chinese host quickly regained his compusure. "Yes. Of course. We should move outside while we can still find a good place to watch." He quickly cleared the water pipe away from the table. Then he bowed and held a hand toward the door.

As they made their way out among the crowd of Chinese men along the narrow street, Ned finally began to feel the glow of the opium. By the time the vanguard of the parade made its noisy appearance, a dull warmth was rising up through him like the tingle of an illicit love. Even the raucous parade became part of the strange, slow thrill.

A throng of blue-suited Chinese men surged through the winding street, banging pans and lighting firecrackers. Above the resulting fog of gunpowder rose dozens of waving poles topped with lanterns and wide-mouthed paper kites. Next came a makeshift cloth-and-paper dragon, bowing its head and undulating to the clacking of the dozens of wooden-soled straw sandals underneath its flapping body. Masked musicians alongside put out a fiendish accompaniment on their cymbals and gongs.

Finally the procession assumed a quieter, respectful air. Three elaborate litters, carried on the shoulders of eight men each, gradually came into view.

Sarah caught Ned's arm and whispered, "There! I was hoping we'd see them if we came tonight."

"What?" Ned's head still hovered from the opium. The sensual touch of Sarah's hand seemed to have lit his whole arm with an alarming intimacy. He managed to focus on the parade. "Who are they, princes or something?"

"No. Slave girls. *Pleasure* slaves!"

The three litters had tasseled roofs and richly brocaded silk curtains drawn back on the sides. Inside each, seated on a pillow, was a young, almond-eyed girl with jet-black hair and painted features. Each girl wore the same style of loose black pants and shirt, all of shimmering silk, and each smiled timidly at the Chinese men lining the street. The girls were evidently the finale of the New Year's parade, for when they had passed, the crowd began to disperse.

"*Slavery* in a free country!" Sarah whispered.

"How horrible!" Minnie said, straightening.

Ned struggled to shake the dreamy arousal warming him from the inside. To prove he could cut through the fog, he laid out as careful a legal argument as he could muster. "I just wonder if you aren't jumping to conclusions. How do you know they're not like Asa Mercer's girls?" Everyone knew Mercer, the entrepreneur who had brought boatloads of Civil War widows from Massachusetts around the Horn as brides for Puget Sound bachelors. "Mercer gets paid for his trouble, but he's a matchmaker, not a slave trader. There's no evidence these China girls are slaves either."

"Ned!" Minnie exclaimed, surprised by his coolness. "Didn't you see the way they looked at the men? They're terrified."

"Of course they are, Theresa, but your husband *does* have a point about the evidence. We don't even know who owns them. And it's going to be hard getting proof of *anything* from the Chinese men." Sarah lowered her voice. "In fact, it would *probably* be safer not to talk about this in the middle of Tiger Town at all." She stood up briskly and straightened her dress. "I suppose it is time we be getting home anyway."

As Minnie was getting into the buggy, Sarah gave Ned a sideways glance. "Go ahead, Judge. Why don't you drive?"

Ned shrugged, took the reins from the clip by the footboard, and positioned himself in the middle of the cushioned seat.

On the ride home, Minnie couldn't help thinking again about the opium. It was a legal drug, but it had a dark reputation. Ned should never have tried it, even at the risk of offending Mr. Kam. Certainly Sarah had gone too far by sampling the smoke as well—a white woman, in China-town, taking such a liberty! Still, Minnie couldn't help feeling a little curious. What kind of effect did opium have? Was there a subtle difference in Ned's manner, a quiet distancing? It was as if Ned and Sarah had begun drifting somewhere she could not follow. The thought made Minnie feel a little left out.

The riding lamp threw its nervous light ahead at the miners' tents along the Canyon Creek road. The buggy itself was as dark as the starless sky. But Ned could feel Sarah's warm presence against his left side—and the soft but deliberate pressure of her breast against his tensed arm.

* * *

Nearly a week later, Minnie was sitting up alone in the kitchen after putting the children to bed when she heard the family cow begin a strange, pained bellowing outside in the yard. For a while Minnie ignored the sound. She was working at the kitchen table by candlelight, correcting her husband's poetry for rhyme and meter. Ned would expect her to be finished when he came home from the office.

Minnie tapped out the rhythm of the verse with her fingertips. Each of the cow's urgent cries made her lose count. Finally she put down her quill in frustration, threw a cloak about her shoulders, and went outside.

As soon as she found the big Holstein in a corner of the yard, straining its round body with each cry, she remembered that it was due to come fresh this month. There was something desperate about the animal's effort, however, that told her the calving would not be as easy this time as it had been the two previous years. She watched a minute, her concern growing, and then made up her mind. The cow needed a doctor. She would have to walk down to her husband's office in the dark to get him to send for help. It would mean leaving the children alone in the house, but they were sleeping, and she would not be gone long.

Main Street had never seemed darker than on that spring evening as she hurried down the hill. A chill wind blew through the bare branches of the aspen along the creek, black against black. Down in the town a few lighted windows cast a dull glow over the empty streets.

Before Minnie could reach the light, however, she was surprised to see a woman's silhouette running across the street ahead of her. At once Minnie stopped, wondering what another woman could possibly be doing on the streets this late at night.

Her astonishment increased when, after following the dark figure through the shadows to the side of the courthouse, she saw it stop and tap furtively on the door of Judge Miller's office.

*   *   *

Ned took a step back when Sarah appeared in his office door. She slipped past him into the room. "Quick, close the door."

"Sary—" he stammered. "What are you doing here?"

She held out a file of papers innocently. "I've brought a statement by one of the Chinese slave girls on her condition. I'm afraid they may torture her if they find out she's complained. The Chinese man who translated it for me can't be trusted to keep quiet. I don't have anyone to turn to but you."

Ned hesitated, watching her eyes. Then he took the papers. "Well, all right. I reckon it'll only take a minute to see if you've got a case or not." He sat at his desk and immediately absorbed himself in the handwritten pages, without even offering Sarah a chair.

She did not seem to mind, but wandered slowly about the office with a thin, satisfied smile. She pulled off her white gloves, one finger at a time, and left them on the edge of Ned's desk. "That testimony is from one of the girls we saw at the parade," she said casually, dropping the shawl from her shoulders to reveal the low neckline of her black dress. "Here's her signature, there," she added, sitting on the desk and leaning slightly forward to point out the Chinese characters.

Ned swallowed. Perfume rose from the cleft between the creamy curves of her breasts. "Sary—"

"I've wanted to tell you how *much* I enjoyed that evening," she whispered, using more breath than the words required. "It made me wonder why we haven't seen each other for so long."

Ned closed his eyes and took a deep breath. "Sary, don't pretend you've forgotten why. When Minnie came it had to be over." He had been so lonely that first winter in Canyon City, working on a mining claim to pay for the house he was building. The distant, strident tone of Minnie's letters had left him feeling even emptier. For a short time, Sarah had offered company and warmth. There had been no pretense of an enduring love. Sarah seemed content to drift through life from one thrill to another. She had already lost interest by the time he told her he was going to Port Orford for Minnie. Since then he had tried to put the whole embarrassing episode behind him. But it was hard to block out such sensual memories. And Sarah had not let him forget. From time to time she had cast him teasing little reminders, as if just to prove that she still had power over him. Now that she was sitting on his desk, Ned's palms had begun to sweat.

"Yes, but it's been four years, darling." She gave him a beguiling smile and ran her finger around a button on his chest. "If the poor lamb hasn't found out our little secret in that much time, she won't know now."

"I—I don't know." He pulled away, but not as far as he had intended.

"All right, then, I'll let you decide." She sat back facing him and untied her hair, shaking it loose in a shining blond stream. Then she cocked her shoulders back. Her breasts pressed against the low neckline of the tight dress, creasing them softly just above the nipples Ned knew would be pink and erect.

"Well, Hiner?"

*   *   *

Ned had to drink nearly a half bottle of whiskey before he could go home that night. As he staggered out into the dark streets, the frenzied howls of coyotes made him shudder. They almost sounded close enough to be coming from the plank house on the hill.

By the time he reached the house the howls had stopped. He was rehearsing a short excuse for working late when he stumbled on the steps and thumped face first onto the porch. He picked himself up, cursing quietly for having ever added on a porch at all. Then he tried the door. To his surprise, it didn't open. He rattled it a bit, but it appeared to have been somehow bolted or barred from inside.

He looked to the window. Sticks of kindling had been propped on the inside sill to bar it closed as well. What on earth was going on?

He stumbled around the house to the side door and began pounding on it with his fists. "Minnie? Are you in there? *Minnie?*"

He stopped short at the sound of suppressed sobs from within. A voice he hardly recognized called back faintly, "Go away!"

"Minnie?"

"Go sleep with *her*," the voice cried.

He stood back dizzily from the door. His thoughts spun about him, hardly letting the significance of her words penetrate. When they did, he swallowed dryly, his face suddenly cold. "Minnie, she's *nothing!* It's over, I swear, I promise!"

There was no reply from within—not even the crying now. He thought of breaking his way through a window with a rock, but he gave it up. What good would it do? There would be no rest waiting for him inside that night. Nor did he feel right about the prospect of shouting her into submission, considering what she seemed to know.

He put his hands over his face and nearly lost his balance. Tomorrow, he thought. Tomorrow she would be more reasonable. Until then he would be better off finishing the whiskey bottle in his office.

After staring up woozily at the stars for a while, as if waiting for them to offer some better advice, he stumbled back to Main Street and down the hill.

* * *

Sunlight stabbed through Ned's office window. Unwillingly, he sat up out of the painful glare and nursed his throbbing head. He couldn't remember—

When he remembered he stood up too fast and cringed, groaning. Gradually he groped his way to the window in the office door. At first it was a little comforting to see the familiar stage pull out from in front of the Eckelhoff Express and disappear down the street in a little haze of dust, just as it did every Friday morning. But then he caught sight of Sarah standing by the express office door—pale, wringing her hands—and a sudden, cold fear swept through him.

He rushed headlong out the back door of the courthouse, taking the steep, heart-pounding shortcut up the hill. As he scrambled up he noticed the vultures circling over the house. And when he crawled under the board fence he saw why: the family cow lay dead before him with its twisted, half-born calf still hanging out, already partly eaten away by the coyotes. White-faced, Ned turned away.

In the open doorway he leaned against the jamb, waiting for the blood to return to his head.

Finally he walked unsteadily into the house. It seemed pointless now to expect any sign of hope inside.

The little cod liver oil bottle behind the bookshelf was missing, of course. It occurred to him that if he had confiscated her "secret" supply of butter money she could never have left, but he let the thought pass.

The bedroom was still orderly, considering the haste with which her clothes must have been packed. The exception was the Bloomer costume that Minnie had worn about the house every few weeks for so many years. The baggy pants lay rumpled in a corner, splattered black with a broken inkwell.

Ned returned heavily to the front room, through the awful silence left behind by his wife and children. Then he put his head on his arms in the middle of the table, and he cried.

It was only when he ran his cold hands over his eyes and sat up that he noticed the papers piled neatly before him on the table. They were his poetry manuscripts, apparently unharmed. He took the top sheet and saw the lovely, looping handwriting across the top—the one thing he would never have anticipated: "Read and Checked, March 15, 1868."

Chapter 20

But because one bough is broken,
Must the broad oak be undone?
                    —Joaquin Miller, *Specimens*

"Theresa!" Minnie's mother called up the stairs of the Dyer house in Port Orford. "Mail from Canyon City."

Minnie took a long breath, but still could not control her anger. "Burn it!" she yelled down the stairs. She rolled little George onto his back, a bit more roughly than she had intended, to change his diaper.

"I won't do anything of the kind," her mother's voice replied. "When you're feeling more yourself, it'll be in the glass cabinet."

Feeling more herself? Minnie didn't want to be her old, compliant self anymore. Her stomach tightened into a knot of rage. For years she had been cheated by the two people she had cared about most in Canyon City. Like an innocent idiot she had tiptoed around the dark secret lurking in Ned's past. Never had she dreamed the hidden truth would be so terrible. An affair with her best friend!

She unpinned the diaper, expecting it would only be wet. But a sudden ghastly stench from a mass of greenish paste left her head reeling. "Oh, Lord." She leaned back for fresher air, held her breath as if for an underwater dive, and then went to work with the washcloth.

Eckelhoff. Perhaps Sarah's betrayal hurt the most. Minnie had wanted a friend, a confidante, so badly in the remote mining town that she had blinded herself to the woman's treachery. She had looked the other way when Sarah falsified express records. She had kept quiet when Sarah smoked the Chinese merchant's opium. And all the time, Sarah had been secretly laughing at her, romancing her husband. The Bloomer costume and the temperance pledges hadn't been signs of moral conviction; they had been excuses to parade about in pants and strike up conversations with men. Sarah had been nothing more than a devious thrill-seeker.

In her anger Minnie cinched the new diaper so tightly that George, who almost never cried, let out a tiny complaining squeal.

"Oh, honey, I'm sorry! It wasn't your fault. You've been so good. You and Maud both." Minnie hugged him close. Then, with her free hand, she gingerly carried the dirty diaper downstairs to rinse it at the washboard outside.

On the way she couldn't help glancing across the dining room to see if the Canyon City letter really was in the glass cabinet. To her surprise it was not a letter, but rather a small package. Her mother had stood it in front of the scrapbook she had collected of Minnie's published love stories from the *Golden Era* years ago. Minnie tossed her dark hair and walked on.

Scrubbing the diaper outside, she decided it was Ned who had hurt her most. Only a man she loved could wound her this deeply. Three times now she had marched beside him into disaster. First he had swept her off her feet to Eugene City, where she had been scorned by his dictatorial parents. Then he had bedazzled her with the literary world of San Francisco, only to yank her away as soon as she had tasted success. Finally she had followed him into the desert of Canyon City, a town with false-fronted buildings and inhabitants to match. There would have to be changes—a lot of changes—before she would listen to him again.

After washing her hands she walked back into the big, still house. A clock ticked. The muffled surf gently roared. The mysterious package waited behind the glass.

"I don't like keeping secrets anymore," she said out loud. The baby goggled at her unsteadily as she opened the glass door of the cabinet. In fact, she did feel a certain relief now that Ned's past had been exposed. How pointless it had been to worry so much about his early California years! All this time she had been looking for The Secret in the wrong place. Now the worst was over. If there were any surprises left, they would almost have to be good.

She opened the package and slid out a thin, unfamiliar paperback book. Its title, printed in large black letters, was *Specimens*. Puzzled, she unfolded the accompanying letter.

Dearest Minnie:

If you are reading this, perhaps I have a chance to convince you how sorry I am, and how much I love you. I made a terrible mistake, Minnie, and can hardly hope to be forgiven. If only we could undo what has happened!

To prepare a fresh start for us I've sold the old house in Canyon

City and moved to this spot, a cabin on Canyon Creek about eight miles south of town. It is quiet and immensely romantic here, with pines, fish, deer, eagles, and the like. Won't you come? You know I would gladly leave Grant County altogether, but as judge my hands are tied, at least until the end of my term in 1870.

Meanwhile I have been briefly to Portland, to see to having my little book of poems printed. The 500 copies cost me $96, and I have placed some of them in a Portland bookstore for sale at fifty cents each. At the same time I saw that Bret Harte and Charles W. Stoddard have both just published their first books of poetry. It seemed like a prophetic coincidence to me, although the odds are that word of my humble *Buke* will never even reach the sage ears of those San Francisco scribblers.

Minnie glanced at the paperbound volume that had been sent with the letter. Its 54 pages held just two poems. The first, which she had never liked, dealt with an Indian chieftain's daughter during the Rogue River Indian War, while the other was a descriptive verse about mountains and streams. She observed with small satisfaction that he had incorporated her corrections.

Then she flipped the booklet shut and stared out over the ocean's slow, white waves, disappointed. The apology was there. But the man didn't yet realize how much pain he had caused. He was still thinking only of himself.

* * *

"I'm not at all sure children can be raised properly without a father's influence," Mrs. Dyer said, washing the dishes while Minnie dried. "Sometimes I think our family suffered from that too, with your father at sea so much. Now I look at you children and just wonder how things might have been different if you'd had the guidance of a firmer hand when you were Maud's age."

Minnie ran her dishtowel over a plate mechanically, watching out the window as her sister Emily, now a young woman, walked across the yard with a young man leading a horse.

"Theresa, are you listening to me?"

"Yes, of course, mother."

"What I'm telling you is that every good husband needs a second chance. If you can't forgive him for a moment of weakness, then you yourself will be to blame for whatever happens to the children."

Minnie set her plate carefully in the cupboard. "I only wish I could be sure it was nothing more than a moment of weakness. He was all I had in Canyon City, outside of the children, and then I found out I didn't have *him*."

"How you talk! Of course you have him. He's your husband, and he works hard to provide for you." Mrs. Dyer warmed up the dishwater with a kettle from the stove, and then put her hands on her hips, facing her daughter. "Just what do you think you're going to do now, anyway, Theresa? Answer me that, what are you going to do? You're welcome here, and the grandchildren too, but you can't stay here forever. Just how are you going to raise those children?"

Minnie laid down her towel and looked again at her sister in the yard, who was laughing silently at whatever her gentleman caller had just said.

* * *

Summer passed, shrouded in the cool fogs typical of the Oregon Coast. When the sun returned in September, Minnie was reading yet another of Ned's letters.

> Every week I apologize, yet your silence seems to say this is not enough. I have sent $200 travel expenses in your name to the Eugene City post office, where it will wait for you until you wish to accept it. Tell me what else I can do!
>
> Incidentally, the express business in town recently sold out after announcing it had not shown a profit for over a year. The Eckelhoffs have since booked on the *Brother Jonathan* to San Francisco. Now the only stage line is based in John Day, down by the Chinese village—a loss for Canyon City, but perhaps a gain for us?

Minnie reread these sentences to savor the news. The demise of the Eckelhoff Express did more to lift her spirits than all the rest of her husband's pleas combined. Her satisfaction was sweetened by an image of Sarah forced out of town in poverty. No doubt her erstwhile friend's habit of stealing from the business' accounts had been the real cause of the bankruptcy. Deceit had caught up with Sarah at last. In a better mood now, Minnie finished the letter.

> I have a surprise here for you and the children, too: something pretty to wear, with feathers and ribbons. Can you guess?
> Your loving husband,
> Ned.

She could not suppress a small smile at this final incentive. Of course it was a ridiculous ploy, but it was just the kind of childish teasing that made it sound like he really might still love her. The thought gave her an unbidden flutter in her chest—a flicker of the old love, tinged with a new uncertainty.

She put down the letter unsteadily, realizing she had already decided to go back. But this time she would lay down solid rules. Quickly she organized them in her mind so she could spell everything out in a letter to Ned. Her first demand would be faithfulness, of course: she would leave Ned for good if he dallied with another woman. Second came the dream of returning to the literary world of San Francisco: as soon as Ned's term expired they would use the money he had saved to move out of the Oregon backwoods forever. Then maybe *both* of them could take a shot at literary success.

Suddenly Maud ran by, letting herself be chased by little George. Minnie called the girl to her side. "Maud, would you like to take a trip?"

"Where to?"

"To see your Papa again."

The five year old clapped her hands and gave a little jump. "Yes ma'am!"

*   *   *

Minnie had just picked up the ten double-eagle gold coins Ned left for her at the post office in Eugene City. She was herding the children out the door when she heard the voice she had been dreading for days.

"There they are!" Margaret Miller cried. She and Hulings were driving up in their old wagon.

"Oh, you poor, dear children!" white-haired Margaret Miller went on, stepping down from the wagon and hurrying toward Maud and George. Her bony hands shook. "We've been worried to death about you! Have you been getting enough to eat?"

Minnie flushed with anger at her mother-in-law's familiar, thinly veiled criticism. As if Minnie didn't feed the children! All the indignities Minnie had suffered in the Millers' household rushed back like the sudden memory of a nightmare. But this time she was determined to stand up to her domineering in-laws. She quickly picked up the little boy and got a tight grip on Maud's hand. "The children are *fine*, Mrs. Miller."

Hulings tied up the team to a hitching rail and strode toward Minnie. "We heard you got in on the stage, so we came right down to fetch you all home." He cleared his throat and pointed to the wagon, but before he could speak again he was overwhelmed by a coughing fit.

Minnie held her ground, her voice edged with steel. "It's very kind of you both to offer your hospitality, but I have already made arrangements to stay at the Renfrew Hotel."

Margaret stopped, obviously taken aback. "Alone? No respectable woman would go spend the night in some hotel when she could stay with—"

"No respectable traveler would impose on elderly relatives," Minnie interrupted pointedly. "I will stay at the hotel with the children until the steamboat leaves on Thursday."

"Three days? In a hotel?" the old woman gasped. "Well, I never!"

Minnie gave her a forced smile, still not loosening her grip on Maud's hand. "You will be welcome to visit us there."

As Minnie walked away with the children, Margaret Miller whispered loudly to her husband, "Are you going to stand there and let that woman just—just *kidnap* the grandchildren like that?"

"I don't like the looks of it much, either," Hulings replied slowly.

* * *

That evening in the dining room of the Renfrew Hotel Minnie felt as conspicuous as Gulliver in Lilliput. The Renfrew was the preferred hostelry of theater people passing through on West Coast tours, and as it so happened, every table but hers was taken by General Tom Thumb's Talented Troupe of Midgets. Nearly two dozen of these little men in gaudy military costumes swaggered about or stood on the chairs, at times flipping plates and spoons with acrobatic nonchalance. Minnie kept up a constant, one-sided conversation with her two wide-eyed children in the hopes of diverting their attention. But the dwarf theater people were far louder and more interesting, arguing in gruff sopranos about the table service.

Before anyone had been served, a clean-shaven man of ordinary adult stature came whistling down the stairs to the hall. He paused a moment on the steps to survey the room, then made his way to Minnie's table.

"Forgive me, Madam—Horatio Hillary Hill—but might I be permitted to share your table?"

Minnie reddened, but nodded her assent, hoping this well-mannered man might more successfully distract the children. He wore an elegant black suit that set off his pale blond hair and delicate features in a manner Minnie liked. She guessed he might be in his late thirties.

"You have two lovely children, Mrs.—pardon me, I didn't catch your name?"

"Miller. Mrs. C. H. Miller, and this is Maud and the little one George."

Mr. Hill beamed at the rosy-cheeked children. Just then there was a particularly raucous shouting and banging of tables from the midgets nearby.

"My, my," Mr. Hill said to Minnie, sitting up taller. "Patience is a virtue at the Renfrew. It seems my miniature colleagues have yet to understand there is but one waiter and one bill of fare."

"Are you with General Thumb, then?" Minnie asked, more disturbed by this prospect than by the evident failings of the hotel.

"No, no. But I am in the theater. I do readings from Shakespeare, primarily."

"How interesting." Minnie now remembered where she had seen the name H. H. Hill—on posters about the town. Imagine, having dinner with a famous lecturer! He seemed such a handsome, cultured gentleman, too, with none of the wilderness crudity that marked Ned. For an instant she wondered what might have happened if she had met a man like Mr. Hill first. The thought left her with a pleasant, heady confusion. "It must be very exciting, traveling and speaking."

"All other professions pale before the thrill of the stage, my good lady," Mr. Hill assured her. "Bringing the works of the poets to life, transporting an audience away from its daily cares. The pity of it is, I despise the travel, and most towns only seem to have patience for a few nights of Shakespeare and another evening of assorted modern bards."

"I admire anyone who would devote himself to promoting other people's verse," Minnie said. Then she lowered her eyes and confessed, "I once wrote a bit of poetry myself. But I'm sure it's all been forgotten by now."

"Really? Was any of it published?"

"Only under a pseudonym, of course." She gave a small, embarrassed shrug. "I was young then. I imagined it would be clever to use an alliterative pen name, so I called myself Minnie Myrtle."

The clean-shaven man dropped his hands to the table with astonishment. "Not the Minnie Myrtle of the *Golden Era*! There used to be something from the 'Sweet Singer of the Coquille' in almost every issue! To be sure it was—maybe two, three years ago, but thousands of people read the *Era*, and if I remember the name, I'm sure they do."

Minnie blushed a deep red. "Do you think?"

"Most certainly." Then his voice became earnest. "Seriously, Mrs. Miller, it doesn't seem right to let your writing be forgotten. We ought to take your poems to the stage. That's the way to really promote your work."

Minnie held her hand to her throat, flattered and a bit startled. "On the stage?"

"You could even read one yourself at one of my programs."

Minnie drew back; he had gone too far. "Really, Mr. Hill, I don't think that would be appropriate." Burlesque dancers and actresses of dubious repute sometimes traveled with theater groups, but no white woman had ever lectured from a public stage in Oregon.

The waiter came with their dinners, and Minnie was glad for the interruption. As much as she enjoyed Mr. Hill's praise and attention, she was tired of being urged to do things that ultimately only led to her humiliation. She had had enough of that from Sarah.

Mr. Hill sighed. "Forgive me. I suppose I must have sounded rather overbearing on such short acquaintance. It comes of being a lecturer, I'm afraid. I suppose you wouldn't even allow me to read from your work?"

"But of course I would. I'd be honored." Minnie touched his hand, intending only to assure him, but when his blue eyes looked up into hers she suddenly felt the thrill of this man's nearness. Her fingertips remained poised on his strong, smooth-haired wrist as if she had been caught stealing candy and didn't know whether to feign innocence or take another piece.

Smoothly he slipped a card from his coat pocket and folded her hand over it. "A ticket to my program tonight at the First Christian Church. I hope you'll accept it as a modest royalty fee for whatever work you permit me to read."

Minnie looked at the ticket and then shook her head with regret. "I'm afraid I couldn't leave the children, and I couldn't go out alone in any case."

"Of course. Thoughtless of me." Then he suddenly brightened. "I tell you what. Why don't I give you a private reading here in the hotel—say, tomorrow afternoon? Something light, that the children would be able to enjoy. It'd help ease the boredom here for me, and it'd give you a chance to coach me in the proper reading of your work."

"Could we, Mama?" Maud asked, her mouth full of mashed potatoes.

"Really, Maud! Don't talk again until you've swallowed." Minnie turned to Mr. Hill and assumed a reserved smile. "I think we'd all be pleased to hear you read tomorrow. We're in Room 204."

When Mr. Hill smiled back broadly, Minnie lowered her eyes to avoid his forthright look. For an instant she regretted what she had done. It was hardly proper for a married woman to allow a man into her hotel room. But they certainly couldn't meet in a public place. And the children would be in the room to ensure everything was above board. Besides, he seemed such a trustworthy gentleman. The reading would merely be a literary diversion to help pass the time until their Thursday steamboat departure.

And yet why on earth was her heart beating so fast?

* * *

Minnie led the children to the river landing on Thursday, smiling to herself. She was not yet so old, or so dull, that she couldn't interest a man if she chose. What a difference there was between Mr. Hill and Ned! Both were men of poetry, but Ned was self-centered and coarse by comparison. Had he ever really read her writings? Mr. Hill seemed to know and treasure every verse she had published.

She herded the children up the gangplank of the riverboat and collected them on a breezy deck bench. Then she looked out across the river and sighed. How was it possible she felt both regret and shame, at the same time? Of course nothing untoward had happened between her and Mr. Hill—the children had always been on hand—but she felt guilty nonetheless. What disturbed her most were her feelings.

She had desired Mr. Hill. She had imagined this strong young lecturer pressing her in his arms—and yes, peeling away her clothing and making tumultuous love.

With a rushing sound of water, the ship's big stern paddle began to churn. The slow throb of the steam engine shook through her. She closed her eyes, remembering his smoldering gaze at last night's dinner. By an unspoken agreement, they had again "accidentally" shared a table. He had held her chair gallantly and ordered wine. Afterwards, as they waited for dessert, he had stretched in his chair, and his shoe had casually touched her own. She should have pulled her foot back at once, but she hadn't. Their ankles had remained nestled against each other, unseen beneath the white tablecloth, for countless minutes. The secret thrill had left her mouth dry.

Still, she had kept her honor. She had withstood the very real temptation of adultery, where Ned had failed. But inside, she knew how weak the wall she had defended really was. Would that knowledge make it harder for her to press her demands with Ned? And would she discover that her love for Ned had dimmed, now that another light had shone upon her? She leaned out to look up the river, more worried than ever about returning to Canyon City.

By nightfall the steamship reached Salem and was forced to dock, since the pilot had no means to navigate the winding river in the dark. Minnie stayed in the rickety hotel facing the dock, where a brass bell rang in the pre-dawn darkness to warn the sleepy steamboat passengers of the ship's imminent departure.

The second day the ship could go no further than the falls of the Willamette at Oregon City. Minnie and the children rode the Navigation Company wagon through the town to the lower river. There an identical steamboat was waiting to take them the few miles on to Portland. They had to wait nearly a week in that village—a settlement ridiculed as

"Stumptown-on-the-Willamette" because its few buildings lay scattered among a vast, optimistic grid of empty dirt streets and recently cleared forest. Yet another steamer took them to The Dalles, where the three-day stagecoach ride began, crossing a mountainous desert track that had become the John Day mining district's primary link to the outside world.

Ned was waiting nervously in a buggy when the stage pulled in on the dusty, nearly vacant street. Maud jumped out and ran to him, squealing, "Papa!"

He whirled the child around, kissed her forehead, and set her up in the buggy. Then, his heart beating in his throat, he turned to meet Minnie with his best smile. She had never answered his letters, except for the note giving the date of her arrival and the new terms of their marriage. How was he to know how to greet her? If he tried to sweep her up in his arms, might she stiffen and push him away? Silently, he swept the air with his hat and gave a deep bow.

Minnie looked over her husband as though he were some distant relative she had not seen since childhood. His hair had begun to thin a little on top. He had lost some weight. But he was still quite handsome—nearly as good-looking, in a rougher sort of way, as the suave Mr. Hill—and he still had a charming smile. Nonetheless, she could not smile back to him yet.

Ned reddened. "I'll say it again, Minnie. I'm sorry. Can't we put the past behind us? Please, at least for the children's sake."

She liked his new, soberer tone. Could it be that he had outgrown the wilder ways of his pony express days?

"We could try," she said. Her intonation made it clear she would be watching him, ready to pounce if he should make a misstep.

"Well, that's a fair start," Ned said. "Don't you want to see your presents?"

Maud hopped up. "I do!"

Ned distributed three hat boxes. The children began eagerly tearing into theirs.

Minnie shook hers suspiciously. "Something with feathers and ribbons, you say, and it's in a hat box? Not much of a mystery, I'd say."

"Look, Mama!" Maud cried, pulling a wild-looking Indian headdress out of her package. Minnie gave a startled gasp.

Ned chuckled, "Well, didn't you guess they were hats? Come on, Minnie, open yours."

"Ned, really!" she said, smiling despite herself. "If you've bought me a war bonnet, I'll never forgive you."

"Just see."

She lifted the lid and withdrew a beribboned, befeathered ladies' dress hat even more elaborate than the one he had given her in Port Orford years ago. "How elegant! I'm not sure I have anything nice enough to wear with it." In fact, the hat was a little too ostentatious for her taste. Perhaps she, too, had outgrown her earlier ways. As a younger woman, she had let him buy off her misgivings with an expensive hat. This time she knew better.

"Reckon you'll have to sew a new dress, then. There's a ball coming up at the French Hotel."

It was a nice added touch—remembering how much she liked to sew and to dance. Minnie felt her emotions teetering as if on a divide, tilting one moment toward the glimmering girlish love this man knew to awaken, then shifting back toward the darker desire of revenge.

"Mama, hurry up or I'll scalp you!" Maud complained, waggling the preposterous Indian war bonnet on her head.

Minnie turned to Ned. "You promise—we'll only be out here one year before moving to San Francisco?"

"Honest Injun." He slapped his arms across his chest theatrically, as if for a solemn vow. Little Maud immediately copied the gesture.

"You two are incorrigible!" Minnie chided, but her smile gave her away.

Ned caught her hand and kissed it. Then he tipped his hat toward the buggy. "Could I interest you in seeing a new home?"

Their new home proved to be nearly an hour's drive up Canyon Creek. For the first five miles the buggy rolled past the detritus of the mines and the all-too-familiar town, with its forlorn clusters of shabby wooden buildings and ragged tents. Then the valley narrowed between craggy, black walls until there was hardly room for the creek and the trail. Finally they entered a broad, green basin high in the mountains. Here the stream had not been dug up by the miners, but flowed clear, meandering through meadows and groves of silver-green quaking aspen. The slopes above were densely forested with Douglas fir—not at all like the sparse cover of juniper dotting the drier hills only a few miles below.

Even Minnie had to admit that this part of Canyon Creek looked less like a desert than any place she had seen in Eastern Oregon. But she asked, "It's a little too isolated for safety, isn't it? They say the farther you live from town the more danger there is from Indian attacks."

"Sounds like you've been reading too many novels. The only wild Indians around here are going to be Maud and George."

Maud turned to her father, adjusting her headdress. "Do you really think I look like an Indian?"

"Prettiest princess in the tribe, isn't she, Minnie?"

Minnie nodded uncomfortably. "Will we have any neighbors nearby?"

"Two ranch families within walking distance. And you're welcome to ride into town with me almost any day to go shopping."

When he pulled up to the cabin, in a grove of tall, orange-barked ponderosa pines a stone's throw from the stream, Minnie saw at once that it was built with the same simple four-room design as the house in Canyon City, with closet-like bedrooms in the back. Still, she withheld her judgment until she had looked through it thoroughly.

To her surprise, it was well equipped with store-bought furnishings. The porch had two bentwood rocking chairs. In the front room she found a roll-top desk and several bookshelves. Presumably, this room would have to serve as both parlor and study. The kitchen proved to be delightfully large, with a pretty blue drop-leaf dining table with four matching spindle-backed chairs. But what really caught Minnie's attention was the large cast-iron wood stove, complete with a built-in oven. Baking proper loaves of bread had been impossible at the earlier cabin. With this stove, it would be a pleasure.

Ned had silently followed at Minnie's side, watching for her reaction.

She turned to him, touched by how hard he had tried to make the cabin cosy. Of course she would lonely at times, so far from a town, but the months would pass and then they would be in San Francisco. She straightened the front of his shirt with nervous fingers. "Oh, Ned, I just hope it works out. No cows or chickens this time?"

He laughed. "No cows or chickens. And I'll be at home more. Being a judge doesn't take much time. I've cut back my private law practice to almost nothing. Oh, and I've started another book of poems."

"Another book already? The bookstore in Portland had only sold a dozen copies of your first one when I was there."

"I know, I know. But this next book will be the one that really makes it for us. Anyway, when I get the itch to write, what can I do? I *have* to write!"

Minnie sighed. "Of course you do."

* * *

Snow sifted down through the pines outside while Ned worked in the cabin's front room with his quill. He blew into his hands to warm them, and then sipped again from his whiskey cup. The stove was burning wood like a locomotive in the kitchen, he knew, but the children were there, and he couldn't concentrate to write with them crying and climbing around. For the first few months it had been pleasant writing in the front room, watching the squirrels outside store away the pine nuts for the winter. Now icy drafts through the loose window frame sometimes blew out his candle. Still, he could bundle up and drink whiskey. The children needed the warmth of the fire more than he did.

He leaned back and called through the closed door, "Minnie? Have you looked at those poems yet?"

He frowned when he couldn't discern an answer among the muffled sounds beyond the door. He opened the door a crack and asked again.

Minnie looked up from a steamy washtub. Maud was standing on a chair, chattering away as she hung wet socks on a line over the stove. George was splashing in a bowl on the floor, pretending the back of a bread pan was a scrub board.

"I'm sorry, Ned," Minnie said. "I can't hear a thing back here. What is it again?"

"The poems. You said you might have time to read them. But it doesn't look like you did."

Minnie dried her hands on her apron and hefted the washtub to the stove to let the water reheat. "I read them before I started the wash." She left Maud with instructions to keep George away from the stove, and took a sheaf of manuscripts off the shelf. Then she followed Ned into his cold room and sank into a chair with a sigh. They had only been living in the cabin a few months, and already Ned seemed to be taking her for granted. When she agreed to come back, should she have added a third demand—something more than faithfulness and the goal of moving to San Francisco? And just how would she have phrased that vaguer, third demand?

Ned leaned forward. "So the poems seemed all right?"

"Oh." She pulled herself back to the subject of poetry. Even if she still wasn't sure how to deal with her husband, at least she knew how to deal with poems. "Well, I didn't have time to check for meter or rhyme yet, but I do have some questions about the plots."

"The plots? What about the plots?"

"Well, for example in this first one, 'Joaquin Murietta,' you've got this Mexican highwayman dying in battle while trying to liberate California from the Americans. I seem to remember there was a thousand-dollar reward out for Murietta once. Wasn't he hanged?"

Ned frowned. "No, actually the California Rangers tracked him down, cut off his head, and brought it back pickled in a jar."

"Then why—"

"Poetic license. He deserves a nobler death."

Minnie looked puzzled. "But you're making Murietta sound like some kind of hero. Who'll want to read that? Everyone knows he was one of the most blood-thirsty killers of all time. When I was growing up parents used to tell their children to be good or the Ghost of the Sonora would get them."

Ned leaned back, stroking his beard. "That's all true, but there's another side to the story, too. California belonged to the Mexicans first, so Murietta was fighting for his rights. He's as much a hero to the Mexicans, I reckon, as John Brown was to the slaves. I'm just cheering for the weaker side, is all. That's the way I am."

Minnie was shaking her head. "No one's going to give California back to the Mexicans. I guess I don't see the point of trying to glorify a bandit." She laid the papers on the desk. "Why not write more of the idyllic poems you used to invent when you rode the pony express? Honestly, I think I preferred them to these blood-curdling melodramas." She couldn't help thinking that a gentle lecturer such as Mr. Hill would never include Ned's new, violent poems in his program. Mr. Hill had seemed so much more at ease with civilized literature. She wondered what had become of Mr. Hill. Was he perhaps reading to audiences in San Francisco by now? Or even New York?

"Did you come up with anything else?" Ned crossed his arms and leaned back, not wanting to show he had been hurt by her criticism. She used to rave about his poems. Had he changed, or had she?

Minnie shrugged. "This next one, 'The Tale of the Tall Alcalde,' has the same kind of problem. Isn't an alcalde a Mexican, too?"

"Not necessarily. It's the Spanish word for judge. Most judges in California are known as alcaldes, whether they're Mexican or not."

"Well, whatever he is, his tale's so improbable that readers aren't going to take it seriously." She looked through the pages. "Here you have him falling in love with an Indian squaw and fighting *against* the whites in an Indian war." She flipped more pages. "Then he's put in jail, but he escapes and goes around murdering sheriffs and miners for revenge a while. And then you have him get a job as an alcalde and live like it all never happened."

Ned stopped short of insisting that it was all true. For once, he had dared to tell her about his life in the California wilderness, if only in the form of a poetic tall tale. She had been prying for this secret for years. In a way, it was a relief to have her ridicule it as an implausible fiction.

The muffled sound of children arguing caught Minnie's attention. "I'd better get back to the kitchen. I'll check through the poems later for rhyme if you want, but I think you'd better look at the plots again first."

Ned sighed as he thumbed through the poem. His years with Paquita had faded to a tall tale he himself could hardly believe. But he would let the plot stand.

* * *

At Christmas there were candles on the tree, with popcorn for the children and brandy for Ned. Even Minnie tried a sip of brandy, afterwards waving her hand wildly in front of her mouth as if she expected to breathe fire.

Maud and George found striped candy and hand-carved willow whistles for them hanging in the tree. Underneath was a little wooden Noah's ark with whittled animals for Maud, and a little bow and arrow set for George. Minnie only found a small note for her, but when she read that it promised her enough cloth for another new dress, she hugged her husband.

"It's just what I wanted," she said, and then added with a whisper, "It's about time I made a maternity outfit, you know."

Ned gave her a puzzled look. "Since when is this?"

Minnie replied coyly, "Oh, I've known for a while. I should be due in late June or July. Aren't you glad?"

"I reckon so." A mixture of pride and alarm left Ned's thoughts so muddled he could hardly reply. He had never grown used to being told he would have a new child. Always he was caught by surprise—first with Cali-Shasta, then with Maud and George. This time he had been so concerned with the fragility of his marriage that he hadn't thought about the possibility of another baby. It was only later, when his mind cleared, that he grew suspicious.

That evening when the children were asleep and Minnie was changing the pillowcases on the big bed, Ned ran his finger down the calendar, counting the months. June was six ahead. Three months ago, in September, Minnie had not been in Canyon City at all. She had been on her way, traveling across the state. He had paid no attention to the letter from his parents then, but now the troubling words came to mind: "Your wife and children did not stay with us here at home, but took a room at the hotel. Hulings says I shouldn't tell you, but there were rumors that Theresa was seeing a man from the theater there. Just a warning, son. I wouldn't trust her . . ."

* * *

Spring came early that year, strewing a colorful fringe of wildflowers in the wake of the mountains' melting snow. One March afternoon Ned took his rifle down from its pegs. He told Minnie he was going to hunt, but in truth he only wanted an excuse to hike through the high country's brilliant meadows.

It seemed to Minnie that everything upset the children that day. Maud broke the ear of her little wooden elephant trying to take it away from her brother. George bruised his forehead on the corner of the table, and they both cried and cried. Minnie, so pregnant with her third child that she only had the energy to sit, let them bury their wet faces in her skirts, wondering to herself just how long she could bear to hear the crying.

Eventually, though, Maud crawled off to her little bed to cry herself to sleep there, and George plopped down on the rag rug. When Minnie was sure he was asleep, she carried him to his corner and covered him up.

After the children were both in bed, Minnie stood in the middle of the kitchen and listened to the strange sound of silence about her. The stove was out, but it didn't need a fire. It was too early to start dinner. The wash had been done yesterday, and the bread at the same time. Maybe she should sew, she thought, but then she remembered she had emptied the mending bag last week. The dress she had been making was done.

Gradually an uncertain, almost naughty feeling came over her. She peered into the front room. Ned would not be back for at least another hour. She walked to his desk. His quill and paper were there as always. She sat down. It had been years, it was true, but perhaps she hadn't really forgotten how to write a poem.

She had just dipped the quill in the inkwell and was looking out the window, trying to come up with a rhythm for her thoughts, when she saw a movement in the trees.

She stood up from her husband's desk guiltily, thinking he had returned early. But then she peered out through the pine branches again and realized that this was not her husband. Whoever it was was even taller than Ned, and wore much shabbier clothes. He was tying a horse to a tree.

Then the man turned toward the cabin and Minnie's heart froze. It was an enormous Indian, with black braids and a hard, red face. He was walking toward the door.

An Indian! Minnie's heart pounded as she turned for the rifle—and saw the empty pegs. She nearly cried aloud. Why did Ned have to take it hunting *today?* Then she remembered the pistol. She pulled out all of the drawers in the desk before she found it.

Of course it was unloaded. For a second the irony flashed through her mind: Ned left it unloaded for the safety of the children, but now, when their lives were at stake, it was useless. Then she heard the porch boards creaking under the Indian's moccasins and thought: no, not entirely useless. She could still bluff.

When the Indian walked in the door Minnie confronted him with the big pistol, holding it in both her trembling hands. She pressed her back against the door to the kitchen, where the children lay sleeping.

"Excuse me, ma'am," the Indian said apologetically, in perfect English.

Minnie had not expected the Indian to talk at all, much less in English, but then she had never seen an Indian at this close range. "Stand back!" She tried not to sound frightened.

"Is this where Ned Miller lives?"

This was too much for Minnie. She let her pistol droop in astonishment before she caught herself and raised it again. "What do you want, Indian?"

"The name's Charley McCloud." The big Indian hesitated, then added, "You can put that pistol down. I wouldn't have just walked in if I'd known Ned had gotten another wife."

Minnie lowered the gun slowly. "A *what?*"

"You see, I lost a pack train and heard Ned had a job as a judge, so I came to see if he could help."

"Did you say—*another* wife?" Minnie's mind stuck on the impossible words.

"I see," Charley said, as if he now understood. His face shadowed with disappointment. "So he does not talk about the Wintu." He reached for the door sadly. "Then do not tell him I was here."

"No!" Minnie said, raising the pistol again. "No, you stay right where you are, Indian. And you tell me about the 'Wintu.'"

Charley looked from the barrel of the big revolver to Minnie's fierce, flashing eyes. His hand dropped slowly from the doorknob. "All right, ma'am. I will."

And so he told her. He told her about his first encounter with Ned at Mountain Joe's California ranch, and about the log cabin Ned built in Now-ow-wa, near the Wintu village. He told her about how Ned had bargained for and married Paquita, the chief's granddaughter. He told her about the years he had lived with Paquita, and about their child. Cali-Shasta, he said finally, was now eleven, still living with her mother on the McCloud River.

Minnie was too stunned to react. Even when Ned returned and slapped Charley good-naturedly on the back, she stood there like a statue, incredulous. Ned took the unloaded gun from her hands with a laugh, guided her into the back room, and closed the door firmly behind her.

Minnie moved mechanically to the kitchen window. She sat against the sill for support. At first the room flushed so hot her eyes burned, and then it ran so cold it left her beaded with an icy sweat. The child in her belly began kicking against her stomach.

The voices in the front room were loud enough that she could hear more than she wanted. They talked about Indian tribes and government agents. They talked about names she did not know. Then they talked about money, and she heard the clink of coins. Shortly after that it was quiet again—as quiet as it had been an hour before—and she knew the Indian was gone. She gripped her hands on the windowsill to brace herself.

"Minnie?" the voice finally came. She heard the kitchen door open gently. "I'm sorry about Charley giving you such a scare. He's just an old friend. I reckon you're curious about him now. We used to—"

"Ned, please *don't*," Minnie said, still looking out the window.

"How's that?"

"I don't *want* to hear any more stories." She closed her eyes and breathed as evenly as she could.

"Minnie, at least let me tell you—"

"*No!*" She turned on him, suddenly red with the anger she finally could contain no longer. "No, you stop and let *me* talk for once!"

Ned drew back at the force of his wife's words. The spiteful side of Minnie he had always disliked seemed to be erupting before him.

Minnie gritted her teeth, struggling to hold back any hint of tears. "Our marriage has been a *lie*, from the first damned day. You already *have* a wife and daughter in California. And I'll bet you treated them the way you've treated me. I work all day long for you, do everything but write your awful poems, and in return you give me *nothing*. When an Indian breaks into the house you give him all the money he wants. But you hoard your salary from me until we practically live like savages ourselves."

She turned to look out the window with her chin held high, as if by finally shouting him down she had freed herself of a burden that had been weighing her down for years.

Ned sighed while he collected his thoughts. Then he replied with the cool, even voice he otherwise saved for the courtroom. "I'm sorry you aren't happy here as my wife anymore, but I don't see the point of your accusing me of being unfaithful ten or fifteen years ago. That was before we had even met. It seems if anybody has a right to complain about infidelity now, it's me."

"*You!* Why *you?*"

"Honestly, Minnie, what else am I supposed to think when I get a letter that says you've been staying at a hotel in Eugene City with a stranger? The only thing *I've* done wrong this past year has been to turn a deaf ear to the people who keep telling me this baby you're carrying belongs to another man."

Minnie gaped at him, aghast.

"Well?" he asked. "Are you able to deny it?"

She threw up her hands in exasperation. "*You're* the one who has dragged our marriage in the dirt—*you're* the bigamist and the adulterer! You've got a lot of nerve to smear *my* reputation!"

"Minnie, I've already suffered more than my share for what's happened, and believe me, I've tried not to bring up these things for your own sake. But now that you've opened the matter, I want an answer. Six months ago at the Renfrew Hotel, did you or did you not share your bed with a man named Hill?"

Minnie stiffened at the accusation. "I am *not* your client, Mr. Miller! I refuse to be cross-examined as if I were some hurdy gurdy house whore."

For a long moment they exchanged nothing but an intense stare, each waiting for the other to draw and fire the fatal shot. Ned searched Minnie's dark eyes, but found only an ugly new defiance and a glare that told him what he already knew: she no longer bore him love. Nor would it have hurt him, if an obstinate spark of his own love for her had not survived, like a smoldering coal in a long-buried campfire. As it was, the worst torture of all would be to be trapped together with this new icy blast until even that one last spark were extinguished.

He drew himself up with a long breath. "All right, Minnie, if that's the way you want it to be. But then there isn't much left of our marriage, is there? As soon as you can get ready, I'm sending you and the children to your mother's in Port Orford."

Minnie grew pale at these words, but her chin remained firm. "Yes, that's your way, isn't it? To solve every problem with a snap decision. And to take away what little satisfaction I could get by leaving you on my own."

"That's not why—"

"No, no," Minnie interrupted, tossing her head back as she went to get her things from the dresser. "There's nothing to talk about anymore. I'm perfectly willing to leave you this instant, so you may as well go hitch up the buggy. Only this time, Ned Miller, I want you to know you can *never* expect my forgiveness. This time I shall *never* come back."

Chapter 21

And you and I have buried Love,
A red seal on the coffin's lid,
                    —Joaquin Miller, "Myrrh"

The summer of 1869 was the hottest Oregon had ever known. Forest fires exploded through the dry woods. Smoke eclipsed the sun for weeks at a time in the Willamette Valley and brought ship traffic on the Columbia River to a standstill. Although clear skies still peered out from above the Pacific, the hills behind Port Orford were ribbons of fire at night, and by day, the east was a wall of boiling black clouds.

From the dormer window of Cliff House, where Minnie lay exhausted with her newly born baby son, it looked as though the entire state was burning. And she thought: Let it burn. She knew she would have to build her future on ashes. From the wreckage of six years of marriage she had salvaged nothing but Maud, George, and the wriggling red infant, Henry. Now she only wished she could burn away the memory of their lying, egotistical father, Cincinnatus Hiner Miller.

But his memory continued to plague her—and not merely because of the boxes of books and clothes that arrived from Canyon City, for these were sent without letters or comments of any kind. Three times in that first year she saw his name in the newspapers. She disliked nothing more than seeing his name in the papers, because it revealed he was not nearly as crippled by remorse as she felt he deserved to be.

The first time was in the *Guard*, a new Eugene City sheet. Minnie had hardly glanced at the paper, but then her mother had found the review, and curiosity forced Minnie to read it through.

JOAQUIN, ET AL.

The above is the title of a volume of poems composed by the Hon. C. H. Miller, Judge of Grant County. The volume is entirely

Oregonian, having been written, printed, bound, and published within this State. The mechanical work in the production of this neat little volume cannot be surpassed anywhere. A careful perusal of the contents proves that the poet possesses true genius and real poetical fire. He is among the poets that are born, not made, and with experience and study, Judge Miller will rank among the first poets of the age. He is worthy to be crowned laureate of Oregon. We cannot give a lengthy notice of each poem, but will briefly say that the little volume is full of sweet flowing numbers and beautiful imagery. Judge Miller is well and favorably known to the citizens of this place and county. Here he received his early education, and here his muse first sung. His many schoolmates and friends will receive *Joaquin, Et Al.* to their firesides as a precious gem from one who possesses a warm and noble heart, and who merits a niche in history among the immortal bards. We welcome *Joaquin, Et Al.* to our sanctum.

Minnie managed a forced laugh. An "immortal bard" with "a warm and noble heart"? Of course they didn't know what kind of a husband he was, but had they forgotten so soon that he had been hooted out of both Eugene City and San Francisco? More likely, the editor was just doing a favor for an old pal. After rereading it, Minnie even thought it was possible her husband had written the frothy review himself. In any case, the new book had been published at the same "vanity" press as *Specimens*, so he had obviously paid up front for what was probably only 500 copies again, and as unsalable as ever.

The second review that came to Minnie's attention confirmed many of her suspicions. The *Overland Monthly*, successor to Minnie's cherished *Golden Era*, buried a comment about the book at the bottom of a department entitled "Etc." Apparently editor Bret Harte had been asked repeatedly by the author for a review, but was only able to say that C. H. Miller's poems exhibited felicity of diction and dramatic vigor in spite of their obvious crudities and dubious taste.

There were no more reviews. The rain-drenched winter came and went, and Minnie was beginning to believe her husband would forever languish in the same obscurity as his books, when his name appeared in the papers a third time, now in connection with a new and altogether unexpected enterprise.

Judge Dyer was sitting by the fire with his pipe the evening he noticed it in the paper. A thick cloud of smoke burst from his bushy gray beard as he pointed at the article with the pipe stem. "Here, Theresa," he said. "Your poet's up in Portland at the Democratic convention. Says he's given up his re-election chance in Grant County to aim for a seat on the Oregon Supreme Court." He clamped the pipe in his teeth and turned the paper over, muttering, "Can't think of a scoundrel more unfit for high office. Still, I reckon there's nothing to be done about it."

It took Minnie several days to decide what needed to be done. Then she put on a prim, dark, businesslike dress and hat, left the children with her mother, and drove the family buggy into town.

There were only two lawyers in Port Orford. She chose the one with the larger office, sat in the chair he offered, and announced, "I wish to file for a divorce."

The lawyer was a grossly overweight man with an enormous fleshy nose like a growth on a potato. He toyed with a paperweight on his desk before he spoke. "Divorce? That's an awful serious business, ma'am. Don't you think you should go home and talk it over?"

"I'm living with my father—*Judge* George Dyer." Minnie's voice was cold. "I have been separated from my husband for nearly a year. For reasons which I deem sufficient, I now want a legal divorce."

The lawyer sighed. He reached a fat hand for his quill and asked wearily, "Your full name, ma'am?"

"Mrs. Theresa Dyer Miller."

He wrote it down. "Husband's name?"

"Cincinnatus Hiner Miller."

The lawyer squinted up at her skeptically. "Not *the* C. H. Miller?"

"What do you mean, 'the'?"

"The county judge running for the Supreme Court."

"Certainly."

He gave a low whistle. "You're going to have one tough case, lady." He stared out the window thinking, and then chuckled. "I wonder if you realize what a suit like this is going to do to his chances for election?"

"That is immaterial." Minnie straightened her gloves. "He has failed to support his children. Unless I have money to feed and clothe the children I will be a burden on my parents."

But the lawyer just watched her with a steady smile.

* * *

"Damn, damn, damn!" Ned paced the floor of the Miller house in Eugene City, reading the legal notice. Then he turned to his frightened parents. "This woman! Why does she want to ruin me?"

Margaret ventured a small voice. "Has she done something awful again?"

Ned shook the offending paper. "A *divorce*. Just precisely now, now that my future hangs in the balance, just now she wants a divorce."

While his parents exchanged startled glances, Ned looked back through the paper. "So. And her lawyer has contacted an attorney named Ellsworth here in town. Very well."

Hulings put in, "You know about law, son. She can't get away with this, can she?"

"Oh, I don't know." Ned's eyes narrowed. "I think if she wants to file for divorce against one of the best lawyers in the state, she'll deserve what she gets. The circuit court just happens to be in session. I believe if I speak with Mr. Ellsworth today, we can move the case to Lane County and clear this matter up within a week or two."

*   *   *

The somber men in the small, wood-paneled courtroom looked as though they might have gathered for a funeral service rather than a trial. The only woman present was Ned's white-haired mother Margaret, who quietly cried into a lace handkerchief in the back row. Ned had planned his case in the heat of vengeful anger, but now he felt a sudden twinge of regret. Minnie had understood so little about the law when she had filed her papers.

The judge cleared his throat. Then he read from the legal paper in his hand. "The complaint filed by Mrs. Cincinnatus Hiner Miller charges that 'the defendant has treated this plaintiff in a cruel and inhuman manner,' and that 'said treatment commenced in 1863 and continued until May 1869, at which time the defendant desired the plaintiff to leave him,' and most significantly, that 'the defendant has on diverse occasions struck the plaintiff and endangered her life.'"

Ned flushed to hear this outrageous charge read aloud in court. Minnie's words renewed his resolve to go through with his plan after all.

The judge glanced up gravely, and then continued. "Furthermore, she states three children issued from the marriage—Maud Eveline, born 1863; George Brick, born 1866; and Henry Mark, born 1869, just this last summer. The plaintiff alleges that her husband 'wholly neglects to provide for the support and maintenance of said children.' As a result she asks this court to grant her the following: first, a divorce according to Oregon law; second, custody of the children that issued from the union; and third, a cash allowance for their upbringing and for her own support, so as not to further tax the resources of the plaintiff's parents."

The judge frowned at Ned. "These are serious charges. I assume you have prepared testimony, seeing as how you have chosen to speak in your own defense."

Ned rose at once. "Your Honor, I feel it is important from the start to deny categorically that I have ever struck the plaintiff in anger as she alleges, and to swear before the court that I have never treated the plaintiff in other than a just and humane manner. During the past year, however, I have refused to live with the plaintiff or to furnish her with the money she desires. If I may be permitted to describe the pertinent events of the last two years, I feel I can amply justify my actions."

"You may proceed."

Ned took up the paper he had spent the past week writing. Minnie had forced him to clear his name. Now he would hurl the facts at her. He read aloud, "In the spring of 1868 the plaintiff visited her mother at Port Orford, and in the following fall she returned to our home at Canyon City, traveling very slowly although the roads and her health were good. I think she was about a month making the journey, although she could easily have made it in less than half that time. Still, it did not arouse my suspicion until three months after her trip, when I learned she was with child and admitted to having been so for a period of three months.

"When I then discovered she had stopped during her trip at the Renfrew Hotel about a week with a man named Hill—a fact which she has not denied—I immediately asked her to go to her mother's. This she cheerfully consented to and did do. I have not treated her as a wife since that time, nor do I intend to do so in the future."

Several of the men in the room nodded understandingly. Margaret had dried her eyes and was listening like an alert bird. Beside her, Ned's father cleared his throat as if to put in a word or two of his own, but then he bent forward, coughing.

Ned wished his parents had not insisted on coming. Margaret had spent most of the week fretting about "losing the grandchildren." Hulings had worried aloud that Minnie's demands for money might bankrupt them all. The tension filling the Miller household had been hard on them both.

After a pause, Ned continued. "In the past year I have not sent the plaintiff much money, since I think she makes a poor use of it. But I have sent her about one hundred dollars worth of clothing, et cetera, for herself and the children, and about fifty dollars worth of books, periodicals, and stationery. As for plaintiff's prayer for money of me, I will state that her father gave her one dollar, or one-and-one-half dollars, I forget which, which was all she had when she married or has received or inherited. I myself have about the same means as when we were married.

"As for the custody of the children, I do not think the plaintiff's mind or judgment is sufficient to properly rear or control them. However, I think her mother is a pure, good woman, and am willing to let her have the two oldest children until they are old enough to place in an academy, and to pay her a reasonable sum not exceeding two hundred dollars annually in gold to keep them, though my mother or sister I think the more proper persons and would gladly keep them for nothing."

Ned laid down the paper and faced the judge. "Finally, I wish to state that I do not claim to be the father of, nor do I desire the custody of the youngest child."

A murmur rippled through the room at this unexpected twist. The judge raised his eyebrows, as if weighing the implications of an illegitimate child. He turned to the young lawyer opposite Ned. "Mr. Ellsworth, do you have witnesses or other evidence to present on behalf of your client?"

"No, your Honor," he said, standing briefly.

"Nothing at all?"

"Mrs. Miller has sent word that she is unable to come to Eugene City for the proceedings. I believe the facts of the case speak for themselves."

Ned was not surprised by Mr. Ellsworth's lack of fervor. There was no proof of Ned's Wintu marriage, and Minnie herself was the only witness who could link him to Sarah Eckelhoff. A young lawyer like Ellsworth would hardly want to risk alienating his colleagues by attacking a well-known barrister without better ammunition.

"I see," the judge said. Then he turned back to Ned. "Mr. Miller, do you have witnesses?"

Ned nodded. He held out a hand toward a young man nearby. "Your Honor, I'd like to call Mr. William Brown of Eugene City to the stand."

When the lanky young man had been sworn in, Ned asked, "Mr. Brown, could you tell the court your profession?"

"Yes, sir. I'm a waiter at the Renfrew Hotel."

"Do you recall seeing Mrs. Miller in the company of a Mr. Hill in the fall of 1868?"

"Oh yes, sir. They were there for a good part of a week. Ate most of their meals together."

"And did Mr. Hill ever talk to you about the plaintiff?"

The young man looked at his hands uneasily. "Well, not directly to me, sir, but I did overhear him boasting about her at the bar."

"What did he say?"

The man's voice dropped. "He said he had slept with her often."

Ned tightened his lips. It had been almost too easy to find this witness. Minnie had been worse than unfaithful—she had been careless. Certainly the waiter had no motivation to lie about what he had heard. Ned asked, "Were those Mr. Hill's exact words?"

Mr. Brown nodded, still not looking up.

"And what else?"

"He said she'd given him money, and that she wanted him to leave with her."

"How did Mr. Hill in fact leave?"

At this point the young man's face lit up. "Oh, he was run out of the county, sir. I knew Hill wasn't just an actor first time I saw him, so I wasn't surprised when he turned out to be a gambler and a thief."

"That will be all, thank you."

The judge shot a glance at the other lawyer. "Mr. Ellsworth?"

The young lawyer stood, looking a little nervous. "Mr. Brown, do you know of your own knowledge that Mr. Hill and Mrs. Miller slept together?"

The waiter stuck out his jaw. "I saw her let him into her private room. And everybody heard him brag about it later at the bar. He was a real talker."

Mr. Ellsworth knitted his brow and sat down. "No more questions."

"All right, Mr. Miller," the judge said. "Who else do you have?"

Ned hesitated, but his mother rose from her seat, waving her hand and prodding her husband. Ned sighed, wishing he could have spared his parents this stress. "Just one more witness, your Honor. I'd like to ask Mr. Hulings Miller of Eugene City to take the stand."

Ned's father, who had been coughing again, looked drained as he repeated the oath and sank to the chair.

"Mr. Miller," Ned began gently. "You are the plaintiff's father-in-law, are you not?"

Hulings nodded silently.

"Did you offer to let the plaintiff stay at the Miller residence when she visited Eugene City in the fall of 1868?"

He nodded again. "Yes, but she stayed at the hotel instead."

"And did you visit her there?"

"We only wanted to see the grandchildren."

"I understand. What did you find?"

The old man grunted. "They were in a room, upstairs." He paused, but then saw Margaret prompting him silently from her chair, and went on. "There were strangers in the room, circus men, who were—who were fondling the children."

"Thank you, that's all," Ned said, sitting down wearily. "No more witnesses, your Honor." Ned didn't know how much of his parents' story was true and how much was a tale invented for fear of losing the grandchildren. His father swore the hotel had been full of dwarves—an improbable tale that Ned had encouraged him to omit. His mother wasn't fit to take the stand at all; she changed her story with every retelling. At times Ned wondered if she were slipping on the edge of senility. She seemed driven by a deep-seated hatred of Minnie that even Ned couldn't understand. He had never wanted to lose Minnie at all.

The judge glanced to Mr. Ellsworth, who only shook his head and looked away.

For several minutes the only sound in the room was the scratching of the judge's quill. Then he blotted his writing. "The court finds sufficient grounds for divorce," he announced. No one in the room expressed surprise, but Ned felt a rush of despair at the words.

"Mrs. Miller shall be granted custody of the youngest child until further order of this court. At Mr. Miller's request, the two older children shall be in the custody of Mrs. Sarah Dyer, the plaintiff's mother, for a period of four years, with a compensation from Mr. Miller of two hundred dollars per annum for their support. Thereafter, Mr. Miller shall have custody of these two children and shall be permitted to place them in school."

When he tapped the gavel, it was done.

* * *

"Two hundred dollars a year." The obese attorney winked to Minnie as he handed her the verdict. "Read the details for yourself. I think we did very well, considering."

Minnie snatched the document from his hand. The further she read, the paler she grew. "But—but we lost!"

The lawyer spread his hands as if in surprise. "An odd interpretation. Very few Oregon women have been granted a divorce at their own request. On top of that you won complete custody of the youngest child and supervision of the other children for years."

"But this verdict suggests I'm an adulteress! Didn't the attorney in Eugene City offer any defense?"

"I think we've delivered excellent results." He chuckled. "Your husband's out of the running for the Supreme Court. Isn't that what you really wanted, Mrs. Miller?"

"Well, of all the simple-minded—!" She huffed in exasperation. "You men!" She turned on her heel and stormed out of the office.

To think Ned had dared to brand her with infidelity—and her own lawyers had said nothing! She fumed with indignation as she drove the buggy back from Port Orford. Perhaps she should have told her lawyer about Sarah Eckelhoff and Ned's Indian wife after all. She had wanted to spare the children from the worst of the scandal. The divorce itself was bad enough. But Ned obviously hadn't cared about the children. He had painted her as a harlot and publicly denounced his own son Henry as a bastard.

Two miles from Cliff House the buggy's thin wheels began slowing in the increasingly sandy track. Minnie's rage had slowed, too, allowing her to wonder what she really had wanted from the divorce after all. Of course she hadn't thought a man like Ned deserved a seat on Oregon's highest court. And yes, she craved revenge. But more than that, she had wanted a chance for her and the children to start a new, independent life together. She had never given up altogether on the old dream of San Francisco. For years she had slaved in Canyon City, helping save money for that sunny future. Now lawyer's fees would devour even the two hundred dollars she had been promised. She would be trapped in Cliff House, penniless and disgraced.

"Oh, damn it!" In her distraction Minnie had allowed the horse to drift to the edge of the lane, where the wheels mired to a stop in the deep sand. She had never used such strong language before, but now she felt like doing it again. "Damn it all!" Angrily she threw down the reins and began walking up the road to look for help.

But then the horse nickered behind her, like a child who did not want to be left alone. Minnie stopped, struck with a sudden, bold realization. Ned might have robbed her of honor and money, but he hadn't left her powerless. She still had her wits and her strength. With a strange new feeling of determination, she strode back to the buggy. She put her shoulder to the wheel and pushed. The vehicle only twisted to one side, deeper in the loose sand.

For a moment she studied the wheel, her hands on her hips. Then another idea hit her, and she almost smiled. Why not steal a trick or two from Ned, if it helped her cause? She stood behind the cart, both hands pushing on its frame, and startled the horse with a fearsome shout.

"*Hyah!*"

The little horse lurched forward, yanking the buggy out of the sand and rattling it down the rutted lane. Minnie picked up her skirts and sprinted to catch up. When she came alongside she grabbed the buggy's fender and leaped into the seat. Then she grabbed the reins—but didn't pull the horse to a stop. Instead, fired by her new, heart-pounding sense of power, she shook the reins. "Hyah!" she shouted again, urging the horse even faster. And she thought: Someday, somehow I *will* get to San Francisco. And I will bring the mighty Cincinnatus Hiner Miller to his knees.

Chapter 22

Fly! Fly . . . where naught is known
Of all that you have won or lost
Or what your life this night has cost.
—Joaquin Miller, *Joaquin, Et Al.*

Time itself seemed to stumble the night Ned won his trial. Without knowing how, he found himself walking through the dust and the cobwebs of the deserted building where he once had edited the *Democratic Register*. The floor creaked where the press had been. Triangles of broken glass hung in the back room's windows. The dust on the desk where he had once sat, writing the angry editorials and the lonely poems, was so thick he could write her name.

He stared at the word in the dust. A beginning and an end. A love letter and an epitaph. He had never wanted to lose her. She had finally roused him to anger, and the anger had given her the divorce. Now that the anger had passed, the spark was still glowing beneath the ash of the night. The maddening, lonely spark that only time might kill. Ned bent toward the desk and blew off the dust, but the name did not disappear.

After that the landslide of days and nights gathered speed. He was sitting on a dark rock on the top of Skinner's Butte, watching gray clouds dim into a sunsetless evening. When the land turned black, the void was there, beckoning from all sides.

Then he was in the darkness of his own bedroom, sprawled across the rumpled quilt on the big four-poster bed, tipping back the bottle with his eyes closed. He reached out uncertainly to the table and closed his fingers around a small, well-bound book. His book. But when he pushed it open, the pages were black. He let his hand drop and waited for the room to spin again.

"Ned?" A fragile female voice through his door woke him up with a start. "Ned? Breakfast is ready." It was his sister Ella.

Wearily he poured a basin of water and splashed his face. The water hung in his beard as he stared at the wild-haired man in the mirror. How many days had it been? Why couldn't he get started? He'd had to pick up the pieces before. Years ago, in California, he had lost Paquita, lost his friends, lost his money, and almost lost his life. Was it worse now? Now, with the lost marriage, the lost children, the lost Supreme Court seat, and the forgotten books? Or was he just getting too old to be starting over from nothing? He went out to the breakfast table as he was.

Ned's mother and Ella exchanged worried glances when he appeared in wrinkled clothes, smelling of whiskey again. After a moment of embarrassment Margaret said, "The morning post had a letter from John in Pennsylvania. He says his dental practice is going so well he's in a position to consider marriage, perhaps even by fall! Isn't that wonderful news?"

Ned stared glumly into his bowl of boiled wheat. He knew what they were trying to do. "Good for John," he said.

There was another silence, and the clank of spoons on bowls. Then Hulings slapped the newspaper with the back of his hand. "Here it is, son—go into cattle! You know the Eastern Oregon range, where to pick up some land. That's the future over there. Just buy a herd here—"

"Pa, please." Ned interrupted with a wave of his hand. "Thanks anyway."

"Suit yourself. Probably passing up a gold mine." He returned to his reading, and was silent for several minutes, but then slapped the paper again. "Say, how about railroads? Now they're building track south from Portland, Eugene City will be a railhead. Says here this fella George Francis Train will be in town tonight to whip up a little enthusiasm. Seems he built the first tramways in London. You see? There's an investment."

Ella perked up at the mention of Train's name. "Isn't he the same one who campaigned for women's suffrage with Susan B. Anthony?"

Hulings drew back with dismay. "Well, I wouldn't know about that. It just says here he works for the vice president of the Union Pacific."

"Ned, he's so famous." Ella leaned across the table toward him. "Won't you help me walk downtown tonight so I can see him?"

Ned looked up at his sister. In the past few years she had grown even paler and thinner. Now there was no disguising the hollow eyes and drawn skin of consumption. She could hardly walk on her own. How could refuse her?

"Sure, Ella," he said quietly. "You bet I will."

Her smile in return succeeded where his parents' talk had failed for days—it began to melt the frost that had withered his interest and ambition. By the end of breakfast that morning he had recovered enough to speculate with Hulings about which street the railroad would be built in when it finally came.

Ned hardly noticed when his sister excused herself early from the table and put on a shawl. She was seldom hungry, and often had chills. But half an hour later, when he couldn't find her to help with the dishes, he wrinkled his brow.

"What's wrong, son?" Margaret asked.

"It's Ella. She's missing."

"What! I saw her go into your bedroom right after breakfast."

"My bedroom?" Puzzled, Ned went to see. The disorder and the empty whisky bottles were still there. But Ella was not. Stranger still, his copy of *Joaquin, Et Al.* was gone.

"Oh my!" Margaret's voice called from the parlor. "She's out trying to walk in the street by herself. Ned, help her!"

Ned bolted outside. His sister was hobbling weakly down Oak Street toward the house. "Ella, for God's sake! Are you all right?"

She took his arm and caught her breath. "Yes, I think so."

"I was getting worried. Where have you been?"

She smiled. "To the Renfrew Hotel."

"The Renfrew Hotel? By yourself?" Ned's thoughts piled up in confusion. The Renfrew was where Minnie had stayed. Why would Ella risk walking so far in her condition? Generally she was sharp as a tack, but Ned had to wonder if her illness had affected her mind. "Ella, what on earth are you up to?"

She started toward the house, still smiling. "You'll see tonight."

"Tonight?"

She stopped, sighed, and straightened his rumpled collar. "Please stop repeating everything I say. Just be ready on time."

"Ready for what?"

"You'll see."

Try as he might, Ned could coax no further explanation from his sister. All day long he pondered Ella's puzzle. He put his whisky bottles away. In anticipation of the evening, he trimmed his hair, bathed, and wore a clean shirt with his suit.

* * *

That night George Francis Train left the audience in Lane Hall bedazzled and agog. Who had ever seen or heard anything like him before? There he stood, resplendent in a white velvet suit with gold trim and lavender kid gloves. Huge diamonds sparkled from his silk cravat and cuffs. He announced, in roaring oratory and whispered rhymes, that he was not merely a candidate for President of the United States, but for President of the World! He pointed his ebony cane at people in the audience, pounded the podium, and marched about the stage gesticulating like a dictator.

Ned had come expecting an explanation for his sister's riddling behavior, but now he gripped the arm of his seat, captivated instead by the bewildering power of this fantastic performer.

Train made little effort to stick to the topic of railroads. He began, as anticipated, describing the driving of the golden spike in Utah that had completed the transcontinental railroad the previous May. But then he launched into a tirade against the anti-progress mentality that threatened the future. Farmers in Lane County were refusing rights-of-way to the railroad even though it would triple their property values. Nonetheless, Train declared triumphantly, daring projects were underway. Railroads were being built through the heart of London, *entirely underground.* French engineers were designing underwater vessels that could terrorize the sea lanes or harvest enough fish to feed the world. Aeronauts were constructing enormous balloons to cross the Atlantic Ocean through the skies!

Train slashed the air with his cane and berated the cowering audience, "While I am speaking here tonight our world is being *rebuilt,* and yet you in Eugene City have yet to *glimpse* the builders! How could you, when greatness can go unrecognized in your very city? In your midst there is an American *Shakespeare,* a *Byron of Oregon!"*

Ned nearly jumped from his seat. George Francis Train was holding up a copy of *Joaquin, Et Al!* Ned looked to Ella open-mouthed.

She gave a small smile. "The Renfrew is where all the visiting lecturers stay."

"But how—?"

She cocked her head, her eyes twinkling.

Train flipped open the book and began reading in a voice charged with dramatic power.

> Lo! when the last pick in the mine
> Is rusting red with idleness,
> And rot yon cabins in the mold,
> And wheels no more croak in distress,
> And tall pines reassert command,
> Sweet bards along this sunset shore
> Their mellow melodies will pour;
> Will sweetly sing and proudly say,

Long, long agone there was a day
When there were giants in the land.

Train spoke solemnly to the hushed hall. "This is the work of Judge Cincinnatus Miller. If it were published in any other land, it would be hailed as the masterpiece of a native genius. Ladies and gentlemen of Eugene City, unless you open your minds and eyes, you will extinguish this and every other spark of genius in your midst before they can go on to kindle the boiler fires that power the imagination of all humankind!"

If there was more to Mr. Train's speech, Ned did not hear it. He felt as though he had suddenly expanded several inches in all directions. And although the hall was only lit by stage candles, he was sure he was luminous, watched by every unseen eye in the hall. George Francis Train had interrupted his speech to declare *Joaquin, Et Al.* the work of a genius. But if he was a genius, what was he doing, idling away in a daze? It was time for him to pull himself together, and to take another running jump into the unknown.

When Train stepped down from the stage to shake hands with the people leaving the hall, Ned was there waiting to thank the flamboyant lecturer for his appreciation.

"Mr. Miller!" Train pumped his hand with an iron grip. "A pleasure. But my advice to you is to take your poetry where it will shake a few more plums from the tree. Go to London, my friend! The literary capital of the world! There they need a good charge of your Mexican bandits."

"London?" The certainty Ned had first put into his voice now quavered.

"Go straight to the top! But don't go whimpering—charge with your saber drawn and your colors flying. That's how you *make* 'em listen, by God!"

Ned walked Ella home with Train's words ringing in his ears. He looked to his sister with awe. "How on earth did you convince him to read my book?"

"I didn't have to convince him," Ella replied, her voice filled with pride. "Your poems did it for me. Don't ever give up on yourself, Ned."

As soon as he was home Ned ransacked the papers heaped atop his cluttered desk. He had gotten the letter from Charles Warren Stoddard less than a week before, but had ignored it then. Now he found it, cleared a bare spot for it on the desktop, and read it over more carefully.

Dear Mr. Miller:
   Pardon the delay of nearly a year in acknowledging the receipt of

your volume of poetry, *Joaquin, Et Al.* I have been on a journey of the South Seas doing considerable writing all this time and only now have returned to attempt to catch up on my correspondence.

Yours is a bold little work, and although I do not recall meeting you at the *Golden Era* office in 1863 as you say, it would be a pleasure to meet you should you happen this way again. I apologize that I cannot be of more assistance in promoting your work, but I wish you the best of luck.

Sincerely,
Charley Stoddard

At once Ned rummaged out a copy of a Portland newspaper to check the schedules. Then he dipped his quill and penned Stoddard the following reply:

Dear Charley:

Thank you for your letter of May 19th, and for your kind invitation to visit you in San Francisco. In fact, I will be in your city for several weeks on my way to London, where I intend to republish the *Joaquin* book. The Oregon steamer arrives June 10 at 11 o'clock in the morning. I look forward to seeing you then and to discussing the poems in more detail.

Sincerely,
Cincinnatus Miller

This time, Ned thought, he was not going to let San Francisco forget him.

Chapter 23

For him I pluck the laurel crown!
It ripened in the western breeze,
Where Saucelito's hills look down
Upon the golden seas.
                        —Ina Coolbrith, 1870

The sidewheeler from Oregon nudged the San Francisco wharf, sending a flock of screaming sea gulls up from the pilings like scraps of paper in a dust devil. Charles Warren Stoddard, wearing a conservative bowler and a plain gray suit, watched skeptically. The cryptic message from Eugene City had aroused his curiosity. Did this unknown Oregon rhymer, he wondered, seriously intend to take his verse to *London*—something none of the literary elite of San Francisco, not even the well-traveled Mark Twain, had dared to do? Or was he perhaps referring to some London other than the one in England?

Stoddard examined the letter again, with its peculiar final note: "P.S. That you may recognize me, I'll be wearing a sombrero—CHM."

Stoddard's fine eyebrows went up and down on his still rather boyish face as he reread the word "sombrero." He had a clear enough picture of the flat-brimmed, floppy felt hats commonly worn by vaqueros in California, but he was having difficulty envisioning this kind of headgear on a *poet.*

He was still scrutinizing the letter's scrawled text for some more probable translation when Ned descended the gangplank wearing exactly this kind of floppy sombrero. Stoddard's eyebrows pumped even more vigorously now, watching the imposing figure stride determinedly onto the dock. The wind caught Ned's voluminous white linen duster, revealing that his pant legs had been casually stuffed into tall, black express riding boots.

"Mr. Miller?" Stoddard asked. He extended a fragile-looking hand.

"Ah, howdy, Charley," Ned responded, shaking the hand heartily. "Well, let us go and talk with the poets."

If there was an appropriate response to this greeting, Stoddard could not find it. Instead he led the way to a bar, ordered himself a double gin and vermouth, and waited to see what his guest would do next.

Ned pulled an elaborate gold watch from his pocket, commented that he never drank before noon, and ordered a glass of water and a toothpick. Then, after cocking back his floppy hat, he clapped his host on the shoulder. "I want you to know I'm much obliged to you for what you're doing, Charley."

"What I'm doing?" Charley struggled to remember what he had promised this man in his letter, but could think of nothing.

"Why, sure, showing me the ropes. Last time I was in town I never even shook hands with most of the poets here. I reckon it didn't hurt any to dedicate my book to you."

"You dedicated your book to me?" Stoddard's eyebrows crawled well up onto his forehead.

"You bet. You mean you missed it?" Ned dug a copy out of his bag and creased it open on the bar to the dedicatory verse, which Stoddard proceeded to read.

> TO THE BARDS OF SAN FRANCISCO BAY
> I greet you on your brown bent hills
> Discoursing with the beaded rills,
> While over all the full moon spills
> His flood in gorgeous plenilune.
> White skillful hands sweep o'er the strings,
> I heed as when a seraph sings,
> I lean to catch the whisperings,
> I list into the night's sweet noon.

"Well, what do you think?" Ned asked.

Stoddard hesitated, searching for words to blunt his initial reaction to this romantic gibberish. "It's very—very *grand.*" He paused again before adding, "I hope you won't be disappointed with the local writers. Actually, it's pretty rare to find them sweeping strings or discoursing with beaded rills. I myself haven't heard a seraphic song for days."

Ned leaned back and laughed. "That's good, Charley. I reckon I'll listen to whatever songs I can get. Who's in town these days?"

Stoddard ticked the names off on his fingers, thinking that this would be the best way to dispel whatever illusions Miller might have about San

Francisco's writers. "Let's see—of course Ludlow, the hashish eater, is back East, and John Muir, the Scottish recluse, is up at Yosemite. Still, we've got Ambrose Bierce, the Civil War casualty who keeps a skull on his desk, and Adah Isaacs Menken, the burlesque stripper who's busy wearing out her third husband. And Ina and Frank, of course."

"Sounds like a likelier bunch of poets than the plowboys I left back in Oregon."

Stoddard sipped his drink thoughtfully. "They're probably as close to seraphic bards as the Coast is going to get."

"Well, then," Ned said, a little impatiently. "I want to make all the contacts I can before leaving for London. Which of these poets do you think we should go talk to first?"

Stoddard looked over the blond-bearded Oregonian again, who was now chewing on his toothpick like a racehorse with a bit in its teeth. When Stoddard had gone to meet the boat that morning he had been prepared to examine this curious poet of the North and then to urge him, in all civility, to take the next boat back to the woods. But now, even though his better judgment told him that would still be the safest thing to do, he felt strangely won by this fellow's reckless ambition and good-natured frankness. It was undeniably the breeziest bit of human nature he had met since his last trip to the South Seas. And the more he thought about it, the more it seemed that Miller's eccentricities might actually help him fit into San Francisco's literary world, particularly if they could distract people from the uncomfortably ornate passages in his poems.

At length Stoddard nodded. "All right. I suppose we could look up Frank and see if he's in."

"Frank?"

"You know, Bret Harte, down at the *Overland Monthly*."

As Ned followed his host to the *Overland's* offices on the Plaza he was troubled by memories of his unlucky introduction to Bret Harte in 1863, when Harte had been a gruff contributing editor for the *Golden Era*. Nor had Harte been any too kind in his reluctant review of *Joaquin, Et Al.* Still, Harte was one of the hurdles he would have to pass if he was to win much support among the California literati before his voyage east. And Harte's door was certainly one that could lead to fame. As they walked, Stoddard recounted just how well Harte had done. Some of Harte's first stories in the *Overland Monthly*, "The Outcasts of Poker Flat" and "The Luck of Roaring Camp," had made such a hit with readers back East that the *Atlantic Monthly* had offered him a position in Boston at the unheard of salary of ten thousand dollars a year. The publisher of the *Overland*, in a desperate effort to save the new celebrity for California, had offered five thousand dollars and a quarter interest in the paper. The University of California had even thrown in the offer of an easy professorship worth three hundred dollars a month, but it appeared that Harte had already decided to take the train east early next year.

This new information did little to allay Ned's fears. Here he was, fresh out of Oregon, where his hundred-dollar-a-month judge's salary had seemed like a luxury, and he was about to meet a man who was going to Boston to accept nearly ten times that sum just for his writing. Wouldn't Harte be miffed that an unproven poet would have the nerve to skip through San Francisco *and* Boston to present his verse at an even higher literary court—London?

He was. Harte remained seated, folding his arms during the introduction. He had gained some weight since Ned met him last, and his hair was streaked with gray, but his drooping mustache and pock-marked face conveyed the same disparaging expression. "So, Miller, what are you up to in San Francisco this time? I see you've stolen the hat off Joaquin Murietta's pickled head—publicity for your frontiersy poems, I assume?"

Ned refused to bend with the blows, even if it meant bending the truth, for Harte had guessed right about the hat far too easily. "The hat? No, no," he replied, chuckling lightly. "I reckon I just got to like wearing it ever since I fought alongside a Mexican friend in the Indian Wars near Shasta. He was the bravest fighter I've ever known—took an arrow in his neck and gave me his hat before he passed in his checks. No, now I'm just on my way to London to see if I can push my poems there."

Harte puckered his mouth to one side underneath his bushy mustache, as though he were deciding whether to disbelieve one, or the other, or both of these stories. "Well. That's all very interesting. You'll pardon my being too busy to chat." He cut Ned off and turned to Stoddard, pushing a dispatch across the desk. "Word's just in from the telegraph that Charles Dickens has died. I'm going to be writing a memorial, but get back in tomorrow before you ship out for Tahiti and we'll talk about running your travel letters."

With that, Harte gave a vague wave of dismissal. Moments later Ned found himself on the board sidewalk with Stoddard again, frustrated both by the editor's arrogance and by the news that his host was apparently leaving town the following day.

Stoddard noticed his sour expression and smiled. "You mustn't think badly of Frank. He's always cool to outsiders."

"Cool? He's downright glacial. Makes you wonder why he published a review of my poems at all."

"Actually, it was Ina who talked him into that one. She seemed to like your little book quite a bit."

"Ina? Who's Ina?"

Stoddard shook his head at the question. "You really do need help meeting poets, don't you? I tell you what—we'll go see her next. I have to sail tomorrow afternoon, but she might have time to show you the rest of our writers' colony."

"Well, I'm sure I'd like to meet her, seeing as she put in a good word for my poems, but I still don't know who she is."

"Seriously? Ina Coolbrith's poems are in the *Overland* all the time. In fact, she has one of the only three keys to the *Overland* office; Frank and I have the others. She is our—how shall I say?—our mutual friend. You'll find she's a very independent sort."

They walked west a half dozen blocks, turned onto Taylor Street, and were soon climbing the steps to Ina's house.

"Charley, how nice to see you." The tall, comely young woman in the doorway greeted them with a musical voice. "And let me guess—your handsome friend is the Oregon poet you went to send back home."

Stoddard and the young woman both laughed during the introductions, but Ned was too taken up with this unexpectedly beautiful poet to join them. She had shining gray eyes and dark auburn hair that fell in ringlets and danced lightly as she laughed. Ned swept off his hat respectfully and gave a deep bow. "I'm honored to make your acquaintance, Miss Coolbrith."

"Well, well." Ina lifted one of her pretty eyebrows at Stoddard. "And you thought he'd be uncivilized. Now come along in. I'm afraid I don't have much in the house to offer you, but perhaps a mug of beer would suit you after the walk from town."

As Ned stepped in past Stoddard he whispered, "Divinely tall, and divinely fair. How could such a woman never have married?"

Stoddard replied with an embarrassed shrug and a mysterious, "Ina is Ina. One doesn't ask why."

Ned had assumed Ina's unconventional suggestion of beer was in jest. He could hardly believe his eyes when she actually brought a foaming pitcher into the formal parlor. She filled three mugs on crocheted doilies atop an oak buffet, clicked her glass against theirs, and joined them in sipping the cool, pale brew—as if it were the most ordinary thing in the world for a lady to share a beer with two men.

She sat casually on the edge of an upholstered chair and crossed her legs, rustling her long, puffy dress. "Now tell me about these plans of yours."

"Well, I haven't worked out the details yet," Ned said, still a bit distracted by the worldly ease of his hostess. Minnie had never been this startlingly self-assured. With Ina, anything seemed possible. "So far my plan is to go to London and republish my book of poems there. Maybe the English will like verse about the frontier. Reckon I won't know until I try."

She set down her beer decisively. "It's an awfully bold scheme, Cincinnatus, but I've got a feeling you're on the right track."

"I feel more confident already," Ned smiled. "After all, I heard rumors it was only your good grace that got my poems this far."

Ina surprised him again by replying without a trace of a blush. "That's true. As soon as I saw your poems I told Frank they were too important to pass over. Oh, he said they were terribly rough and pointed out all the ones that really aren't very successful, but when they do work they're simply thrilling—full of clever images and good stories. I almost think Frank's afraid of competition. He likes to think he has a corner on the market for mining camp tales, you know. It won't hurt you at all to get some other opinions."

Stoddard put in, "He's already asked me to show him every editor and writer in town. I'll be sailing tomorrow, though. How about if I turn him over to you?"

"Of course he needs to be shown about town," Ina said, turning to Ned. "Would you be ready by, say, tomorrow after breakfast?"

Ned gave another small bow and spoke with an air of great chivalrous courtesy. "If the lady would be so generous with her time, I would be delighted to share such pleasant company."

The decision was toasted with several refills of beer, and then Stoddard suggested that it was time to go, especially because he still had to pack his ship's trunk.

As the two men walked through the evening streets towards Stoddard's lodgings on Russian Hill, Ned asked where he might find a room.

"You'll stay with me tonight, of course," Stoddard replied. "If you want to stay there after that, I'm afraid the landlord will be looking to you for rent. Still, it's a nice place, and a good location—not far from Ina's house at all."

Ned cleared his throat but did not speak.

"Charming girl, isn't she?" Stoddard talked forward, as if to the street, while he straightened his cravat. "And quite capable of taking care of herself. She made Frank and me throw out any ideas of jealousy long ago. Just a word of caution anyway. As I said before, she is an independent sort. Bear that in mind, Cincinnatus."

* * *

Despite Charles Warren Stoddard's admonition, the following two months found Ned together with Ina nearly every day, with the result that Ned was soon able to put the memories of his failed marriage and unpleasant divorce almost entirely out of mind. Nor did he long have qualms about his growing friendship with Ina. As it became obvious she enjoyed his company in return, their excursions about the city began to range beyond the limits of editors' offices and artists' studios.

Ned's carefree stay in San Francisco sank into his memory as a succession of sunny scenes, with him in his tall boots and felt hat, and Ina in a light summer dress and parasol. He remembered running to catch a horse trolley just as it began to climb a steep hill, and swinging together into a seat, out of breath. He remembered standing along Montgomery Street amidst a raucous Fourth of July parade, laughing in turn at the absurdity of a man riding a bicycle invention with a five-foot wheel, and at the pomposity of a goose-stepping German brass band from the butchers' guild. He remembered marveling through the glass window of an elegant commuter train at the palm-lined estates of railroad magnates in San Mateo. He remembered racing a light buggy for a few thrilling two-and-a-half minute miles on the road to the ocean, where he and Ina then strolled the Pacific sand, mimicking the dour expressions of the ungainly sea lions on the offshore rocks. He remembered sitting for their portraits at a photographic parlor on Kearny Street, so they could exchange pictures and send copies to Charley in Tahiti. The brown-and-white photographs caught them just as Ned's memories were to preserve them forever: a beautiful young woman and her rakish escort, unattached, smiling, full of far more hope than either of them could justify.

It was only two days before Ned's scheduled departure east that he began to think seriously about the details of the rest of his journey. He and Ina were sitting by the fountain at the Plaza, feeding the pigeons, when she said, "I envy you going to England." She watched the birds wistfully, and then asked, "Do you suppose you'll go straight to London, or see the country first?"

The question caught Ned off guard. He had to crumble bread for the pigeons a while before he could answer. At first it had seemed enough simply to arrive in London and announce his intention to become famous. But now that he had the train ticket to New York in his pocket the whole business seemed less urgent, and considerably more threatening.

"No reason I shouldn't see a bit of the country first," he said at length. "A lot of the great poets aren't from London anyway. I reckon if I stopped by Scotland I could see where Robert Burns and Sir Walter Scott lived. And Byron's buried at Newstead Abbey. I'd want to pay my respects there, too."

"That sounds wonderful," Ina sighed. "Like a pilgrimage to the land of poets. Whatever you do, don't forget Byron. Over there they must think we Americans don't honor his memory at all."

"Why's that?"

"You know, that new book by Harriet Beecher Stowe, *Lady Byron Vindicated,* makes him out to be some kind of monster."

"Oh? What's she say about him?" Ned had heard of Stowe's anti-slavery story, *Uncle Tom's Cabin,* but the Byron book was new to him.

"Just gossip, really. According to her, Byron hit his wife and had some kind of affair with his own sister. Ridiculous! There isn't a scrap of evidence. And Stowe doesn't even bother to mention that he wrote the most moving poetry of all time."

"I've admired Byron since I was old enough to read," Ned said. "I tell you what—I'll write a eulogy and read it at his tomb."

Ina brightened. "What a marvelous idea! I could write a poem too."

"Sure, why not?"

"Wait—I've got an even better idea." She clapped her hands together. "You could take a laurel wreath and hang it over his tomb."

"Excellent! But can you get laurel?"

"That's easy. It grows wild all over the hills across the bay. We could take the ferry there tomorrow and have the wreath before you leave. What do you think?"

Ned met the gaze of her shining gray eyes. "I think it's madness. Let's do it."

* * *

It could have been a fragment of a dream: running through the grassy slopes above Sausalito, surrounded in blue. Above, the endless sky, and below, a sweeping vista from the islands of the bay to the bare shoulders of the Golden Gate and the sparkling Pacific beyond. Running through the scattered, wind-bent trees until she half hid behind a perfect bough of laurel, and he caught her about the waist. A fleeting kiss, and she was free again.

The wreath, however, was proof that the afternoon was more than a dream. On the ferry at sunset, Ina sat on a deck bench, deftly twining the laurel crown from the sprigs on her lap. Beside her, Ned took up several fallen leaves and crushed them for their bitter, spicy perfume. He gazed out at the Golden Gate, which now more than earned its name as the sinking sun lit fires in the clouds beyond the gilt hills.

"That's myrrh," Ina said when she noticed him lost in thought.

"Myrrh," he repeated. "Yes, I know. Kings used it in tombs to mask the smell of death. Odd, isn't it, that the laurels of victory should have the incense of death?"

Ina's hands stopped their work. "It's not so odd. Every victory brings its own defeat."

"I wouldn't have expected you to say something so pessimistic."

"It's true, though. Just look at Byron's life if you want proof. When he became famous in England he was a target for the gossips, and they chased him out of the country. When he went to battle for the Greek revolution people talked of making him king, but he died of an influenza he caught in the field." She sighed, looking at her hands. "That's why I've always loved Byron, I suppose. His life was full of both myrrh and laurel."

"Isn't everyone's? Aren't the lives of all the poets?" Ned tried to catch her eyes, but she looked away, and for the first time since he had known her, she blushed. On an impulse he decided to tell her what her words had brought to mind. "I know I've been through more of the bitter and the sweet than you'll find in any of my poems. Once, when I was a young boy, I loved an Indian girl and lived in a glorious wilderness. Then the Indian wars came and I lost it all. In a way, I'd lived a whole lifetime and died by the age most boys are just leaving the farm."

Ned crushed the aromatic leaves in his palm and held them out. "In Oregon we call this myrtle. Maybe you know the name 'Minnie Myrtle?'"

Ina, who had been listening intently, nodded her head. "I think so. Didn't she once write love stories for the *Era?*"

"Love stories, that's right: bitter love stories. That was my second life. Seven years of bitter myrrh, and it ended just two months ago with our divorce."

Ina looked down. "I'm sorry."

"I was too, for a time. After all, my wife was the one who demanded the divorce. She was vengeful and hoped to ruin me. But I knew enough about law to win the case on my own terms." He looked out across the twilit bay, almost regretting how thoroughly he had defeated his former wife. Minnie's mother had official custody of the two older children, but of course Minnie herself would actually have to care for them. The money he had promised wouldn't be due until the end of the year, and even then, two hundred dollars wouldn't be enough for her to leave her parents' home. She would be tied down forever in the sleepy backwater of Port Orford, as helpless and as hopeless as when he had first met her.

Ned sighed. "In a way, I pity poor, dear Minnie, but I'm glad she won't be able to hurt me again."

Ina raised an eyebrow. "Never write off a woman." She smelled one of the fragrant leaves and smiled.

"What do you mean?" Ned asked. "Do you think Minnie could surprise me?"

"Or I could," Ina said.

"How so?"

She looked him in the eyes. "I'd like to go to London with you."

The statement left Ned staggered. The only possible way to undertake such a voyage together—sharing hotels, trains, and ship quarters—would be as a married couple. And although he had relished every moment of their time in San Francisco, he hadn't allowed himself to consider marriage, partly because the wounds from his divorce were so fresh and partly because of Ina's mysterious air of independence. Ina had carried herself with the grace of an intimate friend, but an unseen wall had always barred him from the intimacy of a lover. Now here she was, virtually proposing to him! Had she only been waiting until she learned of his divorce? He stammered, "Are you serious?"

"I almost wish I were." She tipped her head, her expression a little sad. "It's true enough that I'd like to go try my luck in London with you. But I'm afraid I can't. In fact, I won't ever marry. I'll never be bound by a man, nor chained by society's views. You see, I too am still steering around the shipwrecks of old tragedies."

Ned was still so shaken by her words that he didn't know how to react. "I thought—"

"It's all right," Ina said, taking his hand. "You're strong enough to handle stormy seas by yourself. When I first read your poems I knew you had lived through rough weather. I admire you for having the courage to face up to adversity. My poems are always about simple, transient things—a wild bird's trill, the wind in the grass, the texture of a poppy's petal—but that's only because I'm still trying to shut away the past."

Ned now recalled Stoddard's mysterious refusal to explain why Ina was unmarried, and backed away from the subject of her past gently. "Well, I reckon some things are best forgotten, even for a poet."

"Pain can be hidden, but it should never be forgotten." She looked out across the railing and sighed. "I've thought about this a lot in the past few weeks, because I've enjoyed being with you. I've decided it would be dishonest to let you leave for London without telling you who I really am."

"You're not Ina Coolbrith?" Ned had never known what to expect from this woman. Now he was completely adrift.

"No, I invented that name. I was born Josephine Smith, and my uncle was Joseph Smith, the martyred founder of the Mormon Church."

Ned looked at her with astonishment. "*Josephine Smith?* Then you're secretly a Mormon?"

"I'm not a Mormon, either."

"I—I guess I don't understand. How—"

"My mother, Agnes Coolbrith, was married to the prophet's brother. For five years the Mormons were horribly persecuted. Mobs chased them out of Ohio, burned them out of Missouri, and then massacred my uncles Joseph and Hyrum in Illinois. We were forced to settle on swampy, isolated land. My father died of malaria there. After that my mother was told to remarry under the new Mormon doctrine of polygamy. Instead of submitting, she left the church and later married my stepfather, William Picket, a printer in St. Louis."

A blast from the ferry's steam whistle startled the seagulls off the railing. But Ned's concentration could not be shaken from Ina and her startling history. "So your name is really Josephine Pickett?"

Ina shook her head. "That's only half the story. When I was ten, in 1851, we struck off for California by wagon train. Our wagons broke down in the desert. We only managed to hold them together with rags and ropes. We became lost, and nearly starved while crossing an unnamed pass in the Sierras. Finally we reached the Pacific and settled in Los Angeles, a village near Mexico.

"I grew up there and even wrote a little poetry under the pen name 'Ina.' But I was foolish and took the first proposal I got. I was only seventeen when my husband began beating me for what he said was unfaithfulness. He was so rough I fled to my parents' house. When he found me there he tried to kill me with a butcher knife and a rifle."

"Good Lord. You're not still married to this brute, are you?"

She gave him a thin smile. "No. I've been divorced nearly ten years longer than you have. I moved to San Francisco to hide my past, and I took a new name—Ina, for my old pen name, and Coolbrith, for my mother. Still, a divorce follows inside you like malaria, you know. You never really recover."

Ned shook his head, marveling. "I reckon you've lived as many lives as I have, and it doesn't sound like they were any easier. You're the strongest woman I've ever met, Ina." He admired her all the more, knowing that she had risen above her grim past and the taint of divorce to build herself a free, new life. He too was faced with the challenge of reinventing himself, using the fragments that remained from what seemed like past lives.

He put his hand on her arm. "Despite all you've told me, your real name is Ina. You may have gone through a half dozen other names, but none of them captured your spirit. I never want to know you otherwise than as Ina Coolbrith."

"I'm glad you think so." She straightened and began weaving the laurel again. "At least my name's not as ill-fitting as yours."

He gave her a quizzical look. "What do you mean by that?"

"Oh, that's the other thing I wanted to talk to you about before you set out to meet the poets in glorious old England. How do you expect to climb Parnassus and be crowned of the gods with a name like Cincinnatus Hiner? Heaven knows, Miller is bad enough."

"Perhaps it is a little plain for a poet."

"Miller's plain, but the rest is positively baroque. You should get rid of the Cincinnatus Hiner business at the very least, if you want them to take you seriously in London."

"All right," Ned laughed. "What would you prefer?"

"Oh, I was thinking of something wild and poetic, like your book."

"How about Heine Miller? That's close to Hiner. I'd be the namesake of a radical German poet."

"Now you're the one who's not being serious," Ina chided, smiling. "Why not 'Joaquin,' like your poem?"

"Joaquin?" Ned mused, and for an instant he saw bushy-bearded, old Mountain Joe before him in the ghostly shimmer of a pine campfire, slipping out a whiskey flask as he cackled, "Maybe you're a Joaquin after all."

Chapter 24

I said, with men, and with the thoughts of men,
I held but slight communion; but instead,
My joy was in the Wilderness, to breathe
The difficult air of the iced mountain's top.
—Lord Byron, "Manfred"

Ned left San Francisco on the railroad company ferry, ruefully aware that his fiery optimism about going to London had burned low. As he stood on the deck watching the bold skyline of San Francisco slowly dwindle in the ferry's wake, he tried to cheer himself up.

After all, hadn't he done better than might have been expected so far? He had come to California two months ago with nothing. Now he had several friendships, a tentative agreement with the *Bulletin* to run his travel letters, and at least one solid believer: Ina. Of course he had been disappointed when Ina had declined to see him off—she had talked about the pointlessness of prolonged farewells—but that wasn't the problem either.

He looked over the bow of the ferry toward the distant Oakland wharf where the train waited, breathing steam like a toy Chinese dragon. The real problem, he knew, was both simple and enormous. He was alone again, unknown again, setting out across a continent and an ocean with no addresses in mind but those made famous by poetry, and no letters of introduction but his bundle of manuscripts. To be sure, he was taking George Francis Train's advice—leading a saber charge for fame and fortune against the entrenched forces of the English literary world. But he had just looked over his shoulder and had seen that not one of the American troops was yet following him into battle. Even the bravado inspired by a broad-brimmed hat, a pair of jackboots, and a name like Joaquin hardly seemed sufficient in the face of such long odds.

Ned made his way through the confusion of baggage carts and newspaper vendors on the wharf. A wood-paneled railway car loomed before him through a drifting fog of steam. When he slumped into the hard wooden seat and looked out at the crowd of other people's waving well-wishers, a lump stuck in his throat. For an instant he wanted to jump out, to run north through the woods, to spare himself the terror of such an impossible journey. Here he was, dressed as a backwoods pony express rider, on a train headed away from everything he had ever known. He would have felt more at home trudging into a snowbound wilderness. Who in the civilized homeland of the great Byron would ever believe he was a poet? Did he even believe it himself?

He forced himself to remember Ella, his pale, consumption-wracked sister, who had so strongly believed in his writing that she had defied her laming illness and walked, alone, to present George Francis Train with his book. The single, painful mile she had struggled must have taken more courage than the seven thousand that lay before him now. "Never give up on yourself," Ella had told him. And yet how many times, Ned wondered, had he already walked blindly into the unknown, dreaming of greatness? He had run away to the California gold fields, bought a bankrupt newspaper in Eugene City, and run for the Supreme Court. Each time he had failed. Now he was about to hurl himself into the greatest void of all. Suddenly the entire project seemed insane.

But then there was a jolt, and the train began rolling through the streets of Oakland, the engine bell clanging to warn pedestrians off the line. The ten-day railroad journey across the continent had begun.

At the edge of the town the cars clacked and shook faster until they whistled past the brown hills and dusty orchards at the frightening speed of thirty miles an hour. They did not even stop at dusk, but raced on into the void ahead. Porters lit gas fixtures in the cars as calmly as if it were an ordinary hotel, and then gave the call to prepare for bed. Ned's ticket did not include a berth, and he was far too wrought up to sleep anyway. He spent the night sitting in the parlor car at the back of the train, staring wide-eyed into the hurtling blackness outside while drunken passengers belted out slurred hymns to the accompaniment of a wheezing reed pump organ. Between songs Ned was alarmed to hear the creak of trestles, the rush of waterfalls, and distant echoes of the clattering wheels as the precarious track wound higher into the Sierras.

At dawn Ned sank into a fitful sleep. When he finally awoke, they were already storming across the alkaline wastes of Nevada. A fine white dust blew up from the desert, sifting in at the windows and eddying about the end of the car. The train stopped at a desolate station where men with shotguns patrolled the platform, guarding stacks of silver ingots and warily watching a ragged collection of Paiute Indians nearby. The Indian men squatted in the shade of the station fences while their gap-toothed women hurried to the train to beg from window to window with chipped pots and battered meat-tins.

With a pang of guilt, Ned realized these broken people might be the same proudly defiant Paiutes his company of volunteers had battled near Canyon City only a few years ago. In that short time, their culture had been destroyed. Already, the poems he was bringing to England were tales from a lost age.

Ned opened the bag of food he had brought for himself. He reached bread and dried meat to the brown hands until the train pulled away. The begging women ran alongside through the sagebrush, crying, "Mahsie! Mahsie!" From the blank expressions of the other passengers, Ned realized that he alone recognized this was the old Indian trade jargon word for "thank you." He turned away, saddened and ashamed at the passing of their brave frontier life.

The Indian women's diminishing cries made him think of Paquita, and his eyes grew damp. With Minnie gone and Ina left behind, memories of his dark-haired Wintu wife had begun to haunt him in lonely hours. He could see her on the willow snowshoes she had once made, stooping by a snow-banked creek to fill jugs with icy water. He could hear her musical Wintu words telling tales of the trickster god Coyote as they sat by the cabin fire.

When Charley had come to Canyon City he had said Paquita and his daughter were still at Mt. Shasta, but he had refused to say anything more, insisting that Ned "see for himself." At the time Ned had thought Charley just wanted him to join him on his pack trip. But now he wondered if Paquita and Cali-Shasta needed help. He had always counted on the unsettled wilderness at Now-ow-wa keeping them safe from the changes that had wracked the West. Surely, if an island remained above that ruinous flood, it would be Mt. Shasta. More than ten years had passed since he had promised to return—since he had promised Cali-Shasta that he would "make everything right." Now he was putting off paying that debt yet again, betting everything on a fool's gamble.

The train steamed on into Utah, startling vast flocks of waterfowl from the shores of the Great Salt Lake. At the tidy Mormon village of Ogden, Ned transferred with a crowd of others to the cars of the Union Pacific. For a day they climbed over the Rocky Mountains. Ned sat glued to the window, watching the snowy crags that rimmed the horizon like teeth on a crosscut saw. How different these mountains were from solitary volcanoes like as Shasta and Hood!

Down through Nebraska, along the North Platte, Ned tried to bring back memories of the Oregon Trail he had walked as a boy behind a covered wagon. The great, horizon-stretching plains were as vast as ever, but the old wildness was lost. A wake of sun-bleached animal bones lined the track in piles as much as ten feet tall. The great buffalo herds were gone. Thousands had obviously been shot from the train itself and left to rot. Even now, every jackrabbit and prairie dog scampering away from the rails drew a crackle of target-practice fire from the passengers in the lead cars. Ned felt outraged by the slaughter, but knew the shooters would only laugh at him if he objected.

At Omaha the Union Pacific line ended, and Ned changed to the Chicago & Rock Island. In Chicago, he changed again to the Pittsburgh, Fort Wayne & Chicago. Then he sat three more days in the rattling, lurching cars, wondering just what Joaquin Miller would do when the train finally steamed into New York City, the literary heart of the nation.

As it turned out, the train did not go as far as New York. Instead it stopped in Jersey City, where Ned stepped out of the car and was immediately pushed onto an enormous wooden platform by a crowd of pedestrians and horse-drawn vehicles. Before he was even sure this was a ferry—and not a dock—unseen engines had pushed it into the Hudson River toward the chimneys and church spires of Manhattan Island. The crowd on the ferry seemed to consist of men wearing identical black suits and top hats. The men spaced themselves out across the deck holding their newspapers upright like so many tiny partitions. Ned felt the sting of suspicious glances toward his huge, floppy hat and tall Western riding boots. Trying to be friendly, he grinned broadly to several neighbors and nodded, "Howdy there." But no one answered. The crowd only shifted to give him more room.

Chaos reigned at the ferry landing. No sooner had Ned set down his bag than a tough-looking man said something he couldn't understand and snatched it up. Ned bolted after him in time to see the man toss the bag into a shabby black coach. Desperate to save his manuscripts, Ned jumped in after them. To his alarm, he was given an additional push, the door slammed behind him, and the horse-drawn carriage lurched off down a rough brick street. He pounded on the door, but it appeared to be locked. He shouted to the crowd, but no one seemed to hear.

Finally the coach stopped, the door opened, and a man with a hack driver's cap asked, "Pardon, mister, which hotel did you say?"

In his astonishment, Ned mumbled the name of the only hotel he had ever heard of in New York: the Astor House. The words were hardly across his lips when the coach started rattling onward. He sat back, dumbfounded. Could the whole episode have been his own misunder-standing?

The Astor House was the most enormous structure he had ever seen, with granite columns rising from story to story, seemingly to the sky itself. While he was staring at it from the sidewalk the hackman demanded the preposterous fare of five dollars. Without thinking, Ned dug a ten-dollar gold coin out of his pocket and promptly received a five-dollar bill in change. Then, still dazed, he picked up his dusty leather bag, straightened his floppy hat, and began to walk up the stone stairs. Liveried doormen festooned with gold braid stood on either hand of the great doors, but did not open them. He pushed inside by himself and made his way to the middle of the lobby—a hall so vast and elegant he felt like a pattern in the carpeting. Marble pillars and potted palms reached up toward a huge chandelier, far above.

Ned just stood there a moment, without any clear idea of what he should do next. Then he remembered the five-dollar bill in his hand. Paper money had been so rare on the West Coast that he had never owned any before. As he inspected it, not knowing which pocket he should put it in, and wondering why it was a dirty white instead of green, a pimply-faced bellhop popped up before him, jerked a thumb his direction, and called back to his liveried colleagues, "Hey, look! The cowboy took a rebel fiver!"

Blood rushed to Ned's face. Without a word he picked up his bag, turned about on his boot heel, and strode back the way he had come. This time the doormen held the great portals open wide.

He walked on for blocks and blocks, burning with anger. Finally he threw his bag down and sat on a bench. New York, he thought, was obviously not a place where it paid to look like you had just stepped out of a saddle.

He reached down and pulled his pant legs over his tall black boots to hide them as best he could. Then he took off his rustic, broad-brimmed hat, folded it mercilessly, and stuffed it into the bag. If he could do nothing else here, he would try to save his money for the ship and for London.

*   *   *

The second night in New York he wrote a letter by candlelight in a dingy hotel room:

New York, August 19, 1870.

Dear Ina:

As you can see by the address, I have reached this place, although I am determined to leave it again tomorrow. Tell them at the *Bulletin* not to expect travel letters. I have bought a journal and plan to accumulate my impressions there instead, since I am afraid they are kind of rough. I have tried quite hard to get to see Horace Greeley at the *Tribune*, but he won't see me. Maybe he is not here, but I think he is.

I have bought my ticket, $65, second class, ship Europa, Anchor Line, to land at Glasgow, and will be overjoyed to leave. I don't think anyone who has ever breathed the fresh air of the Pacific could fit in here. At Central Park today I wanted to rest under a tree—a cool, clean tree that looked like it wanted nothing more than a poet underneath and a good rainstorm—and a policeman, club in hand, caught hold of me and shook me, telling me to keep off the grass. Keep off the grass! There was no grass there. If these New Yorkers would come to Oregon they could sit untroubled under the trees, roll in grass that is grass, and rest forever.

The laurel wreath, which I keep carefully, and your photograph, which I keep even more carefully, remind me often of your kindness and encouragement.

Very truly yours,
Joaquin Miller.

The *Europa* was a wooden steamer filled with dour, mustachioed Germans returning to their homeland to fight in the Franco-Prussian war. For two weeks the Atlantic telegraph cable had been alive with the news: France had declared war and had captured Saarbrücken, only to have the surprisingly well-prepared Prussians storm into France along the entire length of the border. Everywhere in the ship men were grumbling in harsh, foreign words. Ned had little choice but to keep to himself. He walked the deck watching for icebergs and porpoises, or wrote in his journal to the ceaseless rhythm of the engines—fifty-two beats of the propeller screw a minute, like the throb of a great, slow heart.

On the tenth day, Irish gulls gave the ship a lazy greeting. Two days later Ireland itself drifted past to starboard, a green checkerboard of stone walls and white cottages. On the fourteenth day they sailed up the Firth of Clyde. Low, rocky islands loomed on either hand. Finally they followed the narrowing river into the heart of a great, gray city.

Ned took one look at Glasgow's crowded, soot-blackened buildings and set off to find the Scotland of verse—the land of bonnie lochs and open braes. He squinted at the sun to check his direction, strapped his bag over his shoulder, and began walking. Robert Burns had grown up in Ayr, and Ayr was south, so south he would go. It was as if Ina's laurel wreath, carefully packed in his bag, were guiding his crusade. He would visit the homelands of the great poets of Scotland and England. Then he would lay the wreath on the tomb of the master: Lord Byron.

By late afternoon he had covered twenty miles. His feet were hot and sore, but at last he was among sheep-dotted hills and stone-walled fields, and the air was refreshingly warm and sweet. When night fell there were no houses nearby, and no trees. Behind a hedgerow, near a friendly brook, he stopped to eat from the bread in his bag. Then, when the stars came out—as beautiful as any he had seen since Oregon—he laid his head on his leather bag and pulled a coat over his shoulders for the night.

For hours he lay awake, caught up in the excitement and the doubts of his first day in a foreign land. He was half a world away from home, as out of place as a coyote in a cathedral. No one here knew or cared that an American poet had landed to conquer the Old World. And what chance did he really have? At the first sight of a city he had fled for open country to sleep in a roadside ditch like a common drifter. But above him the familiar stars twinkled reassuringly, as if to prove that the most distant of goals can shine brightest in the darkest of hours.

In the morning the bells of inquisitive Ayrshire cattle roused him from his damp bed. Ned shook his head to orient himself after stormy dreams. But the dreams had been true—he was in Ayrshire, the land of Robert Burns. As a boy he had read every one of the rustic Scot's poems. He had even stolen the book from his father's shelf the night he ran away to California. Now it was as if he had been dropped into the midst of one of Burns' poetic landscapes.

Four hours of brisk hiking took Ned over the hills to the little coastal village of Ayr. That afternoon he visited the spots made famous by Burns' verse as though they were shrines: Alloway's auld kirk, Highland Mary's grave, and the auld brig spanning the river Doon. Then he rented a room for the night in the village's small stone inn and penned poems long into the night about all he had seen.

In the morning the innkeeper woke him with a tray of scones and tea. "Breakfast, sir."

"Huh?" Ned rolled over, squinted into the sunlight from the window, and slowly sat up. "Oh. Thanks."

The innkeeper hesitated. "The wife said ye were going on to London?"

"I reckon so." Ned frowned as he bit into the scone. He had mentioned London to the innkeeper's wife when he arrived. But the closer he came to the largest city on earth, the more intimidating it seemed. He was glad he had planned to see a bit of the country first.

"Well, it's ten o'clock. I dinna want ye to miss the train."

Ned had already asked in the village about trains. Rail fare was twice as expensive as he had thought. He couldn't afford to ride the entire distance. He waved his hand disparagingly. "Naw, you miss too much traveling by train. I reckon I'll just walk there instead." He drank a slurp of tea; it tasted remarkably good with the dry breakfast bread.

The innkeeper's eyes widened. "Sir? It's nigh on five hundred miles to London."

"Great!" Ned replied, his mouth full with another bite of scone. "Then I'll get some exercise in the bargain."

"Aye sir," the innkeeper said slowly. He began backing out of the room as if Ned might be mentally unbalanced, and a little dangerous. "Aye, that ye would."

An hour later Ned shouldered his leather bag and set out again, this time toward the east. Now his destination was the Tweed, the river of Sir Walter Scott's poetry, ninety miles across the moors and mountains of Scotland. As he walked the rocky dirt roads he kept up his spirits by whistling tunes like "Zip Coon" and "Old Dan Tucker." Scottish women scything wheat in the fields looked up and smiled wonderingly at the strange wanderer.

A farmer leaning against a stone wall took a pipe from his teeth and called out, "Are ye out peddling sewing needles, laddie?"

"No, not a peddlar at all," Ned called back. "I'm a poet, you see."

The man's bushy eyebrows lowered. "A what?"

"A poet! I'm on a pilgrimage to the bards of Scotland."

But the farmer just pushed back his cap and scratched his head. Even when Ned was far down the road, the man still stood there, staring after him.

After five days afoot Ned waded the Tweed and spent an afternoon roaming Scott's estate. There he rested beneath a tree and wrote in his journal, "I have looked over Sir Walter Scott's 'poem in stones,' as he called it. So beautiful, and so sad. Empty as a dead man's palm is this place now." But wasn't that as it should be, he thought, after all the sad tales Scott had written?

That evening he continued three miles to the ruins of Melrose Abbey, famed in Scott's works as a resting place of Scottish kings. For a few coins, a drunken old woman let him in the gate. But later, when he finished visiting the tombs, she was nowhere to be found. Ned shouted and rattled the locked gate angrily. When no one came, he gave up in disgust and began to search for another way out. A chill fog drew up from the river, wreathing the castle-like Abbey in nearly total darkness. For an hour or more he groped among the tombstones and crumbling arches. Finally, resigned to spending a night in the dank ruins, he huddled in a corner under his coat.

For a time he stared glumly out into the cemetery, besieged by self-pity, as if all the doubts and fears that had followed him on his journey were lurking amongst the tombs. The shadows crowded closer, ridiculing his clothes, his books, and his hopeless quest for greatness.

He pressed his eyes closed, trying to call up a mental image warm enough to keep the shadows at bay. Slowly, a campfire kindled in his imagination. Drifting across the flickering vision came the faint, sweet incense of burning pitch. And then the sighing pines and the starlit mountain were there too—as if they really were Wintu spirits from a half-forgotten age, ready to stand by him when he needed them most.

Ned arose in the morning as if from a night of fasting and prayer, miraculously strengthened and renewed. Indeed, as he began to scale the stone wall, he scoffed at the discomfort of his night amidst the kings' tombs. He leaned back his head and startled the sparrows out of the hollow windows of the ruined abbey with a laugh. Then, as if this were his battle cry, he sprang down to the grass and strode off toward the Melrose railway station, ready to meet the giant shadow of Lord Byron. Now it was all that remained between him and London.

*   *   *

Newstead Abbey, Byron's ancestral home, was eight miles by foot from the railway station in Nottingham, and nearly surrounded by the dark fringe of Sherwood Forest. When Ned finally reached the abbey gate he stood before it silently, awed by the prospect of entering the hallowed grounds of the late great poet. Byron, too, had once been an unsung commoner, but had risen to the House of Lords, with the world of literature at his feet. Ned wondered if it were heresy to dream of following in such giant footsteps. But wasn't he himself a Byronic figure, like the tragic hero of the poet's epic, *Manfred*—another tormented loner whose past conceals a dark tragedy?

After a few minutes, however, Ned began to wonder why no other tourists were waiting to pay their respects. There was only an old gate-keeper sitting nearby, reading a newspaper. Ned asked him, "Am I too late for one of the tours?"

"Tours?" the little bald man repled, eyeing Ned suspiciously. "Tours of what?"

"Lord Byron's estate, of course. Isn't this the right place?"

"Aye," the old man laughed, "but he's been dead more than forty years, lad. Nobody comes all the way out here for sightseeing. Where are you from, anyway?"

"America," Ned said dejectedly. He thought of the laurel wreath he had brought from Ina to hang at Byron's tomb. Now he might not be able to fulfill even this simple goal. But how could he disappoint Ina? Remembering that a bribe had worked at Scott's Melrose Abbey, he held out a few coins. "Maybe you could let me in long enough to see some of the places I've read about?"

The man wrinkled his brow. "From America, is it?" He looked from Ned to the coins. "Well, come along then, lad, if it means that much to you."

To Ned's delight, the gatekeeper agreed to leave his post long enough to show him the sights personally. Ned promptly asked to see the tree where Lord Byron had carved his name, the oak he had planted, and the garden where the poet turned up a skull that was later made into a drinking cup for his wine.

Finally Ned said, "I've read that Byron's buried in Hucknall Torkard church. Where on the grounds is that?"

The man gave him yet another odd look. "Why, it's in Hucknall Torkard, to be sure—not on the grounds at all. The village is a mile or two down the dale from here."

Ned thanked the man and set out at once, determined to complete Ina's assignment. The church turned out to be alarmingly run-down, with crumbling mortar between the dark stones of its walls. Scraps of wood patched the broken windows. Inside, the church was as murky and damp as a cave. Ned searched about in the darkness for half an hour before he found the tomb—little more than a stone in the floor. Water dripped from the mossy wall behind it and lay in puddles on the floor. Byron's sister had mounted a small plaque on the wall to inform the world that a poet was buried there, but that was all.

Ned silently shook his head, resentful that the world could forget such a man. After all, it had been Byron's works that he had read and reread through the long winter nights at Now-ow-wa. It had been Byron who had inspired him to charge his own verse with drama and daring. And it had been Byron's example that had made it seem possible for his challenge of the literary establishment to succeed.

He gently unpacked the laurel wreath from his bag, but there was no place to put it over the tomb. Rather than leave it leaning against the wall, in the puddle, he took the wreath with him in search of the church's custodian.

Ned found a white-haired caretaker raking a gravel path outside. Ned explained his plan: would he accept a gold sovereign a year, every year, for nailing the wreath above the tomb and seeing that it remained there?

The man thought a while, looked at the sovereign, and then went to get his tools. As he was driving the nail into the mortar, however, an old woman suddenly appeared out of the pews and pointed an accusing finger at them. "I'll remind you this is a house of worship, not a workshop."

"Sorry for the noise, Mrs. Burdick," the caretaker said, tipping his head to acknowledge her. "The American gentleman here just wants a wreath put up, he does. In honor of the departed."

"What! To honor Lord Byron, that profligate? The way he treated his wife he has no business being buried in a church at all."

The old man drove another nail into the wreath unconcernedly. "I'm thinking he's honored for good reason."

The woman gasped. "You ought to be ashamed of yourself. Remove that wreath this instant."

"Take it up with the vicar if you've a complaint," the caretaker replied.

"I intend to do just that," the woman announced, and stormed away.

When she was gone, Ned shook his head. "Looks like that's going to be a mighty hard-earned sovereign."

The caretaker shrugged. "A bargain's a bargain, I say. And the vicar he's a man of letters too, he is, and a tough nut to crack. If it was all the ladies in the parish wanted your wreath down, I'm mistaken if he wouldn't just nail up another beside it." He leaned against a pew with a distant look. "It's been a long time since Lord Byron sold his estates and left the county, and some in the parish has never forgiven him. But the new vicar, he's from London, he is, and all he says about it is, 'No prophet is without honor, save in his own land.'"

The old man gave Ned a firm wink. "I'll wager we keep your wreath after all."

*   *   *

Four days later Ned finally had time to sit down and write the longest entry his journal yet held:

> *London, October 2, 1870.* Am at last in the central city of this earth. When I came in on the rail I left my bag at the station; paid two pence—great, big coppers, big as five of America's—and took a ticket for it, and so set out to walk about the city. Strange as it seems I walked straight to Westminster Abbey—straight as the crooked streets would let me; and I did not ask anyone on the way, nor did I have the remotest idea where it was. But my heart must have been in that Abbey, going out to the great spirits, the immortal dust of saints and poets gathered there, and I walked straight to where my

heart was. It encouraged me very much—as if by some possible turn of fortune or favor of the gods I may really get there, or at least be on the same road that these giants have journeyed on.

I left the Abbey and walked up Regent Street toward St. Paul's. After keeping on my feet till hardly able to stand, I began to look for a place to stop. I found a woman who had rooms to let, but for some reason she simply shut the door in my face, after forcing me out of the hall.

A public-house here is not a tavern or an inn, and has no lodgings. I tried to get to stop at two or three of these reeking gin-mills. They stared at me, but went on jerking beer behind the counter, and did not answer. At one place I asked for water. All stopped and looked at me. A woman with a baby in one arm, wrapped tightly in a shawl along with herself, and a jug of beer in the other, came up and put her face in mine curiously. Then the men all roared. I was too tired to explain, and so backed out into the street again and went on. I did not get the water. I now learn that one must not ask for water here. No one drinks water here. No public-house keeps it. Well, to one from Oregon, the land of pure water, where God pours it down from the snowy clouds out of the hollow of His hand—the high-born, beautiful, great white rain, this seems strange.

I lost my way in one of the by-streets, and asked how to get out. People were kind and good natured, but they spoke with such a queer accent that I could not understand. At last a little girl of a dozen years, very bright and very beautiful, proposed to show me the way to the main street. She was a ray of sunlight after a whole month of storms. She was making neckties, she said, and getting a sixpence a day; five pence she paid to a Mrs. Brady, who lived at 52 New Street, and this left her a penny a day to dress and enjoy life upon!

"And can I live with Mrs. Brady for five pence a day?"

"Maybe so. Mrs. Brady has a room; maybe you can get it. Let us go and see."

We came, we saw, and settled. I gave Lizzie a shilling the next day to run errands. She went to the station and got my bag, and she put my few things in perfect shape. I think she has some doubts about my sanity. She watches me closely, and I have seen her shake her head at this constant writing of mine. But when she got her shilling, oh! she was happy—and so rich!

Mrs. Brady is about six feet high, and very slim and bony. She has but one eye, and hammers her husband, who drives a wagon for a brewery, most cruelly every night. He is short and stout as one of his beer barrels, and must love his old telegraph pole of a wife anyway, for he refuses to pound her back when she pounds him, although he assured me yesterday, in confidence, that he was certain he could lick her if he tried.

Ned pushed back the journal and reread the last page at an arm's length, contemplating the descriptions of the people he had met in London so far. Of course he knew great writers lived in the city too, somewhere, but how could he find them? He had no Charley Stoddard or Ina Coolbrith here to make his introductions. So far the friendliest person he had met was a twelve-year-old girl.

Ned thumbed through the manuscripts he had stacked on the desk. London was so bewilderingly big it would be easy to lose track of why he had come, and then his small supply of savings would be gone. Once he were penniless this far from friends, his future would be blacker even than Minnie Myrtle's, out in Port Orford.

He let the problem simmer while he drummed his fingers on the desk. At length he settled on a plan. Even if he didn't know how to meet the famed literary figures of London, at least he knew where to find the publishers' offices. He would first try to find a publisher who would put out a book of his verse. If only it could be printed in London he felt sure he could rattle these stolid Britons right out of their overstuffed chairs.

Chapter 25

Where this was written, rhyming is considered a mild type of insanity.
—Joaquin Miller, Preface to *Pacific Poems* (London, 1871)

Ned clutched his bundle of handwritten papers as he hurried down Fleet Street, where most of London's publishers had their offices. Horses snorted billows of steam into the foggy winter air. Smaller puffs drifted from the bowler hats bobbing along the sidewalk. Ned wished he could afford a bowler himself to fend off the chill; since his humiliation in New York he had packed away his ungainly Western hat. He stepped out from the crowd, leaned back to read the publisher's sign above a door, and then went in.

"What's your business?" a square-jawed man at the counter demanded.

"I'm a poet, you see. The name's Joaquin Miller. I've brought—"

"No unsolicited manuscripts," the man growled. "That's the rule and there's an end of it. Good day."

Again Ned was tramping down the street, looking for the signs of publishing houses. He laid his papers before a hollow-cheeked editor at a desk in a second building. The man squinted at the writing. "Joe-ah-quinn?" He shook his head and pushed the papers away. "Leave submissions by the door. We have a boy to sort through them. You should hear from us in three months."

"But I don't have three months," Ned objected. "I'm from America."

"Can't help you about that," the man replied, already returning to other work.

A minute later Ned was outside again. He rested on the rim of the fountain at Piccadilly Circus, clapping his arms to keep warm. Then he went on.

The next editor was younger, and listened attentively while Ned presented his manuscripts and explained his purpose. When Ned had finished talking, the editor gave him a wonderfully sympathetic smile. "You know, I had a cousin who talked just like you once—quite the same queer accent and all. Came back from the States, died of malaria. Pity, really."

Ned stared at the man. "But what about the poems?"

"Oh, we've no use for them, of course. I can't imagine anyone—"

Ned pounded the desk with his fist and stood up, angrily gathering the papers together.

"But you might try the magazine *Fun*," the editor added.

"*Fun? Fun!* Now I reckon you're just trying to pull my leg." Ned strode across the office toward the door.

"Actually, I meant the editor there, Thomas Hood. He's rather fond of Americans and things out of the ordinary and all." The young editor had to raise his voice to make his last words heard across the busy office. "And I certainly did not intend to pull your leg!"

At this statement a dozen surprised faces looked up. The young editor blushed a vivid red as Ned slammed the door.

*   *   *

January 20, 1871. Have completed another poem, "Arizonian," which seems the best so far. I'm putting it on top of my other manuscripts and have decided to call the whole collection *Pacific Poems*, thinking this might make the book more attractive than publishers have found it so far.

February 14, 1871. I am now moved back to old Westminster, where I first entered London. The house on New Street had a large crack and was condemned. The reliable Mrs. Brady said it only had a few months more to stand; that the underground railway or something ran under it.

Now I am right in back of the Abbey. From my garret window I can see the Virginia creepers, which they say were planted by Queen Elizabeth. I hear all the bells of Westminster here, and of Parliament, Big Ben, and all. Not a good place to sleep or to rest, O immortal poets! I had rather rest in Oregon.

March 12, 1871. This last week has made me wonder to what use I have tramped about with my *Pacific Poems* for so long. I think I have called upon or tried to call upon every publisher in this city now. I had kept Murray, son of the great Murray, Byron's friend, to the last. I had said to myself: this man, whatever the others may do, will stand up for the bridge that brought him over. If all others fail I will go to the great Murray.

All others failed, and I went. I marched stiffly up Albemarle Street, boldly entered the publishing house, and called for Mr. Murray. The clerk looked hard at me. Then, mentally settling the fact that I really had business with the publisher, he said: "Mr. Murray will be in tomorrow. Could you return then?"

My heart beat like a pheasant in a forest. For the first time I was to meet a great publisher face to face. "Yes, yes, thank you; I will come tomorrow—tomorrow at precisely this time." And I left the house, crossed the street, took a long look at it, and went home the happiest man in London.

I came next day an hour before my time, but I did not enter. I watched the clock at the Picadilly corner, and I came in just as I had agreed. I think the clerk had forgotten that I had ever been there. For my part, I had remembered nothing else. The great Murray came down—a tall, lean man, bald, with one bad eye, and a habit of taking sight at you behind his long, thin forefinger, which he holds up, as he talks excitedly, and shakes all the time, either in his face or your own.

He took me upstairs when I told him I had a book all about the great West of America. Then he spun about on his heel, and taking sight at me behind his long, lean finger, jerked out the words: "Now, young man, let us see what you have got."

I drew forth my first-born and laid it in his hand. He held his head to one side, flipped the leaves, looked in, jerked his head back, looked in again, twisted his head like a giraffe, and then lifted his long finger:

"Aye, now, don't you know poetry won't do? Poetry won't do, don't you know?"

"But won't you read it, please?"

"No, no, no. No use, no use, don't you know?"

I reached my hand, took the despised sheets, and in a moment was in the street, wild, shaking my fist at the house that had been my greatest hope for so long.

March 15, 1871. Ina has written me a most gentle letter, the gist of which is that I should give up here. Even loyal Ina despairs! And what can I tell her? After all these months in London, not one publisher has given my work a fair hearing. Nor have I managed to meet a single substantial poet—despite my best efforts to be intro-duced to Browning, Tennyson, and Dante Rossetti, the influential Pre-Raphaelite.

Maybe Ina is right. And the truth is, my money is nearly at an end.

If I stay much longer, I won't have enough for a ticket home. But confound it all!

Ned put down his quill and glared out his garret window at the black-suited Britishers walking the street below, who now looked as inhospitable and repetitive as so many ants. And he thought: yes, ants, living in little holes in the ground, living safe little routine lives. Where were the great men in London? The thinkers, the movers, the writers he had hoped to find? In Oregon the men of daring had lived under the open sky, fearless before the power of nature and equal before each other.

He looked again at the little black figures on the street, and tried to imagine a single Mountain Joe storming through their ranks in all his blustering fury.

The image made him smile.

And as soon as he smiled an idea began to take shape in his mind—an idea, and the name of *one* publisher he had not yet gone to see.

At once he went to his closet. He rummaged through the fallen clothes until he found the dusty leather bag he had carried to London nearly half a year before. There, crumpled in the bottom of the bag, was the old, broad-brimmed, floppy felt hat, looking more like an old friend than anything he had seen in months. He beat the dusty hat against his leg, tossed it in the air, and caught it deftly on his head.

After that, he knew exactly what he had been doing wrong. Why on earth should he be trying to mimic the Londoners? That might have worked in Oregon, but here the streets were full of Byrons. He needed to unleash a wilder animal—a deeper, truer part of himself. He needed the living, walking tall tales of Mountain Joe. It was time for a full-scale frontier ambush.

*   *   *

Thomas Hood, the young, red-cheeked editor of *Fun*, looked up in astonishment at his clerk receptionist. "Really, you'd say he's *what?*"

The elderly clerk swallowed, which was difficult enough for him, since his tall, starched collar already strained against his short neck and double chin. "An—an *Indian scout*, sir. One can hear he is an American, and although I am ill-acquainted with their customs, he—"

"I say, Henderson, just tell this Miller fellow to pop in, will you? If he's as American as all that, I'd better have a look at him myself."

"Very well, sir."

Henderson had hardly left before Ned strode in, extending a big hand to the editor. "Howdy. The name's Joaquin—Joaquin Miller."

Hood stood up to shake the hand, examining as he did so the very un-British figure before him. Aside from wearing the old hat, which made Ned's blond hair and beard appear fairly wild, Ned had again stuffed his pants inside his knee-high boots and had tied a red bandanna about his neck. Ned was already half a head taller than most Englishmen, and the huge hat left him towering above Thomas Hood.

"Joaquin, is it? Rather rummy name. What seems to be up?"

Ned pumped the hand heartily. "Mighty glad to meet you, I'm sure. I'm just in from California with some poems about the frontier, you see, and I'm fixing to have 'em printed up here in town. Well, first thing I hear is, 'Look up Tom Hood, pal; he knows more 'bout Americans than anyone in these parts. He'll see to it your stuff gets the right kind of send-off, you bet.'"

An amused smile dimpled Hood's red cheeks. "Well, jolly of you to stop in. I suppose I have known rather a few Americans, but none of them has traveled much in the western section. One gets rather sketchy accounts of war-painted savages, that sort of thing. So what about these poems of yours?"

"Here, read for yourself, pal," Ned immediately replied. He handed him "Kit Carson's Ride" and "Arizonian"—over thirty pages of manuscript—and began rocking back and forth on his heels, waiting for him to read them through then and there.

With an awkward laugh, the editor began to skim lightly over a few pages. Gradually, however, the verse appeared to catch his interest. Even when the clerk interrupted with what he said was pressing business, Hood merely waved him away. Ned waited with his arms crossed, as solemn and silent as a Wintu chief at a parley.

Fifteen minutes later Hood sat back from the poems as though from another world. He wiped his brow and opened his mouth fish-like several times before he actually directed a question to Ned, tapping the manuscript with his finger. "I say, Miller, have you really lived through this kind of thing?"

"Why, I reckon so, or I wouldn't have written it."

"I mean, this business about being caught in a prairie fire and a buffalo stampede—these are things you've really done?"

"Oh, you bet." Ned stroked his beard with the same assuredness he knew Mountain Joe would have shown if someone had questioned one of his tales.

"And the gold mining, and these Indian concubines?"

"I panned gold four years in California, and lived for another two as a brave, taken up by a Modoc tribe." Ned leaned forward with his hands on the desk. "If a poem isn't from the heart, it isn't worth a plug nickel.

That's why I think there's some gold in the stuff I've written, despite all the quartz. Now, where in London do you reckon I can get it published?"

Hood sat back in his chair at this question. "Well, of course *Fun* is hardly the proper market. Still, it might be amusing to set off a little American disturbance somewhere or other—if one could be sure all this business of yours would hold up once the public starts tearing into it." He thought for a moment, then raised his eyebrows as though he had hit on an idea. "I say, what if I challenge you to pop off for a bit, knock back a few, something of that sort?"

Ned understood none of this but the tone of dare. He answered cautiously, "Well, I reckon I'm not too busy, but—"

"Splendid." Hood called through the door. "Henderson!"

The clerk appeared, nervously. "Yes, sir?"

"No more today for me here; I'll be down in the pit."

"Again, sir? Will there be a message if anyone should call, sir?"

"No need for creativity on this one, Henderson. Tell them I've business with Mr. Miller."

"Very well, sir."

Hood donned an overcoat and quickly led the way down the stairs, out of the building, and into a dark cobblestone alleyway. It reminded Ned of the sordid setting for the thugs and pickpockets of a Dickens novel. He followed Hood resolutely, although he hadn't the slightest idea where they were going, and found he was comforted by the observation that, whatever might be in store, he was somewhat larger and stronger than his companion.

A hundred yards down the crooked alley they came to an ancient half-timbered building with a small, indecipherable tin plate suspended in front. Here Hood looked furtively in both directions, then climbed down to a dark door and ducked inside. Ned, however, hesitated. A distant memory had floated to mind—following Akitot into the dark entranceway of a Wintu *cawel* after having delivered several illegal rifles. He wished he still had a bowie knife at his hip.

The instant Ned stepped inside, something cracked against his head. He fell back to the door, and a round of husky laughter resounded from the dim room. While Ned sat on the step rubbing his head, Hood stuck his red-cheeked face out of the darkness. "Sorry about that, chap. I might have warned you—this place was built rather before your American Rebellion, you know, so the ceiling's a bit low. Come on, I'll buy first."

Now Ned could see the cellar contained a public-house. It seemed an unlikely place for a drinking establishment, though, with small leaded windows that refused to let in much daylight, and smoke-stained ceiling beams that sagged to forehead height. Inside, stout men in tweed caps stopped playing darts to watch him. Mindful of this audience, Ned cocked back his big hat, laughed about the bruise on his forehead, and made his way to the bar.

Two large glasses of a peculiarly dark beer were already set up. Hood lifted his and toasted, "To America."

Ned took a drink and gagged, sputtering foam into his hand. "What the devil is this?"

"Why, it's stout."

"But it's damn near *hot*."

"Well, it tastes best when warmed."

Ned pulled a huge bandanna out of his back pocket and mopped his face. He told the bartender, "Look, I'll just have a gullywasher."

"Your pardon, sir?" The bartender gave Ned a curious look. "A gully washer?"

"How 'bout a brandy smash, then?"

The man behind the counter still showed no sign of comprehension.

"Well, maybe you've heard of whiskey?"

A smile of relief spread across the bartender's face. "Aye, there's Scotch."

Ned paid for two of these, pushed one toward the editor with a nod, and immediately drained the other. Only then did he notice that Hood had been watching him from the side with an inexplicably positive expression.

"I say," Hood began. "I'd always heard gold miners were rather more challenging drinkers than the Americans one meets from the Atlantic states." He picked up his whiskey glass, held it as though he were readying himself, and then drained it much as Ned had done. He wheezed and held out a bank note to the bartender. "Bring us a bottle of this Scotch. I believe our friend here rather likes it."

Ned revived considerably at this suggestion, and at the editor's chummy tone. He tossed off his second glass of whiskey with a toast to British generosity, and then inspected the bottle's label critically. "Good stuff, your Scotch. Awful watery, though, compared to corn mash bourbon. Sort of thing we'd drink to wash down soda biscuits back in California."

"I say, really?" Hood chuckled as he poured the glasses full again.

Amid much good-natured banter about drinking habits on both sides of the Atlantic, the libation continued glass for glass. Ned tried two or three times to bring the conversation around to the publishing of poetry, but Hood stuck obstinately to the business at hand. The feeble daylight of the leaded glass windows yielded to the warmer glow of gaslight, and still they were working their way down the bottle.

Finally Hood's nose and cheeks were a flaming red. His head rolled about on his shoulders and his tongue sloshed about in his mouth as he talked. "Awright, Milla, d'ya give up? Ya sure don't look like ya can take much more to me." At this, his eyes rolled back, and his head flopped forward onto the bar.

"Yeah?" Ned responded woozily, grabbing the neck of the bottle and drinking the last two fingers of Scotch without the aid of a glass. He let out a long breath that could have fueled a torch. Then he tried to focus on the editor. Weaving slightly, he tapped the man's head with a knuckle. "Hooder, you in there?" When there was no reply, he motioned to the bartender. "Looks like my pal here's pulled up stakes."

"Tom's out again, is he?" The bartender shook his head. "Well, I'll send round for a constable, but his wife's going to be bloody unhappy about it."

"No, no, no, no." Ned waved his hands in front of his face. "He's just tired, ya see? Tell me where he lives at 'n' I'll get 'im home."

The bartender seemed to prefer this suggestion to bringing in the police, and gave Ned directions in the simplest possible terms. Then Ned shook Hood into a semi-conscious state, took an arm around his neck, and dragged him up the stairs to the gaslit cobblestone alley.

As Ned staggered along, the cool night air and the full moon swimming high overhead encouraged him to a lyrical mood. All the talk of the California mines had brought back memories, too, so when he lurched into song, it was "Forty-Nine"—a familiar tune from his California days. The heads of startled Londoners popped out of windows along the streets during the course of his slurred and somewhat garbled recitation:

> We are wreck and stray, we are cast away,
> Poor, battered old hulks and spars,
> But we hope and pray, on the Judgment Day,
> We will strike it, up in the stars.
> Though battered and old, our hearts are bold,
> Yet oft do we repine
> For the days of old, for the days of gold—
> For the days of Forty-Nine.

Ned dragged Hood up a flight of stone steps to his flat's door and banged the door knocker. Then he straightened his hat and bandanna, thinking rather foggily that he would want to make a good impression.

After a while the door opened a crack. A candle appeared hesitantly, illuminating Ned's bedraggled gold miner's outfit, his bearded smile, and the unconscious Thomas Hood slumped against his shoulder. Suddenly a weird gasp issued from inside the door. A second later Ned was confronted by an insane woman in a dressing gown. She snatched the limp editor into the house with amazing strength, shoved Ned backwards down the steps, and slammed the door sharply.

As Ned picked himself up off the sidewalk, he muttered, "Well hell, ma'am. So much for bein' neighborly."

* * *

Feeling now quite sure he could expect no further help from Thomas Hood, Ned spent the next two days making inquiries about publishing firms that might print his book to order. But the bids were all far more than he could afford. On the third day, in despair, he sat on his bed and laid out every pound, shilling, and penny he owned. All that remained—from the years he had scraped together money as a Canyon City lawyer—was thirty-nine pounds. If he left England at once, he would just have enough to buy a ticket to New York. From there he would have to wire for more from his family.

He tightened his lips at the thought of asking for money from his aged parents. They and Ella had always believed in him. They had wanted him to succeed. They had come to rely on him. He would rather do almost anything than ask them for money.

He paced the room worriedly, wondering if there was some option he had overlooked. Perhaps he could take a job? He remembered the time he had run low on money in San Francisco, and Minnie had urged him to look for part-time work. But what could he do here? England didn't need gold miners or pony express riders. Even his knowledge of American law would be useless. Angrily, without knowing where he was going, he threw open the door—and stood face to face with his landlady.

"If it's about the rent—" he began.

"No, not yet," she said. "This time it's about *Fun*."

"Fun?"

"Aye, just came with the post." She held out a packet. "Didn't know you subscribed."

He grabbed the mail, closed the door, and hurriedly slit open the packet. Inside was a small, wax-sealed envelope and an accompanying letter.

Mr. Joaquin Miller:
Terribly sorry if you suffered any inconvenience on my account

Thursday night. My wife's description of the gentleman who accompanied me home that evening is yet fairly incoherent, but it agrees in certain particulars with your person, to which I say: good show. Tally one up for the stamina of American miners, eh what?

Meanwhile, I am enclosing a sealed note of introduction to "H." Although he is not a publisher, and he is certainly no Rossetti, you may find him helpful in other ways.

Respectfully yours,
Thomas Hood

"H?" Ned wondered aloud. He turned over the little envelope, puzzled. Who on earth was he? And what had Hood written that had to be kept in a sealed envelope? Ned held the envelope to the sunlight of his garret window, but could not make out the writing inside. The address told him nothing. He considered trying to pry off the seal, but was afraid of cracking the wax.

Finally he sat back, eyeing the little envelope suspiciously. It was a peculiar lead to follow. And if he did, he might run so low on money there would be no turning back.

* * *

The stately stone house at "H's" address had marble lions on either side of the step and a brass knocker on the door. A portly butler in a neat black suit and tie answered the door with a dubious "Yes?" The man cast a disdainful glance at Ned's frontier outfit and was about to shut the door when Ned held out the note from Thomas Hood.

The butler turned over the envelope. He raised an eyebrow at the seal. "I see. Would sir be so good as to step into the foyer for a moment?"

"You bet." Ned strode in and crossed his arms.

There was an awkward pause. Ned noticed the butler seemed to be waiting for him to do something more. Finally the servant coughed discreetly. "Might I have your hat, sir?"

Instead of taking off the floppy old hat in embarrassment, Ned decided to see if he could ruffle this stodgy servant with a frontier performance in the style of Mountain Joe. "Sorry, pal," he said, looking the man in the eye. "I'd feel scalped without it. I reckon you'll have to rustle one up for yourself somewhere else."

Ned suppressed a smile as the butler stiffened and his ears turned red.

"I shall take your letter up immediately, sir," the servant replied, emphasizing the "immediately." He vanished with the note and did not return for a good quarter of an hour.

In the meantime Ned occupied himself by inspecting the large entrance hall for clues to the identity of the mysterious "H." The lavish scale of the house and the nature of his reception there had already made it clear that "H" was a much more important person than Ned had at first imagined. He studied the dark portraits of pompous-looking gentlemen on the walls, but as these had no captions they were of little help. He looked in several of the volumes on the bookshelf, but the only name he could find written in them was "Monckton Milnes," which didn't go far toward explaining the initial "H" either.

The bookshelf did have an admirable selection of works by and about modern English writers, including no less than five ornately-bound copies of *The Life of Keats*. On a hunch he took one down. The author was "Mr. Monckton Milnes, The Right Honourable Lord Houghton, D. C. L., F. R. S."

He was pondering the possibility of Houghton—*Lord* Houghton— when the butler's cough made him snap the book shut self-consciously.

"You will pardon me, sir, for asking you to remain in the hall."

"Oh, I reckon so." Ned slipped the book back casually. "Any luck scarin' up this 'H' fella?"

"His Lordship is indisposed at present, sir. However, he indicated he could meet with you tomorrow afternoon while he is at the sportsmen's club, particularly if you should chance to share an enthusiasm for horsemanship. I have printed the address on this card in the hopes that you can read."

Ned passed over the slur and took the card. "He likes riding, huh? Suits me fine. Oh, and see he gets a few of these manuscripts I've brought."

The butler said nothing, but held the sheets dubiously between his thumb and forefinger while Ned tipped his hat and strode out the door.

* * *

Lord Houghton and a mustachioed companion were taking tea on the riding club's verandah when Ned appeared, asking boldly for "H." His Lordship was wearing wide-thighed riding breeches and a red hunting jacket. "I am he," he said, holding up his monocle to inspect Ned's peculiar hat, his bandanna, and the jackboots that had been outfitted with great, jingling Spanish spurs.

"Proud to meet ya. I go by Joaquin," Ned responded, shaking his hand earnestly.

Lord Houghton introduced his companion properly and urged Ned to sit down to join them for tea. "I have read a few of your poems," he said offhandedly. "Several have merit, perhaps. They came quite highly recommended from Thomas Hood, who insists you have personally experienced the content of the poems in the American West. Then I assume you do ride."

Ned tipped back his chair. "Ride? Why, I've ridden the pony express through the wilderness of Idaho, hundreds of miles at a stretch."

"Have you indeed?"

"You bet, and when you ride there you've got to be fighting off Indians and bandits and blizzards too, if you aim to save your skin."

"Ah. And are post riders in America exposed to so many hardships and robberies, then?"

"Well, I reckon so!" Ned said. In the pause that followed he felt the two English gentlemen watching him intently, as if they were expecting some kind of proof. Ned decided to take a chance and oblige them with a tale in correct Western style.

"Why, once I had a shoot-out with the Australian bandit Neil Scott. If it hadn't been for my little Nez Perce pony Niño I wouldn't be alive today."

"Oh?"

Ned spread his hands. "You see, I'd just galloped most of a day with fifty pounds of gold dust from the mines, when all of a sudden the trail was blocked by a fallen tree tall as a horse's back. There was a new trail beat out around it all right, but that little Nez Perce pony didn't want any part of it. I try coaxing her on, but she just keeps sniffing suspicious-like and won't budge. Finally I have to put in the spurs and jump her right over the tree.

"Well, soon as we land there's a clap like thunder from out of the side trail and we're in a rain of bullets. Outlaws had been laying for us all along. I pull out both six-shooters and drop the reins, leaving Niño to find her way out of the gunsmoke while I make it hot for Neil Scott. Off she goes like a shot, heading for the Snake River with the wind splattering blood back from her nostrils. I knew she'd taken some lead, but she galloped on twenty miles to the ferry before she lay down, dead. It was only then, after she'd brought me through safe, that I realized the brave little pony's wounds had surely been mortal from the first."

Lord Houghton's companion had been tugging enthusiastically at his mustache during this story. "Sounds like a smashing good ride, Miller!"

His Lordship was more reserved. "I wonder if after all your experience with Indian ponies you would care to try riding a thoroughbred?"

"Sure. This is a horse race club, isn't it?"

"Well, I imagine one *might* call it that," Lord Houghton said.

The other gentleman exchanged a knowing glance with Lord Houghton before he spoke. "I say, Miller, if you're up to a race, I've five quid that would make it a sporting venture."

Ned detected a certain disturbing smugness in this man's smile. And there was so little money left. Still, he could hardly refuse this dare. He slapped his knee confidently. "You bet. Let's have at it, pard."

When they reached the stables, Ned's competitor mounted smoothly to his horse. By means of imperceptible signals he managed to make his horse walk neatly backwards out of the stable, then step sideways to a path, and finally turn about in place. Then he waited motionlessly for Ned, his chin several degrees higher in the air than seemed absolutely necessary.

The horse Lord Houghton presented for Ned had an oddly bobbed tail and such a shiny black coat that it gleamed bluish in the sun. Ned put his foot in the stirrup, but slipped awkwardly as he tried to swing up. "Whoa, you don't have a saddle horn on this little English rig. Must make it deuced hard to tie up a lariat."

The nobleman appeared faintly amused. "We seem to manage."

They walked to the lawn below the verandah. There Lord Houghton pointed out the course. "First you cross the Misbourn River by the bridge, and then you steeplechase a mile along the bank."

Ned squinted across the deep, sluggish river. "Maybe I'm not looking in the right place. That bank over there's got bushes and fences every hundred yards. Why not race on this side, where there's a clear track?"

Lord Houghton smiled patiently. "A steeplechase consists primarily of jumping bushes and fences. Once that is accomplished, the riders may return as they like."

"Return as you like?"

"Well, yes. You understand it is a rather shorter distance to return over the obstacles, but it is quicker and safer to continue the additional quarter mile to the second bridge and then to return on this side of the Misbourn, since, as you correctly note, this bank is clear of obstructions."

As soon as Ned declared he understood the rules, Lord Houghton retired to the verandah with a pair of field glasses, where he began alerting his fellow club members to what he assured them would be an amusing encounter between one of their most skilled equestrians and an obviously ill-prepared pony express rider from America.

At the starting signal Ned touched his spurs to his horse's flank. Side by side the two horsemen raced across the bridge toward the first hedge-row. The English rider cleared it with a tall bound, but Ned's horse shied. He clutched in vain for a saddle horn to steady himself. As the horse jolted onward he started slipping off, one foot still in the stirrup. Lord Houghton, watching through his field glasses, smiled and nodded to his friends on the verandah.

Ned knew the danger of being dragged by a stirrup. The instant his right foot touched the ground he pushed with all his might and clung to the horse's side. By the time he had clawed his way up into the saddle again, however, the English horseman held a comfortable three-fence lead.

Ned spat into the grass. Then he gripped the reins with a redoubled strength, sank his Spanish spurs into the horse's flanks and let loose a long, terrifying yell that carried far across the river.

"HYAH!"

The thoroughbred shivered at the forcefulness of this strange command and shot forward as though pursued by demons. At the first hedgerow Ned shouted again, "Hyah!" The horse leapt into the air. It landed on the far side with a jolt, but Ned was gripping the horse's mane too tightly now to be shaken loose again.

Fence after fence Ned spurred the horse on, giving the same wild whoop at each jump. When he cleared the last hurdle, however, he saw that the English rider had kept every bit of his lead. The horseman was already at the bridge a quarter mile ahead, about to start the final gallop back to the club.

Gritting his teeth, Ned reined back violently until his horse reared with a piercing whinny. Still in the air, he wheeled the horse about toward the river, and, uttering a hair-raising howl, drove it headlong over a stone embankment—straight into the deep, murky waters below.

For a full minute Ned and his horse disappeared entirely from the view of Lord Houghton's field glasses. A murmur ran through the crowd on the verandah. But then Lord Houghton jumped to his feet, his face pale. "Good Lord, he's still on it! He's swum the Misbourn!"

Ned and his thoroughbred charged dripping up the river's grassy bank just as the English rider galloped past. At once Ned spurred the horse again.

"Hyah! Ya goddam hunk of meat, now move!"

With a mile of clear track to go, he now trailed by only a half dozen lengths. He grabbed off his slouch hat and beat it against the horse's haunches. "Hyah! Hyah! Hyah!" The turf flew up in great clods as he whipped the horse onward, gaining little by little on the still unconcerned English rider. Ned's horse strained at the incessant commands, its eyes red, its coat in a foam of sweat, and its red nostrils flared to gulp the air.

When the English rider finally glanced over his shoulder and saw the apparition charging up behind him, he began applying his riding quirt vehemently, but it was too late. As they raced along the final stretch to the verandah, Ned pulled ahead. The club members rose to their feet in astonishment. When Ned galloped past, a full length in the lead, he greeted the crowd's applause with a hearty wave of his hat.

* * *

In the dark, smoky office of Whittingham and Wilkins, Publishers, Ltd., Ned dropped his manuscripts on the counter and asked how much it would cost to print three hundred copies.

The editor eyed him suspiciously. "Aren't you the same American chap I sent out of here a few months ago?"

"Well, maybe I am, but I'm willing to pay now."

"Turned self-publisher, eh?"

Ned nodded silently. It was a grim admission. His time had run out. There had been a moment, after his heady victory at Lord Houghton's club, when he had hoped the nobleman would help him achieve some kind of literary recognition in London, if only out of admiration for his horsemanship. But Houghton had been cool to his suggestions. Perhaps, Ned thought, he just didn't understand how these things were supposed to be done in England. A week had passed without any word from Houghton, and he could wait no longer. Even the money from his ticket home would run out before long, and then he would be living on the street. Printing and selling the book was his last hope.

The publisher before him thumbed through the papers. "It looks like you've a bit over a hundred pages here. That's, let's see, thirty pounds to set the type and ready the press, and then a pound for every five books after that. Ninety pounds together, then."

"But I don't have near that much money!"

"Very well. Then we shan't print your work. That, my friend, is how it works. Good day."

With a sigh Ned scooped up his papers and left. On the sidewalk he pulled out his gold watch to check the time. But when he glanced at the timepiece a different idea came to mind.

After he had found a pawnbroker's shop, however, a flood of self-incrimination kept him pacing the sidewalk outside. The watch was his one and only physical inheritance from Mountain Joe, bequeathed on the night of his horrible death in the Idaho blizzard. Nor could he forget the day on Mt. Shasta when the old mountain man had shown him Frémont's engraved name on the back of the watch. Joe had been given the watch after serving under that great Western explorer. It was the bequest of frontier heroes, an icon of an unspoiled age.

On the other hand, Ned thought, if the watch was pawned it wasn't exactly sold. A pawn ticket merely raised the stakes in the poker game he was already playing. Wouldn't Mountain Joe have risked as much on one of his horse-trading ventures? And what other chance for success was there left in London? Hood's and Houghton's guarded approval of his writings had not put any poems in print.

At last Ned pushed into the shop dejectedly and laid the watch on the table. "How much will you give me against that?"

The hunched little man put on his spectacles. "Gold?"

"Solid gold. It belonged to John C. Frémont."

"Shh, now, I shouldn't take it at all if it's pinched," the pawnbroker whispered.

"It was a *gift*," Ned responded loudly. "Surely you've heard of Frémont! The man ran for President of the United States!"

"Did he indeed? How marvelous. Twenty pounds."

All the outrage Ned could muster did not make the broker raise his offer. Ned ran his hand over his beard, considering his position. If the watch were checked as security, he would have a month to pay back the money. In that much time the twenty pounds, plus the thirty pounds he still possessed, could pay for a hundred copies of his book—not enough to put copies in the bookstores, but enough to give one to every newspaper reviewer in town. That meant he couldn't make back his money by selling the books. All his hopes would be riding on the reviews. The stakes had risen yet again.

"Well?" the pawnbroker asked.

Ned pushed the watch across the counter. "There's my last ante. Deal me in."

"Beg pardon?"

"I'll take the twenty pounds."

When Ned returned to the publishing house with the money the editor gave him a wry grin. "So? Suddenly you have unearthed some assets?"

"Only enough for a hundred copies. It'll have to do, I'm afraid. And I'll need them as soon as possible."

"The shop's quiet enough, I think we can rush the job. What name shall we use, then?"

Ned pursed his lips. "No name at all. And don't put in any publisher's name, either. If I'm going to have to pay for this show myself, well then damn it, I'll just make them guess for a while."

* * *

Two weeks later, in an old building at 16 Cheyne Walk, near the Chelsea embankment of the Thames, the pre-Raphaelite poet and artist Dante Gabriel Rossetti turned over Ned's recently arrived envelope with a light smile.

"From 'H' is it? Our little town's own dear society poet. I do wonder what he's sent us now?" Rossetti's black hair and olive complexion gave him the appearance of an Italian, but his speech bore only the stamp of a Londoner. He winked to the young model at his side, set down his brushes, and chased a large, brightly colored parrot off his shoulder, causing it to squawk, "Show your legs! Show your legs!"

His dark eyebrows arched as he perused the short note. "A pony express rider from America who dabbles in poetry?" He threw back his head and laughed. "I love it, I love it, I love it! Here, Alice, tell this chap to gallop right in, there's a good girl."

The model narrowly escaped a slap on the backside as she skipped out. She returned shortly with Ned, who extended a big hand in greeting. "Howdy, Mr. Rossetti, it's sure a pleasure meeting—"

"Ah, marvelous, marvelous, marvelous," Rossetti exclaimed, but by-passed Ned's offered hand to give the model several coins. "A bit of tin for your trouble this morning, Alice. Absolutely a stunner, isn't she?" He looked to Ned. "I'm sorry, what did you say your name was?"

"Miller, Joaquin Mi—"

"Ah, Miller, Miller, Miller, of course." The artist put his arm around Ned's shoulder and wheeled him about the studio—a labyrinth of canvases, sculpture, and animal cages. "That's what our charming mutual friend 'H' was saying, that your work is fresh out of the unspoiled wilderness and all that. It's precisely what we're trying to do here, you know? Chuck the conventions, all these inhibiting rules set up by the Raphaelites and the post-Raphaelites, so we can get back to nature herself."

While Rossetti spoke, a small, vaguely bear-like creature had crawled out from a pile of boxes. Now it sat on its fat legs, staring at them inquiringly. As soon as Rossetti saw it, he called out, "Mrs. Hamsby! The wombat!"

Soon a stout, gray-haired woman with a broom bustled out of a door. Using short, frantic sweeping motions, she set to urging the slow-moving marsupial toward a nearby cage. Ned pitched into the effort, but Rossetti merely studied one of the many half-finished life drawings that hung on the studio walls. At news of the wombat's capture he waved his hand. "Capital. Now do see to securing his latch, Mrs. Hamsby, and be so good as to feed the peacock in the back yard. He screeches most dreadfully you know. In fact, I rather think that's why the armadillos have been digging under the wall and distressing the neighbors."

"Right, sir, if you say," the woman agreed begrudgingly in a strong Cockney accent that turned "right" into "royt."

Rossetti glided toward a door. "I'll be in the dining room to see if we can scare up a spot of lunch for the brotherhood when they trickle in. I say, Miller, you'll stay, won't you? That's a good fellow."

The door closed, leaving Ned in the studio with Mrs. Hamsby. He scratched his head, exasperated by Rossetti's manner—and by the strange menagerie that had so effectively prevented him from showing the famous artist the printed copy of *Pacific Poems* he had brought. Despite all of Rossetti's obvious eccentricities, Ned was convinced he could provide entrance to one of the most promising avenues to fame. After all, Rossetti's pre-Raphaelite brotherhood had been successful in promoting the works of Blake, Keats, and Victor Hugo. What seemed even more hopeful was that they had managed to win a small English following for an obscure American clerk, a man by the name of Walt Whitman, whose self-published book of off-beat poetry, *Leaves of Grass*, had been ignored in the United States. And this Whitman fellow had never even met the pre-Raphaelites—he had never been to England at all!

"Beg your pardon, sir," the Cockney maid said quietly. She had busied herself with sweeping and straightening for the first minute, but obviously had something she wanted to say. "Forgive me for speaking out like I am, but I thought as 'ow you looked new 'ere I ought at least thank you for your 'elp."

"Oh, it was nothing."

"Even nothing's something to a maid, sir. You are new, aren't you?"

"Well, yes, I reckon this is the first time I've met Mr. Rossetti."

The woman narrowed her eyes. "You strike me as an honest man, sir, or I wouldn't be saying this, but if I was you I'd leave the whole lot of these artists before it's too late, I would."

Ned looked at the woman with surprise. "Too late? What do you mean?"

"Oh, I've seen queer enough things 'ere over the years to know it's no place for the unsuspecting." Her voice dropped to a whisper. "Take Master Gabriel's poor departed wife. A good girl, Lizzie was, with an honest job in a milliner's shop off Leicester Square, when they make her a model and bring her to the studio. Next thing she's lying in a bathtub stark naked for four days, with nothing but a candle to warm her, so 'e can paint a thing 'e called 'Drowned Ophelia.' A pretty place for an honest girl, and she like to caught her death of cold. But no—'e marries 'er and then 'e breaks 'er 'eart by taking up with some new girl. That's why she drank the laudanum and put 'er poor soul in the 'ands of all that vicious opium and alcohol, you know."

"Are you saying Rossetti's wife committed suicide?"

"I'm not saying nothing, sir. It's what everyone says, and I was 'ere to see what I saw. But that's not all, sir. Master Gabriel gave on to be so full of grief that 'e put the papers with his precious poems in the poor girl's coffin. And then last year they *dug 'er up* just to get the papers back and put them in his new book! It's a ghastly business, sir, and my advice is to steer clear of it while you still can."

Ned frowned, looking at the talkative maid slightly askance. "If it's such a terrible place, how come you don't pack up and leave yourself?"

The maid caught her breath, affronted, and returned to her sweeping. "I get paid for my work, I do. Long as I do an honest day's work, it's not my business asking questions, now is it?"

When the door swung open and Rossetti waved Ned into the dining room, the maid quickly bustled off to other chores. Although Ned actually believed most of what the maid had said, he was not about to let Rossetti's past get in the way of his own literary ambition. A dozen members of Rossetti's brotherhood were waiting for the luncheon in the other room— and whatever their flaws, they were part of the literary elite he had been hoping to meet for so long.

"Ah, Miller, good of you to wait." Rossetti put his arm about him as they walked in toward the other artists. In the process he finally discovered the book that Ned had now practically thrust into his hand.

"And what have you here? A fresh little thing, I see. *Pacific Poems?*"

At this a short, freckled Irishman turned about in surprise. Pardon? Did you say *Pacific Poems?*" He took the volume and flipped to the title page. "Well bless me if it isn't. How did you possibly get hold of one of these? I've looked in every bookstore in the city since the *St. James Gazette* came out this morning."

Rossetti arched his eyebrows. "Have you really?"

The Irishman nodded earnestly. "I have indeed. The *Gazette* made quite a stir about it being anonymous and all; said it reminded them of Browning—except it's about the American West, of all things. Preposterous idea, eh?"

Ned's eyes had grown huge with astonishment. "They thought it was by *Browning?*"

"Yes, of course it's impossible, but they must be impressive poems for all that."

At this Ned threw back his head, sailed his slouch hat across the room, and let out a whoop that made one of the artists drop his teacup with a crash. "I've *done* it, by the holy poker!"

"Good heavens!" Rossetti exclaimed, drawing back. "What have you done?"

"They're *my* poems, don't you see? It's *my* book!" He flung out his arms and took a grandiose bow before the startled group. "Gentlemen, I am *Joaquin Miller!*"

Chapter 26

I am alone, yet not alone. I love society and yet I hate it.
—Joaquin Miller

The young Irish poet from the pre-Raphaelite luncheon waited, his bowler on his knee, while Ned paced the garret room in Westminster, reading through the suggested revision. At length Ned slapped the paper. "Sometimes you leave stuff out and sometimes you stick stuff in, but it doesn't add one bit to the sparkle or the meaning of the thing."

"No," the poet replied, smiling. "It only evens out your meter. You're using anapestic quatrameter in that verse—and it does give a fine hoof-beat rhythm like a galloping horse—but every now and then you've let a five-footed steed get out of your inkwell. That sort of animal leaves tracks on a manuscript only the *Gazette* could overlook. They've given you a nice little break, I'd say."

The stairs outside creaked and there was a knock at the door. "Well, we'll soon see," Ned said, as he went to answer it.

A second, shorter Irishman with a scrub-brush beard stood outside, puffing from the climb.

"Come in, pal," Ned smiled, shaking his hand heartily. "Did you bring the poem?"

"Sure, here it is."

Ned laid out the new text on his desk and read it through, glancing from time to time at the corrections suggested by the first volunteer critic. When he had finished he sank back into a chair, musing. "That is mighty peculiar. I rather disbelieved what you two Pre-Raphaelite boys said about my poems, so I put you both to the same test. And I'll be darned if your revisings of the same passage didn't come out almost exactly the same. Well, there must be something to it, then, after all."

Ned sighed, unwillingly reminded of the times Minnie Myrtle had corrected his verse. The memory jarred. He had always taken her suggestions lightly, unsure his work really needed as much editing as she said. He had thought he wouldn't need such advice once he became famous. But here he was, face to face with genuine success in London, and now it seemed that poor Minnie—marooned in Port Orford—had been right. Even the learned Pre-Raphaelites agreed the poems needed polish.

"All right, I'll listen now," Ned told the Irish poets. "What else do you think I should do before I print up my book again?"

The two Irishmen exchanged a quick nod of understanding. Then the taller one spoke. "First, Whittingham and Wilkins will never do. You'll be wanting a larger publishing house with a better respected name. I've taken the liberty of stopping by the office of Longman, Green, Reade, and Dyer to show them your book and the review." He handed Ned a card. "Here's an appointment with Mr. Longman for next Monday. If you can arrange to be there, I believe you will find him most anxious to meet you."

The first Irishman had hardly finished when the second one took his turn. "I'd say your new book should be longer, too. The first printing had only 119 pages—and thin books do not give the impression of a confident, established poet. I'd recommend filling it out to 300 pages if possible."

"Well, I reckon I've been working on a few things." Ned gave a sigh of resignation. "I could try and get some of them ready if you think it'll help."

"Then there's your title," the first Irish poet spoke up again. "We discussed it a bit at the luncheon. Have you given it any thought since then?"

Ned silently handed them the list of a half dozen names he had worked out the night before.

The Irishmen conferred over this a minute, and then the tall one announced, "I rather like 'Songs of the Sierras' myself. It has a nice alliteration, and the word 'Sierras' has a properly exotic ring."

Ned just shook his head, marveling. "You two seem to have thought of everything."

"There's one more thing, I'm afraid," the short Irishman said, rubbing his stubbly beard. "You're going to need publicity, and a great deal of it too, since there's hardly a soul in London that's heard your name. I don't know how you do that sort of thing in America, but here that means impressing enough of the right people in the city's social circuit."

Ned shrugged. "How am I supposed to do that? I don't know anybody even near a social circuit, unless maybe it's Thomas Hood or Lord Houghton."

The short Irishman smiled to his countryman. "Oh, there's no shortage of teas and receptions. No doubt Rossetti and 'H' will be able to provide you with a few invitations for a start. *Your* concern will be to make sure you're noticed once you're there."

"Noticed?" Ned smiled wryly. "If *that's* all it takes, I reckon I can manage."

"What do you intend to do?"

Ned picked up his big felt hat and spun it on his finger, enjoying the thought of letting the spirit of his old frontier mentor, Mountain Joe, loose once again. "I intend to give them an ambush they won't forget."

* * *

The guests had gathered in little clusters beneath the chandeliers of the drawing room—finely-dressed ladies in low-cut dresses with puffy sleeves and hoop skirts; gentlemen in tailcoats, starched collars, and cravats. At times voices could be distinguished from the murmur of genteel conversation: "... never have met him myself..." "... positively distracted when he wore a leather shirt at dinner ..." "... smokes two cigars at once, but I dare say I hardly believe ..." "... believe? The man's a Munchhausen once you set him off ..."

The conversation hushed when the butler stepped in before the door. Stiffly, the servant announced, "Mr. Joe Quinn Miller."

Suddenly the door flew open and Ned strode in, wearing denim pants stuffed into his top boots, a red flannel shirt open at the collar, and his great, rumpled slouch hat. He tossed aside a toothpick and clapped the butler around the shoulder. "That's *Wah-KEEN* Miller, pardner!"

A heavily bosomed and bejeweled hostess hurried up, smiling strenuously. "Mr. Miller! How charming of you to come."

Ned swept off his hat and caught her hand to his lips. "I bow before you, madam, humbled by your great kindness and beauty."

The matronly woman blushed, obviously pleased by his gallantry. "I must say I've been interested to meet you ever since hearing about your remarkable poems of the Sierras. The papers have been simply full of commendatory reviews."

She then led the way about the drawing room, introducing a dizzying array of many-syllabled names and titles—a scattering of lords, baronets, and duchesses among them. Ned shook the men's hands with a white-knuckled grip and invented lavish compliments for each of the ladies. This was the London he had come to conquer, and he was savoring every moment of it.

"Indeed, Mr. Miller," one of the ladies ventured, "we have just been discussing your narrative of 'Kit Carson's Ride.' I must say I had no idea such a remarkable romance could be developed with an Indian girl."

Ned replied by quoting the verse with a theatrical wave of his arm:

We lounged in the grasses—her eyes were in mine,
And her hands on my knee, and her hair was as wine
In its wealth and its flood, pouring on and all over
Her bosom wine-red, and pressed never by one.

Several of the women reddened and put their hands demurely to their collars. The lady who had spoken first, however, continued boldly. "What I would like to ask is why you have given the poem such a tragic ending. It is certainly thrilling to have Mr. Carson and the abducted Indian fleeing *both* from her pursuing tribe *and* from a deadly prairie fire, but it seems a pity to let the girl's horse stumble at the last moment. Couldn't you have let them both escape to the safety of the river? One wonders about the character of Mr. Carson if he succeeds in saving only himself."

"Ah," Ned nodded. "Make no mistake about Kit Carson, ma'am. He was as brave and big-hearted as they come, but the Indian girl still has to perish, you see. The whole of that noble red race in America is passing away. I reckon it's just in the order of things that none of the Indians in my poems survive."

A sudden memory of Paquita caught Ned off guard. He lowered his head, tight-lipped. This was not part of his performance. He recalled the painful truth behind the tales: his Wintu wife and daughter. And although they were not threatened by prairie fires on Mt. Shasta, that wilderness held other dangers—starvation, freezing winters, and persecution more violent than any of the tales in his poems. For a moment he felt again the guilt of not going back to help his Wintu family. But hadn't he also struggled long and hard? He had scraped together money and written poems by candlelight, fighting for his literary breakthrough. Surely he had earned the right to celebrate his victory.

When Ned looked up he saw that his silence had left the audience somber. Quickly he slipped back into his Mountain Joe role and chuckled. "Besides, if Kit Carson and the girl both live to the end of the poem, there's no story to tell, and if they both die, why, I reckon there's nobody left to tell it."

Everyone laughed and the men nodded approvingly. Then a woman with a lacy collar and a hairpiece like a beehive asked, "Don't you find the American aborigines rather frightening, though—I mean, what with their being incorrigibly heathen and all?"

"Heathen, but far from godless," Ned countered. "The red man's gods are everywhere and in everything. Every redwood and every desert rock is sacred to that devout race."

"Then your esteem of the aborigines is based on an intimate knowledge of their beliefs?" The question came from a stiff figure, whose precise rank in the Church of England Ned could not recall from the introductions. But Ned recognized the man's tone of challenge. Just as Lord Houghton had needed to hear a frontier tale to be convinced Ned was a genuine pony express rider, this cleric wanted proof that Ned knew the Indians' religion. The stodgy doubter had called him out for a showdown in the soiree. Ned turned to face the man.

"You bet, pard," Ned said straightening. "I reckon I'm the only white man alive who's endured the trials to become a Wintu brave."

"Hear, hear," a smiling gentleman nearby put in. He saluted with a glass of gin. "Do tell us how you managed it."

"Well, in my tribe Chief Worrotatot called the shots, picking out the trials I would have to undergo to earn my spirit vision." Ned dropped his voice. The audience hushed to follow his words.

"My first challenge was to scalp a fistful of red fur from the hide of Wemir, the fearsome god of the grizzly bear. And then, surviving that, I was sent forth to take the topmost stone of Mt. Shasta from Kusku, the volcano god who spews fire over the glaciers and forests like red rain from an angry sky. Seven days of fasting followed, with my mind driven mad by the incessant beat of the drums. Finally came the long-awaited dance."

The audience watched, spellbound, as Ned closed his eyes, lifted his arms, and began to step about in a circle to the rhythm of the unseen drums.

"In the sacred ritual," he intoned, "a brave is called upon to throw out the human mask he wears in life, and let the spirit of one of the gods possess his body." Ned's feet thumped harder. "Hi-ya-ya-ya, hi-ya-ya-ya, *wintu wemir cawel wohow, mula yapiton hinna tintin.*" Suddenly his eyes flew open and he stared at the ceiling with a look of terror. He gave the long, eerie howl of a lonely wolf and collapsed to his knees, his arms outstretched.

As he stood up, mopping his brow with a bandanna, the drawing room audience broke into applause.

* * *

"And this wall exhibits representative weaponry taken from the tribes of the African Hottentots," a retired English colonel explained to Ned as he showed him through the high-ceilinged halls of the Savage Club. The colonel had an enormous white mustache and bushy eyebrows that overhung his wrinkled eyes. About the room, other old gentlemen were drinking iced Scotch and discreetly observing the newcomer from their overstuffed zebra skin chairs. A ceiling fan slowly mixed their drifting pipe smoke into a languorous haze.

"Say, don't you fellas have any Indian battle riggings?" Ned asked, tipping back his broad-brimmed hat to scratch his forehead.

"Well, yes, actually, there is a tolerable collection from the Punjab."

"Punjabs? I'm talking about Modocs! Apaches! Now there's some *real* fighters!"

"Ah, *red* Indians. The English Army has left that business up to you American chaps for rather more than a century. Not having any major difficulties, are you?"

"Difficulties? Oh, I reckon I've had my share, all right." Ned spoke loudly enough that everyone in the room could hear. Half the trick of publicity was gathering an audience. The other half, he had learned, was to give them a tale they had never heard before. In London, Mountain Joe's campfire stories were a gold mine. "Why, just a few years back a band of raiding Modocs burned our stockade on the Sacramento and high-tailed it to a hideout in the mountains they call the Devils Crags."

"Audacious of them. Did you attempt pursuit?"

"Well, I reckon so! Thirty of us tracked 'em up to the Crags. Looked like they had two-three hundred mounted warriors from the hoofprints, though, so we crept up on 'em quiet-like and sent a scout to check out the lay of the land. 'Bout evening the scout's horse came streaking back, with the scout tomahawked to beefsteak and lashed to his saddle. Well, we figured since the Indians had smoked us we'd have to stake everything and charge 'em before night fell. White men don't stand a chance against Indians in the dark, you understand.

"We knew the Modocs would be using obsidian-tipped arrows, sharp as razors and sometimes dipped in rattlesnake venom, too, so we wrapped wool blankets around our chests as a kind of makeshift armor. Then we came howling into that Indian camp with thirty pairs of six-shooters blazing, each man shooting left- and right-handed at the same time." Although this tale had been cut from the whole cloth, Ned considered that it was hardly grimmer than the true story of his forced enlistment in the Pit River Indian War, where he had fought against Paquita's brother Akitot. But a proper frontier tale only had to be colorful, not painstakingly true.

"A bully charge! Then you carried the field?"

"I don't recollect quite how we did clear 'em out. I took an arrow in the neck and was left with the dead. Later, when a pardner of mine came back and saw I could still move my eyes, he broke off the feathers and pulled the thing on through by the point. I still wear a beard to hide the damned scar."

"By Jove!" the colonel exclaimed, his eyes lit with enthusiasm. At the same time a number of exclamations were murmured by gentlemen about the room. A crowd gathered to examine the strange American Indian fighter more closely. One man with a long face insisted on posing a number of technical military questions, but even these did not entirely succeed in refuting Ned's story.

At length Ned changed the subject, waving toward a wall covered with mounted animal heads. "You fellas know much about hunting?"

The colonel pointed with casual pride to the head of an enormous Bengal tiger that appeared to have been shot in mid-snarl. "Well, yes, actually this one is my own. Had to hire a thousand navvies to beat the bush for him, you know?"

"A thousand people against one tiger?" Ned asked.

"Yes, it was rather a big operation, wasn't it?"

"Well, I reckon so! Still those are hardly level odds. Now, our black bears back in Oregon may be a mite smaller, but at least when I caught my first one at the age of twelve, *I* did it with nothing but a *rope*."

The colonel reddened, but the others chuckled. One said, "A wild bear with a rope? Come, come, Miller, tell us how. This adventure sounds fully as novel as the last."

Ned mused a moment, planning how he would adapt the bear stories he and Mountain Joe had swapped in Idaho. "All right, it happened this way." He crouched slightly and shook back his sleeves, readying his hands for the gestures the narrative would require. "My family had just crossed two thousand miles of baking desert in a covered wagon, and we'd homesteaded a spread so remote our nearest neighbors were forty miles away. There were wild longhorn cattle in the Willamette Valley where we'd settled—so wild my family had to build a log stockade around the cabin, 'cause the cattle would charge in unison at anything that moved.

"Well, one day my family was working up in the forest and they sent me back to fetch another ax. I just got a good ways out into the prairie when the longhorns started bellowing and snorting to each other. Pretty soon they started charging in a long line, like a troop of double-sabered cavalry sweeping up stragglers in a battlefield. Everything that could run in that prairie just gave a jump and made tracks for the stockade, me included. I reached the gate neck and neck with two coyotes, half a dozen jackrabbits, and a good-sized bear.

"It was plenty lively in there for a while, what with the coyotes chasing the jackrabbits out the cracks between the logs, and the bear clawing after the coyotes until they jumped clean over the top. When things settled down, there was just me and the bear. So I fetched a rope and tied him up. Got to like him, too—even taught him to dance to a fiddle. Poor guy finally died, though, trying to defend us from a ten-foot mountain lion that jumped the stockade. Awful hard to keep them cats out when they smell you're butchering elk for the winter."

Ned shook his head, tight lipped.

"Do you eat a fair amount of elk meat in America, then?" one of the gentlemen asked.

"Oh sure," Ned replied. "They're easy hunting. Folks just wait till a herd starts swimming 'cross the Willamette, then they row out after 'em, lasso 'em by the antlers, and club as many as they need. Saves gunpowder that way."

"Simply astonishing!" the colonel said, shaking his head. He went to pick up a drink from a waiter at the far end of the room. On his way he noticed a visiting American naval officer leaning against a door jamb, watching the group that had gathered around Ned. "I say, you're from the States, aren't you?"

The American captain returned a polite acknowledgment.

"Tell me, what do you make of this 'Poet of the Sierras' fellow?"

The visitor's American accent stood out sharply. "I suppose he's harmless enough. Looks like you're all taking to him pretty strong here in London, too. Still, I just wonder . . ."

"What's that, old chap?"

"Oh, I wonder how an act like his will go over back home."

* * *

London lay sleeping in the pre-dawn hours of a July morning as Ned stumbled back from an all-night dinner with the pre-Raphaelite brother-hood. He pulled out his gold watch, but the gas streetlamps had long since been extinguished, so he merely whistled at its dark disk and put it away. Then he leaned his head back, floated for a moment among the few ball-like stars, and let the memories from the dinner rise up in his mind like bubbles in a glass.

The brotherhood's undisputed master, Dante Gabriel Rossetti, had sat at the head of the table pouring out the red Italian wine. "Come, brothers, surely one of you has a couplet to launch our evening's ship into some felicitous sea."

Of them all, Ned had answered, with a verse from Longfellow:

And the night shall be filled with music,
And the cares that infest the day

Shall fold their tents like the Arabs,
And as silently steal away.

"Good!" the master had said. "Let no one say our Joaquin is not fast in his draw." He had bestowed a smile, and then had lifted his glass. "A toast to the *bambino miracoloso*, who in the space of a single summer has made Americans of us all."

Ned drank to the memory from a whiskey flask in his coat pocket. He raised his flask toward the stars. "Here's to Joaquin Miller, pals."

As he continued on his way, caroming down the dark streets, more of the evening's conversation floated to mind.

"Silence is the noblest attitude in all things," the master had said quietly. "We are but scriveners, for the greatest poets have never held a pen."

"Aye, all the books in the world are too small to hold a single sunset," a voice had responded.

"Heard melodies are sweet, but unheard melodies are sweeter," another had said.

"And yet in every poem there is truth," Rossetti had added. "All religions, said the Chinese philosophers, are good. The only difference is, some religions appear better than others, and the apparent merit of each depends largely upon a man's capacity for understanding it. This is true of poetry, my brothers. All poetry is good. The fault in reading the poems of man, as well as reading the poetry of nature, lies largely at the door of the reader."

Then Rossetti had held his red glass before him, his eyes twinkling. "My toast is: good health to the readers with wit enough to appreciate us poor scriveners." And the glasses had clinked amid laughter.

Ned rounded Westminster Abbey at a tilt. The gray light of dawn had begun to pale the stars, shadowing the church's Gothic facade into a ghost ship of stone. He pulled himself up the stairs of his rooming house by the banister and hung at the top flight. There he tried to focus on an odd white shape leaning ominously against his door. When he trapped the white shape between his big hands, he saw it was a letter.

Ned smoothed the paper out on his desk by the garret window. It was from Eugene City. The handwriting betrayed the years his father had taught penmanship in country schoolhouses, but it also showed a new, disconcerting unsteadiness. Ned rubbed his eyes with both hands, dizzily trying to shift his thoughts to that distant world. Then he took a long breath, and began to read:

Eugene City, Oregon
July 24, 1871

Dear Son:

It is hard for me to write a letter of this nature now, when you are so far from home. Of course your Mother and I have read with great pride the reports of your wonderful success in England. Every newspaper here has had articles about it, although they are often mixed up with the scandalous doings of that bitter woman, Theresa. I thank the Lord she is no longer a part of this family, but I wish she did not feel she had to hurt us yet more. We often pray for the grandchildren—they have been taken away from Port Orford, but we don't know where.

And now I am afraid I have to give you some very sad news, son: our family circle has been broken. Your sister's illness became suddenly worse shortly after the Fourth of July. Three days ago, she passed away. Mother has taken the loss particularly hard. It has been a consolation to us that we were at Ella's side, holding her hand as she left us.

I have not yet told Mother of the letter I received from John today, as I fear this additional tragedy would take away what little ground the poor woman has left to stand upon. John writes that he has suffered an attack: hemorrhaging in the lungs from his old bullet wound. He does not expect to live out the month. Your brother had been so happy since his wedding in December—and now this.

Ned, John's place in Easton, Pennsylvania is terribly far away for the rest of the family. I know you two had a falling out years ago, but please say you will sit by his side in his last days. I am unfit for that kind of travel now, and I have my hands full just taking care of Mother.

Please write back only in my name.

Your father,
Hulings

Ned looked up from the letter, painfully sobered. His beautiful, frail sister Ella was dead. She had believed in his poetry when even he had doubted. His proud, defiant brother, who had never forgiven him for opposing the Civil War, was dying. And what the hell was Minnie up to?

Out his garret window a bloody sun had just crested above the city's sea of chimneys, smoldering with the day's first fires. He had been in England almost a year.

It was time to go home.

Chapter 27

And I the oak, and you the vine,
Clung palm in palm through cloud or shine.
                    —Joaquin Miller, "Myrrh," 1870

Men, who are pitiful oaks of the world,
Lend not your vigor to weakness of mine;
Since one has bidden me stand alone,
I am no longer a clinging vine.
                    —Minnie Myrtle Miller, "Have
                    Mercy," 1871

Minnie was watching the crescent moon through the skewed panes of her one-room apartment in Portland, Oregon. Across the street, the black brick silhouettes of a salmon cannery warehouse and a window-sash manufactory looked as though they were trying to crowd the moon into a dark cage. Through the gap the moonlight danced over the river, slipped past the tall rigging of the ships along the waterfront, and splashed against the signboard suspended below her sagging window: "Wah Sing & Co., Laundry."

Minnie sighed wearily, dipping her quill. But then she only stared at the changing shadows of her slender hand cast across the page by the candle. It was as if the shadows themselves were the poem she was determined to write—the poem that would gather together and seal up the memories of the long winter.

But what could possibly encompass all the bitterness? First there had been the divorce trial, which Ned had wrested from her control and manipulated to his own ends. And then, in December, when the promised child support money had not arrived, she had learned from an acquaintance in Eugene City that he had left the country altogether. The news had set off an argument at the Dyer home. Her mother had excoriated her for driving a good husband away. Her father had thundered back that

Miller was a worthless blackguard who had never deserved as good a woman as his daughter.

The argument had not been resolved. Minnie had long known that she and her three children had worn out their welcome at Cliff House. The next morning she had announced they were leaving for Portland, saying that there would be better schools for Maud in the city. Besides, she had said, her younger brother Robert was an apprentice in Portland; perhaps he could help find them a place to live and some kind of work.

They had arrived in Portland on a dismal January morning, only to discover that Robert had left his job and vanished. After her little money had been lost to hotel bills, she had agreed in desperation to repair clothing at the Chinese laundry in exchange for her room and for two cents' pay for each piece she sewed.

During the months of storms that had followed, the wind had whistled through the boards in the back wall and the rain had dripped through the wooden shingles of the roof. Despite the mountains of mending she had done, there had hardly been enough money each week for a miserable miners' diet of beans and flour. And always there had been the baby crying, and George devising mischief at every opportunity.

Then one day Maud had come home from school in tears, taunted by her classmates and scorned by the teacher because she had been discovered to be the progeny of a *divorce*—a crime often mentioned in the same breath as incest or adultery. Through it all, Minnie had held her head up before the children. Only at night, when she fell into bed exhausted, did she let the tears come.

That evening when the children had finally gone to sleep she had slipped downstairs to ask her Chinese employer for an advance on her next week's earnings. It had seemed the final indignity: having to beg for money from Mr. Wah Sing, the white-haired Chinaman who was mocked by schoolboys on the street as "Mr. Washing" and "Old John Washee."

She had found Mr. Wah in his little back room, holding an upright brush over a large sheet of rice paper. He had immediately put it down when he saw her and had bowed repeatedly. "Mrs. Miller, you are welcome."

"I'm sorry if I disturbed you,—" she had paused, glancing curiously at the red characters he had drawn across a small black-and-white landscape. "I didn't know you painted."

The white-haired man had bowed again. "I paint words, yes. In China we make poem and picture together."

"Really? It's very nice, I think. Have you been painting long?"

Again a bow. "Fifty years I make poems. Twenty years I live in

America. I send poems to China. There people honor the poems of Wah Sing."

Minnie had smiled with a distant look. "You'd never guess it to look at me now, I suppose, but I once wrote poems, too." And at once she had blushed for admitting this to the old Chinese man. However, instead of casting her a scornful smile, he had bowed with serious respect.

"Yes. You write again someday I hope. Maybe you earn more with pen than with needle."

It had almost seemed as though he had already known she was going to ask for money. She had looked into his narrow eyes and had been suddenly flustered when he did not look away.

"Well, I don't know, I—I wouldn't even know where to send a poem anymore, it's been so long since I've looked at a newspaper."

The old Chinese man had then released her from his gaze with a bow. "I buy first issue of new newspaper today. It is women's newspaper, written by woman. Maybe she buy your poems."

He unfolded a poster-size sheet filled with seven columns of tight print. The bold Gothic letters across the top announced, *The New Northwest.*

Minnie took it hesitantly, realizing that by accepting it she was losing her best chance to ask for an unearned advance.

"'Mrs. Abigail Duniway, Editor and Proprietor,'" she read. "Why, I've heard of her—she had the millinery in Albany." She read on thoughtfully: "A Journal for the People. Devoted to the Interests of Humanity. Independent in Politics and Religion. Alive to all Live Issues and Thoroughly Radical in Opposing and Exposing the Wrongs of the Masses . . ."

The ink on Minnie's quill had dried while she had sat by the moonlit window, lost in thought. Now she took a fresh breath, dipped the quill again, and held her hand over the blank paper. She bit her lip, and then began to write.

At first she crossed out line after line, but gradually, as the work with the quill awoke the old skills, the poem she was determined to write finally began to emerge:

PLEA FOR THE INCONSTANT MOON
Queen Moon, thy form was round
Only one month ago;
And with a halo crowned,
Half-draped with clouds of snow.

Tonight we gazed and wondered;
So sadly changed, and soon?

> How was thy fair shape sundered,
> O broken-hearted Moon?
>
> Who so cruel and cold
> As to mar thy regal splendor,
> And make thee crook'd and old—
> Who was the bold offender?
>
> At last we read the secret,
> While she wandered through the skies,
> As we read a woman's answer
> Out of her truthful eyes.
>
> Tenderly, faintly reflected,
> Down from her silvery sheen,
> The spoiler chief was detected;
> The face of a man was seen!

Her long apron smudged with printer's ink, Abigail Duniway stood in the upstairs office of the *New Northwest*, reading the conclusion of the poem that had arrived with the morning mail:

> I will keep his image ever,
> Said the faithful-hearted lune,
> And the white stars said "forever,"
> O broken-hearted Moon!
>
> And she still is weeping, weeping,
> But her tears are so pearly bright
> That mortals, awake or sleeping,
> Mistake them for beams of light.
> —Minnie Myrtle Miller

"That's simply beautiful," Abigail said, shaking her head. She looked again at the Portland address on the envelope and wondered about the author's name. When she cocked her head the sunlight caught her intense, blue eyes and shone on the brown hair she wore up in a neat bun. Although she was a small woman, her every motion radiated strength and self-assurance.

She turned to her husband, who had crossed the room with a cane and had begun to break down a tray of type. "Ben, here's a poem that's been sent in by a 'Minnie Myrtle Miller.' Doesn't that name sound somehow familiar? It almost seems there was a Minnie Myrtle once who wrote poems from down on the coast."

Ben Duniway looked up, revealing a good-natured face supported by a large black beard. "Minnie Myrtle? Sure, she married the Miller boy who used to run the paper in Eugene City. You remember the Millers—when I rode out in '52 to meet your wagon train they were right there in one of the back wagons."

"Oh yes. But they had *several* sons, if I recall."

"This one was Cincinnatus, the same fellow who was in town running for the Supreme Court last year."

"Cincinnatus—" a connection seemed to click in Abigail's mind. She quickly turned to her roll-top desk and thumbed through a stack of telegraph reports. She pulled out a paper and smiled. "Yes, Cincinnatus. I thought I'd seen that name lately. Here's a Cincinnatus Miller from Canyon City who's been writing poetry under the pen name 'Joaquin Miller.' He's published a book in England that's made him quite a sensation over there. Apparently he's been living it up with the likes of Robert Browning, Dante Rossetti, and Lord Tennyson."

Ben Duniway arched his eyebrows. "Son of a gun. Who would've guessed?"

"And think of it," Abigail continued pensively, "the wife of this famous Joaquin Miller is living right here in *Portland*. Why, she's probably terribly well-to-do, and she's certainly creative, judging from her poem."

She turned with an air of decision and handed the letter to her teen-age son, who was bent over a tray of type, mounting the little letters one by one on a composing stick. "Here, Willis. I want this poem set right away and fitted into the front page."

"Yes, Mother."

Abigail continued on to the office door, taking off her apron. She spoke over her shoulder to her husband. "I'll be back in an hour or so, Ben. I'm going to put on my silk dress and look up this Mrs. Miller."

"You are, huh? What if she wants ten dollars for her rhymes? You reckon we can afford fancy poetry?"

Abigail smiled. "That's just what I was thinking. If I stop by to thank her personally, her price may come down a little." She hung the apron on a peg thoughtfully. "Besides, this is a woman I suspect I'm going to enjoy meeting."

* * *

Abigail Duniway looked puzzled as she walked up and down First Street in her blue silk-and-velveteen dress. The address on the envelope was not the hotel after all. It was only a run-down Chinese laundry. In the doorway stood a tired, sunken-eyed woman with strands of brown hair hanging in disarray over her work dress. The woman was carrying a huge hamper of laundry and scolding a small boy in the darkness behind her.

"Excuse me," Abigail ventured reluctantly. "I'm looking for Minnie Myrtle. You wouldn't know where she lives?"

The woman in the doorway turned, speechless for a moment. There was a peculiarly pained smile on her lips and her dark eyes grew damp.

"I'm sorry, I must have the wrong—" Abigail began, about to turn away.

"No, no," the tired-looking woman said, setting down her basket. "It's just I hadn't heard that name for so long." She dried her eyes and lifted her chin. "I am Minnie Myrtle."

The statement left Abigail stunned. "Oh! I—I don't know what I was thinking, I—" She struggled to regain her composure. "I am Abigail Duniway of the *New Northwest*."

Minnie blushed and cast her eyes down. When she looked up again she held out her hand. "We seem to have surprised each other, Mrs. Duniway."

"So we have," Abigail said, and they both let the tension release with a small laugh as they shook hands. "Perhaps I could come in and talk a bit, if you've the time?"

"Oh, I'm sorry, but the room is such an awful mess."

"That's quite all right. Or would you rather discuss your poem here on the step?"

"No, no, of course you're right. If you really don't mind, please do come in."

Abigail followed Minnie up the rickety stairs. She was shaken by what she found. From Minnie's manner and poetry there could be no doubt she was a highly intelligent, gifted woman, and yet for some unfathomable reason she was living in drafty quarters above a Chinese laundry, reduced to serving her guests chicory coffee in a tin cup. What surprised Abigail even more was that Minnie had heard nothing about C. H. Miller's pseudonym "Joaquin," nor of his meteoric rise to fame in England. In fact, Minnie's reaction upon hearing this news was an odd blend of pride and scorn.

"But Mrs. Miller!" Abigail finally interjected impatiently. "How can it be possible that this 'Joaquin' Miller is basking in fame and glory in England while his own wife and children are forced to live in conditions such as these?"

Minnie smiled wanly. "There is a simple answer to that. These are indeed his children, but I am not his wife."

Abigail looked lost. "*What?*"

"Oh, we *were* married for seven years. It's just that the last year of the marriage he sent me and the children away and refused to support us. He was Judge of Grant County at the time, too. I didn't know what else to do, so I filed for a divorce."

"I can't say I blame you."

Minnie refilled the imitation coffee in their cups. "I guess it only made things more complicated. I was granted the divorce all right, but not any money, and the child support for the children wasn't secured, so when he didn't pay I had to earn money myself. I brought the children to Portland and took the only work I could find." Recounting the story put a bitter tone in her voice. "I'm sure he needed all his money to go to England anyway. He always wanted to be famous. Perhaps now he's satisfied."

Abigail set down her cup firmly and drew herself up with indignation. "Mrs. Miller, you have been wronged, and it is time amends were made!"

The ringing tone of these words caused Minnie a moment of panic. She had poured out her story so easily because Mrs. Duniway was such a sympathetic listener. Minnie had forgotten the woman was also a newspaper editor. "You won't mention this in your paper, will you?"

"I think it is *exactly* the kind of thing that should be in my paper! This Joaquin Miller may be famous in England, but that doesn't mean he can run rough-shod over his family here in Oregon. If we women fail to stand up for our rights and the rights of our children, we have no one to blame but ourselves when the Cause of Woman does not advance."

Minnie bit her lip. She had vowed vengeance against Ned for his cold-heartedness, and yet she hesitated to throw her lot in with the Woman's Rights activists. She still felt burned by the treacherous hypocrisy of Sarah Eckelhoff, whose talk of rights had concealed so many wrongs.

Abigail took Minnie's hands. "Believe me, I *know* how difficult it is to stand up in a society ruled by men. My own husband is the kindest man in the world, but fate has not allowed him to provide for me any more than your husband has provided for you. My husband signed as security on a friend's note without my advice, and as a result he lost our farm. Shortly afterward he was crippled by a runaway wagon. Since then I have been forced to stand up, Mrs. Miller, just as I believe you are now. I ran a small boarding school for girls to pay our debts. Then I borrowed money against my own name and opened a hat shop. Now I've followed my convictions and have sold the shop to start a newspaper that will dare to speak out for the women of Oregon. Surely you can see that if women of intelligence like yourself allow themselves to be downtrodden by their husbands, the only message we'll be spreading to the men of Oregon is that they can subjugate their wives and neglect their families with impunity?"

Without giving Minnie a chance to respond, Abigail reached into her handbag and pressed two gold coins into Minnie's hand. "I came here intending to pay you twenty dollars for your lovely poem, but there's an extra twenty as an advance towards the next piece you write."

Minnie stared at the gold. "Forty dollars! What sort of piece do you expect me to write?"

"Whatever you like." The editor leaned back thoughtfully. "Perhaps you could do an article on the rights of women."

"No, no, I'm sorry. I'm not ready yet to march about as some kind of suffragist."

"Well, then perhaps you could do something more specific. Say, a biography of this Joaquin Miller from a wife's point of view?"

This time Minnie hesitated. She could imagine the effect such an article might have, particularly if it mentioned Ned's Indian wife and daughter in California, or his affair with Sarah Eckelhoff in Canyon City. On the other hand, the reasons she had not brought these matters up in the divorce trial still weighed heavily in her mind. She had no hard evidence for either charge. Then, too, people would say it was a breach of matrimonial trust for a wife to bring up things that happened while she was married. And as for the Indian "marriage"—which certainly never was legal anyway—the truth was that she should have been careful enough to have discovered it before she had ever married Ned. Perhaps there would come a time when she would expose the depths of his hypocrisy, but not yet. It was a weapon to keep in reserve.

"I don't believe I could write that kind of article either," Minnie said, placing one of the twenty-dollar coins on the table by Mrs. Duniway. "If you feel it is necessary to balance these reports of my ex-husband's success, however, I will not prevent you from repeating what I have told you today about his treatment of myself and the children since the divorce. Believe me, our suffering at his hands has been genuine."

"I do believe you, Mrs. Miller. And I want you to keep this," she said, pushing the coin back. "Consider it partial payment for your next poem, whatever its subject. In the meantime I intend to see that justice is done. I'm sure there are plenty of fair-minded citizens in this state who will not sit idly by while a woman of your abilities is left in such a position. I can already think of one excellent poet in Salem, Belle Cooke, who could provide you with a better home for the children and enable you to return to your poetry."

Abigail stood up determinedly. "Now I must be on my way. But I promise you, this Joaquin Miller will not be allowed to reap the profits of his cruelty unscathed! I am going to level an editorial broadside at him that will take the wind out of his sails!"

* * *

It did not take long for the newspapers of Oregon to respond to the vitriolic exposé that appeared in the *New Northwest*.

The Salem *Mercury* objected:

> Mrs. Duniway would have it that Judge Miller "deserted" his wife. This is not correct. She "deserted" him and applied for a divorce— and obtained it. We are told that the Judge idolized his wife, but was not in circumstances to live up to her standard of affluence.

The Portland *Herald* countered:

> Judge Miller took with him about eight thousand dollars in gold, leaving behind him his divorced wife and babes, who were found afterwards in this city—almost destitute, struggling bravely against poverty—whom several gentlemen of Portland provided for in their need, as the natural husband and father should have done.

The Baker *Bedrock Democrat* noted:

> Mr. Joaquin Miller, the Oregon poet, formerly of Grant County, has struck a lead in London with his "Songs of the Sierras." He is reported to be the latest pet of the critical and poetical authorship in the town. Judge Miller's wife, we understand, recently obtained a divorce from him, because, as Mrs. Duniway alleges, he spent too much time writing something he termed poetry. Isn't it possible that the former Mrs. Miller was a little nasty?

Back in her office, Abigail threw the papers aside. "Darn them!" she said aloud. Then she reached for a quill and pushed up her sleeves. "Well, we'll just reload and see if our second shot doesn't shake them up a little better." Her new volley proclaimed:

> The time has gone by when a woman of brains may submit, like a whipped spaniel, to neglect, abuse, and misrepresentation from her legal master because the world applauds his doggerel!
> When a man barters connubial constancy and matrimonial honors

for poetic fame we are free to confess that he has paid all that the bubble is worth; and we greatly err in judgment if our bard does not live to see the day when he will realize the fact.

Now the Portland *Bulletin* took up the cause:

> Some Oregonians and Oregon newspapers seem to have an idea that C. H. Miller, otherwise "Joaquin Miller," is in some way a credit to this State. In our view of the case, there is no language strong enough to justly denounce the meanness, cowardice, and villainy of the man who, with his pockets filled with gold, earned in part by the loving and self-sacrificing labors of his wife, will deliberately desert that wife and his own children, leaving them to poverty, beggary, or destruction, and selfishly go out to seek the praise of men and the vanity of the world upon his own worthless head.
>
> California claims this humbug pretender poet, and in the name of all that is good, let that State have the doubtful honor. Miller may be a poet, or he may not be, but he is not a man. He is a disgrace to true manhood. Instead of chanting his praise and sounding his fame, let the press of Oregon, and the editorial fraternity everywhere, unite to show this literary sham up in his true colors.

Even the staid Albany *Democrat* railed:

> C. H. Miller, ex-editor of the Eugene *Register*, and ex-County Judge of Grant County, has published a book of poems and become a man of fame in London. The fact makes us think no more of Miller, but much less of the Londoners.
>
> During the time that he was connected with the *Register* he published one or more serial stories under his own name and called them original. They were, however, stolen bodily from some of the flash publications of that day. After his marriage and after he began to write poetry, this habit of plagiarism was not abandoned, if his wife's testimony is worth anything, and if we do not misinterpret the following quotation taken from her "Sacrifice Impetro:"
> "And he through books and bays
> Delveth for pretty words
> To weave in his languid lays
> Of women, and streams, and birds."
> For this and many other better reasons we don't hesitate to pronounce the belief that this so-called poet is what is termed, in the

vernacular of the coast, a first-class bilk, and that besides the other injuries that he has inflicted upon his unhappy wife, he has filched from the literary jewels and published them as his own.

Abigail sat back in her chair, smiling. She allowed herself a moment to wonder if Mr. Miller knew what the papers in Oregon were saying, and what his reception might be like if he should ever dare to return.

Then she set the papers aside. There were other things to think about. Susan B. Anthony, the famous Woman's Rights activist, was planning a lecture tour of the Pacific Northwest soon to pay her debts from her failed newspaper, the *Revolution*. Abigail, who had been asked to make arrangements for the great woman's controversial tour, knew the coming months would be more than merely busy—they would be a time to test the true strength of the hardy pioneer women of Oregon.

* * *

"Are we really gonna ride a *train?*" little George asked, bouncing about like a jackrabbit on a leash.

"What'd you think—we'd *walk* all the way from Portland to Salem?" Maud replied.

The boy only rolled his eyes. A second later he shouted, "Hey, look!" and ran out one of the two-storied docks on the Portland waterfront to peer in the portholes of a bright crimson barge.

"George, get back here this instant!" Minnie's sharp voice collared the boy. Her intuition told her clearly what manner of business might be conducted in a red-painted barge along the Willamette riverfront. There were plenty of rumors about the bordellos and gambling dens where men were slipped knockout drops and shanghaied out to ships bound for the Far East. It made her shudder just to walk near the two-storied docks. The upper level was used during the spring run-off of snowmelt from the Cascade Mountains, but now, when the river was low, it was impossible to tell what kind of criminal elements were lurking among the barrels and boxes of the lower level. It really would be better for the children in Salem, she thought, living with Mrs. Duniway's friends in a farmhouse.

Minnie carried two-year-old Henry carefully on her hip as she herded the two older children onto the steam ferry. Soon the ferry's engine humphed and hissed, and began winching the scow across on two big cables. Minnie turned to bid farewell to the city whose outpouring of sympathy over the summer had restored her dignity. She was even close to achieving the two goals she had set for herself after the divorce. True, she wasn't yet going to San Francisco to resume her writing career, but taking the train to a poet's house in Salem was a move in the right

A Deeper Wild

direction. And she had laid the groundwork for the vengeance she had sworn against Ned. His day would come.

The squeals of her excited children interrupted her thoughts. "There it is, Ma, I can see the engine and everything!" George tugged on her skirts. Even Maud could not resist making small, unladylike "oohs!" and bouncing up onto her toes at the sight of the railroad depot crowds.

"Come along now," Minnie said as the ferry landed. Beyond a jostling crowd of bowlers and women's millinery, the 4-4-0 locomotive waited, blowing off white steam from a valve and billowing black smoke and sparks from its proud stack. A sooty-faced tender leaned on his shovel in the coal car. From the step of one of the five shiny passenger cars a uniformed conductor called, "'Board!"

At that moment Minnie realized George was gone. A wave of panic caught her. She called out, frantically trying to make her way through the confusion on the platform with both Maud and the baby. All the nightmarish stories she had heard about train travel rushed to mind.

Suddenly a voice asked, "Is this yours?" Out of the crowd in the direction of the engine came a white-haired woman, pulling the boy firmly by his ear.

"George! Thank heavens you're all right." She turned to the woman. "Thank you ever so much."

"I know how hard it is to travel with children. I'm going as far as Oregon City—why don't I just help keep an eye on your three a while?"

Minnie gratefully accepted the offer, and they found seats together in one of the cars. Then the woman introduced herself: "Matilda Jane Fultz, from Farmington, up in the Washington Territory."

"Pleased to make your acquaintance," Minnie said, offering a slender hand. "I am Mrs. Theresa Miller."

The name made the white-haired woman sit back to study her. "Oh, so you're the Mrs. Miller who writes poetry?"

Minnie reddened, but was pleased by the recognition. "Yes, I am."

"And I gather you don't think women should write about politics?"

One of Minnie's poems had suggested as much. "Yes, I like to keep my literature on other subjects."

Mrs. Fultz looked out the window. "Well, you've got a lot to learn, sister."

"I beg your pardon?" Minnie could hardly believe she had heard this woman correctly. "Do you mean about literature?"

"I mean about men."

The woman's effrontery left Minnie at a loss.

Mrs. Fultz still looked out the window. "I read about your troubles,

Mrs. Miller. I'm sorry, but the truth is, you're better off than most."

Before Minnie could reply to this provoking statement a passing porter interrupted, "Lunch is being served in the dining car." At once little Maud jumped from her seat. Minnie caught the girl in time and directed her toward the biscuits she had brought in a bag.

Finally Minnie could ask her white-haired neighbor, "What do you mean, 'better off?'"

"Just that." Mrs. Fultz turned to face her. "Look at me. You probably think I'm sixty." She held up her leathery hands to her snowy white hair and wrinkled face. "Well, I'm thirty-four, not much older than you. But I've had eight children and two husbands. That taught me politics."

Minnie was taken aback; she had assumed this woman was a grandmother. Still, she replied, "I'm not sure what politics has to do with it."

"Then I'll explain. I married my first husband at fifteen to run away from beatings at home. When he died in the mines I had five children to support by doing laundry *cheaper* than the Chinese. My second husband put me to work in a livery up in Farmington. Before long we'd bought three other businesses, and I had to run them all. He finally drank himself to death, but the courts won't give me a dime. They don't trust a widow to own property from her marriage. Instead they take control of everything and dole out a little money for the children's support—not mine, mind you. Now lawyers' fees are eating up the inheritance, and all because the laws are written by men."

Mrs. Fultz shook her head. "Let me tell you, if we women up in Washington Territory get the vote that'll all change and quick. There's a bill already through the legislature for it. Unless the men ax it we'll be able to vote in Territorial elections by November."

"Milwaukie!" a conductor called out. The wheels screeched and people began jostling inside the car as the train slowed alongside another crowded platform.

Minnie knit her brow, thinking about Mrs. Fultz' words. They reminded her of how Ned had manipulated their divorce trial. Perhaps it wasn't just Ned who had been at fault, but the law itself. And then there was Claire Wheaton, the San Francisco landlady whose husband had repeatedly gambled away her business profits because he legally owned everything she earned. Mrs. Wheaton had blamed her troubles on her husband. But wasn't it the injustice of the laws that had left her at the man's mercy?

When the passengers had settled and the train was chugging onward again, Minnie picked up the conversation with her neighbor. "Do you really think it would make a difference if women could vote?"

"A difference? All I can say is, you must have had a soft life, if you trust men to make the rules."

Minnie bridled at this implication. The years she had suffered at Canyon City still stung. "I don't necessarily trust men. And I don't think I've had such an easy life."

"Sounded easy to me," Mrs. Fultz said. "Just compare how I grew up. Both my parents died of mountain fever on the Oregon Trail. Seven of us children were dumped at the Whitman Mission at Walla Walla. Then the Cayuse broke in and killed almost everyone, leaving me an orphan again."

"You survived the Whitman Massacre?" Minnie asked, astonished. As a child she had heard news of that infamous attack. It had left her terrified of Indians for years.

Mrs. Fultz nodded. "Afterwards, soldiers took us children to the Willamette Valley and split us up to whoever'd take us. I was given to a man so mean he used to whip me senseless before leaving the house, just to punish me in advance for the things I might do while he was gone. The truth was, he was only raising me because teenage girls were worth money. Men needed wives if they wanted to get an extra half square mile on their donation land claims. My best friend was fourteen when she was forced to marry a forty-four-year-old drunk. Another girl I knew was married at thirteen—and then her husband burned her alive in an 'accidental' fire as soon as he got his claim. I managed to run away from my foster father in time."

Mrs. Fultz scoffed. "Now you try to tell *me* we women ought to let men run the laws."

Minnie's head reeled from the horrors of the woman's story. Here were hardships and injustices on a scale that *did* make her own life seem sheltered by comparison. And the woman's conclusion now seemed unarguable: if men were capable of such cruelty, why *shouldn't* women demand the right to make more of their own decisions?

"Ma?" Maud's voice from the seat in front of them had a childlike quaver that made Minnie realize with a sudden adrenaline rush of distress the girl had overheard them.

"Will I be married that soon, Ma?"

The girl's words were the catalyst that finally set Minnie's decision. "No, Maud," she said quietly. "Things are changing now." And she thought: how could I allow you, my daughter, to face the same sufferings the women of my generation have endured? Cost what it may, the world must change.

"O-o-o-regon City!" came a cry. The brakes screeched metal on metal.

"This is where I leave, Mrs. Miller," the white-haired woman said, standing up.

Minnie caught the woman's weathered hand before she could go. Mrs. Fultz turned back with a questioning look.

"Thank you," Minnie said. "Thank you and good luck."

A smile wrinkled the woman's face. Then she gave Minnie's white hand a sisterly squeeze and was gone.

* * *

August 20, 1871

Dear Abigail:

Why didn't you tell me Belle Cooke wrote under the name Viola? I remember seeing that name in the *Era* and elsewhere often enough. We are getting along wonderfully. If anything, she is even more gracious and hospitable than you had suggested.

I have been thinking for some time about your offer to work for your newspaper and write Woman's Rights material. I believe now I am ready to accept, if you still want my assistance. Only—what sort of things should I do?

Yours faithfully,
MMM.

August 25, 1871

Dear MMM:

Glad all's well, and welcome to the Cause. As to newspaper work: collect subscriptions at $3 per annum; keep 20%. Have advertisers write to me with copy or cards; rates are in the NNW. Write columns on anything appropriate; more poems, too. And: Susan B. Anthony is arriving in Portland from SF Aug. 31. I have scheduled her to speak in Salem Sept. 15-17, and again at the State Fair the next week. I do expect opposition, and am busy with details. Could I count on you to write up reports of the Salem lectures for the paper?

Sincerely,
Abigail.

P.S.: Have you heard from "Joaquin?"

Chapter 28

I shall sit and I shall see . . .
The sun fall down upon the farther sea,
Fall wearied down to rest, and so retire,
A splendid sinking isle of far-off fading fire.
                    —Joaquin Miller

Ned strode down a corridor of the New York Customs House. His old Western hat was cocked jauntily and his pants were still stuffed into his boots gold-miner-style, but now he now wore a dapper black suit with a velvet collar and a huge gold watch chain. Behind him a porter was struggling to keep up, lugging a large leather bag.

At the customs counter a blue-uniformed inspector with a square gray beard opened the bulky bag. But instead of looking inside it, he peered up at Ned. "You're Joaquin Miller, the writer, aren't you?"

"Yup, I reckon so," Ned chuckled. "How did you know?"

"The reporters have been waiting for you." He tipped his head toward the far end of the hall, where a group of men stood watching from behind a railing. Reluctantly the customs inspector began to search about the inside of the bag. "I've written a few books myself," he said quietly, without looking up. He almost seemed embarrassed by the admission.

"Have you now?"

"Yes. Perhaps you've heard of *Typee?*"

"Type E? Is that some kind of pen name?"

The inspector sighed. "No, that was the book. I never used a pen name—just Melville, Herman Melville." He buckled the bag together and slid it across the counter.

Ned paused, struck with sympathy for the glum man. "Getting a book out is hell, I know. But the paydirt is all in the publicity. Why, when I worked jobs like yours my poems were ignored too. Get out in the spotlight, that's my advice. It won't matter how good your stuff is if you haven't made a *name* for yourself."

Then he left the inspector with a wink and a grin, and strode on to confront New York City.

* * *

"Sorry, gents," Ned said, rising from the plush sofa of his Astor House suite. He held up his hands to the crowd of reporters he had invited to his press conference. "That's all I have time for. I'm meeting with my publisher from Boston in a few minutes, and then I must get back to writing."

Several reporters spoke at once. The loudest asked, "Writing what?"

"Well, it's an autobiography of my life in California—the true story of my experiences amongst the Modocs. I can't tell you anything more about it just yet."

"Could you comment quickly on the reviews in the Oregon newspapers?"

"Sorry, I don't have time to read all the reviews. Now if you—"

"Would you be available for an interview with Horace Greeley?"

Ned held up his hands again. "No, look, I'm sorry. I'm going to be leaving town very shortly on urgent family business, so I'm afraid I'll have to disappoint Mr. Greeley this time. However, I *have* written up a letter you can have him print. It's just a little thing thanking all the friends in England and America who have made my book as successful as it is." He handed a sheet to the *Tribune* reporter and then herded the journalists to the door.

The next morning all of New York was reading the prominently positioned notice from the "Poet of the Sierras:"

To the Editor of the New York *Tribune*. Sir:

As I left England suddenly, barely saying good-bye to a few friends at hand, I have ever since felt like making some public expression of my gratitude to that country for its noble treatment of me and my crude *Songs of the Sierras*, and as the American press has as a rule treated me with similar generosity, and as I am about to return for a time to the Sierras and my home on the Willamette, I take occasion to briefly thank both countries together.

First, let me speak of England, for was she not first to speak of me? Looking back a few months to a venture that now seems to me like a dream I am bound to say that the conduct of that country in holding up my hands when they were not strong, when in fact I had neither money, name, nor influence, appears to me every day, as I recall it, manly and generous beyond calculation. England! the terms of the expression of thanks are threadbare. Permit me to say simply, I thank you!

While the American press has been more cautious and qualified in its reviews, I believe, as a rule, it has been honest and well-meaning. The public is full of good will. The sale of the book proves that, and I have nothing to complain of. I shall return to the Sierras, and the pastoral banks of the Willamette, glad and grateful and with lifted face.

JOAQUIN C. H. MILLER

* * *

"Mr. Miller?"

At first Ned did not hear the woman's voice. He was somberly making his way through the train station in Easton, Pennsylvania, counting back the years to the depths of the Civil War when he had last seen his brother: eight, eight and a half.

"Pardon me, are you Cincinnatus Miller?"

This time he turned and saw a very pretty, very young woman waiting for him.

"Yes," he said. "I'm sorry, do I know you?"

She curtsied in her stiff crinoline dress. "Not yet—and I apologize for stopping you like this. I am John's wife."

"Ah." Ned had known John was married, but he had only thought of it in an abstract way. And now, here she was, in light brown hair, well-mannered, hardly eighteen years old. Perhaps he should have expected her. Of course she had gotten the telegram he had sent to John, and she was the one who had come to meet him. It made perfect sense. And yet something about her was disturbing.

"Then you must be—Sarah?"

"Yes. Sallie."

"Sallie, of course. Tell me, how is John?"

"Not better, I'm afraid."

Ned frowned. "He's at home?"

"Yes, but he's resting. It's not a good time to visit. He had just fallen asleep as I left. A neighbor lady is sitting in to see that he has some quiet."

Ned waited, but that was all the young Mrs. Miller was going to say about John's condition or his reaction to the telegram. "Well, if he's resting, maybe I should just stretch my legs for a while, walk around town till he's up for a visit."

"Yes, that would be well," she said. "Perhaps you would permit me to come with you? The doctor wants me to take some air each day."

"Of course." He was glad for an excuse to put off his confrontation with John, but he still had an uneasy feeling about this polite young wife. What was it?

As they walked through town, Ned's first reaction to Easton was that it was an unsettlingly busy place. Railroads, canals, and rivers converged on the city. The streets were straight, lined with staid elms and maples in fall colors. The citizens were serious-looking Pennsylvania Dutch.

Everything Sallie pointed out on their walk seemed to relate to John. She showed him the Masonic Building, Easton Lodge No. 152, where John was a member. There was the hall of the O. U. A. M., Tatamy Council No. 159. There was the Undine Boat Club. There was John's large dental office in the Centre Square Building—staffed by an assistant during John's illness. On Saturday nights, Sallie said, the better-educated men of the town gathered in John's office for the literary and political discussions of the Easton Lyceum. Through her tour, Sallie conducted herself with perfect respect and humility. Then what was so disturbing?

On the way to John's house on South Third Street, it finally occurred to Ned what it was. Here in Easton, Pennsylvania, he was seeing the kind of life he could have had—the kind of life his family had always expected him to lead.

Would it have been any less pleasant a life than the one he had followed, Ned wondered? John had found an industrious, practical city and had established himself well. He had a solid profession. He belonged to respected civic groups. Now, as John was approaching middle age, he had married a young wife who was as pretty and practical as one could wish. No extravagance. Nothing impulsive. There was a tremendous security in it all—only, he recalled: it was John, and not he, who had the bullet hole in his lungs.

As they neared the gray stone house, Ned's heart beat faster at the thought of that bullet hole, and the unfinished war it represented. How could he say to John that the war was behind them as long as the wound remained?

Through the door to John's bedroom the waiting neighbor lady signaled that he was still asleep. "He must need the rest," she whispered.

"Let me sit with him now," Ned said.

The woman cast a questioning glance to Sallie.

"It will be all right," Sallie replied. "Cincinnatus is his brother."

As soon as Ned took the woman's place at the foot of the bed a shiver of horror ran through him. Propped up on a pillow in the bed was a skeletal face he did not know. The skin was drawn and deathly gray. The closed, sunken eyes were so deeply shadowed they appeared only as dark holes in a skull. But even in sleep the face wore the small, wire-rimmed spectacles that assured him this was John.

For the moment he forgot all his fears of a confrontation. This was his dying brother—the boy he remembered taking him fishing in Indiana, helping him plow in Oregon. He and John—the little brother and the big guy watching out. Always the same, and yet always exact opposites. They had almost reached adulthood before they had realized how different they were. Perhaps that was what made their rivalry so intense. Even now, would John only think he had come to gloat over his fame and success as a poet?

Ned sighed uneasily. A tintype photograph hanging over the bed caught his attention. The metal plate had frozen the old family somewhere in the past: Hulings with his big hands on the back of Margaret's chair, Ella's frail figure a silvery ghost on the shiny tin, little George an impish blur at their feet. And John—a giant standing apart from the others, staring sternly through his spectacles at the camera: at Ned, whose absence in the tintype left the gap between John and the others; at Ned, the son who had run away from the family to the California mines.

Ned lowered his head and saw the stern eyes again, on the pillow, on the bed. The eyes were open.

"So now you have come," John said with a slow, rasping voice that sent another shiver through Ned.

"Would you rather I hadn't?"

"No," John said, not moving his eyes. "We needed to talk, didn't we?"

Ned tried to chuckle at this, but the attempt failed. He looked down at his hands. "I was just thinking of when we were children. We talked to each other so much then people thought we were hatching plots."

"True. And then we stopped telling each other things." John paused, his breath shallow, as if to gather his strength. "I remember when it happened."

"When was that?" Ned wondered which of all the incidents John would choose. The time John secretly joined a radical Republican group at Columbia College?

"When you were seventeen. When I found you climbing out the farmhouse window in the middle of the night. When you hadn't told me you were planning to run away to California."

Ned frowned. "Yes, then."

"Didn't you ever wonder why I didn't wake Pa up that night? Because I *didn't want* him to bring you back." John coughed from the effort these words had cost. Then he managed to continue. "I thought you deserved the beating you would get in California. And sure enough, you came back with your tail between your legs."

John still stared at him. "So I just let the whole thing go until you didn't have the excuse of being a child anymore. I forgot it all until the war."

The war. As soon as Ned had seen the mark of death on his brother's face he had known they would finish the argument they had left suspended in the memory of drizzly watercolor clouds over Skinner's Butte. They had had eight years to choose the words since that wintry day in the midst of the Civil War. And yet Ned now suspected the long preparation had let the once-polished arguments rust into uselessness. The only blade that still shone brightly was the one reserved all this time for him. Looking now at the shell of his proud brother, he decided suddenly to face the bright blade.

"Maybe I was wrong about the war," Ned said, concealing the effort the words cost him.

John did not even blink with his hollow eyes.

Ned looked away from the gaze. If there were emotions on John's face, the horrible mask of his illness left them illegible.

"I know my side lost the war, but that's not why I was wrong," Ned added, more defensively than he had wanted. "You know I always pick the weaker side in a fight if I have to take sides. It's my way of fighting against the fight itself. When war came, I tried to fight against the war itself, but it was too big. That's why I threw in for the weaker side. And that's where I made my mistake. As soon as I stood up for the South I had to forget about the Negroes—and they were on the weakest side of all."

John did not speak for a long time. Finally he said, "Come here."

For Ned, these faintly whispered words carried all the power of a general's order. He stood up and approached the bed.

John lifted one bony fist and shook it feebly before Ned's face. "How can it be?" he asked. "How can it be that your side loses, *over* and *over* again, but you—you always win?"

Before Ned could speak, John broke into a long, rattling cough. Ned took his hand to steady him, and John did not resist.

When he could talk again, John's reedy voice was so faint Ned could hardly hear the words. "I have been wrong, too. You were never less brave than I. But you lost less for your stubbornness. You only lost a war. I lost a brother. And in the end, what does a man have if he doesn't have his own family?"

A lump rose in Ned's throat. He wanted to hold onto John, to keep him from drifting away again. How much family had Ned already lost over the years? First he had been torn away from Paquita and Cali-Shasta in California. Then Minnie and the children. Then his sister Ella. It seemed as if a long, lonely road were stretching ahead of him. Even if fame lined the way with cheering crowds, there was no solace in walking alone. He and John had always belonged at each other's side.

* * *

Two days later, his throat still thick with grief, Ned wrote a letter home.

Easton, Pennsylvania
Sept. 11, 1871

To Mr. and Mrs. Hulings Miller, Eugene City, Oregon.

Dear Parents:

I have sad news to write you. Our John is dead. I send you a paper which contains the particulars. He died at eleven o'clock on the evening of the 9th, very peacefully and in his full mind. He told me to write and say that in his last moments he thought of you all in Oregon. He did not suffer much and died happy and resigned, and said he was going to see Ella in heaven.

I cannot write you a long letter now, but I hope to be in Oregon soon. I may do well on my books. I will send you one.

Adieu, dear parents. God bless you.

C. H. Miller

Chapter 29

What was my troth to him?
A stepping stone at best;
My face was proud and my smiles were sweet,
And his gold could do the rest.
                                        —Minnie Myrtle Miller

Oregon's capital city boasted two thousand inhabitants, and it seemed to Minnie that every one of them had turned out to watch Miss Susan B. Anthony's train arrive. Of course the people of Salem were curious to see what kind of woman would dare to stand up on a stage and lecture about Woman's Rights.

Minnie was wondering too. It had only been a few weeks since she had agreed to write for Abigail Scott Duniway's radical newspaper, and she was still more than a little nervous about the role. As she waited by the tracks she could feel the eyes of Salem upon her, assessing her pleated white dress and the fringed parasol she had brought to deflect the summer heat. She hadn't felt so exposed since she wore her first off-the-shoulder gown to a Port Orford ball as a girl. Everyone here seemed to assume she was a dyed-in-the-wool Woman's Rights activist from Portland—and the truth was, she didn't even know what the notorious Miss Anthony looked like.

Her heart beat faster as she peered down the tracks. Was she really the right person to be taking up this crusade? What did she know about fighting a system built by men? She had lost battle after battle with Ned. Even now the thought of Joaquin Miller, riding the crest of his new-found success, left her apprehensive. She had once vowed to bring him to his knees. That would have been hard enough, but now her motive had subtly shifted from vengeance to a more worthwhile and far more challenging goal. Now she was marching against the entire tradition of men's domination.

A voice behind her laughed. Self-consciously, Minnie turned around. A boy was making his way through the crowd, selling printed sheets. The reporter from the farm weekly chuckled and passed one of the sheets to his colleagues from the daily papers.

Aware that the crowd was still watching her, Minnie stepped in front of the boy. "What are you selling?"

The boy kicked at the dust, then smiled. "Just a purty poem, ma'am. Five cents."

She paid the nickel and took the sheet, but as soon as she looked at it she felt her face flush red.

> THE SUFFRAGIST
> Along the city's thoroughfare,
> A grim old gal with manly air
> Strode amidst the noisy crowd,
> Tooting her horn both shrill and loud;
> Till e'en above the city's roar
> Above its din and discord, o'er
> All, was heard, "Ye tyrants, fear!
> The dawn of freedom's drawing near—
> Woman's Rights and Suffrage."
>
> A meek old man, in accents wild,
> Cried, "Sal, turn back and nurse our child!"
> She bent on him a withering look,
> Her bony fist at him she shook,
> And screeched, "Ye brute! ye think I'm flat
> To mend your clo'es and nurse your brat?
> Nurse it yourself; I'll change the plan,
> When I am made a congressman—
> Woman's Rights and Suffrage."

Minnie angrily crumpled the paper and turned away. But the vicious verse and the smirks of the reporters had left their mark on her pride. Ned had once branded her an adulteress, and that lie had hurt. Only a few months ago, Maud's schoolteacher had called her a tainted woman because she was divorced, and she had seethed with rage. Now a whole new set of lies and insults would be aimed at her for joining the women's movement. How would she fight back?

Minnie peered down the track again, wishing with all her heart that Miss Anthony would come to her rescue and swoop down upon this tormenting crowd like an avenging angel.

As if in reply, the distant wheet of a steam whistle drifted through the heavy summer air. At once every face in the crowd turned. Across the dry prairie, between the island-like groves of oaks, the locomotive puffed larger and larger under its growing black cloud. Again the whistle blasted, this time startling pigeons off the station roof and scattering pedestrians off the Twelfth Street tracks. With a screech of steel and a tremendous hiss of steam the locomotive rolled to a stop.

The crowd did not rush up to the cars. Even Minnie held back—cautious, curious, and a little afraid of disappointment. A few dozen passengers carried their baggage out into the bright August sunshine, blinked in surprise at the hundreds of people, and hurried self-consciously across the platform. At length the car's door opened again. Some of the women in the crowd stood on tiptoes to watch. Finally Abigail Duniway stepped out into the car's doorway. She was followed by an elderly, white-haired woman who acknowledged the crowd with a nod and a smile.

Surprisingly—even to Minnie—the infamous Woman's Rights activist was not an Amazon, not a muscular, masculine crusader in Bloomers. Instead Miss Anthony seemed more like a grandmother on a visit. She was tall and a little ungraceful; she wore her silvering hair back in a conservative bun; her stately dark dress swept the steps. Her eyes had a gentle, yet commanding look that seemed to defy the possibility that anyone could ridicule her in her presence.

Abigail caught sight of Minnie and waved. "There you are, Theresa!" She descended the metal steps and took Minnie's hand. "I envy you the white dress. You look so wonderfully cool in this weather."

"I wish I were," Minnie said.

Abigail turned to make the introductions. "Miss Anthony—Mrs. Miller."

Minnie smiled nervously. "It's an honor. I've heard so much about you."

"And I about you, Mrs. Miller," Miss Anthony replied, giving Minnie's hand a firm shake. "It seems all of Oregon is talking about how you've risen above your husband's wrongdoings. I admire people with the courage to stand up for justice."

Minnie felt herself flush at this praise. If only she could be as brave as Miss Anthony! How did this white-haired woman do it? "I've hired a buggy to bring us to the Chemeketa House hotel."

"Is it far to the hotel?" Miss Anthony asked.

"Almost a mile."

"Let's just send the baggage then," Miss Anthony said. She took a deep breath, as if readying herself emotionally for the repetition of a trial she was regularly required to withstand. "It will be nice to walk after the long ride."

"Are you quite sure?" Minnie could only think of the watchful crowd that would follow them through town.

"Yes." Miss Anthony glanced at the throng, as if reading Minnie's thoughts. "I'm afraid it's important that we be seen. Besides, if I'm not mistaken, the gentlemen behind you are from the press, and we may as well give them a chance to ask their questions on the way."

At this the reporters behind Minnie smiled to each other and got out their notepads.

Abigail took a pencil and a pad from her dress pocket and handed them to Minnie. "I'll hold your parasol if you want to take notes for your article."

"Already?" Minnie knew she had agreed to write an article for Abigail's *New Northwest*, but she hadn't planned to start work until Miss Anthony's official lecture. She had wanted to spend the afternoon as a guide for Miss Anthony.

Abigail whispered, "I think we could use at least one reporter on our side."

Minnie surveyed the seasoned journalists—a rough bunch of whiskered, cigar-smoking men—and traded her parasol for the notepad. "I think maybe you're right."

The walk through Salem might have been pleasant under less tense circumstances. They passed a red brick woolen mill and crossed the clear, swift millrace that powered it. Then they turned down State Street, flanked by saplings and the impressive brick building of Willamette University. Minnie, however, had no time to point out the attractions. She was far too busy keeping up with the reporters' barrage of questions.

"Have you heard," a swaggering older reporter asked, "that the citizens and merchants of the town are sponsoring a free dance to keep people from attending your speech tomorrow night?"

"No," Miss Anthony replied stiffly. "But I shall speak, and I shall be heard."

Minnie felt like applauding, but Miss Anthony needed more than cheers. Instead she put in, "I understand you're renting the large hall at the Reed Opera House?"

The older reporter scoffed at Minnie. "Only after you couldn't get a hall for free. There isn't a church in town that'll let her speak in their building."

Minnie felt a rush of anger—but the charge was true, and she couldn't think of a quick reply.

The reporter turned back to Miss Anthony. "They all say the Bible's against you. What's your response to the Bible verse, 'Wives, submit to your husbands?'"

"The Bible can say many different things," Miss Anthony replied. "Galileo was told the Bible said the world could not move, but the world *does move*. Since the Civil War the verse 'Servants, obey your masters' is obsolete. Your verse, sir, will be next."

Minnie was relieved by how skillfully Miss Anthony had cut the man down. While she was writing down Miss Anthony's response, however, another reporter asked, "What of the argument that men already give women everything they want?"

Miss Anthony nodded. "Yes, they say that. They say we have everything we could want, but when we ask for the vote, they tell us to shut up, keep still, and just *ask* if there's anything we want. What we get *without asking* is wife beating and slavery."

Minnie was quicker with her question this time. "How would you change that, Miss Anthony?"

"With equality. Currently, the fine for beating a wife is ten dollars—a mere slap on the wrist— while beating a man is a penitentiary offense. Even beating a horse is considered more serious."

The *Oregon Statesman* reporter aimed his pencil at her, squinting. "If women vote, won't they have to fight in wars, too?"

"Fine!" Miss Anthony exclaimed. "Let us, then. In ancient Egypt an army once marched into battle with each man clutching a cat. Since cats were sacred, not one drop of blood was spilled. Well, let our soldiers march into battle with their wives and sweethearts before them, and perhaps it will make them less bloodthirsty."

Minnie thought: Why had Ned never thought of such an argument in all the months he had written anti-war editorials? As she walked along, trying to write down the story of the Egyptian cats, she couldn't help but let an entire string of reporters' questions slip past.

One man asked, "What do you think of the proposal that only intelligent women be allowed to vote?"

"I might support it," Miss Anthony retorted, "if the masses of ignorant men were obliged to pass the identical test."

"If women vote," another man demanded, "who will take care of the babies?"

"How long do you men think it takes to drop a ballot in a box?"

The farm weekly correspondent walked ahead to catch Miss Anthony's eye. "Tell us straight out, what you women really want is free love, ain't it?"

Minnie nearly dropped her notepad at the man's insolence. Perhaps a woman of Sarah Eckelhoff's ilk might have used Woman's Rights as a screen for promiscuity, but how could anyone suggest such a thing to this dignified leader?

Miss Anthony drew back her head and scorched the man with a withering glare. "Sir, I am too intensely disgusted by your allegation to comment!"

The reporter cringed as if he had been whipped. He glanced to his colleagues and asked, almost apologetically, "Still, ain't it true that most women don't *want* to vote?"

Miss Anthony raised a long finger like a gun and aimed it at the man's face. "If a farmer is convinced the deer don't want his apples, why should he fence his field? If men are convinced women don't want to vote, why should they deny us the right of suffrage? Of *course* women want to vote. And we *will*, too. In fact, I am meeting this afternoon with the Oregon Supreme Court to argue that the new Constitutional amendments *already* grant American women the right to vote."

This was startling news even for Minnie. All the reporters were rapidly taking notes. Minnie asked, "You believe women can *already* vote? I thought the new amendments only gave Negroes the ballot."

"Do they?" Miss Anthony asked with a smile. "The Fourteenth Amendment says all *persons* born or naturalized in the United States are to be *citizens*. Our laws define a citizen as a freeman with the right of suffrage. That tells me that women either have the right to vote, *or else that they are not persons.* On that basis I intend to cast my ballot in the Presidential election of 1872, and I will take any man to court who should attempt to stop me."

At this announcement, the reporters began shouting questions at the same time. "Are you willing to be arrested?" "Would you vote Republican?" "Could a woman run for President?"

By this time the group had reached the center of town, and Miss Anthony, finally showing the strain her effort had cost, looked wearily to Minnie and Abigail for assistance. At once Minnie stepped in front of the clamoring reporters and held up her hands to silence the men. "I'm sorry, gentlemen, but as you can see we've reached Miss Anthony's hotel. If you have other questions, I invite you to come to Miss Anthony's lecture tomorrow night or to her appearance at the State Fair next week. Now I bid you good afternoon."

As the three women turned toward the hotel's entrance, the gruff, older reporter silently stepped up to hold open the door. Even the farm reporter tipped his hat. Gone were the chuckling and swaggering that had marked these men at the train station.

Minnie marveled at how much Miss Anthony had achieved in just half an hour. Perhaps she had not yet won over Salem, but she had slapped the disrespect out of her most vocal detractors among the press. She had countered every argument with logic and poise. If anyone could give her the moral strength to overcome Joaquin Miller, it would be the great Susan B. Anthony.

* * *

MISS ANTHONY'S LECTURES—OBSERVANDA.

———

By Mrs. M. M. Miller.

———

For the *New Northwest*.

The first night of Miss Anthony's lecture my attention was entirely taken up with watching the speaker, for, be it known, the first, last, and only time I ever heard a woman speak in public was in the "meetin'-house," lang syne, when Aunt Tribulation Fear-the-Lord arose and through her tears, nose, and handkerchief told her "experience."

So the first evening I had eyes and ears only for Miss A.

The following evening I gave her my ears, but managed to bestow my eyes furtively upon her audience.

What I took most interest in observing was the countenances of the gentlemen, who had laid aside that evening their important business matters and come to Miss Anthony's lecture like *lambs to the slaughter*. That my attention should have been bestowed almost exclusively upon the gentlemen may not seem natural; but when I tell you that I had never yet beheld a set of faces so mobile and expressive, so beaming, smiling, and scowling, with all the variable and intense emotions of wrought-up manhood, you will not wonder.

The women were as coolly radiant as though the suttee had never been performed. They were as serene and unruffled as a Quaker's nightgown. It was not their *funeral*.

But the men!

Here sat one alongside of his wife. She had towed him in. It seemed as though if it had not been for the name of it he would rather have stayed at home. He was continually shifting his position, meanwhile casting glances at his wife to see the effect of everything upon her. She looked as happy as a cat with her first kitten.

I have not yet reached that point where I take delight in human suffering (now, if the typos print those last two words *woman suffrage*,

I might as well give up). This man's apparent discomfiture made me unhappy, and I wanted to speak in a voice like Mrs. Winslow's syrup and say, "You shall not be hurted," for I could fancy I saw him dodging imaginary blows; he seemed momentarily expecting that Miss Anthony was going to box his ears.

A phlegmatic old gentleman sat behind me, with his chin resting upon his breast and his eyes closed. *His* play was to be oblivious when Miss Anthony made a point. But cats and old gentlemen are not always asleep when their eyes are closed.

Further on sat a great, benevolent-looking fellow, with his head thrown back and his mouth open, staring as never man stared before. Another style sat bolt upright, never moving a muscle of his body, contenting himself with blinking slowly and mildly at a neighboring chignon as much as to say: "Can these things be and not overcome us?"

But there were a goodly number of happy men there—men who seemed jolly, whole-souled, and willing to accept the truth.

Before me sat two of these sensible men, and their attention and evident satisfaction and appreciation won me; and when the lecture was ended said one of them, with a good-natured laugh: "Let's give her a dollar and tell her to send that book," referring to a valuable pamphlet which Miss Anthony was endeavoring to circulate, and he gave it, and I made a note of it as I passed out of Reed's Opera House, giving to an invisible angel who shifted by me the "God bless you" that was on my lips for Miss Anthony.

SALEM, September 17, 1871

*   *   *

A week later Minnie was hurrying along the oddly deserted midway of the Oregon State Fair, clutching the letter that had thrown all her thoughts in confusion. The side show promoters vented their spiels at the few straggling fairgoers along the dusty lane, urging them one and all to try the Unk Weed Remedy (Oregon's Rheumatic Cure!), to see the incredible two-headed calf, to demonstrate the Home Shuttle sewing machine, to have their photographs taken, or to marvel at the chicken that adds and subtracts. Overhead a hot air balloon rode on a tether, and in front of the agricultural building an ungainly steam tractor was snorting and rumbling as it winched a plow across a field. But even these technological wonders had surprisingly little audience.

Minnie stuffed the letter in her dress pocket. Ned was coming to Oregon!

She hurried on, past a small cluster of people gathered between the barn-like buildings. There, beneath a banner announcing "MRS. FROST Speaks Out For MAN'S RIGHTS," an unpleasant-looking young woman on a crate was shaking her fist and shouting, "Because the Lord God Almighty made man in his own image, every wife has the duty to *revere* her husband, for *he shall be her god!*" The young woman's grating, hoarse voice seemed to pursue Minnie as she went by.

Beyond the buildings lay the camping grounds, where hundreds upon hundreds of white tents dotted a vast field of dry grass beneath scattered oaks. Here and there among the tents Minnie could see women shaking out tablecloths or stirring stewpots over smoldering fires, but only very few. Where were all the people?

Then Minnie heard distant applause drifting over the field. She quickly followed the sound. Behind the largest exhibition hall she found the crowd.

It was an ocean of over a thousand people—men standing with arms akimbo, women with babies on their hips, children ducking behind the skirts. The applause died away like a wave that had broken and run up on the beach a diminished ripple. The mothers hushed their children. From a wagon bed near the barn wall, white-haired Susan B. Anthony turned to the last page of her notes and began again to speak.

Minnie stopped, her worries suddenly held in check at the sight of this thin, elderly woman, who could stand up fearlessly before such a vast audience, armed only with the logic of her firm soprano words.

"Why is it," the voice carried over the sea of heads, "that women schoolteachers are paid just *one-fourth* the salary of men in the same positions? I answer you: it is because women *do not have the ballot.*"

Minnie saw women in the crowd glancing at their husbands, and she guessed their thoughts: were these men *four times* more qualified to raise their children? The idea of Ned Miller—liar, adulterer, charlatan—gaining control over her own children made Minnie's blood run hot.

"Why is it," Miss Anthony's distant voice continued, "that skilled woman physicians are *barred* from their profession while hundreds of masculine quack doctors are being licensed each year to *cheat* and *deceive* the public? Again I answer: it is *because women are not allowed to vote on the laws that govern them.* Why is it that *all but four* of the hundreds of colleges and universities in this nation *deny* women the right to pursue a higher education? Once more I answer: it is because women are also denied the single most important right of any true democracy—the right of suffrage."

Minnie balled her fists, thinking of the unfair advantages Ned had won. He had gone to college where she could not. He had ben employed in high-paying positions when she could not. In a more just world, *she would have traveled to London*—or at least, to San Francisco—and *her poetry might have become famous instead of Ned's.*

"I assure you," Miss Anthony concluded, "any nation with enough sense of justice to grant the power of the ballot to millions of freed Negro slaves *cannot long withhold that essential liberty from its own wives and mothers!*"

A wave of applause swept through the crowd. The tall, white-haired speaker closed her notes decisively and smiled out over the crowd. "And now, citizens, I invite each of you to endorse the convictions of your conscience by stepping forward to order my booklet on Woman's Rights for one dollar, and to subscribe to Mrs. Duniway's informative weekly newspaper, the *New Northwest*, at the modest price of three dollars per year. Furthermore, because of the great fire that has burned for three days in the city of Chicago, leaving tens of thousands homeless, I have determined to dedicate all profits from the sale of my booklets today to the charitable Wisconsin and Illinois relief fund. I thank you."

Minnie clapped along with the crowd, caught up in the spell woven by this indomitable, fiery woman, Miss Anthony. Whistles and cheers punctuated the applause. When the tumult had settled to the hum of talk, Minnie joined the throngs making their way toward the impromptu stage. Nearly half an hour passed before the crowd had dispersed from around the wagon bed, leaving Minnie still waiting.

"Oh, there you are, Theresa," Miss Anthony said. "How did you like my Patrick Henry freedom speech?"

"I wish I'd heard more of it; I was . . . unexpectedly delayed."

"Well, I think we all deserve a rest for a while. Why don't the three of us stroll over to the exhibition halls?"

"All right," Minnie agreed, but without enthusiasm. The letter in her pocket felt like a stone weighing her down. They walked past a barn of bleating black-faced sheep to a hall of quilts, pies, pumpkins, and five-foot sheaves of wheat.

"I've never seen such tall grain," Miss Anthony marveled. "This Oregon is fertile ground—for the Cause of Woman too, don't you think, Theresa?"

"Oh, yes—I suppose," Minnie replied distractedly.

Miss Anthony touched her arm. "Theresa, are you quite sure you're all right? You don't have friends in Chicago to worry about, I hope?"

"No, no, it's nothing." Minnie tried to effect a smile, but without success.

"Come now, it must be something."

Minnie looked down, her voice unsteady. "It's just a letter I got today. A letter about my former husband. He's—he's coming back to Oregon."

Abigail looked up, startled. "Joaquin? Oh my!"

"This is your controversial poet, isn't it?" Miss Anthony asked, wrinkling her brow.

Minnie nodded. "I know I shouldn't be afraid of him now just because he's famous. But he's so spiteful and impulsive. He could do *anything*—to me or to the children. I'm afraid he'll take them away. In the divorce he talked about putting them in a boarding school."

"I understand why you're upset," Miss Anthony said, taking her arm with a sympathetic hand. "I, too, am afraid when I must challenge famous men. But you must never let them think you're frightened. Once a man believes you're weak he is certain to take advantage of you, don't you see? If your poet were to find you like this he probably *would* succeed in taking your children away and telling the world that he's in the right. What you need to do is to meet him on his own ground. Passivity will play into his hands. So take the initiative!"

The words had the same inspirational magic that had won the skeptical Oregon audiences. Minnie lifted her head. "But what can I do?"

"Show him your strength! Why not hire a hall on the day he comes back and give a lecture on 'Joaquin Miller: The Poet and the Man' or something like that? Tell the world your side of the story on stage and he'll be terrified. Why ever let him get the upper hand at all?"

Minnie caught her breath as this suggestion. It seemed, if anything, more frightening than the prospect of meeting Ned again face to face. "But I've never spoken in public before! How could I—Where—"

"You can write, can't you?" Miss Anthony demanded. "Then you can speak as well as anyone. Write out every word you plan to say and rehearse it over and over until you know it all by heart. Put in a few humorous stories, too—if you've lived with him that long you must know some. But don't speak here in Salem; it's too small."

"Then do it in Portland," Abigail added enthusiastically. "I could give you lots of help there."

Minnie looked at the editor with shock. "But Abigail, you've never spoken yourself!"

"I've been intending to start as soon as Susan leaves, but your case takes precedence. People are dying to hear what you have to say about Joaquin Miller anyway. We could hire the Philharmonic Hall and I could run all the ads and promotion."

"Oh my dear Lord," Minnie said, dizzily realizing that the thing could actually be done. "Susan, *where* do you find your strength?"

"I haven't an ounce more than you, Theresa," Miss Anthony replied, giving Minnie a steady gaze. "But the only way we women will ever succeed is by summoning every single ounce of strength we've got."

Chapter 30

The shadows live, and light is dead.
                        —Joaquin Miller

The storm's fury drove the sea gulls north along the Oregon coast. There had been squalls before in that fall of 1871, little puffs of warm rain off the North Pacific that had weighted the rusted leaves off the maples. But the big storm came from the south, late in November, and drowned the land in winter.

The coastal forests swayed like green wheat before each gust of rain. Along the ridgecrests great Douglas firs bent and snapped, sending rapid cannon booms up the valleys. Cormorants, grebes, and murres—attempting to flee only after the storm was upon them—tumbled over the dark brow of Cape Blanco, a stream of hopeless black birds, like sand over the crest of a windswept dune.

The serene gulls glided just ahead of the front. They did not need to flap to watch their shadows race north along the sand. On the second day the gulls reached the Columbia River and knew to turn inland. There they scattered among the strings of barnacled pilings by the salmon canneries, committed to weathering the storm on the river. A steamer passed, but only a few of the gulls followed it farther east, lured by the promise of scraps.

The sidewheeler from San Francisco ran with its engines silent; tightly-reefed sails were enough to give it good speed in the gathering wind. A dozen gulls followed it stubbornly all the way to the Portland docks, like kites tied to its stern railing. Then, finally realizing there would be nothing for them after all, they wheeled away, screaming their disappointment.

* * *

"He's on that ship," Minnie said, looking out the window of her hotel room. Down the street at the waterfront, a sidewheeler was sailing upriver with the wind. "It's him. I just know it."

"Nonsense. They say there's a storm at sea. All the ships are delayed." Abigail Duniway pulled Minnie back to the dresser mirror and held up two dresses before her. "The black. Wear the black, it's elegant, yet sober. It'll tell everyone you're lecturing out of mourning for your marriage."

Minnie turned to her. "Are you sure?"

"Definitely. Wear the black."

"No, I mean about the delayed ships."

Abigail let the dresses droop. "Theresa! We have to be at the hall in less than an hour. Pull yourself together!"

Minnie glanced to the window. She knew Abigail was right. The ship was drifting out of sight, but it no longer mattered. She had to focus her energy if she were to free herself from Ned's shadow. She turned back to her friend. "All right. Give me the black."

"That's the spirit! God help Joaquin if he gets in your way, right?"

Minnie nodded, wishing she could be as confident. "Right."

* * *

Ned strode down the steamer's gangplank to the Portland waterfront wearing the same dapper black suit, the same broad hat, and the same broad smile that had served him so well upon his grand entrance into New York City two months earlier. The Oregon reporters were waiting in the lee of a stacked lumber shipment, clutching their fluttering note pads against the wind.

Ned walked to the middle of the dock and paid the sailor who had carried his large leather bag. Then he put out his arms dramatically and breathed deep the Oregon air. He would wait for the reporters to come to him.

When they did, he took out a sheet of paper and read the speech he had written for the occasion.

"Gentlemen! It is with gladdened heart that I return to the fount of my poetic inspiration! In this past year I have roamed the world, through lands where, when I signed my name 'Joaquin Miller, Oregon,' they had to search for it on the map. And yet nowhere in my travels have I discovered such unspoiled natural beauty and such bold frontier spirit as here in my own homeland. I thank the public, both here and abroad, for the gratifying sales of my *Songs of the Sierras*. Now I confess I have grown weary of the turmoil of society life in London and New York. Since the tragic death of my dear brother in Pennsylvania, I desire more than ever to rest in Oregon."

Then he gave a short laugh to the wind. "There's your statement, boys.

Any questions?"

The reporters looked at each other. One of them asked, "Mr. Miller, do you know where your children are?"

The question left Ned adrift in an unfamiliar sea. "Well—not exactly yet."

"Do you plan to speak out publicly against your wife in response to the charges she's made in the newspapers?"

"Why, no," Ned responded slowly, still struggling to get his bearings.

"Then is it true you left the state with over eight thousand dollars in gold and yet contributed nothing to the support of your wife and three children?"

"For Pete's sake, where'd you hear a tale like that?"

"From Mrs. Miller herself. Do you deny it?"

Ned grabbed at his hat in the increasing wind, buying time to think. What could Minnie possibly be up to, and whatever for? From the reporters' bizarre questions, it appeared she had embarked on a public campaign to spread ruinous rumors about his personal life. He decided it would be safest not to talk about the strange charges at all until he knew more. "Look, boys, I don't know what all my former wife has been telling you. But I want to make it clear that I'm not going to dispute *any* of her statements. The relations between man and wife are so sacred, so holy, that I'd be committing a crime if I were to say anything against her."

Ned smiled again, but not as broadly. "Now let's see if we can steer the questions around to my trip to London."

One of the reporters turned his collar up to the first drops of rain. "All right. We've heard here in Oregon that you wore a brace of six-guns to a lunch with Robert Browning. Another dispatch said you crawled across the floor during one of your readings and bit the ankle of a baroness. Could you respond to these reports for the readers of the *Oregonian?*"

The hostile tone was unmistakable. Ned tacked sharply to deflect it. "Well, let me just say that, looking back now, my venture in England resembles the kind of waking dream that blurs the edge of what is possible."

His evasion did not help. A young, mustachioed reporter raised a pencil almost angrily. "I've got a question about that poem of yours, 'With Walker in Nicaragua.'"

Ned forced a grin. "About time you boys started talking poetry. General Walker was a remarkable man. It took a great leader to fire up the California miners and fight his way to the presidency of Nicaragua."

"But several veterans of that campaign have come forward to say you were never with Walker at all. One of them pointed out that your poem calls Walker a 'tall man' when he was really quite short."

"Tall?" Ned flushed for a moment with anger. Frontier tales were not meant to be questioned. Even in London the press had understood that. "Well, of course I call Walker a tall man. When a poet refers to a 'tall man' he's not necessarily talking about a man of uncommon stature. Here we're talking about a man of uncommon inner strength."

The reporter with the pencil aimed it at him accusingly. "The miner I talked with said he could *prove* you weren't in Nicaragua, because he said you were a squaw man back then, living with the Diggers."

The charge gave Ned a chill of fear. He didn't want his past investigated too carefully. By now rain was pelting the dock, as if to signal the end of the interview. With a tone of finality Ned announced, "I reckon you can read my poems if you want to read about my life."

The black front of the storm finally closed down over them with a roar of rain, and the reporters fled for cover. The one who had spoken last, however, turned to shout back through the gray curtain: "He said Hiner Miller was a horse thief who'd jumped jail and shot a sheriff!"

Alone in the middle of the dock, rain pouring from his broad-brimmed hat, Ned ran a hand across his brow. Then he bent, slowly, to carry his heavy leather bag.

He was suddenly very tired. And he now knew there would be no rest for him in Oregon.

*   *   *

The first hotel he went to that evening actually turned him away.

"No room. Full up, Mr. Miller," the woman at the front desk of the Metropolitan said, turning her back to sort letters.

"What?" Ned asked. Oregon hotels were never full in November. "Are you sure?"

"I'm sure," the woman replied icily. "Why don't you find your children and stay with them?"

"Well, of all the—!" Ned grabbed up his bag and stormed outside. He stood on the porch, below the hotel's sputtering gaslights, and tried to channel his anger. He needed to find out what Minnie had been up to, and soon. A saloon across the rainy street looked like a likely place for information. In Canyon City he had always stopped by the local bar when he wanted to sound out the public's opinion on a case. He splashed through the street's black puddles and pushed open the door.

The only customers inside were old-timers crouched near a smoky pot-bellied stove in the back. Ned dropped his wet leather bag by the polished wood bar and shook the rain off his hat. "A double whiskey," he told the bartender, a burly man with black, slicked-back hair and shirtsleeves tied up around his brawny arms. Ned was about to ask this man if he had heard about Minnie's doings, but to his surprise, the bartender brought up the subject first.

The barkeep brought Ned's drink, broke into a grin, and asked, "Say, ain't you that famous Joaquin Miller fella?"

Ned sighed. "I reckon so."

"They had a drawing of you in the papers. Well, let me tell you, I don't care what everyone says. I think you did the right thing."

"The right thing? How do you mean?"

The bartender leaned forward. "Throwing her out. Them suffragettes are too damn uppity. Give 'em the moon, they want the stars. I say, keep wives in their place. If they get the ballot, they'll vote to outlaw liquor next."

This raised new questions for Ned. He and Minnie had seldom talked about voting rights for women. As far he could remember, she had opposed the idea. In fact, he recalled her throwing away her Bloomer costume in disgust. Ned finished his whiskey with a gulp and motioned for the bartender to refill his glass. "So you're saying, on top of everything else, my former wife's become a suffragette?"

"And how. She's been in an' out of town for months, raking up trouble. Everybody's heard about the divorce, and her job in the Chinese laundry, and her being discovered by the lady editor of that new Woman's Rights newspaper."

Ned frowned as he considered this news. If Minnie had joined the radical woman's movement, it was probably to gain leverage against him. Obviously, he had underestimated her. He had thought the divorce had left her helpless. But vengeance and jealousy must have driven her to desperate measures. "Have you heard what she's done with the children?"

The bartender set the bottle back on the shelf. "I think the papers said they've been moved out of town. Of course I don't believe half what they print."

Ned nodded. "The reporters here seem to be telling all kinds of cock-and-bull stories." It still irked him that they claimed he left for England with eight thousand dollars in gold. He had never had that much in his life. Even now he was living on money borrowed against his first royalty payment in January.

The bartender began polishing the brass along the counter edge. "That's the price of fame, huh? The higher you poke up your head, the easier target you make."

"I reckon so." Ned sipped his whiskey and stared out the rain-streaked windows, thinking. What was it the old man in Hucknall Torkard had said about Byron? "No prophet is without honor, save in his own land." Byron had been great. But Byron had also died young, and in exile, and even now, fifty years later, the newspaper hacks did not spare his memory their simple jokes: "A candle better left unlit—the Byrons' scandal," they said. How long would they talk of Joaquin Miller's scandal?

He glanced at his gold watch and paid up. It was getting late, and he needed to find a place to stay. He could deal with Minnie tomorrow. He hoisted his bag and headed for the door.

The bartender nodded. "So you've decided to go to the lecture after all?"

Ned turned. "What lecture?"

The bartender tilted his head. "Why, I thought that's why you came in here, to wait it out. You arrived just when your wife was supposed to be starting."

"What!" Ned stared at the man. "She's giving a lecture? In public?"

"Right down the street at the Philharmonic Hall." The bartender chuckled. "If you ask me, that lady needs telling off."

Ned tightened his lips. He had not come face to face with Minnie since he sent her away from their Canyon Creek cabin. Now, to put a stop to the lies—and to find out what she had done with the children—he would have to confront her. It wouldn't wait until tomorrow.

* * *

"I remember the day before our wedding—" Minnie stopped short, midway through her speech to the dark crowd in the huge hall. The candles along the walls had suddenly begun to flicker, as if a spirit had entered the room. She fought back a moment of irrational fear.

It had been hard enough for her already, what with hecklers jeering her outside the hall before the speech. Fortunately, the rowdiest sorts hadn't been willing to pay admission. But the audience's silence was unnerving too.

Minnie suddenly recalled the evening Miss Anthony spoke in Salem. Minnie had sat in the audience then, and had gazed about the crowd, reading their thoughts from their expressions. But here the faces were in darkness. Hundreds of eyes were watching her, yet she couldn't tell what these people were thinking. Were they smirking at her in the dark, an Oregon woman on the stage, telling about her years with Joaquin Miller? Were they waiting to disrupt her speech later?

In the front row, in the glow of the stage candles, Minnie caught sight of Abigail Duniway vigorously nodding encouragement.

Minnie took a breath and sallied on; she would have to try to win this audience whether she could see them or not.

* * *

Ned stopped on the rainy street outside the auditorium's ornate cast-iron facade. Grimly, he read the three-inch-tall headlines of a poster on a wooden board by the door:

"THE COMING WOMAN,"
Being an
Explanatory and Entertaining Lecture
by the Renowned Poet
Mrs. Minnie Myrtle Miller
to be held at Philharmonic Hall,
Sat., November 25, at 8:00pm.
Introduction to be given by
Mrs. Abigail Scott Duniway,
Editor & Publisher, the *New Northwest.*
Admission: $1.

Although Minnie's topic sounded suffragist, Ned knew what she was doing. Why else would she have chosen this particular night for her spectacle? He closed his eyes and took a long, steadying breath, the same way he had always calmed himself before taking on a challenge.

He had faced down the outlaws of Idaho and the literary giants of London. But this would be harder: to face down the woman he had loved, the mother of his children. A part of him still loved her; a part of him would always love the brown-haired Sweet Singer of the Coquille. That made his task still more difficult. But Oregon needed to know the truth. He would have to take the stage and explain the facts of their divorce.

He shook the rain from his drooping hat and walked inside to a dark, empty foyer. Then he peered through a curtain into the hall itself. Minnie was alone on the rostrum, standing a little stiffly behind a table in the shallow glow of the stage candles. His heart gave an unexpected lurch; he had forgotten how beautiful she could be. The black silk dress she wore was more attractive and more businesslike than any she had worn during their marriage. White lace set off her petite waist and followed the buttons up her front to a pink knot at her throat. Her slender hands, in white kid gloves, betrayed her nervousness by rolling and unrolling the manuscript before her. For some reason, she had paused uncertainly in mid-sentence.

Then she seemed to catch herself. "As I was saying, I remember the day before our wedding in Port Orford, in 1862."

The familiar voice—the nostalgic words—the elegant black dress—the quiet hall—everything undercut Ned's resolve to bluster onto the stage. Before, he had been able to meet challenges with bravado, by swimming across rivers, brandishing six-guns, or spinning outrageous tales. But this was a different kind of showdown, and he was no longer sure how to meet it. Until he could devise a plan he decided it would be best to listen in on her lecture for a while. He slipped into a corner seat at the dark back of the hall.

On the stage, Minnie continued, "That afternoon I offered to take him rowing across the Elk River to gather shells on the opposite bank. It was so calm I shipped the oars and let the rowboat float down the river in the sun. Unfortunately we became caught in a strong ebb tide that pulled the little boat toward the breakers at the mouth of the river. I struggled hard against it, and with excellent encouragement, too. I remember vividly how Joaquin Miller, the hero of so many later poetic adventures, sat in the bow transfixed with fear, shouting, 'Pull, Minnie, pull for God's sake!'"

A voice in the audience snickered, and Ned squirmed. Should he stop her now, before she told every humiliating story from their marriage? Or should he simply let her make a damn fool of herself on her own? The woman was a ridiculous speaker, rambling on about obscure events.

Minnie continued, "As we drew ever closer to the wild waves despite my efforts, the poet suddenly stood up and pulled off his boots and coat. He was on the point of diving overboard when a wave actually did catch the craft and landed it safely on the beach. Of course, as his newly betrothed, I interpreted his actions as part of a wondrous plan to plunge into the angry surf to save me from a watery doom. Now, however, after several years' experience with him, and especially after reading 'Kit Carson's Ride,' I realize his intentions might have been less complex."

This time several people laughed, and Ned nearly stood up to interrupt. But Minnie stilled the crowd with a sober hand, and he held back a moment too long.

"I must confess," Minnie said, lowering her eyes, "that Joaquin Miller is the most poetical man I have ever seen, or heard, or read of. It is this essence of poetry pervading his life that makes him the marvelous mixture of good and bad that he is. Certainly during the eight years of his life with me he followed single-mindedly a script written by his muses. Whatever he deemed poetic, he would do at any cost. Whatever he deemed not poetic, he shunned. Unfortunately, the raising of children fell under the latter category."

The unexpected honesty in these words hit Ned like a blow to the chest.

"The contemplation of death was a favorite poetical pastime of his," Minnie said. "He always wanted to be burned, Indian fashion, after his demise. He made his will out about once a month, and it got to be amusing to see what varied dispositions he made of his effects at times. The numerous testaments always remembered me, of course. In each of them I was promised precisely one item: the bundle of his love letters."

A few of the women in the audience tittered, but Minnie shook her head. "In truth, those letters were our greatest treasure. They held the memories of that glorious time when we were young, and he was dashing, and I was foolish, and we were so much in love."

To Ned, this touching admission was another unexpected punch. How did Minnie still have the power to twist his emotions so easily? It seemed there were hidden passageways within her character he had never explored, entire rooms he had never known.

Now Minnie shifted her papers, straightened her stance, and let her voice ring through the hall.

"I regret that I am not prepared to give any further information in regard to Joaquin Miller's connection with the Indians. Of course the casual observer, reading the poems that are alleged to be autobiographical, might well conclude that the Poet of the Sierras had spent the better part of his early manhood lounging before various wigwam fires. That may be true, for all I know, or it may not be true. For some reason this was a topic he never discussed with me. However, I *do* recall his mentioning a young woman of his acquaintance who used to wear tar on her face and quills in her nose."

Minnie's deadpan delivery of these lines brought down the house— the men slapping their knees, the women tittering into their handkerchiefs. Ned felt his face flush hot, but how could he counter her? She hadn't actually accused him of anything. Marching up to the stage now would be as much as announcing his guilt. Minnie had laid a cleverer trap than any he had seen in a courtroom.

Minnie continued calmly, victoriously. "He often said this particular woman friend never annoyed him by wanting to go out visiting in the afternoons when he wanted her to stay at home. He always insisted that every man should be absolute master of his own hut—pardon me, I mean, house."

The audience roared with delight, and Ned cringed. The audience was hers. Somehow, subtly, she had won them over. If he stood up now, he knew he would be laughed down. He would have to wait, and win his battle when he and Minnie were alone.

*   *   *

Minnie felt as though she were lifted by the unseen audience. They were laughing with her, not at her! She had written the final page of her manuscript as a humble conclusion. But now she read it with a different tone, instead charging it with the brutal power of irony. "Of course when I speak of Joaquin Miller, I know that I am speaking of one who is greater than I, the latchets of whose literary shoes I am not worthy to loosen. And when I read of his extravagant behavior before the literary lions of London, I am reminded of what he often told me: that perhaps I never really knew him. Well, perhaps I never really did. Perhaps there were *other* women who knew him better! If that is so, I would encourage them to come forward and speak. I would welcome them, and we could mingle our tears together."

The chuckles of the audience showed they had not missed her final jab. Minnie smiled in return and set her notes aside.

"Before I close I feel obliged to add a few words in defense of the course I have chosen. Alas, it is only hard necessity that has driven me to enter the lecture field in the hope of gaining a support for myself and my helpless children. Distasteful as this course is to me, I make the sacrifice gladly in order that my babies might not go hungry. I would also like to thank the newspapers, particularly the *New Northwest*, for their sympathy and assistance in calling attention to this lecture. I also would assure you all that the children to whom I shall now soon return join me in gratefully acknowledging the response of the public."

As Minnie stepped back from the lecture table, the hall filled with prolonged applause. Minnie gave a small curtsy before stepping down. Then Abigail Duniway was on the stage, reading Minnie's poem, "Plea for the Inconstant Moon," as a conclusion to the evening. Again the audience clapped. This time the applause dissolved into talk, and the audience gradually began filing out through the curtains at the dark end of the hall. Minnie nervously received the congratulations of a number of ladies and gentlemen from the audience, who assured her that her lecture had been a success.

After Minnie had shaken the last hand, however, she realized Abigail was gone. Minnie was puzzled and a little hurt that her friend had left so quickly. She put on her hat and coat, her hands trembling with the latent apprehension that follows a time of severe stress. The room was silent, except for the creak of the theater manager's ladder as he went along the walls extinguishing and replacing the candles. This small, gray-haired man stopped in his work to turn to Minnie.

"Fine speech, for a lady."

Minnie adjusted her hat with a nervous laugh. "Thank you."

The old manager frowned. "Say, they all leave you by yourself? I reckon I could see you home."

"Oh, no, no," Minnie laughed again. "I'm just at the hotel, practically next door. I'll be fine." She fidgeted with her gloves, half wishing she had taken up the old man's offer. It was so dark on Portland streets, and there was such a fierce rainstorm that night. What had become of Abigail so suddenly, anyway?

Minnie coughed lightly into her glove; her throat was painfully sore. Then she began walking up the dark aisle. She was almost at the curtains when she heard the quiet voice:

"Minnie—"

The sudden word made her gasp. Then she saw the figure among the shadows of the last row and went pale. Even in the darkness she could recognize the deep eyes and high forehead. She thought of running out to her hotel, but then she glanced back to the theater manager, still working near the stage, and resolved to try to hold her ground. So what if her husband had heard her lecture—hadn't she been wanting to tell him off like that for years? And hadn't Susan B. Anthony warned her that standing up to him was her only chance?

Ned slowly raised himself to his feet. "Well, where are you keeping the children?"

The tired tone of his voice made Minnie's confidence surge. "You think I'd keep them where you could find them? No, they're safely out of town, with a friend you've never met."

Ned drew himself up, his anger mounting. "Minnie, what in heaven's name do you think you are doing?"

"I guess you heard the lecture—I'm doing my best to raise the children and provide them with money, since you have failed to do so."

Now Ned launched his attack, hurling the words at her. "What about the money I've been sending your mother in Port Orford? *She* has custody of the children, you know, not you."

It was a technicality Minnie had almost forgotten, and it put her on the defensive. "Well, you sent so little money, and it came so late." She felt frustrated, hearing the old familiar weakness creep back into her manner so easily.

"Did you imagine I'd just send the entire two hundred dollars at the *start* of each year? Perhaps to *you*, instead of your mother?" Ned paused, knowing from his years as a lawyer that arguments took time to sink in. "Admit it, Minnie. All you're doing with this lecturing is trying to make a dollar out of my success, selling the same kind of sour love stories you used to invent for the *Golden Era*, except this time you're doing it by dragging the memory of our marriage in the dirt."

"Ned Miller!" Minnie's rage rushed to her head and rallied her to counterattack. "I don't need you in any way! Just look at yourself! It's disgusting—to find you hiding in the back of my lecture hall, stinking of whiskey, soaking wet! What could you possibly have that I would want?"

Ned ran his hand over his throbbing brow. Her words had battered his pride, but they were only words. He could still win by crushing her with the weight of the law. "You realize, Minnie, that when you took the children out of your mother's care you broke the terms of the divorce settlement. I can sue and force you to surrender the children at any time."

Fear flashed in Minnie's heart, but then just as quickly there was an inspiration. "Yes, take it to the courts! That's it—get a jury, a good *Oregon* jury. Let the citizens of Oregon decide who would do a sounder job of raising the children, Theresa Dyer Miller or the marvelous Poet of the Sierras! You saw the audience here tonight. *They* will be the ones who condemn you!"

Ned reeled at this blow. She was right! While he was away in London, her campaign in Oregon had obviously won over the press—and enough of the potential jurors that she probably could win her case! With a single stroke she had turned his own legal arguments against him. She had swept away his right to the children's custody as if it were a leaf in a hurricane. "Minnie—" he began, but she cut him short.

"You wanted fame, Ned Miller, but all you've won is infamy. There is nothing for you here—nothing! The children are safe from you forever. And so am I."

Ned felt as though a battered brick wall inside him were crumbling. Why was it they could only talk about the children, anyway—why were they so afraid to uncover the real issues between them: their pain, their love? "Minnie, listen! Shouldn't we—"

"No! No more! *You* go your way and *I* shall go mine!" Minnie tossed back her curls triumphantly and walked out past the curtain. The thrill of victory left her heart pounding away in her chest like a Gatling gun. She held her hat against the storm and ran to the gaslit porch of the Metropolitan Hotel. There she turned and looked back through the rain, afraid that he might dare to follow her. Thank God he hadn't—he wasn't even in sight! Quickly she pushed inside and hurried up the stairs.

But just outside her room she stopped short.

There was light in the crack under her door. She knew she hadn't left an unattended lamp in her hotel room. She had, however, left the door unlocked—a careless habit from her years in Port Orford. Now someone was inside. A burglar? Or one of Ned's cohorts? Perhaps even his parents, come to demand the children?

A year ago—even an hour ago—she would have backed away and gone for help. But now, fired by the courage of her lecture and her confrontation with Ned, she balled her fist and flung the door open.

* * *

Ned staggered into the street outside the Philharmonic Hall. He stared up at the rain, as if looking for direction there. Minnie had won! He might never find out where she was keeping Maud and George. He might never see them again. And the press would have a field day. Tomorrow's papers would tear into Joaquin Miller like wolves after a wounded elk. The news might ripple as far as New York, or even London.

He looked up the street to the saloon where he had left his bag. Tomorrow, somehow, he would have to piece things back together. To-night he needed Mountain Joe's prescription for trouble. Tonight he needed to get drunk.

* * *

As soon as Minnie threw open the door, the hotel room erupted like an enormous magic box. Brightly colored streamers flew into the air. A dozen masked figures sprang out, shouting something Minnie could not understand.

Then a familiar voice behind one of the masks asked, "Surprised?"

"Abigail!" Minnie gasped. "You scared me half to death. What on earth are you doing?"

Abigail peered over the top of her white, circular mask. "It's a mas-querade party. We're the inconstant moons you pleaded for. How do you like our lunar costumes?"

Minnie walked into the room in a daze. A throng of women applauded her, all of them dressed for the party's theme, with white shawls, white gloves, and moon-shaped masks on little sticks. Despite their disguises, Minnie now could tell they were the women she had met and worked with in the tumultuous months since Miss Anthony's visit that summer.

"Care for a moonbeam?" It was her Salem friend Belle Cooke. She pointed to a table of delicacies. "We've white chocolate, white lemonade, and white cheese—it's still a little green, but then that's only fitting."

"I—I'm speechless," Minnie stammered, overwhelmed by the care that had obviously gone into planning this celebration. Here she was, surrounded by loving friends, where only a few moments ago she had faced Ned alone. It seemed as if she had been facing Ned alone for years. Now she was finally safe from him. Could it always have been this way, if only she had found the strength earlier to defy him?

Abigail smiled. "You've given enough speeches for one night, Theresa."

Now it will be our turns to speak out." She tapped a lemonade pitcher for attention. "Three cheers for Minnie Myrtle Miller, who led the way!" "Hip hip—hooray!" The women cheered until the windows rattled. "Hip hip—hooray! Hip hip—hooray!"

"And now," Abigail announced, "I have a special present for our guest of honor."

Minnie held up her hands. "Abigail, you shouldn't. Isn't this enough, just having all of you here? What else could I want?"

"Ah, but I think there is something else." Abigail spun her moon mask mischievously. "Your daughter whispered a secret to me, and I've taken the liberty of making a few arrangements."

"Arrangements?" What could Maud have said?

Abigail held her mask up by its stick as if it were a magic wand. "I've written to a few editor friends. They're thrilled about the idea of having you give a series of lectures and poetry readings after the first of the year."

"More lectures? Oh Abigail, I don't know. Where would they be?"

Abigail tapped her lightly with the mask-wand. "In *San Francisco.*"

"San Fran—!" Minnie caught her breath. Could even that distant dream be coming true? "But Abigail! How could I afford the trip?"

"All expenses paid, my dear."

"And the children?"

"They're welcome too," Abigail laughed. "My editor friends want you to stay and write poems as long as you want."

"Oh, that's wonderful! Abigail, you're amazing!" In her excitement Minnie kissed her on the cheek. Then she spun around and fell backwards onto the hotel bed with her arms outstretched. "San Francisco!"

* * *

Later that evening, when the last of the surprise guests had congratulated her and said good-night, Minnie sat alone in the hotel room, marveling at all that had happened in one short day. Gradually, the whirl of excitement slowed enough that her thoughts came full circle.

She would go to San Francisco with the children, of course. She had succeeded in breaking free. But what would become of Ned?

She blew out the lamp and sat by the dark window, watching the rain pelt the boardwalks and the street puddles below. Once, she had loved him blindly. Maud and George still did. They had begged to come see their Papa arrive in Portland, and she had said no. Of course they were mostly attracted by his gifts, his funny ways, and his flashy, gallant side. But was that so wrong? Those old charms had drawn her as well. Now her eyes were opened. She had won her victory.

Still she wondered: In a more perfect world, might there have been another way? If she had been sketching out the plot of her own love story on paper, what happier ending might she have invented? Perhaps she would have fallen in love again, this time to a man who was right? No—that would be too simple. Or perhaps Ned, suddenly on his death-bed from an incurable illness, would have begged to renew their marriage vows? No—too contrived.

Minnie took a lace handkerchief from her dress pocket and absently cleaned the fog of her breath from the window. What if the rules of the game had been different? Was there a way she could have changed him, taught him compassion, settled him down? Perhaps if they hadn't had to battle for power, she could have saved what was good in him.

She shook her head and sighed. Miss Anthony was probably right. Such a time would only come when women had the right to vote, and were treated as equals. It could be years. It could be never. It was certainly too late for Ned and her now. She might never see him again.

Then suddenly she was looking at him.

She jerked back from the window in alarm. Outside, on the street below, Ned's dark, rain-bleared form had emerged from the door of a saloon. He was standing on the boardwalk in the midst of the storm. Of course he couldn't possibly see her in the hotel's dark window. But her heart raced nonetheless.

Was it fear she felt? No, not fear. Surely her victory had denied him the power to hurt her again. Was it pity?

She watched as Ned walked slowly through the driving rain to the mud in the middle of the street, carrying his leather bag. He stood there bare-headed longer than she thought she could endure. How thin his hair had grown! she thought. *Why* didn't he put on his hat against the rain?

Finally he pulled on the hat and began to walk down the street toward the waterfront. Minnie had to open her window to watch him now. The wind blew drops of rain on her eyelashes and cheeks, but she blinked them away. Had she been too harsh on him, she wondered, or had she only done what he deserved? Surely anything less would have left her at his mercy again. But then—was it cruel not to leave him something?

Her heart was still drumming far too fast when she saw he had reached the docks. He stopped there, now only a small silhouette against the flickering torches of a bright vermilion barge. Minutes passed while he stood on the dock in the fury of the storm. Then he crossed the gangplank to the torchlit ship.

After he had disappeared Minnie carefully closed her window. She sat on the edge of the bed in her empty hotel room. And then, when she cried into her hands, she still was not sure why.

Chapter 31

My snow-topped towers crush the clouds
And break the still abode of stars,
Like sudden ghosts in snowy shrouds . . . .
—Joaquin Miller

Ned awoke to the stench of fish and the sloshing of the Willamette River. Painfully he opened his eyes. Straw and damp rags littered a curved wooden floor. He propped himself on an elbow and blinked at the gray light of a porthole between the creaking decks. The hammering between his temples made it hard to piece together what had happened.

He had argued with Minnie, that much he recalled. He had lost the children—and probably the better part of his reputation in Oregon. He bent forward, cradling his head in his hands. Was this the success he had wanted all these years? It seemed his family was vanishing like untethered horses in the night. If only he had known what fame would cost!

Gradually other memories started to return. After Minnie's lecture he had gone for a drink. That's when he had found the floating saloon on the waterfront. But what then? There had been bottles, loud voices, a piano, and an Oriental girl with marvelous long black hair. She had opened her embroidered jacket, he recalled, to reveal yellow skin covered with ghastly welts and scars. Then the men had come, and . . .

Ned jerked upright. Incredibly, his leather traveling bag was still there, cut open around the lock with a knife. He sorted through the rumpled clothes inside with shaking hands. There had been pitifully little money to steal. Next he remembered the watch. The gold watch. And of course it too was gone.

He lay back into the straw with a groan. Mountain Joe's watch! It had saved him in London. It had his been his shining memory of the unspoiled frontier. He had promised Joe to take it back to Mt. Shasta. Now he had lost that legacy too.

Or had he? The question materialized from somewhere behind him where nothing was. The voice used no words, yet was perfectly distinct, like a flash of understanding in the midst of a dream. The watch had been only a mask! Although the mask was gone, the spirit behind it remained. Now that the clamor of his ambition had quieted he could hear the spirit's low, patient voice calling him back to the mountains. Back to his past to make things right. Back to Paquita. The voice swept away a rockslide of debris, leaving his path miraculously straight and his head clear.

Suddenly he knew what he had to do.

The clouds had lifted when Ned climbed out from the barge and strode purposefully across the dock. Far across the river, against the pink sky of dawn, the distant white cone of Mt. Hood winked at him. A ripple of certainty coursed through him, as if the powers of the mountains were already swirling into his soul. He turned around. His smile swept across the piles of brickwork that were Stumptown-on-the-Willamette, and he laughed. He laughed with the same bold defiance that had shaken the walls of Scotland's Melrose Abbey a year before. Minnie had been right; there was nothing for him here. It was as if the rain had washed away muddy years from his life, exposing an earlier, purer world. What did Portland matter? He was on his way to a truer homecoming now.

* * *

The Stark Street ferryman met Ned with a suspicious frown as he walked briskly up to the Willamette landing. Ned's wet, wrinkled business suit looked as though it had been dredged out of the river during the night. His bedraggled hat and tall miner's boots could have been stolen from an Idaho sourdough. Part of a shirt trailed from the slashes knifed in his leather bag.

The ferryman stood to bar Ned's path. "No one on the ferry without a twenty-cent fare, mister."

"Fare? Tell you what, I'll owe you one," Ned said, and then stopped. "No, hold on a minute." He pulled off one of his big boots, ripped the lining, and turned it upside down over his hand. A fifty-dollar gold slug slapped into his palm. "Trick I learned in the mines," he chuckled.

The ferryman's eyebrows rose. "I'll see if I have change, sir."

When the ferry reached East Portland, Ned caught the day's first train south. The locomotive set off like a snorting bull, charging across the Willamette Valley's prairie through stubble fields, fir groves, and bare-limbed orchards. The steam whistle blasted through the cities of Salem and Albany, and the train rumbled on, over track so new the rails had yet to rust. At Harrisburg the cars rolled across a new Willamette River trestle bridge and stormed down through the bankside cottonwoods. By late afternoon the engine was clanging and whistling its way up Fourth Street in Eugene City, where the rails ended altogether.

"Attention passengers with southbound stagecoach connections," the brass-buttoned conductor called as walked the length of the car. "The stage departs from the front of the depot in fifteen minutes."

Ned stepped out onto the railway platform, suddenly struck with a new guilt. How could he go through Eugene City without stopping to see his parents? The depot was hardly two blocks from the gabled, blue-shuttered Miller house. But he had so little time, and he was determined to leave on the stage. Surely he would be back in a week or so. He could visit his parents then.

Still, as he carried his leather bag to the waiting stagecoach he couldn't help looking back at the house. His sister Ella had once filled that home with her enthusiasm and artistic touch. Now she was gone. And since John's death, an unspoken responsibility had fallen to Ned to watch over their Ma and Pa. The thought twisted the thin knife of guilt.

"Redding?" the driver asked, eyeing Ned's wrinkled outfit askance.

Ned turned with a start. "Pardon?"

The driver sighed impatiently. "I asked if you're going to the California railhead in Redding. Fourteen dollars for the three-day trip."

Ned hesitated. "Actually, I'm headed for an old horse ranch near the headwaters of the Sacramento. Between Mt. Shasta and the Devils Crags. You know the place?"

The driver wrinkled his brow.

Ned tried again. "They've got some springs there with natural soda water."

"Oh, Soda Springs?" The driver nodded. "Yeah, we don't get much call for that stop. Twelve dollars, one way."

Ned paid. The driver flung his leather bag onto the coach's roof rack and pointed Ned to an empty spot in the middle of the back seat.

Before Ned climbed in, however, he took a last look at the town, as if he already knew, deep inside, that he might not be back again soon. Down Willamette Street he could see the signboard for the Daguerrean studio where he had had his photograph taken in the giddy days of his courtship of Minnie. Just beyond, a sign on a two-story brick building announced the offices of the *Register*, the newspaper he had edited in the heat of the Civil War, when every press day had been a call to arms. But it looked to Ned as if the thrills of those early days had faded as the town grew. Even the sandstone ruins of his controversial alma mater, Columbia College, had been hauled away from the hill behind town. He glanced again to the white gables of the house he had bought long ago, in the year of the great flood. He was glad he had paid off his parents' farm mortgage and moved them into town. Eugene City was a good place for them. But he couldn't live here anymore. He couldn't even tell his parents where he was going. This time he could tell no one. He was following the call of a promise, and it had sent him on a journey within himself.

"Going or not?" The driver asked. He swung up onto his front bench and began straightening the six horses' reins. Ned just had time to close the coach's door before the wheels jerked, almost staggering him into an elderly minister's lap.

"Excuse me," Ned said, regaining his balance. He hadn't realized how full the coach would be. The front two benches, facing each other, held three passengers each. There was no aisle back to the third bench, over the rumbling rear wheels. The only way to get to his seat was to ask the people in the middle bench to stand, unclip the leather strap that served as their seat back, and step over.

"For the love of Pete!" the minister's wife muttered as Ned crawled past them in the rocking coach.

All that afternoon Ned sat wedged in the back seat between a stiff, bickering farmwife, who looked as though she had never smiled and never would, and an overweight, sweating salesman, who droned on about how his reaping machines could cut *and* bind into sheaves, while other machines could only cut. By nightfall Ned was ready to crawl out the window to escape them both. When the stage stopped in Cottage Grove for a fresh team of horses, he gladly traded his cushioned seat for the hard wooden bench up front with the driver.

That night, as the coach rattled onward through the forests, the big riding lamps lit the horses' backs and shivered up the wagon road, catching the gleam of raccoon eyes and the statues of wondering deer. Ned leaned back, spreading his arms over the baggage strapped to the roof. He looked up at the huge, dark firs, remembering the other times he had ridden this road with his heart pounding—first with Mountain Joe on his way to the gold mines, and then alone, on his way to marry a poet in far-off Port Orford. Now it seemed as if he were riding back in time, spooling those adventures back within himself. He was returning to the start—to Paquita and the mountain. That prospect made this trip the most uncertain of all. What could he expect to find? His arrival in Portland had been a devastating failure. Did he think he would find any better welcome in the mountains? A dozen years ago an armed posse had chased him out of Northern California. Paquita had still been very young then. Who could say what she would be like now?

All through the second day the stage hardly stopped, rumbling through the settlements of the Rogue Valley. The minister and his wife got off in Jacksonville, but all the other passengers stayed. That evening, with a new driver, the coach finally pulled up to the Siskiyou Mountain summit at the Oregon border. Ned had been anticipating the view across the black canyons of Northern California—as if he needed to reassure himself the mountain was still there, the ghostly white mountain that had held a sure tether on his emotions for so many years. Even though the sun had set, he still expected to see the luminous outline of the peak's great cone rising above the black forests to the south.

The high pass held no such revelation. A cold fog blew in from the starless void ahead. The stagecoach rolled down through it, leaving a wake of windblown sparks from the screaming brakes. Ned gripped the driver's bench to keep from being thrown off on the tight mountain curves. It seemed every moment that they were about to fly off the winding road and smash into the unseen chasm below.

"Could you lean on my braking arm, sir, hard?" the driver asked Ned calmly. Ned quickly added his weight to the brake lever, his heart pounding. Even after they reached the bottom of the Siskiyou grade an hour later, Ned still stared into the dark forests of Northern California, too wrought up with worry and anticipation to sleep.

Dawn broke under seething gray clouds in the dirty, shivering streets of Yreka. Here Ned braced himself against the grim memories of former selves: locked in a courthouse room, riding a calico horse for his life.

"One more day to the O & C railhead in Redding," the third driver of their journey announced, and Ned nodded, although the plan of his silent voice still hung before him, now as much a threat as a promise.

They lurched down Greenhorn Creek, where Ned had once taken the trail to Bill Hearst's mine, and headed across the flats of Shasta Valley. They stopped briefly at a run-down inn among the tamarack for an unappetizing lunch of fried meat, stiff custard, and stale pie. Then the stage plunged into the canyon of the Sacramento River, winding down switchbacks so steep and narrow the driver's whip could hit the tops of the huge sugarpines on the curves below. Mile after mile they rumbled down the canyon—farther than Ned remembered—until they finally passed a row of fruit trees along the road.

"Soda Springs!" the driver called, reining the horses before a long, white, two-story hotel. A jug of water stood on a low stone wall to one side. The driver climbed down and drank deeply from the jug. He wiped his mouth and passed the jug to the passengers. "Natural soda seltzer water," he said. "The hotel folks leave some out here every day for the stage. Advertising, I reckon."

Ned still sat immobilized in his place on the driver's bench, suddenly tormented with fresh doubts about his plan to find Paquita. The years had changed everything so drastically here. Where Mountain Joe's potato patch and brush fence had been, the new hotel stretched out with the ambiance of a European spa. Women in hoop skirts and gentlemen in velvet jackets drank coffee in rocking chairs on the broad verandah. Would his journey simply end with another humiliation—another indignity?

Gradually the passengers left the soda water jug. They stretched their legs wearily, complained about the rigors of the trip, and then slowly returned to their seats. The driver had just climbed back aboard and was about to shake the reins when Ned jerked his bag from the luggage rack and jumped to the ground.

"Hey, where you going?" the driver called.

Ned tipped his broad-brimmed hat and smiled. "Not sure yet. But my fare's only paid to Soda Springs."

The driver scratched his head, then shrugged, and finally drove off with a great clatter of hooves and wheels.

When the stage was gone, Ned turned to face the long white hotel. A chilly wind swept down the canyon, portending a cold mountain evening. The guests on the verandah tightened their shawls and began moving inside. Ned scratched his beard uneasily. Now he just had to figure out *how* he was going to do what he had come to do.

First he got his bearings. If the hotel was really built on top of Mountain Joe's old potato patch, he reasoned, Joe's old cabin ought to be farther back from the river. He walked around the end of the long verandah and smiled. Behind a fence and a patch of manzanita he could recognize the old chimney of river rocks. The cabin logs were dark and mossy with age. Only the doorframe looked new, painted white in a ludicrous attempt to match the hotel.

Cautiously—as if fearful of disturbing the ghosts of another life—Ned knocked. Almost at once, a tall, short-haired man with an ill-fitting cotton shirt and baggy trousers opened the door. The big man squinted at Ned, raised his eyebrows in a peculiar fashion, and suddenly extended a broad hand.

"Ned! So you came."

Ned was staggered. "Charley?"

The man laughed. "You mean you didn't recognize me without buckskins?"

It was true. With his black hair cut short and slicked back Charley looked like a different person, more like a shipwrecked Spanish grandee than a half-Indian muleskinner.

"Reckon I didn't expect to find you here when everything had changed so much. Looks like you've changed, too."

"Me? No, this is just a mask for the hotel people. When they built the new place I asked for a job in the stable. They said I'd have to cut my braids and wear a white shirt. Thought I'd upset the guests." His gray, un-Indian eyes twinkled at this, as if at a private joke. "*Klahowya*, Ned. Come in. We'll talk."

"All right, Charley," Ned sighed, leaving his big hat on as he went in. "I reckon that is what I need to do."

Inside the dark cabin it might have been possible to imagine the last dozen years had not passed. The wall logs Ned had helped notch together in his youth were still stained with smoke and chinked with mud, as he remembered them. The dirt floor was just as shadowy, lit by the crackling pine logs on the fire. And even Charley, once he was sitting cross-legged on his mat, stirring a pot of beans, looked more as Ned had known him.

"Last I recall, you were a judge in the Snake Indian lands," Charley said, looking into the pot on the fire, instead of at Ned. "You dress different now. I take it you're not a judge anymore."

"No. I've published some books. I'm a poet."

Charley stopped his stirring a moment, and then nodded. "And your white wife?"

"We're divorced. She's taken the children."

A pause followed in which Charley only stirred the pot on the fire. They had each summed up their past few years in a handful of words. Each story was a bare tree, waiting for leaves and birds and fruit. But what would it matter to describe the fallen fruit of other years? What mattered more was the hidden growth of each man's roots, and this was harder to know, and still more difficult to discuss outright.

Ned broke the silence. "What news do you have of the tribe?" His tone almost hid his worry.

"The Puyshoos? There have been changes, yes." Charley's words were slow and considered.

Ned flushed with impatience. "Are Paquita and the girl still all right?"

"Yes, I think so." Charley nodded slowly. Then he repeated, "But there have been changes."

"What do you mean?" Ned asked. Why couldn't his old friend simply tell him?

Charley lifted the spoon and then stirred again. "It's three and a half years since we met at Canyon City. That's about when it started. But then

I suppose it started long before that, too."

"What started? Tell me. Please."

"I will," Charley replied, still unhurried. "It started that spring, when Witillahow had a vision. You remember Witillahow?"

"Of course." An image of the thin-chested shaman with his necklace of blue jay feathers stood out in Ned's mind with surprising vividness.

"Well, he said he'd learned how to defeat the evil spirit that takes over white men like Sam Lockhart. Witillahow got ready for weeks. Then he did a long, strange dance no one had ever seen before. After that he collapsed in a trance. The trance lasted three months. Finally he died."

Ned lowered his gaze, embarrassed by his impatience. "I'm sorry. He was a remarkable man. I reckon he never got over Sam Lockhart murdering so many Indians."

"Yes and no," Charley replied.

"How do you mean?"

"The beans are ready."

Ned looked at him blankly. "What?"

"I thought you'd want to eat." Charley dipped a cup of beans from the pot into a bowl.

"Oh, of course. Thanks." Ned took the bowl and spoon, but made no move to eat. "So what about Sam Lockhart?"

Charley blew on his bowl to cool the food. "Well, we got word from some miners in Yreka. They said Lockhart had been wounded about the same time that spring. Lockhart had been sitting outside a stage office in Idaho. It seems a man came up, argued with him about a silver mine boundary, and shot him in the arm."

Ned couldn't help feeling a grim satisfaction from the misfortune of Lockhart, who had nearly killed both him and Paquita. Then he had a different thought. "That was at the same time as Witillahow's dance? Did the tribe think the shaman actually *made* Lockhart get shot?"

"Not at first. But later we heard that Lockhart's wound didn't heal. He ignored it, and it got worse. He had his arm amputated, but the infection still spread. They say the pain got so bad he screamed day and night. Finally, after three months, he died. On the same day as Witillahow."

Ned whistled. "Well, then perhaps—"

Charley nodded. "The tribe was sure. And I don't doubt it. The shaman had great power."

A chill ran up Ned's back, as if from a cold breath behind him—a breath from the unseen voice that had lifted him from the ruins of Portland and delivered him to this cabin. Suddenly all he had felt or heard of the Wintu spirits came back to him, but frighteningly jumbled, like the flutter of night moths. What spirit had been pursuing him—leading him?—and for how long?

Ned put his cold palms on his arms. "Where did Witillahow find his spirit powers? I know you've told me about Kusku and the spirits behind masks, but I've never been able to put it all together. Even when I can feel something I don't know how to reach it."

Charley shook his head. "I wasn't allowed to learn much. Just the legends and the ordinary dances. No one saw the spirit ways as clear as Witillahow, and he never taught anyone how to do it. Without him, we'll probably never know what happened in the rituals—if the dancers became spirits, or the masks of spirits, or the masks of masks."

"Can't you feel them too, sometimes?" Ned asked.

"Maybe. But you and me, we're like blind men guessing at clouds. We can feel their shadow, we can touch their rain. Sometimes we even hear their voices, their thunder. But we'll never know what they really are."

"Maybe the spirits are dying out," Ned suggested.

Charley looked steadily into the fire. "I think spirits are forever, but changing. Like clouds. They'll always be bringing the seasons, moving the lives of animals, keeping the land alive from within. It'll be lonelier for us, though. The shamans were our only eyes to the gods. And now that Witillahow's dead, and so many of the Puyshoos are gone—"

"What!" Ned caught his arm. "What do you mean, *gone?*"

"I told you, it began with Witillahow's death."

"*What* began? You said Paquita was all right."

Charley pulled his arm away and drew himself up. "Eat your beans before they're cold."

Ned sat back. "I have to know what's happened."

Charley watched him silently. Then he dipped water from a bucket and began cleaning his own bowl. As he worked, he spoke quietly. "I was telling you what happened. The tribe had no shaman. The old chief, Worrotatot, sent word to the neighboring tribes. For a whole year the Puyshoos couldn't follow the rituals very well. Finally a Northern Paiute named Wodziwob came. He was a new kind of shaman, a ghost dancer. He said he'd had a different vision. His vision told people to dance huge circle dances and sing special chants. According to him, the dances would eventually make all the white men sink into holes in the ground. Then all the dead people of the tribes would return from the east, riding on the long railroad across Nevada."

"Sounds pretty unlikely. Did the Puyshoos believe any of this?"

Charley set his dishes away and sat back by the fire. "I think they wanted to. Wodziwob was very convincing. He said Witillahow had only destroyed one mask of the evil spirit, and that anyone could see there was still evil among the white men. He said you could only fight the evil by using his dances to get rid of the white men altogether."

"What did you think of him?"

Charley took a deep breath and exhaled through flared nostrils. "I knew he'd make the whites suspicious. In Yreka, people thought the ghost dancers were stirring up the tribes for a big war against the white men. Another Pit River War. So I wasn't surprised last winter when the white government sent soldiers to the McCloud."

Ned's heart was in his throat. "And—?"

"The soldiers got the Puyshoos together and marched them through the mountains to a rancheria, one of those tiny reservations. The snow and hunger were terrible along the trail. The old chief died before they'd gone half a day."

"Worrotatot!" Ned exclaimed. He remembered bargaining with the old chief for Paquita's hand, and following him on a desperate elk hunt in the snow. The old man had seemed indestructible.

"Yes, Worrotatot," Charley said somberly. "The soldiers buried him beside the trail. They wouldn't even build a pyre to release his spirit. When the others got to the rancheria they were given white men's clothes and told to build huts. When spring came they were told to grow wheat. Anyone who disobeyed was whipped."

"But this is horrible!" Ned said, outraged.

Charley went on. "Last summer, the sickness came. It turned out the government agents had given them unwashed blankets from tribes that had died of smallpox. Last week I heard that only twenty-three Puyshoos are still alive on the rancheria."

Ned covered his face with a hand, aghast at the suffering of the tribe. And these terrors had happened within the last year, while he was in London telling stories! If only he had come here instead, perhaps he could have stopped the soldiers—or at least blocked the distribution of infected blankets. But he had been listening to his own voice then, and not the fainter call of the spirits. "So now Paquita is one of only twenty-three."

"No, she's not one of them."

"What!" Ned leaned forward, a shot of fear pumping in his veins. "But you said—"

For once Charley interrupted. "She's alive. She's just not at the rancheria."

"You mean she escaped?" For a moment Ned pictured her running for her life, hiding in the forest, but free.

Charley shook his head. "No, nobody escaped." Then he held out his hands as if to explain. "I didn't have to go because I'm half white. Paquita got to stay behind because she's married to a white."

"Then—" Ned sank back on his stool, following this idea with relief and growing amazement. Paquita had been spared because she was married to him! Even though he was gone, he had saved her. And she still thought of herself as his wife. The concept left him both proud and frightened. Was it possible they could actually live together again, after all these years? Would they even recognize each other? Would he still be attracted to her? And where could they go? He could hardly promote his books while hiding in a wilderness cabin. On the other hand, if he appeared in civilization with an Indian wife and daughter, he would set off new storms of ridicule. Or was there another option?

Ned put his hand to his forehead. "Then Paquita and Cali-Shasta are still living up by Mt. Shasta?"

Charley nodded. "They're the last of the Puyshoos at the old village on the McCloud."

Ned took a long, steadying breath. Charley's news had left him drained. The changes he had discovered in Oregon were as nothing to the cataclysmic new landscape facing him here. He stood up and paced to the far window. Night had arrived, with a cold wind so strong it bent the pines. The voice was still there, calling him closer, calling him back.

"Charley, I'm going to go see Paquita. If I can get a horse I'll leave tomorrow." He turned to face his old friend. "Will you come with me?"

"I wouldn't miss it for the world," Charley replied.

Charley's blunt, wry tone gave Ned the uncanny feeling that Charley had not only foreseen this day, but had known from the first what he had come to do. For a moment Ned remembered the first time he had gone with Charley to the McCloud—the day Charley had translated his request for Paquita's hand at the Puyshoos' harvest festival. The memory was startling, now that he was returning to see her again. But the years had changed everything. The tribe was gone. The whole West was different.

"You haven't changed, Ned," Charley said, as if reading his thoughts. "At least not inside, where it counts. You've just worn more masks than anyone I know."

Ned ran his hand through his hair. "The masks are getting harder to change, Charley. Look at me. I'm thirty-four. I can tell myself I'm just trying another mask on, but it's too late. Now if I take one off I look the same."

"Perhaps," Charley said. "Still, you've lived a whole lifetime since I first met you here at Soda Springs. You must have two or three lifetimes like that ahead of you. Won't they have new masks?"

"Not as many, I'll bet." Ned shook his head and stared into the embers of the fire. "It's like coming down from a mountain. At the top, when you're young, you can start out in any direction you want. If you change your mind you can walk around to the other side with just a few steps. But when you're halfway down the mountain it takes a journey even to change from one valley to the next. Worse yet, the view you once had, the view that let everything fit together in one sweep of the eyes, the view is lost."

Now Ned looked back out the dark window, almost speaking to himself. "And the only way to glimpse that view again is by sending a poem—or a spirit—straight back to the top."

Chapter 32

*This love of the beautiful is my old love—my old lesson.
I have read it by the light of the stars, or away down by
the strange light on the sea, even on the peaks of the Pacific
—everywhere.*
—Joaquin Miller

Charley was blowing the coals of the fire back to life when Ned awoke. Ice crystals glinted from the water bucket beside Ned's bunk. Snow banked the cabin's two small windows with white. The air stood absolutely still, as though sound itself had been buried by the cold night's snowfall.

Neither of them spoke during their breakfast of biscuits and coffee. Then Charley looked to Ned, and Ned responded with a nod: he was ready.

The cabin door pushed back a clean white arc in the fresh powder snow. Outside, in the crisp, early morning of the canyon, the still sunless sky glowed deep blue. Charley led the way to the stables. He broke the ice on the watering trough, indicated with a nod which horses Ned could saddle, and began pitching hay to feed the stock.

The hotel was still asleep when they rode up the trail along Soda Creek, single file, between the flocked pines. Ned clutched the front of his city suit jacket against the bite of morning air; only the warmth of the horse kept him from shivering. Snow capped the rocks in the dark creek, transforming them into sudden white mushrooms.

The world seemed magic that morning. All the mud of the November rainstorms had vanished beneath the gentle white curves of snow. The horses passed through the mists from the hot springs at the head of the canyon and turned east through powdery drifts, climbing toward the pass. Then, at last, the shining white tip of Mt. Shasta began its majestic ascent above the forests, mounting step by step into the blue sky. At the pass the mountain finally confronted them with its full power, blindingly white in the morning sun, with a single cloud-banner streaming proudly from its summit.

As Ned watched, a puff of wind blew a fanfare of snow crystals from the pines and sent it sparkling through the air before the mountain. And he thought: if I have been guided, it has been by such beauty. Surely this was the lesson given to me by Mountain Joe, the lesson that had to be lost to be learned. This was the spirit waiting to lead me through my darkest days.

Now-ow-wa, the valley beyond the pass, was as silent and beautiful as ever—a bold curve of white, suspended between the overwhelming mountain and the forests of cowering foothills. It was an easy gallop of spraying snow down through the fields to Ned's old cabin. There he dismounted and handed his reins to Charley.

A dozen winters of heavy snows had buckled the little log cabin's roof. Logs splayed on either side of the sagging doorway. A pile of straw inside showed that the ruin had been used to store hay. Only the back wall still stood straight, its window framing Mt. Shasta as perfectly as Ned remembered. But in Ned's memory a warm wind was bending a field of blue camas blossoms below the mountain. A girl sat weaving a basket in the sunshine; she tossed black hair from her face and smiled.

Suddenly a gray jay swooped over the snow, squawking away the summery vision. The horses snorted with impatience. Ned returned reluctantly, and they rode on.

The closer they came to the old Puyshoos village, the more nervous Ned became. He remembered the first summer he had lived at Now-ow-wa, dreaming of the beautiful Indian girl he had glimpsed with Mountain Joe. Then he had been terrified of the gap of language, culture, and tradition that lay between him and Paquita. Now another frightening gap loomed between them—a chasm of guilt and time. Would she be old and weathered, like the broken Paiute women he had seen from the train in Nevada when he crossed the country? Would she despise him for leaving her? Would the old Wintu words come back, or would he have to ask Charley to translate, as he had years ago? And what would he say?

At the next ridgetop Ned caught sight of the distant, dark curve of the McCloud. "Does Paquita live in the old chief's *cawel?*" he asked. They were the first words he had spoken aloud that day, and they cut the air like falling icicles.

"There are too many spirits crowding the old Puyshoos village for anyone to live close," Charley replied. "It's like a hundred other villages within sight of Kusku—home only to the masks of Coyote and Woodrat."

"Then the Puyshoos weren't the only tribe taken away by the soldiers?"

"It wasn't the soldiers," Charley said. "It was the sickness. Most tribes don't have enough people left to fill a rancheria. The Army closed its forts because the battle's over."

They rode to the edge of the rimrock, where the McCloud cut its narrow canyon into the high plain. Ned looked down, still picturing in his mind the *cawels,* the barking dogs, the smoke, and the children. But all that remained was a cluster of low mounds, like graves under the snow.

After a somber pause, Ned glanced to Charley.

"It's this way," Charley said.

Now Ned spotted a thin gray plume rising from the edge of the rimrock farther north. A touch of excitement and apprehension made his heart beat faster. The shingled roof of a log cabin shone silver above the brush. He heard the muffled ring of an ax. Ned straightened in his saddle and pulled his broad-brimmed hat firmly even with his brow as if to ready himself for whatever he might find.

As they rode out from the pines he quickly scanned the long, low cabin. Animal skins had been stretched to dry beneath the eaves. The door stood ajar. A long stack of firewood crossed the yard like a half-built wall.

Then he saw her, and his heart gave a sharp double thump. She was chopping wood in the yard, wearing the long, faded calico dress of a poor farmwife. But her every motion carried the grace that had won him long ago. As Paquita swung back with the ax, her dress twisted in curving pleats that showed she was as trim as ever, if perhaps more strongly muscled. Suddenly the ax paused in mid air and she looked up with the familiar dark eyes. Her full hair, pulled back in a long ponytail, was streaked with gray. The bronze of her skin had been deepened by the sun. The marks of maturity seemed to heighten her proud beauty.

She sank the ax into the chopping block. "Kibo. You have come." The English words were accented, but clear.

Ned dismounted slowly and stood in the snow, studying the woman who had been his first love. Obviously she had learned English. But Ned still had trouble finding words. "Paquita, I—" he began.

She shook her head. "They call me now Amanda."

There was a gruff clearing of a throat from inside the cabin. A fur-capped white man with a thick beard appeared in the doorway. "Amanda Brock, mister," he said. The man squinted at Ned and nodded once.

Ned looked at Paquita incredulously. "Who is he?"

Paquita shrugged. "I married again."

The words hit Ned like a cold wind. A moment before, the sight of Paquita had inspired a sudden hope. Now this unexpected gust collapsed that foolish fantasy as quickly as an unstaked tent. "You—you did?"

"Didn't you marry again, Kibo?" she asked.

"For a while, but—" Ned groped for bearings. How could he have overlooked this obvious possibility? Of course Paquita was young enough to start over. She'd only been eighteen when he left. Perhaps because of the child, he hadn't expected her to renounce their Wintu marriage. Certainly he had never imagined Paquita might marry another white man. He turned to Charley reproachfully. "You knew all along she had a new husband."

Charley held up his hands as if to profess innocence. "I told you the soldiers let her stay because she was married to a white. What did you think?"

"Well, I assumed—"

Paquita broke in. "That still I was married to you?" She gave a short laugh. "Long ago I made myself free."

A low growling sound from the cabin caught Ned's attention. With alarm, he realized the noise wasn't coming from a dog, but rather from the bushy-bearded man in the doorway. Ned hazarded a tentative smile. "Howdy. The name's Miller."

The trapper still growled.

Paquita turned to him with a sharp look. "Jim." She spoke the word with a slight rising tone that made Ned wonder if it was a reminder, a question, or a subtle order.

The man scowled a moment. "Reckon I'll check my trap line." Then he took a gun down from inside the door and trudged across the fields through the snow.

When the man was out of sight, Ned breathed a little easier. "Does he treat you well?"

She did not avoid his gaze. "We are happy."

Ned pursed his lips, grappling with the next questions he had to ask. Finally he said, "Do you understand why I couldn't come back to you?"

Again she did not lower her dark eyes. "Yes." But there was a hint of hardness in her look. "Come here, Kibo. There's a thing I wanted to give you. I carried it all this time with me."

Ned stepped forward, uncertain that she would really forgive him so easily, and wondering what she had kept for him all these years. Some of his early writings, perhaps, salvaged from one of his lost journals?

Paquita slowly turned aside, as if to reach for something behind her. But then she suddenly spun forward, swinging her arm with all her weight. Before Ned could flinch, the flat of her hand had caught him square alongside his head with a red flash of pain. She was not a large woman, but the blow knocked him sprawling into the snow.

Ned clutched his burning face with both hands. She had hit him with the strength of a kicking horse, and with as little warning. All the time they had lived together she had never complained. Certainly he had never hit her. What kind of person had she become? To make matters worse, he could hear Charley chuckling.

Ned staggered onto one knee in the wet snow and glared at the big half-Indian. "What the hell are you laughing about?"

Charley shook his head. "I've wanted to do that a few times myself, old friend."

Paquita calmly picked Ned's hat out of the snow and tried it on as if nothing had happened. "Good, it fits. That's a fair trade."

"For god's sake, Paquita," Ned managed to say, struggling back to his feet. "I thought you said you understood why I left." Obviously she had been building up her anger at him for years. Strangely, she seemed relaxed now—as if her rage had passed, like a tidal wave that had finally reached the shore.

"I like this hat," she said, adjusting its brim. Then she walked toward the cabin's door. "Come inside, Kibo."

Ned didn't know what to think. He held a handful of snow to his flaming jaw; the cheek was already swelling where the blow had hit his teeth. He looked to Charley.

Charley's smile had passed. "Only a Wintu woman can hit like that." He tipped his head earnestly toward the cabin. "I'll watch the horses. You'd better go in."

Ned eyed the cabin's door with new misgivings, as if it were the entrance to a mountain lion's den. Still, he had come to talk with Paquita and he wasn't going to turn back now. If anything, the slap proved they did have unfinished business. He brushed the snow off his suit coat and took a long breath. Then he went in.

The cabin's only room was low and dim, lit by one small window and a hearth against the far wall. Paquita knelt by the fire with what appeared to be a stick. When she stood up, Ned saw with some surprise that she had been lighting a cheap corncob pipe—the kind sold at mercantiles. She sat at a table by the window and proudly blew a long stream of spicy smoke at the rafter beams. Then she tipped back Ned's big, floppy hat as if she had worn it all her life.

"Sit, Kibo," she said.

Hesitantly, Ned pulled back one of the heavy, hand-hewn chairs. He didn't think she would hit him again, but he was no longer sure of anything. She had never acted so boldly before. Certainly she had never smoked. The Puyshoos had forbidden women to touch pipes at all.

Ned asked, "Where is Cali-Shasta?"

Paquita puffed out another bluish cloud. "She gets firewood. We talk about her later." Then she leaned forward and offered him the pipe. "Wintu tobacco. Jim hates it."

At first Ned shook his head; his mouth was sore and his head already hurt. But Paquita did not move. She held the pipe before him with both hands. Then Ned recognized the gesture. It was precisely the way her grandfather Worrotatot had held out an elaborate ceremonial pipe to him years ago. That time he had been in a dark *cawel* and Worrotatot had been asking for his help to end the tribe's winter famine.

Ned took the corncob pipe and inhaled the acrid smoke, with its dizzying taste of memories. It was hot and dry, like the scorched summer day when the posse had tied him to his horse and ridden him away from Now-ow-wa. Chastened by that vision, he said, "I know you must hate me for leaving you and Cali-Shasta."

"No," Paquita replied. "You don't know. You never know what I think, what I feel. Even before. You talked only a little Wintu then, and I talked no English. Now you can hear. It's time you find out what a woman thinks."

Ned lowered his head. Perhaps she was right that he hadn't tried hard enough to read her emotions. He had been young, and had thought mostly of his own feelings then. "Well, I used to think you loved me," he said, as if this were an apology.

"I did." Paquita took the pipe back and sucked the stem until the embers glowed red. Then she blew smoke out through her nostrils like an old sailor.

"I loved you," Paquita said firmly. "I'm not sorry."

Ned was relieved to hear her admit this much. "Then why did you hit me?"

Paquita laughed—a deep, slow laugh that put a flash of fire in her dark eyes. "I'm not sorry for that, too."

She pointed a brown finger at Ned. "Your name."

"My name? What about my name?"

"You know what it is?" she asked.

"I'm called Joaquin now."

"No." Paquita waved her finger. "The Wintu name. Kibo. You know what it means?"

Ned knit his brow. He had never really thought about it. On the night of the Wintu marriage ceremony, when Paquita had first called him Kibo, he had assumed the word was just a pair of syllables chosen on a whim. "Does it have a meaning?"

"Yes." Paquita nodded. "It means wolf."

"Wolf." Ned swelled a little inside at the thought. It was a name of honor, of power. But then another thought struck him. "Isn't there a different Wintu word for wolf? Lu— something?"

"Yes, you remember. Lubelas is first word for wolf," Paquita said. "But Kibo is different."

"Different?"

"Kibo is the lone wolf." Paquita pointed out the window with the pipe, as if the animal were there in the snow. "The kibo has no pack. The kibo calls alone. Long and sad. A beautiful call." She blew smoke at the window, fogging a circle of the cold glass. "When you came to the Puyshoos, I knew you were the kibo."

Ned studied her, weighing her words. "The lone wolf. Then you knew all along it couldn't last."

She nodded, still looking out the fogged window. "I knew. I took you anyway. A lubelas sometimes runs with the kibo. Because the kibo's spirit is wild. That short time together is a fall feast. Huckleberries and salmon. The best days. Then winter comes, and the kibo leaves. For the same reason. Because his spirit is wild."

"Then you really aren't sorry?"

"Winter is long. Everyone needs a fall feast to remember." She turned and looked evenly at Ned. "I didn't hit you for me. I hit you for Cali-Shasta."

Ned tightened his lips. "Of course." It was a blow he knew he deserved.

"The tribe is gone. There is no wolf pack. How will Cali-Shasta live? Who will teach her?"

Ned winced; it was a question he hadn't really wanted to ask. "I'm sure you've taught her a lot."

She knocked the pipe's ashes into a tin can on the table and drew herself up. "When you left I taught myself to live. I learned English from the missionary men. Then I married a trapper. That was my plan. Now the tribe is gone, but I still live."

Ned looked at her with respect. Of all the Puyshoos, she alone had foreseen the death march to the rancheria and had found a way to remain at the McCloud. It must have been hard. Even going to the missionaries to learn English must have been a difficult choice. He remembered how little interest she had shown in reading or writing when they lived together at Now-ow-wa. She had always said it wasn't the way of her tribe. "So you decided that you had to become like the whites to survive?"

"No. I only took a white mask," she said, lifting her head proudly. She tapped her heart. "The Puyshoos' spirit lives here always."

"And what about Cali-Shasta?" Ned asked.

"She keeps the spirit too." Then Paquita's face darkened, and she leaned forward earnestly. "But I can't teach her to live. I am lubelas, you see? She is the different wolf. She is the kibo, like you."

"She is the kibo—?" Ned began, wondering what she meant, but Paquita quickly waved her hands to silence him.

"Shh! You hear it?" She cocked her head a moment. Then she stood up and strode to the door. "Come outside. Now."

He followed her to the door. "What is it?"

Paquita only tilted her head toward the mountain.

Ned looked up at Mt. Shasta, unsure whether he should be listening for a spirit, an avalanche, or a wolf. But then he heard a voice slipping down through the thin pine forest. It was clear but distant—a faint but beautiful Indian melody that sent his mind reeling back years and years.

As he watched in wonder, a tall black-haired girl made her way through the trees and stepped into the clearing carrying an armload of lichen-covered branches. There she suddenly stopped her graceful song.

To Ned, she seemed like a fawn startled from the woods. Her dress was of leather. Her smooth, light complexion and simple black braids spoke for her youth. Her high cheekbones, however, gave her face a decidedly grown-up look. For a moment she was still, stopped in mid-song. Then she dropped her firewood on the snow and walked before them, watching Ned as if she already knew who he might be.

"Your father, Cali-Shasta," Paquita said.

Ned was at a loss for words. He hadn't expected to find his daughter grown up to be such a tall, beautiful young woman. Guilt, pride, and wonder churned within him. He added up the years in his head: she must be fourteen!

The girl sized him up coolly. "You are Kibo?"

"I—I'm called Joaquin Miller now." He gave a tentative smile. "You were only two when I had to leave. I don't suppose you remember me. Do I look the way you thought your father would?"

"I thought you'd be older," Cali-Shasta replied. Then she added, "Your face is red on one side. Did my mother hit you?'

Ned opened his mouth but couldn't decide whether to admit or deny the slap. The girl was as bold and brash as he himself had been at that age.

Cali-Shasta nodded. "Mother said she would." Then she turned to Paquita with her head high. "You can't stop me from leaving, Mother."

Paquita glared to Ned. "You see? What can I do? She is a kibo, like you."

"Wait a minute," Ned said, trying to straighten out what he had heard. He asked Cali-Shasta, "You say you want to leave?"

The girl tossed back her black hair. "Of course. I told Mother about it even before Charley said you might come back. What can I do here? Gather firewood? The world is bigger than Mt. Shasta."

"But where would you go?"

"To school," Cali-Shasta said. "I've learned the Puyshoos ways from my mother. I know the tribe's songs and stories by heart. Now I want the knowledge of the whites. If I learn to write, the stories will be safe. "

Ned considered Cali-Shasta's words. The girl was not only fiery, she was sharp-witted. Her knowledge of the Puyshoos' legends and songs was a cultural treasure, and she knew it. If anything could fulfill the promise he had made years ago, it would be to provide schooling for the girl. The question was how? He was at loose ends himself, teetering on the edge of his literary fame. He could borrow more money against royalties, though that was a gamble. But where could he put her in school? Certainly not in Oregon. The newspapers would make life miserable for them both if he took her there. Surely there were other places.

Ned turned to Paquita. "What do you think about her going to a school?"

Paquita took off the broad-brimmed hat and turned it over in her hands, as if it held the answer. "I don't know. Years ago I went to the missionary men to learn English. In my time that was a lot. Maybe now a woman needs more." She looked to Charley. "You talked of a school once."

Charley nodded. "There's an Indian boarding school in Shasta City."

Ned turned to Cali-Shasta. "How about it? Moving to a town like that won't be easy after living on the McCloud. There are so many houses they're stacked on top of each other, two and three stories high. But if you want, I'll take you to the school there and pay your way."

"No." Cali-Shasta replied, crossing her arms. "I won't go."

Ned's face fell. He had hoped the girl would recognize the generosity of the offer, and accept.

"Not to Shasta City," Cali-Shasta said firmly. "Take me to San Francisco."

"What?" Ned stared at her.

"San Francisco is bigger," Cali-Shasta said. "The schools will be better."

Ned threw up his hands. How could he explain the difficulties of this impetuous plan? Here was a girl who had never seen a train or a ship—or perhaps even a book. But it wasn't just the strangeness and the hugeness of the city. Cruelty lurked there, too. He had to make that clear.

"Listen, Cali-Shasta. You're half white, but you're half Puyshoos, too. San Francisco doesn't have any Indian schools. It's simply a different world. It would be a struggle to get you into a white school at all. People there might call you names. They wouldn't trust you. Your life would be very hard."

Cali-Shasta lifted her head. "Was it easier for you, Kibo? Wasn't it a struggle when you came to live with the Puyshoos? Mother says they might have killed you in the Pit River War if it weren't for me. You survived then, so I think I can manage in San Francisco now."

Ned blew out a long breath. The girl had cut through his argument like a chef carving a roast. He looked to Paquita for her advice. "Well?"

Paquita's lips were tight. "Are you sure, Cali-Shasta?"

Ned wished he really could read Paquita's emotions better. Was she worried about the white world their young daughter would face? Was she thinking how lonely this mountain valley would be when Cali-Shasta left? Was she proud of their daughter's courage?

Cali-Shasta nodded. "I'm sure, Mother. I can't stay here."

Ned saw Paquita bite her lip. This time he thought he could guess the words she did not say: They were powerless to hold back their young kibo, hungry for her summer of huckleberries and salmon. And who could deny the girl that beautiful season?

"All right," Ned said. "We could catch the southbound stage tomorrow."

"Tomorrow!" Cali-Shasta exclaimed, startled. "So soon?"

Ned smiled inside to think he had finally surprised her. "Why not? We should leave here tonight if you're going."

"Tonight!" Cali-Shasta's eyes grew wide. She flashed an excited smile to Ned and Paquita—even to Charley and the horses. "I'll get my things together." Then she hurried off into the cabin.

When she was gone, Ned wondered aloud, "Was I like that when I was young? A half-wild wolf pup?"

Charley chuckled. "And just as stubborn."

Paquita put on the broad-brimmed hat and laid her arm around Ned's shoulder. "Teach her the good things of the kibo. Teach her the freedom. The wild song. The spirit."

Then Paquita lifted her face. Were her eyes a little damp? "I think, Kibo, you'll find you've met your match."

* * *

That evening Mt. Shasta's glaciers burned red with the sunset fires of the west. The only cloud streaking the vast sky was a long, fluttering pink flock of sea gulls on their way back to the ocean now that the storm had passed.

Below, crossing the summit of a pine ridge, two horses left their tracks across the smooth, powdery snow. Riding the first was Charley McCloud, his face lifted to the last rays of the sun. Riding the other was Joaquin Miller, his wavy hair loose in the evening breeze. And riding behind his saddle, with her braids thrown back and her arms about his middle, was Cali-Shasta, talking and laughing.

"You told them grizzly bears climb trees?" she giggled.

The Poet of the Sierras half turned to look at her. "Don't they?"

"No! Not since Coyote stole their tails."

"That's right! I'd forgotten."

Cali-Shasta rolled her eyes. "And you're a famous storyteller?"

"Reckon so, Cal. It's just been a while since I was in the mountains."

She shook her head, and her braids swung from side to side. "You've got so much left to learn. I don't know if I can teach it all."

Ned looked ahead with the start of smile, both prouder and humbler than he had ever felt before. "You give it a try, Cal. Give it a try."

Epilogue

When Joaquin Miller arrived in San Francisco in 1871, Ina Coolbrith volunteered to take Cali-Shasta under her wing and enroll her in school. Cali-Shasta stayed in San Francisco and eventually married a Wells Fargo Company employee.

Joaquin himself traveled on to Brazil, England, and Italy. He published popular works nearly every year for the next forty years—books of poetry, opera house melodramas, newspaper articles, and stories.

In 1879 Joaquin married hotel heiress Abigail Leland in New York City. Four years later he moved to Washington D. C. by himself, where he built a log cabin, decorated it with elk horns, and entertained visiting heads of state by giving readings dressed in a mountain lion skin.

He moved to a hillside ranch overlooking Oakland, California in 1887. There he built a chapel-shaped house for himself and a cottage for his mother Margaret Miller. He filled the rambling grounds of "The Hights" with plantings of pine and eucalyptus trees. In the woods he built a funeral pyre platform and erected cement monuments in honor of Browning, Frémont, and Moses.

In 1897, at the age of sixty, he was paid six thousand dollars by the Hearst newspapers to write travel letters back from the Klondike gold rush. He lost parts of his ears and toes to frostbite while mushing in midwinter between Circle City, Alaska and Dawson City, Yukon. Then he went on the vaudeville circuit, reading poems about the adventure while wearing a sealskin greatcoat with enormous gold nugget buttons.

Amanda (Paquita) Brock bore a son to her new husband and lived to old age on the McCloud River, where she died in 1907.

Minnie Myrtle Miller lectured successfully throughout California and Oregon. She settled in Portland, remarried, and continued to fight for women's suffrage.

Maud Eveline Miller, the daughter of Joaquin and Minnie, became a well-known San Francisco actress.

George Brick Miller and Henry Mark Miller were convicted of burglarizing a house in Portland. Henry escaped from the Oregon State Penitentiary, robbed a stagecoach in Ukiah, and was sent to San Quentin on federal charges. In the ensuing uproar, Joaquin briefly left California, saying for a time he intended to escape the shame by becoming a Zen Buddhist monk in Japan.

After many years as the grand old man of Western literati, Joaquin Miller died at the age of 84, on February 17, 1913, at his ranch in Oakland, California.

Few evidences remain today of the Poet of the Sierras. His ranch was sold to the city of Oakland in 1919 and is maintained as Joaquin Miller Park. His cabin in Canyon City has been moved to the center of that small Eastern Oregon town and is preserved as a Joaquin Miller museum. His log cabin in Washington, D. C. was moved to Rock Creek Park in 1912, where it remains to this day. The *Register-Guard* in Eugene preserves the name of his newspaper. Today even Joaquin Miller's most famous poem, "Columbus"—written for the Columbian Exposition in 1892—is rarely included in anthologies of American verse. But the West still echoes with the legends of the swashbuckling frontier poet and the women who shared his life.

Notes

Historical novels vary greatly in their blend of the "historical" and the "novel." While footnotes would be inappropriate in any novel, readers may want to know more about the extent of historical documentation for this work. For that reason I am including notes on the general sources for each chapter, along with a few other observations that may be of interest.

The first seven chapters are based heavily on Joaquin's own handwritten diaries. This early, factual journal of Joaquin's California years, concealed during his lifetime and suppressed for many years afterwards by Ina Coolbrith because of its roughness and occasional crudity, was first published in 1936.

Chapter 1: Mountain Joe's historical foundation lies primarily in the numerous tales Joaquin Miller published about him—as packer, as proprietor of Soda Springs, as a friend to the Indians, and as an old man in Idaho. Considering the freedoms Miller took with such tales, this is admittedly only circumstantial evidence of Mountain Joe's existence. Charley McCloud is a creation of my own imagination.

Nearly all of Miller's names (including Cincinnatus, Ned, Hiner, Agricola, and Joaquin) were used as described in this novel. I have invented only "Kibo." His brothers often called him "Nat."

Chapter 2: Charley's legend of the creation of Shasta is adapted from Joaquin Miller's *True Bear Stories*.

Chapter 3: Joaquin claimed at times that he lived with the Shastas, while at other times he said he was with the Modocs. He probably said he lived with the Shasta Indians (who actually were northwest of Mt. Shasta) because their name was held in higher esteem than that of the "Diggers" (or Puyshoos). His claim that he was with the Modocs (who lived northeast of Mt. Shasta) was certainly for publicity's sake. A Modoc chief by the name of Captain Jack withstood a siege by the U. S. Army for several months in 1872-1873 and killed a general, all of which made the name "Modoc" synonymous with "savage" in the public mind. Joaquin's imaginative autobiography of his California years, published in 1873, capitalized on this name familiarity by its misleading title, *Unwritten History: Life Amongst the Modocs.* Libraries now catalogue the book as fiction.

In fact, Joaquin lived with the Puyshoos band of the Wintu tribe on the south slope of Mt. Shasta. The 119-word glossary of Wintu words in Joaquin's journal is evidence of his stay. This handwritten dictionary includes intimate sexual terms as well as conversational and hunting words, so that it certainly reflects the language of his *mahala,* his Indian wife. Today the tribal name is memorialized by the McCloud River village of Wyntoon, and by the Wintun Glacier on Mt. Shasta itself.

It should be noted that Worrotatot (literally, "The Short One") was in fact the chief of the Puyshoos, but that Akitot and Witillahow are fictional.

Chapter 4: The elk hunt is documented both in Joaquin's journal and in a later published tale.

Chapter 5: Joaquin's reconnaissance mission in the wake of the Pit River Massacre is described in detail in the manuscript journal. His participation in the Punitive Expedition is also certain, verified by several brief journal entries. Bill Hearst and Captain Whitney are authentic; Swede is fictional.

Chapter 6: Several sources verify that Sam Lockhart was in fact one of the few survivors of the Pit River Massacre, that his twin brother did die, that Sam did begin indiscriminately killing Indians in the area, and that he did capture Joaquin approximately as described. The hearing before Judge Rosborough in Yreka is documented.

Chapter 7: Miners of the day have testified that Joaquin worked in Deadwood for Bill Hearst, but the reasons they have given for Joaquin stealing Hearst's horse vary dramatically. Baboon is not documented as being in Deadwood, although he was later in Idaho. The journal entry from 1859 is fictitious, because Miller's journals from 1857 to 1859 have been lost.

Chapter 8: The grand jury indictment is on file at the Shasta County Courthouse in Redding. Neil Scott and Dave English are not documented in California at this time, although Joaquin did escape from the jail with an outlaw.

Chapter 9: Several sources, including Joaquin himself, agree that Joaquin shot Sheriff Bradley, but where and how he did this is unclear. It is only certain that the incident precipitated his return to Oregon.

Chapter 10: Because all of Columbia College's files burned, records are lost that might substantiate Joaquin's assertions that he attended Columbia College and taught school during this period. The letter from

John is hypothetical. Joaquin did, however, go mining with his brother John. Joaquin's younger brother James, who may also have accompanied them to Idaho, played such a small role in this drama that his presence is unmentioned.

Chapter 11: Joaquin's participation in the express business is certain. Isaac Mossman later visited Joaquin at his home in Oakland to reminisce about the venture. Cherokee Bob, Dr. Furber, Sheriff Porter, Hildebrandt, and Baboon were all real people, but Idaho history is so sketchy for this period that many of their deeds fall into the category of legend rather than fact. "Baboon Gulch" has retained its name to this day.

Two of the tall tales told around the campfire are from Joaquin Miller's *True Bear Stories.* The story of Pegleg Smith is a genuine tall tale of the Rockies, the story of Ted McGuire is an oral tale collected by *Oregon Journal* historian Fred Lockley in the 1920s, and the story of the slow echo is based on a Chemeketan campfire tale told by Wally Eubanks of Salem, Oregon in the early 1980s.

Chapter 12: The winter of 1861-1862 was as severe as described. The chase in the blizzard closely follows an autobiographical sketch published later by Joaquin. Scott and English *were* in Idaho, and were hung by vigilantes the following summer, as the newspaper notice in Chapter 13 testifies.

Chapter 13: The largest flood in Eugene's history occurred in the spring of 1862 as described. Extant copies of Joaquin's newspapers testify to his role as editor and proprietor. All of the newspaper quotations and poems are accurate as given. Occasionally they have been shortened or consolidated. Eugene City officially changed its name to the City of Eugene in 1889.

Chapter 14: C. H. Miller and Theresa Dyer courted and married very much as described. Alf Nubia is fictitious, but is based on a character in one of Minnie Myrtle's semi-autobiographical stories published in the *Golden Era.* Minnie's sister Emma has been renamed Emily here to reduce confusion with Ned's sister Ella. The polka lyrics are a folk song of the day that was adapted to several areas around the West, including the Oregon coast. Minnie's assertion that Cape Blanco was the westernmost point of the United States was correct; although Cape Alava in Washington is further west, Washington was only a U. S. territory in 1862.

Chapter 15: General Wright's orders were reported in the San Francisco *Bulletin* and reprinted in the *Register.* Minnie's diaries have been lost, so the entries here are fictional.

Chapter 16: Joaquin Miller's and Minnie Myrtle's literary efforts are documented in the columns of the *Golden Era,* as described. It is not known whether Joaquin met Mark Twain during this time, but Twain was in San Francisco, and Joaquin did meet some of the writers for the *Golden Era*. Twain's remarks are based on his autobiographical book, *Roughing It*. Mrs. Dyer's letter is fictitious.

Chapter 17: Joaquin's letters from this period have been lost, so the excerpts here are invented. His descriptions of the Indian uprising, and of his role as captain of the fifty-four volunteers, however, are supported by several civilian and Army witnesses, although the details of the battle itself vary in each story.

Chapter 18: Sarah Eckelhoff is fictitious. Her outlandish ideas are gathered from newspaper articles of the day. Joaquin kept a ledger of his law accounts during these years, and the ledger has been preserved by the Oregon Historical Society. Of the sundry notes scattered throughout the ledger (including the rough drafts of numerous poems), one note mentions the author's "regrets" and another mentions a "Mrs. E." Some biographers have speculated that Mrs. E was a source of marital friction for Joaquin. There is no proof of such an affair, but there certainly was marital friction during the Canyon City years.

Bill Cain's murder trial and execution are documented both by Joaquin's ledgers and by newspaper accounts. Minnie's 1865 diary entry is entirely hypothetical. Although she did keep a diary, it has been lost along with all her other unpublished papers. The song "The Big Sunflower," hummed by Ned, was actually written three years later in 1868.

Chapter 19: The original owner of the Kam Wah Chung & Company store is not known, but the building was bought in 1887 by Lung On and Ing Hay, who practiced traditional Chinese medicine and supported the dwindling, persecuted Chinese community in Eastern Oregon until their deaths in the 1940s. In the late 1960s, the last person of Chinese descent left John Day. In the early 1980s, the Kam Wah Chung building was restored as a museum.

Chapter 20: Joaquin's letters to Minnie are lost; these two are hypothetical. There is much mystery surrounding the identity of "Mr. Hill," whose name appears in the divorce proceedings.

Chapter 21: The reviews of *Joaquin, Et Al.* are quoted accurately. The divorce proceedings, synopsized accurately here, are on file in the Oregon State Archives in Salem. This is their first appearance in print.

Chapter 22: George Francis Train's speech has been reconstructed from newspaper reports. Joaquin did correspond with C.W. Stoddard, but the text of the letters has been reworked and simplified here.

Chapter 23: Ina Coolbrith and others have described Joaquin's stay in San Francisco. Coolbrith's secret history came to light after her death, although her closest friends knew of it during her lifetime. Several different people have claimed to be the one to have suggested Miller's pen name "Joaquin;" Coolbrith's claim to this distinction is probably the strongest.

Chapter 24: The description of the transcontinental railroad trip relies in part on Jules Verne's *Around the World in Eighty Days*, which describes an 1872 crossing in detail. It is known that Joaquin did write to Ina from New York, and that he signed his name "Joaquin" for the first time in that letter, but the letter itself has been lost. Here it is reconstructed using Joaquin's published journal from the trip.

Unfortunately, the published form of Joaquin's 1870-1871 journal is probably a far cry from the original document, which might have contained many more valuable facts about his trip to England. Once Joaquin became famous and returned to America, he "edited" his London journal for publication and burned the original. The published version has obviously been rewritten after the fact to entertain a reading audience, and includes, for example, an unlikely entry describing a side trip to France between the front lines of the Franco-Prussian War. Nonetheless, the five journal entries given in this chapter are based on the published journal, as are many of his adventures in New York, Scotland, and London.

Chapter 25: Although Joaquin certainly met and was helped by Thomas Hood the Younger, Lord Houghton, and Dante Gabriel Rossetti, the descriptions of these encounters are entirely fictional and the characters themselves have been drawn with a free literary hand. The account given by Mrs. Hamsby of the pre-Raphaelites, however, is factually accurate.

Chapter 26: Little is known of the Irishmen who did, in fact, help polish Joaquin's work at the request of the pre-Raphaelites.

The use of the word "Sierras" in the title *Songs of the Sierras* and in the subsequent moniker "Poet of the Sierras" was perhaps a little misleading, since the volcanic peaks Joaquin wrote about in California and Oregon are not part of the Sierra Nevadas, but rather belong to the Cascade Range. Joaquin later excused the discrepancy by referring to the Cascades as the "Sierra Grande del Norte."

Joaquin later drastically shortened and revised many of the poems in *Songs of the Sierras*—including "Kit Carson's Ride," which, after considerable debate and the threat of litigation by Carson's heirs, was altered to allow Carson to rescue the Indian maiden after all.

Joaquin's antics in London society are well documented. The scenes in this chapter are intended to be representative only. The letter from

Hulings Miller probably did exist in some similar form, but if so, it has been lost.

Chapter 27: The newspaper articles quoted here have been occasionally shortened, but never reworded or invented. The August 1871 letters between Minnie Myrtle and Abigail Duniway are fictional. A meeting between Minnie and Matilda Jane Fultz would have been possible. Mrs. Fultz' life story is genuine, and was recorded by Fred Lockley for the *Oregon Journal* in 1921, at which time she was Matilda Jane Delaney. Incidentally, Washington Territory reneged on its promise to give women the vote shortly before the 1871 election. Suffrage was denied Washington women for two more generations.

Chapter 28: Melville's works were virtually forgotten by 1871, and he lived in obscurity as a customs agent in New York. It is conceivable that he met Joaquin as described. Joaquin's letter to the New York *Tribune*, here somewhat shortened, is actually dated September 22, 1871—thirteen days after John's death. It has been included with Joaquin's interview at the Astor House for the sake of convenience. Joaquin's letter to his parents is based on a similar letter to his brother James, a letter which has survived.

Chapter 29: The poem "The Suffragist" appeared in the Portland *Herald* during Susan B. Anthony's Oregon tour. Anthony's interview in Salem and her speech at the fairgrounds are based on articles appearing in Portland newspapers at that time by and about both Anthony and Elizabeth Cady Stanton. Minnie Myrtle's review of Anthony's Salem speech has been somewhat shortened here. Incidentally, Abigail Duniway campaigned for women's suffrage for forty-one more years before she could witness the governor of Oregon signing statewide suffrage into law in 1912. Susan B. Anthony died in 1906, fifteen years before a Constitutional amendment gave all American women—except, ironically, Native Americans—the right to vote.

Chapter 30: The bill announcing Minnie's speech, and the speech itself, are reconstructed from thorough newspaper accounts.

Chapter 31: Joaquin's stage trip south is based on a description of the same journey by Wallis Nash in *Oregon: There and Back in 1877*. Charley's story of the Puyshoos' fate is fictional, but it is representative of the treatment of Northern California tribes at that time. The ghost dancer Wodziwob, his doctrine, and the white response to him, are all genuine.

Acknowledgments

I am indebted to those who gave me assistance and encouragement during fourteen years of research and writing. In particular, I wish to thank the Eugene Public Library, the University of Oregon Library (for manuscripts in their special collections and for microfilms of nineteenth-century periodicals), the Lane County Historical Museum, Kam Wah Chung Museum curator Carolyn Milnhimer of John Day, former University of Oregon professor of folklore Barre Toelken, the late David Duniway (grandson of Abigail Scott Duniway), Julian Miller of Coos Bay (nephew of Joaquin Miller), and all those who read the manuscript—including Janell Sorensen, Norman Barrett, Talbot Bielefeldt, Barbara Emashowski, Martha Bayless, Brenda Shaw, Mabel Armstrong, Lee Crawley Kirk's Toad Falls writers group, and J. Wesley Sullivan (retired editor of the *Oregon Statesman*). In addition, I wish to thank retired University of Oregon professor of history Edwin Bingham, who directed me to many of the sources for my research, and who was kind enough to check the manuscript for historical accuracy.

I have also relied heavily on Joaquin Miller's many works (listed below), most notably his manuscript journals, which, because they were written for Miller's private records, are virtually free of the imaginative fiction which pervades his later "autobiographical" tales.

The secondary literature concerning the events in this book is much too profuse to acknowledge by title here. However, I have appended a list of Joaquin Miller's principal biographers.

Additional thanks go to Alan McCullough for the author photograph on page 464, and to the Oregon Historical Society for the cover portraits of Joaquin Miller (OrHi 100724, dating to about 1876) and Minnie Myrtle Miller (OrHi 100161, dating to about 1870).

Works By Joaquin Miller

Specimens. Portland, 1868.
Joaquin, Et Al. Portland, 1869.
Pacific Poems. London, 1871.
Songs of the Sierras. London, 1871; Boston, 1871.
Songs of the Sun-Lands. Boston, 1873.
Unwritten History: Life Amongst the Modocs. London, 1873; Hartford, 1874.
The Ship in the Desert. Boston, 1875.
First Fam'lies of the Sierras. Chicago, 1876.
The One Fair Woman. London, 1876.
Songs of the Mexican Seas. Boston, 1877.
The Baroness of New York. 1877.
Songs of Italy. Boston, 1878.
The Danites in the Sierras. Chicago, 1881.
How to Win in Wall Street. By a Successful Operator. New York, 1881.
The Shadows of Shasta. Chicago, 1881.
Forty-nine: The Gold Seekers of the Sierras. New York, 1884.
Memorie and Rime. New York, 1884.
The Destruction of Gotham. New York, 1886.
In Classic Shades. Chicago, 1890.
Songs of Summer Lands. Chicago, 1892.
The Building of the City Beautiful. Chicago, 1893.
An Illustrated History of Montana. 1894.
Songs of the Soul. San Francisco, 1896.
True Bear Stories. Chicago and New York, 1900.
Chants for the Boer. 1900.
As It Was in the Beginning. 1903.
Light. 1907.
Joaquin Miller's Poems. 7 volumes. San Francisco, 1909-1912.
The Poetical Works of Joaquin Miller. Ed. Stuart P. Sherman. New York, 1923.
Overland in a Covered Wagon. Ed. Sidney A. Firman. New York, 1930.

A Royal Highway of the World. Portland, 1932.
Joaquin Miller: His California Diary. Ed. John S. Richards. Seattle, 1936.
Selected Writings of Joaquin Miller. Ed. Alan Rosenus. Eugene, 1977.

Biographies of Joaquin Miller

Wagner, Harr. *Joaquin Miller and His Other Self.* San Francisco, 1929.
Allen, Merritt Parmelee. *Joaquin Miller, Frontier Poet.* New York, 1932.
Powers, Alfred. *History of Oregon Literature.* Portland, 1935.
Peterson, Martin Severin. *Joaquin Miller, Literary Frontiersman.* Palo Alto, 1937.
Walker, Franklin. *San Francisco's Literary Frontier.* New York, 1939; Seattle, 1969.
Marberry, Marion. *Splendid Poseur: Joaquin Miller, American Poet.* New York, 1953.
Frost, O.W. *Joaquin Miller.* New York, 1967.
Lawson, Benjamin S. *Joaquin Miller.* Boise, 1980.

About the Author

William L. Sullivan has written eight books about Oregon, including *Hiking Oregon's History,* a series of *100 Hikes* guides, and *Listening for Coyote,* the story of Sullivan's 1000-mile walk across Oregon's wilderness in 1985. Information about his books and speaking schedule is available online at *www.Oregonhiking.com.*

A fifth-generation Oregonian, Sullivan grew up the son of a Salem newspaper editor. At the age of 17 Sullivan left high school to study at Deep Springs College in the California desert, where his duties included driving cattle on horseback. He went on to earn a B.A. in English from Cornell University and an M.A. in German from the University of Oregon. He and his wife, Janell Sorensen, have bicycled 3000 miles through Europe, studied two years at Heidelberg University in Germany, and built a log cabin by hand on Oregon's remote Siletz River. When not at their log cabin or exploring Oregon trails, they live in Eugene. They have two children, Karen and Ian.